Verdant Witch
Rising

By

Lily Mackenzie Duffin

Wild Things Bloom Press

Published by Wild Things Bloom Press

Edited by Travis Duffin
Book cover by Travis Duffin and Lily Mackenzie Duffin

First Printing, 2026
ISBN: 979-8-9946371-1-1

To my AMAZING beta readers,
Chyenne Arsenault and Jessica Kendall.
Thank you for wandering Velhollow's crooked paths with me, for noticing the places where the branches sagged, and for celebrating the moments when the magic finally behaved. Your care shaped this story as surely as any spell.

For Travis

When the noise around me turned unkind and made me question why I ever began this journey, your voice was the one that didn't waver. This book exists because you were beside me, long after my circle grew smaller.

Lily loves ADH

Prologue

Before she ever knew the word for it, Frankie DiLegna had already begun to bloom. From the moment she toddled barefoot into a summer storm, hair tangled, laughter rising with the rain, she seemed carved from earth and weather. Her eyes, moss-green rimmed with gold, held the hush of forests and the spark of something untamed. Childhood fit her like lichen on stone, soft, stubborn, entirely her own. She wove dandelion crowns with reverence, whispered secrets to trees, and filled her pockets with feathers and stones, small treasures no one else noticed but she knew mattered. While other children traced cursive loops and plinked out piano scales, Frankie studied the language of leaves and the curling script of vines. Her mother tried to starch away the wild edges with collared dresses and silent dinners, but Frankie resisted with quiet ferocity. Mud clung to her heels, wildflowers pressed themselves defiantly between etiquette-book pages, and rocks slipped into the wash from her pockets. Over time, the strained smiles in the household thinned into sighs of disappointment. Her mother's voice became a metronome of reminders and reprimands; her father vanished behind his newspaper, offering little more than a hum. The judgment stung, but Frankie learned to let it slide from her skin like rain off leaves. She understood that to breathe deeply, to bloom fully, she would need nourishment beyond the manicured confines of their home. In a family of blue-eyed DiLegna's who looked as if they'd stepped from the pages of a lifestyle magazine, Frankie stood out like a wild sprig in a clipped hedge. Her curls refused to be tamed; her vibrant eyes were impossible to ignore. Her mother's tight smile came with a barb.

"*Must be a genetic throwback, probably from your father's side. No one in my family ever had eyes that color.*" As if Frankie were an unruly weed disrupting her mother's curated symmetry.

Sometimes Frankie liked to think of herself as a kind of off-brand Cinderella, sans the fairy godmother, sans the wicked stepmother, but add in two emotionally constipated parents who expressed affection through passive-aggressive Post-it notes and a meticulously shared calendar. There was no soot to scrub, just an endless atmosphere of quiet disapproval and living rooms full of furniture no one was allowed to sit on. In her house, emotions weren't voiced, they were suppressed and re-channeled into "productive" outlets. Her mother's favorite form of therapy wasn't conversation, it was retail. A new pair of shoes instead of an apology, a seasonal throw pillow in place of affection. Frankie quickly learned that what couldn't be named could at least be bought and bagged, neatly folded into tissue paper. But she never found comfort in shopping bags or credit card swipes.

She planted her own wild things instead. Herbs in coffee tins, flowers in mismatched pots, weeds left deliberately unpulled because she liked their stubborn cheer. Dirt under her nails suited her better anyway. She bloomed sideways, untamed, curious, brimming with feelings that didn't come with instructions. The world often felt too much, too loud, too sharp around the edges, too full of currents no one else seemed to sense. Emotions rolled off people like heat waves, faint but undeniable. She could step into a room and take its emotional temperature before a single word was spoken. Lies bent the air; sorrow hid beneath smiles. Adults called her oversensitive, teachers said she was too dreamy, her mother scolded her for lacking "thicker skin," as if resilience were something you could knit like a sweater.

But Frankie didn't feel things a little, she felt them completely. Her world was painted in hues unseen by others, a kaleidoscope of emotion that danced around everyone she met. She sensed anger as ember-red heat, kindness as cool river-blue, anxiety as a storm-grey coil in the air. She didn't see these with her eyes but felt them in her bones, pulses of truth carried on an unseen wind. Premonitions stirred gently within her, like reeds bending beneath hidden currents.

Bright artificial light could scrape against her skin like static and silence itself spoke to her, layered and rich. A melody could unravel her into tears, as could a handwritten note or a cedar-scented breeze. She found her reprieve in the natural world. When the house pressed too tightly around her, she crept barefoot to the back yard where ivy crawled like green lace and lavender held the air steady. She carried little jars filled with soil, seeds, and hope, whispering encouragements as though the plants were listening and sometimes, she swore they did. A sprig of rosemary would perk toward her hand. Lemon balm leaves seemed to brighten when she brushed them. She learned early that she was more herself with roots and petals than she ever was at the polished dining table. Her happiest hours were the ones spent alone among her plants. She learned the patience of seedlings, the generosity of compost, the quiet company of bees who never stung her though they stung others. She knew the way the minty sharpness of crushed leaves could soothe her faster than any parental comfort. She memorized the names of flowers instead of the saints her mother insisted she pray to. In those hours, Frankie was never lonely, never wrong or strange, just a girl being met by the world on its own terms, wild, generous, and alive. The rest of the time, she didn't fit. She felt it in the way her classmates whispered about her too-big feelings, in the way teachers sighed when her questions strayed past the lesson plan. She saw it in her father's quiet refusals to meet her gaze, in her mother's clipped praise, meted out like crumbs. She was too much where they wanted less, and too different where they wanted sameness and yet, there was something in her that refused to flatten. Sometimes the ache of belonging elsewhere rose without warning, when she pressed her palm to the earth and swore it pulsed faintly back, or when storms rolled over the horizon and her chest vibrated in rhythm with the thunder. The world seemed to hold secret messages for her, not written in books or spoken by her parents, but carried in root and rain, in wind through tall grass. As she grew, the feeling deepened. Walking home one dusk, she could have sworn her name rode the wind, as though the earth itself remembered her. She never spoke of it, but she never forgot.

Soil and roots had claimed her early. They gave her what her family would not, steadiness, recognition, belonging. And in a world that too often threatened to overwhelm her, Frankie made a choice. She would not dull her edges or carve herself into something easier. She embraced her sensitivity as a gift, and let it guide her toward the hush of trees, toward roots humming deep beneath the ground. Every feeling became a compass, and though she could not yet name it, she knew it pointed somewhere.

Sometimes, in the quietest hours, when the house slept and even the wind fell still, she felt it more keenly. As if someone long gone had left a thread tugging faintly at her ribs, waiting to draw her toward what they had once known. A promise, unfinished, still echoing.

She didn't yet know she was magic.

She only knew she belonged somewhere else.

Somewhere green, and old, and waiting.

Chapter 1

The scent of lavender and loam clung to her hands as she eased open the greenhouse door. Warm air rushed out in greeting, rich with the perfume of damp moss, sun-warmed terra cotta, and a stubborn patch of lemon balm that refused to stay potted. Frankie DiLegna exhaled, slow and steady. Inside the glass walls, time felt pliable, softer around the edges. This was her sanctuary, rows of overgrown herbs, dried bundles strung from the rafters like botanical constellations, and jars of tinctures lined up like tiny potions waiting to become useful. While the rest of the world sped by in urgent, glittering chaos, the nursery moved at the pace of root systems and quiet growth. It suited her just fine. She nudged a rogue vine off the path with the toe of her boot and ducked under a trailing curtain of jasmine. Sunlight spilled in through warped panes, making the dust motes dance, and for a moment she stood still, letting the light catch in her hair and the warmth settle in her bones.

It had been a strange week. First there was the owl that had followed her home, not in a poetic, single feather drifted to the ground kind of way, but in a real, talon-tapping-on-her-bedroom-window-at-midnight way. Then there was the customer who claimed her rosemary plant whispered secrets at night. Oh and the odd way her dreams had started unraveling into something that felt less like dreaming and more like remembering. Frankie didn't mind strange, but this was starting to feel like something else. She reached for the watering can, fingers brushing the familiar worn handle, when a low meow sounded behind her. Chalupa, of course. He sauntered in like a furry monarch, tail flicking with purpose, fur catching the sunlight. He blinked slowly, then hopped onto the bench beside her and let out a noise that sounded suspiciously like judgment.

"You slept late." she said, knowing full well he could understand her. Chalupa just purred and stretched, his spine arching in a slow ripple of fur and bone. His eyes fixed on her, like he saw through her, beneath the garden-stained fingertips and soft resolve, into something buried deeper. That look brought her back, the edges of the moment blurred.

One golden afternoon, when she was no more than eleven or twelve, barefoot in spirit and brimming with wide-eyed wonder, Frankie felt a pull, not the kind you could explain, but the kind you followed without question. Something deep inside her whispered, this way. So she climbed onto her bike and pedaled past familiar corners and manicured hedges, her heart thudding with a strange, giddy anticipation.The breeze tousled her curls, and the wind seemed to sing just for her. With every turn, the world grew quieter, softer, until the last bits of town faded behind her like a dream. Just when her legs started to ache and she considered heading home, the road curved, and there it was. A wooden sign, weathered by years of sun and storm, hung like a secret above the entrance to another world. Willow & Sage Nursery, it read, in curling letters that looked like they'd been drawn by ivy itself.

The moment Frankie stepped beneath the wooden archway, the world felt different, like she'd wandered into the pages of a storybook that had been waiting just for her. The air shimmered around her, thick with scents she couldn't quite name but instantly loved, rosemary and lavender, sun-warmed soil, something sweet like jasmine, and something wilder still, like the way rain smells before it falls. She drew in a deep breath, her chest rising with the scent of green things and endless possibility. Dragonflies zipped through the air like living gemstones, their wings humming like secrets. Butterflies fluttered past her like confetti on a breeze. Ladybugs dotted the leaves like little red buttons, and somewhere nearby, a squirrel dashed across a branch, and a rabbit, soft and round as a dandelion puff, nibbled quietly near the herb beds.

And the plants… oh, the plants. They seemed to notice her, leaves rustled softly, petals turned just slightly in her direction, vines stretched like sleepy cats waking from a nap. It felt like the whole place was leaning in, curious about the girl with scraped knees and acorns in her pockets. Frankie stood perfectly still, eyes wide and heart full. She didn't know what magic was supposed to look or smell like, but if it existed, this was it. She turned a corner and stopped in her tracks, her mouth falling open in a soft little gasp. Before her stretched a path of color and light, towering snapdragons like castles, cheerful daisies bobbing in the breeze, all of it glowing under the golden afternoon sun. Wind chimes sang a gentle tune above her, and somewhere out of sight, water whispered over stone. The whole nursery felt alive, not just with flowers and bees and green growing things, but with something more. A welcoming peace that wrapped around her shoulders like a favorite blanket. She smiled without even realizing it. She didn't know yet how much this place would come to mean to her, how it would root itself in her heart and bloom there for years to come. She saw him then, stepping out of the greenhouse like someone from the kind of storybook where gardens whispered secrets and gentle giants looked after tiny, magical worlds.

Pete Granger emerged with a tray of seedlings tucked under his arm, looking more like a tree that had decided to walk around in flannel than a person. He was tall, giant really, with broad shoulders and arms dusted with soil, like he'd just been carved from the earth. His beard was scruffy and silver, like a soft, slow-moving storm cloud, and his eyes, deep-set and crinkled at the corners, squinted thoughtfully as they landed on her.

For a moment, Frankie didn't move. She was just a kid in a grass-stained shirt, cheeks smudged with the kind of happiness that came from climbing trees and chasing dragonflies. Yet, looking at him, this towering, dirt-streaked man, she didn't feel small, she felt… safe. Like she'd stumbled into the exact right place, even if she didn't know it yet. He didn't speak right away, just looked at her, really looked, the way grown-ups rarely did. Like he was sizing up her roots, checking if they ran deep enough to weather a storm, or maybe just trying to figure out what kind of wild thing had wandered into his world. Frankie stood frozen beneath that gaze, small and scrappy. She didn't know whether to run or stay, she just chewed at the inside of her cheek and watched him back, her heart tapping against her ribs.

"You lost?" he asked at last, his voice rough like a gravel path but warmer than she expected, warmer than the sun on her back.

Frankie shook her head quickly, too shy to meet his eyes for long.

"Just looking," she mumbled, scuffing her sneaker against the dirt like maybe it would swallow her up if she stayed quiet enough. Her eyes kept darting up, curious despite herself. There was

something about him. Like if the world started falling apart, he'd know how to hold it together and in that small, silent moment, something had quietly begun to take root.

He made a low sound in his throat, something between a grunt and a chuckle, as he set the tray down on a nearby bench.

"You know what that is?" he asked, nodding toward a tall plant just beside her, its bell-shaped blossoms swaying gently in the breeze.

Frankie looked at it and lit up. "Foxglove," she said, her voice full of quiet wonder. "It's really pretty, but it's poisonous. You shouldn't touch your mouth after handling it and definitely don't eat it." She hesitated, then added, "But my book said it can help hearts, too. Like medicine."

Pete blinked, the corner of one eye crinkling. "That so?"

She nodded, rocking slightly on her heels. "It's in my wildflower book. I read it twice."

He studied her for a moment, this small, curious thing with windblown hair and dirt-smudged cheeks, and gave a single, approving nod. Frankie's grin stretched wide. He pointed a thumb toward a row of watering cans.

"If you're planning to stick around, you can give those thirsty ones a drink."

And just like that, she was part of something. Pete hadn't asked questions, he simply sensed something in her, and that was enough. Frankie picked up the watering can with both hands, it was heavier than she expected, and followed him without a word. She didn't yet understand how important this day would become. All she knew was that she had found a place to land. Through it all, he watched, never hovering, never pressing, just steady as a trellis beneath climbing vines. He gave her space to bloom, but he noticed everything. Over time he started sending customers her way with a simple "Ask Frankie," never corrected her when she rearranged half the greenhouse or concocted a tea blend no one had asked for. When she filled one corner of the nursery with drying herbs and mason jars full of flower tinctures, he only raised an eyebrow and handed her a better shelving bracket.

When the dust of graduation settled and her future stretched out like an open meadow, it wasn't her parents who laid a path for her, it was Pete. She was scribbling recipes in her journal one warm afternoon, the scent of rosemary heavy on the air, when he shuffled over in his usual flannel, mulch still clinging to his boots. He didn't speak at first, just held out a ring of brass keys, tarnished and warm from his palm.

"I've been meaning to talk to you," he said, squinting toward the sun. "You know that old carriage house? Tucked behind the lavender beds, near the hives? Been sittin' quiet too long. Figured it might suit you."

Frankie blinked, sitting up a little straighter. Pete cleared his throat and dragged a hand across the back of his neck, as if sorting through the right words by touch alone. "I've been repairing it in pieces," he said. "Didn't tell you, I knew you'd just get in the way. But I thought… it was time."

He paused, the sharpness in his gaze softening into something calmer, something weathered by years of watching over her. "I also know your family has never been an easy place to stand," he went on, voice low but steady. "And when you finally stepped back from all of it, I hoped this place might feel like somewhere you chose for yourself, not somewhere you escaped to. You've spent enough of your life tending to everyone else's turmoil. You deserve a corner of the world that steadies you in return."

But it was a thing, this was a huge thing and Frankie felt the weight of it in her hands as she stared at the keys… keys that opened more than just doors.

"I redid the wiring, fixed the roof," Pete went on, a little gruff now. "Even mended that crooked door. It's not fancy, but it's yours if you want it." It was more than a gift. It was an offering. A quiet way of saying, I see you. She flung her arms around him before she could stop herself, startled by the flood of gratitude rising in her chest.

"Alright, alright," he grumbled, waving her off with a mock scowl. "Let an old man breathe."

Then, muttering just loud enough to hear, "You're practically my kid. Least I can do is keep a roof over your head. Just don't fill the place with squirrels and raccoons, alright?"

Frankie grinned, already thinking about the possum family behind the compost bin.

"No promises."

They weren't related by blood, but that hardly mattered. What they shared was something sturdier. Family, Frankie had learned, didn't always come with last names or framed portraits. Sometimes it handed you old brass keys and mumbled something about "just makin' sure the pipes don't freeze."

That key didn't just unlock a door. It opened her sanctuary nestled at the edge of Pete's sprawling kingdom. His land reached farther than most folks realized. Wildflower fields unraveled into orchards tangled with time. Gravel paths glimmered in the late sun. The greenhouses stood like glass cathedrals, catching and cradling the light as though they understood its preciousness.

At the heart of it all, the nursery itself, Willow & Sage. A place so alive it felt like the earth itself had taken a deep breath and started to sing. Flowers bloomed defiantly out of season. Herbs flourished in impossible soil. Locals swore Pete had cut a deal with Gaia herself. Frankie never needed proof. She lived the magic daily. She felt it in the warm weight of soil between her fingers, in the rustle of leaves greeting her by name, in the way the wind shifted just before a customer said aloud what they came for.

This felt like home.

The soft clink of ceramic against wood jolted her back. Frankie blinked as the memory slipped away like tidewater over sun-warmed sand. Chalupa sat exactly where he'd been, tail flicking with exaggerated impatience, as if to say, finished time-traveling? Good, you've got work to do. She exhaled, lips twitching into a smile as she reached again for the watering can, steadier now. The owl. The dreams. That low hum in her chest, thrumming like distant thunder. Something was stirring beneath the surface and if Chalupa knew more than he let on, which of course he did, he wasn't sharing just yet.

"All right, I'm coming," she muttered, voice scratchy with the weight of memory.

She shot the cat a look and lifted the can with a soft grunt. The scent of rosemary and damp soil grounded her fully in the present, though the warmth of the past still clung like sunlight on skin. *Willow & Sage* wasn't just a place she worked, it was where she had taken root and this morning? The air felt thick with possibility.

She finished her rounds with methodical care, checking the soil of her favorites twice, brushing aphids from mint with the hem of her sleeve, and whispering encouragement to a stubborn patch of lemon balm. By the time the sun had fully stretched across the greenhouse roof, her hands were smudged with earth, and Chalupa had long since disappeared, no doubt off to judge someone else's life choices from a windowsill.

Later, with the afternoon leaning soft against the hills, Frankie followed the winding path home. At the farthest edge of the property, beyond lavender fields humming with bees and gardens quilted in herbs and color, stood the old carriage house. Time had softened its edges, the beams bowed slightly, the roof wore a patchwork of moss and stubborn ivy, and the porch steps creaked with charming protest, but still it stood, sure of itself, rooted deeper than most folks guessed. When the wind stirred the trees, the place seemed to sigh, soft, steady, like an old soul remembering how to dream. Inside, her little apartment received her like a long-held breath finally released. Boots were toed off and left by the door, nestled in a familiar heap beside a basket brimming with mismatched scarves and dirt-dusted garden gloves.

In the kitchen window, dried orange slices spun gently in the breeze. A string of copper bells chimed whenever the wind nudged them just right. Frankie hadn't so much decorated as nested, every item placed with memory, intention, or whim. The plants curled and cascaded from every ledge and nook. Lavender swung from the rafters. Rosemary thrived in repurposed teapots. Tiny tinctures lined the windowsill like bottled moonlight. The whole space glowed with quiet aliveness, a home steeped in presence. The kettle went on with a comforting hiss, chamomile steeping in her favorite mug, bright orange with a tiny green frog painted at the bottom, waiting patiently as always to say hello. Frankie settled into the hush like a pebble finding the softest curve of a riverbed. Sometimes she read, sometimes she didn't. More often, she curled up with her legs tucked beneath her and simply listened, to the wind threading through leaves, the beams above murmuring their wooden secrets, the house breathing in time with the night. She spoke to her plants, of course. Lit a beeswax candle that smelled faintly of honey and pine.

Frankie's carriage house felt stitched together from sunlight and second chances. The floorboards creaked in familiar ways. The air always carried the faint perfume of lavender and honeyed tea. The walls leaned in like old friends, warm and forgiving. It wasn't fancy, but it wrapped around her like a story passed down through generations, frayed at the edges and all the more beloved for it. Pothos vines dangled from beams and shelves, their leaves reaching lazily toward the light. Books lived in half-toppling stacks, nestled beside chipped teacups, jars of dried herbs, and a teetering tower of half-used notebooks. Nothing matched. Everything mattered. And when the day had fully exhaled, when the stars blinked into being and the trees stood watch in reverent silence, Frankie slipped beneath her patchwork quilt. Chalupa curled at her feet like punctuation, purring with the contentment of something ancient and satisfied, and she let the quiet draw her under.

That night, sleep came easy; it wrapped around her like something handmade and well-worn, lavender-scented and moon-soaked. The windows were left ajar, just wide enough to welcome the rustle of branches and the gentle song of crickets. Rain arrived like a secret, soft and slow, tapping the glass as though asking permission to enter her dreams. As Chalupa snored gently, tucked into the bend of her knees, Frankie drifted deeper, where waking and dreaming blurred like ink in rainwater.

In her dream, she stood barefoot in the woods, but it wasn't any forest she knew. The trees were the kind spoken of in old stories, creatures of bark and breath from the imagination of the first storytellers, rising impossibly tall, their trunks as wide as cottages, their canopies stitched with a faint silver-green glow, as though the moon had threaded its light through their leaves. The moss beneath her feet was soft and warm, plush as velvet, pulsing faintly as if alive. The air was thick with golden dust, as though the entire forest had been lifted from a forgotten fairytale and set inside a snow globe of starlight.

Fireflies hovered slow and steady around her, lanterns held aloft by invisible hands. She walked forward without knowing why, only that every step felt familiar, like a memory she hadn't made yet. A path unfurled beneath her bare feet, lined with flowers she couldn't name, petals blooming in shades she was certain didn't exist outside dreams. The whole wood seemed to hum around her, watchful, ancient, full of something waiting.

She saw her, a woman stood in the clearing ahead, her back turned. Her long, unruly hair spilled down her back in waves of silver and shadow, shifting like ivy in the breeze. She wore a gown the color of rain and moonlight, and wherever she stepped, blossoms unfurled beneath her feet, soft blue, ghost-white, violet like twilight. Frankie's breath caught, her heart fluttering against her ribs. There was something about the woman, something old and familiar, like a forgotten song she used to hum in her sleep. She couldn't explain it, only that it felt like standing in front of a mirror that didn't show her as she was, but as she might someday be. The woman turned slowly, her movement as fluid as light across water, when their eyes met, Frankie felt the air shift, the world tilt just slightly on its axis.

In that gaze, she saw echoes of herself, a reflection not of who she was, but who she could become. Strength threaded through softness, sorrow folded carefully into grace and beneath it all, a quiet, steady kind of magic. She smiled, a knowing, gentle thing, and extended her hand.

When she finally spoke, her voice moved through the trees like wind through tall grass, low and sure, threaded with kindness and something older still.

"The roots remember, even when the knowing hasn't found us yet."

The words lingered in the air and then the dream began to dissolve, soft at first, like mist unraveling at dawn. Frankie reached out, desperate to hold onto it, the light fractured and the forest folded in on itself, slipping like water through her fingers.

She woke with a quiet gasp, heart thudding hard against her ribs. Rain tapped the window, a soft, steady rhythm, like the dream trying to return. The room was dark, familiar, yet charged, as if the air had been rewound and set humming by unseen hands. At the foot of the bed, Chalupa blinked once, unimpressed. He gave a faint *mrrrp* and resumed his purring.

Frankie sat up slowly, the quilt pooling at her waist. The details had already slipped away, but the resonance remained, a low hum in her chest, a whisper brushing the edges of sense as if the dream still breathed against her skin. She pressed a palm to her heart, listening for what lingered in the quiet. She didn't know what it meant. Not yet. But something had begun.

When she opened her eyes, the cottage sat exactly as it always had: steady, small, and familiar, holding the night's hush like a teacup holds warmth. Yet beyond the window, the garden stirred. Moonlight sifted over the leaves, and the plants responded, blooming in slow, impossible pulses of color, as though her dreaming had seeped through the seams of the world and rooted itself in the soil. Petals glowed soft as lanterns, trembling with a magic that did not belong to night or morning, but to whatever had just woken within her.

Chapter 2

Morning arrived like a slow breath, spilling gold across the edges of Frankie's sleep until the darkness thinned. The dream lingered again, clinging in a way that felt deliberate this time, warm against her skin, bright behind her ribs, a half-formed warning wrapped in wonder. By the time the sky blushed pink and orange over the hills, she had tried to fold it away with all the other nameless things, but its pulse still thrummed beneath her skin, a quiet insistence she couldn't quite shake.

Outside, the world stirred with purpose. Something in the air felt watchful, as if the land had risen early to see what she would do next. The day didn't wait, and neither did the plants. Frankie swung her legs from the bed. At the foot, Chalupa blinked once and offered a grumbly *mrrrp*, the unmistakable sound of a creature who believed he, personally, was keeping the realm in order.

"Yeah, yeah," she murmured, rubbing the soft spot behind his ears. "Some of us have responsibilities, you know. You can be dramatic later."

Chalupa blinked once, slow as a monk to ring morning bells, then tucked his head back down, purr rumbling as if to say, *we'll see about that.*

She didn't bother with breakfast. Mornings like this, when her thoughts felt too loud and she felt too restless, there was only one place she wanted to be. She grabbed her keys, shrugged into her work jacket, and slipped out the door, already picturing the silence of the greenhouse waiting for her. The gravel crunched beneath her boots as she crossed the path lined with thyme and creeping phlox, the cool morning air nipping gently at her cheeks. She could hear the soft murmur of bees waking in the lavender rows, the hush of leaves brushing against each other like whispered secrets. By the time she reached the greenhouse, the restlessness inside her had settled.

The greenhouse felt still when she stepped inside, the world holding its breath in that fragile hour before the day fully shook itself awake. Dew clung to the glass panes like tiny pearls strung on invisible thread, and beams of pale sunlight filtered through the mist, casting soft, dappled patterns across the soil-smudged floor. Everything glowed faintly, the air thick with the quiet hum of things growing, waiting, listening. Frankie moved to the center of it all, where ivy ribbons trailed lazily from above and delicate strings of pearls spilled down in gentle arcs. Moss curled lush and velvety against the driftwood frames, the kind of green that felt older than memory. The air was heavy with the scent of damp earth, blooming orchids, a curl of mint from the herb bench, and something wilder beneath it all, an alive, unnameable note, like the whisper of rain just before it falls. Frankie drew in a slow breath, feeling her chest loosen as the garden settled around her, familiar and steadying in a way nothing else was. It didn't press heavy with expectation or hum with disapproval. This was the only place where the world stopped asking her to be something she wasn't. Her fingers moved in quiet rhythm with the morning, dirt-smudged, sure, shaping green things to lean toward the light. She adjusted the angle of a string-of-pearls vine, its tiny, round leaves catching the soft sunlight like a trail of emerald moons. Her apron wore the map of her morning, streaks of moss, smudges of honest earth, a lavender bloom crushed gently against one hip. Loose curls had already begun to tumble from her messy knot, framing her face in wild, sunlit wisps. She drew in a long breath, letting the scent of growing things settle deep in her chest, letting the hush of it soothe something restless inside her. She reached for a sprig of creeping thyme, coaxing its tiny leaves into place along the driftwood, when the stillness cracked, just slightly followed by a vibration in her pocket. Her phone.

The buzz was soft, but it rippled through the greenhouse like a pebble tossed into still water. Frankie flinched, just enough to break the rhythm. The vines seemed to pause with her, as if even they were holding their breath. She sighed, a breath more weary than annoyed, and wiped her hands on her apron, pressing damp soil into older stains. She already knew who it would be. She could hear the voice in her head, clipped, polished, coated in just enough honey to hide the bite.

Her mother.

It would be another reminder or another expectation to show up scrubbed and smiling, folded neatly into something small and pleasant. Frankie rolled her eyes, thumb hovering over the screen, ready to ignore it like she had all week. When she glanced down, it wasn't her mother's name.

Nono.

Her breath caught, this was both unexpected and somehow... worse. She stared at the name, thumb frozen above the screen. She didn't want to answer. Nono had never been anything but cold and sharp edges, a man who spoke in orders, not invitations. Still, she answered, because she always did.

"Hello?" she said softly, voice cold against the warmth of the greenhouse.

"Francesca." His voice crackled across the line, rough as gravel underfoot. No greeting, no pause, no softness, just the sharp edge of her name, cutting clean through the air like an arrow meant to shatter whatever peace she'd managed to gather. It was nothing new. This was the grandfather she had always known, never warm, never gentle, never anything resembling the soft edges other families seemed to have. Just cold precision, as familiar to her as her own breath.

Frankie's fingers tightened around the phone. "Hi, Nono. Everything okay?"

"I need help Saturday. Early." It wasn't a request, this was a summons.

She swallowed. "Okay... help with what?" There was a pause, too long, too heavy then he said it.

"*Grimwyck.*"

The name dropped between them like a stone in a still pond. The greenhouse seemed to still around her, the vines leaning in, the warm air holding its breath. Frankie's stomach twisted, something cold unfurling beneath her ribs. Grimwyck Manor. If a place could have a taste, it would be like dust and old secrets, heavy on the tongue. The name alone felt like it belonged to another century, like it should only be spoken in a whisper or not at all. Frankie straightened instinctively, her pulse ticking a little faster.

"I thought the family agreed to just..." she tried to keep her voice light, but it snagged anyway, "let it be."

Nono's reply was flat, sharp as a closing door. "It's time. Seven o'clock."

Frankie opened her mouth, a protest already forming, but before she could speak, he added, "Bring coffee."

She huffed out a breath despite herself. "I'll even bring a danish if you're nice."

The sound he made wasn't quite a laugh. More a sharp, dismissive snort, the closest he ever came to anything resembling amusement. Then the line clicked dead, abrupt and final, leaving the greenhouse too quiet, the air too heavy, as though the old walls and older ghosts had all leaned in at once. Frankie stared at her phone. The gentle buzz of bees continued around her, steady and golden, but the sound no longer soothed. His voice lingered instead, that name, *Francesca,* clinging to her like a shadow that wasn't hers.

Grimwyck Manor.

That house wasn't just old and abandoned, it was woven into the town's folklore like a cautionary tale, something you didn't touch unless you wanted to be touched back. It sat at the farthest edge of town beneath a crown of gnarled trees, wrapped in ivy and rumor. The iron gate, always slightly ajar, looked less like an invitation and more like a dare. Everyone had a story about Grimwyck, the whispered kind, passed between friends at sleepovers or over steaming mugs of coffee in the diner. Ghost stories, mostly but to Frankie, it wasn't just the haunted house at the end of the street, it was family. She was the first DiLegna in generations who hadn't been raised within those ivy-strangled walls. Her mother, Corrine, prim, cold, and all sharp edges, had packed up shortly before Frankie was born and never looked back. If Grimwyck came up, her lips would tighten and her voice would turn brittle.

"That house was never meant to be a home," her mother would say, always with a look that ended the conversation before it had a chance to take shape. Her father, Anthony, rarely offered more than a quiet nod in agreement. He was a man of few words and even fewer actions, content to echo Corrine's opinions rather than question them, as though repetition alone might make them true.

Frankie grew up in a beige house where everything felt scrubbed of personality and sealed against change. The walls were clean but bare, the furniture chosen for durability rather than comfort, and nothing was ever allowed to look lived in. Curiosity was treated like a flaw, questions like inconveniences. She learned early that asking about the manor or the family history only tightened the air around her, so she stopped asking. Silence became the house's defining feature, thick and heavy, pressing in from all sides, discouraging movement, discouraging growth.

Grimwyck Manor loomed at the center of that silence, a place she was taught to regard with a mix of reverence and avoidance. It had belonged to her great-grandparents, Eugenia and Milton, and to generations before them, each branch of the family tree rooting itself deeper into its cold stone halls. Eugenia existed in Frankie's memory as a woman of thin smiles and sharper glances, her voice precise and sour, wrapped in lace that never softened her edges. Milton was tall, rigid, and wordless, a presence more than a person, standing watch in every recollection like a marker for something buried and unresolved.

Holidays at Grimwyck were quiet, airless affairs that smelled of harsh cleaners and mothballs instead of cinnamon or pine. The rooms were always colder than they should have been, the furniture stiff and unyielding, arranged more for display than use. Frankie remembered being reminded constantly to sit still, to lower her voice, to keep her hands folded. She was told not to run, not to fidget, not to touch anything that hadn't been expressly offered. Even her breathing seemed subject to scrutiny, as though taking up too much space might disturb something delicate and dangerous.

She did not belong there, and on some level, she had always known it. Frankie was bright where the house was dull, restless where it demanded stillness, alive in ways that place did not allow. Nothing in that environment invited growth or warmth, and she learned to make herself smaller in response, folding inward to survive a space that had never been built to hold her.

When Eugenia passed, Milton followed within weeks, as though the silence had finally swallowed him whole. The once-grand manor folded inward. Curtains stayed drawn. Dust settled like snowfall, slow and constant. And then came the whispers. At first they were just stories, easily dismissed, the kind schoolchildren tell because they want a place to pin their shadows on. But the tales lingered. Sounds in a house where no one lived. Lights in windows long since dark. A shape glimpsed between the curtains, too tall, too still.

Kids dared each other to touch the front gate, shrieking when it groaned. Mail carriers crossed the street to avoid it. Even Frankie, as a child, had learned to pedal faster when passing Grimwyck, holding her breath like silence might make her invisible. It wasn't just ordinary childhood fear. It was a deeper wrongness, a prickle under her skin that whispered look away, even when she couldn't explain why. The manor always felt braced, guarded, as though something inside it was waiting to be found.

Sometimes she had the strangest sense that the house was keeping secrets, holding them close the way a person might clutch something precious or damning. Which made no sense at all. Houses couldn't keep secrets and yet Grimwyck always felt like it did. Now, years later, with the clarity of adulthood and all she had learned since, the question pressed cold against the back of her mind. Had the house been holding its breath, too?

The rest of the day passed in a restless hum, the hours slipping through Frankie's fingers like loose soil. She repotted a dozen succulents, rearranged the ferns, twice, then accidentally drowned the marjoram while her thoughts wandered where she didn't want them to go. Her hands moved on autopilot, but her mind kept circling back, over and over, to the weight of that phone call. Grimwyck echoed like the groan of an old house settling, quiet but impossible to ignore. By the time she finally locked up for the evening, the sky outside had softened to dusky hues of lavender and rose, the last blush of daylight brushing the tops of the trees like a fading promise. The greenhouse behind her stood in silhouette, its glass panes catching the last glimmers of light, the scent of damp earth and green things lingering on her skin. Her stomach gave a loud, unapologetic grumble, a clear protest that she'd skipped lunch entirely. The thought of cooking felt like too much effort, too much noise in a brain already too full. With a sigh, Frankie walked across Pete's property, the path familiar beneath her feet, the hush of twilight settling around her.

Her dusty Jeep waited at the edge of the gravel drive. She tossed her bag onto the passenger seat, climbed in, and rolled the windows down. The cool evening air slipped in immediately, tugging at her loose curls and carrying the faint scent of lavender and damp grass. Behind the greenhouse, Pete was still working, his silhouette steady among the rows. He must've heard the engine because he straightened, wiped his hands on his jeans, and walked over with that unhurried gait of his.

"You heading out?" he asked, voice low and even.

"Just into town," Frankie said. "Won't be long."

Pete nodded, though his eyes lingered on her a beat longer than necessary. "Watch that ridge road," he said, gruff as ever. "Dew settles early this time of year. Makes the asphalt slick once the sun's gone."

Frankie almost smiled. She knew this land, knew how dusk pulled the cold out of the hills, how the moisture gathered in sheets over the pavement, but this was Pete's kind of caring: weather warnings in place of softness.

"I'll be careful," she promised.

"Hmm." He tipped his chin toward her, the closest he came to admitting he worried. "Text me when you're home."

The words came out rough, but steady, his own version of affection, carved sharp at the edges.

She reached out and squeezed his forearm. "I will."

"Good." He stepped back, pretending to busy himself with a stack of pots. "Go on, then."

Frankie eased down the drive, gravel crunching beneath the tires. In the rearview mirror, Pete remained framed in the greenhouse glow, shoulders squared, watching her go the way he always did. He lifted a hand, a small, steady gesture he'd offered from the very first day she arrived here, a quiet ritual of looking out for her. She lifted her own hand in return, a soft wave through the open window. Pete was always there. Always waving her off. Always making sure she got where she needed to go before he turned back to his work. Only then did she let the breeze sweep the weight from her shoulders, just for a while.

The Cozy Cup Diner's neon sign flickered to life in the distance, buzzing faintly like a tired heartbeat against the growing dark. It glowed soft pink and gold, a beacon for the weary, the restless, and anyone who needed a plate of something warm and familiar. The scent hit her before she even turned into the lot, fried bacon, fresh coffee and the unmistakable sweetness of fresh baked pies cooling. Saturday she'd face the ghosts, tonight, she just needed a BLT with perfectly crispy bacon. She might even make it a double. The diner had been a beloved local spot for as long as Frankie could remember. Its vinyl booths invited patrons to sink into comfort, while the chalkboard menu, unchanged for at least a decade, listed classic favorites. Each table boasted a mini jukebox, chrome relics offering three plays for a quarter, a comforting mix of oldies and current hits that somehow always knew just what you needed to hear.

The diner was renowned for its fresh-baked pies, each one proudly displayed in a floor-to-ceiling carousel that revolved with the pomp of a slow-spinning festival ride and just a hint of theatrical flair. Inside, slices rested beneath soft lights: classic apple with its sugared lattice crackling lightly at the edges, maple pecan rich with a thick caramel-set topping that promised trouble, and the famous chocolate chip cookie pie so decadently stuffed it probably should've come with a permit and a warning label.

Two smaller carousels graced the counter, each no taller than Frankie's shoulder and twice as charming. One was shaped like an old carnival wheel, its tiers painted in faded reds and creams, holding slices of berry crumble, peach ginger, and a lemon custard so bright it practically winked. The other was a polished chrome number from the sixties, all retro curves and soft teal accents. It showcased miniature pies: cherry hand pies with glossy tops, tiny key lime tarts piped with clouds of whipped cream, and cinnamon-sugar apple pockets still warm enough to fog the glass. Frankie could never resist them, not that she ever tried. Pie wasn't just dessert; it was a full-fledged food group, the backbone of her personal food pyramid, and possibly her primary love language.

Sliding into her usual booth by the window, she took in the soft amber lighting and the comforting hum of conversation that blended with the clink of plates and the gentle sizzle from the kitchen. The place felt like an embrace, sweetened by sugar and nostalgia. Right on cue, Marcy, her favorite waitress and, in Frankie's opinion, a low-key oracle with a psychic link to caffeine cravings, appeared table-side with the coffee pot before Frankie could even open her mouth.

"Long day?" Marcy inquired, arching a penciled-in brow.

Frankie sighed, nodding. "You could say that."

Marcy poured the coffee, the rich aroma mingling with the diner's ambient scents, and tucked her order pad back into her apron. "Your usual?"

"Please and if you can convince the kitchen, extra crispy fries?"

Winking conspiratorially, Marcy replied, "I've got my ways."

She turned and disappeared with the kind of graceful efficiency only seasoned diner staff seemed to possess. As Frankie waited, her gaze drifted to the pie carousel. Something about it always pulled her in, the slow, steady rotation, the way each slice appeared like a tiny reveal in a story she hadn't quite read yet. The tiers turned with soft clicks, offering up glossy berry fillings, sugared crusts, and steam-fogged glass, and Frankie found herself watching them the way some people watched ocean waves. Predictable, soothing, a small promise that something sweet still existed in the world. She made a mental note to save room for a slice. After all, it had been that kind of day.The front bell jingled, and Frankie's stomach dropped before she even turned her head. That laugh, sweet and sharp at the same time, like a meringue with a vinegar bite.

Cathy Russo.

Cathy had been a longtime friend of Frankie's mother, though "friend" was a generous term. She was more of a social climber with a syrupy smile and a mean streak dressed in pastels. Frankie kept her eyes on her coffee as Cathy swept into the diner, pastel-clad and over-perfumed, with her daughter Stephanie trailing behind like a nervous duckling. They didn't notice her at first, until Cathy's gaze swept the diner and landed on Frankie's booth like a heat-seeking missile.

"Oh, hello, Frankie," Cathy chirped, her eyes skimming Frankie's attire. "I see you're still embracing that... earthy style."

Frankie's smile tightened. "Hi, Cathy," she said, voice sweet with a dash of venom. "I see you've decided to bring back Pepto-Bismol chic. Bold move."

Cathy's grin widened, oblivious to the jab, as she slid into the booth behind Frankie's.

Stephanie followed with a strained smile and eyes that refused to meet Frankie's.

"You know," Cathy said, her voice pitched for maximum projection, "I always say a woman should take care of her appearance, especially if she's still trying to catch a husband."

Frankie took a deliberate sip of her coffee. "Well, Cathy, some of us are more interested in cultivating our minds than hunting for husbands," she said lightly, but with an edge. "I've got a stack of books waiting for me, a thriving plant collection, and a cat with abandonment issues who expects me home every night. But thanks for the life advice."

A few amused glances flicked her way from other tables, locals who were well-acquainted with Cathy's unsolicited commentary and Frankie's withering comebacks. Frankie turned to Stephanie and offered a warm smile, her voice softer now.

"It's really good to see you Steph, I was just about to ask if they let you out unsupervised, but then I saw her." She tilted her head toward Cathy with a mock conspiratorial grin.

Stephanie let out a sudden laugh, quiet, surprised, and real. It slipped out before she could stop it. Cathy's head snapped around, eyes narrowing at her daughter like she'd just giggled during a funeral.

"Sorry," Stephanie mumbled, straightening quickly, but a flicker of amusement lingered in her eyes. Frankie gave her a tiny wink.

Cathy, oblivious, waved a hand. "Oh, Frankie. Always the *free spirit.*"

Frankie chuckled, lifting her coffee cup in a mock toast. "Guilty as charged."

But Cathy wasn't finished. She leaned in like she was about to share a juicy secret.

"Have you heard? Stephie's getting married in the spring. A lovely boy, very respectable. He's the Chief Financial Officer at a major firm. Not one of those... creative types." She didn't have to look directly at Frankie for the message to land.

Frankie snorted softly. "Imagine that," she said, voice syrupy with faux admiration. "A man who can balance the books and crush souls in one package. Nice." Stephanie made a small choking sound, quickly muffled by her napkin.

Cathy's eyes narrowed ever so slightly, but she pushed on with a brittle smile. "I'm just saying, some of us have responsibilities."

Frankie opened her mouth, then closed it. This wasn't new. Cathy had been lobbing passive-aggressive grenades at her since junior high. Still, today's barbs landed a little sharper than usual. Luckily, Marcy appeared like divine intervention, armed with a plate of food.

"One BLT with fries, extra salty, just like your soul," she said with a wink, setting the plate in front of Frankie.

Frankie grinned, the tension draining from her shoulders. "Who needs a husband when I've got you bringing me food, Marcy?"

Marcy laughed, a bright, genuine sound. "Darn right."

She turned to Cathy's table, her tone slipping into a more professional register. "Can I get y'all something, or are you just here for the floor show?"

Cathy's smile thinned. "Two sweet teas."

"Coming right up," Marcy said, and sashayed off.

Frankie dug into her fries, savoring the crisp crunch. Cathy muttered something about "standards slipping" and "manners," but Frankie tuned it out. She wasn't here to make nice. She was here for fried food and quiet, and maybe, just maybe, to shake off the weirdness of that phone call. She'd nearly finished eating when Cathy struck again.

"You know," she said casually, "I heard your grandfather is finally dealing with the old house. Such a shame, really. That property could've been worth something, if it hadn't been so let go."

Frankie paused mid-bite, watching as Stephanie shifted in her seat, just a tiny adjustment, the kind that signaled a maternal embarrassment was incoming.

"Mom," Stephanie said at last, the word long and thin, laced with polite exasperation like she was holding back an eye roll by sheer force of will. It was the softest rebellion imaginable, hardly more than a spark, but it still made Frankie bite back a smile. Stephanie could navigate a crisis with perfect poise, yet one dramatic comment from her mother turned her into a frazzled debutante trying not to combust.

But Cathy was rolling now. "Of course, some people don't understand the importance of legacy. Of keeping things nice. You let things go, they rot."

Frankie set down her sandwich and turned slowly. “You’re absolutely right,” she said sweetly. “Things do rot, especially when they’ve been full of crap for decades.”

Cathy blinked, Stephanie choked again. Marcy returned just in time, setting down the two sweet teas with the flourish of a bartender delivering a shot to someone who’d just lost a bet.

“You good, hon?” she asked Frankie.

“Better now,” Frankie said, eyes still on Cathy.

Marcy smirked. “Well, let me know if you need anything else. I’ve got a fresh pie cooling in the back, blueberry. I can box a slice for the road.”

Frankie softened. “I’d love that.”

Marcy nodded and wandered off, humming under her breath. Cathy muttered something to Stephanie about “bad influences,” but Frankie didn’t care. She finished her dinner, paid her tab, and accepted her boxed pie with a quiet “thank you” that meant more than Marcy probably realized.

Stepping out into the cool evening air, Frankie tilted her face to the sky. Dusk had softened the edges of the world, painting the horizon in hazy shades of lavender and gold. The first stars blinked gently to life overhead, like someone had stitched tiny lanterns into the fabric of twilight. A breeze stirred, brushing her curls across her cheek and carrying the scent of fresh-cut grass and honeysuckle. It wasn’t just the end of a day, it felt like the moment before a page turns. She made her way to the Jeep, the air crisp against her skin, the pie warm against her palm. The engine rumbled to life, steady and familiar, and she rolled down the windows to let the night in. The winding drive back to the carriage house never failed to soothe her, the roads curved gently past open fields kissed with the glow of fireflies. Crickets played their nighttime song from the tall grass, and the occasional hoot of an owl echoed through the trees. She let her arm rest against the edge of the window, fingers trailing the wind as the headlights brushed over patches of wildflower and the gravelly lane leading to Pete’s land. It was quiet out here, peaceful in the way only places wrapped in trees and memory could be. The lavender fields whispered under the moonlight as she passed, and in the distance, the soft hum of bees lingering late at their hives seemed to fold into the night

By the time she reached the carriage house, the stars had multiplied above her, crowding the sky in twinkling constellations. She parked beneath the leaning oak and stepped out, her boots crunching lightly over the path worn smooth by years of her coming and going. She unlocked the door, and the moment it creaked open on its slightly crooked hinges, she was met with a throaty meow of greeting. Chalupa, with his one crimped ear, a souvenir from a long-ago encounter with either a particularly bold squirrel or a wayward garden hose, emerged from the dim hallway like a furry loaf of disapproval wrapped in affection. He blinked up at her, tail flicking once before weaving himself between her legs in figure-eights, purring like a tiny engine that ran on smug satisfaction.

"Hey, buddy," Frankie murmured, setting her pie box and bag down on the entryway bench and crouching to scoop him up.

His fur was warm and slightly fragrant, carrying the faint, comforting scent of cat nip from the potted plant he liked to nap beside in the windowsill. She pressed her cheek to his head and exhaled slowly, grounding herself in the soft, familiar weight of him. She nudged the door shut with her hip and leaned back against it for a moment, letting the quiet of home fold around her. Outside, the wind rustled through the trees like an old lullaby. Inside, everything held its breath, the tick of the wall clock, the creaking of the rafters and the scent of herbs still lingering in her clothes. It was peaceful, it was hers still, something stirred in her chest, a quiet flutter, like the wind shifting before a storm. A knowing. It wasn't loud, not yet, just a whisper at the edges of her thoughts, the kind of feeling that didn't announce itself with trumpets but with a held breath. Like a door had opened somewhere out of sight. Like the trees had paused their rustling to listen. Something was coming. She didn't know what, or when, or why, but whatever it was, it was already on its way.

With a sigh, Frankie walked into the kitchen. She reached instinctively for her favorite mug, the bright orange one with the tiny green frog grinning up from the bottom, and spooned in a heap of chamomile. As the kettle began to hum, the faint scent of apple blossoms drifted through the room, stirring the edges of her thoughts. A few minutes later, she settled onto the couch, quilt tucked over her legs, steam curling from her mug in slow, ghostlike ribbons. Chalupa, ever the sentinel, curled beside her like a striped comma, his purr low and steady, as though he were trying to soothe the entire world into stillness. She traced her fingers along his warm back, letting memory creep in. He'd been her scrappy little shadow since childhood, found behind the greenhouse on a rain-slick afternoon, all knobby limbs and oversized yowls. From the moment she bundled him in an old towel and tucked him under her coat, he'd decided she was his. Over the years he'd grown rounder, grumpier, more opinionated, but never any farther from her side than he absolutely had to be. But tonight, even Chalupa's familiar weight couldn't chase away the unease coiling at the base of her spine. Thoughts of Grimwyck slipped through the quiet like cold fingers, and Nono's voice echoed in her mind, gruff, clipped, final, dragging the past behind it like a shadow that had never quite learned to let go. Frankie sipped her tea slowly, willing the warmth to settle the unrest gathering under her ribs.

The house settled into evening, lamps lowering to a softer glow. Frankie was aware of the quiet in a way she couldn't explain, wondering whether the unease clinging to the room belonged to nothing more than darkness… or to the beginning of a something she couldn't yet name. She drew a slow breath, held it, then released it, letting the silence rest where it would.

Morning would come. Of that she was sure. But she knew, with a certainty she didn't trust, that it wouldn't come easily.

Chapter 3

Saturday morning arrived with a silence that clung to everything. Mist draped across the hills like a shawl, softening the edges of the world until even the trees seemed unsure where they ended. The air felt thick, expectant, like it, too, was holding its breath. Frankie took the back roads, the winding ones lined with trees that leaned just a little too close, as though listening. Her thermos of coffee steamed in the cupholder, and a brown paper bag of still-warm pastries sat on the passenger seat, fragrant with cinnamon and sugar. A peace offering, maybe, or just comfort food for a long-overdue confrontation. The trees here were taller, older, their limbs knotted as if they remembered more than they let on. The road narrowed until it felt less like she was driving it and more like it was funneling her, quietly, intentionally, toward something she wasn't entirely ready to face. She turned down the long-forgotten drive, tires crunching over fallen branches and last year's leaves, the kind of debris that only gathers when no one has come calling in far too long. Wild grass swayed on either side, brushing the undercarriage as if trying to slow her down… or hold her in place. The temperature dipped when she passed beneath the final arch of trees, a sudden pocket of cold that prickled her skin. The birds, lively just moments before, slipped into a hush.

Grimwyck Manor came into view. It didn't loom, it lingered. Tall and stone-faced, the manor looked less like a house and more like a secret someone had tried to bury under ivy and forgetfulness. Vines clung to the façade with slow, patient determination, crawling up the walls as though carrying stories no one had asked to hear. The windows were streaked and shuttered, reflecting nothing back. The porch sagged at one corner, and the wrought-iron fence leaned forward, not in welcome, but in weariness, as though even it had grown tired of standing guard over whatever waited inside. The yard, once trimmed within an inch of its life, had surrendered completely to chaos. Azaleas exploded in tangled pink and fuchsia, blooming like they'd been waiting for a rebellion. Moss softened the crumbling stone path, and thorny vines twisted through rusted trellises like nature was trying to reclaim every inch. It was beautiful, in that haunting, forgotten sort of way. Like something that had been waiting too long to be remembered. Frankie pulled the Jeep to a stop and stepped out, the quiet folding around her like a too-heavy coat. The air was damp, laced with the scent of wet stone and old roses, and everything felt... held. There he was, already waiting on the porch like a gargoyle carved from old grudges and older disappointments.

Nono stood with his arms crossed, his scowl set in granite. "You're late," he barked.

Frankie raised the thermos like a trophy, then gave the paper bag a little shake so the danish rustled inside.

"It's 6:55," she said brightly. "You said seven. I brought the strong stuff. And a cherry danish."

He grunted. Classic Nono. She stepped onto the porch, the boards groaning beneath her boots, loud in the early hush. Frankie eyed the vine-choked stone and shuttered windows.

"You sure about this?" she asked, half-grinning. "Still time to let the raccoons sort it out. I hear they work cheap."

Nono didn't answer, he just stood silent with his keys clenched tight in his fist, his posture suddenly rigid. His shoulders, always a little stooped with age and gravity, now held a tautness that made her pause, like something invisible had pulled him tight from the inside out. For a moment, he didn't move, not a blink. Just... still.

Frankie tilted her head, the smile fading from her lips. She'd meant to lighten the mood, to crack through his usual grumpiness with a bit of her usual charm but the way he was looking at the door, like it wasn't just wood and iron but something heavier, something waiting, sent a cold whisper through her. Then he turned and she caught his face in profile, his eyes, normally stern, held something else entirely now. Not fear, but recognition. Her chest tightened. She'd never truly felt at ease around Nono. He wasn't the cookie-baking, lap-offering kind of grandfather. He was sharp edges and clipped words. He showed up with expectations, not hugs. But this... this was something unfamiliar. The way he looked at the house, then at her, as if seeing her and seeing it in the same breath, made her feel like a piece on a board game she hadn't agreed to play.

"It's just time," he said at last, his voice low and scraped raw, like the words had clawed their way up from somewhere buried deep, someplace that hadn't seen light in years.

Frankie's playful thoughts of raccoons dissolved instantly, swallowed by the sudden weight in his tone. A chill threaded down her spine, slow and deliberate, and though she couldn't say why, her grip tightened on the thermos as if it might anchor her to something solid. Something about the way he said it... She suddenly, deeply, wished she hadn't come.

The front door creaked open like it wasn't quite ready to let them in, the hinges let out a long, complaining whine, the kind that made Frankie wince and glance back. A breath of air whooshed out from inside, stale and dense, and that old smell that clings to forgotten attics and boxes no one's dared open. It hit her like a dusty curtain, and Frankie took a step back, coughing lightly into her elbow.

"Well, that's inviting," she muttered.

It didn't feel like entering a house, it felt like stepping into a memory. One not her own, but someone else's, tucked away in a drawer for too long, curled at the corners and fading at the edges. Every surface was draped in drooping, dust-tinged sheets that stirred faintly in the breeze from the door, rising just enough to hint at the furniture sleeping beneath. High-backed chairs. Curved settees, ornate lamps with tassels long out of style. Ghostly shapes of a life once lived. The air was thick with the scent of mothballs and old paper, of wood slowly forgetting its shape. Light trickled through the heavy curtains in tired streaks of amber, catching on floating dust like gold caught mid-fall. Frankie walked into the foyer, each step creaked under her boots sounding louder than it should've. She trailed her fingers along a shrouded sideboard, raising a puff of dust before settling back into the quiet. It clung to everything, walls, portraits, silence. Nono didn't wait, of course he didn't. He just moved with the mechanical detachment of someone clocking in at a job he hated, just another item on the list to cross off. He paused only to jab a finger toward the room off the main hall.

“Start in there,” Nono said flatly, jerking his chin toward the nearest doorway. “Sort what you can, trash, donate, keep. If you’re not sure, ask.”

And with that, he vanished down the corridor, his footsteps swallowed by dust and old wood, like a shadow retreating into the bones of the house. Frankie lingered at the threshold of the parlor, squinting into the dimness. A heavy rug sprawled across the floor, its pattern so faded it looked more like the ghost of flowers than the real thing. The fireplace sat cold and hollow, its iron grate laced with cobwebs that caught the light in the muted light like forgotten lace. The silence between her and Nono wasn’t new, it had always existed in the space between spoken words and unspoken expectations. But today, it felt heavier. Denser. Like it was no longer content to be ignored.

She began to sift through the boxes. Old books with cracked spines, yellowing sheet music curled like fallen leaves. A music box that chirped out half a tune before giving up entirely. Nono had moved to the adjoining room with the kind of gruff, exasperated energy reserved for stubborn lawnmowers and people who talked too much. Every so often, he grunted about “junk” and “waste” like he was arguing with the ghosts. Frankie sorted through stacks of brittle, sun-bleached volumes and shook her head.

“This family never met a book they didn’t love,” she muttered under her breath. “It’s like a library and a mausoleum had a baby.”

The collection was strange, eclectic in a way that felt more intentional than accidental. The shelves groaned beneath the weight of everything from crumbling leather-bound Bibles to well-thumbed volumes on obscure theologies and forgotten folklore. Books on herbal remedies sat beside heavy tomes of Renaissance poetry. A slim volume on Norse runes leaned against Shakespeare’s complete works, its spine cracked with use. There were books on alchemy, guides to the language of flowers, essays on the philosophy of nature, and tucked between them all, dog-eared copies of Tolkien and Wilde. It wasn’t the kind of collection someone built casually, it was the kind of library stitched together by someone looking for answers, as if each book filled a hole, patched a gap, or tried to make sense of something too big to hold. She ran her fingers along the uneven spines, the dust clinging to her skin like ash. The air smelled faintly of old paper, lavender, and a breath of something old, soft as dust stirred from forgotten corners. A draft curled through the parlor like a long-held breath finally exhaled, soft, but deliberate. It ghosted past Frankie's cheek, cool against her skin, and tugged at the corner of a moth-eaten blanket draped in the farthest corner of the room. The fabric stirred just enough to catch her eye. Beneath it, a glint that didn't belong, that waited. She stilled as the room pressed against her, her heartbeat suddenly too loud, too present. The air around her thickened, heavy with something unspoken, something watching. The rest of the parlor, brittle furniture, yellowing books, memories stacked like dust, blurred at the edges. It was as if the house itself was holding its breath again, waiting for her to see. Before she realized she'd moved, she was crossing the room, each step as though some invisible thread had wrapped around her spine and was gently pulling her forward. Her fingers brushed the frayed edge of the blanket. She tugged it free. It slipped away with a soft sigh, pooling at her feet like surrender.

There it was, the chest crouched in the corner, silent and forgotten, like a secret too old and heavy to name. Its wood was unlike anything Frankie had ever seen: dark, rich, and faintly glowing in the gloom, its color shifting with the light, deep earthen brown to green-black, like moss beneath moonlight. Twisting runes curled across its surface like vines, forming a language she didn't know but somehow felt. The corners and hinges gleamed with heavy, ornate metalwork etched in looping symbols, not merely decorative but protective. This wasn't just a container. It hadn't been built to hold something. It had been built to keep something in.

Frankie knelt beside it, her breath shallow, fingertips hovering just above the lid. The wood radiated warmth beneath the dust, unexpected and oddly familiar, like a melody she hadn't heard in years but still knew by heart. A low hum unfurled beneath her skin, steady and patient, like something old stirring awake at last. She hesitated, the weight of the moment pressing around her, then curled her fingers around the latch and lifted the lid. The hinges groaned with age, and something else. The sound was almost a sigh, as though the chest itself were finally releasing a breath it had held too long. A scent drifted out, soft and earthy, tinged with lavender and something older, deeper. It smelled of pressed violets, rain-soaked stone, parchment, and forgotten dreams. It smelled like memory. Inside, the chest was lined with velvet so dark it seemed to drink the light, a spill of ink swallowed by shadow. Bundles of letters lay nestled within, tied in faded ribbons the color of old roses, their edges curled like dried petals. A faint trace of lavender clung to the fabric, as though the scent had been pressed into it long ago. Some envelopes bore names in looping script, others only initials, still guarding their secrets. A few brittle photographs peeked from beneath the stacks, faces half-smiling, half-lost, staring out from another time.

Frankie's gaze skimmed until her hand stilled. One photograph lay near the top, its edges worn thin from years of touch. She didn't know why, but her hand moved anyway, reaching as if drawn by a magnet. The air shifted, the parlor itself seeming to lean in, listening. Somewhere in the silence, a floorboard popped, sharp as a held breath breaking. Her fingertips brushed the glossy paper, and her breath caught. The woman in the picture stared back with a smile edged in wild mischief and something fiercer beneath, as though the photograph had failed to cage her spirit. Her curls tumbled in unruly waves around sharp cheekbones, her posture easy, almost careless. But it was her eyes. The instant Frankie met them, the world lurched. A jolt snapped up her arm, sharp and electric, the photograph alive in her grip, thrumming with a heartbeat that wasn't hers. Her chest tightened, her vision blurred, and the room tilted into silence until only the rush of blood filled her ears. Even the steady tick of the mantel clock seemed to vanish. Goosebumps rippled along her arms and with that, memory rose.

She had seen this woman before, not once, but over and over, since childhood. In the woods of her dreams, beneath silver-lit trees that whispered without wind, the figure had always waited. Frankie didn't dream often, but when she did, it was her. The woman appeared when sorrow pressed too hard or loneliness hollowed her out, slipping into Frankie's dreams as if summoned. Her presence was steady, soothing, protective, comforting in the way fairy godmothers were meant to be. Yet there was always something more, a shimmer of knowing in her eyes that made it feel less like chance and more like purpose. She could almost hear it now, that dream-forest rustling at the edge of her hearing, as though leaves stirred inside the very walls of the house. She could almost see it too, a wash of silver light glimmering at the corner of her vision. The woman's hair tangled with starlight, her eyes vast, impossibly old, impossibly kind.

More fragments surfaced. The scent of lilac where no flowers grew. Dreams that clung to her waking hours with the weight of truth. Wildflowers too bright. Moss glowing faintly at dusk. Mushrooms cupped like lanterns. And as a child, stranger things still, a dandelion puff that refused to scatter, vines creeping closer overnight as though angling toward her window, shadows leaning just slightly toward her, as if they were listening. She had always told herself it was imagination, the mind of a girl weaving stories into the world. Now, surrounded by the silence of the parlor, those fragments pressed closer. The air smelled of beeswax and dust, of rain-soaked stone and faded lavender sachets tucked away in drawers. The old clock ticked once more, slow and solemn, each beat a reminder that the room itself was watching. The house seemed to carry the same weight, thick, waiting, impossible to ignore.

This old mausoleum of a home had always unsettled her, its silence heavy, its shadows pressing until she longed to flee. But this wasn't that. This beckoned her closer. It wasn't menace, it was invitation. And instead of dread, Frankie felt an ache to stay, to peel back the layers, to understand. Yet beneath the pull was something sharper, like a current too strong to resist, one that might sweep her under if she strayed too far. Frankie knew the spark in that gaze wasn't chance, it was recognition. A thread had been drawn taut across time, and she didn't understand it yet, but she felt it in her bones, something unseen had shifted. The first stone had fallen, and the ripples were racing outward. Somewhere beneath that awe, a whisper lingered… once begun, such ripples could never be called back.

The silence thickened, pressing in until every breath scraped loud in Frankie's ears. Her pulse stumbled, uneven. A prickle crawled along the back of her neck, sharp as static. She didn't need to see it to know, someone was there. Watching. The room hadn't changed, and yet it had; the hush no longer felt empty but occupied, swollen with a presence she couldn't name. She could feel eyes on her. The fine hairs at her nape lifted. A shiver slid down her spine, and she froze, every muscle taut. The house itself seemed to notice her stillness. The walls held their breath, the velvet hush too deep. Somewhere in the rafters, wood groaned, low and tired, as though shifting under a hidden weight. A draft stirred from nowhere, faint and cool against her skin, though every window was shut tight. It was impossible to tell if it was the house leaning close, or someone inside it.

Her throat went dry, her tongue sticking to the roof of her mouth. She wanted to run, but the weight of that unseen gaze pinned her in place and before she could stop herself, she spoke into the silence. She swallowed hard, unable to look away.

"Nono?" The word left her cracked and thin, a whisper carrying too much. Behind her, footsteps halted, heavy and final. When he stepped into the doorway, his shadow stretched long across the floor, thick and weighted enough to raise the fine hairs on her arms. His gaze dropped to the chest, then to the photograph in her hands. His scowl faltered, not into softness, but into something far more dangerous. His face fractured, his jaw locking, and in his eyes, a flash of naked, unguarded truth.

"*Put. That. Back.*" His voice came slow and icy, every word deliberate. He advanced, not quickly, but with the inevitability of a door swinging shut forever.

"Who is she?" Frankie's voice cracked, raw with the hollow ache tearing open inside her, a wound she hadn't known she carried until this moment.

Nono's hand reached out, then stalled, dropping uselessly. His eyes clung to the photo as though it might scorch the air itself.

"Aoife," he said at last, the name brittle, almost broken. "My wife. Your grandmother."

Frankie reeled, breath snagging as though the air itself had thickened. The mood in the room deepened. "My... what? But I thought... "

"You thought wrong."

Her head shook, disbelief pouring through her, voice breaking. "Why have I never heard of her?"

She studied the image again, slower this time, as if it might shift under scrutiny. The resemblance was undeniable. The same eyes. The same set of her mouth. A familiarity she had spent her whole life assuming was coincidence.

"I look just like her."

The realization settled unevenly, carrying both relief and something closer to grief. For once, Frankie didn't feel like the wrong baby had been brought home from the hospital. For once, she wasn't an outlier in her own family, wondering how she'd ended up shaped so differently.

It wasn't funny. But it was grounding. Proof, at last, that she hadn't come from nowhere.

"But I do," Frankie whispered, fierceness burning through the tremor in her voice. "I need to know."

His temper cracked, sharp and final. "Enough."

He slammed the chest shut, wood crashing against wood, the echo booming like thunder in the silence.

"This doesn't concern you."

"It concerns me if I'm part of it!" Frankie surged to her feet, voice ringing, her hands trembling around the photograph. "Nono, what happened to her?"

"Leave it be, Francesca."

Without another word, he bent to lift the chest. His movements were stiff, as if his body resisted the act even as he forced it forward. His fingers gripped the sides too tightly, as though the box might sprout wings and fly from his grasp. In his haste to lift the chest, Nono didn't secure the lid properly. As he hoisted it, a small bundle, neatly tied with a faded ribbon, slipped silently from the chest and landed on the floor. The bundle lay there, half-hidden against the worn rug, while he moved toward the door, the chest clutched tightly in his arms.

Frankie's eyes snapped to them, Nono either didn't notice, or he pretended not to. Before he could turn back, Frankie moved, pushing the small stack of papers and photographs behind the curtain in one smooth motion. She kept her posture casual, but every part of her buzzed with the weight of what she'd just tucked away. He muttered something under his breath and disappeared down the hall. The moment he was gone, Frankie let herself breathe. She turned back to where the chest had been, her gaze landing on the corner where the bundle had fallen. She reached behind the curtain and pulled the neatly tied stack of letters, bound with an old, faded ribbon. A few photographs were tucked on top, Frankie's fingers traced over the top photograph.

Aoife.

The resemblance was unsettling, like looking at her own reflection, blurred and softened by time. It wasn't just the wild, dark curls or the cheekbones. It was the eyes, Frankie's eyes. Warm and watchful, bright and defiant, carrying a spark of something unruly beneath the surface. The same eyes that had always set her apart in family photographs, the same eyes she'd caught in the mirror her whole life and wondered why they didn't match anyone else's. Everyone in her family had those cold, sharp DiLegna eyes, icy blue, like polished glass. Eyes that looked through you, not at you. But not this woman, not Aoife.

Aoife's eyes were the same shade as Frankie's, deep, earthy, with that unmistakable flicker of something alive, something curious and quietly wild. For the first time in her life, Frankie felt it, a thread stretching across time, tethering her to someone who looked back at her not with judgment, but with recognition. A face that didn't ask her to shrink or smooth her edges. Growing up, she had never known her grandmother. There had been no stories, no photographs on mantels, no whispered memories passed around at family gatherings. Nothing. Her parents had perfected the art of omission, their silences carved clean and final. Frankie had learned early that some things in her family didn't exist, not because they weren't real, but because they were erased for connivence of some else's narrative and now, here was Aoife, staring back at her. Laughing. Alive. A woman Frankie might have belonged to. Her fingers drifted to the bundle of letters, tracing the edges of the ribbon. The discovery didn't just feel important, it felt like the missing pieces of herself had been waiting in the dust and shadows all along.

She slid the bundle of letters and photographs into the hollow of her stack of books, the ones she'd already set aside to take with her. She tucked them deep beneath the worn spines, her movements quick and careful, as if the walls themselves were watching. The sound of footsteps snapped her back to the present, heavy, deliberate. Nono reappeared in the doorway, his gaze sweeping over the piles she hadn't yet touched. He grunted when he spotted the boxes she'd packed.

"That's what you're taking?" His voice was clipped, but she caught the flicker of something like suspicion in his eyes.

Frankie wiped her hands on her jeans and shrugged. "Yep, just the books."

Nono snorted, shaking his head like she was the biggest fool he'd seen all day. "You don't have enough of those already?"

"Apparently not," Frankie said, forcing a smile, keeping her tone light. He gave her a sharp look at that, but said nothing, just turned and walked back down the hallway.

By the time Frankie loaded the last of the boxes into the back of her Jeep, the early evening light had started to soften, the sun sinking low enough to stretch long shadows across the gravel drive but somehow, Grimwyck still managed to hoard its darkness. The old manor slouched at the edge of the estate, its stone silhouette heavy and brooding, even as the sky blushed with the last light of day. Above the hills, clouds had begun to gather, thick and heavy, curling like smoke on the horizon. The kind of clouds that didn't just promise rain, but something restless riding in on the wind.

Frankie paused at the driver's side, one hand resting lightly on the doorframe. The stack of books she'd hidden the bundle of letters in had been the first thing she packed, tucked safely beneath worn spines of poetry, folklore, and theology, disguised as harmless clutter. She hadn't dared give Nono the chance to glance twice. Whatever truths those letters carried, they were hers now. Her gaze flicked back one last time, catching the manor's empty windows, the way the ivy curled around the stone like claws. The wind kicked up, tugging at her curls and rustling the trees around her, like the house itself was whispering something she couldn't quite hear.

She knew, deep down in her bones, that today hadn't just been about dusty books and forgotten heirlooms. She'd pulled something loose back there, something tangled and hidden that no one wanted her to find. And now that thread was unraveling, quiet and steady, like a tapestry coming undone, and she wasn't about to stop pulling.

By the time Frankie wound her way down the narrow gravel path toward Pete's farm, the sky had darkened to a bruised violet, storm clouds stacking like an argument waiting to boil over. The first drops began to fall, soft, tentative taps against her windshield, like the sky testing its weight. The storm hadn't arrived yet, but it was coming, pressing at the edges of the horizon and curling beneath her ribs. It wasn't just the weather. No, this was something else too. A different kind of storm, one she'd set in motion the moment she'd cracked open that chest. The kind that didn't just shake the windows, but rearranged everything it touched.

She pulled up beside the carriage house just as the wind began to howl, sharp and cool, carrying the sweet, sharp scent of rain. The little house stood sturdy beneath the heavy sky, its moss-covered roof and weathered beams bracing against what was coming. Frankie moved quickly, unloading the boxes one by one, her boots thudding against the porch steps, thunder rolling low in the distance like a promise. By the time she dropped the last box beside her bookshelf, the first fat drops had turned to sheets of rain rattling the windowpanes.

Her gaze flicked toward the stack. She didn't reach for them. Not tonight. Her fingertips twitched, out of habit more than intent, but she pulled her hand back before it could betray her. She'd already cracked something open today, already tugged one thread too many. The conversation with Nono, the drive to Grimwyck, the way the house had seemed to breathe around her... it had all scraped the inside of her ribs raw. Touching those papers now, letting their ghosts spill out, would only split her open further.

There was a heaviness at the base of her throat, the kind that comes when old memories stir without being invited. She wasn't sure if she felt exposed or protected by keeping her distance, maybe both. But she knew one thing for certain: tonight wasn't for unearthing ghosts. Tonight belonged to the storm. By the time she sank onto her worn sofa, the sky had unraveled completely. Rain lashed against the windows in silvery sheets, wind curling around the eaves like restless fingers searching for a way in. The old carriage house creaked and sighed with every gust, its beams shifting like bones settling into sleep, as though even the walls were bracing for whatever the night meant to bring.

Frankie cradled a steaming mug of herbal tea, one of her own calming blends, laced with chamomile, lemon balm, and a whisper of lavender. The scent wrapped around her like a lullaby, the warmth seeping into her palms, grounding her as the world outside rattled and roared. She tugged her quilt higher around her shoulders just as Chalupa leapt onto the couch with a soft *mrrrp*, circling once before curling into the familiar hollow at her side.

Thunder rolled low across the hills like a memory returning, slow and heavy. The storm was wild and sprawling, a symphony of chaos, but inside, everything was still. The kettle clicked in the background. The candles flickered. The storm, fierce and unrelenting, curled around the carriage house like an old friend, asking nothing of her except to listen....and Frankie wouldn't miss a second of it.

Chapter 4

By morning, the storm had passed, but it hadn't gone quietly. It tore through the night like a creature unchained, howling through eaves, rattling glass, flinging branches like bones. Now the world lay raw and breathless in its wake, as if the land itself was waiting to be sure it was safe to exhale. The air outside Frankie's window clung close and wet, thick with the scent of overturned soil, rain-soaked cedar, and something faintly electric, as though the sky still held the storm's fingerprints. The garden was a study in aftermath. Rain dripped steadily from the roof in rhythmic plinks. Water pooled in every hollow. The lavender, once proud, now slumped like it had seen too much. Leaves lay plastered to the ground like fallen thoughts. The trees stood darker, heavier, their bark swollen and bruised. Overhead, clouds dragged slow and low, muttering as they went.

Inside, the light was thin and pewter-gray, filtering through the lace curtains in hesitant strands. It made the room feel suspended, neither day nor night, just that peculiar in-between where time wobbled. And beneath it all, beneath the soaked earth and battered branches, something pulsed. A hum, low and uncanny, curled under her skin, as though the night had cracked open something deeper than sky. Frankie moved slowly through her little carriage house, the wooden floors creaking beneath her bare feet. Chalupa blinked lazily from his perch on the armchair, stretching like a shadow unwinding itself before tucking back into sleep. The air inside carried the scent of the night before, rain-dark wood, crushed rosemary, a trace of lavender sweetening the edges. Usually, those smells settled her, stitched her back together after long days. But not this morning. Something threaded beneath the comfort of it all, a pulse, soft but insistent, curling under her ribs like an echo she couldn't shake.

Her eyes drifted toward the stack of books by the wall and the bundle of old letters tucked safely inside. In the gray morning light, they seemed to hum with their own gravity, alive in a way she couldn't explain. Last night, she'd let the storm speak for her, let the thunder drown out the weight of what she'd uncovered. But now the silence held the room like a held breath, and those letters tugged at her thoughts like a thread she could no longer ignore.

She crossed the room, poured herself a mug of coffee, the rich, bitter scent grounding her in a way nothing else could, and made her way back to the living room. The storm had left the world washed clean and quiet, but inside her, everything still buzzed like a plucked string. Chalupa flicked his tail once, his eyes sharp and watchful, like he already knew what she was about to find. She lowered herself onto the floor, crossing her legs in the soft spill of morning light stretching across the worn floorboards. The mug of coffee rested warm in her palm while her other hand hovered just above the stack of letters, hesitant, almost afraid to touch them. She let her fingers trail over the ribbon one more time, the fabric thin and fragile beneath her touch, like it might crumble if she pulled too hard. When she finally tugged the knot loose, it slipped free without resistance, falling open like it had been waiting for her all this time.

Dozens of pages spilled beneath her fingers, each one written in looping, careful script. The ink had faded to soft browns and honeyed sepia, the edges worn thin like old petals. Some words were smudged, blurred as if they'd been traced over too many times, or written in a hurry by someone desperate to get the words out before they disappeared. Tucked between the folds were photographs, small, curled at the edges, their images softened by years of handling. Faces she didn't recognize. Places she couldn't name and pieces of a life that had been hidden from her, pressed between paper and time.

She glanced down at Chalupa, he blinked back at her from his spot on the rug, tail curled neatly around his paws, his eyes half-lidded and knowing, like he was waiting for her to stop stalling. When she didn't move right away, he let out a soft, pointed *mrrrp*, that little sound he always made when he thought she was overthinking things. Almost like he was saying, *Well? What are you waiting for?*

Frankie set her coffee aside, as she drew the first letter from the stack. The paper felt delicate in her hands, feather-light and soft at the edges. A faint scent clung to it, rosemary, lavender, and maybe black pepper, something both odd and familiar. At the top of the page, the date was decades old. Her thumb brushed over the salutation, her heart thudding quietly in her chest. It was addressed to *The Family DiLegna.* This wasn't just dusty family history folded into brittle pages. This was something private, something personal. Something no one had ever meant for her to find. She glanced toward the window. The light outside had turned gray, the clouds low and unmoving, pressing heavy against the hills like even the sky was waiting. Carefully she unfolded the letter, the ink stretched across the page, faded but still legible. Each word felt like a voice reaching out from far away and finally she began to read.

> *To the Family DiLegna,*
> *You'll no doubt read this with tight mouths and closed hearts, thinking you've won. That you've broken me. That you've driven me out like smoke from your grand halls. You'll fold this letter the way you fold your smiles, neat, sharp, and without feeling. Hear me now, and hear me true… you did not silence me, you never could. Collectively, you tried to press the wild from me as if it were nothing more than creases in old linen. You tried to bind me in stillness, to carve the voice from my spirit. But I was not made for silence. I could never fit inside your cage of polished wood and whispered judgment. What you called sin was only spirit. What you named shame was joy in its purest form. So mark these words, and mark them well. By moon and marrow, by fire and seed, Anthony's first, and only, child will be a daughter. You will see my eyes staring back at you from her face. The fire of my blood will burn in her veins, and she will walk barefoot where I was told to kneel. She will speak the truths your prayers could never chain. She will not bow. You may try to lace her into silence, but silence will shatter. You will call her unruly and ungrateful. You may name her wild, defiant, or difficult. Call her what you will, it changes nothing. In*

spirit, in spark, in blood, and in bone, she will find her way. You can try to deny me, but I'll rise again in the one you cannot bind, the one who carries me forward. She is not yours. She is the reckoning.
~A

Frankie's eyes locked on the final words as though they'd been carved into stone. The letter burned with defiance, every sentence sharp and alive, like a spell etched in ink. It didn't end sweetly or neatly. The words landed heavy, reverberating through her chest like a struck bell. Frankie's fingers curled tighter around the fragile paper, her heart thudding unevenly. She looked back to the photograph, the wild tumble of curls, the bright, untamed eyes, the smile that didn't ask permission. Aoife's face. Her face... my face. The realization hit Frankie like a blow to the gut. For a long moment she could only stare at the photograph, shaken by the familiarity etched in its fading lines. Then her gaze drifted back to the letter resting in her lap. Its presence felt heavier now, alive somehow, as if the photograph had only been the doorway and the words themselves were the threshold.

This wasn't simply ink on a page. It was a promise, an oath stretched across generations so tightly it seemed to hum, as though the paper remembered every hand that had ever touched it. A word from her Irish folklore course surfaced, one that had rooted itself in her memory long after the lesson ended: binding, the old kind, the kind that wasn't just a promise but a force. Something stranger, older, a vow forged with such fierce intent it bent the world around it, spell and burden braided so tightly they became one.

She had always found the idea both mesmerizing and unsettling, in the oldest tales, a single spoken promise could shape destiny, outliving its maker and threading through bloodlines like a quiet, patient tide. Words sharpened with purpose could wait in the shadows for generations, certain as bone, steady as breath. And now, staring at the script before her, she felt that truth stir again, quiet, inevitable, and far too close. Then her breath stilled, beneath the first bundle, her fingers brushed another envelope. She froze. This one wasn't to the family, wasn't some stiff, impersonal address. In a looping hand, it simply read, *To my darling girl.*

Her pulse stumbled. Frankie hadn't even been born when Aoife left town. She knew that much in the way children notice what adults hope they won't. Once, flipping through her parents' enormous wedding album with idle curiosity, she had studied the endless parade of relatives and friends, the stiff lines of DiLegnas posed for posterity. And there, on her father's side, something was missing. No mother of the groom. No soft-faced woman beaming at her son on his wedding day. The absence had struck her even then. It was as if Aoife had already been cut out, erased cleanly before Frankie had ever drawn breath. Not forgotten, forgotten was too gentle. Erased. As though she had never existed at all.

So how? How could this woman with her face, have written words that waited across decades for her? Questions tumbled over themselves, sharp and relentless. How had Aoife known there would be a girl? How had she known she would come looking? She could feel it humming in her palms, as though the ink itself was alive, carrying Aoife's intent like a low, steady pulse. The paper felt warm, thrumming faintly with energy, as though it spoke her name in a language deeper than words. She was drowning in questions, but she didn't doubt the one that mattered most, this letter was meant for her.

Carefully, she opened the envelope and her finger traced the salutation. It was in the gentle curve of those letters, she felt something she'd never been given at home: tenderness, belonging. For the first time, she wasn't the odd sprig in a manicured hedge, forever trimmed and set aside. She was part of a story that welcomed her wild edges, that let her grow as she was. The realization ached deep, sharp and sweet all at once, like roots pushing down through stone. And beneath the warmth of it, a quiet shiver passed through her, as if knowing that to belong here, to this legacy, would carry both gift and burden. Pete had been steady soil. Chalupa, her sardonic anchor. But this, this was blood-deep, root-deep. A warmth that didn't ask her to earn it. It overwhelmed her so completely she had to set the paper in her lap for a moment, palms open, breathing like someone bracing against a storm.

Aoife hadn't just disappeared one day from the manor with no word, it was planned and she'd left a seed behind, a prophecy. You can try to bury me, but I'll grow back in the one you can't control.

Now here Frankie was, decades later, sitting cross-legged on the floor, holding those words like a match in dry tinder. For a long time, she didn't move. The house seemed to hold its breath around her. When at last she unfolded the letter, her hands still shook.

Oh, my darling girl,
I pray to the Goddess that this finds you well and ready. If you're holding this, then I've wandered off to a path most folk can't see. But don't go thinking they've won. Aye, they may have shut the doors behind me, whispered my name like a curse, tried to tuck me away like an old ghost best forgotten, for wild things can't be erased. Leaving Grimwyck Manor was written in the marrow of me long before I ever understood the why of it. Never turn your back on destiny, love. If these words have found their way to your hands, then the winds are shifting, and the old world and ways are stirring again, as are you. There was a time I thought love might soften the ache, the restless pull in my soul, the call of something ancient and untamed. Oh lass, your grandfather seemed like a dream in the beginning, bright, charming, so full of life. I wanted so badly to belong in his world, I folded the wildest parts of myself away, tucked them quiet like dried herbs in an old drawer. I thought his love might fill the hollow places. But dreams are tricksters, mo chroí, and love built on silence never lasts. Behind the smiles, he was stone, cut from the same chill as the ones who raised him. When your father was born, I hoped some warmth might return, but the cold only deepened. Now you, you are something else entirely. You've felt it, haven't you? That quiet buzz under your skin, the tug in your bones that has no name. Trust it. That's your own wild calling, rising. When the time comes, you'll see with eyes unclouded, truths stranger than reason, older than rules. Some will seem too wild to be real. Lean in anyway. Inside this chest are the first pebbles on

your path. I wish I could give you the whole map, but some truths aren't meant for paper. If this letter were to fall into the wrong hands, the consequences would stretch farther than you or me. The answers will come when the earth is ready to whisper them, and not a moment before. Trust the shimmer at the corner of things. Trust the questions that don't come with answers. Trust what doesn't fit. The ones who taught you to doubt yourself never understood but you will. Each step is meant for your eyes alone. Know this, mo chroi, you are more powerful than they ever dared imagine. The thread that runs through me runs through you, strong and ancient. You are the one who will break what they tried so hard to bind. You are the wildflower bursting through the stone and you feel the shift as the world holds its breath, you won't be alone.

I'll be waiting, where the wild things bloom…

~Aoife

Frankie sat cross-legged on the rug, the letter trembling slightly between her fingers. The words felt alive, humming beneath her skin like a melody she almost recognized. Her heart stretched too full with something she couldn't quite name: fear, wonder, or something softer and heavier than both. She read the final lines again, her eyes snagging on the unfamiliar phrase…*Mo chroi.*

She mouthed the words aloud, tasting them. *Mo chroi* . Her laptop sat open on the coffee table. Leaning forward, the letter still clutched in one hand, she typed the words into the search bar. The translation bloomed on the screen, simple and small, but it knocked the air from her lungs. *Mo chroi … my heart.*

Before she knew it, tears slid hot and silent down her cheeks. No one had ever called her anything so endearing before. Not her parents, not her grandfather who she'd spent her whole life trying to make herself small for. But this woman, this wild, untamed woman she'd never met, had written across decades with words stitched from love and longing. For the first time in her life, Frankie felt like she had roots. Her fingers curled gently around the letter, cradling it like something fragile and sacred. In her mind's eye,

Aoife smiled back at her, curls wild, eyes bright, a spark fierce and free. Frankie wiped her cheeks, drew a shaky breath, and sat back on her heels. Aoife's words sent a chill through her, not from fear but from the undeniable pull of truth woven into them.

"The chest?" Frankie murmured, the word slipping out like a secret. She pictured the chest Nono had carried away so quickly, as though it burned to touch. What was inside?

Driven by sudden need, she gathered the bundle of letters, tucked them carefully into her bag, and stood. Chalupa meowed from the coffee table, round body planted like a judgmental sentinel, tail flicking as though he disapproved of her haste.

"I'll be back soon," Frankie promised.

He didn't move, just fixed her with that wide, unblinking stare that said you'd better. So she stepped closer and slid her fingers beneath his chin, scratching the soft spot he guarded like treasure. His tail slowed, then stilled, his eyes half-lidding as the tension melted out of him in a single purr. Only when he finally leaned into her hand, the way he always did when he decided she'd earned temporary forgiveness, did she straighten again.

"Hold the fort," she whispered. Chalupa blinked once, approval granted, for now.

Outside, the world felt hushed, caught between night and day, the air damp and cool in her lungs. Her fingers tightened on the steering wheel as her thoughts churned. Nono had snatched that chest like it held the meaning of life. Minutes later he'd returned empty-handed, too quickly to have carried it far. He hadn't left the house. Which meant it was still there, hidden somewhere he thought she'd never look.

The gravel crunched beneath her tires as she pulled into the drive. Morning fog still pooled low across the yard, blurring the edges of the trees. Nono had said he was staying with her parents for now. The manor had been dark for months because the electricity still hadn't been restored after a lightning strike over the summer. Maybe that was what had finally pushed him to start clearing out the old place, an excuse to rid himself of its shadows once and for all.

Climbing out, she inhaled damp earth, wet leaves, and something older, like a root cellar left to rot. The grass brushed high against her calves as she crossed the yard, heavy with dew, tugging at her jeans like grasping fingers. Grimwyck loomed above her, its roofline jagged against the paling sky, chimneys leaning like tired old watchers worn thin by decades of weather. Ivy crawled up the stone as though trying to drag the house back into the earth, and the shutters sagged at odd angles, like broken eyelids too weary to stay open. The house didn't sit so much as crouch, brooding, and Frankie had the uncanny impression it knew exactly who was creeping up its lawn.

The front door, thick oak blackened by time, was locked, of course. It always was. She gave it a jiggle, rolled her eyes, and whispered, "Naturally. Because breaking into your family home should come with added complications."

She rounded the side of the house, boots squelching softly in the wet grass, narrating under her breath like she was in a low-budget spy film.

"Phase two, window entry. Totally foolproof. Nothing says professional like face-planting into a dust cloud."

The guest room window waited there, tucked beneath a sagging gable. Its panes were opaque with grime, streaked by years of rain that had carved crooked rivulets down the glass. The paint peeled in curling strips, and the frame sagged like it, too, had given up. This was the room they'd forced her into as a child, never hers, only a container. Even in daylight it had felt oppressive. Now, in the thin gray hush of dawn, it looked more like a lid waiting to be shut. Her fingers found the familiar worn ledge. She grunted, braced a shoulder, and jiggled the sash until it groaned in long, offended creaks.

"Yep. Stealthy." A puff of dust billowed out, choking her. She waved it off with a cough. "Don't make me beg," she muttered at the stubborn frame. One last shove and it screeched open, the sound so loud it made her flinch. "Perfect, announce me to the neighbors. '*Hi, just breaking into my family mausoleum, don't mind me.*'"

She hauled herself up, one knee hooked over the sill, narrating her own disaster under her breath. "And here we have the graceful infiltration technique known as… the flailing carp."

Her boot snagged on the frame, her elbow clipped the wall, and she toppled forward, landing with a thud that rattled the floorboards. Flat on her back, staring up at the cracked ceiling, she whispered, “Nailed it. Cat burglar of the year. Definitely born for espionage. Watch out, world, I’m a menace to unsecured windows everywhere.”

The house gave no reply. It only listened, silence pressed heavy and intent against her ears. Not empty silence, but waiting silence. She sat up with a wince, dusting herself off. Her jeans wore a new streak of grime, her sleeve bore the mark of an elbow-shaped collision, and her pride was somewhere back outside in the wet grass.

“Flawless entry,” she muttered. “Truly, MI6 should be calling any day now.”

She stood, scanning the guest room. It was almost exactly as she remembered, wallpaper faded into dull florals, furniture stiff as if posing for judgment, the same scratchy quilt crooked on the narrow bed. A humorless smile tugged at her lips.

“Always so charming,” she said, brushing her fingers across the dusty dresser. The surface left a gray film on her fingertips, which she wiped absently against her jeans. “Still feels less like a bedroom and more like a timeout in purgatory.”

This room had always been a container, not a refuge, and standing in it again only reminded her of how unwelcome she had been within these walls. But charm, or the lack thereof, wasn’t why she was here. Somewhere in this house, Nono had stashed that chest. She remembered the way he’d clutched it, his knuckles white on the handles as if the wood itself burned. Minutes later, he’d returned empty-handed, his scowl sharper than usual. He hadn’t had time to carry it far. Which meant it was still here, hidden in Grimwyck’s brooding silence, tucked into some corner he thought she’d never search.

Whatever Nono had locked away, whatever he had hidden in such frantic haste, carried the heavy, aching weight of a secret left to rot too long in the dark. The house seemed to sense it, too. Every creak, every shifting plank pressed in around her, as if the walls themselves were holding their breath, waiting to see if she would dare pry open what was never meant to be found.

But why hide it at all? The question wormed through her thoughts. She remembered the way his face had cracked, just for a fleeting, unguarded moment, when he’d caught her holding Aoife’s photograph. A flicker of something raw and haunted, smothered almost before she saw it. It had been gone in an instant, but the echo of it clung to her now. Had the chest been concealed because some truths, once dragged into the light, refused to go back quietly?

The air thickened as she stepped into the hall, her footsteps light against the warped floorboards. The parlor lay just as it had yesterday, half-packed boxes stacked like barricades, lamps abandoned on the floor, furniture shoved against the walls. Dust drifted in her flashlight beam, stirred only by her breath. She paused, retracing the memory of Nono storming through this room. From where he'd stood, there were only two places he could have gone in the brief span he'd been away, the pantry or the garage. The pantry yielded nothing but bare shelves, cloudy jars, and cans decades past expiration. She shut the door softly, then turned toward the garage. The door stood slightly ajar, its edge tilted just wide enough to reveal a seam of blackness. The gap felt less like an invitation and more like an eye, watching her from the dark.

Her throat tightened. "Marco," she whispered.

"Polo," she answered herself.

The garage smelled of rust and oil and beneath it a trace of something floral. Odd. Shelves sagged under jars of nails, brittle paintbrushes, rusted tools, and tangled cords. Her footsteps echoed across the concrete as she swept her flashlight over the clutter, boxes stacked like forgotten promises, garden tools leaning against the wall, a busted lawn chair sadly sagging in the corner. Then her light caught a faint scuff mark in the dust, a trail dragged toward the back wall. She followed it with her flashlight until it found the thin cord dangling from the ceiling.

"Of course," she breathed, rolling her eyes. "Straight out of a horror movie."

The cord was just out of reach. Frankie sighed and jumped once, fingertips grazing. Again, closer. On the third try she caught it, giving a sharp tug. The attic stairs unfolded with a groan, a puff of dust and cobwebs spilling into the air. She climbed carefully, each step complaining beneath her weight. Dust motes spun in her flashlight beam like tiny ghosts. At the top, the light swept across low beams and a cluttered expanse of chests, boxes, and furniture draped in sheets. A rocking chair slumped in the corner, its paint flaking, its curve skeletal. Then a scent curled through the air, sharp and distinct enough to stop her cold. Verbena, rosemary and rue. Not the faint ghost of dried herbs forgotten decades ago, this was alive and insistent, braiding together into something whole. The fragrance threaded over her tongue with the weight of meaning, verbena for clarity, rosemary for remembrance and rue for protection and for truth.

She knew these plants, not just their names, not just their uses, but their language. Frankie was educated and well versed in all of it, the phytochemicals and alkaloids that made valerian root calm the nerves, the salicylates that gave willow bark its power to dull pain, the antiseptic oils locked inside thyme. She had a master's degree in botany to prove it, countless hours spent with textbooks and lab notes. But it had never only been science. The courses she had loved most were the electives: homeopathy, folklore, ethnobotany. The places where the science blurred with story. She remembered sitting up late, seed catalogs scattered beside folklore texts, tracing how cultures oceans apart had once come to the same conclusion, juniper and nettle planted near a barn to protect livestock, rowan branches tied above doorways to keep away ill luck. Even rosemary, beyond its oils and resins, was said to anchor memory. Old stories claimed that students in ancient Greece braided it into their hair before exams, a small hedge against forgetfulness, a way to keep the mind sharp and steady. Frankie had always loved that idea, the way knowledge and belief braided together, science and superstition twining like roots beneath the surface, unseen but inseparable.

Her mind still balked at the idea of a spell. That felt like a step too far, didn't it? Spells belonged to storybooks. Frankie didn't believe in theatrics. She believed in the soil. In the way seedlings leaned toward her voice. In the way sage eased a fever and verbena softened a restless mind.

For years, she had stood behind the nursery counter, watching people assemble their quiet rituals piece by piece, rosemary for thresholds, lavender for sleep, mugwort for dreams, fennel for protection. Most customers barely noticed her, but some did. Women with silver hair and knowing eyes. Young people clutching notebooks, hungry for something they couldn't yet name. They spoke to her easily, as if sensing she would understand. And she did. Frankie listened. She gathered their stories and half-spoken beliefs as carefully as she catalogued her seeds, storing them away without judgment. One woman, in particular, had leaned across the counter one spring afternoon, her hands stained with soil and silver rings glinting in the light. She tapped the flats of herbs Frankie had arranged and lowered her voice, as if the plants themselves might be listening.

"These three go together," she'd said, sliding verbena, rosemary, and rue into her basket. "Clarity, remembrance, protection. Put them in the earth side by side and you'll see what truth wants to rise."

She had smiled politely then, chalking it up to charm, but the words had stayed with her. And now, in the dim attic, that same braid of scents hung thick in the air. This wasn't random. Not after all her studies, not after all her dreams. It wasn't a spell, not exactly. It was intention and deep in her bones, she knew that intention had been waiting for her.

The attic pressed in around her, no longer a room but a threshold. Shadows peeled back as light fractured like glass struck from within. In a heartbeat, the rafters and boxes, the scent of rust and wood rot, all of it dissolved around her. Beneath Frankie's feet, the boards melted into living earth, moss springing soft underfoot, pulsing faintly as though it had its own heartbeat. Around her, a meadow spread in every direction, wildflowers spilling like paint across the horizon. Blossoms bent and swayed in a breeze she could feel but not hear, a silent rhythm threading through the field. Above, the sky stretched vast and indigo, pricked with stars so bright they throbbed like living hearts, their silver light washing the meadow in a spectral glow. The air was heavy with rosemary, sage, and sweetgrass, braided with something older still, a fragrance that hummed of memory, of places half-remembered and never named.

Then she saw her.

Not a ghost, not a wisp of imagination, but solid, radiant and untamed. Long silver-gray curls spilled down her back, streaked with moonlight and storm clouds, tossing in the wind like something feral and free. A marigold skirt brushed the tops of the flowers as she moved, bright as fire against the indigo night. Her shirt was plain white linen, sleeves rolled, worn from use and utterly unpretentious. She looked like someone who had lived deeply, without apology. Barefoot in that wild tangle of color and wind, she carried the poise of someone timeless, stitched from earth and sky alike. To Frankie, it was both a mirror and a memory, a vision of who she was and who she might yet become. Her pulse thundered as though every breath she had ever stifled had risen all at once. She could see herself in the curve of that smile, in the tilt of that head, in the quiet strength shimmering beneath her skin. The meadow sharpened, as though it wanted to prove itself real. The figure was no longer a suggestion but a true presence, moving closer, each detail undeniable.

Aoife.

She wasn't translucent or wavering, she was vibrant, wild, alive. Her silver-gray curls tumbled freely, caught in the wind like banners. The marigold skirt flared around her, her linen shirt plain and ready. She strode forward, and the flowers leaned with her like old friends. Frankie's breath caught. This was no dream. This was recognition made flesh. Aoife's eyes met hers across the meadow, moss-green, flecked with amber, the very same as Frankie's. She didn't speak at first. Instead, she lifted a hand, palm up. As if summoned, the entire meadow bowed. Petals rippled in a graceful wave, the hum of the earth deepening beneath Frankie's feet, steady as a heartbeat.

"You've always felt it, haven't you?" Aoife said at last, her voice soft and low, like water slipping over ancient stones. "That pull. That knowing. The way the earth hums to you when no one else is listening."

Frankie swallowed hard. "Yes… but why?"

Aoife stepped forward, vines curling gently around her fingers as if eager for her touch. "Because it's who you are, mo chroi . Who you've always been. The gifts you carry are not by chance. The natural world leans toward you for a reason." Her eyes softened, her voice a tether of love and truth. "You've always had one foot in the wild, haven't you? Always felt the hush beneath the noise, the things others miss, the things they fear."

The stars bent closer, burning brighter, as if the sky itself leaned in to listen.

"When you're lost, when the path grows dim," Aoife murmured, "find where the wild things bloom. That's where this begins, love."

Frankie's heart beat like wings desperate to lift.

"The clock's begun," Aoife continued, her voice threaded with both time and tenderness. "This moment, these choices, they are not happenstance. They are threads, all of them, being woven into something greater than you can yet see. And the weaver..." Her gaze lifted skyward, then returned to Frankie. "The weaver is watchin'."

The meadow thrummed with unseen rhythm, but Aoife's edges began to glow, then fade, her form dissolving like mist caught in morning sun. The stars flared behind her, tugging her gently back into their embrace.

"Wait!" Frankie cried, her voice breaking. "I don't understand, what am I meant to do?"

The vision wavered. Aoife's answer came faint as a breath, yet it carried like a vow stitched into the marrow of the earth, "You already know. Just listen for the hum beneath your feet... and follow your heart."

She was gone. The meadow shattered like glass, stars winking out, flowers collapsing into ash, and the hum of tall grass folding into a silence so sudden it ached in Frankie's ears. She blinked, and the attic rushed back around her, the sagging beams, the sour reek of wood rot, the heaps of furniture draped in yellowed sheets. But the room was not the same. The silence had changed. It was no longer hollow. It pulsed, low and patient, like something breathing just beneath the floorboards. As if Aoife's words had sunk into the bones of Grimwyck, stitched into its timbers and stones.

The air pressed close, heavy like rain just before a lightning strike. Shadows pooled deeper in the corners, listening. Every creak of the rafters sounded deliberate, not settling wood, but reply. The stillness was not passive; it remembered. It carried the weight of her grandmother's presence, half-blessing, half-warning, a reminder that this house had always held more than it cared to reveal. The hum she had felt in the meadow vibrated faintly beneath her boots, threading up through the warped floorboards like a heartbeat that wasn't hers. The air clung damp and close, tinged with rosemary and smoke, as though the meadow had left its breath behind. Her flashlight beam jittered across boxes and chairs, shadows twitching at the edges of vision. She told herself it was dust, only nerves, but the silence pressed back with intent.

The beam swept farther, and there it was, crouched in the farthest corner. It sat waiting, as though the hum in the floorboards had been leading her straight to it. Aoife was gone, but the air still carried her presence, threading whispers between shadow and silence. Frankie crossed the attic, dust spiraling in her wake, the hush pressing in like held breath. She crouched, resting her hand on the lid. The wood was warm, as if it had absorbed every secret it contained. But the warmth faded almost at once, slipping away like sunlight behind a cloud. The attic leaned in around her, shadows stretching too far, too eager. It felt like the house was watching.

"No way I'm doing this here," she muttered.

Gripping the metal handles, she hoisted it up. It was heavier than its frame should allow, not only wood and brass, but burden. She moved for the stairs, every creak of the floorboards sharp in the stillness. The attic seemed to hold its breath as she descended, step by straining step, until she finally crossed the threshold into the early morning light. She carried it across the gravel drive, the weight tugging at her arms but grounding her, something solid in a world tilting sideways. The Jeep waited beneath the crooked oak, its limbs clawing at the sky. With effort she slid it into the back and braced herself against the bumper, lungs burning, pulse still quick.

The old manor house loomed behind her, its sharp roofline jagged against the sky. The windows stared blank and unblinking. The morning was unnaturally still, no birdsong, no wind. She climbed into the Jeep, closed the door, and the sound cracked through the silence like a gavel. Grimwyck didn't look abandoned. It looked like it was waiting.

The Jeep rumbled down the drive, gravel crunching under its tires. Instinct tugged, and Frankie glanced into the rearview mirror. That's when she saw it, a faint ripple in one of the upper windows. She braked hard, squinting. A glow pulsed there, golden and steady, where no light should be. It didn't flicker like electricity, it breathed, slow and deliberate, the heartbeat of something waking. From behind the glow, a figure emerged. A silhouette, still and silent. No features, only a shape that mirrored her own tilt of head, her own lean forward, like a darker version of herself reflected back. Then, faint and humorless, a chuckle slid into her thoughts, not through the air but straight into her skull. The glow flared once, enough to carve the suggestion of a shoulder, a head, leaning closer. Then it snapped out, leaving only blank glass. Frankie blinked. Once. Twice. The window stared back at her, empty sky and cold stone. But she knew, it had seen her and it had recognized her. Her foot hit he gas. and gravel spat under the tires. She didn't look back again. The silence inside the Jeep was not empty. It pressed in gently, warm and humming, as if the air had shifted its attention toward her. Then, soft as breath against her ear, Aoife's voice slipped through her thoughts, *You've always felt it, haven't you? That pull. That knowing. The way the earth hums to you when no one else hears a thing.*

She had tried to explain that feeling away for years but something had cracked open today, and it would not be sealed again. Her eyes flicked to the mirror. The chest sat in the back, quiet but not harmless, whatever it carried was not content to stay buried. By the time she turned onto the winding lane that led home, the lavender shimmered silver-green in the morning light, their blooms swaying like old friends whispering her back. Something in her loosened, like an exhale after holding her breath too long. She parked and let the engine die. She circled to the back, brushing her fingers along its worn handles. For a moment she didn't lift it. Instead her gaze wandered upward, past roofline and lavender, to the sky. Clouds drifted like tufts of carded wool across a pale quilt, edges stitched in gold and in that stillness, something stirred. Not sound, but a whisper brushed the edges of her mind,

Where the wild things bloom, you'll find me.

Chapter 5

The front door clicked shut behind her with its familiar soft thump, sealing the outside world in lavender and old wood. The air inside smelled faintly of sun-warmed pine, rosemary from the windowsill, and the ghost of last night's chamomile tea. Frankie shifted the chest awkwardly in her arms, its brass handles pressing into her palms. It was still warm from the sun, heavier than it had any right to be, as though it carried more than wood and velvet inside. Chalupa pranced towards her, tail high, but the moment it crossed the threshold, he stopped dead. His ears flattened, his whiskers fanned wide, and his tail ballooned like he'd just spotted a snake, or worse, a mole elbow-deep in his stash of nursery catnip.

"Whoa." Frankie staggered and set it down on the braided rug with a muffled thud. "Easy, drama king."

Chalupa didn't move, he was crouched low, glaring at the intruder, as if it had hissed first. Frankie straightened, rolling her shoulder, and gave him a wry look.

"It's just an old box. You saw me carry it in. No haunted vibes, no… "

A sound cut her off. The chest gave a low hum, soft at first, almost beneath hearing. It was less a noise than a vibration, like a cello string drawn tight and plucked in some hidden chamber of the house. The sound shivered up through the floorboards and into Frankie's bones. The fine hairs on her arms lifted and she froze. Chalupa growled, a low, steady rumble reserved for things he didn't trust. He padded in a slow circle around the intruder, tail flicking, eyes locked as though expecting it to spring to life. Frankie backed up a step, her pulse quickening.

"Okay," she muttered, "not haunted. Just… residual vibration. Maybe the ride shook something loose. Maybe it's got… bees. Angry antique bees."

Chalupa didn't dignify that with a glance. He swatted at it, claws flashing, a sharp warning to whatever was inside. The hum softened, as if it had heard her. As if it were listening. Frankie rubbed the back of her neck, unsettled, her gaze still pinned to the box.

"Perfect," she whispered. "A box with opinions. What's next, chanting in Latin?"

The chest just sat there.

"You better not be cursed," she muttered, taking a cautious step back. "I do not have the bandwidth for cursed, not today. Not with rain in the forecast and a cat who treats me like the help at a bed-and-breakfast."

The words hung in the air, meant as a joke, but they didn't land the way she hoped. The silence pressed in, as though the house itself were holding its breath to hear what she would say next. Frankie rubbed her arms against the sudden chill, wishing she hadn't given her nerves a voice. Jokes were armor, and this one had clattered uselessly to the floor. Behind her, the kettle sat cold on the stove, long forgotten. The plants by the window gave a little shiver as if someone had leaned in close and whispered through the screen. The chest didn't move, didn't rattle or creak, but the air around it felt... off. Not wrong, exactly, just the kind of charged that made your skin prickle and your inner voice go, hey, maybe don't poke the possibly haunted heirloom today.

Chalupa still crouched low beside it, tail coiled tight, ears pinned back, like a feline gargoyle on alert. Guarding something sacred or glaring at it for existing. It was hard to tell with cats. Frankie forced a brightness into her tone, backing toward the kitchen with the unconvincing grace of someone pretending they hadn't just made eye contact with an ominous, humming box.

"Tea," she announced. "That's what normal people do when faced with cosmic oddities, they make tea." She kept one eye on the it the entire time, like it might grow legs and bolt. The cupboard squeaked when she opened it, her favorite mug, waiting like an old friend. The act of filling the kettle, setting it on the stove, gave her hands something to do.

"You know," she muttered to the kitchen in general, "this is exactly how horror movies start. Single woman. Creepy object. Cat with opinions."

The kettle gave a faint rattle, not quite a boil. Chalupa didn't move. Frankie sighed and turned back toward the chest, mug abandoned, hands shoved in her cardigan pockets to keep them from fidgeting. She walked slowly across the room, her gaze never leaving Chalupa, or the box.

"I know what you're trying to say," she said softly. "But it's alright. Whatever this is..." She crouched in front of it and placed a hand on its lid. It felt warm and was vibrating ever so faintly beneath her fingers. "I can handle it."

Chalupa didn't blink, his tail tapped once against the floor. Like punctuation on a warning. Outside, the breeze had quieted, as if the garden itself had paused to listen.

Frankie exhaled slowly and reached for the latch. It clicked open beneath her fingers with a soft, satisfying snap. The lid creaked as it lifted, stiff with age, like an old door unused. A breath of air rose up from inside, warm and dry, steeped in the scent of cedar wood and pressed flowers. It smelled like old letters and Grandma's attic, like something sacred wrapped in linen and time. The kind of scent you couldn't bottle but dearly wished you could, familiar and tender, like the quiet of a library where every shelf breathes stories, and even the dust feels meaningful.

Inside, everything had been placed with a kind of quiet care, tucked and folded like someone had hoped, maybe even trusted, that the right person would find it one day. The silence in the room shifted in that strange, quiet way when you stumble into something meaningful and don't yet know why. Outside, the lavender bowed in a soft, synchronized ripple, stirred by a breeze that passed through like a thought barely spoken. The rosemary at the window stood perfectly still, its leaves silver-tipped in the afternoon sun. Frankie didn't move. Something about this moment settled. Like the first note of a song you somehow already know.

Her gaze flicked to Chalupa, who had inched closer without her noticing. He was crouched low by the hearth, tail wrapped snug along his side in a tense little curve, paws tucked beneath him like he was bracing for impact. His ears twitched, eyes sharp and unblinking, fixed on it as though it might leap up, start tap-dancing, or spontaneously combust. The look he gave it was the same one he reserved for squirrels with poor decision-making skills or moles foolish enough to trespass in the nursery beds. Frankie reached inside. Chalupa gave a low, suspicious grumble, but he didn't stop her. Her fingers brushed something soft, and she drew it out with care, a journal. The leather was warm against her palms, worn to velvet in places. Its corners curled like leaves pressed too long in an old book, and the spine was gently cracked, as if it had been opened and closed so many times it knew the rhythm by heart.

On the front, in looping script, was a single name.... *Aoife*. The name looked back at her like it had been waiting. She didn't know this woman, hadn't known she existed until yesterday, but now, here it was, written like a quiet answer to a question she hadn't thought to ask. She traced the letters, slow and tentative, as if touching them too firmly might erase them. This wasn't just a journal, it was a doorway. She drew it to her chest and shut her eyes. There was no thunder, no rush of revelation, just a soft ache, tender and odd, like missing a place you'd never been but always somehow belonged to.

Chalupa gave a little grunt that might've meant "*well, you've come this far.*"

Frankie peeked at him and whispered, "Alright, let's see what else she left behind."

She set the journal gently on the rug. Beneath it, nestled like secrets in layers of time, were more pieces. A scarf came next, thin silk, worn soft with age, embroidered with tiny stars and twining vines that looked like they might keep growing if you stared long enough. Frankie smoothed it flat, smiling faintly. It felt like something made for twilight walks through heavily scented gardens, soft, familiar, and meant to be worn by someone who trusted the wind to guide them home.

Something pale caught the light. Chalupa, who had been quietly observing, let out a dramatic sigh, the kind that said.... *Finally*. He marched forward with purpose and batted at the edge of the silk scarf, then sat back with a pointed flick of his tail, staring at Frankie like she was the slowest student in a very magical class. She blinked at him.

"What?"

Another paw swat, this time with more flair and the scarf fluttered to the side, revealing the corner of something tucked just beneath it.

"Oh, now you want to help," she muttered, reaching down.

Her fingers met paper, thick and fibrous, the kind that held its shape even after being carefully rolled and stored for ages. The texture was rich, almost velvety beneath her fingertips, the edges slightly frayed, as if time had gently brushed against it but never worn it down. It felt purposeful in her hands, deliberate, like something meant to last. Like something that had waited. She unrolled the paper slowly, her hands moving with a kind of reverence she hadn't meant to show. The page unfurled with a soft *shhhh*, like it had exhaled after being held in too long.

A map, the ink had faded in places, worn by time and maybe weather, but the lines were still legible, clear enough to read, but soft enough to suggest age. They weren't machine-perfect. No grids or coordinates. No tidy roads with numbered exits. These lines curved with intention, drawn by a human hand, someone who had cared, deeply, about what they were charting. Immediately, she could see it was unlike any map she'd ever come across. There was a rhythm to the way it had been drawn, a quiet grace in the flourishes of ink. Each ridge and valley flowed with natural ease, rendered with delicate strokes that seemed to echo the landscape itself. The rivers curved like silver threads stitched into parchment, winding patiently toward places unnamed. Little inked illustrations peeked out from corners and edges, a stag beneath a tree, a moon cradled in clouds, what looked like a fox curled up beside a circle of mushrooms. It was as if whoever had drawn it hadn't just mapped the land, they had captured its spirit.

There was no compass rose, no tidy key. Just a sprawl of curling script that twined across the page like ivy curling through lattice. It wasn't printed or typed. It looked drawn, by a hand both practiced and patient, the letters looping and dipping in a rhythm all their own. Nestled among them were little symbols, spirals and stars, slender crescents tucked between curling lines like secret punctuation marks.

A decorative border framed the entire page, scrollwork and curling vines twined together like something that might've grown there if paper could bloom. Tucked among the tendrils were tiny creatures, a moth with lacy wings, a sparrow mid-song, and, because of course, what looked suspiciously like a cat with wings.

Frankie sat back slowly, her palm still resting on the map like it might whisper secrets if she just stayed still enough. She glanced to the side, Chalupa was watching her and not in his usual blink-slowly-and-pretend-you're-bored way. No, he looked almost ... smug as if he'd known this moment was coming and had simply been waiting her out. Like if he could talk, he'd say something infuriating like ... *about time*.

Frankie narrowed her eyes at him. "Well, that's... mildly unsettling." Chalupa just blinked again. "Don't get any ideas," she muttered, brushing her hands on her leggings. "You sprout wings and you're moving to the greenhouse."

He yawned, stretched with theatrical ease, and curled his tail around his paws like the very picture of innocence, except for the look he gave her. One that suggested, in no uncertain terms, he'd been waiting for her to catch up. Frankie turned her attention back to the map. It still lay open, the creases soft from age, the ink a little faded but unmistakably sure of itself. What caught her next was in the lower right corner. Instead of a legend or compass rose, a sprawl of looping script curled across the parchment like ivy left to wander. The letters weren't from any alphabet she recognized, but they didn't feel foreign either. They felt old, like something passed down in stories murmured by firelight. Nestled among the script were tiny symbols, spirals, stars, crescent moons, and sigils that looked more carved than drawn. Glyphs that seemed to hum, not loudly, but just beneath the surface of awareness.

Her eyes lingered on the largest of the markings, an intricate knotwork design, lines folding over themselves, weaving into a shape not quite symmetrical, but deeply balanced. It reminded her of frost on windowpanes or the wrought iron of forgotten garden gates. A strange feeling curled in her chest, not recognition, exactly, but the sense that something inside her had paused to listen. She leaned in, letting her eyes follow the paths again. The usual details were there. Mountains, rivers, the sprawl of forests, but among them ran a different kind of mark, faint, dotted lines that slipped between landmarks like whispers. They wound through valleys and across ridgelines, dipped beneath trees and skirted lakes, never quite direct, never quite random.

Frankie tilted her head, tracing the dotted trails with her fingertip. They weren't roads. They drifted across the map with no regard for topography, slipping between forests, skimming rivers, crossing through valleys in quiet defiance of logic. But there was a rhythm to them, a deliberate weaving.

Ley lines.

The word surfaced from a dusty corner of her memory, one of those half-believed things from a college folklore class, tucked between tales of selkies and second sight. Earth's hidden threads, they'd called them. Invisible currents of energy said to connect sacred places, thin spots in the world where the air buzzed just a little differently, where the skin between what is and what might be wore thin. And on this map, all of them, the whole web of fine, dotted lines, seemed to pull toward one place.

Near the center of the page, nestled deep in the folds of the Appalachian Mountains, a small circle had been inked darker than the rest, a single point, etched with certainty and beside it, in that same looping were five words.

Where the wild things bloom

Frankie's breath caught. The phrase struck her like a chord hit just right, in Aoife's letter. She'd written those very words... *I'll be waiting where the wild things bloom.* Her fingers hovered above the ink, trembling slightly. The weight of it bloomed behind her eyes, behind her ribs. This wasn't just a map. It was the answer to a promise. A thread stitched from pen to paper to flesh and bone, across years, across silence. She scanned the map again, heart thudding, and found a second notation, smaller, barely legible, nearly swallowed by the folds and timeworn creases. It was penned in a different ink and hand, *Verdant Sanctum*.

The words settled in her bones like a bell tolling from a distant chapel, one she couldn't see, but could feel. She didn't know what it meant, but the word sanctum carried a hush to it, a kind of sacred weight. A sanctuary hidden beneath wild bramble and time, waiting. Whatever it was, wherever it led, that was where the map pointed to where all the wild currents of the earth converged. Frankie sat back slowly on her heels, palm still pressed to the map as if it might anchor her. Her fingers trailed over the symbol once more, tracing the line between that darker dot and the words beside it. This was no accident.

"She meant for me to find this," she whispered, as if speaking it aloud would make it more real.

She folded the map with reverence, smoothing the creases with both palms like sealing a letter to fate. She tucked it into the journal, her fingers brushing the edges of the scarf, the old dried flower pressed between pages, the life she hadn't known had been quietly waiting. This wasn't the end of a search, it was a beginning. An open door, a thread leading toward whatever the Verdant Sanctum was and the wild things, wherever they were, they were calling.

For three days, something quiet and insistent inside Frankie had taken root and begun to grow, like a vine curling toward sunlight, threading itself through everything she touched. Her carriage house, once a calm haven, had become a cluttered maze of open books and crumpled notes that sprawled across every surface like ivy. Letters and journal pages from Aoife's chest were fanned out on the dining table, their faded ink glowing under the warm pool of lamplight. Maps, some freshly printed, others worn thin with age, overlapped in a chaotic patchwork. Articles blurred together until the words unraveled, forum threads led to dead ends, and even the modern maps she pulled up felt sterile compared to the soft, hand-drawn one stretched across her table. The air smelled of old paper and the sharp tang of black tea she kept forgetting to drink.

The laptop screen glowed dimly amid the chaos, tabs blooming across the browser like restless weeds, archives, obscure folklore blogs, forgotten corners of the internet. Her fingers moved constantly, restlessly, from keyboard to brittle parchment, cross-referencing names, places, fragments of songs, and Aoife's looping notes. At the greenhouse she moved on autopilot, hands busy but mind elsewhere. Surrounded by seedlings and the scent of damp soil, she'd drift into stillness, staring off as if her thoughts had taken root someplace far away.

Pete noticed. Of course he noticed, he always did. That afternoon, he caught the way her hands lingered a little too long on the ties of her apron before she reached for her keys. From behind the counter, he tilted his head, one brow quirked. His voice, when it came, was easy, careful.

"Everything alright, Greenling?"

The nickname fell into the air soft as moss underfoot. He'd called her that almost from the start, like the word had always been hers and he'd just reminded her of it. *Greenling*. The little shoot reaching for light. The sound of it tugged her out of herself for a moment. She glanced up, and though her smile was small, it was real. Pete's mouth curved into one of those crooked almost-smiles of his, the kind that didn't ask for answers but promised he'd be there when she was ready.

"Yeah," she said, a touch too quickly. "Just working on a project. You know me, can't leave well enough alone."

Pete's expression didn't change, but something in his eyes sharpened. Then, as she turned to leave, he spoke again, quieter this time, like he was passing along a secret.

"Sometimes," he said, "the roots we ignore run far deeper than we think and the wildest things often bloom in the places we least expect, when we stop looking for what we already are."

Frankie stopped short, glancing back at him over her shoulder. "That's... oddly poetic coming from you," she said, attempting to keep her voice light. "You've been spending too much time talking to the plants."

He only offered a small smile before turning away, busying himself with the tray of seedlings as if he hadn't said anything at all. Still, his words lodged in her mind, quiet, persistent, impossible to ignore. Frankie carried that echo with her as she crossed the gardens that afternoon, past greenhouses and herb beds where rosemary and lavender bowed in invisible currents. Even amid the familiar routine, the steady murmur of bees and the damp scent of soil followed her like a soft undercurrent, a reminder in the rhythm of the path beneath her boots.

By the time she reached the carriage house, the words hummed louder. Frankie pulled her Jeep into the narrow, lavender-lined drive, one she called home for so many quiet hours, and shook her head at the memory of Chalupa, perched like a disapproving little lord in the passenger seat, having leapt into her lap mid-drive when an oversized grasshopper crashed the windshield. The memory made her smile then, but now, even that levity felt in tune with something... more. The feeling followed her inside, clinging like mist. Even after she'd changed into her softest sweater and brewed a fresh pot of tea, it lingered, curling into the corners of the carriage house, settling behind her ribs like a promise not yet spoken. Hours slipped by unnoticed. The clock on the wall ticked steadily past two in the morning. Stacks of books flanked her laptop like small fortresses. Her tea had long gone cold beside her elbow, untouched. Scribbled notes formed a haphazard constellation across the tabletop, arrows and circles linking words like threads in a web. Her eyes burned from staring at the screen too long, the hum in her ears having turned into a dull roar of frustration.

Frankie's chin rested heavily in her hand as she scrolled aimlessly through yet another archive site, the words blurring together on the screen. Her eyelids felt like sandpaper, her thoughts looping back to the same place... Where the wild things bloom. She rubbed her temples, the ache behind her eyes pressing in and that's when Chalupa made his move. Without warning, he leapt ever so gracefully onto the table, scattering a pile of papers with a careless flick of his tail. Frankie barely reacted, too used to his habit of weaving himself into her workspace like an entitled paperweight. But tonight, he didn't curl up or settle in. He walked deliberately across the table, his tail twitching with purpose, then stepped squarely onto her keyboard.

"Hey!" Frankie half-laughed, half-scolded, reaching out to nudge him. "Seriously? I'm trying to figure out my destiny here, buddy."

Chalupa didn't move, instead, he padded deliberately across the keys, his paws tapping out a jumbled string of characters. The screen flickered but before she could shoo him off, his back paw landed firmly on the Enter key.

Frankie sighed and reached to pull him away, but froze when her eyes flicked back to the screen, a new search result blinked at her. The page title read:

**The Wild Bloom Conservatory,
Forgotten Conservatory of the Appalachian Highlands**

"The Wild Bloom," she whispered aloud, the words curling over her tongue like something familiar. Chalupa finally sat down, curling his tail neatly around his paws and blinking at her like he'd just done her a favor.

Frankie clicked the link, the page loaded slowly, its formatting clunky and outdated, but the words and images were clear enough. A flood of information filled the screen, old photographs, scattered articles, snippets from local history blogs and digital archives. As she scrolled, a photo appeared that made her breath catch. The structure stood tucked deep in the hills, a latticework of weathered iron and streaked glass, tangled with vines and crowned with creeping moss. The surrounding garden burst wild and untamed, bright patches of flowers blooming defiantly between cracks in the stone paths, as if nature itself had reclaimed the place.

It looked like something out of a dream. Her pulse roared in her ears as she leaned closer, scanning every detail. The longer she looked, the more extraordinary the place became. It wasn't just old, it was legendary. Truly hidden away along a forgotten stretch of the Appalachian Mountains, the Wild Bloom Conservatory was said to sit at the convergence of multiple ley lines, the same lines marked on the map folded on her table. According to forgotten newspaper clippings and whispered folklore, the land beneath it pulsed with an energy few could explain. The air around the greenhouse was said to hum faintly, charged with a subtle, living pulse like a heartbeat in the soil. Locals spoke of the plants that grew there, species found nowhere else, flowers that glowed beneath the moon, vines that curled toward voices, petals that shimmered in rhythm with the wind. Some claimed the conservatory wasn't just a greenhouse; it was alive, a place that noticed who walked through its doors. For some, it welcomed them, for others, it didn't. Frankie scrolled farther, her pulse pounding louder with every line, until one small quote caught her eye.

> **"The Wild Bloom Conservatory isn't just a place, it's a secret kept by the earth itself. Hidden beyond the reach of ordinary maps, its gardens breathe with ancient magic, moonlit blossoms, whispering vines, and petals scented with forgotten dreams. Some say it rests on the old ley lines, where wild energy stirs beneath the soil. You don't find the Wild Bloom, it calls to you."**

The words flared in her mind like a struck match, igniting the thread she'd been chasing for days, where the wild things bloom.

Her gaze dropped to the map still stretched across her table, the delicate, hand-drawn lines weaving like lattices across the parchment, the tangled web of ley lines converging in the folds of the Appalachian mountains. Her eyes traced the dark circle inked in the center, the same one she'd stared at so many nights without answers. She glanced back at the coordinates listed in the article, her heartbeat drumming louder with each beat. She cross-referenced the numbers against Aoife's map, her fingers trembling slightly as she followed the lines again, this time, knowing what to look for. The coordinates matched. Not perfectly, but close enough to make something inside her tilt and settle all at once, like a puzzle piece clicking into place.

She looked down at Chalupa, who had finally curled into an impossibly round, over-proofed loaf beside her keyboard. His tail wrapped neatly around him, his green-gold eyes half-lidded but glinting with a suspicious alertness, like he'd been pretending to nap just long enough for her to figure it out on her own.

Frankie stared at him, that quiet thrum rising again, a breathless laugh slipped out, shaken and small. "You're something, little man," she murmured, wonder softening the edges of her voice. "You knew."

Chalupa's ears twitched, blinked once, slow, deliberate, maddeningly smug, and let out a low *mrrrp*, like he'd been holding onto that secret just long enough. Frankie sat back in her chair, staring at him as he settled deeper into his curl.

"How?" she whispered. "How do you know all this?"

He didn't answer, of course. Just sighed through his nose, the picture of cozy indifference.

But the flick of his tail against the table's edge felt almost like punctuation. As if the question wasn't if he knew... but how much he'd already decided not to tell her.

For the first time in days, the ache behind her eyes eased. She'd found something solid, more than a scatter of vague breadcrumbs. The map, the message, that steady pull deep inside... all of it pointed here: *To the place where the wild things bloom* and now she knew where to begin. By the end of the week, her mind was made up.

Morning light spilled pale and soft across the kitchen, casting long golden slants through the windows and onto the chaos that still claimed every corner of her apartment. Books lay cracked open beside half-drunk mugs of tea. Dried flowers curled beside stacks of dog-eared papers. The map remained spread across her table like a compass she hadn't dared fold away, but this morning, she wasn't cross-referencing the notes in the margins of Aoife's journal. She was staring at her phone, her thumb hovered over the call button, still and unsure, before she finally let out a breath she hadn't realized she'd been holding, and pressed.

Pete answered on the third ring, his voice warm and familiar, like he always sounded when the greenhouse was quiet and the morning air still smelled of damp soil.

"Hey, Greenling, what's up? You find another sad fern for us to nurse back to life?"

A soft smile tugged at her lips despite the tightness in her chest. "Not exactly, Pete," she murmured. "Actually, I… I need to talk to you about something."

There was a pause on the other end, the quiet stretch of it longer than usual. She could almost picture him leaning back in his worn chair, mug of chamomile tea in one hand, his tie-dye T-shirt faded soft with age, one eyebrow raised like he always did when he knew something important was coming.

Pete let out a quiet breath, almost a laugh, but not quite. "I know that tone," he said, voice like the rustle of leaves. "Like a storm's brewing and you've decided you're going to walk straight into it."

Frankie swallowed and tucked her free hand into her pocket. "I need to take some time off," she said quietly. "I can't really explain why… but I need to take some time off."

Another pause, this one heavier but when he spoke again, his tone had shifted, softer, steadier, like something weightier sat just beneath the surface.

"Well," Pete said, his voice taking on a quiet gravity, "there comes a time when a person must stop tending the same patch of soil and step into the wild, to see what blooms in places they've never dared to go." He paused, and something older wove into his words, steadier, deeper, like a thread pulled tight through generations. "Just remember, Frankie… once you take that first step, the wild doesn't let you go, not really. It marks you in ways you won't understand until much later." He let the silence stretch just long enough before continuing, more softly now. "The wild things grow where roots run deep. Even when you can't see them, they're still there, waiting. And when you're out there, in the stillness, when the path seems to vanish... remember, you're never as alone as you think." A breath and then, like an afterthought wrapped in ancient knowing. "The wild has eyes, Frankie and it's always watching."

Frankie's voice softened, and something quiet flickered behind her words. "Thank you, Pete," she said.

It wasn't just gratitude. Something in her had shifted. She wasn't used to this kind of care, gentle and unwavering, the kind that didn't come with expectations or conditions. Not from family. Not from anyone, really. But Pete... Pete had always been different.

"I'll see you when I get back," she added, softer still, as much a promise as a whispered hope that she'd return changed, not lost.

"See you soon Greenling, be safe." Pete said, his voice calm and sure. Then, after a beat, lower now, almost to the roots of things, "Take heart, you're a wild child of the earth, the world has a way of bending toward those brave enough to listen."

The line clicked softly as the call ended, but Pete's words lingered, *You're a wild child of the earth*. Simple as they were, they rang through her like a bell, gentle, but impossible to ignore. It wasn't just what he'd said, but the way he'd said it, like he was naming something she'd always been but hadn't yet seen for herself.

Frankie stood in the quiet of her carriage house, sunlight filtering through the windows in golden bands, warming the floorboards beneath her bare feet. The space felt different now. Not unfamiliar, just... deeper. Like the ordinary had shifted slightly, revealing edges she hadn't noticed before. The table beside her, cluttered with books, old letters, scraps of paper and dried herbs, no longer looked like a mess. It looked intentional. Like a life being stitched back together. Her half-finished cup of tea sat forgotten, the steam long gone, but the scent of lemon balm still clung faintly in the air. Aoife's journal lay open where she'd left it, nestled against the soft curl of a letter she must've read a dozen times by now. The ink was fading, the paper yellowed, but it all felt alive, like memory pressed into pages, waiting for the right hands to hold it.

The stillness around her wasn't empty. It felt expectant. As if the house itself had taken a breath and was waiting to see what she'd do next. Frankie inhaled slowly, letting it settle into her bones. She felt... changed, like she'd crossed an invisible threshold and couldn't quite name it, but she knew she wouldn't go back. She glanced down at the things she'd gathered without quite realizing it. They didn't look like much, just small, familiar scraps of her life, but together, they felt like more than coincidence. Like intentions she hadn't known she was making.

A square of beeswax cloth, soft and faintly scented with honey, lay beside a smooth river stone, cool in her palm and streaked with a single white line, like it had carried a message across time. A length of frayed twine, still curled from its last knot, brought to mind bundles of herbs and late summer mornings in the greenhouse. Tucked near the edge was a sprig of mugwort, tied with sun-faded thread, its scent earthy and grounding, like it had been waiting to be chosen. And somewhere between it all sat a feather, striped and bent at the tip, pulled from the pages of a book she barely remembered reading, but couldn't bear to let go.

She hadn't meant to collect any of it. Somehow, her hands had known what her heart was only beginning to admit, she wasn't just packing for a trip. She was preparing for something older. Something that had already begun. With quiet care, Frankie folded the cloth, wrapped the mugwort, and slid the stone and feather into the side pocket of her pack. Each piece settled into place without resistance, as though it had always known where it belonged. When she stepped back, the table looked lighter. Not empty, just... ready, and so was she. From his perch on the windowsill, Chalupa watched the entire process with the disdain of someone unimpressed by human inefficiency.

"Oh, don't start," Frankie said, not even looking up. "You know your things are next."

He offered a single, pointed blink, slow, judgmental, and thoroughly unconcerned. Still, when she crouched beside his bag, the tabby leapt down with an air of exaggerated resignation and padded over, tail swishing like a fluffy, plumed metronome. Frankie laughed and pulled his things together, a collapsible water bowl, every can of his fancy pâté, because he refused to eat the same flavor twice in a row, and his treats. She tucked in his favorite fleece blanket, soft and embarrassingly pink, stolen from her bed years ago, and the tiny plush cactus toy he only played with when no one was watching.

"There," she said, satisfied. "I don't think I forgot anything."

Chalupa sniffed at the bag, then looked up at her like he was considering a formal complaint. Frankie crouched down and scratched gently behind his ears.

"Yes, I packed the good treats and yes, I'll stop for nuggets on the way out of town. Happy now?"

He let out a quiet *mrrrp* that sounded suspiciously like *fine*, then turned in a slow circle and sat regally beside the tote, as if granting his royal approval.

Frankie laughed. "Bossy little gremlin." she murmured, but her fingers lingered for a moment longer in his fur.

She straightened slowly, her gaze drifting across the room one last time. Morning light spilled through the windows, soft, golden and stirring dust motes that shimmered like stars suspended in amber. Everything looked just as it always had, familiar and warm, cluttered in the way that made it hers. But the air felt different now, laced with the hush that comes just before a beginning. At the threshold, she paused and let her eyes linger on the little carriage house, the ivy-laced walls, the sun-drenched window seat, the overgrown lavender just beginning to bloom beneath the sill. The only home she'd ever truly claimed. The place that had held her gently, fiercely, until she was ready to let go.

"I'll be right back," she said as her fingertips brushed the doorknob. As she pulled the door closed, a breeze stirred through the quiet, low and steady, laced with wild herbs and damp cedar. It moved like the forest itself had drawn breath, slipping over her skin, tugging gently at her sweater, winding around Aoife's scarf at her neck like a benediction. A silence followed, ancient and sure, older than weather.

Outside, the air was sharp and sweet, charged with something electric. Like the sky before a storm, or the breath just before a spark takes hold. She inhaled deeply, and it filled her with more than air. It filled her with possibility. Dew jeweled the grass beneath her boots. The trees leaned overhead, whispering to one another in the early light. Then came the gust, rising from the ground itself, as if the land had drawn breath and let it go in quiet encouragement, *Go on now, child. She waits.*

The whisper threaded through the wind, low as thunder nesting in the earth, soft as leaves shifting in unison. Frankie froze, breath caught, as though the world had paused to bear witness. The scarf stirred at her throat, the fabric worn thin with age, still holding the faintest trace of rosemary and something warmer she couldn't name. Once hidden and forgotten, it now felt as though it had been waiting for her all along. Wrapped close, it was an embrace she hadn't known she needed, a tether to a woman she was only beginning to understand.

"I heard you," she murmured. "I'm going."

The wind softened, rustling the grass, lifting the trailing edge of the scarf in one last flicker of motion, and then stilled. For a breath, everything held, then the world exhaled. A bird called once from the hedgerow, and the moment loosened its grip. The quiet gave way to motion, the creak of the gate, the faint ticking of cooling stone, sunlight stretching across the gravel path as the day edged forward. Frankie turned toward it, her boots whispering through the dew-slick grass.

Her Jeep waited beneath the crooked limbs of the old oak, its windshield dusted with dew, glittering like a scatter of stars in the slanting light. Frankie loaded their bags into the back, her canvas pack, the tote with Chalupa's food and blankets, the bundle of journals and maps wrapped carefully in twine. She opened the passenger door and slid Chalupa's carrier into his fleece-lined booster seat, the one reserved only for longer journeys. Elevated just enough for him to scowl at the world as they passed it by. The harness clicked into place with a snap, a trace of catnip still clinging from their last road trip.

Frankie smoothed a hand over the top of the carrier. "It's a long ride," she murmured. "So no shoulder acrobatics this time, alright? You nearly gave that toll booth attendant a heart attack."

Chalupa gave her a long, deliberate blink followed by an irritable flick of his tail, then tucked himself into his usual loaf, clearly exhausted by the emotional toll of departure.

She smiled, "Yeah, yeah. Settle in, buddy. You've got the best seat in the house."

Rounding the Jeep, she slid into the driver's seat. From within her journal, Aoife's photograph peeked out, wild curls, that knowing smile, eyes bright with secrets and starlight. Frankie looked at her grandmother's face, her voice barely more than a breath.

"You really did plan all this, didn't you?"

She turned the key, the engine rumbled to life, low and familiar. Her gaze shifted to Chalupa, now dramatically sprawled in his perch, tail twitching with seasoned disdain.

She laughed softly, easing the Jeep onto the gravel road. "Just remember to keep the sass to a minimum mister or no chicky nuggets." He gave her a look that could only be described as long-suffering.

The sky ahead stretched wide and rose-gold, light spilling across the windshield like a quiet promise. She glanced at the map between the seats, then back to the road. Her breath steady and heart sure, this wasn't just a road trip. This was a beginning, with a mystery beginning to unfold, a stubborn cat riding shotgun, and the mountains rising like a promise in the distance, Frankie DiLegna was finally on her way, toward the wild, the wonder, and whatever it was Aoife had always known she would one day seek.

The wild things were waiting.

Chapter 6

The world had blurred into motion and hum. Frankie blinked, but the scenery stayed soft around the edges, just shades of green and gold slipping past the windows like watercolor on wet paper. Her hand rested on the wheel, steady enough, though she hadn't registered the last town, or the one before that. She was somewhere between here and there, lulled by the rhythm of the road and the sleepy weight of late morning sun. The highway curved, wrapped in trees that seemed to lean closer the farther she drove. Shadows danced across the windshield in leafy patterns, and somewhere behind her, a song she hadn't meant to hum slipped from her lips and vanished into the air. She wasn't quite dreaming, but she wasn't entirely awake, either.

Chalupa snored from his fleece-lined booster seat, curled into an offended crescent of fur with his tail draped dramatically over one eye. He hadn't spoken since breakfast, unless you counted the deeply aggrieved chirp he made when she took a turn too sharply and his view of the passing cows was momentarily obscured.

She reached down with one hand to adjust the map nestled beside her on the passenger seat, her fingers brushing over its soft, creased surface. It was Aoife's map. She let her fingertips rest there a moment longer, drawn to the faded glyph tucked near the base of a painted mountain range. Her phone buzzed, sharp and sudden, lighting up the console tray with all the subtlety of an angry hornet.

"Ugh," she muttered, brushing a curl out of her eyes as she reached for it.

The screen flashed: *Mom*. She hit decline without hesitation.

Three seconds later: *Dad*. Another quick tap, decline.

Then: *Aunt Grace*.

She groaned. "For the love of fresh donuts and passive-aggressive voicemails," she muttered, swiping the notification away. "Did they form a phone tree while I was packing?"

Honestly? Probably. It was a small town, people noticed things, people talked and Frankie had left early enough that Mrs. Donnelly from the bakery had definitely seen her Jeep pull onto the main road. Mrs. Donnelly saw everything. By mid-morning, her mother would've heard a cheerful, "*Oh, your daughter left awfully early today, heading out of town.*" delivered with the nuance of a crowbar.

Once her mother knew, the next number she'd dial was Pete's. Pete, bless him, curse him, never dodged Corrine when confronted. He didn't gossip, but he also didn't lie. So when her mother demanded, "*Is Frankie with you? Did she leave town?"*

Pete had probably given his usual brand of blunt honesty. "*She said she had to take care of something*."

That would be it, short and absolutely guaranteed to light her mother's hair on fire. Her mother wouldn't call that helpful. She'd call it deceitful by design, the kind of evasiveness she believed only happened when people were "*conspiring*." From there, the rumor train didn't just leave the station, it barreled out like it had someplace urgent to be, long before Frankie even reached the county line.

The phone went quiet for a beat, just the soft chime of new voicemails stacking like warning bells. Frankie exhaled, long and slow, and let her gaze drift back to the map in her lap. Maybe they'd finally gotten the hint and she could enjoy the rest of the drive in peace. A minute passed, then another and then, *Buzz*.

The sound cut through the quiet like a strike of flint, sharp enough to make her flinch. The name glowing on the screen made her breath hitch.

Nono.

Her thumb hovered, motionless. She didn't decline, not this time. If anyone knew she was up to something, it was him. He always knew. And if Pete had said even half a sentence in the wrong company, Nono would have heard it before the words cooled. Frankie flicked on her blinker and eased the Jeep onto the gravel shoulder. The tires crunched over loose rock, dust curling in the mirrors like breath from something old and watching.

She stared at the glowing screen, then she pressed *Accept.*

"Francesca." A pause. "I sincerely hope this isn't what it looks like."

She blinked at the forest beyond the windshield.

"Lovely to hear from you Nono."

"Don't be flippant," he said, the warmth gone before it ever had a chance to reach her. "Tell me you aren't driving halfway across the country chasing someone else's shadow."

"I'm not chasing shadows," she said, her voice steady but clipped. "I'm just following a thread."

There was another pause and then a sigh, sharp and deliberate.

"You always were too curious for your own good," he said. "But this isn't a storybook, Francesca. Whatever romantic nonsense you've conjured about finding answers out there, it will end poorly."

Her grip tightened around the phone. "You don't even know where I'm going."

"Don't insult us both." His voice dropped, low and laced with quiet authority. "Turn around and come home. This game you're playing… it's not yours to finish."

A flicker of unease passed through her, but she didn't let it show. "Funny, you never seemed all that concerned before."

"You didn't think I'd notice when you disappear?" His words snapped like brittle wood. "You're on a path meant for someone else. Leave it be."

Frankie stared out at the trees, jaw tight. "You don't even know what path I'm on."

"Don't I?" His voice shifted, still calm, but colder now, as if his patience had reached its edge. "There are names better left forgotten. Places better left untouched. If you knew what was waiting at the end of that road, you'd never have started down it.

She shook her head, eyes narrowed. "Then tell me, for once in your life, just say it plainly."

Silence. The kind that filled rooms and graveyards.

"I'm telling you plainly," he said. "Come home… now!"

Frankie gripped the phone tighter. His words had that same clipped authority she remembered from every childhood holiday, every stiff Sunday dinner, when his disapproval could fill a room without raising his voice.

“I’m telling you to turn around,” Nono said, the edge in his tone cutting through even the quiet of the forest beyond her windshield. “This isn’t a path you’re meant to follow. Let it lie.”

She didn’t answer right away. From his end of the line, he said nothing further. He didn’t need to. The silence was weighted, as if he already knew exactly what her silence meant, because he did. She wouldn’t turn around and he was counting on it. Instead, his voice returned, cool and final.

“You’ve been warned Francesca,” he said, voice fading into something almost… tired. Then, with the finality of a door slamming shut, he added, “Whatever you think you’ll find, it won’t be what you’re looking for.”

Click.

The call ended.

Miles away, in a room long abandoned by footsteps, but never by purpose, the silence didn’t fall, it settled dense and knowing. The phone was placed down with a soft click. Outside, the wind curled around the eaves of the old manor like a cat retracing paths it had walked a hundred times before. The house was supposed to be empty, it looked empty. But on the third floor, where the glass had once shimmered with strange, unnatural light, where Frankie had glimpsed a figure standing silent in shadow, something still lingered. The room held no purpose now, no furniture save for the chair, no flame but the one that flickered far below and yet, the presence remained, unseen and watching. He sat unmoving in the high-backed chair, half-lit by the hearth’s gentle fire. Only fragments of him caught the glow, an eye that reflected too much light, cheekbones angled just a bit too sharp. The rest melted into shadow, as if the room itself refused to fully reveal him.

‘*She was going. Of course she was’,* he mused. She always had a fondness for paths veiled in fog. The more one warned her, the more certain she became that forward was the only direction that mattered. It wasn’t rebellion, not really, it was instinct, the kind of truth that lived in the marrow. A compass spun by something older than reason, always pointing toward the unknown. He didn’t smile, but there was a tilt to his stillness, as if the air around him had gone very still in approval. The fire crackled softly, its light pooling across the rug like spilled honey, but the shadows behind him held fast, reluctant to let go.

She had taken the bait without ever knowing it was set in motion now, pulled by threads invisible to her eye, but not to his. Once she crossed the threshold, the story would begin to truly unfold, just as it always had, just as it must. The manor groaned around him, wood and stone shifting like the stretch of an old beast disturbed mid-dream. This house had never been only walls and roof. It remembered. And it waited. He laced his fingers together, the firelight catching on a ring that hadn't left his hand in centuries. It gleamed faintly, green gold. *Verdant.* Let her run. Let her believe it her choice, the leash held strongest when the animal believed itself free. From the rafters above came the soft whisper of leathery wings. From beneath the floorboards, a slow creak, like breath caught in the lungs of something long buried. The shadows in the corner of the attic stirred, waiting.

"Good girl," he murmured to no one. Then the room fell still again, and outside, the wind scraped against the shutters, then fell away. The silence that followed was not absence but anticipation.

Far away, beneath a different sky, in a Jeep gone quiet beneath towering trees Frankie stared at the phone in her hand. The echo of her grandfather's voice still clung to the air, curling like smoke after a fire, sharp at the edges, sweet with something that didn't belong. Her grip tightened around the phone. The Jeep sat quiet around her, the engine off, the windows fogged slightly at the corners where breath and morning met. The faint scent of pine and cracked vinyl lingered in the air, threaded through with the cooler undertone of forest stone and wet bark. The seat creaked faintly beneath her, like it too was waiting for her next move. She exhaled, the breath catching on its way out. Chalupa blinked at her from the passenger seat, one ear flicking.

"Well," she muttered, slipping the phone back into the console, "that was vaguely terrifying." Chalupa just yawned. "Yeah. I know, let's get moving."

She shifted the Jeep out of park and eased back onto the road, but her thoughts were still trapped in the stillness her grandfather had left her with. The road narrowed as it curved sharply around a bend, trees pressing close. Shafts of light slanted through the canopy above, catching on the dust her tires kicked up, turning it gold for a moment before it vanished.

Frankie leaned forward, squinting through the windshield. The forest had grown stranger here. Wilder. The trees weren't just growing, they were looming, their branches bent in strange, sweeping arches overhead. Vines stitched their trunks together like threads pulled through thick cloth. Somewhere in the underbrush, something chirped a note that wasn't quite birdcall. Chalupa let out a dramatic snort from his crate in the passenger seat, his tail flicking with theatrical flair.

"Oh, please," Frankie muttered. "You're not the one trying to navigate some moss-eaten forest road without cell service. You've got treats and a blanket. I've got tire pressure anxiety and a dashboard compass that thinks south is a suggestion."

He blinked at her, unimpressed.

The road dipped sharply, then curved around an outcrop of slick rock. This was it. She turned up the drive, the Jeep bumping gently along the uneven path. The trees parted slowly, sunlight spilling through in fractured beams. And then she saw it.

Her breath caught. The conservatory looked like something out of a dream stitched together with wild intention. Its arched iron frame twisted into delicate floral shapes, worn with age but standing proud. Glass panels shimmered with age-old fractures that caught the sunlight in glimmering prisms. Vines wound themselves lovingly over every surface, leaves gleaming with moisture that hadn't come from any raincloud. Flowers spilled out along the stone path, bold and unapologetic in their bloom, colors too rich, too strange, to be ordinary.

It was... stunning. Alive, yes, but not in a pulsing, mystical sense. Alive in the way something ancient and well-tended always was. Everything, every strange phrase, every riddle, every map edge and half-finished thought, had pointed here. And then she saw it, half-obscured by trailing vines and soft green shadow, a wooden sign stood just off the road. Weatherworn, etched with curling script, the gold lettering faded but still legible beneath the moss.

The Wild Bloom Conservatory

Nestled in the hollow of the mountains, the structure rose from the earth as if grown rather than built. Wrought-iron ribs curved over domes of aged glass, their surfaces dappled with ivy and time. Climbing roses spilled over the archways in tangled profusion, blooming in impossible hues, peach, wine, palest gold.

Frankie eased the Jeep to a stop and shifted into park. The engine hummed beneath her like a heartbeat, steady and waiting. Her hands stayed wrapped around the wheel for a moment longer as she stared at the conservatory, her chest rising and falling with disbelief. Then she turned off the ignition and a loud, irritated meow cut through the quiet. She looked at Chalupa in his booster seat, his tail flicking with righteous indignation, the very picture of a long-suffering passenger finally reaching his destination. As the self-appointed *Passenger Princess*, he'd grown increasingly cranky every time the Jeep dipped below thirty-five miles per hour, offended, clearly, by her cautious mountain driving.

"We're here," she said, her voice thick with wonder and something close to awe. She unbuckled her seatbelt and reached into the carrier, lifting Chalupa out, he settled into her arms like a reluctant football, soft, round, and entirely unimpressed. He flicked his tail, eyes narrowing as if he could already smell the weirdness in the air.

"Oh, don't look at me like that," Frankie muttered, holding the door open with her foot.

She stepped out into the small gravel lot and gently set Chalupa down, where he immediately settled into a loaf of judgment. Reaching back inside the Jeep, she grabbed her bag from the floor of the passenger seat and slung it over her shoulder. The air here felt different, fragrant and full, like it had steeped for years in moss and morning light.

The Conservatory sat nestled in a wooded hollow, cradled by forest and sky, unbothered by time. Ivy clung to its weathered frame, vines threaded through rusted iron and aged glass that shimmered softly in the dappled sun. The door loomed ahead, arched and ornate, its wrought iron tangled in twisted vines and old leaves, as if the forest itself was reluctant to let it go. Frankie's boots crunched along the path. She scooped Chalupa back into her arms; he tolerated it with a put-upon sigh, tail flicking irritably at every shift in her grip. At the door, she paused. Warm, humid air wrapped around her like breath. The scent hit first, green and layered, damp earth, citrus peel, sap, and crushed petals. Sound followed, the rustle of unseen leaves, the soft patter of water, the gentle hush of something breathing just out of sight, a lullaby made of living things.

From between a row of fern-laced tables, a man emerged with the soft swish of flannel and the faint jingle of something metallic. He was small and wiry, his gray curls erupting in wild directions like a dandelion gone to seed. His boots were caked in mud, sleeves rolled to the elbows, and his apron bore the signature of a dozen minor catastrophes: leaves, soil, and a long, suspicious streak of something bright purple. He looked, Frankie thought, like a garden gnome who had wandered off from a fairy tale and taken up part-time work in botany.

"Ah!" he said brightly, spotting her. "A visitor. The frogs were right again. They told me something curious was headed our way."

Frankie blinked. "Sorry… the frogs?"

"Oh yes," he said, as though what he'd said made perfect sense. "They don't always agree on the specifics, but they're rarely wrong about the weather. Or visitors. Or Vietnamese cinnamon shortages." He squinted at her, as if trying to decide whether she was weather, a visitor, or a cinnamon shortage.

Frankie's lips curved despite herself. There was something about him, unbothered, deeply rooted, like a creature who had lived too long among leaves to be surprised by much of anything.

"Well," she said, shifting Chalupa to one arm as the cat blinked lazily at the greenery. "I suppose I'm the visitor sort."

She stepped forward into the filtered light and extended a hand. "Hi, my name is Frankie DiLegna, and I'm really hoping you can help me."

At that, the little man straightened, eyes sharpening behind the laughter. "DiLegna you say." he repeated slowly, tasting each syllables. "Well now, that's a name with deep roots." He tipped his head, curls bouncing. "If you ask me."

He swept into a bow so dramatic it nearly dislodged the trowel jutting from his pocket. "Darrow Quinlan. Keeper of this greenhouse. Occasional gardener of oddities, full-time protector of things most people can't pronounce. That's Darrow, like sparrow, but with a *D*."

Frankie, still holding Chalupa, managed a wary half-smile. "I'll never forget it."

"Exactly!" Darrow declared, popping upright with a flourish. "The kind of name that demands attention yet leaves people whispering, *'Who is this Darrow? A poet? A rogue? A man who knows far too much about fungi?'"*

Before Frankie could answer, his gaze shifted. His laughter dimmed into something steadier when he noticed the bundle in her arms. A recognition passed over his face like wind through tall grass. Chalupa, as if on cue, gave a throaty chirp and sprang from Frankie's hold, landing squarely on Darrow's shoulder.

"Hey!" Frankie lunged instinctively, but Darrow only lifted a steadying hand. The cat balanced there as though it had been his perch all along.

"Well," Darrow murmured, reverence folding around the word, his eyes locked on Chalupa's. "That's a hello if I've ever felt one."

Chalupa leaned forward and pressed his forehead to Darrow's, deliberate, unhurried. Frankie froze. Her cat did NOT do that. Not with strangers, honestly not with anyone.

Darrow's palm rested lightly against Chalupa's back, his fingers parting the fur as though he were laying hands on something sacred. He closed his eyes, exhaled like a priest before an altar, then grinned, wide and boyish.

"Ah, you have guarded her well," he said, not to Frankie but to the cat. "Kept her tethered when the wind might've carried her away."

Chalupa, infamous for swatting at new people, leaned harder into the touch, purring like a saw through cedar. Darrow's laughter bubbled over, curls bouncing as if in applause. "Not just a cat. No, no, no. You, my fine whiskered fellow, are a sentinel! A sage! A furry archivist of fate!"

He wagged a finger. Chalupa blinked slowly, unimpressed, then nudged Darrow's hand with the imperious air of royalty finally deigning to accept tribute.

"See that?" Darrow stage-whispered. "The tail flick of confirmation. Scholars spend lifetimes chasing omens. Me? I watch the cats."

Frankie gawked. "Okay... what is happening here?"

Darrow at last tore his gaze from Chalupa and fixed it on her. The mischief in his expression folded into something older, steadier. Behind the sparkle, she glimpsed the shift of branches older than the forest, a quiet that felt like the hush before dawn. He studied her as though she were a sunrise he hadn't expected to see again. Then he beamed, triumphant.

"You," he said, voice bright with delight and anchored in certainty, "are Aoife's granddaughter."

Frankie's mouth fell open. "I... wait. I never said anything. How do you even know her name?"

"Proof!" Darrow flung his hands skyward, nearly toppling a pot of thyme, and caught it at the last second with a sheepish grin. This caused Chalupa to jump to a nearby table. "Child, your face is proof. Those eyes, Aoife's eyes! Sharp as green glass and twice as untamed. And that chin, ah, saints above, stubborn as oak roots. I'd wager my boots on it!"

He leaned toward Chalupa again, stage-whispering, "And this distinguished gentleman agrees, doesn't he? Yes, yes. Another tail flick of cosmic confirmation."

His voice dropped suddenly, reverence threading through the exuberance. For a moment, all the joy fell away, leaving something rooted, solemn.

"Aoife," he breathed, tasting the name as if it were memory itself. "The Greyvale still remembers her, stone, soil, river, root. Power like that doesn't fade."

Greyvale. The way he said it thrummed through Frankie like a struck bell, resonant and strange. She brushed it off as the name of this eccentric town, but it settled deep in her, rippling outward, too heavy to ignore. Later, she told herself, she'd untangle why it lingered. For now, she tucked it away.

Darrow steadied himself against a vine-wrapped post, fingers trembling faintly, then smiled. "Now there's a name the earth remembers. Moss remembers her. Water remembers her. She was the kind of soul storms bow to and stones lean toward, hoping to listen." Then, with sudden cheer, he flapped a hand at the hedges. "Come along, before the leaves start eavesdropping. Nosy things. Gossip worse than sparrows."

He led her towards a small table tucked beneath a trellis woven with trumpet vine and evening primrose, two teacups steaming as though they had been waiting for her all morning. Chalupa followed trailing at his heels. Frankie hesitated only a moment before following, boots brushing moss-damp stone.

“So… you really knew her?” she asked again, softer this time.

“Knew her?” Darrow threw his arms wide. “Child, I knew her like moonlight knows still water. She danced, and the world leaned closer. Oh, Aoife!” He laughed again, not mockery but awe, the name itself filling his lungs.

As they reached the table, his tone shifted, reverence pulling taut around his words. He spoke as though unlocking a door that had long been sealed.

“As shadow knows the sacred flame,
She walked where older powers claim.
Her path was hidden, veiled in green,
A name once whispered, now unseen.
She bound the storms and stilled the tide,
Left runes in bark and roots beside.
Not lost, no, never lost to time,
She is the pulse beneath the rhyme.”

The words moved through Frankie like light through stained glass, fractured but radiant. Her heart ached with the truth of them. For the first time in her life, her grandmother wasn’t erased. She was remembered, revered even. Darrow’s grin softened but stayed bright, his eyes glistening.

“She wove through soil and smoke and silence. Magic, Frankie. Not stagecraft, not parlor tricks. The true kind, the kind that waits in roots and rides the wind. That remembers what was promised before you were born.” He pressed his palm to a vine-wrapped beam. The wood glowed faintly, soft as first dawn. “And now, here you are. So I ask you, once and only once, did you come to awaken what never truly sleeps?”

He brushed his fingers against a bloom, and it unfurled at his touch, shimmering, as though the flower itself leaned in to hear her answer.

“Magic is real,” he said simply. “Not glitter, not glamours. The true kind. Bound in breath and stone, in rot and bloom, in bond and break. It lives in the hush before a name is spoken. It walks where light and dark contend. This is the oldest war, fought not with swords but with memory, with will, with love… and with you. You didn’t come here for stories, Frankie DiLegna. Something woke, and now it sees you.”

The vines above them rustled faintly, as if remembering her, and his voice gentled. “This conservatory is more than what it seems. It’s a keeper of what had to be hidden for safety. Aoife shaped it as sanctuary. I... was left to tend it, to wait, to guide when the winds changed.” He studied her face, his expression a braid of mischief and tenderness. “And they have changed. You carry her echo. I see it in the tilt of your smile, in the way you glance over your shoulder like the world itself is about to whisper. You’re not here by accident, my girl.”

He stepped closer, curls wild, eyes alight with something older than excitement. “There is good... and there is undoing. Light, and what would smother it. What Aoife stood for, what you may one day guard, isn’t just herbcraft or whispered charms. It’s creation and rot. Love, and the thing that would unmake it.”

Then, as if shaking himself free of the heaviness, he grinned again and gestured to the table. “Come, come, tea won’t wait forever.”

With a little flourish, he twirled his fingers. A shimmer danced in the air, and a wedge of golden cheese appeared in his hand, utterly ordinary, except it hadn’t been there a heartbeat ago.

“For the sentinel,” he intoned, breaking off a section and offering it to Chalupa, who had jumped up onto the table.

The cat sniffed once, then accepted it with the gravitas of royalty, whiskers twitching, before purring his approval.

Frankie squinted at the mossy table. “Did you just... conjure cheese?”

“Only a modest cheddar,” Darrow said, utterly pleased with himself. “Would’ve been rude to startle you with a brie.”

Frankie blinked. “Okay, but that’s magic. Real magic. And you used it... for a snack?”

“Of course,” he said with a shrug. “What else would you do with ancient power in a greenhouse at teatime?”

She opened her mouth, closed it again, then shook her head. “I thought there’d be more... sparkles, a chant, I don’t know maybe fog. Not just poof... cheese.”

Darrow’s curls bounced as he laughed. “That’s the thing about real magic, love. It doesn’t show off. It makes itself useful, and occasionally delicious.” He placed the remaining cheese reverently beside the steaming cups, as though he had offered her a key instead of dairy. “All the grand enchantments in the world aren’t worth much if you can’t feed your guests.”

Chalupa, mid-nibble, sneezed. A puff of silver mist hiccupped from his whiskers, briefly taking the shape of a rabbit before vanishing into the air. He licked his paw, settled into a loaf, and ignored them both, perfectly pleased with himself.

The pot of steeping tea was fragrant with thyme and orange blossom as it sat. For a long moment, neither spoke. The greenhouse held its breath with them, and outside, something unseen shifted, softly, but with purpose. As if the world had just turned one quiet degree closer to the truth. Then, with a sudden, shimmering shift in tone, Darrow opened his arms wide and sang with a lilt like wind through lattice.

“*Magic is real, though it hides in the hush,*
In root-bound riddles and nettlebrush.
It stirs in the seed and speaks through the rain,
In the ache of the old and the joy born of pain.
Not stage-light trickery, nor sleight of hand,
But breath of the forest and bones of the land.
It binds what is broken, it hums what is true,
And sometimes it waits… for someone like you.”

He lowered his arms, the last note settling like pollen on the air. The vines above them gave a soft rustle. He caught his breath and looked at her with something steadier than whimsy.

“You’ve felt it, haven’t you?” he asked. “The way the air shifts, the way the world leans in.”

Magic echoed through Frankie, tolling far below thought. “Magic?” she whispered. The word felt strange in her mouth, heavy, holy.

Darrow nodded, stepping closer. He brushed a hanging vine; its leaves curled toward his palm as if they knew him. “Not the storybook kind. The kind that endures. That listens. That weaves itself into root and rain and rhythm. Flowers blooming through frost. Moss covering old names. The hush before a truth is spoken.”

“I… I don’t understand,” she said, breath unsteady.

“You don’t need to,” he answered, warm as sun on stone. “Not all at once. If you’re brave enough to look beyond what you’ve been told, you’ll start to see it.” His voice dropped, low and sure.

"Magic isn't memorized. It's how the realm remembers you. It's already in you, Frankie."

"Then why didn't I know?"

"Because the world teaches you to forget," he said, wind-soft.

"Magic is the song beneath the noise. You've been humming it your whole life without knowing its name."

Something long-buried unfurled inside her like a seed finding light. "Is it... dangerous?"

"It can be," Darrow said. "Like day and night, seed and ash. It heals or harms by the hand that holds it. Fire warms or burns. Water nourishes or drowns. Love saves or undoes. Magic's the current, you decide its course." He let the truth settle. "If you stay rooted in kindness, listen to the things that grow, it won't lead you astray."

Chalupa made a sound that wasn't quite a meow. Frankie exhaled; the world hadn't only shifted around her, it had shifted within her.

"You're not here by accident, Frankie DiLegna," Darrow said. "Plants bloom at your touch. Animals trust you without reason. Your heart knows before the world tells you. That was never coincidence." His eyes warmed, solemn. "Once awakened, it doesn't go back to sleep."

The herb-scented air pooled like honey around the little nook, a chiminea breathing quietly, mismatched chairs, one patched with quilted cushions, the other draped in a chamomile-soft throw. Frankie sank into a seat, Chalupa curling into the crook of her arm. Across from her, Darrow poured tea into scuffed mugs that clinked like old friends, every motion reverent, as if he were brewing ceremony as much as leaves.

He reached for a cup and held it out to her, and Frankie froze. It was orange. Bright, warm, orange and when she glanced inside, a tiny green frog grinned up from the bottom, its paint worn soft with time. It matched her favorite mug at home exactly, the same warm orange glaze, the same tiny green frog grinning up from the bottom, even the same tilt to its painted smile. A soft shimmer of recognition swept through her, not fear, but a bright little spark of delight, the kind that feels like the world winking back at you. Darrow only smiled, whether oblivious or indulging her, she couldn't quite tell.

He lifted his own mug, the one that read **Herb Your Enthusiasm** in faded green letters, and gave her a wink.

"Now," he said, settling back into his chair, "let's talk about the *Grrrrr.*"

Chapter 7

Frankie blinked. "The what now?"

Darrow's spoon tapped the porcelain with the easy rhythm of an old song. Steam coiled between them like breath from something ancient and waking.

"*The Grrrrr,*" he said, softer now, as if the word itself might bite if spoken too loud. "Deep wildness. The part of you that rises when the world pushes too hard."

He set the spoon aside, palms open as though cradling an ember too hot to name. "Most folks, when the storm turns mean, they hunch their shoulders. They brace, grit their teeth, try to outlast it. But the Grrrrr?" He shook his head, curls bouncing. "The Grrrrr doesn't shrink. It opens. It lifts its chin to the wind, stares the fury in the eye, and says, 'Come in then.' It takes what was meant to undo you, every bitter word, every lash of weather, every threat, and pulls it inside, reshaping it, turning it into fuel."

Chalupa let out a low, skeptical chirp, flicking his tail like someone unimpressed with Darrow's dramatics.

"Don't sass me, sentinel," Darrow said cheerfully, waggling a finger at him.

Chalupa blinked, unimpressed, then gave a grand stretch and flopped onto his side, belly up, as if to say, *Yes, yes, I embody the Grrrrr daily, peasant. Continue*. Darrow grinned and leaned back, his voice dipped lower, steady as a drumbeat.

"Resonance, not resistance. You don't fight the storm, you tune yourself to it. You take its howl into your soul until your bones ring with it, until your strength and its roar are moving together. Then it isn't breaking you; it's singing with you."

The air between them seemed to thrum with the weight of it. Darrow leaned closer, voice now nearly a whisper.

"The *Grrrrr* doesn't destroy; it transforms fear into fire. Pressure into strength. The ache that was meant to bow you becomes the heat that lifts you. That thrum in your bones when something's coming? That's the Grrrr. It doesn't ask you to survive the storm, Frankie. It dares you to rise with it."

He lifted his mug, took a thoughtful sip, and set it down again with deliberate care.

"Chaos is inevitable," he said. "Especially once you start tangling with magic. It's not tidy, not polite. It leaks into places you least expect, like a vine pushing through stone, or nettles sprouting in the middle of a rose bed." His eyes gleamed, bright with mischief. "And sometimes, the ones who carry it aren't what you expect, either."

Frankie arched a brow. "Not what I expect how?"

"Oh, child," Darrow said, leaning in conspiratorially. "The quiet ones glow after dusk, the stubborn ones mutter at moss on cloven hooves, and if a cloaked stranger offers you soup in the woods? Best take it. Just... don't ask what's in it."

Frankie frowned. "Why not?"

"Because they'll tell you," he said solemnly, wagging a finger. "And once you know it's beetle broth with nettle dumplings and a dash of distilled moonshadow, you'll never sip stew again without suspicion." He gave her a sly wink. "It's never really about the soup anyway. The meal is the message. They steep meaning into every spoonful, the ingredients are just the story's disguise."

Chalupa let out a long, theatrical sigh, then curled more tightly into Frankie's lap with the kind of regal disdain only a cat could manage.

She glanced down. "Let me guess. You've had worse?"

A slow blink and a pointed *mrrrp*. Then, as if to punctuate his verdict, he tucked his head beneath his paw like royalty retiring from court.

Frankie huffed a laugh. "Next you'll tell me Bigfoot is real."

"Real as rain," Darrow said gravely. "Formal name's Brannach Ó Woodwilde the Third, but he prefers Steve. Smells like cedarwood and lightly scorched hope. Surprisingly philosophical, too, if you catch him post-nap. Signs everything with his initials, B.O.W., but if you ask what it stands for, he'll tell you it's just Steve."

"Steve?" Frankie repeated.

"Showed up at a Winter Solstice potluck once," Darrow said, eyes brightening like he'd been waiting for someone to ask.

“Brought a beet tart and a pocket-sized book of poetry titled Meditations on Fog. Sat through half the evening, critiqued the fiddle player for being ‘emotionally dishonest,’ then slipped out before dessert. Vanished. Left behind a folding chair, a suspicious footprint in the hummus, and, this is the kicker, every single lighter in the place went missing.”

Frankie blinked. “Wait... what?”

“Gone. Every last one,” Darrow said. “Steve’s mastered the ancient art of the Irish goodbye. One moment he’s sighing about atmospheric melancholy, the next, poof.” He threw up his hands in a gesture so dramatic Chalupa startled. “Gone like mist on a kettle.”

He leaned in, lowering his voice conspiratorially. “And the beet tart? Delicious. Unsettlingly so. Like it knew things.”

Then, with a theatrical sweep of his hand, he straightened and recited:

“O noble fog, thou moody curtain,
Veiling truths I wasn’t asking for,
Wrap me once more in damp indifference,
For I am but a soggy metaphor.”

Frankie nearly spat her tea, coughing on laughter. “Please tell me that’s published.”

Darrow nodded solemnly, as if swearing it on sacred moss. “Limited run. Lichen-embossed covers. Very exclusive market.”

She laughed again, the sound bursting bright before softening into something gentler. “This should be impossible, and yet...”

Darrow didn’t press. He only smiled, tender and knowing, as if he’d seen this exact bloom before: disbelief loosening, curiosity stirring, wonder beginning to lift its head.

“If I ever meet a Bigfoot named Steve,” Frankie said dryly, “I’m hiding in the first hollow tree I see.”

“Reasonable,” Darrow agreed with a sage nod. “Mushroom folk adore hollowed-out trees, cozy little parlors, excellent acoustics for gossip. They’re fiercely loyal once they’ve claimed you. But beware, whatever you do, don’t get roped into their trivia nights.”

Frankie tilted her head. “Trivia nights?”

“Oh, ruthless,” Darrow said, his curls bobbing as he leaned in with mock solemnity. “Imagine arguing with someone who can remember what sprouted, bloomed, and withered three hundred years ago. They'll recite the rainfall of entire centuries, debate spore migrations, and cross-reference mushroom poetry until you question your own birth date." He shuddered theatrically. "Once lost a match because I forgot the exact year nettle beer went out of fashion in Greyvale. It was 1687. They'll never let me live it down."

Frankie laughed, sharp and helpless, until her shoulders shook. "I am absolutely not ready for any of this."

Darrow's grin widened, but softer now, warmer, as though her laughter had been the answer he'd wanted all along. "No one ever is," he said, his tone still light but carrying a thread of something truer beneath it. "That's the trick with magic, it doesn't wait for permission. It just arrives. Expect the unexpected."

The brightness lingered for a heartbeat longer, then mellowed. His gaze steadied, less sparkle now, more weight, like roots sinking under soil. Silence gathered between them, not empty but alive, the kind that listens. Frankie felt it fold around her like moss, urging her toward questions she hadn't meant to ask.

Her voice came low, fragile. "Why are you telling me this?"

Darrow's smile softened again, the boyish mischief dimming into something older, tender as candlelight.

"Because you're about to need it," he said gently.

The air shifted. The greenhouse seemed to inhale, leaves stirring though no breeze moved. The scent of lemon balm sharpened, rich as though the plants themselves leaned in to hear. Something was circling nearer, not danger, not yet, but change, the kind that tilts the world and never waits for anyone to be ready.

Frankie's breath trembled. "And if I fall flat on my face?"

"Child, please." Darrow leaned forward, velvet-thunder in his voice. "Of course you'll fall. That's how you learn where your wings are." He cradled his mug like memory itself. Steam rose between them, curling like something sacred. "The oak isn't tall because the wind is kind. It stands tall because the wind comes, again and again, and still, it reaches."

His voice slowed, deepened, the shift complete now, all whimsy tucked into reverence. "So fall. Fall like rain, honest, heavy, necessary. Let the ground teach you. And when you rise, rise taller in the places that cracked. Wilder in the places they tried to tame."

Then, softer still, a thread of starlight. "You don't have to know how to fly yet. You only have to leap. That's when you'll fly."

Chalupa chirped, approving. Something unknotted inside Frankie, weight she hadn't known she carried easing at last.

"You want to understand the magic?" Darrow asked. "Let it move through you. Muddy your boots. Tangle your hair. It lives in showing up, not being perfect." He tapped the table once. "Aoife left you a map, yes. But magic is what flares when the map runs out, the fire in your bones when the path goes dark. I don't need your whole story to know your spirit. You come from Aoife's line. Iron in your blood, wild in your soul. You were born to bloom where others break." Above them, a blossom unfurled, slow, deliberate. A leaf drifted down.

"The storm doesn't wait for those who hesitate," he murmured. "But it listens to those who dare to move with it. You don't fight the tempest, love, you learn its rhythm. You step in. You sway when it pulls. And if you're brave enough... you dance."

Frankie's smile was quiet and sure, eyes bright. "Alright. I guess I need to learn to dance."

"That's the spirit, lass," Darrow said, raising his cup.

A low hum slid through the glass panels of the greenhouse, as if the place itself exhaled. Warm tea grounded her; jasmine and sun-warmed soil wrapped around her like a favorite sweater. Darrow leaned in, voice leaf-soft.

"You're standing at the edge of something rare, a reckoning wrapped in moss and moonlight. It won't wait for permission. It will stretch you, show you wild corners you've forgotten how to name. When it's done, you won't just know who you are, you'll feel it. In your bones. In the way the air listens when you walk through it." He glanced toward the ivy, a shadow passing behind his smile. "We haven't much time," he murmured.

Frankie leaned forward, brows drawn. "What do you mean?"

He stirred more honey into his tea with the worn handle of a thyme sprig, the motion slow and thoughtful. "There's a stirring," he said at last. "Something old waking up. It's been waiting quietly in the roots of the world, and now it's rising fast."

She swallowed. "How soon?"

He met her eyes, the glint of mischief gone, replaced with something weightier. "Sooner than we'd like. And there's so much inside you that isn't new, it's simply waiting to be remembered." He set his cup aside and looked toward the low-burning chiminea, flames dancing like small, secretive things. "Your grandmother... she knew this was coming. Not just the danger, but the call it would place on your name." Frankie's breath caught, the edges of her understanding shifting.

"There are beings," Darrow said, voice low, "not of fairy tales, not of bedtime myths. Real ones, keepers of wild places, of old truths the world has forgotten. They are called the *The Forgotten*. The ones who never truly left, even when the rest of the world stopped believing. Fae-born, elemental, ever-shifting. They walk between what is and what was." He turned to her fully now, gaze gentle, as though placing something precious into her hands. "Your grandmother is one,."

Frankie blinked. "What?"

"She came from their world. It's where she truly belonged." His voice warmed with memory. "She tried to live with one foot in both worlds. Married your grandfather. Tried to quiet the call for something wilder, for the sake of love, for the sake of family. But that kind of calling... it doesn't go quiet. Not forever." He let the words settle, then added, "The wild doesn't ask for half of you."

"In the end," Darrow continued, "she returned to the only place that had ever felt like home. And now, that same call is stirring in you. Have you ever felt homesick for a place that you've never been? That's the call."

Frankie didn't speak, she didn't need to. The pull in her chest, the ache for somewhere she couldn't name, said enough.

Darrow watched her for a long, quiet moment, something soft and solemn in his eyes. Then he gave a small nod, as if something unseen had just been confirmed.

"All right then," he said, his voice low with meaning. "It's time."

Darrow rose from his chair and stepped away, the soft rustle of leaves following his movements as if even the greenhouse was paying attention. He returned with a wrapped bundle, the fabric worn but carefully folded.

"You follow her trail," he said simply, placing it before Frankie on the table.

Frankie unwrapped it slowly, her fingertips reverent, as though the fabric itself might whisper secrets if she listened closely enough. The cloth was a deep, mossy green, soft as velvet and stitched at the edges with a thread that shimmered faintly in the light, like ivy kissed with morning frost. Nestled in the folds, cradled like something sacred, was a compass, unlike any she had ever seen. Its casing was a dark, burnished bronze, worn smooth by age and touch, etched with tiny, intricate patterns that seemed to dance the longer she looked at them. The glass face curved slightly, catching the light and scattering it like ripples on a still pond. Inside, no familiar cardinal points marked the directions, only West, etched in delicate, curling script that pulsed softly with golden light, as if it were written in sunlight itself. The rest of the compass was filled with strange, ancient glyphs, beautiful, enigmatic markings that shimmered like moonlit ink. They moved ever so slightly, shifting in place, as if breathing. At the center, the needle spun once, slowly, thoughtfully, then stilled, pointing firmly west. The glow beneath the glass deepened, a soft heartbeat of light that seemed to respond to her presence.

Darrow's voice broke the silence, low and sure. "It doesn't point to where you are going," he said, "only to where you're meant to be… if you're willing to follow."

Frankie turned it over in her hands, the warmth of it blooming against her palms. "And if I lose the path?"

Without a word, Darrow reached into the folds of his well-worn apron and brought out a tiny glass vial, no larger than a thimble. Inside, silver flecks danced in suspension, swirling like frost caught in candlelight.

"Stardust," he said softly. "From the Verdant Sanctum, gathered on a night when the veil between the realms thinned to a thread. If the path dims or your heart clouds with doubt, sprinkle this across the compass. It will show you what's been hidden, even from yourself."

Frankie took it gently, the vial cool and weightless in her palm. She opened her satchel and withdrew the folded map, setting it on the table so she could tuck the stardust into a narrow pocket sewn along the lining. As she did, the compass slipped free from its resting place and landed with a soft tap on the map's surface. The response was immediate as a hush settled around them, the kind that makes moss seem to breathe. The runes along the map glowed faintly, like fireflies behind parchment. The single etched line pointing west warmed to a gentle gold. The compass needle quivered, turned slowly as if waking from a dream, then came to rest, not just pointing, but anchoring, its tip aimed squarely at a tiny, hand-drawn mark.

Darrow leaned in, his breath slow and quiet. He smoothed one edge of the map with a touch that felt more like memory than motion. His fingers paused near the lower corner, where a rough sketch waited. A canyon, jagged and wild, rose from the ink in layered strokes, like the jaws of something vast and ancient yawning open beneath the sky. It didn't feel like a map anymore. It felt like a warning whispered in old wind. Beneath the sketch, curling in a delicate hand, a single line curved along the base of the canyon.

Where stone meets sky, and wild things thrive, the truth begins.

The greenhouse quieted around them, as if it too sensed something was unfolding. Even the vines held their breath, leaves drooping in still reverence. Frankie reached into her satchel without thinking, drawn by a feeling more than thought, and pulled free her weathered road atlas. The pages fluttered open like they knew where to go. She laid it beside the older map. Side by side, the two maps looked like opposites. One crisp and printed, smelling faintly of ink and dust. The other soft-edged and strange, sketched with memory more than accuracy. One spoke in names and roads, the other murmured in symbols and star. They didn't match, but like twin melodies sung in different keys, they began to harmonize. A river bent like a crooked elbow. A fork in the road, splitting like a trident. Twin hills labeled The Sister Stones on the atlas curled like sleeping animals on Aoife's map, sketched beneath a crescent moon. Frankie's fingertip slid west, across ridge lines and weathered paper, following a trail of hunches and hope, until it stopped.

A name, faint, nearly erased was there. The longer Frankie looked, the clearer it became, as if the ink itself had been waiting for her, slowly waking from its long slumber to greet the one it had been made for.

Shadewind Canyon

The words deepened on the parchment like a long-held breath finally released. As her gaze settled on them, the compass at her side flared with a gentle warmth. The runes glowed like fireflies beneath water, soft, pulsing, alive. The map and the compass, each strange on their own, had become something greater together. Like a lock and key finally turned.

Darrow stepped away from the table and began moving through the greenhouse with quiet purpose, as if each step stirred the space into deeper stillness. He gathered supplies with the ease of a ritual long-practiced, plucking oddities from hidden drawers, mossy shelves, and vine-wrapped cubbies.

"Every journey needs a few essentials," he murmured, more to the room than to Frankie.

First, he retrieved a small pouch of dried starfruit slices, golden and sweet,

"These are said to keep the mind sharp and the spirit from drifting when roads grow long." He added a twist of moon salt wrapped in waxed linen, "Good for keeping shadows at bay and revealing hidden truths when sprinkled at a crossroads."

From a carved wooden box, he lifted a river stone etched with a sigil that shimmered faintly in the light. "This one hums near deception," he said. "Trust it when your gut wavers."

Next came a glass vial of foggy violet liquid, wild thyme elixir. "To calm nerves and embolden the heart. One drop under the tongue when fear starts speaking louder than your instincts." He tucked in a bundle of green thread bound with rosemary and vervain. "For protection," he said. "Woven on the last full moon with fingers that know what loss feels like."

Lastly, he placed a weathered feather, iridescent and long, with an eye-like spiral near the tip, between the folded fabric at the top of the satchel. "This belonged to a sky-watcher," Darrow added, a little smile ghosting at the corner of his mouth. "It'll remind you to keep your eyes open. Sometimes what you're meant to find arrives from above, not ahead."

Frankie watched, wide-eyed and quiet, her hands curled around the glowing compass as if it were the only steady thing in a world that had suddenly bloomed open beneath her feet. Darrow turned to her, offering the satchel with both hands.

“These are more than supplies,” he said gently. “It’s memory. Intuition. Trust. And just enough magic to get you started.”

Then, chaos. From across the room came a rustle, a snap, and the sharp flick of leaves. Chalupa let out a furious yowl, leaping three feet into the air. A giant Venus flytrap had clamped onto the tuft of his tail and refused to let go.

“Chalupa!” Frankie rushed forward just as the cat spun in indignant circles, dragging the leafy predator like an unwanted dance partner.

Darrow knelt, chuckling as he gently pried the plant free. “Don’t mind her. She’s dramatic, and she prefers her snacks with sass.”

Chalupa fixed them both with wide, wounded eyes and a tail puffed to tragic proportions. He submitted to being scooped up, but not without sighing so theatrically it could have wilted daisies. Clearly, this journey was already beneath him.

The greenhouse door creaked open on its own, spilling a ribbon of golden light across the mossy threshold.

“I think your greenhouse is telling me it’s time to go,” Frankie murmured, watching the vines near the frame sway as if in agreement.

Darrow nodded, eyes bright with quiet certainty. “You’ve got what you came for, for now. But paths have a way of circling back, lass. I’ve no doubt we’ll cross again.”

She paused with one foot on the threshold, something unsaid rising sharp and insistent behind her ribs. Darrow stood framed in vines, one hand lifted in farewell.

“Trust the pull,” he said. “And remember, magic is wild. Let it muddy your boots.”

Frankie smiled faintly, map in hand, compass aglow, her cat glaring like a storm cloud contained in canvas. Her heart felt impossibly full. She was standing at the edge of something unnameable, like the hush between pages, the kind of stillness that could shatter into wonder or reshape everything and beneath it all bloomed a single, impossible thought, she might actually find her. After a lifetime of silence and shadows, she could be at the beginning of a road that led not only to magic, but to Aoife. A living thread, waiting to be found.

The air around her stirred, leaves rustling in a language just beyond knowing. Her fingers curled tighter around the map and the compass, two halves of a key long separated. The path ahead wasn't lit; there were no signs, no guarantees. Only a glowing compass, a weathered map, and a pull that thrummed in her blood like a forgotten song rising back into its chorus.She didn't know where the road would lead. Wild, wondrous, or dangerous, she would meet it on her own terms, with her heart open and her steps steady. Frankie crossed the threshold, and the world leaned forward to meet her. Behind her, Darrow's voice carried after her like a heartbeat stitched into the wind, "*Trust the pull. Trust the wild. Trust the fire in your blood.*"

Chapter 8

The road stretched ahead, weaving through landscapes that shifted like a dream. Rolling green hills gave way to sprawling plains, and eventually, the dusty reds and oranges of the high desert. The compass on the passenger seat pulsed faintly, its runes glowing like embers. Beside it, Chalupa sprawled with the indifference of a king, his tail flicking lazily as Frankie muttered under her breath. She glanced at the rotund tabby, he responded with an unimpressed meow, his eyes narrowing in feline judgment.

"You sir, are living your best life, aren't you? Chauffeured across the country while I chase… what? Destiny? Magic?" Frankie let out a low laugh, the sound edged with disbelief. The tabby blinked once and yawned, utterly disinterested in her existential crisis and let out a *mrrrp.*

"Hope you're happy," she said, glancing at the compass. "You've taken me places AAA wouldn't dare mark on a map."

The compass had guided her down backroads so hidden they barely seemed like roads at all, weaving through dense forests that whispered secrets in the rustling leaves and over narrow bridges that groaned under the weight of her car, each creak a reminder of the uncertainty beneath her. This wasn't just a journey to some far-off canyon; it was a crossroads, a test, a thread unraveling to lead her to a truth she couldn't yet see. Frankie knew this was more than a road trip, it was the beginning of something that would upend everything she thought she knew. Yet, the enormity of it all escaped her grasp, a puzzle still locked behind a door she didn't yet have the key to. Doubt curled around the edges of her resolve, whispering questions she couldn't answer. Would she even recognize what she was meant to find when she found it? The runes on the compass pulsed faintly, steady and rhythmic like a heartbeat, as if urging her to trust the path even when her faith faltered.

Her phone buzzed on the console, Corrine DiLegna flashing across the screen. Frankie hesitated. She'd been dodging her parents' calls since leaving, but silence wouldn't make the questions or the disapproval disappear. With a deep breath, she tapped the green button.

"Francesca," her mother's voice snapped through the line, sharp and cold, as if scolding her daughter was muscle memory. "Where are you? Your grandfather said you've quit your job and taken off on some... whim. Do you have any idea how irresponsible that is?"

Frankie white knuckled the steering wheel, her patience already worn thin with her family right now.

"Hello, Mother," she replied coolly, sarcasm dripping from each word, which only fueled her mother's irritation.

"Don't take that tone with me," Corrine snapped. "You can't just run away every time life doesn't go your way."

"I'm fine, mother. I just needed a change of scenery, that's all." Frankie said, trying to keep her voice even.

"Really?" Corrine's brittle laugh cracked through the phone like ice breaking. "Frankie, this isn't how adults handle their problems. You can't just quit your job and disappear every time something doesn't go according to plan."

"I did not quit my job, and I'm not running away," Frankie shot back, her frustration bubbling to the surface.

A long silence followed, as Corrine formulated her retort. Frankie could almost hear the slow, deliberate turn of thoughts on the other end of the line, as if her mother were assembling a disapproval bouquet stem by stem. It was familiar, the cold pause, the quiet edge. Every time Frankie had veered from the family's polished path, choosing soil and sunlight over spreadsheets, tending to herbs instead of hosting dinner parties, it had been met with the same response, a sigh, a silence, a subtle snub that lingered longer than any argument. But this silence... it felt different. Not her mother's usual brand of clipped disapproval or tight-lipped sighs. No, this was quieter. Calculated. Like the still moment before a summer storm breaks loose and turns all the leaves upside down.

Outside the car, the wind stirred, light but odd, curling through the trees in a way that made the shadows stretch too long for the hour. Frankie shivered and glanced at the compass. The compass on the seat beside her gave a faint pulse, its glow warm but insistent, like a firefly nudging her thoughts. Frankie glanced down at it, then at the road unspooling before her like a stitched path through a storybook. A breeze stirred the tips of the trees lining the narrow backroad, and for a moment, the air inside the car seemed to still, as if the world itself was holding its breath. She shifted her grip on the wheel, the silence pressing in, not just from her mother's voice, but from somewhere older, deeper, like something lodged in the bones.

"A change of scenery," Corrine repeated, her tone clipped and cold. "Honestly, Frankie, do you even hear yourself? You're throwing away your potential. Running off to who-knows-where with no plan, no structure, it's exactly what we were afraid of. You're just like *her*."

Frankie's stomach flipped. "What is that supposed to mean? *Her?*"

"You know exactly what it means," Corrine snapped, brittle now, like glass straining under a hairline crack.

Frankie's voice rose, the dam finally fracturing. "How could I know? No one ever talks about her. You never say her name, you pretend she never existed, "

"She disappeared." Corrine's voice was sharp. "She left when your father graduated and never came back. I only met her a handful of times, and even then, she was… strange. Always chasing some whim, she lived in her own world and expected everyone else to follow her into it."

Frankie gritted her teeth.

"She thought rules didn't apply to her. Your grandfather tried to help her, tried to keep her grounded, but she wouldn't listen. No one ever understood why he married her in the first place." Then Corrine's voice dropped, quieter, almost soft. "It's why I worry."

Frankie drew a slow breath. The woman her mother described had always felt like a ghost shaped from disapproval, a figure made of absence and judgment rather than truth. But Darrow's words flickered through her like warmth through frost. Aoife had been vibrant, untamed, threaded with light and magic. A woman who planted secrets the way others planted herbs, leaving breadcrumb trails for the one person who might someday follow.

"And now," Corrine continued, her tone cooling, "Dom says you've been digging into her past."

A ripple of unease moved through Frankie, sharp and unwelcome. Of course Nono had told them. He'd been the first to twist the story, polished enough to sound plausible, empty enough to disguise the rot beneath. He had told her parents Aoife had simply left. No reason. No farewell. Just disappeared. A vanishing act wrapped in insinuation and tied off with silence, and no one questioned it. Not because it made sense, but because it was convenient. They'd let Aoife evaporate like morning mist, no grief, no outrage, forgotten so thoroughly it was as if remembering her had been forbidden. But now Frankie could feel the edges of another story beginning to show through the cracks. There was Dom's Aoife, unstable, selfish, a cautionary tale, and then there was Darrow's, bright and wild, full of mystery and mischief, the kind of woman the forest remembered and the vines still leaned toward. It struck her as slightly absurd, she was choosing to believe a stranger in a dirt-smudged apron over her own blood and yet... she was. Because Darrow's Aoife felt real. She felt like sunlight breaking through a shuttered window. Like the answer to a question Frankie hadn't known she'd been asking her whole life.

She stared out the windshield, the compass pulsed faintly on the seat beside her, then flared, a shimmer of green and gold that danced across the worn leather. As if it had heard the thought. As if it were answering her in its own quiet way, keep going. She was done inheriting other people's versions of the truth. She was going to find Aoife, the real Aoife no matter what it took.

"And what exactly do you think you're going to find?" Corrine demanded. "Do you think this will make you happy? That any of this will fix what's broken?"

Frankie's voice came low, but clear. "I don't know, Mom. But I need to find out."

There was a pause, then a long hiss of breath, half sigh, half disappointment. "You don't even know what you're looking for, you're just like her, you know. Foolish. Stubborn..." But the words broke off and in the quiet that followed, Frankie's mind reached backward, past silence, past shame, and brushed against a memory she hadn't dared to hold in years.

She was sixteen again, locked in her room after another explosive argument with her parents. It had started the same way it always did, Corrine's sharp, clipped tone slicing through Frankie's defenses with accusations of "wasting potential." The fight had spiraled into shouting, and Frankie had stormed into the bathroom in tears, grabbing a pair of dull scissors. She'd shaved one side of her head in a fit of rebellion, leaving jagged tufts that took months to grow back. At the time, it had felt like reclaiming something of herself, a small act of defiance against the constant pressure to be someone she wasn't. But what stayed with her most wasn't the haircut or the fight, it was the argument she'd overheard afterward. She had been sitting on the floor, her back pressed against her bedroom door, when her father's low, anxious voice filtered through the crack.

"What if she turns out like her?" he had asked, his words heavy with worry.

Corrine's response had been cold. "Then we'll handle it. We won't let her ruin herself the way Aoife did." Frankie hadn't known who Aoife was at the time. She'd only known the words stung, branding her as something careless, something that needed to be contained.

Now, as the memory surfaced again, things started to click, slowly, stubbornly, like puzzle pieces that had always been there but refused to fit until now.

"Mom," Frankie said, her voice a little shaky but edged with something new, determination. "Why did everyone act like Aoife was so awful?"

The silence on the other end was thick and heavy, the kind that held more truth in it than any answer ever could. Frankie's grip on the wheel tightened. Her pulse kicked up, thrumming just beneath her skin.

Finally, Corrine sighed, sharp and tired. "Aoife walked away, Frankie. From everything. From her family, from real life, from the things that actually mattered. She was flaky, unreliable, always chasing some whimsical dream or other."

"Whimsical dreams?" Frankie echoed, her brow furrowing.

"She believed in fairies, Frankie. *Fairies*!" Corrine said, the word laced with derision. "All of that metaphysical nonsense. Your grandmother lived in a world of make believe because she couldn't handle reality."

Frankie's throat tightened, anger sparking in her chest. "And that's why you hate her? Because she believed in things you don't understand?"

Corrine's sharpness returned, slicing through the connection like a blade. "Because she left," she snapped. "She left your grandfather, your father, her whole life, for what? To live out some bohemian fantasy? You're too young to understand what that kind of selfishness does to a family."

More silence but when Corrine spoke again, her voice was quieter but no less sharp.

"She embarrassed them, Frankie. Your grandfather, your father... me. Do you know what it's like to watch someone take everything they've been given and throw it away? To watch her behave like a child, humiliating herself, and by extension, the family? She wouldn't bend, not even a little. The more they tried to help her, to make her... normal, the more she pushed back."

Frankie swallowed hard, her mind churning.

"Maybe," she said slowly, her words cutting through the tension, "you're just upset because she got away, she's free."

Corrine 's sharp inhale was audible even through the static of the line.

"That's ridiculous," her mother said, but the brittleness in her voice betrayed her.

Frankie pressed on, the words tumbling out before she could stop them. "Nono and Dad tried to change her, did they? '*To clip her wings*', to make her fit into this perfect little box of what a DiLegna should be. And when she refused, when she left, it wasn't just her choice you couldn't handle. It was the fact that she chose herself. Are you afraid I'll do the same?"

"Francesca." Corrine's voice was tight, defensive.

"Am I wrong?" Frankie challenged, her voice rising. The silence that followed was so thick it felt like it might swallow her whole.

When Corrine finally spoke, her voice came quiet and brittle, like frost stretched thin across glass.

"You're just like her," she said.

The words weren't loud, but they landed with the precision of a blade-sharp, uninvited, and laced with something layered:

bitterness, fear… and maybe, just maybe, the faintest thread of envy. But most of all, they carried finality.

Then the line went dead.

Frankie stared at the screen, stunned.

"Seriously?" she muttered.

She tossed the phone onto the passenger seat, but the words lingered anyway, clinging to her like woodsmoke. A slow ache unfurled beneath her sternum. She'd once read that a girl's first bully isn't the kid who knocks her down on the playground, it's the one who tucks her in at night. Corrine had never needed to raise her voice. Her quiet was a blade all its own. Affection came sparingly. Approval, rationed like a prize she was never meant to win.

You're just like her.

Was that meant as an insult? Or had her mother, without realizing, brushed too close to a truth sacred enough to hurt? Frankie leaned back against the seat, a sigh slipping from her like a thread pulled from something unraveling. The words echoed inside her, circling, tugging, refusing to settle.

Just like her.

In their house, blame had filled the spaces where love should've lived. Silence had built the walls. And Aoife's name, never spoken aloud, hadn't even been allowed the dignity of being a ghost. She'd been rewritten into a cautionary tale and buried under layers of quiet shame.

Until now.

Frankie's gaze dropped to the compass on the seat beside her. It pulsed once, green-gold and steady, as if it, too, had overheard and was answering in quiet defiance. Its glow echoed something fluttering inside her, soft, rhythmic, alive.

A soft *mrrrp* rose from the passenger seat. She turned to look and found Chalupa watching her, eyes bright, still, ancient in a way cats are when they're waiting for you to catch up to what they already know. There was something behind his gaze, something more than curiosity. As if he could see the storm beginning to form inside her and was waiting to see whether she'd let it pass… or walk straight into it.

Frankie let out a breath that felt like a beginning. "I'm starting to think," she murmured, "that being like her might actually be the best thing I've got going."

The doubts that had clung to her like burrs, quiet, needling things, began to fall away with each passing mile, shaken loose by movement and momentum. The old fears, of being too much, too wild, too impractical, had been stitched into her since girlhood, whispered between the lines of every withheld smile and measured sigh. But now, they were softening, unraveling thread by thread in the hush between one breath and the next.

Outside the window, the world unfurled in a blur of color and light, a living watercolor swept past by time and wheels and will. Trees bent in the wind as if to watch her pass, hills rolled gently like a lullaby she hadn't known she needed. For the first time in a long while, perhaps ever, Frankie didn't feel misplaced. She felt like she was returning to a part of herself she'd never been allowed to name, let alone nurture. A self woven from green things and quiet magic, from stubborn roots and songs no one else could hear. She wasn't just moving toward a destination, she was moving toward a girl with her name who had never been trimmed to fit or quieted to please. A girl who had waited quietly beneath the weight of years, untamed, unforgotten, biding her time until the world grew soft enough to let her rise. Frankie wasn't just moving forward; she was moving inward, toward something truer. Towards this magic, toward the version of herself no one had ever dared to envision, except, perhaps, Aoife and now, at last, she was ready to meet that becoming.

Her gaze drifted to the compass. Its runes pulsed brighter, casting pale, silvery patterns across the dash like moonlight through branches. The symbols shimmered, then shifted, like a language beginning to remember itself. And for a breathless second, Frankie nearly understood. It felt like the echo of something she'd always known… and was only now beginning to hear.

Up ahead, something changed. The road hadn't ended, but it no longer looked the same. It's edges shimmered now, wavering like heat rising from sunlit stone. But this wasn't heat, it was… invitation. The landscape unfolded in slow motion, like a secret deciding it was time to be seen. Trees leaned back just slightly, giving space, as if acknowledging her arrival. And the light… the light pooled golden and thick, honeyed and strange, bending around her like the world itself had taken a breath. Frankie blinked hard, a dirt path unfurled ahead, narrow, winding, and undeniably there. She could have sworn it hadn't been. But now, it looked as though it had always been. The compass in the passenger seat pulsed, stronger this time.

"Alright," Frankie muttered, tightening her grip on the wheel.

"Magical GPS, don't let me down."

The change was subtle at first, like a curtain lifting, like breath held then released, but it was impossible to ignore. The world shimmered at the edges, and reality bent quietly into something older, something watching. The trees rose taller with every bend in the road, arching overhead like a cathedral woven from bark and breath. And the leaves, the forest didn't burn like autumn, it bloomed. A riot of impossible color, alive with something older than seasons. The air shimmered faintly, like stardust suspended in a hush. Frankie's breath caught as a butterfly, large as her hand, drifted past the windshield, its wings glowing with blue fire, every movement unhurried, eternal. To her right, a meadow unfurled, wildflowers swaying in a rhythm she couldn't hear. Frankie eased the Jeep to a crawl, eyes narrowing at a flicker of movement among the blooms. A rabbit. No. Not a rabbit. Antlers rose from its brow, delicate and branching like spring twigs dipped in sunlight.

"Is that …" she gasped. "Is that a jackalope?"

She blinked hard. It was still there. The creature stood motionless, ears alert, antlers catching the light like something pulled straight from the margins of a folk tale. Then it turned its head slowly and met her gaze. Its eyes were strange, too deep, too old, like it remembered everything that had ever happened in this place and maybe even what came next. Then, without a sound, it turned and disappeared into the tall grass, vanishing as quickly as it had come. Frankie stared at the space where it had been.

"Okay," she breathed. "So. Jackalopes. That's… a real thing now." Chalupa, now curled like a comma, cracked one eye open, regarded her, then promptly resumed his nap. "Oh, don't even start," she muttered. "You sleep through everything and I'm the one who looks crazy?"

The compass pulsed once in her hand, low and steady. At the same moment, the Jeep's headlights flicked on. She startled slightly. The beams cut through the quiet woods ahead, bright and focused, even though the sun still glowed high in the sky. Frankie stared at the glow stretching ahead of her.

"Seriously?" She reached for the switch and flicked it off. The lights stayed on. She tried again. Still on. They hummed, steady and indifferent.

She dropped her hand into her lap. "Jackalopes and magical headlights. Sure. Next up, a squirrel in a cloak handing me a cookie." Chalupa stretched, yawned, and turned his back to her. Frankie exhaled and looked out at the road ahead. And then, it shifted. No warning, no sound. Just a change, subtle but certain, like something beneath the surface had risen. She eased the Jeep to a stop. Behind her, the road still looked like it always had, sunlit, familiar, edged in wild grass. But ahead?

The world had tilted toward something unseen, gone strange at the edges.The light thickened, golden and slow, like dusk being stirred gently into the trees. Shadows stretched longer. Wildflowers pooled in the hollows between roots. The sky above shimmered faintly, not quite morning, not quite night. The air itself seemed to soften. The trees had grown taller, much taller, and arched overhead like guardians leaning in to listen. She sat very still. One hand still resting on the wheel. The other curled protectively around the softly pulsing compass.

"Okay, now what?" she whispered, then she saw it.

In the center of the clearing ahead stood a wooden signpost. Weathered but unbowed, like it had been waiting exactly where and when it needed to be. Four arrows jutted from its center, each pointing in a different direction. The names carved into them shimmered faintly, as if resisting being fully read. They didn't belong to any place she'd ever heard of, yet... they didn't feel unfamiliar.

Eversky

Hollowroot

Thistledown

West

The compass pulsed once more, steady and certain. Frankie leaned forward, eyes narrowing as the arrow marked West glowed faintly in the strange, golden light. Something landed on the hood of the Jeep with a solid *THUD*. Frankie jolted back with a yelp. A massive raven stood there, feathers shimmering like oil-slicked obsidian. It blinked once, slow and unimpressed, like a cranky librarian who'd just caught someone dog-earing a sacred scroll.

"Uh… hi?" Frankie managed, her voice an octave higher than usual. "Can I… help you?"

The raven tilted its head. Its feathers rustled like velvet curtains just before a performance began. It opened its beak, but before it could speak, Chalupa launched himself from his fleece-lined booster seat like a furry cannonball. His tail exploded into full bottle-brush mode, ears flattened, and he let out a hiss so sharp it might have sliced through glass.

"Chalupa!" Frankie cried. "We do not attack wildlife!"

The raven gave a disgruntled huff. "Control your furred footstool."

Frankie blinked. "Did you just…?"

"Furred footstool?!" Chalupa spat, his fur bristling. "You overgrown feather-duster!"

The raven fluffed its wings in contempt. "Glorified nap mat."

"Peck-happy sky goblin!"

"Enough!" Frankie slapped the steering wheel, eyes wide, breath ragged. "What is happening?! Chalupa… you're talking?!"

Her cat, the loaf of fluffy sass she'd had forever, who judged her outfits, hogged her pillow, and shed exclusively on black clothing, sat primly in the passenger seat, licking one paw with cool detachment.

"I mean," he said, pausing only to smooth his whiskers, "I always could. You just weren't ready to hear me."

Frankie's mouth opened. Closed. Opened again. Words abandoned her like spooked pigeons. "You've… always… been able to?!"

Chalupa gave the faintest shrug, the kind that somehow managed to drip condescension. "Honestly, you weren't exactly built for a full magical breakdown at thirteen. You barely survived algebra."

Frankie pointed at him, pointed at the raven and back to him. Her voice cracked. "You've been sitting on this for years, and now you're trading insults with a talking raven?!"

The raven fluffed his feathers, beak lifted with regal disdain. "I do more than talk. I guide, observe and frequently deliver inconvenient truths."

"Oh, perfect," Frankie groaned. "Mystical *and* smug."

The bird tilted his head, eyes glinting. "You're adapting quickly. That's promising."

Frankie collapsed forward, pressing her forehead to the steering wheel. Her groan rattled the Jeep's interior like a trapped spirit escaping.

"I am going to need wine," she muttered. "Copious amounts."

She lifted her head, turned slow and cautious, to face the raven gleaming black against the hood. Her breath snagged and held. For a moment, even her pulse seemed to forget its rhythm. Frankie's laugh broke out thin and wild, the kind of sound people make on the ledge between fear and hysteria.

"Right. Of course. My cat talks, and now there's a cryptic raven that thinks this is a taxi."

Chalupa, loaf of judgment that he was, only flicked his tail, his eyes glinting with the long-suffering patience of someone forced to supervise chaos. The raven shifted, claws rasping lightly against the Jeep's metal, wings half-mantled as though he might launch straight through the glass. His eyes fixed on Frankie, sharp and molten.

"Do you feel it yet, the hum?" he asked, voice low, as if it belonged less to the bird and more to the night itself.

Frankie stilled, sarcasm dissolved before it could leave her tongue. Because yes, she felt it. The hum had been there before, faint and nagging, like a second heartbeat she could almost ignore. But now it pressed against her from all sides. The Jeep's interior was dense with it, buzzing in her ears like bees crowding a hive. It coiled beneath her ribs, threaded down into her fingertips, drummed through her bones like roots knocking against stone. The steering wheel vibrated faintly under her palms, or maybe that was her hands trembling.

Neither cat nor raven offered explanation. Chalupa held her gaze, his eyes steady, unblinking, a quiet weight that said you're not imagining this. The birds feathers shimmered with oil-slick iridescence, his stare cutting through Frankie as though she were a lantern with no secrets left inside and in that silence, she understood the truth and that unsettled her more than either of them speaking aloud.

Frankie blinked, pulse hammering in her ears. "Okay… right. Introductions are needed, I guess."

Her throat felt dry, but she lifted her chin anyway. "I'm Frankie DiLegna."

She gestured to the passenger seat, where Chalupa lounged smugly like royalty surveying his court. "And this is Chalupa, who, it turns out, has apparently been holding out on me for years."

Chalupa offered a slow blink, then licked his paw as if to say finally, recognition. With deliberate grace, the raven dipped his head in a low, formal bow. It wasn't showy, it was regal, an act that felt centuries old, as though he had bowed to queens, to gods, and now, to her.

"I am called Nyx," he said, voice resonant and velvet-rich, drawn from the hush that follows thunder. "*Sentinel of the Turning Ways. Watcher of Thresholds. Occasional Ambassador to the Gloaming and the other In-Between Realms*… and most certainly not a common raven, thank you."

The words didn't just echo; they rang, softly, like a tuning fork struck in the heart of the forest. They seemed to bend the air, shifting it. Frankie felt them settle into her skin like ash or ancient ink, truth written straight into bone. Nyx's feathers stirred in the breeze, whispering like pages in a book older than memory.

Frankie stared, breath shallow, sarcasm forgotten. "It's… an honor to meet you, Nyx," she whispered, the words trembling with a reverence she hadn't expected.

The raven's posture shifted, elegant as wind threading through silk. He extended one glossy wing in a sweeping arc and bowed again, this time lower. The light caught him just right, casting an iridescence like spilled ink under a moonlit sky.

"The honor, Frankie DiLegna, is mine," he said, voice like a twilight bell. "The threads that led to this moment have been long in the weaving."

Her throat tightened. The words came out hushed, reverent despite herself. "Are you… one of the Forgotten?"

Nyx tilted his head, feathers catching prism-spun light, rippling over him as though the air itself bent to his presence. The motion was unhurried. His gaze held hers, steady and unreadable, until the silence itself seemed to deepen around them. At last, his voice broke it, low and resonant, like wind riffling through the pages of an ancient book.

"It is... complicated." A pause, weighted, careful. "I have walked their paths, flown their skies. I have spoken their names in places where names do not linger long. I am not of their blood, no. But I have been entrusted with their truths."

He shifted slightly, the sheen of his feathers flickering like ink under starlight. When he spoke again, his voice carried the gravity of vow and the intimacy of confession.

"I serve their will... and now, I serve you."

Frankie blinked, caught off guard by the gravity of his words.

"Me?" she echoed.

Nyx hopped across the hod and over the mirror to the passenger door.

"This path you walk, it wasn't meant to be walked alone. Aoife saw to that. She left behind more than just maps and journals," his voice deepening with quiet reverence. "Aoife set things in motion long before you were ready to walk this path. Trusted allies, hidden guides, guardians placed like stars along a constellation she hoped you'd one day follow." He tilted his head slightly, black eyes gleaming beneath the prism-spun light. "I was one of those placed. When your journey began, so did mine."

Frankie's brows drew together, realization hovering just beyond reach. Nyx continued, his tone steady but not unkind.

"I've watched from the edges until now, but the road ahead won't be walked in solitude. Your grandmother made certain of that. So yes, I'm coming with you."

Frankie stared at him, stunned. "You're... coming with us?"

"Yes, didn't I just explain that?" Nyx said, his voice rich with certainty. "You'll need more than a compass to understand where it's pointing, besides...", his beak tilted in what could only be described as a smirk, "someone has to keep that cat humble." He gave a slow, ceremonial nod, as if sealing an unspoken pact. "There are truths waiting in the shadows, threads that will try to tangle you. You'll need help to stay untangled."

His tone shifted, drier now. "And frankly, I'm not interested in sitting on the sidelines. I'd prefer a front-row seat."

He dipped his head with the elegance of an old-world envoy. "You'll need a guide, someone who knows the Turning Ways, who can read the signs in dark and starlight, who understands how the veil bends... and when it might snap and, let's be honest, someone with better taste than your current travel companion."

From the passenger seat came an indignant yowl. Chalupa, still perched in his fleece-lined booster like a fluffy loaf, gave Nyx the kind of glare that could curdle cream. Then, with all the drama of a silent film villain, he reached down with one paw, unlatched his own buckle with a flourish, and leapt into the backseat.

"I'm not sitting next to that feathered windbag," he grumbled. "He can have the front seat. I'll be in the back where no one's shedding feathers in my water bowl."

He stomped a tight, deliberate circle, twice, before collapsing onto Frankie's crumpled jacket and the emergency blanket she always kept back there. With a theatrical sigh, he began kneading both into what could only be described as a personal throne, tail flicking like punctuation.

"Yes," he murmured, mostly to himself, "this has better energy. Less beak, more blanket."

With a single beat of his wings, Nyx hopped down and settled neatly on the now-vacant passenger seat. He gave a regal shimmy, feathers flaring until they gleamed like starlight caught in obsidian.

"Much better," he declared, adjusting his wings with the smug satisfaction of someone born for stage lighting.

Frankie mused, "This is my life now," the words slipping out somewhere between disbelief and reluctant wonder.

She stared through the windshield at the shimmering road ahead, then sideways at the theatrically solemn raven now occupying the front seat of her Jeep. A talking cat. A sharp-tongued bird. A glowing compass. A map that seemed to breathe. Somewhere along the way, reality had packed its bags and left her at the edge of a story she hadn't agreed to tell, but couldn't seem to stop living.

Outside, the forest hadn't changed, not exactly, but it leaned closer. Branches curved and shadows stretched into questions, and the air tasted of iron and rain, thick with a secret aching to be spoken. Behind her lay the road of the life she thought she knew. Ahead… it gleamed like a promise half-whispered, half-dared. Her eyes dropped to the map, then to the compass pulsing faintly on the seat between them. Chalupa flicked his tail with smug indifference, while Nyx settled with the gravity of a herald waiting to announce destiny.

Frankie exhaled slowly, her grip tightening on the wheel until her fingers cramped. "So… what now? Do we wait for a burning bush, or does destiny just leave Post-it notes these days?"

Nyx's beak tapped the glove box, each strike deliberate as a gavel. "*West* is calling."

The compass flared in answer, green light spilling across the dim cabin, pooling like breath too long withheld, finally exhaled in a single, irrevocable yes. The glow didn't just illuminate, it pulsed, steady and insistent, as though the compass itself carried intent.

Frankie let out a shaky laugh, part surrender, part awe. "Of course it is," she whispered, because how could she argue with a raven and a compass conspiring in unison, especially when the compass seemed the most certain of them all?

She shifted the Jeep into gear and gravel crackled beneath the tires like bones giving way beneath time. The trees leaned close around the road, tall and solemn, their crowns whispering together as if conspiring. The map beside her shimmered faintly, its lines glowing like fractures of light, alive with a secret pulse. Then something stirred between the trees ahead. Not deer. Not shadow. Something that watched. The weight of unseen eyes pressed against her skin until her pulse stumbled. The compass surged again, sharper, quicker, its glow beating like a second heart, urgent, alive, as if it too had seen. The road thrummed beneath her tires, heavy with promise and peril both, the certainty of a threshold that, once crossed, could never be undone. Beyond that bend, her life was already changing, stretching into something stranger, vaster, older than she had ever dared to imagine. As the forest swallowed the last of the light, Frankie felt it settle over her like a vow, the world she had known was gone. What waited ahead was wilder, older, inevitable a nothing would ever be the same.

Chapter 9

The forest deepened, trees arched overhead, their crowns weaving together like cathedral vaults, shadow and starlight laced through every branch. The air shifted and a breeze moved through the canopy, damp with moss and threaded with something sharper, like the breath before a storm. Nyx perched on the dashboard, feathers gleaming.

"This path was never meant to be stumbled upon," he murmured, his voice pitched low, almost conspiratorial.

Frankie checked the rearview mirror. Chalupa had sprawled across her coat like a tyrant on a throne, one paw dangling with exaggerated despair.

"I regret everything," he muttered, eyes narrowing at the shimmer ahead.

Frankie smirked. "We've barely started. Don't go full drama llama on me."

Chalupa huffed, lifting his head with offended dignity. "Measured dread, not drama. " he corrected. "Entirely different category."

She shook her head and glanced at Nyx. "Do either of you ever say anything that isn't cryptic?"

Nyx didn't so much as blink. "Where would be the fun in that?"

On the seat between them, the compass pulsed, green and gold spilling over the dash. Its glow wasn't steady, it breathed, patient and alive, like it was choosing when to let its secrets be known. Frankie loosened her grip on the wheel. The road was no longer just road; it was an invitation, a riddle, a summons. The canopy began to thin, and the hush of forest gave way to something wider. The air shifted, pine giving way to dust and sun-warmed stone. Hills rolled out before them in slow, deliberate waves, wildflowers spilling across their slopes in impossible hues. Each bloom shimmered faintly, colors sliding between rose-gold and silver-lavender, never quite still.

The sky above arched vast and dazzling, clouds drifting like opal fire, their edges burning with mother-of-pearl light. Frankie took it all in, and it filled her like a chord struck clean, deep and resonant.

"This," she whispered, wide-eyed, "is... incredible."

Chalupa stretched luxuriously, tail flicking. "You're lucky you're seeing it," he muttered, eyes slitted in feline satisfaction. "Most beings never do."

Frankie blinked, still drinking in the glimmering expanse. "Seeing what, exactly?"

Nyx let out a dry caw, feathers ruffling. "The *In-Between*, this is where what's hidden lives just beneath the skin of your world. It's always been here. You just couldn't see it, until now."

"The In-Between is the..." Frankie repeated, the word tumbling off her tongue like a forgotten lyric finally remembered.

"It's the space between worlds," Chalupa explained, tone unusually solemn. "A seam woven thread by thread. Where magic and memory and the things humans stopped believing in still breathe."

Nyx gave a thoughtful nod, feathers catching the light like ink spun with stars. "Some of The Forgotten make their home here," he said quietly. "They were never banished. The world simply stopped believing in them. So they slipped sideways, into the quiet, into the thresholds, into the places where wonder still lingers like mist before morning."

His voice deepened, threaded with memory.

"They are not fairy tales. Not figments. The Forgotten are real. Fae-born. Elemental. Ever-shifting. They tend the wild places, cradle the old truths. They are the ones who never truly left, even as the world built over their hollows and named their rivers after men. They walk between what is and what was, and sometimes, when the veil thins, they guide what might yet be."

A silence fell between them. The forest seemed to lean in.

"I remember stories of your grandmother," Nyx said, his tone softer now, the cadence of someone honoring the dead. "Aoife is one of the rare ones, born of the edge, but not content to stay hidden in it. She walked boldly between the worlds. She mended what others ignored. She helped keep the balance.That's what the

Forgotten do, Frankie. They don't demand worship.They offer help, quietly and often unseen."

Frankie's breath hitched. "She was one of them?"

Nyx nodded once. "Not all who are Forgotten choose to fade. Some choose to stay near. To raise gardens and young. To leave behind seeds instead of shadows."

He looked at her then, not as a messenger, but as something older.

"And now," he said gently, "one of those seeds has sprouted."

She turned her gaze back to the road, which curved gently past a crystalline stream glowing faintly beneath a canopy of willow boughs. The water shimmered like it remembered older moons. Along the bank, figures moved, slender, liminal, not quite human, not quite shadow, darting at the edges of sight. They were too swift to be clearly seen, more felt than known, but their laughter rose on the breeze, silvery, light, and ancient as birdsong echoing through a dream.

Frankie's voice trembled, barely above a whisper. "It feels like... like I've crossed into a place that was waiting for me."

Chalupa licked his paw with practiced indifference, then paused, eyes gleaming with something older than mischief.

"Because you have," he said simply.

And she had. In the way the wind stirred the air as if carrying her name. It wasn't déjà vu, this wasn't a memory. It was older than that, deeper. The air thickened for a breath, and Frankie saw her, just beyond the willows. A figure cloaked in green and gold, haloed in soft light. Not fully there, not quite solid, but unmistakable. Her face turned toward Frankie, solemn, knowing, then vanished like sun through morning fog. Frankie blinked, her breath catching. This place didn't just welcome her, it recognized her. As if the earth remembered the shape of Aoife's footsteps and now stirred to greet her granddaughter. The same blood, the same call, the same wild inheritance whispered through the trees and into her bones. Every glinting ripple of the stream, hummed with quiet recognition. It wasn't familiarity, this was belonging. Frankie tightened her grip on the wheel, steadying herself. This wasn't just a detour through magic. It was a homecoming no one had told her to expect, and yet somehow... Aoife had always known she'd come.

The road dipped again, light filtering through the branches like memory made visible. For a moment, no one spoke, even Chalupa had stilled, ears twitching but silent. The air held as a church right before a prayer, waiting. Then Nyx, still as a statue carved from ink, turned his head.

"The Forgotten don't leave doors open by accident," he said, his voice low, threaded with something ancient. "They placed guardians along the way. I'm one of them. This path, your path, it's been in motion for a very long time."

Frankie swallowed hard. Her fingertips brushed against the glowing compass, warm to the touch and still pulsing in green-gold rhythm with each bend in the road. She felt it like a heartbeat, answering something in her own.

"So this isn't just some magical detour..." she said softly, eyes fixed on the winding road ahead.

"No," Nyx said, perching higher."It's the space where truth waits. The closer you get to it, the more the veil thins. You'll see. The colors sharpen, the air sings and the impossible begins to feel like the natural order of things."

The hills deepened in shade as they passed, a stream now glinting like it carried shards of stars, a fox with too many eyes blinking from beneath a tree whose bark was carved with ancient runes. Every turn revealed something more strange and beautiful than the last. The forest wasn't fading into the horizon. It was folding around her like a storybook opening, page by page.

Frankie smiled faintly, watching as another jackalope bounded across the road, its antlers catching the golden light like twin crescent moons. It glanced at her before disappearing into the brush. She just laughed.

The road ahead still shimmered and she let out a long breath, "Okay, but I still don't understand why I suddenly have a talking cat and a know-it-all bird as road trip buddies."

"Enchanted companions." Chalupa corrected. "And I'm here because you'll always need me, obviously."

Nyx scoffed. "Need you? Oh please, if anything, I'm the only competent one here. You're the equivalent of a magical houseplant."

"Say that again, featherbrain!" Chalupa growled, his fur puffing up.

"Enough!" Frankie snapped, her patience fraying. "Focus, both of you. Enchanted companions, fine. Now what exactly am I supposed to be looking out for in this magical in-between?"

Nyx clicked his beak, adopting a tone that suggested he was delivering a lecture to a particularly slow student. "Oh, the usual. Sprites, trolls, the occasional pixie swarm if we're unlucky. And whatever you do, avoid stepping into a fairy ring, they might look enchanting, but they're traps in disguise."

Frankie raised an eyebrow, her unease growing."Traps? What happens if you do step in one?"

"Let's just say fairies believe in subtle warnings," Nyx replied, his voice dripping with condescension. "Step into a fairy ring, and you're likely to find yourself dancing their merry little jig for what feels like hours, or days. When they're done with you, you might find you've lost weeks, months… or worse."

Her stomach twisted as she scanned the landscape, spotting a circle of mushrooms nestled among the tall grass.

"That's horrifying," she muttered. "Why would they do that?"

Nyx's eyes gleamed as he regarded her. "Why not? Fairies are tricksters by nature. What's a bit of suffering to them when they can have their fun?"

Chalupa yawned dramatically, sprawling across the blanket like a cat who believed he'd invented lounging, his tail swishing in lazy theatrics.

"The fairies only mess with those foolish enough to ignore the signs. It's basic magical literacy, really. If you see mushrooms in a perfect circle, maybe don't go tap-dancing through them."

Chalupa rolled his eyes. "Honestly, trolls are worse. No subtlety, all brute strength and zero brains and they always want something ridiculous. Shiny buttons, marbles, a haiku written in moon dust."

"At least fairies have flair," Nyx added with a sniff. "They'll charm you, dance circles around your sense of reason, and steal your socks while complimenting your haircut. You won't know whether you've been robbed or romanced."

Frankie groaned, rubbing her temples. "Great. Swindled by fairies, mugged by trolls. I'm starting to feel like a walking cautionary tale."

She raised an eyebrow, leveling a look at the dash. "So… you'll give me a heads-up before I get fairy-footed into oblivion?"

Nyx gave a solemn nod, then dipped into an overly grand bow, one wing arched like a velvet cloak.

"Consider this your first formal lesson," he intoned. "Stay vigilant, human. Magic doesn't forgive ignorance, and it tends to prank it mercilessly."

Chalupa gave a long sigh, licking his paw with regal nonchalance. "Darling, if I told you everything all at once, your mortal brain might short-circuit and leak out your ears. Best to pace the revelations."

Nyx gave a dry caw from the dash. "Rumor has it, he also thinks he was royalty in a past life."

"I was," Chalupa sniffed.

Frankie shook her head, a half-laugh catching in her throat.

"Great. I'm traveling with a regal cat and a raven with a superiority complex."

"We prefer 'legendary guide' and 'winged truth-bringer,'" Nyx said smoothly, preening a feather and Chalupa just smirked.

"Wonderful," Frankie muttered, her voice thick with sarcasm. "Any other magical creatures I should be worried about?"

Nyx tilted his head thoughtfully. "Well, there are kelpies, but they tend to stick to lakes and rivers. Then you've got will o' the wisps, which will lead you straight off a cliff if you're too trusting."

"Oh, and goblins," Chalupa added, stretching again. "Greedy little pests, but manageable, if you keep your wits and never wager anything sentimental."

Frankie stared ahead at the road, which shimmered like liquid gold, the colors deepening into strange, hypnotic patterns that made her question whether the forest was moving, or she was.

"This is starting to sound less like a magical adventure," she muttered, "and more like a survival guide with sarcastic footnotes."

"Welcome to the in-between," Nyx said dryly. "It's beautiful, yes, but it's also not for the faint of heart."

As if on cue, the compass pulsed again on the dashboard, its glowing runes blooming outward like fireflies caught in a slow, deliberate dance. The symbols shifted, casting lacy reflections that sprawled across the windshield, the seats, and the seams of Frankie's coat like a secret only the forest and the stars could read.

Then, with a soft click, her dashboard lights flickered like candle flames in a breeze. The turn signal blinked on of its own accord, ticking like a heartbeat as it indicated a narrow road that hadn't been there a breath ago.

Frankie blinked. "Is my Jeep… possessed?"

"Hardly," Nyx said with a click of his beak. "The compass is guiding you, trust in it."

She gave him a dubious glance, then turned to Chalupa. He met her gaze with rare solemnity, his usual flippancy replaced by something older, wiser, ancient, even.

Chalupa didn't blink. "Believe in yourself, Frankie," he said, voice quiet but unwavering. "You've got this."

A breath passed through her like wind through grass, stirring everything loose inside. The air itself had shifted as well. It crackled faintly, charged and humming like the world had just taken a deep inhale.

"Alright," she muttered, easing her hands back onto the wheel. "Let's see where this rabbit hole leads."

Nyx cawed once, a note of dry approval. "Now you're beginning to understand."

The Jeep rolled forward again and the narrow path yawned wide to greet her, framed by wildflowers that glowed like living lanterns. Their petals changed hue with every blink, coral, indigo, celadon, rose-gold, painting the hillside in hues too strange for daylight. The trees arched overhead in reverent silence, their bark shimmering silver-blue and laced with glowing moss that curled like ink. Leaves glittered with dewdrops that hadn't come from rain, each one catching the light like a tiny prism. The air was thick with bloom and shadow, and something else, something that felt like being remembered. She turned to ask what that even meant, but the road ahead rippled like the surface of a pond. It folded once, shimmered, and then straightened in an entirely new direction, one that hadn't existed a moment ago. The Jeep lurched to a sudden stop, sending Chalupa tumbling off the seat in a disgruntled sprawl of paws and tail. He hit the floor with a soft thump and a sharp hiss, fur puffed to full affronted volume.

"Oh, rude!" he snapped, untangling himself with wounded dignity. "What's the meaning of this?"

Frankie gestured vaguely in Nyx's direction without taking her eyes off the road.

"Don't look at me, ask the our new feathered friend. He's the one with all the cryptic wisdom."

Nyx, entirely unfazed, gave a single nod toward the shimmering path that had appeared as if on cue. His voice dropped to a velvet murmur, like a riddle about to unfold.

"That's why."

Frankie squinted through the shifting light, then sucked in a sharp breath as something massive emerged from the watercolor haze. It lumbered forward with deliberate weight, each step thudding like a timpani drum roll from the center of the earth. The creature was mossy and hulking, with skin like lichen-covered stone and glowing amber eyes that didn't blink nearly enough. And then she saw the staff, honest to gods, it looked like he'd uprooted a small tree and decided it was a fashion choice.

"Troll," Chalupa announced, deadpan. "And a tall one, too."

Frankie gawked. "Wait, like a real troll? Not the kind who lives in his mom's basement, types in all caps, and picks fights in the comments section about pineapple on pizza?"

Chalupa snorted. "This one probably hasn't ever seen a pizza, but trust me, he still has opinions."

Nyx added, "This one can also throw a boulder the size of your Jeep. So ... choose your words wisely."

The troll cocked its head, blinking slowly like a confused mountain trying to remember why it walked into a room. Then it tapped its massive staff against the earth with a *thoom* that vibrated through the air like distant thunder or the warning knell of some ancient gate.

"Traveler," the troll rumbled, stepping forward, his moss-covered shoulders creaking like old trees in a storm. His voice had the depth of distant earthquakes, a sound that seemed to resonate through the ground and rise into Frankie's bones. "You have arrived at the *Threshold of Wyrmroot Crossing*. None pass without proving their worth."

Chalupa groaned. "Wonderful. Expect riddles, emotional monologues, and an unsolicited opinion on your aura."

The troll stopped just before the Jeep, his enormous hand unfurling slowly and tapping two fingers on the driver's side window, tap tap, like a polite avalanche requesting entry.

"Roll it down," he intoned, his amber eyes glowing softly beneath a crown of ivy and stone. "I won't shout. That would shatter your windows and half your mind."

Nyx gave a low whistle. "At least he's considerate."

Frankie slowly rolled the window down. The troll leaned in, his breath earthy and cool, carrying the scent of wet wool and forgotten rain. His face was worn and wise, like it had seen ten thousand dawns rise over ten thousand different mountains.

"To pass," the troll said, his voice low and gravel-thick, "your familiars must face a riddle. You must offer something of yourself."

Frankie shifted in her seat, her fingers still curled tight around the wheel.

"Like what?"

"A truth," the troll replied solemnly, the moss in his beard swaying gently with each word. "A truth you've not yet to name."

The troll did not smile. He did not blink. The silence around him thickened like steam in a sauna, heavy, expectant.

"Answer my riddle," he said, "and speak your truth. Only then may you pass."

He raised his gnarled staff and struck the earth once more.

Thoom.

The sound rolled outward like a bell through fog, and for a breathless second, the ground beneath the Jeep shimmered, etched with soft glowing runes that blinked in and out of visibility like fireflies caught mid-thought. The troll closed his eyes and began, voice low and rhythmic like something remembered from the bones of the earth,

"*I have towns but no houses, forests but no trees, rivers but no water, a place where what's found is only ever imagined. What am I?*"

Silence followed, heavy and humming. Frankie opened her mouth, then closed it again. The words felt familiar, like a dream she'd almost caught once but couldn't quite hold.

Chalupa squinted, tail twitching. "Well, it's not a haunted postcard," he muttered.

Nyx tilted his head. “Towns without houses, forests without trees. It’s conceptual, not literal, think broader.”

The cat’s ears flicked once, sharply, then he sat up straighter, suddenly very still.

“It’s a map.” he said at last, his voice unexpectedly gentle, as though he feared he could be wrong.

The troll’s eyes opened, slow, heavy, and full of something ancient. He blinked once, deeply, like a mountain taking note. Then his mossy head turned to Frankie, his gaze settled, patient and unmoving.

“Now your offering, your truth.” he said, and the silence that followed was laced with magic and with waiting.

All eyes turned to Frankie now, Nyx’s sharp and knowing, Chalupa’s unreadable but steady, the troll’s ancient and unblinking. And the truth, her truth, stood quietly at the threshold, no longer hiding, only waiting to be named.

Frankie’s brows drew together. “My offering?” she asked, her voice barely more than a breath.

The troll nodded once, the movement slow and deliberate. “Your familiars answered the riddle. Now the toll is yours. Truth, spoken aloud.”

She shifted in her seat, heart pounding in her throat. “What kind of truth?”

“Something real,” the troll said. “Something buried, but not dead. The road will know the difference.”

Around them, the earth answered. Soft at first, then rising into a low, humming vibration. Roots pulsed with light beneath the moss, and glowing runes uncoiled like snakes made of fire and memory, circling the Jeep in a ring of starlit breath. The air thickened, reverent and charged. Even the wind seemed to pause, leaves holding their breath. Inside the Jeep, the dashboard lights flickered once, then steadied, casting strange, shifting glows across the interior like candlelight in a chapel. The compass pulsed in quiet rhythm. Outside, the runes circling the troll’s staff shimmered upward, delicate and deliberate, like fireflies tracing a story in a language long forgotten. Frankie sat very still, her breath catching at the edge of her ribs.

She swallowed hard and found her voice. “I’ve never really belonged anywhere,” she said, and the words emerged with the softness of something long-carried. “Not with my family. Not at school. Not even in my own skin, sometimes.” The runes responded with a gentle flare, pulsing like a heartbeat heard through water, steady, unhurried, ancient. “I’ve always felt too strange, too much… or maybe just not enough. Like I was made with the wrong blueprints, like the world knew how to move and I was always half a step behind it.”

Her throat tightened, but she didn’t stop. “I learned to smile right, to talk just enough, to shrink when I should’ve burned brighter. But none of it ever fit. Not really. I always felt like I was wearing someone else’s life, stitched from other people’s expectations.”

The light around the troll brightened, but he didn’t speak, he simply waited. Frankie’s voice trembled, but she pressed on.

“So I guess this is what I’m hoping for. That this road, this whole wild, terrifying journey… maybe it leads somewhere I do belong. Somewhere that doesn’t make me feel like I’m broken or pretending. I want to believe there’s a place for people like me. Somewhere I make sense, somewhere I don’t have to apologize for who I am.” Her words hovered in the air, raw, unpolished, and full longing.

The troll was still for a long moment, his eyes unreadable beneath the mossy fringe that curtained his brow. Then, with a rumble that echoed like distant thunder through stone and root, he bowed with a slow, reverent grace.

“Truth accepted,” the troll rumbled, his voice deep and weathered, threaded with something older than time itself.

The runes flared once, gold and bright, then slowly seeped into the moss and soil, dissolving like dew at dawn. The circle unraveled, symbols fading one by one, as gracefully as falling petals. But the troll didn’t vanish with them. He tilted his great head toward Frankie, moss shifting along his shoulders like something waking. His eyes, once dull as stone, now held a faint shimmer, ancient, knowing, as though he were seeing her from a height far beyond the clearing. A soft tremor passed through him, subtle as a falling leaf. The moss along his arms loosened into threads of green light. His stony skin began to fade, becoming more like mist caught in the shape of a giant. Frankie blinked, and for a heartbeat, it looked as if a second silhouette stood behind him, some older essence stepping forward.

"Witchling, you seek a place to belong," he said, voice low and rough. "But the map doesn't make the path, the walker does. Step as though you believe, and the road will rise to meet your feet."

Then he began to go. Almost inwards, as though he were returning to the very bones of the forest. Light sifted off him in quiet streamers, drifting into the earth, the roots, the branches overhead. His form diminished, softened, until he was little more than a suggestion of a shape, a memory of weight. The clearing brightened around him, vines lifting, leaves stirring as if welcoming him home and then, he was gone. No burst of sound. No gust of wind. Just absence, warm and reverent, like a guardian stepping back into the place he had always belonged. Only a patch of moss remained, richer and greener than before, humming faintly with the echo of his departure.

Nyx tilted his head, feathers catching the light. "Well. That was unexpectedly profound... especially for a troll."

Frankie blinked. "Witchling?" she asked, the word tasted unfamiliar. "What does that mean?"

Chalupa flicked his tail. "I'd say it suits you."

She glanced at him in the rearview mirror. "That's not an answer."

Outside, the road waited in quiet stillness. Frankie paused with her hands on the wheel, letting the moment settle, letting the aftertaste of the dreamscape fall away. Chalupa shifted in her lap, and the faint rustle of his whiskers was enough to nudge her forward.

"Alright," she murmured. "Let's keep going."

She guided them back onto the road, the Jeep rolling ahead at an easy crawl. For a few breaths, everything held the same strange glow as before, soft, unreal, as if the world hadn't quite finished deciding what it wanted to be and then something shifted.

The dreamlike shimmer that had wrapped around them began to unravel. Wildflowers that moments ago had burned with impossible vibrancy now faded to ordinary meadow hues. The leaves lost their sheen. Even the sky seemed to drain of its molten brightness, the brilliance bleeding away like a painting wiped with a damp cloth. A subtle hush fell across the landscape. What had felt enchanted only moments before now felt… watchful.

Chalupa curled tighter into his blanket nest with a sigh and yawned. "Well," he mumbled, his voice muffled by fluff, "that was a mood swing."

Nyx ruffled his feathers and muttered, "This realm's nothing if not dramatic."

Frankie stared out at the road, which still shimmered faintly under the weight of whatever came next. She glanced at the compass, its glow now dimmer but steady, pulsing in quiet rhythm like a heartbeat under the dash.

"Alright," she murmured. "What's next?"

Nyx straightened on the dashboard, eyes narrowing as he scanned the path ahead. "The road will show you *human*," he said, in that familiar cryptic tone, "when it's time."

Frankie arched a brow, side-eyeing him. "Okay, can we talk about that? You keep saying '*human*' like it leaves a bad taste in your mouth. Maybe dial it back?"

Nyx tilted his head, his feathers catching the last of the strange light, a ripple of emerald and blue flashing down his back.

"Would you prefer 'flesh bag'? Or perhaps 'biped with questionable instincts'?"

Chalupa snorted, his tail flicking in lazy amusement. "I vote for 'flesh bag.' It *is* accurate."

Frankie groaned and rubbed her temples, the gesture theatrical but weary. "You two are impossible. Just… call me Frankie. You know, my actual name?"

Nyx puffed up, feathers flaring in mock contemplation. "Hmm….fine, Frankie it is. But only for the sake of civility, not because I've grown fond of you or anything ridiculous like that."

Chalupa stretched luxuriously and curled into a perfect smug pretzel. "Right. Totally not because she threatened to boot you out the window."

"I did not," Frankie said, genuinely scandalized.

"You absolutely rolled the window down and looked directly at him," Chalupa said, his tail flicking with infuriating delight. "He squawked like a kettle."

"I was airing out the Jeep from your freeze-dried tuna snacks," Frankie shot back. "They smell like something that expired in a shipwreck."

She laughed, and it caught her off guard. The knot in her shoulders began to loosen, her breath easing as their absurdity chipped away at the quiet weight inside her. It wasn't just banter, it was a ridiculous, bickering tether holding her steady while the world outside slid further into the strange. She leaned back slightly, fingers resting on the wheel, eyes drawn forward. The air had cooled. The shimmer of magic, once flickering like candlelight, had softened, quieter now, but still present. Not gone. Just older. Watching.

A hush crept in, winding through the trees and threading into her thoughts. Her companions bickered quietly as she refocused on the road. The compass pulsed softly on the dashboard, a fading heartbeat of magic, steadying her in the stillness. Its glow no longer swirled, just held, like a candle braced against the wind, anchoring her to something just beyond reach.

"What's happening?" Frankie asked softly, the words barely brushing the air. Her voice held the hush of someone speaking in a cathedral, reverent and a little afraid.

"The veil is closing," Nyx said from his perch on the dash, his feathers dimming from opal shimmer to dusk-gray. "This was never meant to last. It's a threshold, a breath held between worlds. You stepped through a door most don't even see, but doors close. The magic folds itself away, veiled again. Hidden where only the right kind of knowing can find it."

Frankie blinked slowly, the trees outside had begun to change, not all at once, but in quiet, aching ways. Leaves that once caught light like stardust now drooped at the edges, dry and curling, their delicate lines brushed with gold that flaked away like old paint.

The sky had gone pale, drained of its color like a watercolor rinsed too long. The wind through the open window no longer carried the scent of citrus blossoms and spell-light. It smelled like pine sap and sun-warmed stone. Like something older. Earthbound. Settling in.

Chalupa's ears twitched as he sniffed the shifting air. "Feels like someone blew out all the candles in the universe," he murmured. "I liked it better when the breeze smelled like sugar violets and thunderclouds."

Frankie's hand drifted to the compass beside her, still pulsing with a faint, steady light. Warm. Alive. She curled her fingers around it like it was the last thread tying her to that other place, the wild place. The place where the rules bent, and the road bloomed with impossible things.

"So... what does it mean?" she asked quietly.

Nyx didn't look away from the road, but his voice softened, the edges of it laced with something older than memory.

"The Forgotten made the Veil to keep the ordinary from unraveling," he said. "And to protect the extraordinary from burning too bright. What you saw, what we passed through, it's real. Just not meant for always."

Ahead, the road dulled, the shimmer in the distance fell away like an illusion shedding its costume. Pavement pushed through browned grass. Magic pulled back like a tide.

"I didn't want it to end," she whispered, more to the fading moment than to anyone in the car. Then, she felt it. The tug, a quiet pull just ahead, gentle but insistent. Something was waiting.

Nyx's head tilted sharply. His feathers ruffled, catching some current that hadn't reached them yet.

"Pull over," he said, his voice threaded now with a note of quiet urgency, something between warning and wonder.

Frankie glanced at him. "Why?"

His gaze flicked toward a weathered turnoff ahead, half-hidden beneath a bough of arching trees, their leaves just beginning to gild with autumn.

"Because," he said, softer now, "some doors don't open unless you step out to meet them."

Frankie didn't say anything. She eased off the road, fingers still curled around the pulsing compass. The Jeep rolled onto the gravel shoulder with a sound like breath catching. Shadows spilled across the ground, long and soft as velvet, and even though the shimmer had faded, her heart lifted. The path beyond the trees looked like it had been waiting for her. She opened the door, and it was as if the land finally sighed... *There you are.*

Chapter 10

The moment her feet touched the ground, the hush deepened. She felt the kind of stillness that settles over long-abandoned rooms, or fields where something important once happened. A breath held underground, just before a seed splits open. Behind her, the Jeep gave a soft metallic sigh as the engine cooled. A bird chirped once in the canopy above and then thought better of it. Frankie stood still. The air had changed, cooler now, threaded with the scent of dry grass, brittle bark, and the faintest trace of ash. It smelled like a place that had gone quiet long before she arrived.

She stepped forward. Sunlight filtered through thinning branches in thick, golden beams, catching the dust around her like swirling mica. It made everything look softer than it was, weathered wood, peeling bark. Light moved slowly here. Like it was remembering how. The air pressed close, as if the land itself had turned to look at her. The compass pulsed once in her hand, warm and quiet, like a breath against her palm. Too much had happened for doubt to follow her now. The shimmered roads. The jackalope. The forest that whispered in root and shadow. The raven. The way Chalupa spoke and stared at things she couldn't see. Through it all, the compass had been her thread, pulling, never pushing. Offering direction, not answers and somehow, she'd learned to trust it.

Beyond the trees, the ground sloped into a shallow basin, ringed in worn stone. There, nestled in the bowl of the land like something misplaced and long unclaimed, lay a town or what was left of one. Wooden buildings leaned together like old neighbors trading secrets, their plank walls silvered by sun and softened by time. The paint had long since fled, leaving bare boards that blurred at the edges in lavender haze. Tattered curtains hung limp in windows where no breeze stirred, some shifting, slow and deliberate, in a way that felt too aware to be chance. At the far end of the lane, a chapel sagged into itself, its steeple cracked but still reaching skyward, stubborn in its devotion, as if it hadn't quite accepted how long it had been forgotten.

"Something's watching us," she mused.

Nyx circled once overhead before landing on a weathered stone marker. His feathers ruffled against a wind no one else could feel.

"I have no doubt," he said, voice low. "Step carefully. Magic runs deep in ground like this, and sometimes, it answers back."

Frankie moved farther into the deserted street. Somewhere behind one of the dark windows, a curtain fluttered. The heat pressed in, dry and close, but it didn't feel natural. It felt like something old was exhaling around them. She scanned the sun bleached lane, eyes catching on the saloon crooked at the far end of the square. Its timbers leaned but hadn't collapsed, and something about it felt... aware. As she watched, the double doors creaked, just slightly, then eased open another inch, like an invitation whispered in wood. No wind stirred, no breeze touched her face and yet, high above, a curtain shifted in an upper window. Slow, too slow, not like fabric caught by air, but like something watching had moved it on purpose.

"Not wind," Nyx said quietly, eyes narrowing. "Whatever that is, it saw us first."

Chalupa squinted toward the saloon. "Feels like it's waiting for a proper hello."

Frankie walked toward the saloon. Her heart kicked up, nerves, not fear. The saloon door groaned beneath her palm, and as she pushed it open, she braced for shadow. Instead, warmth spilled out to meet her, cinnamon and clove, the scent of something freshly baked. Inside, teacups clinked like someone had only just set them down. The room bloomed with color. Where she expected decay, she found a high-ceilinged space lit by chandeliers strung with ivy and soft, twinkling lights. Mismatched tables were draped in lace, each one teeming with teapots, saucers, and delicate floral cups. Ornate chairs circled the tables, their cushions plump and waiting.

And the people? Frankie blinked, at every table sat older women, each one dressed more extravagantly than the last. Their hats, fascinators really, were works of art. One wore a nest of mechanical butterflies that flapped golden wings in perfect clockwork rhythm. Another sported a miniature pirate ship, complete with glittering waves spilling from the brim. A third's fascinator glowed with a crescent moon, surrounded by tiny spinning planets.

Nyx perched on Frankie's shoulder and gave a low whistle. "Well, this is... unexpected."

Chalupa sniffed the air, his ears twitching with interest. "I smell moon-crusted trout cakes," he said, his tone almost reverent.

A small pixie darted toward them, her wings shimmering like dragonfly scales in the light. She hovered just in front of Chalupa, clutching a delicate moon-crusted trout cake layered with glittering purple slaw and something vaguely fish-shaped that sparkled faintly at the edges, comically oversized for her tiny hands. The pixie's wide eyes sparkled as she studied him, her voice filled with curiosity.

"Well, aren't you an unusual familiar? I've never seen a one like you before." She circled him slowly, trout cake in hand, as if trying to unravel some great mystery.

Chalupa flicked his tail, clearly enjoying the attention.

"Unusual? I prefer exceptional," he said with a dramatic stretch. His gaze drifted to the tasty treat, his whiskers twitching. "I hope that's for me."

The pixie giggled, holding the trout cake just out of his reach. "Perhaps, if you behave yourself."

Before Frankie could speak, a woman with bright pink hair and a fascinator shaped like a peacock's tail strode toward them, her bracelets jangling as she gestured toward an empty table.

"Well, don't just stand there gawking, dear," the woman said with a smile. "Come in, come in! Sit, sit! You're late, but we forgive you."

"Late? Late for what?" Frankie asked, bewildered, as the woman ushered her toward the table.

"For tea, of course," the woman said with a laugh. "And whatever comes after."

Nyx ruffled his feathers and hopped down from Frankie's shoulder, perching on the back of one of the chairs.

"They seem friendly enough. What could possibly go wrong."

Frankie hesitated but finally sat down, Chalupa hopping onto a cushion beside her. The woman with the peacock fascinator returned with a silver tray of finger sandwiches, strawberry scones, and a steaming pot of tea.

"Now, darlings, I suggest you eat first. It's always best to approach one's destiny with a full stomach."

Frankie picked up a sandwich hesitantly, watching as Nyx and Chalupa dove in with surprising enthusiasm. Around them, the women chatted animatedly, their voices blending into a harmonious hum of conversation. Frankie caught snippets here and there.

"...the ley lines are especially strong this year..."

"...poor dear was nearly trapped in a fairy ring..."

"...and then the goblin ate the map! Can you believe the nerve?"

One of the women rose, her fascinator a delicate clock, its tiny hands forever frozen at 2:15. She drifted toward Frankie with practiced ease, eyes bright with curiosity and something sharper beneath it.

"Tell me, dear," she said, her voice low and lilting, "how did you come to be here, sipping tea with the likes of us?"

Frankie nearly choked. She set her cup down too quickly, porcelain clinking against the saucer. "I ... uh ...stumbled across the town," she said, the words tumbling out half-formed. She glanced toward Nyx, then Chalupa, searching for rescue.

Nyx did not offer it. Instead, he cleared his throat, a crisp, formal sound and stepped onto the table. His talons clicked softly against the wood, precise as punctuation.

Frankie blinked. "What are you doing?"

He did not look at her. He lifted his head, feathers catching the low light, dark wings settling with ceremonial stillness. When he spoke, his voice carried a gravity that had not been there before.

"Behold," Nyx intoned, "Francesca DiLegna. Direct descendant of Aoife Ní Talún Caelith, High Warden of the Verdant Line. Daughter of the earth. Firstborn female of her bloodline in generations. A rarity among rarities."

The room seemed to contract around them.

Frankie's breath caught. "Wait," she said softly. "How do you know that? I didn't even know that."

Nyx did not pause. "She is a living thread in the weave of magic itself," he continued, voice unwavering. "Woven with intention. Bound not by accident, but by purpose. If knowledge is held here that pertains to her seeking, let this gathering bear witness. Speak now, and let truth rise beneath destiny's gaze."

Silence fell, not polite, not awkward, but absolute. Teacups hovered mid-lift. Fans stilled. The low murmur of conversation drained away as if swallowed by the walls themselves. The women exchanged glances, something unspoken passing between them, curiosity giving way to recognition.

The woman with the clock fascinator leaned forward, her earlier mischief gone. What remained was assessment. Calculation.

"Well," she said at last, her voice quieter now, edged with weight. "That changes matters."

Frankie stared at Nyx. Then at the women. Her heart hammered, caught between disbelief and the dawning realization that she had just crossed a line she hadn't known existed and there would be no stepping back over it.

"What does that mean?" she asked, her voice small yet urgent.

The woman adorned with the rose fascinator spoke next, her tone calm but heavy with meaning.

"It means, child, that you are not merely a wanderer stumbling into fate's path. You carry a lineage steeped in power, a legacy not easily ignored. Your presence here is no accident, it was written long before you knew to follow the signs."

Frankie's fingers brushed against the compass in her pocket as if seeking reassurance.

"I don't understand. I'm just... trying to figure out why I'm here."

Peacock fascinator lady stood gracefully, the feathers of her headpiece catching the light and shimmering like the wings of an enchanted bird. Without a word, she glided to a corner of the room where an unassuming bookshelf leaned precariously against the wall. She paused, her fingers hovering over a row of worn spines, and then plucked a thick, ancient tome from its place. From the concealed hollow cut deep into the book's heart, she drew forth a rolled map, its edges lit with a thin shimmer of phosphorescent script, cold as starlit frost. She cradled it in both hands, reverent as if it were spun of starlight and memory, and crossed the room with the gravity of someone delivering a long-buried truth. With measured grace, she placed the map before Frankie, her gaze sharp as broken glass.

“You shall find your answers,” said the woman in the peacock fascinator, her voice textured like wind through heather and stone, soft, but with an unyielding edge. “But let this settle deep in your marrow … The truths you seek will not rise easily.They require trust, trust in your own knowing, in the unseen threads that pull you forward.Trust in the leap that comes when the world tilts toward destiny.Without it, the path remains closed, curled tight like a blossom awaiting spring.”

Frankie inhaled, the air catching on her ribs as she unrolled the map. Its markings glowed faintly, like rain-slick lichen beneath moonlight, the lines flowing and curving as though inked by wind. The paper itself felt impossibly heavy, denser than it should be, as though holding the weight of prophecy. The woman leaned close, peacock feathers quivered atop her fascinator, catching stray glimmers of invisible light. Her voice dropped, gentler now, but no less anchored.

“The cave you seek lies here.” she said, tracing a single fingertip across curling glyphs until it rested on a softly glowing spiral, nestled within thorns and waves. “It waits, buried in stone and time. But it will not open to mere curiosity. It opens only to the called.”

Frankie’s fingertips hovered near the glowing spiral as she looked up, her breath shallow. The jeweled plume of the woman’s fascinator refracted light into dazzling prisms, like a veil rippling between worlds. Still, she held her gaze, eyes that held storm and flame, forest and ash.

“A cave?” Frankie asked. Her voice was even.

The woman tilted her head, her smile curving like the arc of a crescent moon. “This is no simple hollow in the earth. It is a threshold. It keeps what the world learned to hide, what time layered over and forgot how to name, and what only you can bring back into the light.”

Frankie’s brow knit, her hands tightening on the parchment.

“That’s… vague.”

“As it should be,” said the woman, her tone like dusk settling over wild hills.

“To name the future is to unravel it. The cave holds what you seek, or what has been seeking you.”

Frankie’s mouth twisted. The map glowed faintly in her hands.

"Not exactly helpful," she muttered, her frustration surfacing. "Would it kill someone to give me a straight answer?"

The woman's smile deepened, her eyes softening with something like compassion. A faint breeze stirred the bright plumage of her fascinator, though the room remained still.

"Answers are not handed down like heirlooms or recipes," she said. "They bloom when they are ready. When you are ready." She traced the edge of the map, her fingers light, as if stroking a memory. "The cave is tied to Aoife Ní Talún, whose roots run deeper than most dare to dream. It was carved with purpose, steeped in ancient magic. It is a sanctuary for truths too powerful to live above the soil. It is not simply waiting to be found... it is waiting for you."

Frankie's throat tightened. Her eyes drifted over the map, the symbols glowing like dew on old oak leaves. The weight on her shoulders didn't vanish, but it shifted, less like burden, more like belonging. Nyx spoke at last, voice a gravel-toned echo.

"What waits inside is no trinket or tale. It will test your courage, your clarity, your ability to stand in shadow and still name the light. Fail, and it will remain stone." The peacock fascinator woman leaned closer again, her feathers brushing the map's soft illumination. "You seek a cave because your story begins there. It's not a place, Francesca, it's a revealing."

Frankie's voice faltered as she stared at the glowing point.

"How do you know it's really meant for me?"

The woman's smile turned wistful, edged with an ancient certainty.

"We are more than keepers of tea and clever conversation, child. We are weavers, keepers of memories, and lore-bearers. The veil speaks, and it has whispered your name."

Nyx, perched solemnly at the table's edge, gave a ceremonial nod. His voice took on the cadence of ceremony. "Your wisdom is acknowledged, but our time shortens. What must she do when she reaches the cave?"

The woman with the clockwork fascinator leaned in, her expression serious beneath its whirling moons and golden gears.

"When the moment comes, leap. The cave's magic favors no hesitant heart. Step forward even if your fear howls, magic does not reward caution."

A quiet settled over the room. Candlelight swayed, casting soft halos that danced along the lace and porcelain. The tea parlor, half dream, half memory, seemed to draw inward, like it was holding its breath. Frankie pressed her palm flat against the map.

Nyx's voice rose from the stillness, low and certain. "What you needed has been given. What comes next... is yours to claim."

Frankie glanced from the raven to Chalupa, then to the women with their whimsical, impossible fascinators. Around her, the glow dimmed, the lamplight fading like mist lifting at morning's edge.

"These women are not what they seem," Nyx murmured, his tone woven with reverence. "They guard what time forgets. Their truths are planted, not handed over. Let them take root."

Chalupa licked a paw. "Also, the scones changed my life. Take some to go."

One of the women chuckled and handed Frankie a small pink box tied with ribbon. "Award-winning strawberry scones," she said. "Enchanted for strength... and wisdom."

The woman in the peacock fascinator stepped forward once more, her feathers catching some invisible light as she studied Frankie. Her expression held no urgency, only a knowing stillness.

"When the wind turns without warning, and the ground beneath you feels too quiet, listen for the echo that doesn't belong. That will be your moment."

Frankie opened her mouth, but the woman merely touched two fingers to her own lips, as though sealing the rest of the message in silence.

"Some truths don't arrive in words," she added softly. "They bloom in the pause after."

They stepped out into a world that felt less solid than before, the saloon door sighing shut behind them like a storybook closing. None spoke as they headed back to the Jeep. As Frankie slid behind the wheel and Chalupa claimed his spot on the dash, Nyx swooped in with dramatic flair, landing on the headrest like a suspicious butler arriving late to a séance. Frankie glanced back once and the saloon unraveled into stillness, its structure peeling away like the end of a dream, dissolving into the breeze. The women vanished with it, as if they'd been conjured by strong tea and sheer attitude. In her pocket, the compass gave a slow, contented thrum, less lost, more smug.

Nyx fluffed himself up. “Excellent. Nothing says ‘you’re on the right track’ like a building evaporating.”

Chalupa stretched luxuriously, tail flicking like a metronome of mischief. “Please, we have scones, cryptic advice, and only mild existential dread. That’s a win in my book.” He licked a paw, then sighed with theatrical weight. “Although I do wish I’d grabbed a second box.” He paused, glancing at the space where the saloon had vanished.

“Quick question,” he said, squinting. “Was that a nexus… or a vortex? Because on one hand it felt like the universe handing us a magical breadcrumb, and the other felt like we narrowly avoided being drafted into an interdimensional knitting circle.”

Nyx didn’t blink. “Either way, you would’ve found a way to nap through it.”

Frankie snorted. “Please. He’d be the group leader of the circle by lunch and convince them to add snack breaks and ceremonial napping.”

Frankie started the engine, and the Jeep gave a low, uncertain growl. She glanced once more toward the spot where the saloon had stood, but the building was gone, dissolved into a hush of dust and memory. Only the faintest shimmer hung in the air, like the aftertaste of magic.

As they drove on, the road narrowed as the trees began to thin, their trunks growing crooked, as though uncertain whether to lean in or flee. Even the shadows seemed to hesitate, clinging loosely to branches before giving way to open light. Conversation faded, replaced by the low hum of tires over gravel and the rhythmic flutter of Nyx’s wings. The magic from the saloon lingered like perfume, subtle but insistent, clinging to their skin and humming in the seams of the air. Then the Jeep gave a hiccup, just a soft stutter, barely enough to notice. But Frankie noticed.

“What’s going on?” she asked, her voice threading into the hush. “It’s acting strange.”

The raven straightened, feathers ruffling like stirred ink. He eyed the compass, gaze narrowing. “Pull over. Now. Something has shifted.”

Frankie guided the Jeep off the narrowing trail, tires crunching over dry gravel until they rolled to a stop on a patch of sun-bleached stone. The engine sputtered once, then fell silent. Ahead of them, a massive dust devil uncoiled from the earth like a spirit made of grit and heat, tall as a house and spinning lazily across the trail. It roared to life without warning, cutting a crooked path just yards in front of the Jeep. Loose pebbles skittered against the tires, and dust lashed the windshield in a sudden storm of amber and gold. Inside the cab, the light fractured through swirling grit, throwing warped shadows across the seats. Heat blew through the vents, dry and mineral-rich, thick with the scent of scorched stone and something older, sunbaked sand, ghost sage, and the faintest hint of metal. It tasted like ash and copper, gritty on the tongue, raw in the throat. Frankie leaned forward slightly, her breath caught, less from fear than from the feeling that something enormous had just turned to look directly at them.

Chalupa hissed from his perch, fur puffed so wide he looked twice his usual size, tail fanned like a warning flag. His ears flattened, and his eyes tracked the whirlwind with sharp, unblinking precision. Nyx hunched, talons digging into the headrest, feathers flared and trembling like something ancient had just passed over them. The dust churned louder, rising like a breath drawn sharp, then, just as suddenly, it collapsed. The whirlwind unraveled with a dry, sighing hush, scattering into the sky as if it had never been. The world went still and when the last grains settled, everything had changed.

The moss-draped roots, the cool green hollows, gone. The trees had vanished, giving way to a stark horizon of stone and hush, as if the forest had stepped back and left only its shadow behind. The air was brittle now, edged and arid, scented with scorched earth, sunbaked thyme, and the memory of ghost sage. Even time felt thinner here, stretched taut as parchment near flame.

Frankie opened the door and stepped out slowly. What lay before her wasn't any desert she knew. This one shimmered with heat, the sandstone ridges rising like sleeping beasts, backs curled and wind-scored. Crumbling arches stood like the bones of forgotten gates. Narrow canyons twisted out in every direction, each one a half-told story, carved into dust and shadow. It was fierce. Stark and breathtaking in the way of something that had never asked to be found, only endured.

She turned a slow circle, awe chasing disbelief. "There's no way we've come this far already," she whispered. "We were just in the mountains. This… this is a desert."

"Indeed," Nyx croaked, landing with a soft clatter of talons on the Jeep's hood. His wings folded with the sound of feathers brushing sand and silence. "You've heard of the *Extraterrestrial Highway* in Nevada?" Frankie nodded, her gaze still caught on the shimmering ridgelines. "Well," Nyx said, tilting his head, "this isn't that. This is older. You've been traveling a magical thread, tucked between the seams of the world. A road the waking mind no longer knows how to follow."

She blinked. "So you mean a shortcut?"

Nyx's eyes glinted. "More like a magically charged bypass, a back-alley whisper the stars never meant to share. A current beneath everything, quieter than roads, older than memory. Time and distance blur along it. It doesn't take you where you want to go. It takes you where you're meant to arrive."

Frankie looked at the Jeep, half-expecting it to retroactively flash a warning light. "I never even stopped for gas…"

"Exactly," Nyx said, a note of satisfaction threading through his voice. "The moment you truly began this journey, the rules of the ordinary world stopped applying. You've been traveling through the folds, those hush-hollows where magic gathers and time forgets how to behave."

"So I didn't just cross the country," she murmured.

Nyx met her gaze with a slow, solemn nod. "You did, and more. You crossed a threshold shaped by the Forgotten."

A grunt interrupted them as Chalupa dropped from the Jeep with a soft thud, tail flicking like a slow spell. He narrowed his eyes at the horizon.

"Well. The veil's thinning, the land remembers your name, and I'm still expected to walk in sand. Glorious."

Frankie let out a breath of laughter that caught even her by surprise. She turned her gaze back to the ridgelines, burnt-orange and rose-gold beneath the sinking sun, the sandstone glowing beneath the hush of memory. It should have felt strange, but instead, it felt like something long-lost had finally clicked back into place inside her.

“I didn’t know where I was going,” she said softly, her voice carried more by the wind than her lips. “But I think… I’m here.”

The compass stirred, it didn’t just pulse this time, it breathed. A warm glow unfurled from its center, spilling over her fingers like golden milklight. Threads of luminous green curled from the edges, vine-like and delicate, as if the compass had bloomed in response to her voice. The metal, once cool, was now warm, alive, its hum low and steady, like the purr of something that had finally found its place.

Frankie stilled. The glow flickered once, then steadied, casting dappled light across her palm like sunlight through leaves and for a moment, it felt as though the land itself was answering. The wind shifted. It moved around them in whispered currents, curling around the red stone as if it carried secrets. Ahead, the canyon yawned wide, red rock and amber shadow, wind threading through narrow mouths like secret songs. Heat and silence, stitched together by possibility and somewhere out there, a cave waited. In her hand, the compass gave one final, gentle thrum, then quieted, as if satisfied she finally understood where to go. Frankie curled her fingers around it, not for direction, but for the echo it stirred inside her, warm and steady, as sure as breath. At first she thought it was just a strange trinket, but now, the pulse of its magic felt like a conversation. She’d stopped asking how it worked. Stopped questioning why it found her. Somewhere between jackalopes and Nyx’s gaze, she’d started listening instead. The compass didn’t point north, it pointed true and that was enough.

Reaching into the Jeep, she grabbed her satchel and stuffed the map and the rest of the items she felt she would need into it. She stepped forward, the ground beneath her crunched softly, sun-warmed and fractured, scattered with flecks of mica and tufts of sage green, the kind of plants that bloom only where the earth remembers how to hold hope. It felt like the land had been waiting with quiet certainty, like it had always known she would come.

As she continued to walk the trail narrowed, carved deep into the rock, flanked on both sides by towering canyon walls that curved inward like ribs. Their surfaces were sun-warmed and wind-smoothed, veined with mineral streaks the color of old clay pots and burnt sugar. The sky disappeared above her, swallowed by the height and bend of stone. Only narrow shafts of light slanted down, turning dust motes to drifting gold. She ran her fingers along the rock as she passed, a dry, warm like skin left too long under summer light. The scent of sun-heated sandstone mixed with something older, the faint tang of iron, the green bite of sage clinging to crevices where no roots should grow. The deeper she went, the quieter it became. Her footsteps barely echoed now, muffled by sand and shadow. Even the breeze held its breath.

She'd been to the Grand Canyon, crowded lookout points and postcard views, but this was nothing like that. This place didn't announce itself. It didn't rise up in grandeur for cameras or awe-struck tourists. It revealed itself slowly, like a secret kept too long, and far too lovely to share with just anyone. And yet, even in its secrecy, it was breathtaking. The stone walls curved like sculpture, painted in ancient hues, rose, rust, ochre, colors no photograph could catch. Light filtered down in quiet ribbons, softening the edges of shadow. It didn't need a crowd to admire it. It didn't want a camera. It was beautiful in the way wild things are beautiful, when they think no one is watching. The land didn't rise to meet her, it opened, slow and solemn, like petals long folded and as she rounded a bend where the stone darkened to deep russet, the light shifted. Not dimmer, just... different. Like something ahead was thinner than it should be.

The canyon trail had lied. From above, it had looked manageable, charming, even. Like the kind of place you might wander into on a postcard hike before. But once inside, it became a sandstone labyrinth with the temperament of a trickster god. Passages narrowed into slits so tight Frankie had to turn sideways, exhaling to squeeze through as her shoulders scraped against stone. Her satchel caught on outcrops. Her arms were already collecting bruises and scratches that would resemble abstract art by nightfall. Then, just as suddenly, the walls fell away, spilling them into airy chambers where wind and color moved like breath. Sunlight poured through high cracks above, painting the stone in copper and rose, like some ancient cathedral carved by erosion instead of hands. Wind sang through the gaps in strange, shifting tones, haunting melodies too precise to be chance. Frankie hitched her pack higher, the compass warm and pulsing at her side. Sweat gathered along her hairline, and her wild curls clung damp and heavy against the back of her neck. But she wasn't tired, not in the way she'd expected. The canyon air crackled faintly against her skin, electric and alive, like the land was whispering in a language just beneath hearing, she didn't understand it yet, but she knew she was meant to.

Chalupa trotted ahead along the sun-bleached path, tail high, ears twitching with every distant sound. "First sign of a giant lizard or a growling heat shimmer, I'm out."

Frankie blinked. "What's a *growling heat shimmer*?"

Nyx shifted on her shoulder, feathers ruffling in the dry air. "An unfortunate desert phenomenon. Think mirage meets mild hostility. Best avoided."

Chalupa nodded solemnly. "Exactly! I don't do predatory illusions, that's where I draw the line."

Frankie smirked, the image already resurfacing. "Remember that time in the greenhouse? You got startled by a beetle the size of my thumb, knocked over two trays of seedlings, and took out the compost bucket with your tail."

Chalupa sniffed indignantly. "It buzzed at me."

Nyx clicked his beak. "Ah, the fearsome Battle of the Beetle. Truly, bards will sing of your bravery."

Frankie smiled, the sound of their bickering oddly grounding, even here, in a place that felt increasingly like a dream spun from heat and shadow. Towering hoodoos and arches loomed overhead, sculpted by time and wind and something older. Inlays of copper and deep indigo threaded through the stone, pulsing faintly with a rhythm she couldn't quite hear but somehow felt deep in her bones.

She slowed, eyes drawn to a narrow spire where the light bent unnaturally. For the briefest moment, it seemed to blink, not with eyes exactly, but the sense of eyes, buried in the rock. Watching.

Aware of their presence.

Frankie paused mid-step, her breath catching in her throat. "Is it just me," she asked softly, "or is something watching us?"

Chalupa's ears twitched flat as he narrowed his gaze toward a nearby ridge. "I'm telling you, it's giant lizards. This place screams '*reptilian ambush.*'"

Nyx let out a slow, feather ruffling sigh from her shoulder. "What is it with you and giant lizards? Did one steal your food bowl in another life?"

“I don’t have to explain my trauma to a bird,” Chalupa replied coolly, his tail flicking. “I know what I know.”

Frankie bit back a laugh, the tension easing slightly. “You two are something,” she said. “Not sure what, but something.”

Still, her eyes returned to the spire. The sensation hadn’t faded, if anything, it had deepened. Whatever presence lingered out there, whether made of stone or something stranger, wasn’t hiding. It wanted to be noticed. Or perhaps… it was deciding if they were worth noticing in return.

“What do you think it is?” she asked, voice low.

Nyx’s feathers shimmered slightly in the filtered light. “Hard to say. This land was a crossroads long before maps remembered its name. And places like this?” He glanced toward the cliffs. “They draw the things that drift between, things without names, who prefer to be forgotten.”

“Nameless, sentience watching from decorative sandstone.” Chalupa muttered.

Frankie took a breath, grounding herself, whatever was watching them, it hadn’t chased them off.

“Let them watch,” she murmured, lifting her chin. “We’re not here to hide.”

They pressed on, following a narrow trail that dipped into a shallow pocket canyon carved by time and wind. The light shifted here, cooler, filtered through steep red walls streaked with iron and ash. Their footsteps echoed softly, swallowed quickly by the silence that clung to the stone like lichen. The air smelled of sun-baked minerals, dry earth, and the sharp, green edge of sagebrush. Small cacti clung stubbornly to narrow crevices in the rock, their spines catching the light like tiny needles of glass. Clusters of rabbitbrush and low-growing succulents hunched in the shade of boulders, their roots buried deep in search of water long gone. A dusty breeze stirred the canyon floor, carrying with it the scent of sandstone and something older, like time exhaled. It slipped through the gorge with the quiet of a forgotten lullaby, a voice too ancient to form words but too present to ignore. Here and there, the light shimmered oddly, bending around nothing, as if the air itself was layered. Colors shifted when no one was looking, and a faint chime rang once, far off, with no clear source. A hummingbird hovered over a blossom that hadn’t been there moments before, its petals glowing faintly violet, then vanishing the instant it was touched by shadow.

Chalupa trotted ahead, nose twitching, then paused to sniff a curious spiral pattern etched into the canyon wall.

"This place gives me the heebie-jeebies," he muttered. "Too quiet ... sacred."

Nyx, still perched on Frankie's shoulder, gave a low croak. "Places like this don't forget what passed through them."

They slowed at the bend where wind whipped stone gave way to a hidden clearing. Rising from the earth stood three towering sandstone spires, elegant, timeworn, and regal. Their peaks curved inward, joined by a slender natural bridge that arched between them like fingers brushing in prayer, or a vow never broken. Light spilled across the stone in slow, shifting patterns, and for a moment, the world seemed to hold its breath. Each spire was distinct, yet they leaned inward slightly, as if sharing a secret only they remembered. At their crown, a delicate arch stretched from one to the next, a fragile bridge binding them in silent communion. Light filtered through it in golden strands, casting shimmering patterns on the ground below like woven thread.

> *"Three sisters guard the pass where the veil thins.*
> *You'll know them by the way*
> *the wind quiets, as if even the canyon holds its*
> *breath. They mark the place where*
> *choice meets calling, where I last turned back, and*
> *knew I could not again."*

Back in her carriage house, those words had been a mystery, jotted in the margins of a weathered journal, fragments of someone else's life. Frankie remembered sitting cross-legged on the floor, papers scattered around her, the meaning just out of reach. The phrase had haunted her, but only now did it hum with resonance.

Here, in this parched gorge, the air had shifted. It stilled, as if the canyon itself had gone quiet in anticipation. No birds. No insects. Even the wind, which had whistled through the cliffs only minutes ago, had vanished. She didn't know how she knew, she just did. Frankie stopped mid-step, a ripple of something deep moving through her.

"That has to be it," she whispered, sitting on a rock.

Her hand slid into her pocket, fingers curling instinctively around the compass again. It pulsed once, firm and steady. Solid. A heartbeat not her own, but somehow familiar. She was learning to listen to it now. To feel the subtle differences, the twitchy flicker of hesitation, the sharp jolt of danger, and this, the quiet, resounding thrum of recognition. On her shoulder, Nyx shifted, feathers rustling against her jacket. Without a word, he hopped down and reached into her satchel and withdrew the folded map with his beak.

With a flick of his head, he let it unfurl. Frankie didn't need to consult it. Her gaze had already locked ahead, where the three towering spires of sandstone loomed at the canyon's narrowest point. She stood and took a slow step forward. At first, they appeared to be nothing more than strange rock formations, wind-carved, sun-scored, shaped by time and weather. But then she saw it, presences in the rock. One spire leaned, tall and questing. Another stood firm and grounded. The third was cleaved down the middle, parted like something that had been forced to reveal its inner truth. They weren't just rocks, they were guardians.

"The Three Sisters" she murmured.

Nyx glided down to a boulder beside her. The heat shimmered around his talons.

"This isn't just a landmark," he said. "The Sister Stone marks the boundary between illusion and what's left when illusion fades. Those who walk past them are remembered."

Frankie stood still, staring up at them. She didn't feel afraid. What she felt was something more dangerous, certainty. The wind quieted, as if the canyon itself had gone still to listen.

Chalupa paused mid-sniff, his tail flicking once as he squinted up at the archway. "So we're walking through magical rock guardians into the unknown?"

Frankie didn't answer right away, she stepped forward, her gaze lifted to the towering spires joined in silent communion overhead. The hush in the canyon deepened, and a strange stillness bloomed inside her, as if some old thread had tugged taut between her past and this moment. She spoke without thinking, the words rising from somewhere far older than memory.

"They mark the place where choice meets calling."

The phrase lingered in the air like a spell, or perhaps, like a promise remembered. She blinked, startled by the way the words had felt in her mouth. Like something buried in bone and blood had simply… surfaced.

Chalupa didn't offer one of his usual snarky remarks. Instead, he looked up at her with a curious stillness, his green eyes catching the canyon light.

"You speak like one of the other realm," he said, his voice low, rough with something almost reverent. "You don't remember it yet, but it remembers you."

Frankie looked at him, startled. "What are you talking about?"

He didn't elaborate. Instead, he simply nodded once- dignified, proud. "You'll know soon enough."

From his perch on the boulder, Nyx gave a small tilt of his head, his feathers rustling like parchment.

"Not all knowledge comes through study, Frankie DiLegna. Some truths are inherited- and yours has been waiting."

The wind stirred again, softer this time, almost like a breath released. Frankie stepped forward, beneath the stone sisters, beneath the sky gone silent, and the canyon opened before her. Without waiting, she stepped forward, beneath the arch, under the watchful gaze of the sisters, and the canyon narrowed. They walked in silence for a while, the compass in Frankie's hand pulsed with a steady rhythm, confident, almost content. She paused beside a canyon wall veined with shimmering streaks of color, rose gold, violet, ochre, like the cliffside had been painted by some ancient, tipsy deity.

"Okay, that's beautiful," she whispered. "Can you not appreciate geological beauty?"

The compass flickered, not shyly. Frankie frowned at it.

"What?"

It gave a stronger pulse, then dimmed, like it was sulking.

Chalupa tilted his head. "I think you confused it."

"Confused it how? I stopped to look at a rock."

Nyx, still perched overhead, replied, "It's not about the rock. It's about the path. That thing only glows when you're moving in the right direction."

Frankie narrowed her eyes at the compass. "So if I stop to admire something shiny, it throws a tantrum?"

Another flicker, this one pointed.

Chalupa snorted. “It’s like a magical bloodhound with control issues.”

“Fine. I’ll keep walking, but one of us needs to learn boundaries.”

The compass gave a long, low pulse. Frankie sighed and turned back to the path. The canyon walls began to rise on either side, stretching higher with each step until the sky above narrowed to a thin ribbon of pale blue. Sunlight filtered down in slanted beams, catching on stone etched with a thousand years of wind and water. Swirls of ochre, rust, deep plum, and pale gold layered the sandstone like the folds of ancient tapestries, shifting and alive in the changing light. Strange vines wove themselves through the fractures in the rock, their tendrils glowing faintly in unexpected colors, soft reds and dusky pinks, glimmers of cobalt and violet, like filaments of bioluminescent thread stitched into the canyon’s ribs. With every step, the canyon seemed to deepen, its silence thickening, the air folding inward as though the stone itself had begun to listen. It was breathtaking, yes, but beauty in a place like this was never just for looking. It could enchant, disarm, lead you in circles until you forgot why you’d come. She kept her gaze steady, even as the walls bloomed with color, ochre and rose and violet swirling like brushstrokes on a giant canvas. Wonder tugged at her senses, drawing her toward every glimmer and glow but she tightened her grip on the compass, steadying herself with its quiet rhythm. Stay present, she reminded herself. Don’t get swept away by what only looks like the way forward.

Chalupa’s ears twitched. “Things are getting weirder, I swear that bush just looked at me.”

“It did,” Nyx replied coolly from his perch. “Try not to stare, it’s considered terribly rude.”

The path narrowed until it disappeared entirely. Ahead, the canyon split into two narrow clefts, both veiled in shadow, both carved in the same elegant curves, twin passages that seemed to breathe. At first glance, they were identical. But the longer Frankie stared, the more wrong that felt. The sameness was too perfect, too deliberate. There were no markings. No breeze. No birdsong. The rock formations on either side loomed like ancient sentinels, their surfaces etched with whorled patterns that flickered faintly in the low light, spirals and loops and jagged glyphs that pulsed under the stone. It didn't look like erosion. It looked like language. On her shoulder, Nyx shifted, his talons flexing through her shirt. The rustle of his feathers was like pages being turned by unseen hands.

"Well, that's ominous," he murmured, voice low and strangely reverent. "A fork in the canyon, just a coin toss between destiny and disaster."

He said it like a warning, but also like a quote, something remembered. Something he didn't entirely trust. Chalupa crept forward and sniffed at the left path, tail twitching, his fur puffed ever so slightly.

"They smell the same," he said, ears angling back. "Which is suspicious. I don't trust symmetrical doom."

Frankie didn't answer. The words slipped past her like fog. Her gaze had dropped to the compass in her hand. It glowed softly, but the glow was no longer passive, there was a rhythm to it now, a flickering heartbeat she could feel beneath her skin. The needle began to spin deliberately, like a thought forming mid-sentence. The compass was attuned to something inside her, something old and stirring. It wasn't showing her the way because it couldn't, because this place didn't want to be navigated. It wanted to be answered. A subtle pressure moved through the air, like a sigh from the canyon walls. The ground beneath her felt too still, like it had once moved and might again if she chose wrong. The twin clefts before her shimmered, barely perceptible, like heat-haze layered over a dream. For one suspended instant, they seemed to flicker between reality and something just beyond it, like mirrors reflecting not light, but intention.

She felt it then, a whisper, a feeling, curling at the edge of consciousness. One path thrummed like blood in her ears, the other pulled from somewhere deeper, a place so deep, she hadn't known was there until it responded. She didn't understand how she knew, only that she did. It wasn't knowledge in the way she was used to, it wasn't something she'd learned, or read, this was older than that.

This wasn't a crossroads, it was a veil. She was at a threshold between states of being, between who she had been and who she might become, if she dared step forward. The air itself shimmered faintly, as if it were holding back something just beyond sight. The canyon felt thinner here as though one more breath, one wrong move, might tear it open and let the impossible spill through.

The moment stretched wide and strange, each second felt elongated, dreamlike, as though she were suspended inside a question that had been waiting centuries to be answered. This step wasn't meant to be found, it was meant to be claimed, by only those worthy. It was a truth she hadn't known she carried, until the canyon asked and something within her answered. And in that instant, the compass in her hand shivered. The glow that had spun uncertainly now steadied, pulsing once, twice, then dimming into a slow, reverent flicker. It wasn't pointing. It was acknowledging. As if whatever ancient force had laid this path was watching too, and the compass was its nod of approval. It didn't want to guide her. It wanted to see if she'd step.

The canyon answered without hesitation. The wind rose in a sudden a howl torn from the bones of the earth. It circled them in a spiral of dust and ash, petals lifting from the ground like forgotten offerings. The air grew sharp, electric, crackling with static, thick with the scent of scorched stone, broken juniper, and something older. Something feral. Shadows stretched long and thin, trembling as if afraid to touch the ground. The temperature dropped and the ground beneath her feet shuddered with a warning.

Before her, the stone between the twin paths rippled. Then, without ceremony, it disappeared. What remained was a ledge, narrow and sunlit, suspended above a void that pulsed with impossible light. Below, a pool churned with energy. Alive with memory. A river of dream stuff threaded with violet and gold, silver and shadow. It moved with intention. It breathed like a question waiting for its answer.

Nyx's voice came, low and reverent. "The cave doesn't just open," he said. "It asks."

Frankie's throat tightened. "Asks what?"

"If you'll leap," he said. "If you'll trust what hasn't yet revealed itself: the truth, the magic, the path waiting just beyond sight. If you'll trust who you're becoming."

Chalupa edged closer to the ledge and peered over with narrowed eyes. "I don't like pools that shimmer like they know something. Definitely not regulation canyon water."

Frankie turned to him, a nervous laugh catching in her throat. "So I just... jump?"

"Not jump," Chalupa corrected. "Leap. There's a difference, one has doubt, the other has guts."

Then, like a thread being pulled taut, the canyon held its breath, from somewhere not far and not near, a voice rose.

"You've come so far, mo chroi . Believe in yourself and all things are possible.."

Frankie's heart skipped. "Aoife?" she whispered, spinning around but there was only wind.

The canyon was empty, no movement, no sign of life, save for Nyx and Chalupa beside her.

Chalupa's ears twitched. "You heard that too, right?" he asked, his voice unusually quiet.

Nyx didn't answer right away. He just looked ahead, eyes distant, as if listening for something he didn't quite dare name. He then stepped forward, his feathers catching the glow.

"This is your moment. The veil thins here. What lies beyond... is not for the hesitant."

Frankie's breath caught. Aoife's voice had faded like mist at sunrise, but in its place, another memory surfaced. Darrow's voice, steady and warm, echoing from that greenhouse full of sun and growing things, *"Of course you'll fall. But when you do... that's when you'll learn to fly."*

She hadn't understood then. Now, standing at the edge of the impossible, she did. It wasn't about avoiding the fall, it was about trusting what waited beyond it.

Frankie looked down at the pool of light churning below. Not water or fire, no this was something older. The compass in her palm pulsed once, steady and calm. This wasn't about certainty, it was about faith. Faith in the unseen, the unknown, and most of all, faith in herself.

She turned one last time, gaze landing on Chalupa and Nyx. "You two coming?"

Chalupa narrowed his eyes, tail flicking. "Not leaping into glowing soup is how I've lived this long."

Nyx dipped his head, solemn. "This path was always yours to walk alone. But we'll be there when you land."

A flicker of hesitation passed through Frankie the weight of knowing that the next step was hers alone. The ledge beneath her boots thrummed with life, ancient runes flaring in rhythm with her pulse. She could feel it everywhere now, in her throat, in the charged air that wrapped around her like breath held tight. Magic wasn't just surrounding her anymore. It was moving through her. The wind curled inward, close and deliberate, like a hush before a symphony begins. Light streamed upward from the glowing chasm below, ribbons of violet, silver, and gold spiraling through the air like smoke made of starlight. Her hair lifted from her shoulders, caught in the rising current. Her fingers tightened around the compass, still warm and steady in her palm.

What if I fall? The thought whispered and from somewhere unseen, the wind replied, *Then you'll fly.*

Frankie stepped forward, one foot and then the other. The ledge trembled beneath her, but held. Then, with a final breath, the canyon split open like a curtain drawn wide, and she leapt. The world vanished and she tumbled into brilliance. Light exploded around her, golden, blinding, wrapped in wind and scent and sound. The rush roared past her ears, a river of starlight that sang in languages she didn't know but somehow understood. The air carried the scent of lavender and smoke, of moss, of something like memory warmed by sun. Her stomach dropped. Her arms flared wide. The roar softened to a hum, the hum to a song and then, stillness. Her feet found ground. Cool, damp earth greeted her, faintly glowing with bioluminescent moss that pulsed like breath beneath her. The silence that followed was not empty, it was sacred. The air shimmered with the scent of moonflower and stone, threaded with the electric hum of old, waiting magic. A stream of water, bright blue and laced with silver light, wound through the cavern, its ripples scattering star-shaped reflections across the walls. The cave itself soared overhead in sweeping arches, its walls lined with crystal and shimmering minerals in colors that defied naming. Some glowed with inner light. Others reflected her image back to her, not as she was, but as she could be. Here and there, glowing fungi bloomed like lanterns, their petals unfolding with the rhythm of breath. Strange trees with translucent leaves swayed though no wind touched them, casting shadows that whispered across the stone.

At the other end of the cavern, where the light gathered like morning pressed against the veil of dreams, stood a woman. She wore a long, flowing skirt layered in hues of forest, dusk, and river stone, colors that didn't shout but breathed, soft as moss, grounded as soil. It looked as though she had gathered the palette of a twilight garden and sewn it into folds. Her blouse was loose cotton, sun-washed and embroidered with winding vines and tiny, deliberate stars. A scarf slipped from her shoulders, its edges hand-stitched with threads the color of moonlight and milk thistle. Dozens of mismatched bracelets jingled softly at her wrists, glass, wood, hammered copper, old silver, each one telling a story in its texture. She wore no shoes, only soft leather slippers that looked shaped by years of walking barefoot through morning grass. Her hair was a crown of wild silver and storm-grey curls, cascading down her back in waves that defied time or taming, like she had never once asked it to behave. And her presence... her presence was like warm bread and rosemary, like earth after rain, like songs you don't remember learning but still somehow know by heart.

She reminded Frankie of the old women in tucked-away mountain towns, the ones who brewed lavender honey in their kitchens and read tea leaves between garden chores. Beautiful in a way that had nothing to do with polish or youth and everything to do with soul. Aoife's smile, soft, radiant, utterly unguarded, wasn't just recognition. It was belonging. It was every lullaby Frankie had never been sung, every story left half-told and folded away in forgotten boxes. It was the ache she had carried her whole life without a name. That smile felt like home and her eyes, moss-green flecked with gold, fierce and endlessly kind, were Frankie's own. A quiet awe swept through her, widening the moment until it felt too full to hold. Joy bloomed in her like wildflowers after rain, fragile, unstoppable, reaching for every bit of light it could find. And from somewhere deep inside, a place she'd almost forgotten, hope stirred and lifted its head, alive again.

"Aoife," she whispered, the name trembling from her lips like a prayer finally answered.

Her grandmother stepped forward, arms already open, her voice wrapping around her like light and love.

"Welcome home, my darling girl."

Chapter 11

She was the woman from Frankie's dreams, no ghost, no shadow, but real, radiant, untamed, alive. The one who had called her here. As she stepped forward, the crystals flared brighter, sending ripples of amethyst and gold racing across the cavern walls. The air shifted too, laced with crushed herbs and storm rain, as though the earth had exhaled in recognition. Even the ground beneath Frankie's boots pulsed once, deliberate and steady, like the planet's heartbeat rising to greet her.

Aoife stood as if she had always belonged here, woven into the light, stitched into the silence, waiting only for Frankie to arrive. Her skirt whispered dusk and dawn across the crystal-dusted floor. Bracelets chimed faintly, each note carrying laughter and grief in equal measure. Her hair spilled wild, silver and storm-gray threaded with moonlight. Her face bore the lines of a life lived deeply, etched by joy, carved by sorrow, softened everywhere by love. But her eyes, moss-green, flecked with gold, stopped Frankie cold. She knew them as intimately as her own reflection. The one inheritance her family could never erase.

A sound broke loose, half laugh, half grief, and for a heartbeat she thought the world itself might crack beneath the enormity of it. All her life Frankie had carried an unnamed ache, a hollow where belonging should have been. Now, in this glow, the ache shifted, answered. This wasn't chance. This was the thread tugging at her since childhood, the hum beneath her skin she had never been able to name. The world hadn't broken open; it had fallen into place. Aoife was nothing like the polished DiLegnas. She was wild. And standing before her, Frankie didn't feel like a girl stumbling into magic, she felt like someone who had finally come home.

"Aye, you've wandered the winds to find me, love," Aoife said, her voice lilting like a lullaby remembered from a dream. The words wrapped around Frankie like sunlight through lace, tender, familiar, impossibly safe.

Frankie stepped forward, each movement careful, as if crossing into a secret she'd carried her whole life without knowing it. When Aoife's fingers brushed her cheek, the touch was featherlight yet grounding. It wasn't only affection, it was recognition, a tether, the quiet beginning of something sacred. The cavern breathed with them as crystals flickered in sympathetic light. A low hum rippled through the stone, deeper than sound, older than memory. Frankie drew in a trembling breath, awe pressing in like dawn.

"Oh how I've waited so long for you," Aoife whispered, her voice rich with love and threaded with longing that seemed to stretch across lifetimes.

In the silence that followed, something clicked into place, like a key turning in a lock, or a thread finding the fabric it had always been meant to complete.

Frankie's voice cracked, raw with awe. "I can't believe this is real."

Aoife pulled her into an embrace. A fierce, bone-deep hug, full-bodied and unashamed. It didn't just steady her, it claimed her. It rooted her and the cavern answered with light swelling like dawn, as if even the earth itself was relieved they had found each other. For a long moment Frankie didn't move, afraid that if she let go the woman in her arms would dissolve like a dream. But Aoife's presence was solid, grounding, warm as sunlit soil. When they finally pulled back, Frankie's breath hitched again. Her eyes traced every line of Aoife's face, greedy to memorize it all at once, starved for what she had been denied her entire life. She had imagined this meeting a hundred ways, but none prepared her for the weight of belonging pressing so suddenly, so sweetly, into her being.

The words slipped out before she could stop them, half laugh, half confession. "I don't know what to call you." She shook her head, her mouth quirking in a crooked smile. "'*Nana*' just... doesn't fit. You don't feel like a '*Nana*.'"

Aoife's chuckle came soft and mischievous, carrying the music of wind teasing through tall grass. "No, I don't suppose it does. I'm not exactly the 'Nana' to your Nono, am I?" Her eyes twinkled as if the thought alone amused her.

"You could call me Máthair Mhór," she added after a beat, the Gaelic rolling off her tongue like a lullaby shaped by wind and sea. *MAW-her WOHR*. The words seemed to ripple against the cavern walls, rich and lilting, as though they'd been spoken here before.

Frankie tried the phrase under her breath, awkward at first, the syllables unfamiliar yet strangely comforting, like humming a tune she didn't know she knew.

"It means 'great mother.' But..." Aoife tilted her head, smile softening. "That's a bit much, yeah?" She gave a small shrug, bracelets chiming faintly. "I think just Aoife will do for now. The rest will come when it's ready."

Something in Frankie eased at that, the tight coil of longing loosening into something warmer, steadier. Aoife. It felt right. The name itself carried the weight of legacy, of roots, of truth long denied but finally returned.

Aoife's hand slipped into hers, callused and gentle, and the simple touch bloomed inside Frankie like spring breaking through frost. For the first time in her life, she didn't just feel seen, she felt claimed.

"You carry the fire of the wise women who came before you," Aoife said gently, her voice laced with the soft cadence of old songs and sea winds. Her gaze lingered on Frankie's face like she was reading a familiar story in a new language. "Their strength runs in your blood, sure, but it's the earth's own rhythm I hear beating loudest in your heart. You're not just an echo of their legacy, love, you're the next verse in the song. One only you can sing."

She reached out, tucking a strand of Frankie's hair behind her ear with fingers as steady as the roots of an oak. Her eyes crinkled at the corners, warmth spilling out like golden light, but there was something else, too. A flicker beneath the surface. Like thunder in a clear sky.

"There's so much I need to show you, Frankie," she murmured, her tone softer now, threaded with something tender and urgent. "So much I've waited to teach you. But time... well, time's slippery here. It doesn't play fair and we've much to do."

Her smile faltered, just for a breath, and in that moment Frankie saw it, grief, old as stone and pride, fierce as flame.

"That fire in you..." Aoife said, voice barely above a whisper, "it rattled them you know, your grandfather, your parents. They didn't understand what you carried, so they tried to snuff it out. Fit you into a world too small to hold your light." She shook her head, her bracelets clinking like tiny wind chimes.

"But you weren't born to be tidy, my girl. You're stardust and soil. Wild magic. That rhythm you feel, that hum under your skin, it's the land. The old ways. The heartbeat of everything that remembers."

Then her smile returned, wide and fierce as a fire catching hold. "And that spark they feared? That song they couldn't silence? It'll serve you well, you mark me. Where we're headed, you'll need every bit of it. So don't shrink, Frankie. Don't dim it. Let it burn. Let it sing." Her voice dropped lower, full of quiet wonder. "You made the leap, love. The cage is behind you now and the sky's ahead."

Frankie let out a breath she didn't realize she was holding, eyes still locked on Aoife's.

"This is wild," she said softly, almost laughing. "It feels like I've known you my whole life… even though we just met."

Aoife's eyes softened, stormy eyes lit from within, she rested her other hand over Frankie's. "Because our blood remembers, lovey," she murmured. "The earth remembers and so do we, some bonds run deeper than time and realms."

But before she could respond, the soft patter of footsteps echoed from the tunnel behind Aoife, followed by a familiar voice.

"Well, it's about time," Chalupa muttered, his tone dry as ever. He sat primly atop a glowing rock near the stream, tail flicking like a metronome of mild impatience. "You leapt through a swirling cosmic void and still managed to be fashionably late."

Nyx perched beside him, one wing tucked, the other lazily preening. "Patience, feline," he said, eyes flicking toward Frankie. "She has made the leap. That is no small feat."

Frankie blinked, the weight of the moment colliding with their presence. Her heart softened.

"You're here!"

Chalupa gave a dramatic sniff. "Who else is going to keep you from falling into enchanted wells and talking to suspicious shrubbery?"

Nyx inclined his head. "We said we'd be there when you landed and here we are."

Aoife's gaze drifted down to Chalupa as she stepped back from Frankie, and something in her expression shifted, softened, like sunlight breaking through cloud. A silence fell over the moment, warm and still, as if the air itself had turned sacred. Frankie felt a lump rise in her throat as she watched the look pass between them, something deep and wordless, ancient and tender.

Chalupa, for once, didn't have a quip ready. He stood motionless, tail curled neatly around his paws, his usual swagger gone still. Then he stepped forward and leapt onto a nearby rock. His eyes met Aoife's, steady and bright in the cavern's glow, and for a heartbeat it felt as though time itself was holding its breath.

"Hello, old friend. Welcome home," Aoife murmured, her voice thick with emotion. She leaned forward, resting her forehead gently against his. The gesture wasn't just affection, it was communion, steeped in memory, gratitude, and trust. "Thank you for watching over our girl," she whispered, her words like a benediction.

Chalupa closed his eyes and leaned into her touch with a grace that felt almost regal. The sharpness he usually wore dissolved, revealing something older. Then it began. The sound rose from deep within, not anything Frankie had ever heard from him before. It began low, a vibration that thrummed through the stone beneath her boots. Then it layered, deepened, split, tones folding over each other, harmonies stacking in ways that made no sense and yet rang true. It was music without instrument, language without words. It was the groan of roots twisting underground, the sigh of branches bending in ancient winds, the echo of rivers carving stone. It was creation and memory braided into sound.

The vibration filled the cavern, not loud but absolute. Frankie felt it in her ribs, in her teeth, in the blood moving through her veins. Crystals along the walls didn't just glow, they bloomed in response, answering in light. Dust lifted in spirals, carried by a breeze that hadn't been there a moment before. Even the air itself seemed to thicken, charged, alive. Nyx, who always had a retort, a jab, a sharp edge ready, fell silent. He tilted his head, feathers shivering as though trying to shake off a storm. His eyes narrowed, not mocking this time but reverent, as if the sound itself demanded his stillness.

Frankie turned toward him. "What is that?"

Nyx didn't answer right away. His gaze stayed locked on Chalupa, the silence between them weighty. Finally, he spoke, his voice low, almost hushed.

"That," he said, "is a *Rootsong.*" The word dropped heavy in the air, like a name and a prayer at once.

"It's older than language," he went on, each word careful. "A song the land remembers. Few can call it now. Fewer still survive it." His eyes flicked toward Frankie. "You don't stumble into a Rootsong. You're chosen by it."

Aoife had not moved. Her forehead still pressed to Chalupa's, but now her lips moved faintly, as though she were echoing the sound in silence. The crystals swelled in rhythm. The cavern itself seemed to lean closer. Frankie realized with a shiver that it wasn't just Chalupa singing to the land, it was the land singing back.

When Aoife finally pulled away, she smoothed her hand over his fur, her touch reverent. Chalupa's eyes opened slowly, steady and bright, and in them Frankie saw not the cat who snarked and swaggered, but something ancient, watchful, deliberate, vast. Aoife turned then, brushing a loose lock of hair from Frankie's cheek with a touch light as breath.

"He's been with you for a reason, love. His path was never separate from yours. It was always intertwined."

Frankie's heart thudded, full of awe and a belonging so deep it seemed etched into her bones. Chalupa blinked slowly, then turned to Aoife with a look that was equal parts fondness and familiar exasperation.

"She wasn't exactly a model charge, you know," he began, his voice low and velvety, tinged with an air of exaggerated martyrdom. "Years… years, I've spent trying to teach her not to have a full blown meltdown every time a plant withers. Let me tell you, even now? We're still firmly in *work-in-progress* status."

Aoife turned to Nyx, her expression softening with deep respect. The shift was subtle but reverent.

"And you, Nyx," Aoife said gently. "Thank you for guiding her here. Your wisdom and vigilance have been invaluable." She inclined her head, the formality of the gesture making Frankie blink.

Nyx fluffed his feathers, the deep blue-black shimmer of his wings catching the faint light like polished obsidian. His beak clicked once as he gave a slight, dignified bow.

"The task was a necessary one," he replied, his voice imbued with a regal cadence. "Her path is intertwined with far more than she yet understands, I could not fail."

"You never have," Aoife murmured, her voice soft yet full of weight. "Your place in this realm, and beyond it, is no small thing, Nyx. I would be honored if you stayed. I fear we'll have great need of your gifts for what lies ahead."

Nyx tilted his head, his eyes glinting like shards of midnight sky.

"I will stay," he finally said. "There is much yet to unfold."

Frankie's gaze flicked between them, as awe tangled with disbelief. The familiar edges of her reality felt blurred, remade. Chalupa, her sarcastic, sunbeam-hoarding feline who had been by her side for as long as she could remember, and Nyx, the sleek, shadowy raven who had appeared in her life like a riddle with wings. Only now… neither of them looked quite the same. There was something different about them, more than just the setting or this magic humming through the air. Chalupa sat straighter, his emerald eyes catching the glow of the cave like cut glass, thoughtful and sharp. Nyx stood nearby, perched on a ridge of stone with an easy grace, his feathers gleaming like oil and obsidian. He watched everything with the quiet intensity of someone used to seeing the world unfold in patterns no one else could see. They weren't just companions anymore. They were… more. Guardians. Guides. Something out of myth, peeled back into the real. Frankie blinked, trying to reconcile it all.

"So, let me get this straight," she said slowly, rubbing her forehead.

"You", she pointed at Chalupa, "have been watching over me most of my life and you," now to Nyx, "just show up out of nowhere and know things you shouldn't, and now you're both some kind of ancient magical guardians?"

Chalupa gave a long, theatrical sigh, tail flicking as he stretched out with the practiced drama of a cat who had waited just long enough to be properly smug about it.

"Took you long enough," he said, ears twitching like punctuation.

Frankie raised an eyebrow. "You could've said something earlier."

Chalupa tucked his paws beneath him, eyes gleaming. "You weren't ready."

She crossed her arms. "And how did you know that?"

He gave a slow blink. "If I'd started talking back in the carriage house, or the nursery, what would you have done?"

Frankie snorted. "Probably chucked a shoe at you and blamed it on a rare phytotoxin reaction."

A satisfied snort, then, "Exactly. You had to believe it first, not with your head, but with the part of you that remembers where you came from."

She narrowed her eyes. "Convenient excuse for keeping secrets."

Chalupa gave a dramatic sigh, as if burdened by the weight of wisdom. "It's not secrecy, it's narrative pacing."

Nyx landed nearby, wings folding neatly as he perched on a low crystal outcropping. "I wasn't there for your childhood," he said, voice cool, "but I've been watching for longer than you'd guess."

Frankie looked at him sideways. "Wow. That's not unsettling at all."

Nyx blinked once. "I find directness saves time."

Chalupa flicked his tail. "Ignore him. He's still convinced 'mysterious silence' counts as charm."

Nyx tilted his head, feathers gleaming. "Says the house cat with a flair for dramatics and selective hearing."

Frankie huffed a breath that was half a laugh. Their banter was ridiculous, but familiar now, still, something twisted in her chest.

"All this time," she said, more to herself than them. "I thought you were just… my cat."

Chalupa's voice dropped lower, losing its usual teasing edge.

"And I was. But also more. You didn't need to know all of it then, you just needed someone to be there."

There it was, that quiet truth, slipping in sideways and landing deep.

Aoife's voice was warm and grounding. "These two," she said, her gaze flicking between Nyx and Chalupa with fond amusement, "have been more than guardians. They've been your tether to the truth you didn't know you were seeking."

Frankie hesitated, trying to piece everything together. "I have so many questions."

Aoife's smile deepened, and her soft laugh rippled through the air like a lullaby. "There'll be time to untangle every one, my girl. But for now, let this be enough, you are not alone on this journey."

She stepped closer. When her hand settled on Frankie's shoulder, the warmth of her touch spread like sunlight after a storm, grounding and lifting all at once. Something inside Frankie, tight for so long, began to ease, just a fraction, but enough to feel the shift.

"Aye now, love, you are exactly where you're meant to be," Aoife said, her voice calm and sure. "Surrounded by those who believe in you... and will guide you."

Frankie blinked, tears stinging the corners of her eyes. Her throat tightened beneath the weight of Aoife's words. She drew in a breath that wavered, overwhelmed by the quiet strength in her grandmother's gaze. Aoife radiated a wisdom and resilience that felt ancient, like roots sunk deep in the earth, steadying her, holding her, reminding her that she didn't have to carry everything alone. She gave Frankie's shoulder a gentle squeeze. When she spoke again, her tone dipped into something solemn and sure, the words pulsing through the room like a heartbeat in the stillness.

"Now, my girl," she said, "we begin."

Something hummed softly from Frankie's pocket. She slipped a hand inside, fingers closing around the compass. It pulsed, quiet and steady, like a heartbeat she hadn't known was hers. When she drew it out, its brass shell glowed with a faint warmth, and the weight of it in her palm felt less like a tool and more like a tether.

Aoife's gaze caught on it, and her eyes shone with something old and full of memory. "That compass," she said softly, "was mine once. I gave it to Darrow to hold, long ago for you."

Frankie blinked. "You knew I'd find my way there all along?"

Aoife stepped closer, brushing a lock of hair gently from Frankie's cheek. "Aye, I hoped you'd find it, and that in finding it, you'd begin to find yourself."

Frankie looked down at the compass in her hand, her voice thick with feeling. "It helped me more than I can explain. But... what if I hadn't met Darrow?"

Aoife's eyes sparkled, lips curving into a wry smile. "Och, do you think that was the only clue I left behind? The only person I trusted with something important?" She raised a brow, all gentle mischief.

"Come now, love, give me a little more credit than that." Aoife nodded toward the compass still resting in Frankie's palm. "There were others. A few more breadcrumbs tucked in that old chest, you'd have found your way here, one way or another."

Frankie opened her mouth, a dozen questions fluttering at the edge of her thoughts, but something in the air stilled her. This was the hush of something sacred unfolding. The hush before a seed dares split open beneath the soil. Aoife stepped away, she did not raise her arms or mutter charms under her breath. She only stood, spine straight, hands at her sides, and exhaled, as if she were letting go of something she'd carried for centuries and the world answered.

Light spilled from her in soft waves, first barely visible, like morning mist catching sunlight, then growing clearer, purer. It rolled through the canyon like water through roots, silver-white and threaded with lavender and gold. Crystalline striations along the walls bloomed awake at her presence, lighting up in resonance, amethyst, indigo, sunlit rose. The stones seemed to breathe. The air grew warmer, thicker with scent, wild thyme, sweet myrrh, and something older, green and aching.

Frankie's skin prickled as the light brushed against her, not just seen but felt, like fingertips trailing across memory. Beside them, the stream stirred, the water stilled for a heartbeat, then began to shimmer. Stars surfaced, spinning in slow celestial spirals, each one pulsing as if to the rhythm of a heartbeat older than time. A constellation floated free and drifted toward them. Frankie watched it hover, weightless and impossibly close, before it dissolved into the air and vanished. Aoife's cloak lifted slightly, caught in a wind that hadn't been there moments before. Her hair shimmered faintly in the glow, loose curls dancing like they, too, remembered what she was. She looked at Frankie as something older, wilder, and true.

"This is where your true path begins, love," she said softly. "Where the story meant for you begins to find its way home."

Frankie turned slowly, trying to understand, her voice low and awed. "You're doing this."

Aoife smiled, the glow still tracing the edges of her like moonlight clinging to dew. "I'm only opening the door, mo chroí. The path, that's yours to walk."

As if summoned by her words, the path beneath their feet responded. Beautifully colored lights unfurled with each step, blooming in quiet spirals that rippled outward like blessings. The walls were ochre deepening to rose quartz, threaded with inlays of green that ebbed in rhythm with something ancient and awake. Frankie slowed, she reached out and touched the stone, it was cool, but a warmth stirred.

It welcomed her as someone long expected. The air sharpened with clarity, scented with wild thyme, moss, crushed petals, and the faint trace of rain-soaked stone. Glowing mushrooms clustered at the trail's edge, casting gentle halos of turquoise and violet across the sculpted walls. Overhead, slender beams of golden light slipped through narrow cracks, scattering like sunlight through cathedral glass. Dust danced in the glow, tiny specks of gold suspended in honey.

Frankie turned slowly, wide-eyed, her voice barely a whisper. "It doesn't feel real."

Aoife smiled, a soft, secret smile. "Aye, it's real. Been here longer than the mountains. Hidden away, waiting for the right hearts to remember how to find it."

Their footsteps softened, as though even the ground understood the sacred hush. Then, without warning, the narrow passage widened, and the world unfurled. Frankie halted, breath caught. Before her stretched a vast subterranean expanse, a hidden realm cradled beneath stone and time. Towering trees rose from crystal-laced soil, their trunks rippled with pearl and opal, arching toward a vaulted sky that shimmered with light. Leaves flickered in hues of flame-gold, twilight violet, and bronze, catching the glow like stained glass suspended in dream. From their branches hung fruit that glowed like stars held in cupped hands. Pools dotted the mossy floor, clear as glass, reflecting constellations she'd never seen and skies that didn't belong to the world above. Far overhead, the cavern walls glittered with enormous crystal geodes, amethyst, sapphire, moonstone, rose-gold, casting rippling color like a living aurora. Soft-winged creatures drifted through the canopy. Frankie didn't know their names, but something in her remembered them, as if they'd been pulled from the edges of childhood dreams and stories never spoken.

Aoife stepped beside her, her voice low and reverent.

"Welcome to Velhollow."

Chapter 12

The world shifted the moment she stepped inside. It wasn't just the air, though that had changed too, sharper now, laced with petrichor, wild thyme, and something bright and crackling, like ozone woven through stone. No, it was deeper than scent. It was the way the land itself seemed to pause… and turn toward her. It felt like being noticed, like being called home. This wasn't a cave or some secret hollow. This was a realm shaped by memory and moonlight, vast and quietly alive, breathing with the rhythm of something older than seasons, older than speech. Above her, the ceiling arched high and endless, like the spine of a sleeping god curled beneath the mountain. Crystal shards streaked through the rock, flashing with hints of lavender, amber, and blue fire. Light spilled through jagged seams overhead, sacred and stranger than sunlight, casting dappled radiance over stone ridges and winding canyon walls worn smooth by time and fae memory.

The veil between worlds didn't just feel thin here, it pulsed, alive with old magic, as if the entire realm inhaled with her and held its breath. Trees unlike any Frankie had known rose from the moss-veiled floor in quiet majesty. Their trunks gleamed in shades of copper and ivory, smooth as carved bone. Leaves circled gently overhead like dancing flame, ever-shifting through colors of dusk, wildfire, storm. Some rustled softly, even without wind, like they were whispering to one another. Low-hanging fruit glowed from their branches, cool, bioluminescent orbs in pale green, coral, and indigo. They looked like stars mid-bloom, as if constellations had drifted too close to the ground and decided to stay. A silver river curved through the valley floor, wide and slow, its surface catching the ambient glow and casting it back in ripples of mirrored light. The stars reflected in its waters didn't belong to any sky Frankie had ever studied. These constellations were older, unfamiliar, maps of a world within a world. Around the river's edges, clear pools shimmered like portals, mirroring strange inverted skies, where galaxies wheeled in directions that made her bones feel hollow and reverent all at once. Time bent here, not forward or back, but deep. Even the dust motes shimmered differently, drifting like golden leaves caught in still water, suspended in air so hushed it felt ceremonial. They glowed faintly, like the breath of forgotten stories rising again to be heard.

Frankie's breath caught in her throat, held captive by wonder. Beside her, Aoife stepped forward, her skirt brushing through moss with the sound of pages turning, like a spell being spoken into the roots of the world and in that breathless quiet, something in Frankie shifted. The weight she always carried, of not belonging, didn't vanish, but it softened, as if the land itself had reached inside her and said, *You're not lost, you've arrived.* It wasn't just awe she felt, it was true recognition. A gentle reorientation, like her compass had always pointed here, and only now did she realize it. Before a single word was spoken, something old in her had already answered back.

Frankie turned to Aoife, her eyes wide and shimmering.

"How is this even possible?" she whispered.

Aoife's gaze lifted to the vaulted ceiling above them, where golden light spilled like breath through jagged seams in the stone.

"The mountains have kept her like a secret," she murmured, voice threaded with something older than wonder. "Velhollow wasn't built. She was remembered, tucked gently into the bones of the world." She began to walk, her footsteps soft against the moss-carpeted path. Her voice followed like a hush.

"This realm lies beneath the noise, sealed beneath the hum of wires and the weight of clocks. No maps can find her. No road leads here. This place was born from memory and root, from rhythm and stillness. She is untouched by the surface world, and yet she remembers it all."

Their path curved deeper, lit by soft golden moss and quartz that swelled with quiet life. Overhead, ancient trees stretched tall beneath the earth, their canopies brushing crystal-dusted ceilings. Pools of silver water mirrored constellations that had never graced the skies above, galaxies unknown to humankind, spinning in gentle defiance of surface logic. Frankie's steps slowed, each one sinking into silence like a note into velvet. The air felt alive. She could feel it against her skin, thrumming faintly at the edge of awareness, as if she were walking inside the breath of something ancient. She looked around in wonder, the silver-threaded river, the soft-glowing trees, the glimmering moss beneath her feet. The colors here didn't shout, they shimmered with intention, as if the whole place had been waiting for her without urgency, but with certainty. The world above had always felt too fast, too loud, too sharp. But here... here, nothing asked anything of her, yet, she didn't feel adrift.

She felt welcomed.

"It's like..." she began, voice thin with awe, "a storybook come to life. Completely untouched by the world I know."

Aoife turned to her, her voice threaded with something ancient and luminous, shimmering faintly between sorrow and hope. "This place has always lived in you. Not in thought, but in bone. In the stillness between heartbeats."

Something shifted inside Frankie, like a door she hadn't known existed had quietly opened. She had no words for it yet, but the feeling was unmistakable. As if her soul had been trying to return here for years without knowing the way. She looked again, slower this time. At the soft light. The silence that felt full instead of empty. The quiet, uncanny sense that no part of her, no grief, no wildness, no wound, had to be hidden here. Aoife gestured toward the grove, the bioluminescent trees, the crystal imbedded within the stone was breathing with ancient light, the shimmer of unseen spells suspended in still air.

"This is our home," she said, voice low with reverence. "A refuge for magic, and the misfits it shapes. The ones too wild, too strange, too much to survive under the harsh light of the above world. Witches who wouldn't bend. Seers who saw too far. Creatures born of dreams and half-remembered stories, forgotten by a world that stopped believing. Velhollow remembers them all."

She paused, the light catching in her silver braid like fire in thread. For a moment, she looked half-rooted herself, grown from the stone and story of the place.

"It holds them," she whispered. "And it holds us."

Then her gaze returned to Frankie, steadier now.

"It's also a beginning," Aoife murmured. "A pulse beneath the world that says, you belong. Even when the world above forgets how to recognize you."

Her voice shifted, still gentle, now threaded with something wind-worn and spell-bound, like a tale pressed into bark or sung into stone. It carried the hush of forgotten halls, the hush before truth.

"This was never chance, Frankie," she said, eyes glinting like lichen in moonlight. "You weren't caught in a current, you *are* the current."

She paused, gaze drifting as if reading from a tapestry only she could see.

"There are threads in this realm, threads older than kingdoms and names. The Verdant line runs through them still, quiet but unbroken." Her eyes flicked toward the trees, then back to Frankie. "And where that line flows, the land begins to stir."

Aoife stepped forward, brushing her fingers over a glowing vine as gently as breath.

"The old magic has been waiting, asleep in the roots. But now... now it turns its face toward you. And not everything that stirs will be pleased."

She looked at Frankie, her gaze holding no fear, only something fiercer. "The wild remembers. Before your feet ever touched this earth, the path was already humming beneath it. Etched into root and stone, into the dreaming of the mountain herself. The old tales, never written, only sung or kept close in bone, they spoke of a returning. A stirring. The threads were woven before your first breath."

She turned then, toward the bend in the canyon where the light thinned and the moss deepened, lush, velvet-dark. A green so rich it seemed to drink the glow from the air. It clung to the stone like memory, thick and ancient.

"Even here," she murmured. "where sunlight forgets to reach... the story waited for you."

"Magic doesn't sleep," she said softly. "It waits and listen and it remembers and lately..." Her eyes narrowed. "It's been restless beneath the stillness. Something in the bones of this place has begun to stir."

She turned back to Frankie, gaze steady and full of quiet thunder. "You didn't stumble here. You were called, not by name, but by essence. The mountain felt the tremor before the surface cracked. And magic, in all her wild wisdom, answered. Through you."

Silence folded around them then.

"That ache you've carried," Aoife said at last, "that pull you could never name, it wasn't longing, Frankie. It was recognition. It was the story finding its thread again." She reached out, brushing a stray curl from Frankie's brow with the care of someone touching a relic. "And now that you're here, the telling can begin. Not the way it was told before, but the way it was always meant to be."

Then, suddenly, she grinned and clapped her hands, mischief glinting in the corner of her eyes. "Now come! We've lingered long enough. The Hub's just ahead, and you haven't truly seen magic until you've stood at Velhollow's heart."

Chalupa stretched luxuriously, tail held high, and trotted after her with regal indifference. "If this path leads to lunch, I'm in."

Nyx sighed, wings giving an exasperated flutter. "If it leads to peace and quiet, I'll eat my own feathers."

Their voices echoed playfully down the stone corridor until the air began to shift, quieter now, thicker, laced with a hush that felt expectant. The path eventually narrowed into a slot canyon, the walls rising high and close, their surfaces worn into sinuous curves. Strange things grew here, ground-hugging plants with waxy leaves, slender stalks that shifted hue in the dimness. The air smelled of damp stone, crushed herbs, and something older, like root cellars and held breath. Water trickled unseen, threading through the rock in a slow, melodic rhythm. Lavender, gold, and pale green shimmered along the canyon walls, refracting, like sunlight passing through mineral deposits. Light moved like stained glass, though no glass framed this world.

The ground stirred. It began as a subtle vibration rising through the roots. Then it deepened into rhythm, slow and steady, like a distant drumbeat carried through stone. Not quite sound, more a memory underfoot. It pulsed upward, through her soles and into her calves, bypassing thought entirely. Frankie slowed, the vines swayed gently, though no breeze stirred. Ferns unfurled along the path, their undersides silver-dusted, catching the ambient glow. Each frond seemed to reach toward her, curling softly, as if in greeting.

Above, no sky waited, only the vast, vaulted ceiling of the cavern, arched like the ribs of some slumbering giant. Crystal inlays caught and fractured the breath of the place into ribbons of pale gold and ghost-blue. Thick, gnarled roots threaded through the stone like ancient fingers. Some pulsed faintly, others sparkled. Every ripple seemed to lean toward her, murmuring in a language too old for words. She had entered as a visitor, but something in the soil, something in the shimmer of light and the pulse beneath her bones, made it clear. She was expected.

Compelled, she reached out. Moss clung to the canyon wall in soft whorls, beaded with dew and flecked with glowing lichen. She hadn't even touched it yet, but already, warmth stirred with recognition. When her palm met the stone, light unfurled beneath her hand, a soft glow curling outward in the shape of a rune, woven deep into the wall's inner stillness. It pulsed once, low and steady. Then, one by one, other sigils blinked into being, blooming in a slow cascade of color, as if the canyon had been waiting. The path ahead began to glow, step by step, revealing a thread of breath-like magic. Overhead, vines uncurled and bloomed with silver flowers, each blossom opening in sync with the rhythm of the runes.

Aoife's voice came soft, almost reverent. "It answers your presence," she murmured. "For Velhollow knows its own blood. When one long-fated returns, the land does not merely welcome, it bears witness."

The air buzzed faintly, like the world holding its breath. Frankie tasted something strange on her tongue, iron and honey, pine and memory. Even her heartbeat shifted, falling into rhythm with the thrum beneath her feet. The corridor ahead unfurled like a ribbon of light, winding into a wide, spiraling descent. Glowing stones marked the path, and the walls shimmered as the mountain welcomed them.

Aoife extended a hand, her face lit with quiet pride. "Come," she said gently. "It's time."

They passed beneath an archway of starlit vines and golden moss, and the quiet around them shifted, deepening into something hushed and expectant. The silver river beside them slowed, its surface smoothing into a glassy calm that reflected the glowing roots above like an intricate web of light. The air gathered a charge, scented with moss and something older, like the memory of a thunderstorm resting in the stone.

Aoife slowed, her gaze lifting to the vaulted ceiling where crystal strands shimmered like captured starlight. She paused there, utterly still, as though listening for a heartbeat hidden in the rock. When her fingers brushed the wall, the stones brightened beneath her touch, answering her in a soft, pulse-like glow.

"There are places," she said softly, "where time forgets to move forward, old magic gathers, and secrets sleep deep, this is one of them."

A soft gust stirred the moss above them, and with it came a sound like chimes ringing through water, clear, delicate, impossible.

Frankie raised a brow. "So what is The Hub, exactly? Sounds like a trendy coffee shop."

Nyx gave a dry flick of his wings. "It's not a coffee shop. Though with everything that stirs there, you might wish it served espresso."

Aoife's voice deepened. "The Hub is where threads begin to gather, long before your name was ever spoken. It's a confluence, like the hidden place where rivers meet beneath the soil, quiet, unseen, yet powerful enough to shape stone."

She stepped forward, eyes drawn to the moss-lined path ahead. "It's not just a place, it's a crossroads. A living threshold. The kind old stories whisper about, where choices echo, where magic waits with its breath held. And only those the land deems worthy are permitted to pass through."

She turned back, voice lower now. "It may look like beauty, but beauty is the least of it. The Hub isn't decoration, it's decision. A loom in the mountain's core, drawing forward the frayed strands of fate and letting you glimpse the pattern they might form. It doesn't command, it beckons. Doesn't dictate, it reveals."

Her gaze held Frankie's. "It shows you what hums beneath your skin, what stirs in your blood when the world falls quiet. It lets you feel the weight of paths not yet taken, their cost, their promise." She paused for a moment as if lost in thought.

"It," she continued, "is older than names, older than even asking. It's where paths converge before anyone knows they've been walking them. Where magic pools like mist in a hollow, waiting for the right breath to stir it. It listens. And if you're willing... it lets you listen back."

She turned fully to Frankie then, voice soft but unflinching. "It won't hand you answers, love. But it may show you how the world might shift, depending on where you step next. And sometimes... that's all the guidance we ever get."

Silence followed, weighty as stone, then Chalupa sniffed. "Well, if this were a coffee shop, at least it'd have muffins, maybe one that didn't hum with ancient intent."

Nyx clicked his beak. "If the muffin hums, you just eat around it."

Frankie looked around, the shimmering walls, the silver-still water, the flowering archway behind them. It all felt impossibly alive, like standing inside a dream that knew it was being dreamed.

"But how does it know my thread?" she asked quietly.

Aoife met her gaze, her Irish lilt deepening. "Ah, love... the old magic knew ya the moment your hand touched the veil. You don't just carry your own thread, you carry the echo of a pattern that was foretold, long before our grandmothers' grandmothers ever opened their eyes to this world. Wasn't written in books, no, it was held in the hush of trees, in the breath between stories. A thing remembered by the land itself, waitin' for the one it named... to step into her place."

Frankie's breath caught. "Foretold?"

Nyx shifted on the ledge. "She means the prophecy."

Prophecy.

The word dropped between them like a stone into still water. Even the river seemed to still, its mirrored surface catching flecks of light from the ceiling above. Aoife didn't speak at first. She simply nodded and beckoned Frankie forward.

"You must see it for yourself."

They walked in comfortable silence, the path curved inward as the canyon walls gave way to a vast, circular chamber, coaxed from the mountain itself, as if grown from memory and magic. The air cooled, perfumed with damp stone, old rain, and something sweet and ancient, like myrrh left too long in moonlight. Above, long, translucent leaves hung in clusters from the cavern ceiling, neither plant nor crystal, but something between. They pulsed faintly, alive with bioluminescent breath, like jellyfish ebbing in slow rhythm.

Frankie slowed, breath catching on wonder. Every alcove cradled a marvel stranger than the last, seed pods of glassy amber, fossilized mid-bloom, their petals caught in perpetual unfurling; stone shelves inscribed with runes that shimmered and rearranged as she looked at them, reluctant to stay legible for long. A hollow stump, sealed in quartz, glowed from within, its heart alive with drifting spores that rose in slow spirals, like smoke from sleeping roots. Droplets hung suspended in the air, each one cradling a flickering mote of light. Tiny constellations, caught mid-breath, as if the stars themselves had paused to listen.

It was the structure at the far end that drew her forward. A single column of quartz rose from the center of the chamber, towering and radiant. Its surface was threaded with golden shoots of light that pulsed faintly, carrying something deeper than a breath, a heartbeat, the passage of time. Hovering just above its crown floated a tapestry, vast and weightless, cradled by breath or intention, its edges rippling on currents no eye could see. Frankie stepped closer, and her pulse slowed to match the stillness around her. The tapestry shimmered like woven spell-work, threads of silver and deep, ancient green, of moonlit indigo and soft, earthen umber. Gold, so pale it looked like dawn's first light was somehow spun into thread, caught the light and held it like a promise. The patterns didn't remain still. They shifted, slowly, like reflections in moving water, like memories rising from beneath the surface, revealing only what one was ready to see.

Then, near the center, an image began to surface. A woman, kneeling at the edge of a grove. She wasn't embroidered, she emerged from the tapestry itself. Her hands pressed lovingly into soil, vines curled around her arms, blossoms unfurled at the hem of her cloak, blooming into being.

It wasn't beauty that stole Frankie's breath, it was the way the grove listened. Leaves tilted toward the woman's fingers. Moss brightened beneath her knees. Even the shadows stilled, as if the entire forest had paused, waiting. The land didn't just surround her, it knew her and something in Frankie stirred. A memory rose, quiet but sharp, the seedlings in the nursery leaning toward her hand before she touched them. Vines that brushed her hair when no wind stirred. She had dismissed it, coincidence, breeze, her own imagination. But now, as the tapestry shimmered in its slow, dreamlike rhythm, something clicked into place.

"She's... part of it," Frankie whispered, voice tremulous. "The land responds to her. It... remembers."

The tapestry pulsed softly. Frankie's breath caught. She didn't know how she knew, but she did. A sense of familiarity echoed through her, deep-rooted. The forest didn't follow her. It answered her. Just as it had answered the woman in the weave.

The images began to shift again, wings lifting, rivers curling around stone and root, constellations flickering into being in the corners of the tapestry. The woman's form dissolved into the forest, but the feeling remained, a quiet pull, steady and alive.

Behind her, Aoife stepped forward, her voice folding into the hush like mist into moss. "It's woven by the seers of Velhollow," she murmured. "A record of what has been... and what stirs now."

Frankie didn't respond, she was watching as the tapestry transformed again.

A great tree rose, its trunk split clean in two. One half bloomed with impossible light, the other burned with fire that licked toward the stars. Cloaked figures stepped through smoke. One held a broken crown. Another scattered seeds like starlight into ash.

"How is this moving like that?" Frankie asked, her voice barely more than breath.

Aoife's lips curved faintly. "You're in Velhollow, lovey. Little here behaves the way the world above expects." She turned her gaze back to the shifting threads. "The tapestry responds to lineage... to purpose."

She stepped closer, voice shifting into something wind-worn and reverent, as though drawn from the soil itself.

"Some say that when the Balance begins to fray, and the edges of the world grow thin, one will rise, bound to root and storm, heart-tethered to the land beneath. And beside her, a guardian of shifting form. Together, they will awaken the Verdant Path, a promise whispered into the soil before the world even knew it needed saving."

The threads stirred in quiet rhythm, weaving and unweaving, memory breathing through fiber and light. Frankie stood still, her eyes lifted, watching images ripple across the tapestry like reflections over water. She didn't understand the full meaning of what she saw, not yet. But she felt it, a knowing older than thought, older than story. Aoife's voice came again, low and steady, laced with a cadence that felt older than language.

"What I'm about to speak has never lived in ink. It's passed in fragments, carried on breath, dreamt in quiet minds, and sung by the old trees when the wind leans just so."

As she stepped closer, something in the air shifted. Words no longer felt spoken, more like a spell that flowed like water. Frankie stood still, eyes lifted to the tapestry as its images stirred like echoes across still water. She didn't yet understand what she was seeing, only that it stirred something elemental inside her. A recognition older than thought, a call without origin or destination. Aoife looked to Frankie once more, steady as stone.

"This is the prophecy, love. Bound to root and the green fire core. To us." She then began the summoning. What left her lips was not shaped by voice, but by earth and echo. Half-song, half-silence, the words came slow and sure, uncoiling from the mountain's bones as if they had waited there, buried in stone and time, for the right breath to speak them back into the world.

"Beneath the endless, skyless glow,
Where unseen rivers of magic flow,
Two paths converge, destined to meet,
Where ancient earth and wild hearts beat.

One bound to witches' roots, to green life's bloom,
A healer's hand to chase back gloom.
One shifting form, unbound by name,
A fleeting shadow, a flickering flame.

In shadow's dance and nature's grace,
Together they'll mend the fractured space.
By bloodlines woven, by fates aligned,
A bond shall rise to heal, and bind.

Where twilight lingers and veils wear thin,
Their journey starts, but won't begin
Without the leap, the trust, the fall,
When courage dares to heed the call.

Yet even light must walk through night,
Where wrong feels right and truth takes flight.
A choice must come, a price be paid,
Where hearts are tested, and lines are frayed.
The dark will rise to claim its due,
With poisoned charm and paths askew.
And she must stand where good men break,
To save the world or be the quake.

In shadow and light, their strength will grow,
To face the tide, to ebb and flow.
Two souls entwined, a single thread,
To hold the balance where all may tread."

The words settled around Frankie, absorbed like rain through cracked earth. She stared at Aoife, at the shifting tapestry, at the moss-bright floor that now felt too sacred to stand on. Her thoughts spun like wind-scattered leaves.

"I'm not sure what it means," she whispered, her voice fraying at the edges. "This prophecy… how could it be about me?"

Her throat tightened.

"All of this is so new to me," she went on. "I didn't grow up in this world. I've never cast a spell." Her voice caught. "I'm just a girl who talks to plants, I cry at sad commercials and I haven't worn matching socks ... ever." She laughed, one hand pressing to her chest as though trying to hold herself together. "How am I supposed to be part of some ancient magic? How could I belong to anything like this?"

Chalupa let out a dramatic sigh, the kind only a long-suffering, overqualified magical familiar could conjure.

"Oh, please," he drawled. "You've been *witching* half your life and didn't even know it."

He hopped onto a ledge, tail flicking, and began grooming his paw with theatrical flair.

"Your tinctures, your tonics, your endless herb-laced lotions, half the village smells like rosemary thanks to you. You brew peace into tea, stir comfort into honey. You so much as glance at a wilted basil and two days later it's blooming like it's competing at the county fair."

Frankie opened her mouth, but he lifted a paw.

"And don't even get me started on the harvest market, you told everyone to wear boots because you had a '*weird feeling,*' and then came the hail, plum-sized, no less. Whole square turned to slush, and we were the only ones dry and smug."

He gave his tail a smug flick. "Face it, you've been *witching* for years. You just didn't know the word for it."

Frankie blinked, uncertainty still etched across her face, but beneath it, something warmer had begun to stir. She turned back toward the glowing threads above her, eyes full of questions she didn't yet have language for.

Aoife gave a low, knowing hum. "Aye love, he's not wrong, you know," she said gently, her gaze still fixed on Frankie. "You've followed the thread of your magic all your life, even without a name to call it. Some spells don't need circles or candles, they live in instinct, in the way you listen to the wind or know what a heart needs before it asks."

She stepped forward, a gentle glow trailing through the moss, and her voice lowered, rich with quiet purpose. "There is lore," she said, "of a witch not named, but known. A figure the old ones never dared to carve in stone or ink in script. She was spoken of in seed and star, in smoke curling from sacred fires. No face, no name, only presence, like a hush in the trees before a storm." Her gaze lifted toward the tapestry, its threads glowing gently as if warmed by morning light. "They say the earth stirs when she draws near. That she belongs to the Verdant line... the bloodline that winds beneath mountain and river, threaded through generations like ivy through old stone."

She turned back to Frankie, voice low and steady. "That bloodline is ours, love. And the one they whispered of, the witch the world aches for when the wild grows restless and the bones of magic creak, she does not arrive from outside the tale. She rises from within it, drawn by need not will."

Aoife stepped closer. "I was but a flicker of that magic, a glimmer, a seed-light. But you..." Her gaze softened, eyes shining with quiet awe. "You are the Verdant Witch rising into your power."

Frankie swayed from the enormity of all of this. Aoife reached for her hand. The words struck like thunder, Frankie's throat tightened, her thoughts scattering.

"But I'm just... me."

Aoife smiled gently, eyes warm with knowing. "Aye," she said. "And so was every seed before it broke open and reached for the sun."

Nyx spoke. "There is more," he said, voice suddenly low, as if the shadows had shifted and were listening. "A shifter walks beside her. Bound by an older magic. A thread spun before time had breath. Fated. Balanced. Written into the weave."

Frankie just blinked. "A shapeshifter… like, a real one? Not just some bearded lumberjack who owns too much flannel and gets weird around full moons?"

The words felt ridiculous even as she said them, but somewhere beneath the swirl of disbelief, something quiet and certain inside her stirred. In a world where tapestries breathed and cats made prophecies, maybe even the flannel-clad wolfman was real.

"Oh, dahhhling, not just any shifter," Chalupa chimed in, his tail flicking with performative disdain. "*The* shifter. Tall, broody, emotionally complex. Probably has haunted eyes and a tragic backstory involving mist and moonlight. Broods while chopping wood. Broods while boiling tea. Broods while tying his boots with heroic intensity."

Nyx gave a long-suffering sigh. "He is correct," he said, dry as bark. "But understand this, he is not an accessory, he is an anchor. Where she is growth and bloom, he is shift and shadow. The path does not open to her alone. It opens because they walk it together."

Chalupa sniffed. "Still broody. Bet he smells like pine needles and unresolved tension."

Aoife's voice folded back into the hush like the settling of snowfall, quiet but unmistakable.

"Let them jest," she murmured, her eyes never leaving Frankie. "Even laughter can carry truth."

She stepped forward once more, and the air around her seemed to hush with her. "I felt the Verdant hum in our blood, in my veins. For a time, some wondered if I might be the one. But I was meant to remember and guide." Her voice deepened, wrapped in moss and moonlight. "You, love… you are meant to awaken and rise."

A rush moved through Frankie, wild and quiet, like wind threading through tall grass. Something ancient was stirring within her, not as a burden, but as birthright.

Aoife turned once more to the tapestry, her voice soft, as though the mountain itself were listening. "Velhollow rests beneath the veil of forgetting, hidden where the world no longer looks. Woven into bedrock, steeped in shadow and time. It reveals itself only to those the land remembers. And through its roots runs An Fhírinne Ceilte… the Hidden Truth. The breath beneath breath. The pulse beneath silence."

A silence followed, thick as twilight, humming with things unsaid. "These aren't just prophecies," she said at last. "They're awakenings. They bloom when the world begins to fray at the edges. And always there is one who stirs the old magic awake."

Frankie felt the truth settle, like the first green after frost. Aoife gestured toward the dim passage ahead, where light shimmered faintly like the glint of memory.

"Velhollow is where that story begins to shape itself. A place older than maps. It does not give answers, Frankie, it reveals the threads. It lets you listen to the questions that live beneath your skin."

From behind, Chalupa muttered, "If this were a coffee shop, at least it'd have muffins."

Nyx, every feather radiating deadpan disdain, "And knowing Velhollow, they'd hum lullabies and float three inches off the tray."

Frankie laughed, because what else could she do? She was the Verdant Witch rising and the world had just begun to stir.

Chapter 13

A flicker of light shimmered ahead, slipping down the moss path, soft, pulsing, like the heartbeat of something ancient just waking.

"We're running short on time, love," Aoife said gently. "And you've more to learn than most."

Frankie stood still, as if the earth had shifted under her without a sound. Nothing looked different, yet everything felt changed. She was no longer just watching the world turn strange, she was part of why it might hold, or break.

"She won't have long once the dark threads begin to pull," Nyx murmured, stepping forward, wings drawn close. His voice was quiet, like wind slipping through hollow trees.

Aoife nodded, her gaze shadowed. "Aye, we've already felt the tremors. The veil grows thinner by the day, and the balance with it." Her voice lowered, as if the mountain itself leaned in to listen. "This isn't myth, love, it's a warning and whatever's coming, it's stirring faster than any of us hoped."

Frankie's fingers curled around the hem of her coat, grounding herself in the familiar fabric. The air around them seemed to hush, waiting.

"What's coming?" she asked, her voice unsteady. "And what exactly is the veil?"

Aoife turned toward her fully, and for a moment, she looked like something older, weathered and wise, made of memory and stardust. "The veil is what keeps the realms apart," she said quietly. "The living and the dead. The seen and unseen. Light and shadow. Magic and the wild, unbridled force that waits beyond it. It's what keeps the dark from swallowing the rest."

She stepped closer, her skirts whispering over the mossy stone. "But the veil is fraying. And when it thins, the balance unravels. Magic begins to shift, to rot in places, to turn on itself. There are forces that thrive on that unraveling, ancient ones.

Forgotten by most. Remembered only by those of us who've spent a lifetime listening to the land."

Aoife's words fell like stones into still water, each one sending ripples that lingered. "You've seen the beautiful things," she said, her voice gentling. "The glory of this cavern. The tapestry woven with starlight and memory. The hush of the trees when they listen. You've felt the shimmer of a healing charm, the warmth of magic blooming in your hands. The kindness in it. The grace."

She paused, her gaze steady. "But that's only part of it, love. Magic isn't only light." Her tone darkened, not harsh, but honest. "It casts a shadow. And when the balance slips, even beauty can be twisted. Wonder becomes weapon. Memory becomes madness. Growth turns to rot."

She bent, touching a glowing leaf. It flared bright beneath her fingers, then faded. "There was a time when we could hold the line between the realms. When witches like me, like you, stood as stewards of the threshold. But that time is slipping. And the world is hungry for power again."

Frankie shook her head. "But I'm not, I'm not ready. I don't know what I'm doing. I talk to plants. I make salves for bee stings. I forget to water my rosemary." Her voice cracked. "I'm not trained for this. I don't even know where to begin."

She paused. "And if I can't stop whatever this is?"

Aoife didn't answer at once. She looked toward the glowing walls, where the shadows swayed like old ghosts listening in.

"Then the unraveling begins," she said finally. "First at the edges, then the roots."

Chalupa stretched. "You've already faced a hundred tiny apocalypses. Remember when Mrs. Dunkin's garden got root rot and you resurrected it with compost tea that smelled like feet? Or when Becky Munroe's twins wouldn't sleep for three days and you brewed that sleepy-time syrup? She shared it with her book club, and they all passed out mid-chapter, snoring into their cardigans with half-eaten muffins in their laps. One of them dreamt she'd eloped with a selkie."

He began grooming a paw with exaggerated calm. "And don't get me started on the 'rash butter' incident. Three jars of mystery balm later, and old Mr. Rutledge was eczema-free, could dance a jig, and insists he now understands crows."

Chalupa flicked his tail. "You've been tossing around quiet magic for years. You just call it 'intuition' and tuck it in tins labeled 'soothing blend.'" He shot Frankie a glance, equal parts affection and judgment. "You've got grit, a green thumb, and that unnerving weather sense. You once told everyone to bring ponchos to the Midsummer picnic because it was 'too quiet.' No one listened, then the clouds rolled in like the sky had opinions."

Chalupa gave a satisfied sniff. "So no, you're not fumbling toward some grand destiny. You're the girl who brews clarity into nettle tea and instinct into honey. The universe just finally caught up." He bumped his head lightly against her knee. "And you've got me. Plus Aoife and Nyx, I suppose, though he's more feathers and foreshadowing."

Nyx didn't respond, just fluffed his feathers and blinked.

Chalupa turned smug. "If anyone's going to keep the world from unraveling, it's the witch with the mismatched socks."

Nyx finally spoke, voice soft but steady. "Trust the journey, human. This story's only just beginning."

Aoife's voice warmed. "Aye, love. Trust what you carry, and what carries you."

Frankie drew a slow breath and for the first time, the weight of what was coming didn't feel like a cliff's edge, it felt like a door.

"I'll try," was all she said and that was enough.

Aoife's smile was full of quiet pride. "That's all the realms ask."

Chalupa flicked an ear. "Ah, excellent. Vague deadlines and cosmic jeopardy. My favorite."

Nyx gave a slow blink. "Some of us take impending ruin a bit more seriously."

Chalupa didn't even look at him. "And some of us have been through five apocalypses and learned to pace ourselves."

Frankie groaned. "This is my life now? Magical prophecy, a shapeshifter, and you two bickering until the end of time."

Aoife chuckled and rested a hand on her shoulder. "The path will test you, but these two will keep you grounded, in their own ridiculous ways."

Chalupa smirked. "You're welcome."

Nyx sighed. "Think of us as chaotic guardians of your arcane destiny."

Aoife stepped closer, her voice low, laced with quiet enchantment. “It's the odd ones, love, the companions you least expect, that end up guarding your heart the fiercest.” She cast a knowing look toward Chalupa and Nyx, the corner of her mouth lifting. “The path ahead won't always be clear. It may twist, vanish, or double back. But it knows you. It remembers the shape of your spirit, even when you forget. It will lead you home.”

She laid her palm against a lichen-laced stone, fingers stilling, as though feeling for something just beneath the surface. “Stay true to what tugs at your spirit, even when it makes no sense. The earth doesn't shout. She doesn't rush. She weaves in silence, pulling every thread toward what has always waited for you.”

Turning back, Aoife's eyes shimmered, quiet wonder wrapped in something older than words, like the hush before a story begins. “Velhollow isn't like the world above, love,” she said gently. “Time curls here. It lingers. It listens. What's meant for you won't go amiss, not in a place like this. It arrives when the soul is ripened by the waiting. Not a moment too soon… not a breath too late.”

She let her hand drift over a bloom that opened at her touch, petals glowing soft as fireflies. The earth itself seemed to lean closer.

“Even if your heart feels uncertain,” she went on, voice low as the hush between verses, “the magic will know when you're ready.”

Then, with a sideways glance and the barest arch of one brow, she added, “And perhaps… that readiness draws near.”

Frankie blinked, but Aoife's gaze was already drifting toward the deeper part of the path ahead, where the runes began to shimmer a touch brighter.

“Your anam cara,” she said, almost like naming a charm, “may not be far now. The land has a way of bringing soul threads close when the time is right.”

She smiled then, half-knowing, half-wild, and turned without another word, letting the mystery settle between them like soft mist in the hollow.

“Anam cara?” Frankie echoed, the words slipping from her lips.

Aoife nodded, slowly. “Aye, a soul friend,” she said, voice low and wrapped in wonder. “The one who sees you truly, as you are, and as you were always meant to be. Not ahead of you, not behind, but beside you. Step for step and if your path stays true, he'll find you... just as you are finding yourself."

Frankie's breath caught. "So... he's out there?" she whispered. "Walking toward me?"

Aoife's smile curled, soft and sly. "Not toward you, love. He's walking his own winding path. But with time, and trust, and a little magic... your paths will cross. Just not always when, or where, you expect." She leaned in slightly, her voice dipped in mischief. "Remember, Velhollow isn't the world above. The usual rules, the usual clocks... they don't hold here. This place lives by older rhythms. Stranger ones. Learn to see it as it is, its wonder, its shadows, and most of all, learn to trust yourself in the seeing."

She reached out and curled her fingers gently around Frankie's. "And when it happens, when you feel it, don't doubt it. Don't try to make it small enough to fit what the old world taught you to expect. Here, the heart often remembers before the mind can make sense of it."

A comfortable quiet bloomed between them, and beneath their feet, the ground cover shimmered gold, pulsing slow and sure like the heartbeat of something ancient. A breeze curled around them, edged with petrichor, impossible, and yet undeniably real. The silence wasn't empty, it was full of waiting.

Up ahead, the path began to glow like dusk yielding to starlight. Runes blinked to life across the stone, their soft pulse syncing to a rhythm older than time itself. Gold and silver wove together in delicate patterns like constellations trapped in moss. The air thickened with anticipation, like the moment before music begins. Then the path unfurled, petal by glowing petal, and the realms opened their heart.

The Hub.

It stretched before them like a secret the world had kept too long. A vast chamber carved by time and magic, its stone walls lined with living crystal casting soft waves of green and deep violet. Overhead, the cavern ceiling curved high like a cathedral of earth, laced with bioluminescent vines and glowing spores that drifted like stars fallen from their constellations. At its center stood a lone tree, not tall, but immense in presence. Its bark was iridescent emerald, laced with molten gold etched in runes that shifted when looked at too long. Roots fanned outward like a web of ley lines, threading into the earth in every direction. Its branches reached upward, leaves whispering in a breeze that didn't belong to this world. Magic gathered here, not solely in spells or sparks, but in breath, in memory, in knowing. As they stepped deeper into the chamber, the magic stirred. Glittering creatures blinked into being, motes of light with wings, tiny beasts made of moss and dew, orbs that giggled and darted like will-o'-the-wisps. A cluster of floating blossoms whirled past Frankie's cheek, their petals buzzing in harmony. A glimmering creature drifted down from the cavern ceiling like a soap bubble stitched from moonlight, trailing glitter and the faint sound of chimes and… was that humming? It landed squarely on Chalupa's head and immediately began weaving his fur into something vaguely ceremonial.

Nyx, perched above, let out a dry click. "Looks like you've been claimed by a whisper-sprite. Odd, they usually prefer moon moss lichen."

Chalupa bared a single fang. "If I wake up as a decorative amulet in another realm, I expect an immediate rescue."

Aoife chuckled. "Och, relax, it likes you."

The creature let out a delighted squeak and tucked a dewdrop between Chalupa's ears like a crown jewel.

"You're being accessorized," Nyx said dryly. "Embrace your destiny."

Frankie grinned. "Honestly? It's kind of cute."

Chalupa sighed like a martyr. "I was once a terror of the Shadowlands. Now I'm…*cute*."

Laughter echoed softly, rising into the high-vaulted cavern like smoke from a wood fire, light, warm, and utterly out of place in such a space, and yet… not unwelcome. Threads of light wove through the walls like wild embroidery come to life. Frankie stood wide-eyed, as a cluster of floating seedpods spun past her head, giggling in bell-like tones before bursting into trails of glitter that rained down and vanished midair.

"Did those floating dust bunnies just giggle?" she asked, brushing sparkles from her lashes.

"It's pollen from the gigglebrush vine," Aoife said, utterly serious. "Rare and highly contagious. Don't inhale too much or you'll be giggling for a week."

Frankie arched a brow, watching the last of the glittering pollen disappear. "You're making that up."

Aoife only smiled, eyes twinkling with mischief. "Am I?"

They walked on, laughter still clinging to the air like dandelion fluff. But as they moved deeper into the chamber, the mood began to shift, subtly at first. The sparkle of the gigglebrush gave way to something quieter, more intent. Frankie's steps slowed without meaning to. Every leaf, every ripple of light, every hush in the air felt purposeful now, as if the mountain were listening. Runes along the path blinked awake, flaring in rhythm to her steps, as though the very stone was greeting her.

The path curved again, just slightly, and with each step more of the veil seemed to lift. The air wavered, warm and restless, like heat rising off a sun struck road, bending the space ahead until it opened into something ancient and luminous. What had looked like solid cavern walls now thinned and drifted aside like a curtain of light, revealing a hidden clearing beneath the vaulted boughs of the Hub, and at the center of it stood a fox.

It didn't walk into view, it just *became*. One moment, there was only shimmer and glimmer, the glint of light on air. The next, the fox coalesced from it, as though the magic had been waiting for the shape of it to form. Its coat was russet fire brushed with silver, like autumn leaves caught in moonlight. The tips of its ears flicked as if listening to a language older than sound. It looked real, solid and breathing, but something in its bearing betrayed the truth, this creature had been born of magic, not biology.

The fox stood poised beneath the tree, haloed in the soft glow cast by drifting ivy and threads of pale light curling through the air. Its eyes were golden-amber, flecked with something old and remembering. When they met Frankie's, the moment tightened, quiet and unbroken. As the fox's gaze deepened, the runes along the path brightened in response, their glow rising like a low-held breath. Overhead, vines stirred despite the stillness, and a silver blossom slowly opened above them, releasing a delicate dust that drifted down in a soft, dying sparkle before dissolving into the air. Then the it moved, fluid, silent, certain.

Frankie didn't dare breathe. Wonder held her still, wide open in a way she hadn't known she could be. When she lifted her hand, the fox stepped forward without looking away, and touched its nose to her palm. Warmth opened along her arm, spreading through her like a thread drawn taut across years and story, pulled into place at last. Her pulse steadied, answering the quiet thrum rising from the ground beneath her feet, and for an aching heartbeat she felt the fox's presence settle into her. *Recognition.*

Then, as swiftly as it had come, it began to fade. Its form loosened, unraveling like fine silk touched by sun, thinning into golden strands that lifted and drifted upward like dandelion seeds carried on a sigh. And when it vanished, it left no footprint, no trace, only the deep certainty that something true had taken shape around her. The silence that followed was not empty. It was full, charged, waiting, alive. Frankie didn't speak. She couldn't. She had been seen. Not just by Aoife, or the Hub, or the land, but by the wild itself.

Nyx let out a low whistle. "Well," he said, wings fluffing, "that was either a profound spiritual reckoning or an exceptionally dramatic way to say hello."

Chalupa yawned. "I don't do connections. If I ever dematerialize, it'll be to escape brunch, not bond with anyone."

Frankie blinked, the awe still lingering like an afterglow, but a smile tugged at the corners of her mouth.

"Okay," she murmured. "So that just happened."

Aoife watched as the last shimmer of the fox dissolved beneath the roots of the Hub, her gaze lingering on the space it had vanished from. A silence clung to the air.

"Well now," she murmured, voice threaded with something ancient. "A Kitsune. You don't often see them walking the world." Her eyes met Frankie's, alight with quiet wonder. "They're keepers of in-between spaces, shapeshifters, tricksters, protectors and like all true magic."

She stepped forward gently, as though careful not to disturb the breath of the moment. "The veil here is thinner than lace, love. Sometimes it vanishes altogether. That's why fairy tales cling to places like this, because they remember. Because they're true. Magic doesn't need belief to exist... but it blooms when seen."

Her voice softened, woven now with something both tender and unshakable. "Every culture holds stories, foxes with firelight in their eyes, women born of root and storm, children laced with stars. The world didn't conjure those tales to pass the time. It's remembering, bit by bit, in lullabies and half-spoken dreams, in the hush before thunder and the wind that forgets to be still."

She nodded toward the place where the Kitsune had stood.

"That fox didn't come to charm you, or test you. It came to bear witness and to warn."

Frankie stiffened slightly. "Warn about what?"

Aoife's gaze didn't waver. "That the world is shifting. That something long-buried has begun to wake. Old magic, warped by time and silence, starved for purpose. The Kitsune felt it, just as Velhollow has. Just as the all wild places always do."

She turned fully now, her expression fierce with love and something older, resolve etched into the lines of her face. Beneath Frankie's feet, the earth shivered with golden light, no longer gentle, but restless. It didn't swirl like a welcome, it coiled like a question. The stone gave a single, quiet thrum, as though the mountain itself had drawn a breath and waited to see what she'd do next.

"The Hub knows you," Aoife said, her voice low and deliberate. "Not just who you've been, but who and what you're becoming. It remembers your rhythm, your roots, the magic woven into your blood before your first cry. It doesn't just recognize you, love, it's placing its hope in you."

The chamber around them seemed to respond. Runes shimmered in shifting patterns. A harp stirred in the unseen. And above them, ivy bloomed in slow motion, as if waking from centuries of sleep.

Aoife stepped closer, grounding her words with the hush of truth. "You won't be ready all at once. But the road ahead will not wait. That muchness in you, the part too wild, too radiant, too much for the world above? That's not a flaw. That's your compass."

She reached gently for Frankie's hand, her fingers warm and steady. "Velhollow didn't call you here to watch, love. It called you to rise."

Frankie didn't answer right away. At her feet, the light flickered like fire catching on autumn leaves, and she felt an ache she hadn't known was there until now. Since discovering magic was real, it had hovered at the edges of her awareness like a secret begging to be named: glowing ivy, floating teacups, pollen that made you laugh before you knew why. It had dazzled her, wrapped her in the warmth of finally belonging somewhere, of being wanted by something ancient and beautiful.

But this... this was something else. Her gaze drifted to where the Kitsune had vanished, its silence still echoing in her bones. Magic, she was starting to understand, wasn't just starlight and song. It had weight. It had teeth. A shadow that stirred when the balance tipped. Her palm still tingled from the fox's touch. She pressed her hand to her chest, steadying herself against a feeling she couldn't name, an unraveling, quiet but insistent, like a thread tugged loose from the inside. Not fear exactly, but something colder. Older. As if a door had creaked open in the dark and something was waiting on the other side.

She looked down. The glow at her feet pulsed low and slow, like embers dreaming beneath a blanket of ash. It wasn't just light, it was rhythm, ancient and alive, like the stillness before a storm or the breath of soil before spring. The ground felt watchful, as if it carried a heartbeat of its own, and was reaching gently for hers, searching for the same wild thrum beneath her skin. And suddenly, all those little things she used to do, hanging herbs above the sink, tucking rosemary into the soles of her shoes, sweeping clockwise to chase out bad luck, felt like lullabies sung to calm a storm. Sweet intentions, yes. But fragile. Small. Like dandelion charms whispered against a rising tide.

"What if I fail?" she whispered, not to Aoife, not even to the mountain, but to the fear blooming quiet and wide inside her. "What if I can't do what's needed?"

Aoife's voice came low. "The Kitsune didn't cross the veil and show himself for nothing. When beings like that appear, it means the world is shifting. Old magic is waking and not all of it welcomes the light." She reached for Frankie's hand, grounding her with a touch soft as breath, sure as earth. "You will get things wrong. That's not a maybe, it's a certainty. But failing isn't the same as not trying. Magic doesn't ask you to be perfect. It asks you to show up anyway. Bruised, unsure and stubborn as ever."

She tilted her head, eyes kind but clear. "You think The Hub and Velhollow chose you because you knew what to do? No, love. It chose you because you don't. Because you'll care enough to try, even when it hurts. Even when it costs you."

She paused, her gaze sweeping the chamber like she could feel every heartbeat the stone had ever held. "Velhollow didn't call you here to be flawless. It called you to be whole. To be you. That wild, radiant part of you, the muchness others tried to quiet, to trim, to tame, that's not your flaw. It's your way through."

She let go of Frankie's hand only to press her own to the ground beside them, fingers splayed. "The Kitsune saw it. The mountain knows it. And the magic?" She smiled, slow and certain. "The magic remembers."

Frankie turned to her, voice barely more than breath. "My whatness?"

"Your *muchness*," Aoife said, smiling gently. "That wild, bright, too-much-not-enough wonder you tried to silence. The spark that never dulls, no matter how much the world asked you to shrink. The magic here recognizes the magic in you, and it sees your potential." She tilted her head toward the tree. "You've come this far. Now let it know you."

Frankie stepped forward and the air shifted. It felt wild, charged and breathless. Magic curled up from the ground in delicate tendrils, winding up her boots, her legs, her spine, wrapping around her. Aoife's voice came gently from behind, low as a lullaby. "Go on, love, let it know you, lay your hands on it, no spells, no words. Just you, as you are."

Frankie just nodded as she reached out, she placed her hands against the heartwood, feeling the warmth beneath her palms, as if the tree itself had a heartbeat and the realm responded. A low note rose through the chamber, through the stone, through her bones, resonant, ancient, full of recognition. Light ignited beneath her palms, racing across the bark like fire-water, threading into the runes, the canopy, the walls. Green and gold surged in every direction, fierce with knowing. The tree answered as a radiant wave of living magic burst outward, sweeping the chamber in arcs of brilliance. Glyphs awoke in its wake, stags crowned with stars stepped across the stone, wolves howled at blooming moons, vines unfurled in impossible bloom. The ceiling lit up in constellations, redrawing the sky in wild patterns. Beneath her, the roots shifted in welcome, reshaping the earth to make space.

The Hub had accepted her.

Frankie hands were still pressed to the trunk, but the warmth had changed. It no longer ran only through the tree. It had moved into her now, steady as the beat of her heart.

"I think it likes me," she whispered.

Aoife stepped to her side, voice shining with pride. "Aye, love," she said. "The Hub doesn't accept just anyone."

Frankie turned slowly, the chamber unfolding around her like a world remembering its own story. Color flowed across the stone, soft and vivid, and for a suspended breath she felt less like a visitor and more like she had stepped directly into the inner workings of a legend. She wasn't walking through a tale. She was part of its turning.

Then the air shifted. Light tightened inward, steadying like candle flames bracing for a coming change. The warmth that had curled around her slipped back, cautious. Watchful. The runes along the path flickered, not in fear, but in attention, settling into a quiet tremor. Even the great tree drew itself inward, its leaves whispering against each other though no breeze moved. A sound came from the far end of the chamber, low, deliberate. A rustle that meant intention, not accident. From the thick hush, a figure stepped forward.

Tall. Shadowed. Certain. He crossed the threshold of the dim light, and the space itself seemed to take a breath. He was enormous, just shy of seven feet, his frame all storm-hewn strength and effortless control. Built like something shaped by wind, stone, and the memory of thunder. Power didn't radiate from him; it rested on him with quiet certainty. His movements were precise, held, almost feline in their restraint, as if he knew exactly what he was capable of and chose gentleness instead. His face was striking, sharp, beautiful, almost too perfect until she saw the faint scar over one brow. Not a flaw, but a truth. Something earned. Something survived. And his eyes, silver-blue, steady, otherworldly, caught her and held her still. They didn't simply look at her. They recognized her. His hair fell in dark waves threaded with copper, and his eyes... those eyes held storms that had learned patience.

Magic stirred between them, answering itself across the space. A pull, instinctive and electric, like two halves of a long-silent chord finally hearing the other's note. His hair, shoulder-length and wild, carried threads of muted gold and copper that caught the chamber's glow. Faint runes lay along his collarbone, not calling attention, just present, as though they had always been part of him. Frankie stepped back without meaning to, her boot catching uneven stone. She stumbled. He moved before thought could catch up. Strong hands, steady, warm, caught her with impossible gentleness. The touch sent a rush of heat across her skin, not painful, but startling in its clarity, like someone opening a door inside her she hadn't realized was locked. For one suspended heartbeat, the world narrowed to the space between their breaths. Then Aoife stepped forward, not breaking the moment, but anchoring it.

"Frankie," she said, her Irish lilt warm with pride, "allow me to present Griffon Thorne, Warden of the Wild Thresholds, bound by oath to the Royal Guard."

Frankie turned fully toward him and everything shifted again. Every book she'd loved as a child, every sketch of heroes she'd drawn in secret, felt suddenly like it had been preparing her for this exact man standing in front of her.

Aoife's voice wove softly through the charged quiet. "A guardian of the forgotten ways. Born of old magics, shaped by storm-light and root-song. He has walked where silence keeps its own counsel, through hollows the wind dares not name. He speaks the language of stone and shadow, and the storm listens when he calls."

Frankie barely heard her because Griffon Thorne, this impossible man, this living myth, had turned his full attention toward her. Oh and the way he looked at her... it hit with the force of weather shifting, grounding and electric at once. He inclined his head in greeting, simple, devastating in its quiet grace.

Aoife's smile softened. "Griffon," she said gently, "this is my Frankie."

Griffon turned to face her, the shift in his attention was seismic. Magic leaned forward. His eyes, silver-blue and glinting with the echo of moonlit wilds, found Frankie and held her there, steadfast and unwavering. For a long moment, he said nothing then bowed his head with the kind of respect that didn't feel rehearsed. When he spoke, his voice was deep like the sound of distant thunder rolling through the bones of the earth.

"*Francesca Caelith*," he said, and the name struck the air like a spell spoken in its true tongue, rich with power, older than stone. Each word unfolded with deliberate grace, echoing like an ancient chant in a temple long forgotten. "*Granddaughter of Aoife Caelith, Blood of the Verdant Line, Keeper of the Balance.*" Each title landed like a stepping stone across some invisible threshold, a bridge between what was and what will be. Then he added, his voice deepening.

"Also, the Verdant Witch that is rising, called by the wild, claimed by the weave. A force reborn to mend what others have broken." The golden threads in the air brightened, bending toward her as though drawn by her very presence. The chamber seemed to lean in, listening. Frankie felt it too, that undeniable hum beneath her skin.

Frankie's breath caught at the sound of her name, not DiLegna. The way Griffon had spoken it... *Caelith*. It rang through the chamber like the chime of a long-forgotten bell.

Slowly, she turned to Aoife, her voice catching like wind in the trees.

"Why did he call me that?" she asked softly. "*Caelith...* Is that your name?"

Aoife stepped toward her, her gaze threaded with knowing and tenderness, as if she had waited lifetimes for this moment. Her voice, when it came, was low and lilting, steeped in old magic and echoes of moss-wrapped stone.

"Aye love, in the ways of our kin, names are not given, they are remembered," she said, lifting a hand and brushing her fingers just above her heart, where magic pulsed like a secret trying to speak. "They are not simply passed from mother to child like heirlooms of silver and bone. No, names in our bloodline are the breath of the land, the memory of the stars. They are bound to soul and soil."

She stepped back, her skirt whispering across the stone, her eyes bright with a fierce, ancestral light. "*Caelith* is the name of the line, the name whispered by river and root, known to wind and wild. It threads back to the *First Mother,* to the dawn of the old ways, when witches did not borrow power, but walked it."

Her voice dipped, as the cavern itself seemed to lean closer.

"Here, you are *Francesca Caelith*, child of the Verdant Line, named by the land, by the old spells, by the very breath of the in-between. The world does not speak such names lightly, love. The stars knew it before you were born, now, so do you."

As Aoife spoke, the chamber responded, the quartz walls brightened, beating in time with Frankie's heartbeat. The vines above unfurled with a whispering sigh, their blooms turning toward her as if recognizing something old-rooted. Petals glinted in hues of green and gold, catching the golden light and scattering it like rain through sun. A soft wind brushed through the cavern, carrying the scent of wild thyme and blooming hawthorn. The water in the crystal pools rippled outward in soft, widening rings, reflecting the glow of cavern-light caught in their depths. Shapes of stone and root swayed gently across the surface, bending into unfamiliar patterns as the ripples moved on. Beneath her feet, the ground answered with a low, steady warmth, subtle, like the earth acknowledging her step. It wasn't bright or showy, just a quiet recognition, as though the land had opened an old memory and found her name inside it. She was known, and the world beneath remembered.

Aoife said nothing, her smile shifted, not just with pride, but fierce with love. The kind that rises when you've watched someone bravely become what they were always meant to be. Griffon's gaze never left Frankie, and in the space that followed, Frankie felt something settle through her like a door swinging wide open. Everything she had known was ending, and somehow, impossibly, everything was just beginning.

Aoife folded her arms across, her gaze still resting on the pair.

"The Hub never mis-weaves," she murmured, her voice like wind through ancient trees. "It always draws the right threads together."

Chalupa flicked his tail, his tone dry as starlight on stone. "How curious that Griffon Thorne, of all creatures, just happens to pass through The Hub on the very day Frankie crosses over."

From his perch above, Nyx let out a low, melodic caw that echoed like fate striking a distant bell. "Almost like the forest got tired of waiting and gave destiny a little push."

Aoife's gaze lingered on the two figures before her, her eyes reflecting something old and knowing.

“Well then,” she said softly, magic curling beneath the words like smoke from a hearth fire, “two paths that once wandered alone… seem to have found their convergence.”

She didn’t look surprised, but there was a tenderness in her expression, the quiet awe of someone watching the first leaf fall at the start of a long-awaited season.

Chalupa arched a brow at her, whiskers twitching with amusement. “Come now, old friend. Be honest, did you nudge the loom?” He padded a few steps closer, tail flicking behind him. “You’ve got that look. The one you get right before the universe rearranges itself and you pretend it’s coincidence.”

Her eyes glittered with mischief, but she shook her head, slow and deliberate. “Not even I can touch the weaving, The Hub chooses whose threads are pulled, and when.”

Nyx snorted, clearly unconvinced.

Aoife smirked. “Aye, the magic chooses. I merely… light a candle now and then. Whisper a little encouragement to the wind.”

Chalupa narrowed his amber eyes toward the pair. “Think they understand what’s just begun?”

Nyx gave a slow shake of his wings, his voice light as falling ash. “Not even a flicker.”

Aoife smiled, soft and wistful, the kind of smile worn by those who’ve seen fate in motion too many times to call it chance. “Ah, but that’s how all the great stories begin, isn’t it? Two souls who don’t yet know they’re walking the same thread… until the world shifts beneath their feet.”

She looked once more at Frankie and Griffon, standing together beneath the quiet thrum of ancient magic. “And this?” she whispered, voice threaded with wonder. “This was always meant to be woven. Thread by thread, just like this.”

Chapter 14

Lady Aoife Caelith," Griffon said, his voice low and certain. "*Mistress of Tempests, Guardian of the Sacred Vale, Guardian of the Verdant Line and Ally to all the shapeshifter clans.*"

He gave her a crisp, formal nod, sharp enough to have come straight from a council hall and then abandoned all formality in an instant. A grin split across his face as he stepped forward and swept her into a fierce, bone-rattling hug that lifted her clean off her feet.

"And," he added in a mock-conspiratorial murmur as he set her down, "the woman who swore she'd check my cottage for gremlins whilst I was gone. Tell me, did you actually do it, or did those little terrors turn the pantry upside down again?"

Aoife let out a sharp laugh, swatting his arm. "They only make mischief when you try to bribe them with the wrong snacks, you overgrown *Stonewing*."

Griffon bent down with a grin and scooped Chalupa into his arms, cradling him like someone who'd done it countless times before.

"Well, well, well … If it isn't the most opinionated familiar in all the realms. Still pretending you don't like being picked up?"

Chalupa gave a sniff of theatrical disdain. "Still stomping around like a centaur in a tea shop?"

Griffon chuckled. "Stop acting like you weren't curled up in my cloak every winter for a decade."

Chalupa narrowed his eyes. "Your cloak was lined with phoenix feathers, don't flatter yourself."

Griffon scratched just behind his ears, and Chalupa melted against him with a traitorous sigh. "I missed you too, grumpy," Griffon murmured, his voice soft now. "It's been far too long."

A beat of stillness followed, then a sudden rush of wind swept through the chamber as a shadow streaked overhead. *Nyx*. The raven circled once, his wings slicing through the quiet like prophecy remembered. He landed on a jagged ledge above them, his glittering eyes fixed on Griffon. A low, keening cry escaped his beak, sharp and final. Griffon looked up toward the ledge, his gaze catching on the raven perched in stillness. The moment their eyes met, something subtle shifted in him, an almost imperceptible pause, like a chord vibrating just out of reach.

"And who's this sharp-eyed shadow?" he asked, voice edged with curiosity.

Nyx launched into the air with a beat of his wings, gliding down in a smooth arc before landing neatly on a curved root nearby.

"I am Nyx," he said, his tone as crisp as his feathers. "Endlessly useful and frequently unappreciated."

Griffon raised a brow, the corner of his mouth curving ever so slightly. "Charming introduction."

Nyx preened a wing with exaggerated care. "I have layers."

Griffon studied him for a beat. "There's something about you…"

Nyx shrugged his wings. "It's the cheekbones."

Griffon chuckled again, but the sound faded into something quieter. "Can't shake the feeling we've crossed paths before."

They didn't speak again, but something unspoken passed between them, almost like an understanding. Aoife watched the exchange, her expression unreadable but shining with something deep and ancient.

"Seems The Hub wasn't finished weaving after all," she murmured.

Chalupa gave a groan and flopped onto a nearby mossy stone. "Lovely, does this mean we're stuck with both of them?"

Frankie let out a breath that was half a laugh. "Okay. So… shapeshifters are real. That's fine, no really that's great. I was mentally prepared for werewolves, maybe a bear, possibly even a squirrel." She turned toward Griffon, gesturing at him vaguely. "But what's a Stonewing?"

Aoife answered before he could. "Stonewings are more than shapeshifters, they're guardians of ancient paths. Myth to most now, but once, they stood watch at the edges of the world, where the veils thinned and the wild crossed into the waking." Her gaze shifted to Griffon, something reverent in her voice. "They were born of sky and stone, lion-hearted and eagle-eyed."

Griffon's expression remained quiet, as Aoife spoke.

"Stonewings can turn to living stone when needed, to withstand what others cannot, to shield what must endure. He doesn't just fight with claws or flight, he becomes the mountain itself. A sentinel, the stillness itself that watches."

Frankie stared, wide-eyed. The idea of someone who could fly like a storm and still root himself like a cliff was... overwhelming. Her voice was barely above a whisper, tinged with disbelief. "Ok, so you're a witch and shapeshifters are real? I thought they only existed in steamy romance books."

Aoife chuckled, the sound warm and low, like the murmur of a brook cutting through ancient woods. "Aye, they are very real, my girl, as are so many other extraordinary beings you've yet to encounter. I help them, guide them, heal them, and occasionally, scold them when their egos threaten to outgrow their wisdom." Her gaze flicked briefly to Griffon, whose faint smirk betrayed no argument.

"We stand where we are needed, no matter the cost," Aoife continued, her voice softening into something luminous, her storm-green eyes alight with purpose. "My girl, there is so much for you to learn, much I long to show you." Her smile widened, unguarded and radiant, filling the space between them with a warmth that made Frankie's heart ache. "The world is boundless and its magic even more so. You've only grazed the opening notes of its ancient symphony. I cannot wait for you to hear the full orchestration."

Griffon inclined his head, his silver-blue eyes softening as he regarded Aoife. His voice quiet, but with deep admiration. "The balance you protect isn't just woven into the magic, it's in the lives you touch, the choices you shape. The realms owe you more than they will ever know."

Aoife's lips curved into a faint smile, her eyes glinting with wry amusement. "Well, Griffon, if you keep this up, I might actually start believing your flattery." Her tone light but edged with dry affection. The two exchanged a glance thick with unspoken history, memories that needed no retelling.

Griffon turned to Frankie then, his gaze gentling without losing its gravity. "It does seem," he said, "that the winds have carried me to this moment."

Aoife stepped forward, her voice soft but sure. "The winds always carry you, Griffon Thorne, always arriving when least expected. A gift or a curse, depending on who you ask."

Griffon inclined his head once more, a flicker of something solemn passing behind the calm. "I go where I am needed," he said, his voice low and steady, touched with something older than memory. "The winds began whispering of a rising, and so I heeded their call."

He stepped forward, his shadow stretching across the golden-lit floor like a herald. Around him, the runes etched into the stone brightened for a heartbeat, a quiet acknowledgment, as though even the Hub recognized what he carried. "At first, it was a murmur, a disturbance in the ley lines, like something ancient stirring in its sleep. But then it grew stronger. The balance had shifted… as if something had opened its eyes."

He looked briefly to Aoife, his gaze threaded with quiet memory. "I followed a pull I couldn't ignore, I didn't know where it would lead, only that I had to go. The Hub, I trusted, would carry me to where I was most needed. Funny that this took me back right back where I began. "

Aoife's expression softened, pride flickering in her storm-green eyes. "Never try to reason, just listen, especially when the threads begin to stir." she murmured.

Griffon turned to Frankie, the light around him dimming as if even the cavern paused to listen. "I crossed fractured ley lines," he said quietly. "Places where the world's hidden seams had split. open, where the veil thinned and magic swirled, feral and unanchored. The land was wrong there, the wind spoke in broken tongues, even the light bent strangely."

He rested a hand on the satchel at his side. He withdrew a small, cloth-wrapped bundle from his satchel and slowly unwrapped it. Nestled inside, surrounded by folds of worn linen, lay a carved palm-sized deep green stone, streaked with silver-blue striations that shone like moonlight on water.

"I found it in the Hollowing Deep," Griffon said, his voice low. "Buried beneath collapsed stone and roots older than reckoning. The air there was wrong, too still." His fingers brushed the stone. "I wasn't looking for it… but it knew I was coming."

Aoife stepped forward slowly, her eyes fixed on the relic. "The Hollowing Deep?" she whispered, disbelief laced with awe. "That place's name hasn't passed my lips in a hundred years..."

Frankie's head snapped toward her. "A hundred years?" Her voice pitched upward. "Wait, how old are you?"

There was a pause. Aoife and Griffon exchanged an amused look. Aoife smiled faintly, the kind of smile that had known many seasons.

"Time is... different in Velhollow, my girl."

Griffon gave a soft huff of agreement. "Especially if you forget to watch it."

Frankie blinked at them. "That's not an answer."

"It's the only one you're getting for now," Aoife said, her tone teasing.

Griffon tilted his head toward Frankie, his voice like a quiet echo. "Velhollow doesn't move with the world above."

Frankie opened her mouth, then promptly closed it again. Aoife chuckled softly, then turned back to the relic.

"That's the Severstone," she said, her voice low. "A relic of binding magic. Forged when the weave first began to tear, when magic fractured and nearly collapsed.

Griffon nodded slowly. "It stirred the moment I touched it. Like it remembered its purpose."

"No," Aoife murmured. "It remembered who it was meant for."

Griffon offered it to her, palm open, she didn't touch it. Her gaze swept the runes, recognition flickering in her storm-green eyes. "This is no weapon. It's a blade for threads, not flesh. Old binding magic, crafted during the First Sundering, when the world came undone and had to be rewoven." She met his eyes. "It's meant to sever corruption before it infects the loom."

Frankie's brow furrowed. "What does that mean?"

Aoife's voice grew softer. "It means... if magic becomes too twisted, too frayed, it cannot be healed, only cut. This relic doesn't destroy, it ends the damage before it spreads." She looked at Frankie now, her gaze solemn. "It's a mercy few have ever been trusted to hold."

Griffon nodded. "I didn't know what I'd need it for... not until I saw you." He turned to Frankie fully, the glow of the relic catching the gold in his eyes. "I thought this journey would take me far from home. But it led me right back here, to this moment and all of you."

The stillness deepened. "I've seen what happens when magic collapses. When balance fails. Lands where rot silences the soil. Where even memory fades and hope thins like old thread. And if your rising falters, witchling, if you fall, those places won't remain buried." He paused, the silence around him as heavy as his vow. "They will come again and this time, they will not stop."

Aoife looked between them, something ancient stirring behind her eyes. "The relic found you, Griffon, because it knew you'd bring it to where it was meant to be. To her."

Griffon drew in a breath, steady and sure. "I won't let the weave fail," he said. "If she falters, I will catch her. I will stand between her and whatever tries to unravel what must endure."

Aoife's gaze softened as she turned to Frankie. "Then come, my girl," she said gently. "The path calls. And now, we walk it together. As we go deeper," she said softly, "Velhollow will begin to test you. Not out of cruelty, but out of care and curiosity. It does not offer power without purpose. It listens. It remembers. It weighs the truth of who you are against the truth of what is needed."

Frankie glanced toward the path ahead, where the golden light curled like a question yet to be asked. Aoife continued, her voice a low. "There are places in this realm that mirror your fears. Places that call to your hidden knowing. You may see things that aren't what they seem. Or worse, things that are exactly what they seem, and demand more of you than you've ever given."

Griffon said nothing, but the tension in his jaw confirmed it.

"You carry great magic, Frankie," Aoife said, reaching out to gently brush a hand over

Frankie's shoulder. "But it is not the spell work or the sigils that Velhollow will test. It will test your heart. Your courage. Your willingness to walk into the dark carrying light you're not yet sure you have." Frankie's breath caught. Aoife smiled faintly, though her eyes remained serious. "But, my dear girl, you won't be alone. Not anymore."

She turned, the hem of her skirts whispering over the glowing stone as she stepped forward. "Come. The veil grows thinner the deeper we go and time, here... well, it's never been much for patience."

Frankie cast a wary glance at Chalupa, who padded silently up to her, his fur catching faint glimmers of the cavern's light. His eyes darted toward every shadow and flicker, his tail twitching in calculated vigilance. Above them, Nyx swooped low, his dark wings slicing through the golden glow with predatory grace. The raven's sharp eyes followed Frankie and Griffon's every movement, narrowing as if issuing a silent warning.

They moved forward in solemn rhythm, the weight of Aoife's words still settling over them. Frankie's steps slowed as her gaze drifted to the cavern walls. Threads of golden light crisscrossed through the quartz, their glow steady and alive as if the stone itself remembered long-buried stories. Interspersed within the rock were ribbons of ore, streaked with iridescent color, tiny flecks of silver catching and scattering the light like distant constellations.

Aoife spoke, her tone steady and reassuring. "Velhollow recognizes those who belong here, those whose destinies are tied to its magic. But don't mistake belonging for ease. Velhollow tests as much as it welcomes."

Frankie's gaze darted to a nearby pool of water. Its surface rippled with light, casting reflections of distant skies, constellations she couldn't name shifting as though alive. She stepped closer, drawn to its strange beauty, the air cooling as though the pool itself breathed. A faint hum reached her ears, a melody layered atop the cavern's steady rhythm. The water deepened, revealing shadows that twisted and flickered, their forms just beyond comprehension.

Griffon stepped up beside her, his voice quiet but firm. "Velhollow is vast, ancient, and untamed," he said, his amber eyes fixed on the pool. "It feels your curiosity, your intentions, and sometimes… it tests you before you're ready."

Frankie stepped back, her cheeks flushing as she looked up at him. "It's… it's like it's alive," she murmured, struggling to put her feelings into words.

"It *is* alive," Griffon replied, his voice softening. "This realm is more than just magic. It's memory, history, and possibility woven together. It sees you." His smirk tugged at the corners of his mouth, his usual cynicism tempered by her unguarded awe.

Aoife, watching them both, gave a small chuckle. "You'll learn, my girl," she said, her tone laced with both pride and warning. "Velhollow isn't meant to overwhelm, it's meant to remind us of our place. We are not its servants, nor are we its masters. We are its stewards, its children. For you, Frankie, it could be home."

Frankie nodded slowly, her chest swelling with an ache she couldn't name, as though the cavern's rhythm had reached inside her and stirred something long dormant. Every step forward felt like a new discovery, yet the beauty around her carried an edge of tension, a reminder that not everything here was as it seemed. She began to notice small details she hadn't seen at first, tiny, luminescent insects darting among the glowing leaves, their movements leaving trails of light like falling stars; delicate plants swaying as though moved by an unseen breeze. Stone archways carved with ancient runes spiraled upward, each symbol radiating faint warmth as they passed.

As they turned a bend in the path, the soft golden glow of the cavern deepened, illuminating a low cluster of flowers nestled against a wall of quartz. Their petals pulsed with each breath of air, blushing from violet to teal to a warm, blushing rose, like they were reacting to the very presence of magic. Aoife slowed, one brow arching as the blooms pulsed softly beneath the crystalline canopy.

"Ah... now these are rare," she said, her voice dropping into a tone of fondness "*Glowbells*. They only bloom for those attuned to Velhollow's breath."

Frankie stepped closer, her eyes wide, her hand half-lifting.

"They're beautiful."

"They are," Aoife agreed. "And temperamental. Would you like to try something?"

Frankie's head snapped around, her expression bright with surprise. "Me?"

Aoife smiled, a spark of mischief glinting in her storm-green eyes. "Aye, you. Don't look so shocked. You're part of the song now, remember?"

Frankie giggled nervously. "Okay... yes. What do I do?"

Aoife pointed to one of the blooms, its petals shifting through soft bands of color, delicate as breath moving across silk.

"Repeat after me, slowly ... *Gléasta le solas, éirigh i mbláth*."

Frankie tried to mimic the words, stumbling slightly over the sounds. "*Glee-ah... glaesta... wait, gléasta le solas... air-ig... im blah?*"

"Good," Aoife said cheerfully, stepping back. "Now just breathe with it. Let the words move through you, not from your head, from here." She tapped her own chest, just over her heart.

Frankie turned to the flower again, inhaled deeply, and repeated the phrase, more confidently this time. For a heartbeat, nothing happened. Then the flower stirred, its petals catching a sudden swell of color that deepened all at once, as if waking from a long breath.

"Oh!" Frankie gasped as a soft glow rose from her palm, warm and humming, like static and stardust. But the magic didn't stay politely in her hand. It flared outward in a sparkling arc... and struck Chalupa full in the side.

There was a poof and then.... sparkles.

Silver sparkles.

Everywhere.

Chalupa let out a strangled yowl and staggered backward, his sleek fur now dusted with glittering starlight that clung to him like enchanted confetti.

"Frankie!" he snapped, his voice crackling with outrage. "What. Have. You. Done?"

Frankie clapped both hands over her mouth, eyes wide, a helpless giggle slipping out. "Oh no, I'm so sorry! I didn't mean to bedazzle you!"

Nyx swooped down and landed on a low vine with a perfectly timed flutter of wings. He tilted his head, then let out a dry caw of pure judgment. "You've turned him into a disco ball. Glorious."

Aoife coughed behind her hand, barely suppressing a laugh. Chalupa narrowed his now-sparkling eyes.

"Fix it. Now. Or I swear by the moss gods, I will sleep on your pillow... wet."

Frankie let out a gasp that turned into a snort, her hands flying to her mouth. "Oh my! I didn't... you're so sparkly."

She dissolved into giggles, eyes tearing up as she tried, and failed, not to laugh harder. Even Aoife's lips twitched before she shook her head, stepping forward with a practiced flick of her fingers.

"Alright, alright, before the cat declares war on your bedding." She muttered something under her breath and tapped Chalupa's head lightly. The sparkles flicked once, then rose in a slow spiral, thinning into the air and fading away like breath on cold glass.

Chalupa gave an exaggerated shake and sniffed. “Finally. Some dignity.”

Aoife turned to Frankie with a knowing smile. “Let that be your second lesson, magic is always listening, and sometimes, it plays.”

Frankie beamed, still breathless with laughter. “That was amazing.”

Aoife chuckled. “Not bad for a first spell… though next time, try not to enchant the familiars.”

Nyx swooped closer, his sleek black wings slicing through the golden glow of the cavern. With a swift motion, he plucked a tuft of glittering fur from Chalupa’s coat before the glittering effect could fade completely.

“Oh, come now,” the raven said, perching on a nearby ledge. His beak clicked as he held the tuft aloft like a trophy. “It’s not every day I see a cat outshine the stars.”

Chalupa’s eyes narrowed dangerously, “Ravens and shiny things,” he muttered darkly.

Aoife suppressed a laugh as she glanced at Nyx, amusement glinting in her eyes. “Leave him be, Nyx.”

Chalupa scoffed, as he shot the raven a scathing look. “I’ll have him plucked and simmering in a stew.”

“This is why we practice, my girl,” Aoife said, though her amusement was evident in the way her eyes twinkled.

Chalupa sniffed indignantly, giving his fur an exaggerated shake. “Practice somewhere else next time.”

Frankie bit her lip to keep from laughing and Chalupa padded ahead, his ears twitching as though catching sounds too subtle for human ears.

“Still sulking, are we?” Nyx called from above, his shadow slicing through the golden light as he soared overhead.

“I’m not sulking,” Chalupa retorted without breaking stride, “I’m recovering from being turned into a disco ball.”

“Still, a very fluffy disco ball,” Nyx shot back, swooping low to perch on a nearby rock. He ruffled his feathers and continued. “It was a moment of brilliance, pun fully intended.”

Frankie stifled a giggle as Chalupa shot the raven a glare. “Laugh it up, bird. Your time will come.”

Nyx replied airily, his dark eyes gleaming. "I'd wear it better, of course."

"Enough, you two," Aoife said lightly, though a sharp edge of authority underpinned her tone. "Velhollow doesn't tolerate discord for long. If you stir its ire, it has its own ways of quieting things... and trust me, you don't want to test them." That silenced the bickering at once, though Nyx let out a final, amused caw before spreading his wings and taking to the air.

As they ventured further, the cavern opened into a vast clearing, its ceiling arched impossibly high and adorned with crystal formations that shimmered like frozen starlight. The formations caught and refracted the golden glow of Velhollow, casting kaleidoscopic patterns across the floor that shifted and danced with every movement. It was breathtaking and otherworldly, but the vastness of the space carried an edge of foreboding. The air felt heavier here, thick with ancient power that pulsed in time with the faint hum of the crystals. Frankie's eyes were drawn to every flicker of light. Her gaze fell on a carved rune glowing faintly on the cavern wall. Its lights were erratic, flickering like a dying ember, as though calling to her. She hesitated for a moment, then stepped closer, her curiosity pulling her forward. The rune's edges were intricate, spiraling into patterns that seemed to shift subtly under her scrutiny. Compelled, she extended her hand, her fingers tracing the rune's intricate patterns. Its edges seemed to glow and shift beneath her touch, as though alive and breathing with an ancient rhythm. The moment Frankie's fingertip connected with the rune, a sharp jolt of energy lanced through her hand, streaking up her arm like fire and ice. She gasped, stumbling backward as a cold unlike anything she'd ever known swept through the air. The golden glow of the cavern dimmed, shadows pooling like spilled ink. A low rumble coursed through the air, growing heavier with every second. The rune flared once, twice, then fractured into a spiderweb of cracks, releasing a tendril of darkness that lashed out with a guttural snarl. Frankie doubled over, gripping her arm as the shadows surged forward, breath hitching at the impact.

"*Francesca!*"

Griffon's voice rang out like thunder carved from stone, deep, commanding, impossible to ignore, as he stepped instinctively between her and the writhing dark. His silhouette cut a sharp figure against the chaos, shoulders squared, every line of him etched with calm, unyielding resolve. The stone beneath their feet began to hum, a low, resonant sound that vibrated up through their bones. Something ancient stirred in the walls, as if the mountain itself was waking to bear witness. Frankie froze, the scent of scorched air swirled with something older, ozone and lichen, fire and wind.

Something primal surged in the air. Griffon's body tensed, gathering the storm to him. Strands of golden-red hair sparked to life, lighting up like embers caught in a gale. Energy rippled along his arms, his skin alive with shifting light, like sunlight dancing through molten quartz and then… the shift. Wings burst from his back, vast and breathtaking, stretching wide with a sound like stone cracking and wind catching all at once. Each feather gleamed like hammered gold threaded, massive enough to stir the cavern's still air into wild motion. His form grew, leonine and deadly, rippling with sinewed grace. Talons unfurled from his hands, obsidian-curved and glinting with inner heat. His face lengthened, reshaped, no longer human, but fierce and intelligent. A beak took form, edged with firelight, gleaming like a blade kissed by a forge. A crown of feathers and flame flared along his head and spine, a mane alive with fiery motion and then living stone. Griffon's form solidified, gray marbled with gold en flames, a living monument carved from the mountain itself. He stood unmoving, timeless, as if the earth had dreamed him into being and named him guardian….a massive gargoyle come to life.

Frankie stood wide-eyed and wordless, heart beating like a bird caught in a storm. Every part of her stilled, breath caught in awe, in something deeper, something that felt like the truth of an ancient story stepping off the page. Griffon's eyes snapped open, silver-blue, storm-lit, fury and calm burning there in equal measure. The shadows recoiled instantly beneath his gaze, unraveling under the weight of him. The cavern bloomed with light, crystal walls flaring like stained glass set aflame.

Above, Nyx streaked through the air, a blur of dusk and starlight. His wings cut the charged atmosphere, sharp as memory. Then he saw Griffon and something deep stirred. It was recognition and in that instant, the decades upon decades of wandering, the restless crossing of realms, the dreams half-remembered and prophecies half-heard, all of it coalesced into a single, blazing certainty. He hadn't been lost, he'd been waiting. His purpose had always been this, flying beside Griffon, guarding the guardian. With a cry sharp as breaking sky, Nyx descended, drawn like a star to its rightful orbit. He landed on Griffon's shoulder with grace, talons settling like a vow.

He was home.

Griffon turned, meeting Nyx's gaze with silver fire and for a heartbeat, the world stilled, runes flickering, magic pausing mid-breath. Something passed between them. Feather meeting flame and the unspoken bond snapped into place, not chosen, but always fated. Just as Chalupa had always belonged to Frankie, Nyx now knew he was meant to fly with Griffon.

Suddenly the air shifted and the light dimmed, drawn inward. Warmth fled to the edges. A scent rose, scorched metal, wet stone, a storm unearthing something it shouldn't. The floor beneath them vibrated, off-rhythm, wrong and from the far edges of the chamber, the shadows stirred. They didn't charge, they gathered and waited then, the silence broke. A crackling rose from the stone, like the air itself flinching. The shadows moved with cold purpose. Like smoke with weight, they surged toward a single point.

Frankie.

The shadows veered midair, drawn to her like hunger with a name. Tendrils slithered, curled, reached. The air shivered with unspoken pressure, too sharp for sound, too ancient for mercy. Frankie tried to move, but her body betrayed her. It wasn't pain. It was something older. A force that slipped past flesh, bypassed muscle, and bit deep into will. Her magic cinched in her chest like a breath held too long. Her knees buckled. She fell into the light like an offering laid bare. She couldn't run, she could only watch the dark come for her as the shadows lunged. But Chalupa was faster. He leapt forward with a hiss that sizzled like oil on fire, his fur bristling, eyes twin embers in the gloom. He didn't hesitate. He flung himself between Frankie and the dark, tail lashing like a live wire.

"Over my dead furry body," he growled.

The shadows hissed back in reply, recoiling, circling, but Chalupa pivoted with them, sharp and defiant. Behind him, Frankie remained frozen, breath caught between awe and terror. Still, he held the line. The shadows gathered again, tighter now, denser, calculating. They swelled like storm clouds tasting lightning. A crack split the air, like bone, like bark, then the first tendril lunged and Griffon met it mid-strike. Flames curled around his talons. He tore into the darkness with fierce, blistering precision, each movement fueled by a purpose that would not yield. Nyx dove beside him, slicing through shadow with wings that moved like vengeance made flesh and they moved as one. They didn't fight, they danced the storm back. Still, the darkness came. Dozens now, born from the places between places, drawn to blood, to prophecy, to power not yet claimed. They whispered along Frankie's skin with hunger.

Aoife stepped forward. No longer soft-spoken, no longer cloaked in starlit mystery. She was fury wrapped in moonlight. Her hair rose with the wind, silver strands alight with charge. Bracelets clinked like warning bells before a quake. She lifted her arms. The runes blazed gold. Light spiraled from the stone like it remembered its own name and then, her voice. Gaelic, old as the sea, spilled like molten gold. A spell. A summons. A storm.

"*Solas i gcroí, cosc ar an dorchadas, Filleadh ort féin, gan cumhacht anseo…*"

The words rang like iron through water, familiar and foreign. Beside her, Chalupa didn't blink.

"*Light in the heart*," he translated gruffly, never taking his eyes off the fight. "*A ban on the dark. Return to yourself. You've got no power here.*" His tail flicked. "And no, she's not asking nicely."

Light bloomed, a kaleidoscope of colors, vibrant and wild. It poured from Aoife's hands rootlike and radiant, weaving through the chamber like fire-wrought lace. They caught the shadows mid-lunge, and this time the darkness screamed. The spell bound them, pinned like night beneath a rising dawn and the ground answered. The shadows were pulled inward, folding, breaking, unraveling with howls swallowed by the mountain's breath. Then silence. Aoife lowered her arms, exhaling like she'd just extinguished a star and Frankie could move again, but she didn't. Not yet.

The thrum beneath her steadied, but Frankie's bones still carried the echo of the dark. Her chest ached where the shadows had lingered too long, probing as if they meant to unmake her from the inside out and her palm, still tingling, held the place where the Kitsune had touched her. It burned soft and deep, like a coal hidden beneath ash. Like a seed beginning to split. Something stirred beneath her skin now, wild and quiet and wholly alive. A path not set before her, but opening from within. At her feet, the light gathered once more, slow, steady, pulsing like a heartbeat. Griffon moved, one step forward, slow and deliberate. His great wings, still dusted in firelight, folded behind him, and the golden heat threading through his limbs began to dim. The glow along his skin softened, pulling inward. His body, once massive and mythic, began to contract, sinew tightening, feathers withdrawing, stone giving way to flesh. Fire became breath. Beast became man. It wasn't violent. It wasn't even sudden, it was amazing. A shifting back into skin that still held every echo of what he had been. Frankie just stared. The memory of his transformation burned behind her eyes. He had been legend made flesh. Now he was just... standing there. Breathing like nothing had happened.

He caught her mid-stare and smirked. "Ah," he said, smooth as ever. "You're wondering about the clothes."

Frankie blinked. "I ... what?"

He nodded, solemn. "It's a common concern. Most assume shifters return... less clothed."

She opened her mouth. Closed it. "I wasn't ... I didn't ... "

Griffon placed a hand over his heart, bowing with exaggerated gravity. "Lady Francesca, I accept your unspoken admiration."

Nyx cackled, a sound of pure mischief.

Frankie groaned. "Someone dig me a hole. I'm just going to live in it now."

Chalupa rolled his eyes. "Oh, come on. He explodes into muscle and myth and you're not even a little curious?"

Frankie dropped her face into her hands. "Please. Stop."

Griffon let the moment linger just long enough for her soul to attempt spontaneous evaporation, then added with a glint in his eye, "Who am I to deny a lady her imaginings?"

Her cheeks were blazing, her brain had short-circuited and there was only one logical response.

"*Abracadabra!*" Frankie blurted, squeezing her eyes shut like a kid playing hide-and-seek. She stood there, rigid, silently bargaining with the universe. If there was any lingering cosmic magic hanging around, now would be a great time to kick in. Invisibility? Temporary vaporization? She wasn't picky. Nothing happened. Cautiously, she cracked one eye open. Griffon was still there. So was Aoife. And Chalupa, who blinked slowly like he was trying to decide whether to laugh or lecture her. Even Nyx tilted his head, watching from his perch with what could only be described as amused skepticism.

Frankie sighed dramatically. "Okay, fine. I don't know any spells. I just thought if I said abracadabra with enough enthusiasm and wished really hard, maybe, poof, the ground would open up and swallow me hole. But clearly, that's not how any of this works."

Chalupa gave a theatrical sniff. "Well, that was bold."

Nyx fluffed his feathers. "And mildly impressive."

Frankie groaned and dragged her hands down her face. "I'm going to need a do-over on this entire day."

Mercifully, Griffon's tone shifted, softer now, warmer. "I'm only teasing you, Frankie," he said, the formal edge falling away like a weight lifted.

He reached out and gently touched her hands where they still covered her face. The contact was light, but it carried weight, a quiet heat that moved through her like the first stir of spellfire. A spark leapt between them. Small, but undeniable. Like something in the deep had taken notice and marked the moment. For a heartbeat she didn't move, the world narrowing to that single point of contact. Her fingers shifted, just enough to let her eyes meet his. The smirk was gone. He looked at her as if she'd startled him, as if she were rare, unexpected, and worth the pause. Like, despite the chaos around them, he truly saw her and had no intention of looking away. Her cheeks were still warm, but her heartbeat had settled into something quieter, steadier. She lowered her hands slowly, unsure what to say, but no longer hiding.

Magic threaded through the space between them, soft and weighty, like a held breath waiting to become something more. The moment stretched, golden and still, until the cavern exhaled. Light shifted overhead, subtle, certain, as though the earth itself had sighed and settled. The crystalline walls answered with a gentle radiance, their brightness easing into something warm and even, like lanterns burning low after a long storm.

Aoife's voice broke the silence, calm and resolute. "Aye, you've seen a sliver of what Velhollow can do," she said, her gaze sweeping over them, steady and grave. "Don't mistake that for the whole of it. This was only the edge, what waits beyond is far deeper, far darker."

Frankie's brow furrowed, her focus reluctantly breaking from Griffon.

"The magic here," Aoife continued, "isn't a tool. It's a force. It doesn't serve us, it studies us. It waits. It listens to see if we're worthy of what it guards."

Her eyes drifted briefly to Griffon, a flicker of amusement there, threaded with the kind of fond irony that only comes from knowing someone deeply. After all, Griffon had always wielded immense power, but finesse hadn't always been his strong suit. She'd watched him blaze his way through problems better suited to subtlety, and more than once, magic had swatted him like a cat would a brash kitten. The corner of her mouth lifted ever so slightly before her gaze shifted to Frankie and softened.

"Strength without wisdom is as dangerous as shadow without light. Magic demands balance, and so must those who carry it."

Nyx ruffled his feathers, his eyes still scanning the edges of the cavern. "Well," he said, tone dry, "next time the ancient magic tests us, I'd appreciate a heads-up. Maybe a memo."

Chalupa stretched out with an exaggerated sigh, tail flicking.

"Please. You'd just spend the extra time preening."

Nyx tilted his head. "And you'd use it to nap harder."

Chalupa didn't miss a beat. "Preparation through rest. It's called strategy, featherbrain."

Nyx gave a sharp caw of amusement. "Here I thought it was laziness in disguise."

Before Chalupa could fire back, Aoife cut in, not even glancing up. "If either of you starts tallying imaginary battle honors, I'll gladly volunteer you both as magical scarecrows for the next rootling migration."

Chalupa blinked. "You're joking."

Aoife arched a brow, her voice like steel wrapped in silk. "Try me."

Frankie barely heard them, her focus had drifted, caught by the figure standing a short distance away. Griffon was running a hand through his ember-kissed hair. The others might have relaxed, the fight behind them, but not him. Something still clung to him, a power that hadn't fully quieted, an unsettled charge in the air around him, subtle to most but impossible for her to ignore.

He was himself again, no monstrous wings or flame-wreathed claws, but the memory of what he'd become lingered like heat on stone. She could almost feel the echo of it, the earth beneath his feet thrumming like it knew him, no, like it belonged to him. She took a breath, stepping closer. Her voice was low, hesitant, but honest.

"Griffon... what is a Stonewing? Other than..." her lips curved despite herself, "Wow. You're more than just a shapeshifter, aren't you?" *More than a shifter*, the words hung awkwardly between them. *I actually said that out loud. Smooth, Frankie. Next I'll ask him if he glows in the dark.* It was true, he wasn't just a tall tale come to life, he was more. The kind of more that shifted the ground beneath your feet, that made the world feel deeper, older.

Griffon turned, slowly, his silver-blue eyes meeting hers. There was a stillness in him. He didn't speak right away. The space between them seemed to hold its breath, the magic of the place drawn tight, listening.

"I'm a protector," he said at last, his voice low.

Frankie stepped closer, her curiosity rising like something drawn to light. "A protector of what?"

His gaze didn't falter. "Of balance," he replied. "Of the threads that hold light and dark in check. When those threads begin to fray..." His voice dropped. "Someone has to keep them from unraveling everything."

Nyx cawed from his perch, his voice cutting cleanly through the quiet. "He's leaving out the best part, as usual. Protectors like him?" He tilted his head, feathers ruffling with theatrical flair. "They're not just guardians when the balance tips too far, they're also destroyers. That's the part people like to forget."

Griffon cast a sidelong glance up at the raven, his expression unreadable.

Frankie's pulse quickened. Something in Griffon had shifted, barely, but enough to unsettle her. His calm wasn't complete; it held an edge, like a blade she could sense but not see. He looked at her too long, too carefully, as if trying to decide whether to offer an answer or protect her from it.

The weight of his gaze landed like a touch. She opened her mouth, unsure what she meant to say, but Griffon lifted a hand. His voice dropped, quiet but threaded with something he wasn't ready to name.

"You have questions," he murmured. "I see them in your eyes." A beat passed, charged, deliberate. "But not here. We'll talk later."

The words struck deeper than she expected. Her cheeks warmed, traitorous and immediate. What did he mean? The prophecy? Her strange, awakening magic? Or the way he seemed to look at her, as though she'd knocked something loose inside him? Something alive fluttered through her chest, nerves and curiosity tangled with a spark she didn't dare call hope.

Nyx fluttered his wings with a pointed huff, cleaving the moment cleanly in two.

"Well, if everyone's done brooding dramatically into the middle distance, can we please get moving?"

Chalupa, stretched out in a perfect portrait of feline superiority, flicked his tail. "Someone's feeling bossy again."

Aoife exhaled slowly. "You're both lucky Velhollow doesn't smite for ego. Now move."

Griffon smiled, just enough to break the tension. "Velhollow doesn't wait," he said, voice low and sure, before turning and striding ahead.

He moved with purpose, each step deliberate, like a warrior answering an ancient call. The subtle shift in the group was immediate, without needing to be asked, they followed. He wasn't commanding, he simply led. Frankie lingered a step behind, her thoughts spinning like wind-caught leaves. Something in her chest tightened with the weight of everything she didn't yet know. The way Griffon moved, silent and certain, stirred something deep in her. Whatever truth he carried, whatever fire lived behind that steady gaze, it felt close enough to touch, but cloaked in shadow. The air began to change, warmer, wilder. The stone walls narrowed, then gradually opened, as if the earth itself were exhaling. A breeze curled down the tunnel, brushing against her skin like fingers through silk, lush with moss, loam, and the ghost of flowers long extinct.

Then they stepped through, and the world changed. The forest beyond felt alive and welcoming. Leaves shifted with soft color as though brushed by dusk light, their edges catching faint hints of silver and gold. The canopy above moved like water touched by slow wind, strands of pale luminescence threading through the branches as if the cavern light had woven itself into the leaves. The underbrush glowed with gentle bioluminescence, petals lit from within like small lanterns. Flowers unfurled as they passed, turning toward them with a quiet attentiveness, blooming in silence to a rhythm that felt ancient and patient. Magic lived in the air. It threaded through every tree and stone, every sound and hush. It wound through the roots like memory and drifted on the breeze like a song gathering the courage to be sung.

Griffon didn't pause. He walked as though the forest recognized him, the path easing open under his stride with quiet familiarity. Frankie followed, wide-eyed, the world unfolding around her like a secret finally allowed to breathe. This wasn't just a new place, it felt like stepping into the pulse of something ancient and awake. Color moved through the leaves in soft waves, brushing the air with a warmth she could taste at the back of her tongue, rich, wild, electric, the way summer smells just before lightning splits the sky. Every leaf, every shift of air, every soft gleam of bioluminescence tugged at something deep inside her, a place that felt startled and called at the same time.

Frankie could feel it, beneath her skin, in her bones, this was where her real story began.

Chapter 15

The first few steps felt like crossing into a dream. Frankie moved slowly, her boots barely making a sound against the moss-soft earth. The light here didn't fall so much as it flowed, curling through the trees like spun gold, dappling her arms, catching in her hair.

Everything felt impossibly vivid, as if the world had been turned a fraction closer to true. Colors deepened, shadows breathed, and the space around her carried a quiet alertness that brushed against her skin like a hand guiding her deeper. Scents unfurled richer than anything she'd known, wildflowers she'd never seen before, crushed herbs warming the air, wet stone cooling it again, and a sweet, spiced note that stirred something in her chest she didn't have a name for. Even the air tasted different, crisp and green, like it had been steeped in secrets and handed to her gently.

Frankie turned in a slow circle, wonder rising so sharply it almost unsteadied her. It felt like stepping into the first page of a story she'd somehow always belonged to.

"This can't be real," she whispered, almost afraid that speaking aloud might break the spell.

"Aye," Aoife said gently, her voice near her shoulder. "It's as real as you are. Though I'll grant you, it rarely feels that way at first."

Frankie nodded, but her thoughts were far from steady. There was a hum beneath her skin now, low and lovely, like a current threading through her body. She didn't know if it was Velhollow's magic or her own beginning to wake, but she knew with aching certainty that she wasn't the same girl who'd first followed her grandmother into the mountain. The Hub had been breathtaking, yes, powerful, ancient, echoing with purpose, but this? This was different. It didn't announce itself here, it just was. It existed, quiet and woven into every petal and breeze, every birdsong and shadow. It wasn't spectacle, it was presence. This was the part of Velhollow where magic wasn't rare. It was ordinary. And that made it more wondrous than anything she'd seen. This wasn't the beating heart of the realm, this was its soul.

Up ahead, Griffon slowed his pace and glanced back. "Stay close," he said, his voice dipping into something quieter, almost intimate. "The paths here like to wander if you let them."

Frankie tried to answer, but the words snagged. The forest wasn't just alive; it was aware, every leaf and root seeming to lean in, watching, listening. And somehow, she felt more exposed under its gaze, more visible, because Griffon was watching her too. When she reached his side, she noticed Nyx perched on his shoulder, unusually silent. His head tilted, eyes sharp and intent, but Frankie barely registered the raven. Griffon was close, close enough that she could feel the warmth radiating from him, close enough that the air between them tightened, charged with something she didn't have a name for yet. She took a steadying breath. The forest might have been watching…but so was he.

Chalupa trotted beside her, tail high, expression unreadable. Even he didn't break the calm that had settled over their small group. Velhollow recognized him, as a returning guardian. Aoife followed, and the wind shifted to greet her, brushing her hair with petals as if remembering the shape of her soul.

The air rippled around them with mischief. From the blossoms overhead burst a flurry of sprites, tiny, radiant beings no larger than Frankie's thumb, their wings iridescent and fast as dragonflies, their laughter light enough to chime. They moved like living stardust, flitting through the air in dazzling spirals. One tugged boldly at Nyx's tail feather with a delighted squeak, while another zipped forward and, with laser precision, looped a curling vine into a glowing halo and plopped it squarely on his head. A third zipped past his beak with a trill of glee, leaving behind a glittering trail of mischief and pixie dust.

Nyx flailed, wings jerking. "Uncalled for! Absolutely undignified!"

"They're just saying hello," Aoife called, grinning outright. "That's how they greet newcomers they find interesting."

Frankie laughed. "So this is what a warm welcome looks like?"

"I prefer a nod and some personal space," Nyx muttered, fluffing his feathers with indignation.

Chalupa trotted past, deadpan. "At least they didn't weave bog moss into your tail. That's how they greeted me last time."

"They braided a vine into my feathers," Nyx snapped. "This is not a hello, it's harassment."

"They're flirting," Griffon added helpfully, completely straight-faced.

Nyx froze mid-flap, scandalized. "I beg your pardon, I think not!"

Chalupa yawned. "Tell that to your leaf crown and glitter trail, Tinkerbell."

A chorus of giggles burst from the branches as the sprites whisked off, leaving behind sparkles, squeaks, and one very ruffled feline guardian. From the high boughs overhead, the glen awakened. A thousand sparks of life descended, sprites twirling through the air trailing silver dust, seed-spirits drifting like feathers on hidden currents, tiny petal-moths beating wings of gauze. They swirled around Frankie in a bright, playful storm, joy disguised as flight.

One bold pixie zipped up and tapped her nose with an exuberant "boop," dusting her in gold. Another tucked a flower behind her ear. A third spun a garland of glowing vine-threads and draped it across her shoulders, as though crowning her in mischief and light. Frankie went still, truly still. Wide-eyed. Breath suspended between awe and disbelief. Then something shifted. Not sound or light. But tremor, soft and deep, rising from beneath the earth like a long-held breath finally exhaled. It spread through the chamber in gentle waves of green and gold, brushing the air, brushing her.

Every sprite froze at once, their tiny wings halting mid-beat as though the air itself had paused. Glitter hung suspended in the sudden hush, and the entire glen seemed to draw in a single, held breath. Then, slowly, one after another, the sprites bowed. Their wings lowered, their small heads dipped, and a ripple of quiet recognition moved through them like a shared understanding.

They weren't bowing to Aoife.

They weren't bowing to Griffon.

They were bowing to her.

Frankie went still. "What…?" she whispered, the word barely finding shape as the meaning of the moment pressed in around her. Then it hit, an unmistakable tingling rising from somewhere deep within, a warm current flickering awake like a long-silent answer finally returning home.

The Kitsune's mark still lingered on her palm, faint but persistent, like an ember that refused to cool. Aoife's spell had not created anything new; it had only revealed what had always been there, waiting beneath her skin for the moment it could finally breathe. Awareness spread through her in a quiet rush, alive and startling. Colors sharpened at the edges. The earth beneath her steadied, gathering itself with calm assurance, as though the forest had shifted its weight to stand closer to her side.

The small faces lifted toward her were not filled with awe. They were filled with knowing. Recognition moved through them as one, clear, unhesitating, and old beyond measure, etched into every bowed head, every lowered wing, every held breath. It was not reverence. It was acknowledgment. Something tightened behind her eyes, sharp and overwhelming. Frankie swallowed, her voice unsteady not with fear, but with the weight of being seen at last.

"They know who I am?" she asked softly, wonder and disbelief threading together.

Aoife stepped beside her, never taking her eyes off the kneeling sprites. When she finally spoke, her voice carried a softness shaped by years and memory. "Aye, love."

She pressed a gentle hand to Frankie's back.

"The magic knows its own… and the land never forgets."

Frankie couldn't speak. Around her, the magic swirled in welcome of belonging, homecoming written in root and bloom, in soil and sky.

"They recognize your thread in the great weave," Aoife added softly. "And now… they wait.To see what you'll grow from it."

The moment lingered, suspended like the last note of a song. Then, slowly, the forest resumed its rhythm. Lights lifted, blossoms softened their glow, and the tiny spirits that had danced around Frankie melted back into vine and petal, leaving only the hush of belonging in their wake.

Aoife placed a gentle hand on Frankie's back. "Come now, Love, this way."

The path cleared ahead, woven from root and moss, its curve soft as breath. They walked side by side, no longer a caravan led through the unknown, but a family returning to the heart of something older than memory. The trees thinned around them, parted with quiet welcome. Shafts of soft violet light streamed through the canopy, and the air carried the scent of sage and blooming things. A breeze stirred the ferns, curling around their ankles like an affectionate animal. Griffon didn't take point again, he didn't need to. The forest knew him, as he knew it. He walked with ease, as if the land itself bent to greet him. Chalupa walked ahead, ears twitching, every step ringing of recognition. Even Nyx dipped his wings as he glided beneath a low arch of woven branches, the glimmer of mischief replaced with quiet awe. Then she saw it. Nestled in a glade rimmed with silvergrass and glowing mushrooms stood Aoife's cottage, half-hidden beneath a lattice of flowering vines and moonleaf ivy. The stone walls pulsed with a quiet light, as though warmed from within. The thatched roof shimmered with dew and starlight, and wind chimes of bone and crystal whispered from the eaves like distant lullabies. Smoke curled from the crooked chimney, trailing into the lavender sky in lazy spirals. Aoife's smile was quiet and full.

"Home," she whispered. She pressed her hand to the wooden door, her fingers tracing a sigil that glowed briefly, gold on weathered wood. The door clicked and swung inward.

Aoife turned, hand still resting on the threshold. "Come, child," she said, her voice threaded with warmth. "The forest has greeted you. Now let me do the same."

Together, they stepped inside.

Frankie paused, the scent of jasmine and ancient herbs wrapping around her. Something pulsed at the edge of her senses, a deep, steady hum that welcomed and tested all at once. It wasn't threatening, just aware. As though the cottage, like the forest, was sentient in its own quiet way and deciding whether to let her all the way in.

Behind her, Chalupa gave a pointed flick of his tail. "If this homecoming doesn't include dinner soon, I may start chewing on the furniture."

Aoife turned, her hand still resting on the threshold, and arched a brow. "You always were dramatic."

"I'm underfed and over-magicked," Chalupa huffed, brushing past Frankie's ankles. "Someone owes me something roasted and preferably smothered in gravy."

Frankie bit back a grin, the tension in her chest loosening. Aoife's home was a living tapestry of memory and intention, steeped in earth and time, stitched together with love and magic. The moment she'd stepped inside, the air wrapped around her like a favorite sweater, warm with woodsmoke and lavender, sharp with rosemary and citrus peel, softened by rosehips and dried moss. It was like every season had settled in the corners, harvest and bloom, snow and sun, woven into the very bones of the place. This wasn't the thrill of discovering someplace new, it was the quiet, undeniable knowing of coming home. Griffon, wordless and efficient, stepped back outside. A moment later, the door creaked open again, a crisp whisper of night air curling in behind him as he returned with arms full of cedar and pine logs. He added them to the hearth fire without a word, the embers flaring to life with a low, purring crackle that painted the walls in amber light.

Aoife glanced over her shoulder, her voice a hush that felt like it had always belonged to this space.

"Look around," she said gently. "This place will tell you what you need to know, if you listen."

Frankie moved slowly, as if afraid to break the spell woven through the air. Her fingers drifted along the edge of a worn armchair, its fabric faded but soft with memory. She brushed over the carved legs of a table etched with time, the runes and rings of a hundred brewing sessions barely visible beneath layers of polish and use. Her hand lingered on the long, stained counter in the center of the room, its familiar shape, its worn grooves echoing the one in her own little greenhouse back on Pete's land. A breath caught in her throat.

That old carriage house had been her refuge, the first place she'd ever felt wholly herself. But this... this felt like walking into a story that had been waiting for her, patient and sure. Above, bundles of herbs hung in thick braids from the rafters, sage and sweetgrass, mugwort, lemon balm, nettle, and others she couldn't name. They swayed slightly as if stirred by an unseen breeze, releasing their scent in quiet sighs. Twining through the beams and curling around the shelves, silver ivy pulsed with a soft glow, its leaves delicate and luminous. From the hearth, the fire crackled low and content, flames shifting colors, flashes of blue, green and silver, as though it responded to the rhythm of the room. The shelves were lined with glass bottles in all shapes and sizes, some milky and translucent, others deep green or smoky plum. Cork-stoppered vials winked with their own light, labels curling with age and scribbled in a looping, spidery hand. Frankie tilted her head, reading their names like poetry, *Thistle's Whisper, Rue's Shadow, Moonmelt, Foglace.*

They glowed softly when she passed, as if acknowledging her presence. Beyond the tall-paned windows, the forest of Velhollow carried its own quiet magic, light bending through the glass in drifting mosaics of violet, amber, and soft green. The colors slid across the floorboards like spilled ink catching the sun, shifting with every breath of the room. Trees swayed in a rhythm untouched by wind, and somewhere deeper in the wood, a bird released a single, clear note that rippled straight through her bones. It was more than beautiful, it felt like the world holding its breath for her. Frankie didn't just see the magic, she felt it. In her skin, her breath, deep in the marrow of her bones. This was no display, no curated charm, this was a life, a witch's life, honest and untamed. Lush, practical, and wild with intention. As she stood there, breathing it in, something inside her softened and settled, like a key turning in the right lock. She wasn't an outsider here. She didn't have to ask permission to belong, she already did. Behind her, Chalupa stretched across a bench near the fire, paws tucked, eyes half-lidded in feline contentment.

"Finally," he sighed. "A working hearth, a promise of food, and walls that don't whisper my name when I'm trying to nap."

Aoife smirked. "Still so dramatic."

"I am," he declared, "an artist of coziness. Respect the craft."

Dinner was simple, hearty, and perfect. Root vegetable stew with a hint of clove and garlic, fresh-baked herb bread, and roasted apples dripping with honey and thyme. Chalupa inhaled his with scandalous enthusiasm and immediately began petitioning for more.

Nyx, perched above on a rafter beam, muttered, "Here I thought cats had dignity."

Chalupa licked a paw. "You're mistaking my efficiency for a lack of manners."

Griffon sat near the fire, broad shoulders haloed in the hearth's amber glow, his attention drifting between the flames and Frankie in quiet, steady intervals. Every time his gaze returned to her, something in her steadied... and something else fluttered, warm and unfamiliar, as though her world had tilted toward him without asking permission.

Aoife poured tea that tasted like warmth wrapped in memory, like sleep brushed with sunrise. The scent drifted through the room, soft and sweet, curling around the mismatched chairs and worn quilts as though reminding them all that this place was meant for rest.

Silence settled, but it wasn't empty. It was comfortable, lived-in, the kind that gathers between people who don't need to fill the air to feel close. Frankie let herself sink deeper into the chair, the heat from the fire washing through her like a weighted blanket fresh from the dryer. Her mind, knotted tight since the attack, began to loosen thread by thread.

Griffon shifted, just a fraction, and the movement drew her attention like gravity. He wasn't watching the fire now. He was watching her. Not intensely, just openly, quietly, like someone memorizing the shape of a moment they didn't want to disturb. A slow warmth unfurled in her chest. She looked away before she forgot how to breathe.

Aoife crossed the room, her fingers brushing along the spines of old books until one softened beneath her touch. She eased it free, a grimoire weathered by decades, its vellum pages cushioned with pressed flowers and ink blurred into gentle strokes. When she opened it, a puff of lavender and old paper rose like a sigh. Held in Aoife's hands, the book felt less like an object and more like a story finally ready to be told. She brought it to the center table, the rune-etched wood still warm from the day's light, and set the grimoire down with an affection that needed no ceremony. It felt like placing a cherished memory where it could be shared.

Frankie drew her knees up into the chair, wrapping her fingers around the warm mug. Griffon's gaze brushed her again, light as a fingertip tracing the rim of a glass, and she felt it settle over her like a quilt. For the first time all day, she didn't just feel safe. She felt seen, truly seen, and welcomed in a way that reached deeper than logic. As if this house, this fire, these people had opened a space with her name already carved into it. She felt at home and that, somehow, was even more disarming.

"This one's gentle," she said, flipping through the pages until her finger landed on a passage. "A whisper-spell. The first most hedge-witches learn. It doesn't command. It listens."

Frankie leaned closer. The spell was written in curving script, ivy-like and ancient.

Whisper-Spell of the Listening Green

Leaf to root and stone to seed,
Hear my breath, attend my need.
By hearth-smoke curl and moonlit thread,
Speak the truths that go unsaid.
Mist to branch and moss to flame,
Carry now the ancient name.

From a rack above, Aoife selected a few sprigs of pale, curling herbs, blue-silver leaves with downy edges, and began to gather the ingredients with quiet precision, a twist of dried citrus peel, a pinch of hearth ash, a sprig of blueleaf, a silver thread looped like a promise, and a thimble of softly glowing moonwater. Each was laid out in a crescent around a single smooth crystal that sat nestled in moss and thyme, opalescent and quietly alive with flickering light.

"Would you like to try?" Aoife asked, her voice low and melodic. "Now is the best time. The forest greeted you, it's only polite to greet it back."

Frankie blinked. "You mean… me?"

Aoife arched an eyebrow. "Unless there's another witch hiding behind you with performance anxiety."

Frankie glanced over her shoulder just in case. Nothing but a sleepy Chalupa and a chair that looked mildly judgmental.

"This is not about control," Aoife said gently. "It's about presence. Let the land know your heart."

Slowly, Frankie stepped forward. The hearth's glow painted the table in soft gold, casting flickering shadows across the worn wood and rune-carved edge. The crystal at the center pulsed faintly as her hand hovered over it, as if it were appraising her intentions, checking her vibe before letting her sit at the magical table, so to speak. Around her, the room seemed to exhale. The shadows leaned in. The creaks in the floorboards stilled. Even the air went quiet.

Aoife extended a wand with quiet intention, simple yet startlingly beautiful. Slender and intricate, it was carved from rose and rowan, the twin woods spiraling together in a natural helix as if they had grown toward each other with a shared purpose. Their grains caught the firelight in warm bands, one soft as dawn, the other rich as dusk.

"This is for you," Aoife said, her voice gentle but certain. "I crafted it for you long ago. The wood wouldn't settle for any other purpose." She brushed her thumb along the spiral of rose and rowan, her eyes softening. "I knew you'd find your way to it when the time was right. Magic never rushes its own."

Frankie reached out and the instant her fingertips brushed the wand, something inside her went utterly still, as if the noise of the world had folded itself away, leaving only this one, crystalline moment. Her breath caught without her noticing. The hush around her deepened and when her fingers curled fully around the wood, recognition unfurled through her like a soft, inevitable tide. A long-missing piece sliding quietly into place.

She closed her eyes because the sensation was too profound to dilute with sight. The wand steadied in her grasp, meeting her touch with a subtle certainty, aligning itself with something deep and long-hidden within her. Warmth traveled through the wood and into her palm, intimate and sure, like someone speaking her name in a voice she had always known but never fully heard. A low hum rose through the wand, answering a rhythm she hadn't realized lived inside her. It wasn't a spark of newfound power, it was recognition. As if the wand had been waiting for her skin, her magic, her presence… waiting to breathe again.

Power threaded upward in a slow, claiming sweep, not overwhelming but becoming, settling beneath her skin with the quiet confidence of something returning home. The wand balanced against her palm perfectly, its weight familiar in a way that made no sense and every kind of sense. An extension of her. Her fingers tightened, and the wand responded, deepening its resonance, a soft vibration trembling through her grip as if whispering ... *There you are*. Understanding washed through her with startling clarity. This wasn't a gift. It wasn't an heirloom. It was hers as if had always had been.

She opened her eyes slowly, and as her other hand brushed the runes etched along the table, the symbols stirred awake. One by one, their curves warmed to life, catching faint glimmers of light like embers coaxed into steady glow. They carried meanings older than anything she could name, but she felt their intention as surely as breath. A soft vibration moved through the table, grounding and alive. The herbs arranged around the crystal responded, releasing their scents, bright rosemary, clean citrus, warm earth, unfurling like memory rising in gentle waves. The crystal at the center deepened with light, blooming from within in a steady radiance. It wasn't just illumination. It was attention.

Chalupa, curled near the hearth, lifted his head. His ears perked. Even he could feel the shift, his gaze flicking between the wand and Frankie with rare, solemn understanding. The wand sang for her. The magic listened and somewhere deep within her, something rose to meet the call

Frankie's eyes closed again from a gentle pull inside her, the kind that felt like remembering a song she used to know by heart. The current flowing through her was warm as dawn, steady and sure, threading through her like a memory resurfacing after years in the dark.

This wasn't spellwork.

This was recognition.

This was coming home to herself.

When she opened her eyes, Aoife was already watching her, a quiet smile softening her face.

"You've had the knowing all along, love," she said, voice warm with certainty. "It's in your roots. I knew you'd feel it when the moment called to you."

Frankie swallowed, the room settling around her in a new, vivid way. "I... I felt it." Her voice trembled, not with fear, but with something bright and astonishing. "It's like the wand knew me before I knew myself.

Aoife nodded gently. "Aye. And now you're finally meeting each other properly."

That grounded Frankie just enough for the world to tilt back into something she could breathe through. She let out a shaky laugh, wiping at her eyes even though she wasn't sure when they'd grown misty.

"It's not that different from mixing tea bundles," she mused, the humor thin but real. "Just… more moonlight. Fewer labels."

Aoife's smile widened, and then she laughed, her pride unmistakable. "Exactly that and far better company."

A tranquility settled around them like the forest outside had drawn near to listen. The fire crackled low, casting warm gold across the runes carved deep into the old wood. Frankie glanced down at the gathered ingredients, simple things, beautiful things, and felt her breath catch. Her hands weren't trembling anymore. She closed her eyes to better feel.

One breath in… the scent of rosemary, citrus, and old paper.

One breath out… the soft hum of the wand in her hand, alive and warm.

She pictured roots growing beneath her boots, anchoring her in the moment, and she opened her eyes slowly. The hearth light danced along the edges of the crystal, flickering with quiet invitation. Then, like she'd always known the words, not from books, but from bone, Frankie began.

She laid the blueleaf first, its curled edges catching the firelight.

"Leaf to root and stone to seed…"

Then came the ash, feather-soft, scattered in a crescent moon arc.

"Hear my breath, attend my need…"

She uncoiled the silver thread with care, its gleam delicate and steady, and looped it into a spiral. The salt followed, sprinkled in three neat arcs, her hands moving with grace.

"By hearth-smoke curl and moonlit thread…"

She dipped her finger into the moonwater. It gathered against her skin in a cool, pale bead, slid free, and touched the crystal with a quiet drop that felt less like sound and more like a whispered yes.

"Speak the truths that go unsaid…"

The last line rose from somewhere deeper than thought, older than voice. It left her lips like breath shaped with intention, carried on something she did not yet understand.

"Mist to branch and moss to flame…

Carry now the ancient name."

The spell didn't flare or crackle. It received her words, steady and attentive. The crystal deepened in color, light unfurling from within its core like moonrise breaking through water, silver laced with green, soft but certain. The radiance flowed outward, slipping across the table and over the herbs, the salt, the braided thread, as though the land itself was offering quiet agreement. Beneath her palm, the runes carved into the wooden surface awakened. They didn't move, yet warmth gathered beneath their lines, outlining each symbol with gentle light. The curves brightened like gold glimpsed beneath a canopy of leaves, alive with meaning and response.

Overhead, the bundles of drying herbs rustled softly. A breeze moved through the room, gentle, cool, and carrying a scent that did not belong to the fire or the tea. Cedar. Rain. And something sweet enough to catch at the edges of thought. Violets, perhaps. Or something that wanted to be violets. Even the shadows eased back, their outlines softening as the air brightened. The wand in her hand grew quiet, settling with a warmth that felt less like magic and more like company, steady, present, sure. And the crystal at the center of the table held her gaze, its surface catching more than firelight. It reflected something of her, a new clarity she hadn't known she carried.

Beyond the window, the forest answered. Leaves shifted. Light flickered through the branches in a slow, measured rhythm, neither wind nor chance, but something deliberate. It felt like a breath released, a quiet murmur slipping through the trees. Like the land was whispering back.

Aoife didn't speak at first either. She just watched her granddaughter, pride pooling in her eyes like moonlight in a bowl. Then, softly, with a smile blooming slow and sure,

"There it is," she said. "Now you're listening. The rhythm isn't yours alone. It's shared. That's the secret."

Frankie let out a long breath, her shoulders softening. Her hands no longer trembled. The light from the crystal danced in her eyes.

"I think it heard me," she whispered.

Aoife nodded. "Aye, child. And I think it liked what it heard."

From the hearth, Chalupa lifted his head, unimpressed. "Hmph. Never doubted her for a second."

Frankie just laughed, the sound bubbling up from somewhere deep. There was still so much she didn't know, so much ahead... But in this moment, she knew one thing for certain, *She belonged here*. The laughter faded into a hush, the kind that comes only after something true has been spoken.

Aoife stepped around the table, the firelight gilding her silver hair, her smile both quiet and fierce. "The first spell is always nerve wracking," she murmured. "Not because the magic resists you. But because you resist yourself. But you didn't, you listened and trusted what you felt, that's all magic ever asks."

She reached for the grimoire, her fingers brushing the timeworn leather with the tenderness one might offer an old friend.

"Let's try another," she said gently, holding the book out to Frankie. "This time, you choose. Let the pages speak to you."

Frankie hesitated, her fingers hovering just above the cover. As she opened it, the pages fluttered, soft, almost coy, like the rustle of wildflowers in wind. One page twitched, then another. A long, low sigh escaped from somewhere in its spine. Or was it a chuckle?

From above, Nyx let out a suspicious chirp. "That book just made a noise. Books shouldn't make noises."

"It breathed," Frankie whispered, stunned.

"Maybe it's hungry," Chalupa offered dryly from his sprawl near the hearth. Frankie's lips twitched despite herself.

Aoife, unbothered, smiled like someone who'd long ago made peace with the eccentricities of spellbooks. "Don't think, Love. Feel. Let it find you."

Frankie nodded, inhaling deeply. The scent of thyme and something citrusy-green curled around her as she closed her eyes. She reached inward, toward the steady hum she'd begun to recognize, like the memory of rhythm beneath her skin. The magic wasn't loud, it was quiet like a heartbeat waiting to be heard. She opened her eyes and turned the next page and everything promptly went sideways. One moment, she was humming with intention. Then the magic slipped through her fingers like a trickster's laugh. The crystal on the table flashed, once, twice, then detonated in a burst of glittering chaos. Shards of shimmering light shot out like enchanted confetti, raining over the table, the floor, and most of all Chalupa.

Frankie staggered back with a strangled yelp. "Oh, for crying out loud on a broomstick!"

The grimoire snapped shut with a sound that suggested it was either smug or scandalized.

Chalupa, now sparkling like a very disgruntled disco ball, glared from under his glimmering fur. "Wonderful, I've been bedazzled. Again! Do I look like a party favor to you?"

Frankie stared at the mess, then groaned. "It's like a unicorn sneezed in here."

Nyx swooped down and landed delicately on the edge of the table. "You're not wrong. But to be fair, it was quite spectacular."

"You would admire a magical detonation," Chalupa huffed.

Aoife, still smiling, stepped beside Frankie and rested a steady hand on her shoulder. "Magic's not a pet you train. It's a storm you learn to dance with. You're doing just fine, Love."

Frankie buried her face in her hands. "Fine? I just turned the kitchen into a faerie rave."

"First spells are meant to surprise," Aoife said, her voice warm with knowing. "If it all worked perfectly on the first try, we'd all be too proud to learn anything."

Chalupa flopped back down, glitter cascading from his fur in slow motion. "The first rule of magic," he intoned, "is to beware glitter bombs after dinner, it takes so long to clean up."

Frankie peeked out from between her fingers, eyes narrowing.

"You're impossible."

"Accurate," Chalupa said, smug.

Aoife waved a hand, and the shards of fractured spellwork swirled upward like glittering motes caught in a breeze, gathering themselves neatly into a small bowl.

"Now," she said, "try again. Gently. Don't command the spell. Invite it, let it trust you."

Frankie exhaled, her nerves smoothing just slightly, squared her shoulders and stepped back to the table.

Nyx flapped his wings, dropping down next to Chalupa and trying to shake off the glitter clinging to his feathers. “Ugh. Why is it always glitter?”

Chalupa, stretched luxuriously near the hearth, didn’t even open his eyes. “What is it with magical mishaps and glitter bombs?”

Nyx gave a long-suffering sigh. “It could be worse.”

Chalupa cracked one eye. “Yeah?”

Nyx tilted his head, deadpan. “It could be raining toads.”

Chalupa shuddered. “Don’t. Last time I saw that, it took three baths, two spells, and a sage smudge to get rid of the smell.”

Nyx gave a grim nod. “Warts in the strangest places.”

Chalupa muttered, “You bring the worst visual imagery.”

“Thank you,” Nyx said brightly, preening a glittery wing. “I try.”

A soft rustle of movement drew Frankie’s attention, Griffon had crossed the room without a sound. He stopped beside her, tall and quiet as ever, his presence grounding. Without a word, he reached out and gently brushed a scattering of glitter from her shoulder, then from the curls near her temple. The motion was unhurried, his fingertips careful as they swept the last sparkling specks from her cheek.

“You’ve been claimed by the chaos,” Griffon murmured, a smile ghosting across his lips as he brushed a trail of glitter from her shoulder.

Frankie blinked up at him, her heart still thudding from the spell’s spectacular failure. “It didn’t just misfire,” she said, breathless. “It launched a full-scale enchanted fireworks display.”

“I noticed,” he said, his silver-blue eyes catching the light, just enough to glint with quiet amusement. “A dramatic one, even by magical standards.”

His thumb passed gently beneath her eye, sweeping away one last fleck of shimmer. The touch was light, but it landed with weight, as if even the smallest moment between them held meaning. Frankie stood still, held by the warmth of his presence. Something stirred in her chest, the quiet ache of being seen. She smiled without meaning to, caught in the peace that lingered between them. Griffon's hand lowered, and he stepped back with an air of reluctant grace.

"I think I'll head to my cottage," he said, voice dropping to a low drawl. "Assuming it's still intact. You were keeping an eye on it, weren't you, Aoife? Or did the gremlins finally unionize while I was away?"

Aoife didn't look up from the bundle of herbs she was tying. "I lit the hearth, set a few wards, and left three charms glowing on your doorstep. It should be safe but they missed you."

Griffon raised a brow. "Noted. I'll bring a broom and a peace offering."

Then he turned back to Frankie, his steps unhurried. His expression was quiet, but in his gaze there was a steadiness that hadn't been there before, something watchful, wondering. He reached for her hand. When his fingers brushed hers, the room seemed to soften.

"Goodnight, Francesca," he said, voice rich and warm. "I stepped through the Hub thinking I was at the end of a long road... but now I wonder if it was only the threshold." His thumb traced lightly along the side of her hand, grounding, sincere. "The threads are stirring," he added, eyes locked with hers. "And I find myself wondering what shape the world might take... with you at its center."

Frankie didn't answer, she couldn't. The warmth in his voice wrapped around her like a promise, unsteady perhaps, still finding its shape, but real. He bowed slightly, all old-world grace, and pressed a kiss to her knuckles, tender, deliberate, and lingering just long enough to steal her breath. Without ceremony, Nyx flew up and landed on Griffon's shoulder as if it were the most natural thing in the world.

Griffon gave him a side glance. "You're coming?"

Nyx blinked slowly, settling in. "Clearly."

They didn't need to speak further. The quiet between them was its own kind of conversation, easy, intuitive, understood.

Griffon turned back toward Frankie, his voice low and certain. "Rest well."

Then he was gone, the door clicking softly shut behind him. The silence that followed wasn't empty, it was full of warmth, of potential, like the pause before a page turns. Frankie stood still, breath caught somewhere between wonder and something weightless.

From his spot near the hearth, Chalupa let out a long-suffering sigh. "He always leaves like he's got a theme song playing behind him. I hope the gremlins short-sheeted his bed and spelled his soap to smell like boiled cabbage."

Frankie snorted, covering her mouth. "Chalupa!"

"What?" he blinked. "I'm just saying. Nobody gets to be all that *and* smell good."

A quiet chuckle escaped Aoife as she reached for the table. Her voice, soft but steady, returned the focus. "That's enough for tonight, pet. You've done well. Now let's get you to bed before the walls start humming and Chalupa tries to hex the teapot."

"I heard that," Chalupa muttered from his place near the hearth. "I stand by what I said, teapot's are shifty."

Aoife ignored him with grace honed over centuries and turned toward a hallway framed in driftwood sconces. Their glass globes glowed like bottled starlight.

"Come now, I've your room ready."

Frankie followed, her exhaustion suddenly pressing in like a woolen blanket. Chalupa padded behind them with the air of royalty who had waited too long for turndown service. They passed a crooked grandfather clock that ticked to its own peculiar rhythm and a narrow gallery wall of stitched sigils and pressed wildflowers, each framed with care, as though someone had captured the seasons mid-breath. A breeze, scented faintly of lavender and old oak, slipped through the hall as if leading the way.

Aoife paused at the end of the corridor and laid her hand on a carved wooden door. "Go on, child," she said, her voice soft and threaded with quiet knowing. "This room has waited for you longer than you'll know."

She pushed the door open, and Frankie stepped into a dream. The room glowed with a light all its own, warm, golden, alive. The walls were painted a gentle moss green, brushed with vines that curled around windowpanes as if they, too, had grown up longing for this view. Above, the sloped ceiling bloomed with hand-painted wildflowers, foxglove, poppy, meadowsweet, like someone had scattered the memory of spring across the beams.

Frankie paused, her eyes tracing the delicate stalks of foxglove trailing across the ceiling. She was suddenly reminded of the first time she met Pete, years ago, standing in the greenhouse at Willow & Sage Nursery. He'd grinned and launched into a half-hour explanation, talking with his hands, dirt still under his nails. That moment had changed everything. She hadn't known it then, but that was the first time she'd felt seen. The memory wrapped around her gently, familiar and grounding. Now, she stood beneath the painted flowers in a room she had never seen but somehow belonged to. It was a sign, a thread woven through memory and magic, a quiet, certain reminder that she was exactly where she was meant to be. She smiled softly, brushing her fingers across the carved edge of the doorframe as if to anchor herself in this new place that already felt steeped in belonging.

Bundles of dried herbs, lavender, mugwort, chamomile, hung from the rafters, swaying slightly in a breeze that wasn't there. The air smelled of rosemary, old paper, and something sweet and spiced, like honey stirred into cider. A canopied bed sat nestled against the far wall, cloaked in patchwork quilts stitched from the colors of dusk and bonfire. Cushions in faded floral and linen had been tucked just so, like someone had taken the time to remember what softness meant.

An antique wardrobe stood quietly near the window, its doors painted with delicate wildflowers and spirals of ivy, as if the forest itself had lent its hand. Aoife stepped beside it and rested her fingers against the worn wood like greeting an old friend.

"These are for you," she said gently, opening the doors. "Natural fibers, dyed with roots and bloom, stitched with care, and waiting for the one they were meant to fit. Waiting for you, Frankie."

Inside, garments in soft, earthy tones hung in graceful folds, dresses dyed in dusk-blue and moss green, shawls as sheer as spun fog, linen skirts the color of river stone and fallen petals. Frankie reached out and brushed her fingers along one, a long-sleeved tunic the warm rust colors of late-autumn. The fabric was soft and cool beneath her fingertips, and the moment she touched it, something shifted in her chest.

"They're beautiful," she whispered, barely trusting her voice. "It's like... like they were made from the seasons."

Aoife's smile deepened, her voice turning soft. "Aye, Love. That's exactly what they are. Stitched by hand under moonlight and dawn, dyed with bark and bloom, wind-washed and sun-dried. These threads remember. Woven with nettle and patience, lined in quiet spellwork. They breathe with the earth and soften with use. They're not just for wearing, they're for becoming."

She stepped closer, brushing her hand fondly along a nearby sleeve. "You're spring's hope, summer's bloom, autumn's fire, and winter's stillness. Verdant witch to your bones, and the land knows it. It's only right your second skin remembers too."

Frankie's fingers lingered in the folds of a twilight-blue shawl, its fabric light as mist. A silence settled in the room, a pause filled with meaning. Like the cottage itself had exhaled, satisfied. She looked around at the painted beams, the quilted bed, the fragrant bundles of herbs above her, and felt the same quiet rhythm inside her chest, she belonged here. Somewhere in the stillness, Chalupa gave an exaggerated huff and launched himself onto the bed with the confidence of someone who had always known he belonged in velvet and quilts.

"Finally," he announced, circling once. "A room that respects my status."

Aoife lingered in the doorway, her silhouette haloed in the warm light from the corridor. She glanced toward the window, and a knowing gleam sparkled in her gaze.

"You'll want to crack it, just a touch," Aoife murmured, her brogue deepening as she rested her hand on the window frame. "There's a storm moving through the lower caverns, first in many moons. Velhollow's storms don't claw and rage the way surface storms do. They travel like visitors with purpose."

Frankie turned, one hand still resting on a folded dress of pine green. "You can sense it even down here?"

Aoife's smile curved, small and knowing. "Aye, love. The land shifts when something wakes beneath it. Storms down here carry messages, not tempests. Tonight's has a mind to greet you... and I'm inclined to let it."

Frankie crossed to the window and eased it open. Cool air slipped in like a secret carried on damp wind, sweet with the scent of wet leaves, dark soil, and pine steeped in gathering twilight. It held the quiet pressure of something approaching, steady, deliberate, watchful. Somewhere deep within the subterranean groves, thunder rumbled like a distant drum, more earthbound than skyborn, as though the cavern itself was clearing its throat.

Outside, the forest held unnaturally still. Branches barely stirred, though the breeze threaded through them. The indigo-dark sky pressed low over the trees, close enough to touch, close enough to listen. The hush settling over the clearing felt too deliberate to be chance, like the land had paused, waiting to see what the storm intended.

Behind her, Aoife stepped close, her presence soft as moss under bare feet. She tucked a stray curl behind Frankie's ear with a tenderness shaped by years of love carried quietly.

"You are the Verdant Witch, Frankie," she said, voice warm but edged with certainty.

"Born of root and rain, breath and bramble. The land knows you, even if you're only beginning to hear it."

She pressed a kiss to Frankie's brow, part blessing, part protection, part farewell.

"Rest now, love. Much lies ahead, and the dark that moves beyond these trees is swift. It knows the thin places. It walks where the light loosens. It enters without waiting for welcome."

With that, Aoife slipped into the hall, her shadow trailing behind like smoke and moonlit moss, the soft creak of old floorboards the only sound she left behind.

Frankie changed slowly, selecting a nightdress the color of wild heather bloom. It smelled of cedar, clean linen, and that soft, charged coolness the world holds right before the rain breaks. By the time she reached the bed, Chalupa had already claimed his spot at the foot, curled in a perfect loop of feline contentment, tail twitching in sleepy rhythm.

She slipped beneath the quilts, cool to the touch and heavy with comfort. The fabric wrapped around her as though the forest itself had stitched every seam, waiting for her return. Rain began to fall in earnest, not the surface kind, but subterranean rain, soft and deliberate, drumming against the carved stone outside in a measured rhythm. The sound felt ancient. Wild. A song of water on root and cavern, of old magic stretching in its sleep. Thunder answered from the depths with a low, resonant exhale. Wind brushed her cheek through the cracked window, carrying the scent of green things waking in the dark, magic gathering beneath the soil like breath before a word. Frankie closed her eyes, heart full and oddly weightless, letting herself sink into the cradle of warmth and storm.

Outside, the air moved in steady rhythm with the forest's quiet breath, each drop a soft heartbeat against the night. Within the cottage, something subtle shifted, as though the threads of fate had begun to realign, slow and certain in their awakening. And far beyond the treeline, where shadow and rainwater wove together in dark, silken currents, something ancient stirred. It drifted through the gloom with deliberate ease, drawn to the faint new light gathering around her. It did not threaten, nor did it press closer. It simply watched, patient as stone, attentive as a turning tide, waiting for the moment she would sense it watching back. A whisper drifted through the night, soft as breath along bark, carrying a tone that felt older. It brushed the air with quiet recognition, as though the land itself had leaned close to greet her in its own forgotten way.

Thunder rolled once more, measured and deliberate, the sound carrying through the cavernous world like the steady drum of something magical taking breath. Frankie had loved storms her entire life, their wildness, their music, the way they shook loose the things she didn't know she was holding. But here, in Velhollow, they felt different. Older. Primal. As if the storm wasn't simply weather, but a presence with its own intent, its own memory, its own quiet eyes turned toward her.

The whisper folded into the night, slipping through the trees with the ease of a creature that knew these woods by heart. It lingered at the edge of the night, waiting just beyond the veil of dreams, steady and sure, ready for the moment she would open her eyes to it.

Chapter 16

The hour that passed for morning in Velhollow had not yet fully arrived, but Frankie was already awake. The cottage rested in a hush unique to the realm, a quiet that came not from darkness lifting, but from the world pausing between breaths. The lamps along the stone corridors beyond the walls glowed low and steady, their light softened as if even they were reluctant to intrude.

Magic stirred faintly in the air, subtle as a string brushed and left humming. Frankie could feel it now, not pressing, not demanding, simply present. Aware. Not watching her so much as acknowledging her wakefulness, like the house itself had noticed she'd opened her eyes and was waiting to see what she might do with that small, deliberate choice. She sat at the long wooden table, the grimoire spread open before her, its pages softened by time into a gentle, weathered curl. The ink caught the early light in soft glints, the kind that seemed to breathe rather than shine. As her fingers traced the looping script, the words rose in her mind with a cadence that felt older than morning, older than the quiet room around her. She mouthed them silently, tasting their rhythm, letting them settle through her like a remembered song finally reaching its last missing note. The book carried a presence she couldn't name, faint, watchful, keen. It felt less discovered and more returned to, as if her hands had once known these pages in another lifetime. A subtle energy gathered beneath her touch, steady and patient, the sense of meaning coiled within the margins like something waiting to be woken. The grimoire didn't just hold knowledge, it held invitation and every line leaned toward her as though it recognized the shape of her magic rising to meet it.

Frankie had chosen something simple, so she thought. A little charm to brighten the room, and maybe impress the smug furball currently stretched out nearby. But spells, she was about to learn, didn't much care about what seemed simple on paper. She'd barely finished the final syllable when the charm reacted like it had been personally offended. Light burst from the crystal in a brilliant flare, golden, crackling, and far too enthusiastic. A loud *POP*!

Followed, sharp and final, like a cork launched into another dimension, and then the curtains burst into flames as if they'd been harboring pyromanic ambitions this whole time.

And Chalupa?

He had screeched an earsplitting sound that could only be described as the unholy blend of a shrieking old woman and a child discovering that monsters under the bed were, in fact, real. It was the very definition of panic wrapped in fur. He'd launched himself off the windowsill like a creature betrayed, tail puffed to comical proportions, paws scrabbling for purchase as he skidded across the floor in an undignified blur. Frankie had shrieked too, mostly out of guilt, as she lunged for the nearest cup of water, dousing both the flame and half the table in a dramatic splash that smelled faintly of lavender tea and … panic.

Chalupa reappeared moments later on the top shelf, eyes wide, fur puffed into a disgruntled pompom, looking every inch the victim of a failed magical assassination attempt.

"I'd really rather not be set on fire before I've had my first breakfast," he muttered, fur still puffed. "Next time, just announce your intentions to ignite the furniture."

Frankie winced, patting at the scorched edge of the curtain. "Sorry?"

With a dramatic huff, Chalupa turned his back on her entirely, spine rigid, radiating betrayal. Clearly, he was reevaluating every decision that had led him to this shelf, this cottage, this life. She was determined to try again now, a grounding charm this time. Basic. Steady. The magical equivalent of a weighted blanket and a cup of tea. It was meant to root her to the earth, help her feel the quiet rhythm beneath her skin. Frankie inhaled, slow and shaky, trying to match the rhythm of her breath to that faint hum she was sure she could almost feel. Her hands hovered over the table, trembling slightly. The magic was there, she could sense it, just beneath the surface of everything. Present, but watchful, like a wild animal at the edge of the trees, curious, waiting to see if she'd flinch.

She closed her eyes, tuning out Chalupa's melodramatic muttering from above. It was just her now, well, her and the magic to fly solo. The crystal flickered faintly, like it, too, was questioning her readiness. She stared at it, jaw clenched, fingers curling against the table's edge. Her pulse was frantic, her breath uneven. Every sigh from above landed like a personal jab. She'd tried. She was trying. But the magic was slippery, too vast, too quiet, and entirely uninterested in her expectations.

Creeeak.

The back door swung open on its iron hinges, groaning like the cottage itself had decided to wake up. A rush of crisp morning air spilled into the room, curling around her like a cold breath against warm skin. It swept across the hearth, teasing the embers into a faint glow, and replaced the scent of smoke with pine, wet moss, and something brighter, something alive, wild and untamed. With her concentration lost, the crystal dimmed to nothing, and just like that, whatever thread she'd been clinging to snapped.

Frankie exhaled with frustration, her hands falling into her lap in quiet defeat. "Brilliant," she muttered. "Absolutely brilliant."

A flutter of wings cut the silence. Nyx swept in through the open door like a shadow laced with starlight, circled once, then landed with a soft thump on the mantle. He ruffled his feathers, cocked his head at the charred curtain, and let out a low whistle.

"Well, I see the drapes have been sacrificed in the name of magical excellence," he said dryly. "Shall I alert the local coven council about magical mishaps or just the fire brigade?"

Frankie groaned. "Too soon, Nyx."

He clicked his beak. "If your goal was dramatic flair, consider it achieved. The scent of scorched linen is really setting the mood."

Chalupa emerged from behind a basket with singed whiskers and a look of eternal betrayal. "I've lived through storms, spectral skirmishes, and that incident with the exploding sourdough starter," he muttered, leaping gracefully to the bench beside her. "But this?" He flicked his tail at the still-smoking curtain. "This is where I draw the line. I am a familiar, not firewood."

Frankie buried her face in her hands. "It was a tiny charm."

"A tiny charm with big ambitions," Chalupa sniffed. "Next time, aim for illumination without the immolation."

Then came the sound of boots across wood and Griffon stepped through the doorway like the morning had summoned him directly. He moved as if the room made space around him. Without a word, he crouched beside her, folding his broad frame until they were eye to eye. His presence didn't push or press, it grounded. A steady warmth, like stone heated by the sun. He glanced once at the scorched curtain, then back at Frankie, a hint of a smile tugging at the corner of his mouth.

"Could've been worse," Griffon said. "My first spell scorched an orchard and permanently offended a goat."

Frankie stared. "Offended?"

"Deeply," he said. "Won't make eye contact to this day."

She snorted, the magic may have fizzled, but at least she wasn't alone in the magical mishaps. Her eyes stayed locked on the crystal, now just a lump of dull quartz and dashed hopes but his nearness made it hard to wallow. When she finally glanced at him, he was watching her, not with pity, not even amusement, but with something far more dangerous, belief.

"You don't have to wrestle with it," Griffon said, voice low and easy. "Magic's not something you conquer. You just have to show up where it lives and say hello."

Frankie swallowed, the corners of her mouth twitching like she wasn't sure if she was about to laugh or cry. She hadn't exactly failed, but she hadn't nailed it either. Everything still felt new, like trying to dance to a song she didn't quite know the rhythm of. What if she kept stepping on the beat? What if the knowing just...never showed up?

"What if I can't?" she murmured. Not giving up, just genuinely unsure.

Griffon didn't miss a beat and a grin tugged at one side of his mouth. "You will," he said, like it was the most obvious thing in the world.

For a moment, the space between them shifted. It wasn't the magic, not exactly. It was something quieter, something that gathered in her all at once, slowing the rush inside her until everything felt steady for the first time since she began. She didn't have to reach for it anymore or chase it down. It had already come forward to meet her. She waited, and in that waiting, something within her eased. The tension she'd been gripping so tightly loosened, unspooling like threads drawn gently free. For the first time, she didn't feel as though the magic might slip through her hands the moment she touched it. She wasn't fumbling now, wasn't forcing anything. The crystal beneath her palm held a calm, steady hum, rooted and sure. A slow breath left her, soft and full of wonder. She exhaled again, longer this time, her fingers relaxing as the moment settled around her.

"Alright," she murmured, her gaze drifting back to the crystal, its light faint but patient. "Let's try this again."

This time, the crystal didn't waver. Its light grew with a steady beat, gentle, assured, like a presence waking after a long and listening quiet. Frankie inhaled, steady now, her breath syncing to something deeper. She wasn't reaching anymore, she was meeting it. The magic wasn't a force to grasp, but a rhythm, alive and ancient, waiting for her to hear it. She let herself sink into that hum, the hush of the cottage walls, the soft tick of time stretching. There, beneath it all, the magic answered. The crystal's glow returned, brighter, bolder. It thrummed in harmony with her breath, with the pulse in her wrists, like a song she didn't know she knew but had always been hers.

A laugh bubbled up, light and breathless. "I can feel it," she whispered. "I can really feel it."

Beside her, Griffon's smile was slow, sure, like dawn creeping over the edge of night. "There," he murmured. "Now you're getting it."

Her heart lifted, joy threading through her like sunlight. "I think I am," she breathed, eyes wide with wonder.

"You are." His voice softened, but the strength in it held. "It's not just about trusting the magic, Frankie. It's about trusting in yourself."

She blinked, emotion catching her off guard. Relief unfurled in her chest, chasing out the last of the doubt.

"So," she said, a wry smile playing at her lips, "do you charge for magical pep talks, or is this part of the hospitality package?"

Griffon's grin tilted, slow and shameless. "Oh, I'll collect," he said, his voice low and warm, eyes dancing over her face. "Eventually. Might take it in tea, trouble, or stolen moments, but I'll collect." Her breath caught, just a little, but her smile held. She didn't need to ask what he meant. "Until then," he added, softer now, "don't forget what that felt like. That spark? That was all you."

Across the room, Aoife stood in the doorway, silent, unseen. Her eyes softened as she watched them, Frankie's face alight with wonder, Griffon close but steady, guiding without holding. The crystal's glow bathed them both, casting flickers of light across their faces, across the walls where shadows danced. Her heart stirred, an old ache mingling with hope. The threads were weaving, slow and sure. Perhaps slower than the world could afford, but weaving nonetheless.

"So much to learn and so little time." she thought. But in this moment, she allowed herself a smile. They were finding each other and the magic... it was listening. Then the air shifted like the room itself had inhaled. A ripple stirred across the space, subtle and strange, bending the light like heat over stone. Shadows curled inward, gathering with slow intent around something unseen. Even the vines along the windowsills paused, as if the whole cottage had leaned in to listen.

Aoife entered the kitchen like she'd stepped out of a memory, her presence quiet but certain, the silver braid down her back catching the slant of dawn and flaring like starlight. Her gaze slid to the table and the world seemed to stop. Frankie turned slowly, the hairs along her arms rising, her breath catching. There, in the center of the old wooden table, lay something that hadn't been there before.

A scroll.

It had not been delivered or set down. It had appeared. The scroll rested on the table as though it had risen from the wood itself, drawn up from grain and shadow rather than placed by any hand. It was tightly wound, bound with a narrow strip of leather that caught the candlelight in pale, silvery echoes, less like ornament and more like dew clinging to bark at dusk. It was not paper. The surface was thicker, denser, bearing a subtle grain like pressed wood or cured hide, dark and ridged beneath her fingertips. It held warmth, faint but unmistakable, as if something within it breathed slow and patient.

Frankie hadn't seen the scroll appear, no one had. One blink, one breath, and it was simply there, waiting, awake, and undeniably meant for her.

"That wasn't there," she whispered, her voice barely a thought.

Aoife stepped closer. "Aye, love," she murmured. "I know, but it is now."

Griffon edged in beside her, his shoulders tense, his eyes locked on the scroll like it might bite. "Did it just appear?" he asked, low and wary. "Or did someone summon it?"

Aoife shook her head, slow and deliberate. "No one summoned this," she said, her voice low with a certainty that settled rather than soothed. "This was not called. This is the kind of magic that arrives when it chooses to be known."

Chalupa hissed low in his throat, fur bristling along his spine.

"Old magic," he muttered, eyes fixed on the scroll. "The kind that remembers too much." His tail flicked once. "And I'd very much prefer it remember someone else."

Nyx clicked his beak once, wings giving a restrained flick. "On this rare occasion," he said coolly, "the cat is correct."

Frankie's hand hovered near the scroll, caught between reaching for it and pulling away. When her fingertips grazed the edge, the room answered with a soft, low hum, like a chord struck on an ancient instrument. The scroll stirred in reply. It unrolled with purpose, spreading across the table as though it had been waiting for breath and touch to wake it. Symbols spread across its surface in curling lines of gold, weaving themselves into the shape of a great tree. Roots dove deep into the page, spreading wide like they sought the very heart of the table beneath; branches climbed upward in sweeping arcs, tangled in what looked like distant constellations rendered in fine, luminous ink. The parchment's surface, dark, ridged, almost bark-like, seemed to shift with each breath Frankie took, the golden lines brightening in answer. The tree was no longer a symbol or a thing to be interpreted. It was in motion, changing even as she watched, its form deepening and unfolding with deliberate intent. Bark darkened, roots pressed farther into the earth, and branches stretched as if answering a call older than language. This was not an image meant to explain meaning or decorate a story. It was an act of becoming, a living force stepping into itself, claiming space, weight, and purpose in the world.

Drawn by a pull she didn't fully understand, Frankie let her hand drift closer. The moment her fingers hovered above the golden canopy, the tree brightened from root to crown, as though recognizing her presence, aligning itself to the quiet cadence moving through her.

"What is this?" she whispered, unable to look away.

Aoife didn't answer at once. Her hand floated above the scroll as well, careful, almost cautious, as if she feared disturbing something with a will of its own.

"This scroll is the Verdant Oath. A relic older than ink or word, born when magic was breath and the world still spoke in roots and rainfall. Back when our line didn't cast spells... but tended them. Guided them. This is a living vow," she continued, voice steady, "woven from the first roots of our family. It wakes only when the balance falters... and only for the one meant to restore it."

Something deep within Frankie warmed, slow and sure. The tree on the page brightened again, its branches gleaming with the suggestion of fruit, its roots stretching toward her without crossing the space, reaching not for her hand, but for something unseen and quiet inside her.

It knew her and it had been waiting.

Beside her, Griffon stepped closer, steady as ever. His presence was grounding, quiet as stone and just as true. When he spoke, his voice was low, certain.

"The Verdant Oath carries the weight of those who came before... and the promise of what still must rise. It calls now because it remembers what lives in you."

Frankie turned toward him, caught by the certainty in his gaze. Something passed between them, unsaid but undeniable.

Aoife's voice broke the hush, gentle and unwavering. "Magic doesn't wait for readiness, love. It moves when it must and now... now it's time for you to remember what the land has never forgotten."

The scroll answered. A low rhythm moved through her, steady and old, like footsteps finding their way along a forgotten path. This wasn't merely magic, it was memory, inheritance, a lantern lit in her lineage. The Verdant Witch was rising. And the earth, along with every realm above, below, and between, wild and waiting, rose to meet her.

The runes shifted again. The tree's roots stretched outward, curling into new shapes. Frankie didn't know the symbols, not with her mind. But her heart recognized them. Her blood recognized them. They beat through her like a vow whispered before language ever learned to form a word. Aoife inhaled sharply. Frankie caught the flicker in her grandmother's eyes, recognition not of what had been, but of what now bent toward them.

The scroll's rhythm changed. Sharpened. Symbols reorganized themselves, the great tree folding inward until its branches spiraled into a sigil glowing like mist lit by firelight, a curling flame crossed by wind, encircled by thread.

Aoife stepped forward, her voice low but sure. "It's begun. The call is clear."

Frankie pulled her gaze from the scroll. "You can read it?"

"Aye... in a way," Aoife murmured, eyes still tracing the shifting light. "Not in words, but in how the magic moves. This isn't just a telling. It's a sending." She turned to Griffon, the strength returning to her voice. "The Oath doesn't reveal itself without reason and that sigil... it marks the path of the Unbound."

Griffon's expression darkened with recognition. "This is old magic," he murmured. "Older than Velhollow itself."

"Older than any kingdom," Aoife agreed, "and bound to the earth's first breath. To those who swore to keep it balanced." Her eyes met Frankie's. "This is where we must go."

Silence fell again, deep and expectant, like the world itself had stopped to listen. Frankie felt it in her heart, a thread tugging her forward into darkness, into truth. The unknown no longer waited at the edges of her story. It had entered the room. Griffon turned to the window, where a thin slice of dawn crept through the ivy-stained glass. When he looked back, his expression had shifted, softer, yes, but touched with something ancient. Something that felt like memory waiting to be lived.

"The last time Zyphirion stirred," he said quietly, "was during the Sundering, when ley lines cracked, and magic broke loose. Even then, he didn't act, he warned."

He paused. "He's not like us," Griffon continued. "Zyphirion is a hermit in the truest sense. He sees everything. Knows everything. He gathers knowledge the way others gather breath. His sanctum is carved into the quiet between worlds, filled with relics of ages lost and languages the earth has buried. He keeps record of things forgotten... and things never meant to be found."

Griffon's gaze sharpened, the weight of history pooling behind his eyes. "Time folds around him. He waits, but never idly. He observes, remembers and even judges." He turned to Aoife. "She needs more than riddles from us, Aoife. She'll get enough of that from Zyphirion." His gaze drifted to Frankie, steady and sure. "She walks a path written long before her first breath. We owe her truth, not just echoes."

Aoife's eyes sparkled, her voice warm with affection. "Careful, Stonewing. You're sounding almost poetic. Should I be worried?"

Griffon's lips curved, the hint of a smile beneath the weight he carried. "Even stone can speak when the winds shift."

A breath passed between them, Aoife's smile lingered, fond and sure, before she turned back to Frankie. Her nod was slow, her eyes never leaving her. Aoife let her fingers drift over the unfurled scroll, and the room seemed to lean closer, as if listening to her speak.

"The shadow we face isn't new," she said quietly. "It has been weaving itself through the roots of this realm for longer than most remember. What you felt during the attack, those fragments, are pieces of a larger hunger. They were searching. And now that they've brushed against your magic, they'll try again."

The words landed heavy in the space between them, thick with meaning. Frankie swallowed, the memory of those dark tendrils prickling through her like a cold echo.

"Searching for what, exactly?" Her voice was soft, but steady.

Aoife met her gaze with something fierce and sorrowful braided together. "For the one who carries the old signature," she said. "For the witch whose magic rises from root and rain, the one the land called home the moment you crossed its threshold." Her hand briefly touched Frankie's cheek, brief, but grounding. "They were seeking you, love. Not by name. By nature."

Frankie felt the truth of it slip through her like a key turning in a lock she hadn't known she carried. Across the table, Griffon watched her, really watched her, with a focus that felt like touch. No teasing now. No smirk. Something deeper.

"The deeper we go," he said, voice low and steady, "the closer we draw to the oldest parts of Velhollow and the darkness knows it. Whatever stirs out there..." His jaw tightened. "It wants what you are becoming."

Frankie met his eyes, something warm and unsettled sparking between them, recognition, yes, but also a pull, like two currents deciding which one would move first. She didn't look away, and neither did he. Aoife cleared her throat softly, though a thin smile flickered at the corner of her mouth.

Aoife's eyes met hers, and something fierce and unspoken passed between them, pride, fear, hope, all braided into a moment she had carried in her heart for years. "The path has already begun," she whispered, her voice like silk wrapped around iron. "You felt it when the scroll woke. When the air leaned toward you. When the forest listened. His sanctum lies beyond the Veil of Cascading Stars, where no road dares to stay steady and no map remembers its lines. You don't find Zyphirion unless you've been summoned." She stepped closer, the weight of old magic settling around her like a mantle. "And you have been, Frankie. The turning has started. The first thread of your destiny is already in motion." Her gaze softened, though the truth beneath it did not. "Whatever waits beyond that veil... it's tied to who you are becoming. And there is no turning back now."

Chapter 17

Frankie didn't move. She stood at the edge of the table, her hand hovering just above the scroll as though touching it might unravel the entire world. Light pooled beneath the vellum surface in a steady, unnatural glow, far too calm for the storm building inside her. The cottage felt caught in a single held breath, every shadow tightened, every candle leaned inward, as though the room itself was waiting to hear what she'd say next.

"Will someone please tell me what's happening?" Her voice came out rough with confusion she could no longer disguise. "Everyone keeps talking about veils thinning, old magic waking, some… role I'm supposed to play. But none of it adds up. I feel like I've been dropped into a story written in a language I don't speak."

Her gaze flicked between them, searching for anything solid, anything she could hold on to. Aoife breathed out, slow and careful, like she was sifting through memories older than the walls around them.

"The signs have been gathering for moons," she murmured. "Quiet, but insistent. Dreams that cling when they should fade. Shadows that stay too long in the corners. Birds migrating toward lands where no sun has shone in an age. These aren't accidents, love. They are warnings. Whispers. Threads pulling taut."

Frankie swallowed. "Warnings of what?"

Griffon moved then, a shift so subtle she felt it before she saw it. He stepped closer, the low heat of him brushing her shoulder, a quiet strength anchoring the moment. When he spoke, his voice vibrated through the floorboards, deep as a drumbeat.

"When the veils give way, it won't be gentle," he said. "What's kept at the edges will try to cross. Forgotten hungers. Old shadows. The things that reached for you last night?" His jaw tightened. "Those weren't lost fragments. They were scouts."

Frankie's breath stuttered. "Scouts for what?"

“For whoever commands the darkness tugging at the veil,” Aoife said softly. “It probes where the world is thin, testing the defenses of Velhollow. When it sensed you, when you lit the chamber with your magic, it took notice.”

Frankie felt Griffin watching her then, intensely, quietly, like he saw the storm gathering behind her ribs and wanted nothing more than to stand between her and whatever came next. Griffon’s gaze lingered on her, steady and unguarded in a way she wasn’t sure he allowed with anyone else.

“You’re not an omen, Frankie,” he said softly, the words shaped like something he’d carried longer than he meant to admit. “And you’re no lock to be turned or warning to be heeded.”

He stepped closer, close enough that she could feel the warmth rolling off him, slow as rising embers. Close enough that the forest itself seemed to still.

“You,” he murmured, voice dipping rough and low, “are the shift the dark has dreaded. The change it can’t outrun.” His eyes, gold warming toward amber, held hers without flinching. “It reaches for you because it senses what you’re becoming… even before you do.”

Something fluttered in her chest. She was terrified and hopeful all at once and when Griffon, leaned in just a fraction, his breath brushed her cheek like a promise waiting for courage. Warmth unfurled inside her as fear, awe, and something else entirely tangled together while he held her gaze a heartbeat longer than was strictly necessary. The tension was thick enough that even Nyx seemed to notice, he hopped from Griffon’s shoulder to the table and muttered.

“Well, this escalated quickly.” Chalupa flicked an ear, unimpressed. “I told you. Everything about her screams ‘*main character energy*.’ I should get hazard pay.”

“I shall, of course, take the higher vantage,” Nyx said, settling onto Griffon’s shoulder with a precise adjustment of feathers. “One sees more from elevation.”

Chalupa sniffed indignantly. “You’re a bird. You literally have wings.”

Nyx shrugged. “Yes, but why fly when you can travel in style?”

Frankie’s nerves settled, just slightly, beneath the ripple of humor, beneath Griffon’s steady gaze, beneath the weight of

Aoife's certainty and somewhere inside her, quiet but undeniable, something ancient began to turn.

Chalupa leapt from his perch and strutted across the floor, tail high and voice full of indignation. "If we're heading into some ancient lair of doom and riddles, someone better be packing snacks." He sniffed at Aoife's bags with exaggerated suspicion. "If any of these contain bacon, I demand first rights."

Nyx arched a brow. "You'd eat a cursed root if it smelled like bacon."

"Bacon *is* bacon," Chalupa sniffed. "You wouldn't know refinement if it bit you on your feathery behind."

Aoife didn't look up. "Keep bickering and I'll turn you both into glowing dormice and set you loose in the Labyrinth of Whim."

Frankie smiled despite herself. Even with the air so charged, the bickering felt grounding, real. She moved to her pack, laying it open on the table. She reached for the satchel she'd carried from her carriage house, inside were her dried tea bundles and a grounding stone she'd found by the creek that first strange morning. She turned it in her fingers briefly, remembering the way it had glowed faintly in her palm, then tucked it away once more. Then her hand brushed the old leather journal, the one that had started this whole journey. The one that whispered of strange lineages and family magic long buried. She hesitated, then slipped it into her bag… just in case.

Aoife stepped in close and handed her a heavy wool cloak, the kind woven for deep forest travel. "You'll need warmth," she saids simply. "It gets colder near the Veil."

Frankie slung it over her arm, but Aoife had something else. From the folds of her satchel, she drew a slender glass vial filled with a liquid that swirled in muted hues, somewhere between honeyed amber and soft new spring moss, alive in a way no ordinary potion ever was.

"This is *Moonfire*," she said, placing it gently into Frankie's hand. "Born of frost beneath a full moon, sealed in glass before it could vanish. It burns through illusion, fear, and shadow. But it's wild, don't trust it unless you must."

Frankie turned the vial, watching it catch the light. "So… magical napalm in a perfume bottle. Got it."

Aoife smirked, unfazed. "Better wild and dangerous than defenseless."

"We'll need more than rations and bandages where we're going," Griffon said, eyes scanning the table.

"Best to prepare for the unexpected," Aoife replied, slipping a carved sigil into Frankie's bag. "And hope both the forest and Zyphirion favor us."

Frankie nodded and tucked the pouch away with the rest of her carefully chosen supplies. The satchel was nearly full, charms wrapped in velvet, sprigs of warding herbs, a bundle of crow feathers tied with copper thread, each item placed with intention, each one carrying a quiet echo of its purpose. She reached to fasten the flap when her hand brushed something warm beneath the fold.

Not fabric.

Not leather.

Something… that felt aware of her. Not in any way she could name, no movement, no shift of air, but the moment her fingertips touched the hidden shape, a faint warmth rose to greet her, steady and deliberate. It wasn't heat from the fire or from the packed supplies. It felt… directional. As if the object beneath the layers had paused and taken notice of her. A prickle stirred along her palm. An impression, subtle but unmistakable, the feeling of walking into a room where someone was already waiting for her. Her breath slowed, the space around her growing still. Curious and drawn toward it despite herself, she eased the layers aside. What she found at first was only a smooth length of wood, no longer than her forearm, unassuming, polished by time. But the moment she lifted it free of the satchel, the wood warmed, brightened, and stretched. Not violently or with a sudden jolt. It grew, lengthening in her hands like a branch remembering its true shape, unfurling to its full size with a quiet, natural certainty, as though this was its rightful form and the smaller shape had merely been a way of resting. Frankie stared as the markings carved along its length brightened under her touch, responding with a soft, steady glow, as if acknowledging her.

Chalupa flicked an ear, unimpressed. "Of course it likes you. Everything in this realm does. Before anyone gets ideas, if it starts following you around like a lost puppy, I'm not sharing the bed."

Griffon turned toward Chalupa, the weight of long-suffering patience written across his face. "Sharing the bed?" he said, dry as stone. "As I remember, you barely tolerate anyone near your cushion."

Chalupa's whiskers twitched in offended grandeur. "That's called having standards," he sniffed. "And I am not sharing my sleeping spot with an enchanted stick making eyes at her, or with a wandering giant who forgets how big his elbows are."

A quiet huff escaped Griffon, real, unguarded, quickly smothered. But when he turned back to Frankie, the humor in him shifted, softened, into something deeper, something he didn't bother to hide. His gaze followed the curve of her hands, wrapped around the staff warming beneath her touch, then lifted, slow and deliberate, until it met her eyes and held. The stare wasn't casual, it wasn't polite and it wasn't subtle in the slightest. It was the kind of look that landed with weight, deep, searching, impossibly steady, as though he were seeing the shape of her future superimposed over the girl standing before him. As though he saw the woman she was becoming, the force she hadn't even realized she was stepping into. As though he was already reckoning with what that might mean for him.

Frankie felt it hit her like warmth rising from deep earth, quiet, sudden, unbalancing. Her fingers tightened on the staff without meaning to. Her breath stilled. It was too much and not enough all at once. Griffon's jaw moved, not tense, but restrained, the careful tether a man uses when he's standing at the edge of a precipice he both longs for and fears stepping over.

Chalupa groaned dramatically. "Oh stars, there it is. The stare. The one that makes the room smell like trouble with really good hair."

"*Chalupa*!" Frankie hissed, mortified.

But Griffon didn't look away. "When magic turns toward its counterpart," he murmured, voice low and warm, "it doesn't pretend not to notice."

The air thinned, as though the walls themselves leaned closer to listen. Then, without meaning to, Griffon let something flicker behind his eyes. A thought. A truth.

She's the one the realm has been waiting for and gods help me... I've been waiting too.

He drew in a subtle breath, anchored himself, then finally spoke aloud, directed toward Chalupa, but with his gaze locked entirely on Frankie. "It isn't merely reacting," he said softly. "It's answering her."

Chalupa flicked an ear. "Oh great. We're courting enchanted lumber now. A golden age for romance."

Frankie shook her head, fingers tightening instinctively around the warm wood. "I didn't... I didn't ask it anything," she whispered, confused and breathless.

Her voice trembled on the edges of awe. "So what is it answering?"

Griffon's gaze moved to her, steady, warm, unbearably gentle. "Whatever it heard in you." he mused.

Frankie almost laughed, but the staff warmed again beneath her palm, steady, deliberate, as though it recognized something she hadn't yet put words to.

His voice dropped lower, intimate, steady, meant for her alone. "It doesn't choose lightly, *Lady Francesca*."

The words landed inside her like a spark housed in stone, small, sure, carrying heat long after the moment passed. Neither of them moved. Aoife stepped forward, breaking the tension just enough to let the air flow again, though her voice carried the gravity of something older than memory.

"The Staff of Thorneval," she said, "was carved from heartwood that blooms under starlight once in a century. It remembers every hand that has guided it, and shapes itself to the one it belongs to. A guide when you are lost. A shield when you are hunted. A weapon when no soft path remains."

But even as Aoife spoke, Griffon's gaze lingered on Frankie like an unspoken vow he hadn't yet found the courage, or the right moment, to name and Frankie felt something in her begin to bloom.

Frankie curled her fingers more firmly around the staff. Its weight grounded her, but the warmth moving through the wood felt almost like relief, like it had been waiting for her touch, waiting for this moment. Awe pressed close, bright and unbalancing, and she instinctively reached for humor, the familiar tether that kept her steady when wonder grew too large.

“So…” she murmured, trying for lightness even as her voice wavered, “basically a magical multi-tool?”

Chalupa slapped his tail against the floor with dramatic outrage. “Fantastic. She’s cracking jokes. That means something’s gotten under her skin.”

Griffon’s mouth shifted, not quite a smile, but almost, and the small, subtle change sent a ripple of heat up Frankie’s neck. She looked back down at the polished wood for grounding and instantly wished she hadn’t. For one startling, impossible heartbeat, the reflection staring up from the staff wasn’t hers. It was her face, but transformed, sharpened, stripped of softness. Her eyes burned a deep, feral green shot through with shadow, as if lit from within by something untamed. A crooked smile curved her mouth, sharp with intent, predatory, assured, the expression of someone who commanded storms instead of weathering them. Power radiated from that version of her, not borrowed or found, but claimed, rooted in depths Frankie had never dared imagine. It wasn’t a stranger. It was a possibility. She blinked, once, hard, and the image dissolved. Only her own face remained, wide-eyed and shaken, the ghost of that other self still clinging to the edges of her thoughts.

Aoife was looking on, not startled. Waiting, as if a truth she’d carried alone had finally stepped into the open. She stepped closer, laying a steadying hand on Frankie’s arm, her voice dipping into something old and sure, shaped more by knowing than comfort. Aoife’s fingers tightened just slightly, grounding her.

“What you saw,” she murmured, “isn’t a warning of what you’ll become, it’s a reminder that your power holds more than one truth. Verdant magic grows and it devours. It heals and it breaks. It answers the hand… and the heart behind it. Light casts its own shadow, and even a tree that blooms beneath starlight anchors itself in deep earth. The staff will answer you as you are…”

Her gaze softened, with pride, with fear, with recognition. “And as you might become.”

Frankie swallowed, trying to steady the swirl inside her, the awe, the fear, the strange pull of possibility. The staff warmed again, gentler this time, as if acknowledging her confusion and choosing patience over pressure.

Behind her, Chalupa gave a theatrical snort, tail lashing.

"Remember that twenty-in-one gardening contraption you bought? The one with the fold-out spade, corkscrew, saw, and whatever else they crammed into it? You nearly lost a finger trying to prune roses and open a bottle of wine at the same time."

Heat flared in Frankie's cheeks. "That was one time and it mostly worked."

"Mostly," Chalupa echoed, his tail flicking with feline amusement. "Until it collapsed mid-use and you screamed at it like you found a mouse in your sock drawer."

Aoife hid a smile behind her hand, shoulders trembling with a laugh she didn't let fully escape.

"Well," she said gently, eyes glinting, "I trust that the staff is sturdier than your... gardening gadget."

Frankie adjusted her grip on the staff, half in awe, half in disbelief. The runes shimmered faintly, as though humoring her.

"Let's hope so." she muttered.

Nyx clicked his beak. "And what of me? Should I just hurl insults and hope the monsters die of embarrassment?"

Aoife tossed him a small pouch without looking up.

"Windseeds. They'll carry your warnings farther than your wit ever will."

Chalupa gave a short, affronted sniff but said nothing, nose twitching as though he already distrusted the pouch's rustle. His attention shifted when Aoife slid a thick, leather-bound tome into Griffon's pack. Its cover looked like bark that had been pressed flat and polished, etched with grooves that pulsed faintly, as if they'd once been roots.

"What's that?" Chalupa asked, tail curling, voice wary.

"The Veilroot Codex," Aoife said. "A book to be listened to, not read. It hears the forest. When you're lost, it will show the way forward. Not always the way you want, but the way you need."

Frankie felt a shiver thread through her as she took it all in, the tools, the charms, the quiet gravity of each gift. This wasn't packing. It was outfitting a myth, every piece humming with stories that had begun long before her. Even the air seemed thicker, expectant, as though the cottage walls knew the weight of what was being gathered within them. At last, Griffon moved to the door and pulled it open. A breeze slipped in, sharp with pine and memory, cool with secrets. The forest stirred beyond the threshold, vast, waiting, no longer quiet.

"It's time," was all he said.

Frankie glanced once more around the cottage. The hearth flickered low, shadows bending in farewell. On the table, the scroll still glowed faintly, stubborn as an ember. The magic in her chest thrummed in answer, no longer foreign, no longer silent. She turned to Aoife. She stepped close, cupping Frankie's face in both hands. Her palms smelled faintly of rosemary and ash.

"Trust yourself," she murmured. "The forest will challenge you. But it will cradle you too. Listen to it, and it will not let you stray."

Frankie drew a breath, feeling the air settle around her. Her hand tightened on the staff, the runes answering with a faint shimmer.

"I'll find the path," she said, and it didn't sound like a vow.

Aoife's smile deepened, fierce and ancient, carrying the weight of a hundred winters. "No, love," she said softly, though her voice rang like iron. "You won't find a path. You'll forge your own and the world will remember where you've walked."

With that, they stepped across the threshold, and the forest exhaled. Far beyond the village gates, deep in the unseen reaches of the subterranean realm of Velhollow, something ancient stirred, its attention turning toward her with the slow inevitability of tides beneath stone. But here, at the realm's surface layers, where cottage paths met cobblestone streets, the world opened in a way that is straight from the story books.

What stretched past the cottage wasn't a town, nor a glen, nor anything she'd ever known. It was revelation, pure and startling and alive. A realm carved by roots and myth, expanding far below the reach of daylight into forests older than memory, into caverns laced with rivers that glowed blue as sapphires, into mountains hollowed with secret passageways, into glens where moonless light grew from the stone itself. And somewhere beyond all that, deeper still, lay worlds she couldn't yet imagine, untapped layers of land and life and magic that hummed like distant heartbeats. But first, the village. Frankie took one step forward and the town seemed to rise to meet her. Velhollow's village was not built; it was grown.

Homes of living wood and stone curled together like they'd sprouted overnight from the earth's imagination. Vines climbed their walls, shifting color as though painted by passing moods, emerald melting to sapphire, then to burnished rust, leaves fluttering with secrets in the still air. Roof gardens spilled over in waterfalls of thyme, honey-bloom, and strange luminescent flowers that brushed her cheeks when the breeze carried them close.

The cobblestones beneath her boots glowed faintly where she stepped, lit not by spell or device, but by the moss threaded through their cracks, moss that brightened in soft spirals as her weight passed over it, like the village recognizing her footfall. Lanterns hung from arching posts and drifted freely above the streets. They resembled Victorian gas lamps, iron-framed, glass-paned, but inside them danced fireflies, spell-light, and drifting flecks of color that rose and fell like tiny floating suns. Their light cast ripples across the stone in hues of rose, amber, and moss-green, shifting gently with each change of air. There were no wires. No signs buzzing with electricity. No neon glare or heavy hum. Not even the faint drone of distant engines. Velhollow did not thrum with machinery, it breathed with life.

Frankie hadn't realized how violently loud the modern world was until suddenly she stood inside a world without it. No traffic hiss. No digital pull at her thoughts. Just the fullness of sound that wasn't noise at all, birds calling from hidden rafters, river water slipping under polished bridges, the flutter of small wings overhead, a baker's low hum as she kneaded dough behind an open door.

The smells hit next, bread rising in stone ovens, warm spice drifting from market stalls, herbs crushed underfoot, wild fruit ripening in rooftop gardens, and something richer, older, impossible: the scent of earth after rain, though the cavern sky held no clouds. Her pace slowed. Velhollow wasn't quaint, it wasn't charming. It was alive. A place that had never forgotten what the surface world had let slip through its fingers. They passed a market square where fae musicians played flutes fashioned from spun glass. Their notes rose like mist and curled into shapes, birds, blossoms, tiny dragons, before unraveling on the breeze. A woman with hair like woven sunlight drifted past without ever touching the ground. Another, sitting cross-legged on a woven mat, spun threads of daylight between her fingers, weaving skeins that glowed like molten gold.

In a nearby fountain, water arced and shifted, forming fleeting images, a fox, a handful of falling leaves, a star. A man with a beard braided in feathers tipped his hat as they passed.

"Mind the whispering ivy, miss. It likes to eavesdrop."

Frankie turned to look, and the ivy promptly rustled as though it had been caught mid-snoop. Her laugh escaped before she could stop it, breathless, disbelieving, and was swallowed by the village's gentle hum, as though the place had been waiting for that sound.

Frankie spun in a slow circle, heart thundering, eyes burning.

"How… how does this even exist without anyone above knowing?" The words escaped her in a whisper, half-wonder, half-bewilderment.

Aoife smiled, warm and knowing, her voice carrying that easy certainty only Velhollow-born witches ever seemed to have.

"Aye, love. Velhollow is no accident. She's hidden because she chooses to be. A realm carved from ancient magic, a haven for those who never fit the above-world's rules. Humans, fae, shifters, sprites, every creature the world forgot or feared finds shelter here. It's freedom, not secrecy, that built this place. Magic keeps us veiled from wandering eyes. No one enters unless the realm lets them, and the realm only lets in those it means to."

Frankie's breath hitched, not from fear, but from sheer disbelief.

"So anyone here… they're meant to be here?"

Aoife nodded. "Every last soul."

Griffon stepped beside her, grounding and steady, the quiet heat of him slipping through the noise of her wonder. "It's a lot," he murmured, voice low enough for only her. "But it's yours to learn."

Frankie swallowed hard, her senses roaring with color and scent and the wild hum of life around her. Something loosened inside her, a tightness she'd carried so long she'd forgotten it had a name. Belonging. For one suspended breath, prophecy quieted. Fear retreated and wonder bloomed. Velhollow didn't just open before her. It opened for her.

Velhollow unfolded like a living tapestry, forest, river, village, cavern, and sky all stitched together beneath the earth in ways no map could hope to hold. It wasn't merely subterranean; it was layered, vast, a realm spiraling downward and outward into reaches she could not yet imagine. Through cracks in the crystalline ceiling, sunlight refracted in glimmering threads, pouring warmth where no sun should fall. Underground rivers wound silver-bright through mossy ravines. Groves of impossible fruit trees glowed softly from within, roots drinking from hidden aquifers warmed by ancient spells. Far below, deeper than sight, Frankie sensed caverns she had no language for, places where time moved strangely, where legends slept.

Life flourished without a single wire or engine, as if the land itself had chosen to keep breathing the old way. The scent of bread, fresh, yeasty, bright with herbs, floated from a stone bakery hollowed into a hillside. Gardens spilled over rooftops and terraces, lush with vegetables the shape of twisted stars, blossoms that opened and closed with the rhythm of human footsteps, vines that hummed when the wind passed through.

A bright, breathless wonder rose through her, lifting the dim places inside she'd almost forgotten. "It's like stepping into the story every child wishes were real," she whispered, the words tasting half like disbelief and half like coming home.

Chalupa darted toward a food stall, paws barely grazing the cobblestones.

"Do NOT eat that!" Aoife shouted after him, laughing. "It'll have you singing Viking drinking songs, off-key, for days!"

Nyx swooped low overhead, wings slicing through air scented with honey and fir resin. He angled toward a man wearing a cloak made of iridescent fish scales that rippled like shifting tides.

"Oh," Nyx crooned, "I absolutely need to know where he found that."

They moved deeper into Velhollow's heart, and Frankie could hardly keep pace. Magic wasn't subtle here, it wasn't shy or hidden or whispered. It walked openly. Vines climbed the sides of houses sculpted from living wood and stone, their leaves shifting in color, emerald one moment, deep rust the next, as though stirred by some quiet emotion. Floating lanterns drifted above the pathways, bobbing gently in the breeze, casting soft halos of violet and gold.

A creature stepped from the crowd, a man shaped from bark and bone, broad-shouldered, with antlers sweeping up like autumn branches. His eyes, deep and ancient, considered her. Not with suspicion. With appraisal. With recognition. He gave a subtle nod, then slipped back into the throng.

Before Frankie could breathe, a youngling darted from a cluster of glowing ferns, barefoot, bright-eyed, hair wild as pollen fluff. She pressed a sprig of lavender into Frankie's palm. The petals buzzed softly, tingling against her skin.

"For luck," the youngling whispered, then vanished, her laughter light as chimes in the breeze.

Frankie cradled the lavender sprig as though it were a fragile promise, its petals humming faintly against her palm. The village around them still glowed with marvels, floating lanterns, wandering motes of light, vines whispering their colors, but the warmth in the air began to shift. Like a room cooling when someone slips away. She felt it first in the way conversations thinned. Laughter clipped short. Eyes lingered a fraction too long. The magic itself seemed to withdraw by degrees, drifting higher, dimming its glow as though uncertain of her place beneath it.

Griffon noticed the change before she gave it voice. He watched the light leave the lanterns nearest her, watched a trio of sprites step wide around her as if brushing against the hem of her coat might cost them something. And then he saw Frankie, her shoulders going still, her breath catching around the lavender sprig she held like an anchor she wasn't sure how to use yet.

"*She's not one of us,*" someone murmured.

"A Greyvale walking freely, dangerous."

"Too soft. Too untrained. Too above."

Frankie's fingers tightened around the sprig, the magic in it fluttering like a frightened bird. She turned her head just enough to find Griffon in her periphery, a small, instinctive movement, seeking steadiness, perhaps, or simply the nearest thing that didn't pull away. Griffon felt something inside him brace, the way the land does before a storm. A quiet, protective gravity unfurled in him, slow and certain.

Then the goblins appeared. Two small figures, perched atop warped crates in a narrow slip of alley, half-wreathed in mossy shadow. Their eyes gleamed like wet glass, their grins sharp as chipped quartz. They froze mid-squabble when Frankie passed, their attention snapping to her with the keenness of scavengers scenting a story. The first leaned forward, nostrils flaring.

“Greyvale-born,” he croaked. “Soft and thin. Let’s see how long she lasts before the woods devour her.”

The second chittered, a broken laugh. “Unless she’s got her gran’s spark hiding in those bones. Might vanish quick once the dark starts prowling.” Their voices twisted through the lantern-light like smoke, high, sharp, gleeful in their cruelty.

Frankie flinched, nothing dramatic, just a tiny tremor that passed through her like a shiver of rain. But Griffon caught it. Of course he did. “What… what exactly is the Greyvale?” Frankie asked softly. “Is it a place? Or… a person?”

The uncertainty slipped out before she could catch it, not fear exactly, but the disorienting sense of realizing she was missing a word everyone else seemed to share.

Aoife moved, her hand settling at Frankie’s elbow, warm and anchoring. “Not here, mo chroí,” she said under her breath, already guiding her a step aside. “They like to turn questions into sport. We’ll speak of it when there aren’t teeth in the listening.”

The goblins snickered behind them, voices dissolving into the dark. Frankie didn’t look back, though Griffon did, and the look he gave the goblins carried enough warning to send even the boldest of them scrambling. They walked on, but the air around Frankie still felt bruised. Griffon saw it in the way her steps faltered, in how her shoulders drew tighter beneath the weight of a name she had never heard before.

The word *Greyvale* echoed in Frankie’s thoughts, turning over and over like a stone warmed by the sun and only now lifted. It wasn’t fear that unsettled her, but recognition, the quiet ache of realizing there had always been a question she hadn’t known how to name. Griffon watched it dawn on her, the subtle shift in her expression, the way her shoulders held as though something inside her had finally found its outline.

Frankie drew a slow breath, steadying herself. “I didn’t choose to be from there,” she said quietly. “Or to be… whatever they think that makes me.” The words weren’t defensive. They were honest.

Aoife’s response came without judgment, her voice warm with old knowing. “No,” she said, meeting Frankie’s gaze. “None of us chooses where the seed first takes root. But we do choose whether we grow crooked in the shade… or reach for the light when we find it.”

Griffon's voice dropped low, meant only for her. "Where you came from doesn't decide who you are down here." She lifted her eyes to him and he held her gaze. "And it certainly doesn't decide what you become."

Something unspoken moved between them then, soft, deep, impossible to name but impossible to ignore. Even Chalupa, nibbling on a pastry in the distance, paused just long enough to groan. "Oh stars above... he's doing the gaze again. Someone fetch me a blindfold."

Frankie flushed. Griffon didn't look away, and the magic around them, hesitant moments ago, began to warm and gather again, like light returning to a dimmed room. In his eyes she saw no doubt no hesitation, no echo of the whispers naming her outsider. He looked at her as though she were something the realm recognized, leaned toward, awaited.

"Let them talk," he said softly, the words settling warm between them. "They see where you came from. I see where you're going." Hope moved through her, quiet and fragile, but fierce enough to unsettle her balance. She held his gaze a moment longer than she meant to and then they walked on.

The path curved gently, narrowing between two great roots before widening in a sudden breath of space. The trees stepped back as though parting for someone expected, not merely passing through. Light changed, softer, older, the kind that felt like dawn and dusk woven together. And then she saw it. A single monolith rising from the forest floor, tall as a tower and worn smooth as riverstone. The air around it thickened, humming with a stillness that was not silence but waiting.

Frankie slowed. "Griffon... Aoife... what is that?"

This time Aoife answered without hesitation, stepping shoulder to shoulder with her, her voice hushed. "The Stone of Vehlan, love."

Frankie blinked. "Vehlan?"

"Aye." Aoife's eyes softened with both caution and awe. "Old as the first breath of magic. Some say older still. It marks the heart of Velhollow's ley-thread... the place where destiny listens closest."

Frankie stared. The stone was neither beautiful nor frightening, yet it was both. It drew her with a quiet gravity that felt frighteningly familiar, like the first pull of a tide she didn't know she was standing in. Griffon watched her carefully as Aoife continued, her voice woven with memory.

"This place doesn't reveal itself to just anyone. Most who travel these paths walk right past without ever seeing it. But when the stone wants to be seen… it appears."

Frankie's fingers tightened around her staff, the wood warming beneath her hand in a slow, insistent answer. The hum inside her deepened, swelling like a note rising from deep water.

"What does it do?" she whispered.

Aoife's expression shifted. "They say the Stone of Vehlan listens to the truth beneath your skin. It shows you what threads bind you, past, present, and those still unwoven. Light as well as the dark and the shadows and everything that lie between."

Frankie swallowed. "What if someone touches it?"

"If you touch it," Aoife murmured, "it shows you who you might become… and who you could be, if you lose your way."

Frankie looked on and Griffon stepped closer, not touching her, simply near enough that she felt anchored. "Not everyone is meant to see their whole truth," he said quietly. "Some aren't ready. Some never are."

Frankie didn't respond, she couldn't. All around them, quietly the people of Velhollow had gathered. Sprites perched on twisted branches. A wisp drifted near the roots, its glow dim and thoughtful. A man with antlers tipped his head in slow acknowledgment, while a cluster of cloaked figures stood still as carved stone, watching with unreadable eyes. Every one of them looked at her. Not with hostility or with kindness, either, just expectant. The forest leaned in. Even the light itself seemed to bend toward her, softening around the edges as though asking a question she did not yet know how to answer.

Frankie's hand tightened around the staff once more. "I feel it," she whispered. "It's calling to me."

Aoife laid a steadying hand on her arm, warm as sunlight through leaves, her reply was soft. "That's because it is."

The air around the stone shifted, as if the realm itself lingered in the space between one breath and the next.Then Velhollow exhaled. Magic skimmed across the clearing in a gentle, shimmering ripple that lifted the edges of Frankie's hair and scattered motes of light like startled fireflies. The forest shifted, branches rustling as though something small and sprightly darted through the shadows, eager to be part of whatever came next.

The moment broke, softly, inevitably, and then … *POP!*

A whirring blur of wings, a tiny figure shot into view, narrowly missing Frankie's nose.

"*Pardon, pardon!* I am late, but only fashionably so!" he exclaimed, his voice light and lilting, thick with a charming French accent.

Frankie blinked, stepping back in surprise as the pixie hovered before her, no taller than her hand, yet somehow carrying himself with the confidence of a king. His iridescent wings caught the light in quick, liquid flashes of blue and gold with every rapid flutter. He wore a waistcoat stitched from velvet petals and dewdrops, the tiniest buttons glinting like stars. A perfectly curled mustache framed his impish grin, and his dark eyes shone with bright, unmistakable mischief. Sweeping his arms wide, he spun into a dramatic mid-air bow, nearly tumbling headfirst from the flourish.

"Benoît Flècheplume, *Keeper of Enchanted Whimsy*, and your most humble service!" he announced, as if the world had been waiting for him alone.

Before Frankie could reply, he waved a dismissive hand toward the wary onlookers, his wings buzzing with indignation. "Bah! Do not listen to them, *ma chère*," he said with a theatrical roll of his eyes. "They are like old bread, dry, and far too crusty."

Frankie couldn't help the laugh that bubbled out. "It's… nice to meet you."

"Nice?" Benoît gasped, clutching his chest with theatrical offense. "*Non, non!* It is *extraordinaire*!"

He twirled midair, scattering a few glittering feathers like celebratory confetti, then leaned in with a wink that carried the weight of someone greeting a moment he'd been waiting ages to witness, like this tiny sliver of time was a page torn straight from an old fairytale.

"Imagine it, the wind shifts, the veil thins, the stories ripple. You, here, finally listening to the magic instead of calling it a dream."

Chalupa padded over with a skeptical flick of his tail. "Still handing out destiny like party favors, wing-boy?"

Benoît darted a loop in the air with a smirk. "Ah, *mon ami*, someone must keep the sparkle in the story."

"You're one enchanted acorn short of a tree," Chalupa grumbled.

"Ah now, enough," Aoife said. "Fifty years is a long time to be chewing the same old bone. I'm surprised you've any teeth left."

Frankie blinked, looking between them. "Let what go?"

Benoît brightened. "Ah! A masterpiece of illusion. I enchanted his fur once, glowed emerald in the moonlight. *Très chic.*"

Chalupa narrowed his eyes. "I was the laughingstock of half the forest."

"The other half was inspired," Benoît countered, utterly unbothered. "You lit up the glen like a very surly lantern."

Aoife shook her head with amused exasperation. "He's never forgiven you."

Frankie's laughter lingered as they walked, loosening the tightness that had knotted beneath her skin. Benoît drifted along at her shoulder now, his wings scattering flashes of color across the path like falling shards of stained glass. He cleared his throat with the gravity of someone preparing to make a royal proclamation.

"If you intend to reach Zyphirion's *clairière*, his glade, within the forest's quiet heart, without the path deciding you look like a snack," Benoît announced, fluttering closer with exaggerated gravity, "you will require a guide."

He tilted his head, eyes gleaming. "Someone the forest already knows. Someone it hasn't tried to eat yet."

Chalupa snorted. "So definitely not you."

Benoît placed a hand dramatically over his tiny chest. "How dare you, *monsieur*. I have navigated these woods since before you were a whisper in your mother's whiskers."

"Still not a brag," Chalupa muttered.

But Benoît sailed on, gesturing grandly toward the wild-spun world around them.

"You have not truly seen Velhollow yet, *ma chère*. There is a glade where the tea leaves read you back. Ask kindly and the willows share stories your soul misplaced. And the scarves woven near the river?" He clasped both hands to his heart. "Spun from morning mist. They follow the wind, but only if you flirt with them properly."

Chalupa padded ahead, tail flicking. "Or ignore them completely. Enchanted scarves love a challenge."

Benoît gasped, horrified. "*Mon dieu*. Heathen."

Aoife hid a smile. "Flirting scarves aside, Benoît, do you truly know these woods well enough to lead us?"

The pixie stopped midair. His posture straightened; his wings slowed to a faint, glimmering drift. For the first time, the jest fell from his face, replaced by something steadier. And deep-rooted.

"*Madame*," he said softly, "the pixie clans owed fealty to the

Verdant line long before memory learned to speak it. When your kind walks these woods, the forest listens differently."

Frankie just looked on.

Benoît bowed midair, small, graceful, earnest. "It would be my honor to escort the Verdant Witch. Not because the paths are dangerous, though they are, but because it is our way. We guide the green-blooded when they rise."

A tiny, wry smile touched his mouth. "And you, *ma chère*, have begun to rise."

Chalupa groaned. "Wonderful. She's got enchanted lumber flirting and now ancient pixie fealty."

But Griffon had gone still. Not tense, something quieter, deeper, like stone settling after a tremor. He stepped slightly closer to Frankie, close enough that she felt the heat of him like a quiet shield at her side. His gaze flicked to Benoît, not with distrust, but with a kind of knowing respect earned only through shared history.

"The pixie clans don't offer loyalty lightly," Griffon said, his voice pitched low. "Not after what happened in the Deep Warrens. Not since the Sundering of Thorns."

Benoît flinched, barely, but enough for Griffon to see it. The pixie's wings stilled mid-beat, their bright, jewel-bright colors dulling as if shadow had passed over them. When he spoke, he leaned closer, his voice no more than breath and memory.

"Ancient grief," Benoît whispered. "Ancient debt."

Frankie's brows knit, concern threading through her voice.

"What happened there?"

Griffon exhaled slowly, the sound low and controlled, as if releasing something long held. "The Deep Warrens were once a refuge," he said. "A place beneath the roots of the world where the pixie clans gathered when the surface turned hostile, when wars and hungry magic made the open air unsafe. They trusted the stone. Trusted the wards. Trusted the promises made by those who swore to guard the passages." His jaw tightened, just slightly. "Those promises failed." He did not look at Benoît when he continued, but his words were careful, reverent.

"During the Sundering of Thorns, the Warrens were breached. Dark magic was drawn down through forgotten veins of the earth. Entire clans were trapped, sealed in, or worse, left unprotected when the wards collapsed. Pixie blood fed the stone that night. Their songs were cut short. The realm survived, but the pixie folk paid the price."

Benoît's wings trembled once before resuming their slow, measured rhythm. "We lost elders," he said softly. "Children. Keepers of old light. And we learned what trust costs."

Frankie swallowed, the weight of it settling into her chest. "So their loyalty..."

"Is never casual," Griffon finished gently. "When pixie-folk turn toward someone, it is not curiosity or convenience. It is remembrance. It is a choice made with the ghosts of the Deep Warrens watching."

He finally looked at her then, really looked, and something in his gaze unraveled far more than his words ever could. There was protection there, and resolve, shaped by a history he rarely named aloud. Griffon understood what it meant for the pixie clans to align themselves with someone again. Their loyalty was bound to old wounds carved deep into Velhollow's past, to blood spilled in darkness so others might walk in light.

When Benoît drifted closer to Frankie in quiet allegiance, Griffon moved too, instinctive, subtle, a half-step that placed him nearer without him fully choosing it. It wasn't duty that brought him there. It wasn't caution. It was something older, something that settled into his bones before thought could interfere, as if the land itself had leaned and he had followed.

Frankie felt the air shift, warm and charged, and she looked away first, startled, unsure of what had sparked between them so suddenly, so unmistakably. Her breath caught, the moment brushing too close to something she wasn't ready to name.

Griffon didn't look away.

He stood where instinct had drawn him, his presence steady, grounded, the space between them tight as the moment before a spell takes shape, when the world holds its breath, waiting to see what will be spoken aloud.

"Pixie loyalty matters," he said softly. "They don't pledge themselves lightly. When they turn toward someone, it means the old magic is stirring around that person. It means the realm itself has begun to choose."

His gaze remained on her, unwavering, as if he already knew the weight of that truth, and the cost that would follow it.

Frankie swallowed, her voice small and unguarded. "Choose what?"

Griffon's expression softened, something tender creeping through the gravity in his eyes. "Which paths open for you," he said. "And which dangers start moving in your direction."

His voice lowered, carrying an honesty that left no room for doubt. "Their loyalty is a sign, Frankie. A powerful one. It means you're stepping into a story the realm remembers, and some parts of that story have teeth."

Her breath hitched, not in fear, but in the strange, quiet certainty that she was being seen in a way she had never been seen before. Griffon stood close as if the realm wasn't the only thing choosing her.

Benoît spun once in a sparkling ribbon of light, his wings scattering glitter like celebratory sighs. "We depart before the paths decide to tango with themselves again. You will follow me, *oui*?" He wagged a tiny finger at Frankie. "No wandering. No touching strange vines. No singing to roots unless you have a death wish." He tapped his chest proudly. "Though you, *ma Sorcière Verdoyante*, my Verdant Witch, perhaps you could survive it."

Chalupa sighed. "We're doomed."

But Griffon kept his gaze on Frankie for one breath longer than was polite, long enough to say without words: *I'm here. Whatever comes next, I'm here.*

From the shadowed path ahead, a woman stepped into view, cloaked in layered feathers that caught the dim light like oil sliding over stone. Her presence carried the hush of ancient places, the kind of silence that lingered in catacombs and sealed groves, where memory waited in the dark. Her eyes, dark as obsidian and just as sharp, found Frankie and held her in place as surely as a pin pressed to a map.

"Child of the Greyvale," she said, her voice a blade wrapped in velvet. "You walk among roots that remember betrayal. Magic may let you pass… but it never forgets a wound."

Wind hissed through the leaves with no breeze to stir it, a soft creaking groan echoed from somewhere deep in the trees, wood stretching, or warning. The forest didn't move, not exactly, but it shifted its attention, like something ancient had just stirred and taken interest. Before anyone could speak, she turned and vanished into the trees, her cloak rustling like a thousand autumns passing at once.

Benoît fluttered closer, wings slower now, his usual gleam dulled but not gone. "Well," he murmured, his voice a low ribbon of sound, "that one had a tongue like nettle wine steeped in old grudges. Perhaps next time we send Chalupa to greet her. He has a certain… rugged diplomacy."

Chalupa grunted. "I'd rather chew glass."

Nyx dropped from a high branch, feathers whispering against the air. "She wasn't speaking just to you, Frankie. She was speaking to all of us. The forest remembers everything, especially the things we'd rather it forget."

Chalupa, unable to drop this particular bone continued. "You know, they never liked me," he grumbled. "Even as a kitten."

Aoife, who had been watching the trees, turned with a dry glance. "They don't trust creatures born of cleverness and mischief. Too many of your kind wove riddles into roots… and tore them loose before the truth took hold."

Benoît gave a quiet laugh, but something in it was different, warmer, heavier. He touched Frankie's shoulder with a hand light as a whisper.

"Don't let it settle too deep. Yes, magic forgets nothing and trust must be earned… but it remembers kindness, too."

Frankie nodded slowly, the words anchoring her even as the forest whispered around them.

Nyx landed nearby, silent, eyes sharp. "Velhollow doesn't trust easily." he quipped. "Not until you prove you belong."

"Even then, love," Aoife added, "they'll test you, sometimes just for fun. That's the old magic, wild, wary, and not free from whimsy. It knows the cost of missteps."

Griffon had taken the lead again, eyes sweeping the path ahead. "Keep watch. The forest knows what you fear, and it's never shy about showing it to you."

Frankie nodded, adjusting her grip on the staff. The trees had shifted again, subtly. The air had turned metallic, like cold iron laced through fog. This path didn't welcome blindly.

Benoît's voice came again, lighter now, a thread of humor weaving back into it, though softer than before. "The trees," he sighed, wings catching the shifting light. "So full of mystery. They guard the old ways like dragons curled around ancient hoards, silent, watchful, and slow to trust."

He twirled midair with a self-satisfied hum, then added with a mischievous smirk, "If they had any taste at all, they'd have made *moi* their guardian. A touch of brilliance wouldn't kill them, *non*?"

Chalupa let out a growl that was almost a sigh. "You'd give a headache to a stone. You're like a cursed gemstone, flashy, and impossible to bury deep enough."

Nyx dropped onto a low-hanging branch, his wings settling like dusk. "Most of those end up in a hag's pocket or the bottom of a lake. On purpose."

Benoît only grinned wider, utterly unbothered. "Ah, *mais mes chers amis*, my dear friends, who else lights the way through shadow quite like *moi*?"

Frankie laughed, the sound cracking through the tension like sunlight through fog. Aoife sighed and muttered something about "peacocks and pixie dust," but kept walking. The forest watched them go, leaves whispering like parchment pages turning, toward whatever came next. Their laughter, fading into the hush beneath the trees. The path narrowed. Roots coiled like sleeping serpents beneath their feet, and the air shifted, cooler, and heavier with silence. The deeper they walked, the stranger the quiet became. It wasn't just the hush of an old forest, it was listening. The very trees seemed to lean inward, no longer content to merely observe. These trees weren't just old, they were ancient sentinels of the first magic, from before spellwork had names or rules. Up ahead, a low rumble stirred, deeper than thunder from the bones of the earth, and the group stilled. Frankie gripped her staff, the carved runes glowing in time with the unseen rhythm beneath her skin. The light built steadily, a heartbeat that wasn't hers.

"What is that?" she whispered.

Aoife slowed, her hand brushing something unseen inside her satchel, her face taut with memory. "It's not the Veil," she said. "This is older."

The sound rose again, a deep, resonant roll. The forest stilled with it as shadows thickened between the trees. Frankie's heart beat faster, but not from fear. It was something else, like that uneasy feeling of being watched.

Benoît hovered close, wings whispering softly. "Some places in Velhollow, *ma chère*... they do not guard the way. They measure you."

Frankie's eyes caught on the archway ahead, just visible, yet alive with a faint glow, as though the stone itself were rousing from sleep.

"What does it see?" she whispered.

Nyx's feathers rustled. "It sees through you. It knows what you carry."

Aoife stepped closer. "This is truth-magic. The arch opens only for those who stand before it as they truly are. Lie to it, or to yourself and it will know."

Griffon's jaw tightened. "And if it... doesn't like what it finds?"

"The forest will decide," Aoife said, her voice low. "And the forest does not offer second chances."

Benoît drifted nearer, his voice gentler than before, touched with something almost solemn. "This place, *ma chère*... it asks for honesty, not in word alone, but in spirit. It wants to see the you beneath every mask."

Frankie's breath thinned. "But what if I don't know who that is yet?"

He floated closer, wings catching the light in soft, opalescent flashes. "*Mais oui,* you do," he mused. "You simply fear the answer."

The arch brightened, gold spreading across bark and stone like dawn spilling through branches. Frankie steadied herself, heart lifting and sinking all at once. Instinctively she looked to Aoife. Her grandmother met her gaze, and gave a single nod. Griffon did the same, his eyes anchoring her with quiet certainty. No words were needed. The message passed between them clear as sunlight through leaves: *You're not facing this alone.*

Benoît's voice came gently, the hush of velvet and candlelight. "*Ferme les yeux, ma chère*. Close your eyes… and let it come, all that is needed is a single moment. Small, perhaps, but heavy with truth."

Frankie obeyed, lashes falling shut. The hum of the arch moved through her like a river beneath ice, deep, insistent, inevitable. The forest fell away. The light behind her eyes dimmed, then bloomed into an old, forgotten memory.

It was Tuesday. Meatloaf day.

The cafeteria always smelled wrong on meatloaf day, like ketchup trying to disguise something it had no business covering. Frankie sat at the long table under the buzzing lights, swinging her legs, waiting for lunch to be over. Outside the high windows, the sky hung low and gray. Rain tapped down in fine pinpricks, not enough to make puddles, just enough to turn the air earthy, like worms and wet leaves.

She'd brought Albert in her lunchbox.

Albert was a frog with wise, watchful eyes and bumpy green skin, and Frankie thought he was the most magical thing she'd ever found. She'd built him a temporary moss bed in a yogurt cup, damp and earthy the way frogs liked it. She'd been careful. Thoughtful. She couldn't wait to show the others. Maybe they'd laugh in a good way. Maybe someone would say, "Cool frog," or ask to hold him.

When the lunch bell clanged and the room erupted into noise, Frankie flipped open her lunchbox right there at the table.

Albert blinked.

That was when it all went wrong. One girl screamed. Chairs scraped back hard enough to shriek. A few kids recoiled like the frog might leap across the table and explode. A teacher rushed over, face tight and sharp, and snapped, "Put that away. Now. Before someone gets ideas."

Ideas of what, Frankie never knew.

She closed the lunchbox slowly, carefully, like she might hurt him if she moved too fast. Albert went back into the dark.

Frankie shrugged like it didn't matter. Like she hadn't expected anything else. But something inside her folded in on itself, small and light. Like Albert. Packed away where he wouldn't bother anyone.

Later, when they were sent outside for recess, the drizzle had settled in for good. Frankie stood near the fence, lunchbox still clutched in her hands, cuffs of her jeans muddy, hair puffed and frizzed by the damp. She looked down at herself and saw what they saw.

The weird girl.

The one who brought frogs instead of dolls. The one who never got picked first. Or second. Or third. The one who hovered at the edge of games, pretending not to care. The other girls looked like her mother, smooth hair, small voices, practiced smiles. Frankie never did. Standing there in the rain, Albert quiet in his makeshift home, she understood something with a clarity that surprised her.

She wasn't like them and she wasn't going to be. No matter how hard she brushed her hair flat. No matter how carefully she smiled the way her mother taught her. No matter how quiet she tried to make herself. That day, in the drizzle, she stopped trying to fit into something that had never wanted her in the first place.

She wasn't a mistake. She was just the wrong shape for their box. Stars don't fit neatly. They have edges. Strange points. They shine anyway. And Albert, tucked safe in the dark, was proof of that.

Her eyes opened, bright with something fierce, her voice rose into the hush, clear and unwavering, like wind cutting through stone. "I was never meant for that world," she said. "I stood in silence. Lived in shadows. The magic isn't just around me, it's in me. It always was."

And with that, the gateway didn't simply glow, it stirred. A deep hum rolled through it, the kind that felt older than stories, as if the carvings had been waiting for someone to call them back to life. Then the light rose, bright but not harsh, wild yet strangely welcoming. Gold and pale fire wove through every etched line, racing along the runes as though recognizing the moment they had been crafted for. The trees responded first. Their branches leaned in, leaves catching the radiance like a quiet salute. Even the air gathered itself around her, alive with that charged stillness that comes just before the world decides to change. Symbols lifted from the arch in slow, deliberate arcs, bold, certain, alive with purpose. Not a hesitant glow, not a half-waking flicker, but truths stepping forward to meet her. They spun like constellations clicking into place, flaring with meaning older than memory. Around Frankie, they circled, not judging, not testing, just knowing. Then, soft as breath, they aligned into a perfect ring, a crown of flame and silver thread suspended above the gateway. Not to challenge her… but to welcome her through.

Beneath Frankie's feet, the earth answered with a low, steady thrum, as if the ground recognized her presence and rose to meet it. The runes along her staff brightened in response, no longer simply warm but attentive, tuned to her like a living chord. They sensed the crack inside her, the uncertainty she carried, and held fast. From somewhere deep below, a vibration stirred, a quiet acknowledgment, a note that wasn't sound so much as certainty. Velhollow itself, vast as myth, seemed to speak her name without a single word. Then the light shifted and the symbols along the arch narrowed to fine lines of gold and withdrew into the stone, their brilliance softening until the entire gateway settled into a deep, waiting hush. The flames beside it shrank to steady embers. The stillness that followed was full, deliberate, as though the forest had reached its conclusion: *Yes.*

Without force or fanfare, the gateway parted. A pale path revealed itself on the other side, threading into the woods in a clean, unwavering line, quiet as memory, sure as fate. It offered no assurances of safety or ease. But it opened. It accepted her. It knew her, and it stepped aside to let her through. Behind her, Benoît hovered in the dim glow. His wings muted to soft color, his usual sparkle gone, replaced by a hush she had never heard from him.

When he spoke, it was with a gentleness shaped by awe rather than mischief. "*Voilà*, … the forest has made its choice." he said. "It knows you now, *ma chère* and more than that… you know yourself. And you are more than enough, *oui*?"

Frankie turned to him, still unsteady, the truth she'd spoken echoing through her like a bell struck deep. "How did you do that?" she asked, her voice frayed with wonder.

He smiled, small and sure, curved with time and memory.

"There are few of my kind left," he said. "We are *Seers of the Turning Paths, Whispercrafters.* We don't summon visions, we listen for what already sings in your bones and help it find its voice." He floated closer, wings barely stirring the air, his gaze warm and unwavering. “But I did not do this alone,” he added gently. “You let yourself be seen. You did the hardest part.”

Aoife stepped forward, her gaze softened by recognition. “You never said.”

Benoît gave a shrug, light as spun sugar. “Ah, but did you ever ask, *madame*?” A wink, a glint. “Besides, mystery is so much more flattering than explanation.”

Frankie studied him, really studied him, not as a flicker of whimsy or a flash of mischief, but as something rare, loyal, and unmistakably true. “So… you came to help me find my truth?”

Benoît’s expression softened. The usual mischief dimmed, replaced by something steady and strangely solemn. “*Oui, ma chère.* You’ve walked far. I wished to be certain you reached this moment.” His voice lowered, the tone of twilight settling across still water. “I believed you would and I wanted to witness it.”

The clearing held its breath as the path beyond the gateway glowed pale and unwavering, waiting like a question that had outlasted centuries.

Benoît drifted back, wings catching faint light in fleeting flashes. “But this,” he said gently, “is where I turn aside. The road ahead does not open for me. I follow wonder, and wonder rarely stays in one place.”

Frankie’s chest tightened. “You’re not coming with us?”

He offered a wistful bow. “*Non, non.* I am no bearer of destiny. I am the spark, *ma sorcière verdoyante…* not the flame.”

He pressed a hand to his tiny chest, sincerity softening every bright edge of him. “But *mon dieu*, how fiercely you will burn.”

With a whirl of iridescent wings, he ascended, leaving a drifting trail of soft color in the air behind him, like joy imprinting itself on the dark.

“*Et souvenez-vous*,” he called, voice thinning into the canopy, “joy is armor. Do not let the shadows persuade you.”

Then he vanished, quick as thought, quiet as a wish. Frankie turned to Aoife, then to Griffon. Their nods were quiet vows, steadfast, unshaken, meant to be carried into whatever came next. The forest stilled around them, expectant. She drew a breath that felt both borrowed and entirely her own and stepped toward the gateway. It did not close, instead, it held open, bright, intentional, as though the realm itself had paused to watch her cross, turning a hidden page not touched in generations. A faint current brushed her cheek, neither warning nor welcome, but a promise that the story from this point on would not move gently. Frankie stepped forward and walked into the waiting light, toward a path that would change everything she thought she knew of magic, destiny, and most all… of herself.

Chapter 18

The light beyond the gateway was not warm, it was cool and clear as moonlit water, and just as untouchable. As Frankie stepped through, the air shifted around her, thinning as though the very atmosphere weighed and measured each breath she took. Nothing here had grown wild the way the rest of Velhollow had. This place had been shaped with intention, tended by hands or forces long vanished. Even the trees stood differently, tall and narrow, their silver-veined trunks smooth as if rubbed by centuries of quiet devotion. They didn't sway, they watched. The path tightened underfoot. Roots webbed across the soil, coursing with faint currents of magic deep below the surface, ancient currents of power moving like forgotten rivers. Ahead, the trees arched inward, not swaying, not bending from weather, but shifting of their own will, forming a narrow throat of wood and shadow. The hush thickened with every step, heavy as expectant silence before a truth is spoken aloud. No one talked. It wasn't fear, it was respect for whatever waited here, something older than Velhollow's name, older than its stories.

Frankie's staff glowed softly in her palm, its light no longer coaxing, no longer uncertain. It felt steady now, as though it understood more than she could name and was holding that understanding for her until she was ready to carry it herself. Her fingers brushed Griffon's as the path narrowed. He didn't speak, just threaded his hand through hers, firm and grounding. Not romantic, more of a silent promise to be a presence at her side that asked for nothing and offered everything that mattered.

The forest pressed closer. The air thickened with a strange awareness, brushing her skin. Her thoughts were testing her in the quiet, patient way of something that had outlived ages and still endured. She felt it sift through her intent, searching for cracks in her resolve. Then the trees ahead twisted. Deliberately. Their trunks curled inward, bark spiraling, roots tightening like clasped fingers. A gateway took shape where no opening had existed before, crooked, uneven, purposeful. A threshold created in real time, as though the forest itself had decided to let them through.

Aoife slowed, raising a hand to the warped bark. Faded runes pulsed beneath her fingers, shifting like thoughts passing under skin. "This place," she murmured, "is choosing how to receive us."

Griffon moved forward, jaw tight. "Then we shouldn't make it wait."

The ground softened under their steps, a faint give like earth unsure whether it wanted to bear their weight. The air deepened, charged, not sound, but sensation, moving through them in a way that felt like a warning wrapped in welcome.Behind them, the trees stayed open, but the gate ahead, whatever shape it had taken for them, altered again, the form dissolving as if it had never been wood at all. The forest was rearranging itself and it was doing so with them inside it.

"Does anyone else feel that?" Frankie whispered.

Her voice barely broke the air, but it carried like a thought she couldn't keep to herself. A chill slid down her arms, raising the fine hairs along her skin. It wasn't cold, not really, but a pressure, like the air had thickened just enough to make her lungs notice. Her pulse ticked louder in her ears. She didn't know what she felt exactly, only that something had shifted in a way the body understands before the mind does. The forest was no longer simply quiet. It was listening, and deciding.

Griffon's answer came low, sharp. "We're not alone."

They instinctively drew together, their steps smaller now, tighter. The mist crept in closer, thickening like breath turned visible. It stole the outlines of the world, softening edges, swallowing movement. Every root, every shadow seemed to stretch the wrong way. The light changed too, flickering as if unsure whether it wanted to stay, then it came like a dark whisper. It slithered across the clearing like smoke spun into thread, curling through the trees and winding between their ankles with the quiet insistence of something that had always been there, just waiting to be seen. It was more a feeling than a sound. A breath against the skin of the world. Like the forest had inhaled and forgotten how to exhale. Frankie felt it before she saw it, something in her bones stilled, then pulled tight, like a string ready to snap. The mist parted as if from intention, purpose.

Then it surged. A figure tore forth from the dark, a thing not made, but unmade. Born of smoke and shadow, its form refused to hold shape. It flickered in and out of focus, like it belonged to a different plane entirely, one the forest itself didn't want to acknowledge. Its edges twisted like liquid smoke, writhing and recoiling in a ceaseless dance of undoing. Where it moved, the air thinned, and the warmth drained from the world. It didn't walk. It glided. Its steps made no sound, but each one carried the weight of something ancient and wrong. Its eyes found her, twin coals, lit from within by something more hunger than fire. They locked on Frankie like a claim.

She didn't have time to think as the magic tore through her before thought could catch it, pure, instinctive, and untamed. It surged up her spine and down her arm like lightning through wet bark, blistering with purpose. Her fingers jerked upward, and the energy leapt free, a blinding bolt of white-gold light. But it wasn't aimed or shaped and it definitely wasn't controlled. The magic veered hard to the left, missing the creature entirely. It struck a nearby tree with a crack like the sky splitting in half. The chest exploded down the middle, splinters flying like shrapnel, the sound echoing through the clearing in a riot of thunder and splintered wood. Leaves shrieked in protest. Bark peeled back like skin. The impact was raw and brutal.

Frankie staggered back, hand still outstretched, heart hammering like hooves on stone. The magic had come so fast, like it had been waiting, pacing just beneath her skin, too wild to be patient any longer. It had surged through her in a flash, fierce and blinding. It felt like hers, yes, but only in the way a wildfire might belong to the match that struck it. It hadn't listened. It hadn't asked. It had simply come roaring out.

Now, standing in the crackling silence after the blast, with the shattered remains of a tree smoking beside her, she understood something cold and clear, power didn't care if she was ready. It didn't wait for certainty. It didn't coddle the cautious. It came when it was called, and sometimes, even when it wasn't. She had summoned it, and it had answered, but it would not be gentle. Not until she learned to hold the reins. Not until she learned to ride it, shape it, wield it, not merely survive it.

The creature didn't flinch. It advanced, slow and sinuous, gliding through the mist like it was made of the same stuff. Its form coiled and uncoiled, smoke and shadow pulling itself into the shape of menace. It had no mouth, and yet it seemed to smile, a cruel, patient smile that needed no face to be understood. It didn't rush her. It didn't strike. It watched, like a cat toying with something small. Like it had seen this kind of power bloom and falter before. Like it had waited for exactly this moment, her moment, knowing she would break the silence with more magic than control.

"Focus!" Aoife's voice cracked through the air like thunder over stone, sharp and commanding.

She raised her hands in a blur, and golden light bloomed at her fingertips, spiraling outward in a web of glowing thread. With a flick of her wrist, a radiant shield burst into being just as the creature lunged. The impact struck with the force of a battering ram, darkness crashing into light. The shield shuddered but held, golden sparks scattering into the mist like startled fireflies.

For an instant, the clearing burst into gold and shadow, colliding, clashing, then the light tore itself apart. Griffon moved before the silence could return. Heat rolled from him in waves, bending the air, distorting it like desert glass. His body cracked, loud, raw, like a mountainside breaking open. Stone pressed upward beneath his skin, reshaping him with the force of something that had been waiting far too long to rise. Fire ran through him brightening with each breath, each beat, each surrender to the power calling him forward.

He grew taller, fiercer. Skin darkened into volcanic rock traced with molten lines. Wings tore free from his back, vast, jagged, obsidian-edged, unfurling like a storm unchained. Earthen armor rippled across his form, locking into place with the deep groan of shifting earth. His claws formed like forged blades, drawn straight from the world's molten heart. His eyes, once storm-silver, now burned with a brilliance that felt older than fire itself, like the first spark that ever dared to ignite.

With a roar that shook the canopy, Griffon surged forward. His wings cut the air in a storm-hard sweep, carrying him straight into the creature's charge. Claws tore through smoke as flame collided with shadow. The creature shrieked, a jagged, breaking sound, like ice fracturing beneath molten stone, but it did not fall. It twisted sharply, folding in on itself before snapping outward again like dark silk caught in a sudden wind. Tendrils lashed toward him, thin as needles, fast as instinct. They curled around his strike and whipped toward Frankie.

The forest reacted first. Trees groaned, a deep, primal sound, leaning toward one another as though forming a shield. Branches lowered in sweeping arcs. Leaves caught the shifting light like forged metal. Ivy rushed across the ground in tight coils. Vines dropped from the canopy in snapping lines, tangling through the mist. Flowers burst from the underbrush in frantic color, gold, violet, red, opening wide as if to catch whatever threat broke through. The forest didn't merely resist, it rose as the earth heaved beneath Frankie's boots, a swell of root and soil lifting as if it meant to bear her upward and away. But she didn't step back. Something inside her broke open instead, wide, fierce, undeniable. The staff flared bright, runes along its grain answering her as naturally as breath. Her inhale hitched.

Magic surged through her in a single, unbroken sweep, no longer wild or scattered, but gathered at last into its true shape, flowing with the certainty of a river that had finally found its rightful course. Light burst from her hand in a cascade of color: sun-gold, storm-silver, foxglove violet, the deep green of new leaves pushing through dark earth. It poured from her like heat rising off stone after rain, rich and alive, a force too long held back. The clearing flooded with scent, crushed mint, bruised herbs, the metallic tang of a storm gathering on the horizon. Her magic didn't wait for permission. It rose as a tide and she rose with it.

The mist recoiled, the tendrils hissed back. Even the shadow faltered, only for a breath, but it was enough. Its smoky form twisted, blinking in and out of shape, no longer certain of its hold. It had seen her now, not a girl with borrowed magic, not just a conduit, but as the Verdant Witch. The shadow reeled back, flickering and uncertain for the first time. But it wasn't done, not yet. Frankie's magic had shaken it, not destroyed it, and the clearing pulsed with unfinished threat. The mist twisted tighter around their ankles, and the trees groaned low, warning of something older still stirring beneath the soil. Frankie's chest heaved, the staff still glowing hot in her grip, but her hands trembled. Power like that didn't leave her untouched, it rang through her bones, humming, wanting more, too much more.

Aoife stepped to the edge of the clearing, her breath steadying as the air around her crackled with pressure. The veil was thin here, stretched to breaking. She raised her hands, palms lit with quiet fire, and closed her eyes. When she spoke, her voice was low and sure, wrapped in words older than speech, meant to bind, to banish.

"*By root and flame, by blood and star,*
unravel where the shadows are.
By bone of earth and sky once sworn,
return to dark, unshaped, unborn."

The earth rumbled low beneath their feet, a sound like thunder held in the chest. Light sparked along the runes in her cloak, blooming gold one by one. Mist peeled back from her presence and the air bent inward, listening.

"*By breath withheld and name unspoken,*
let the seal of stillness now be broken.
I call the ward. I wake the flame.
Be gone by truth. Be bound by name."

From her fingers, light unfurled, green and silvern and the figure shrieked as the spell wove through it, binding it in threads of glow and grit. It twisted, tried to flee, but the light held fast. Aoife's voice dropped to a final, resonant truth.

"*You do not belong here. Be gone!*"

The final words struck like iron.The shadow began to unravel, peeling away thread by deliberate thread until only a sliver remained, taut and watchful. Contained, but not gone. Aoife swayed, catching herself. Her breath came rough, hands still lifted in the shape of the spell.

"Now!" she said, meeting Frankie's eyes. "I can hold it, but I can't seal it. That part falls to you."

Frankie's throat tightened. "Me? But I don't... "

"Aye, but you do," Aoife said, guiding Frankie's hand forward. "Stop thinking. Let yourself feel. The magic already leans toward you."

The moment Frankie's fingers brushed the glow, the world shifted. The light didn't flare, it deepened, turning lush and wild, green fire threaded with silver. It slid across her skin like cool water poured from a hidden spring, bright and alive. A force rushed through her, not violent, but vast, as though the forest had poured part of itself into her hands. It didn't wait for commands. It responded, swift, certain, instinctive. Magic wrapped around her fingers like ivy waking at rainfall, it bloomed. Her heartbeat steadied into its rise, her breath falling into the same quiet rhythm. The shadow recoiled, shrinking as though it recognized the strength gathering in her touch and wanted no part of it.

Frankie stood at the center of it all, light spiraling from her hands in bright, living currents. Aoife stepped back, not in retreat, but in trust. The spell, once held by another, now settled fully into Frankie's grasp, waiting for her hand alone to shape its end. The moment she let go of fear, something inside her answered. The knowing wasn't in her mind. It was older, bone-deep, breath-bound. The magic didn't need words. It needed will. She released it, raw and instinctive. A sound rose from her throat, low and wild, woven with wind and root and memory. It moved through the clearing like the forest speaking through her. The light didn't grow brighter, it grew truer. Green and silver twisted into something ancient, something nearly forgotten. Her power didn't command. It called.

The shadow twisted back, blinking with a dozen eyes, all narrowing at once. This wasn't just magic, this was Verdant magic. Green magic, this was the forest listening. The light shot from Frankie's palms, piercing the creature like ivy through stone. No violence. Just truth. The shadow screamed. It buckled, convulsed, then unraveled thread by thread into smoke and silence.

Frankie staggered, hands still glowing faintly as the power receded like a tide, quiet but not gone. Her body felt hollowed out and humming, as if something had passed through her and left its mark. The stillness wasn't empty, the trees bowed as leaves hung motionless as the air itself paused and Frankie, standing in the quiet, finally understood, she hadn't wielded the magic. She had become it. Then, from the silence, Aoife's voice came steady and low.

"This is a test, Frankie, the old magic sees all… and it judges."

Frankie turned toward her, dazed. "What do we do?" she whispered.

But before Aoife could answer, the shadow re-emerged and laughed. It wasn't human, more a sound that belonged to bones and burial. The ground lurched, the sky twisted. Trees bent backward, their limbs clawing toward something unseen tore through the clearing, a ripple with no center and no end. Light fractured. Then darkness fell. Frankie stumbled, reaching out, but found nothing.

No Griffon. No Aoife. No Chalupa. No Nyx.

Just silence.

She spun, heart thudding. "Aoife? Griffon?"

Her voice echoed. It sounded strange, warped, like it had to drag itself through water and shadow to be heard. The sound returned twisted, thinned, as though the world itself no longer remembered her name. What came back wasn't comfort, it was the realization that she was alone. The silence wasn't still, it pressed in on her skin and coiled behind her eyes, soft at first, then insistent. The air thickened, heavy with the scent of ash and something faintly sweet, like overripe fruit just starting to rot. The ground beneath her shifted, no longer solid, no longer certain. The forest had vanished. There were no trees, no stars, no path only shadow without shape. The darkness wrapped around her like smoke with weight, curling cold fingers into her thoughts. It didn't scream. It whispered. *You don't belong. You were never enough. You've only ever been pretending.*

Each thought landed like a drop of ink in water, spreading fast. Doubt was first, then came dread. Her pulse raced, but her feet felt rooted in something deeper than earth, something old and waiting. Every fear she had ever buried stirred now, slow and certain, rising like fog from a field left untended. She tried to summon the light again, the green and silver that had bloomed from her hands, but nothing came. No warmth. No shimmer. The magic had gone quiet. Or worse, it was watching. From the void ahead, something began to take shape.

A mirror.

It rose from the dark like a breath drawn from the bones of the earth. It was made from something older than metal or glass, something that pulsed with a memory too ancient to name. Its surface shimmered like oil over water, shifting beneath an unseen moon, alive with a light that didn't reflect. Frankie stood still as it emerged, watching herself form within its shifting surface. But what stared back wasn't quite her. It had her eyes, her mouth, her bearing, but the gaze was off. Slower. Steadier. Like it remembered something she hadn't lived yet. There was weight behind those eyes, heavy with knowing. It wore her face the way ivy wears stone, closely, but never truly part of it. Then the surface rippled, and the mirror began to change. Her reflection flickered, then fractured, not shattered, but transformed. One moment she saw herself as she was, the next as someone else, a version she had never met.

The First… The Fire

She moved like a tempest barely restrained, her steps scorching the unseen ground. Heat shimmered off her skin like breath from a forge. Her eyes were wild, too bright, too sharp, as if flame had learned to see. Her lips curled, not in a smile, but in challenge.

"You think you can wield it?" the Fire hissed, her voice crackling at the edges like burning leaves. Flames danced at her heels, crawling toward Frankie. "You think power bends to kindness? To hope? This power will eat you alive and when it does, they will all burn with you."

Frankie stepped back, throat tight, the heat was clawing at her. She could feel the magic within her stir in response, hungry. The Fire's magic was seductive, intoxicating, like a storm begging to be unleashed. But it wasn't just danger, it was rage without shape, power without care. The mirror rippled again.

The Second… The Void

The fire guttered, swallowed by cold and the clearing dimmed. The next figure emerged in silence, barely formed. Her body wavered, her edges flickering like smoke in a windless room. Her eyes were empty, but not blank. They held despair, wide and deep and unmoving.

"They know," the Void murmured, voice stretched thin, unraveling like thread. "They see your doubt. They expect you to fail. Why try?"

Her words sank like stones. Frankie felt her knees threaten to buckle, the chill seeping in past bone. It wasn't the words, it was the weight behind them, the exhaustion, the ache of carrying too much for too long. This version of her had drowned in it. She had stopped fighting, not out of defeat, but out of certainty that there was no longer anything left to win. Frankie tried to speak, but the words turned to ash in her mouth. The mirror pulsed and then, the final figure stepped forward.

The Third... The Nothing

She came slowly, her presence unhurried, eerily calm. She moved like someone who no longer feared anything, because she had lost everything worth fearing for. Her face was Frankie's, perfectly mirrored. But her eyes were hollow. Unlike the second version, these eyes were just empty. She smiled with quiet indifference.

"It doesn't matter," the Nothing whispered. Her voice was soft. Gentle. Like the hum of the world before a storm breaks. "You will try. You will give your heart, your strength, your name... and still, it will not be enough. Nothing you do will stop what's coming. Nothing you love will stay. Nothing you fight for will ever truly be yours."

She stepped closer. She left no trace, no heat. Just a cold, settling finality. "The world is made to take. One day, you'll learn to stop giving."

Her voice sank into Frankie's chest like iron. They seeped in like smoke, slow and suffocating and for a breathless moment, Frankie couldn't tell if they came from the figure before her...or from the dark place inside herself that had always feared they were true.

Wouldn't it be easier to stop? To let go? To feel nothing at all?

"You are weak," said the Fire.

"You will fail," said the Void.

"You are worthless," said the Nothing.

All her doubt, all her self criticism, every mistake, flooded into her thoughts. Living a life feeling separate from others she thought she was supposed to feel close to. In that separation she found strength and with that forged her own path in life.

"I'm not letting my fears decide who I am!" Frankie said with fire in her soul.

The words rang out like a bell, true and undeniable. The mirror shuddered as a tremor rippled across its surface, deep and elemental. Cracks ran through it like lightning, and from them surged a blinding golden light. It spilled outward in jagged bursts, searing through the gloom. Then, with a sound like the sky tearing open, the mirror collapsed inward, folding into itself and dragging the shadows with it.

Griffon was the first to appear, stepping from the treeline like a shadow reclaiming form. His movements were controlled, but the tension in his shoulders betrayed him. He didn't draw his blade, not yet, but his fingers hovered near the hilt, as though some part of him still expected the earth to split open once more.

Aoife followed close behind, her long skirt sweeping like mist behind her. There was no urgency in her steps, only gravity, as though she, too, recognized the shape of the moment and had no desire to interrupt it. Her gaze flicked to Frankie, then to the space where the mirror had shattered. Her expression was unreadable.

Above them, Nyx circled once, then landed in a high branch with unnerving silence. He did not move again, nor did he did he blink. Chalupa came last, emerging from the dark as if he'd been watching the entire time. His paws touched the earth with caution, testing it like something had shifted in his absence. The fur along his spine stayed raised, his tail swaying in slow, deliberate arcs.

A heaviness settled over the clearing, slow at first, like dusk creeping into the corners of the world. The trees, once passive witnesses, now stood like sentinels, bracing for something they had always known would return. The light dimmed unnaturally. Beneath the earth, something stirred, deeper than stone, older than bone. Leaves stilled mid-fall. Branches arched as if listening. Even the smallest creatures vanished, swallowed by silence. But this was no peaceful silence. It was a stillness born of fear. Within this stillness a figure emerged.

The world seemed to fold inward around him, reshaping to make room for what should not be. Shadows clung to him like living robes, shifting and coiling with purpose, like smoke learning how to devour light. Around Frankie, the light recoiled, shrinking into the trees like startled creatures fleeing a storm. Shadows thickened, drawn to the hollow's center, slithering across the ground in slow procession. Beneath her, the earth pulsed, a warning written in tremors. Roots twisted back into the soil as she stood there, and from the heart of that dark convergence, he came. The figure's shape refused certainty. One moment, he was cloaked and towering, the next, vast and winged, then serpentine, slipping through the air like ink dropped into water. He seemed forged from void and memory, and the world around him warped and shimmered, uncertain whether to hold him or spit him out.

Then, he spoke.

"I have waited for this moment, *Francesca.*" His voice was a contradiction, silk over stone, soft yet flayed with steel. Each word threaded beneath her skin, lacing into her being like a poison she had unknowingly harbored, now stirred awake. The shadows curled at his feet were not cast, they were part of him. They pulsed with an unnatural rhythm, consuming light and sound, a moving absence that swallowed reason.

"Who are you?" Frankie asked, but the words broke in her throat. They cracked on the air, thin as frost under boot. The figure tilted his head, a slow smile unfurled across his face, as though delighting in something only he could see.

"Ah," he breathed, savoring the shape of her voice. "You ask... and yet, you already know the answer." His words wrapped around her like a spell, heavy with a power that predated language. "You feel it, don't you?" he murmured, taking a step forward, though the ground never marked his passage.

"For now, I am *Veyrath*. But that answer," he said, his voice curling dark at the edges, "won't serve you and your curiosity, will it?"

Veyrath's form shifted again, fluid, wrong. Shadows behind him writhed and rose like wings, or smoke, or both. The shapes refused logic. Refused stillness.

"Names are for the weak," he whispered, each word slithering close. "For those who must make the world small to bear it." His eyes gleamed, bright as stars smothered by night.

"Everything you are," he said softly, almost gently, "everything you've clung to... it is unraveling."

He leaned forward, not with his body, but with his presence. It pressed into her thoughts, winding deep, like something half-remembered from a dream that had never ended.

"You came seeking truths?" His voice coiled tighter now, thick with weight. "Truth does not always comfort." He then spoke the words that weren't quite words:

"*Blood bound and blood betrayed,*
Through verdant line your path is laid.
One hand gives, the other takes,
The roots you seek are the ones you break.
A shadow's gift, a truth concealed,
The seed of power, once revealed."

The cadence was mesmerizing, like a chant half-lost to time. It coiled through her thoughts like incense smoke, heavy, curling, refusing to fade. She didn't realize she'd taken a step toward him until a single word broke the trance.

"Frankie." Griffon's voice, low, steady, and sharp as stone, cracked through the illusion like cold air through fog.

She blinked, and the spell unraveled and, Veyrath was gone. No flash of light, no sound, just sudden absence. As if the space where he had stood had sealed itself shut, unwilling to admit he had ever been there at all. But his voice still echoed in her bones. He hadn't come to destroy her, not yet. This wasn't mercy. It was strategy. A first move, calculated and cold, in a game older than memory itself. The clearing hadn't settled. It felt wrong now, too thin, too still. As though the world had stretched to let something ancient through... and hadn't quite returned to itself. Beside her, Chalupa stood rigid, fur bristling, ears flat to his skull. His gaze fixed on the place where Veyrath had stood.

"There's something about him..." Chalupa murmured, not to her, but to the trees. "Like I've seen him before, in a dream that I couldn't wake from."

Frankie nodded slowly. "I felt it too. Like I knew him, but that's not possible... is it?"

Aoife didn't answer at first as the color drained from her face, in realization of something deeper than fear. Recognition laced with dread. Her head tilted slightly, as if listening to something far below the soil.

"Aye, something in him..." she said at last, her voice thin, reluctant. "It knows me or I know it." She shook her head once, slow and uncertain, like even the denial required strength she wasn't sure she had. "His true self is cloaked but underneath that magic, something... familiar. He's not just powerful," she whispered. "He's threaded into something older than we have language for. He isn't new to this world. He's returning to it."

She stopped, the silence that followed wasn't empty. Her eyes narrowed with the unbearable effort of remembering something she was meant to forget.

The forest shuddered, it wasn't a sound at first, it was a sensation, a tightening, like a breath held too long. The very air grew still, charged, as if every branch and blade had turned inward, bracing for something they couldn't name. The trees seemed to draw back, an invisible recoil that passed from root to canopy in a ripple of unease. Then came the groan, a wooden exhale torn from the oldest trunks. It vibrated through the earth and echoed in the hollows like grief too long unspoken. It wasn't loud, but it was wrong. A sound that didn't belong, as if the world had hiccuped, had cracked along a seam it wasn't meant to show. Bark tensed. Leaves curled slightly at the edges. Even the wind seemed to forget itself, pausing mid-motion, as if the forest had remembered something it never wanted to feel again. High above them, a thick branch twisted violently and snapped. Splinters rained down through the canopy. There had been no wind, no touch, just the sound of something breaking that shouldn't have. The very air shimmered with pressure. The clearing distorted, reality warping at the edges. It felt like something unseen was tugging at the threads of the world, like a seam pulling open. Then, near the treeline, a knot of dark energy bloomed. It pulsed once, visible, like a heartbeat caught in open air, and vanished as quickly as it had come, leaving the clearing sharp-edged and breathless.

Frankie staggered back, the chill still clinging to her skin. "What was that?" she asked, her voice tight.

Aoife's head lifted, eyes narrowing. The air had changed. Magic, when woven, left behind traces, a tremor, the scent of ozone, a whisper in the wind. But this had none of that. Her fingers moved through the space where the rupture had opened, sifting invisible threads.

"No one cast a spell," she said, voice low. "That wasn't spellwork, that was something else."

Griffon tensed beside her, his hand drifting toward his blade. "Then what was it?"

Aoife drew a breath, slow and cold. "A wild slip," she said at first, but her voice wavered, then hardened. "No... not just that. It was too clean, too sudden."

Her expression darkened. "That was a Faldoran Fracture."

Griffon's brow furrowed. "I've only ever heard about those. I thought they were myth."

"Not myth," Aoife murmured, her gaze still locked on the trees. "Just rare, and never harmless. A Faldoran Fracture isn't a miscast spell. It's a break in the ley. When the threads of magic that run beneath the world begin to fray or twist, they bleed into the open with no will to guide them. Magic escapes its pattern. It lashes out, wild and unformed."

Griffon's jaw clenched. "Do you think Veyrath caused it?"

Aoife didn't answer at first. Her eyes lingered on the place where the knot of shadow had pulsed and vanished, where the air still felt too thin and too still.

"Not caused," she said finally."Called or stirred but he didn't tear the veil, but his presence was enough to loosen it. The Fracture wasn't his attack, it was his echo."

Frankie felt a shiver race down her spine. "You mean... just by his showing up?"

"The magic here is old," Aoife said. "It sleeps, mostly. It minds its roots and its sky and doesn't trouble itself with passing folk. But Veyrath? He disturbed it, his presence made the magic recoil. That rupture we saw, that was the forest reacting to something it couldn't hold. Something that shouldn't be here." She looked to Frankie, her eyes gone storm-dark. "The land noticed him before we did."

Griffon's voice dropped. "And if the land keeps noticing?"

Aoife's lips pressed together, her voice barely above a whisper. "Then we're walking in his shadow. And wherever his shadow falls, the world forgets how to hold itself together." Her fingers curled into fists and released, as though resisting the urge to touch the ground. "That's the danger with magic that comes from beneath the roots. It doesn't ask. It seeps. It slips its leash just to make room for what doesn't belong."

She turned toward Frankie again, the weight of what she'd said settling in the space between them. "The forest didn't wait for words. It remembered him. The Fracture we saw wasn't some spell gone wrong. It was the land flinching. The weave pulling taut, then tearing under pressure. That break wasn't aimed at us. It wasn't meant to strike. It was the world trying to hold itself together, and failing."

Frankie didn't respond. She didn't have to. The cold still clung to her skin, and Veyrath's voice still lingered in her bones. He hadn't come to end anything. He had come to begin it. To set the first domino in motion. To test the seams of the world, just to see what would unravel. Her fingers gripped her staff tighter, the riddle still circling her thoughts like a tether too tight to shake. Just as the silence began to stretch into something unbearable, Chalupa let out a sharp huff beside her. His tail snapped against the underbrush.

"Okie dokie," he announced, far too loud. "We nearly got eaten by the Babaman. I vote we stop for snacks."

Frankie blinked, caught off guard. "The what-a-man?"

Chalupa turned toward her, eyes wide with mock horror. "Of course you've never heard of Velhollow's finest bedtime terror, *The Babaman*?" He dropped his voice to a stage whisper. "The shadowy menace who creeps out after dark to gobble up younglings who won't sleep, or who sneak extra honey cakes when no one's looking." He flicked his tail for emphasis. "Fae mothers swear by him. One mention and hatchlings tuck themselves in without complaint." He gave a solemn nod. "They say he especially likes the ones who don't brush their teeth." Then, with dramatic flair, he fluffed his fur. "Teeth like rusted scythes. Claws that click when he's near and breath that smells like spoiled root stew and burnt cabbage. Grown folk laugh, until he shows up, all shadows and snarl."

Nyx fluttered overhead, wings rustling as he snorted. "Next you'll say the *Cabbage Hag* is real too."

Chalupa didn't miss a beat. "She *is!* Steals socks and leaves week-old cabbage in their place."

Frankie opened her mouth, then shut it again. The fear was still there, but Chalupa's ridiculousness grounded her. It reminded her that she was still here. The world hadn't ended, not yet. The Babaman could wait, Veyrath could not.

The air around them had already shifted, threaded through with something older, stranger, an awareness that didn't belong to the forest alone. This was no longer just a journey. The unraveling had begun. They moved on, their steps hushed against the leaf-softened path. Overhead, the canopy stirred as if exhaling secrets.

Chalupa trotted ahead, tail lowered, ears flicking at every sound. His posture had changed, no longer the lazy, snarky guardian of before, but something honed, ancient, and watching. His eyes held no humor now, only knowing. Behind him, the trees leaned closer, their shapes taller, their shadows longer than they had been just moments before. Each branch seemed to stretch toward them, listening. Beneath their feet, the forest floor pulsed faintly, too faint to call a tremor, but not quite still. The path narrowed and the light dimmed and somewhere, deep beneath root and stone, something turned in its sleep, something that had waited long enough.

Chapter 19

Frankie didn't know when the silence had changed, only that it had teeth. The forest wasn't watching anymore, it was listening and taking note. Every step forward felt like moving across something's breath, like the world itself had gone still to hear what she might do next. Behind them, the light faded like a door quietly, irrevocably, closing.

Griffon walked beside her, silent and steady, but it wasn't ease he wore, it was control. The kind sharpened by danger, coiled just beneath his skin. His hand hovered near hers, not quite touching, but close enough. A tether, if she needed it. Up ahead, Chalupa came to a halt. His tail dropped low, spine taut, ears swiveling like fine-tuned instruments. The air had changed. It thickened like something old was remembering.

Nyx swept down from the trees and landed hard on a gnarled branch. His feathers flared, his body tense. Watching.

Frankie's voice barely rose above the hush. "What is it?"

Chalupa didn't answer right away. He lowered his head and sniffed, slow and deliberate. When he finally spoke, his voice was quieter than usual, stripped of its usual bite.

"It's close and it's not pretending anymore."

Aoife appeared behind them, her expression hardening as she scanned the woods. "Velhollow's waking things it once buried," she murmured. "And not all of them should be disturbed."

Frankie stepped forward, her boot pressing into soft earth. It beat beneath her like a second heartbeat, and her own began to race in time with it. Beside her, Griffon moved, shoulders tight, jaw clenched, eyes scanning the trees like they were about to shift and bare their teeth. The calm he wore was a mask. She could feel the strain humming beneath it.

"What?" she asked, her voice more breath than sound.

He hesitated. Then, quietly, "You're shaking."

She looked down. Her fingers trembled, barely, but enough for him to see. The shadow's presence still echoed inside her. Deep, bone-held fear.

"I'm fine," she muttered, though it didn't sound like truth.

Griffon didn't press. Instead, his fingers brushed hers, soft, almost unreal. The touch was grounding. When she looked up, his eyes were already on her. Steady. There. He didn't speak, but the silence between them felt solid. Rooted. His hand lingered near hers as they walked, brushing knuckles each time the path bent or narrowed, as if reminding her, I'm still here.

Around them, the forest pressed closer. Shadows pooled beneath towering trees, and light filtered down in long, slanted beams. The trail narrowed to a thread. No birds called. No breeze stirred. Even the wind seemed to hold its breath. Behind them, Aoife caught up, saying nothing, her gaze distant and tilted to the canopy, as if listening for something too old to name.

Then Chalupa broke the silence, tail flicking with familiar sass.

"So... we're still doing the whole 'marching toward uncertain doom' thing?"

Griffon didn't turn. "We don't have a choice," he said simply. And the forest, as if in agreement, closed just a little tighter around them.

"We do," Aoife murmured gently. "We just don't like any of them."

Frankie exhaled slowly, only then realizing she'd been holding her breath. "So how can Zyphirion actually help us?"

Aoife didn't answer right away. Her gaze drifted to the forest ahead, where the trail narrowed into shadow and the light wavered with shapes that never fully revealed themselves. When she finally spoke, her voice carried a depth that felt worn by years and sharpened by knowing.

"Because what's coming isn't only Veyrath, love. It runs deeper than any single name. The Veil between realms is thinning, and something is tugging at its threads from both sides. If it gives way, if it collapses entirely, the balance that holds every realm together will collapse with it."

Chalupa let out a low, growl. "So we're looking for a magical tailor?"

"No," Aoife said. "We're looking for the one who remembers how the cloth was woven in the first place." She continued walking, her boots sinking slightly into the earth, the hush of the trees crowding closer. "Zyphirion is unbound, not just by title, but by nature. He was never meant to live within the laws that govern us. He was made to stand in between them. He remembers the old magic, before it was sliced into schools and categories, before it was shaped to serve us, rather than the world. He doesn't serve prophecy. He doesn't fight wars. But he sees where the cracks begin… and sometimes, if you're lucky, he shows you where not to step."

Griffon's voice came low and sure behind her. "He can sense where magic has twisted. Where it's breaking. He might not stop it, but he can show us the true shape of the unraveling, what's feeding it. What's still hidden."

"He sees the fault lines," Aoife said. "In the Veil. In us. In the world." Her eyes met Frankie's then. "And if anyone can show us how to hold the realms together, how to walk forward without shattering the rest of what's left, it's him."

Frankie frowned, her mind turning over what they were saying.

"So he's not giving us a spell or a weapon."

"No," Aoife said. "He gives understanding. And direction. He shows you the truths you need to face, even when they terrify you. Especially then."

"Sounds exhausting," Chalupa muttered. "Does he at least hand out snacks?"

Nyx cackled from above. "No snacks. Just riddles and existential dread."

Despite herself, Frankie huffed a laugh. But deep in her chest, something shifted. The idea of meeting a being who saw through everything, illusion, fear, even hope, made her skin prickle. Yet, under the discomfort was something else. A feeling she couldn't name, like stepping into water that was colder than expected, but exactly what you needed.

"So we're walking into the unknown," she said slowly. "To find a legend who might not help… but might show us what we've been blind to all along."

"Aye," Aoife said. "And through that, find the path that hasn't yet been written."

Griffon stepped ahead, his voice calm but edged with weight. "Because if we don't find him, we'll be chasing shadows. Fighting fire with no source. And when the Veil breaks..." He paused, gaze sharpening. "There won't be a second chance."

Chalupa sighed. "Great. No pressure."

The wind shifted, stirring the leaves with a sound like breath caught between worlds. Frankie knew, ready or not, the forest was watching. Around them, the world began to change. Subtly at first: the light cooled, the hush thickened, and the path beneath their feet narrowed until it felt less like a trail and more like a memory they were walking through. The trees arched overhead like the ribs of a vast cathedral, ancient and alert. But it wasn't just the landscape shifting. The very nature of the space felt different. They weren't being guided forward, they were being drawn inward.

For a while they walked without speaking. Their steps softened into the carpet of damp leaves, and the quiet that wrapped around them thrummed with something just beyond hearing. Branches rustled overhead, faint and deliberate, like whispers traded in a language time had forgotten. The air grew heavier, not with threat, but with recollection. It felt like stepping into a place the world had once buried... yet never stopped remembering.

When Aoife finally spoke again, her voice didn't just carry through the stillness, it belonged to it. The tone she used was not meant for idle talk; it was the voice of someone calling forth history from the core of the earth. The others slowed without thinking, drawn in by the weight of it, by the sense that what she was about to say mattered in ways even she might not fully understand.

"Long ago," Aoife said, her voice shifting into a cadence that seemed to pull the very shadows closer, "when the veils between worlds were thick with starlight, Zyphirion stood as a sentinel where time frays. He wasn't born so much as woven into being, a watcher, a keeper, meant to hold the boundaries between realms intact. He guarded the seam between what is and what should never touch."

The others said nothing, their breaths fogging faintly as the air cooled, the trees pressing inward.

"But something changed," Aoife went on, her voice hushed. "No one agrees on what it was. Some say he saw too much, glimpsed a truth too vast, too terrible. Others believe he broke his oath, defied the very laws that gave him form. There are even those who whisper that he chose compassion over order, and it undid him. Whatever it was, he cast off his bindings, shattered the runes that anchored him, and vanished into the folds of forgotten magic. He walked into myth."

Frankie's throat was tight. "And now we need him," she whispered, almost to herself.

"Aye," Aoife said, nodding. "Because whatever Veyrath is stirring… it's older than the first spell ever spoken. Older than prophecy. Zyphirion may be the only one left who remembers the beginning well enough to tell us how to stop the end."

She slowed then, her eyes lifting to the canopy above, where the trees began to thin and the light softened into a strange, silvery hue. "The Veil of the Cascading Stars is no ordinary place. It's liminal, half in this world, half in the next. It's hidden deep within the oldest rootlines of the forest, where the soil remembers the first moon and the sky folds inward like a breath held too long. It's where what is and what was lie side by side, thin as threads of spider silk. That's where he'll be."

A sound drifted from the trees, too soft to name, too deliberate to dismiss. Branches creaked without wind, leaves shivered though the air stood still. Something moved between the trunks, unseen but aware, as if the forest itself had turned its gaze toward them, listening for the next step they dared to take.

Chalupa walked ahead again, shaking his head with theatrical dread. "Just a quick jaunt through the unknowable void," he muttered. "What could possibly go wrong?"

Frankie didn't laugh, but her lips twitched in spite of herself. They walked on and the forest changed. The light thinned into silver strands, bending at odd angles through the branches. The air grew cold and expectant. Then the trees dissolved away and there was only this, this place beyond naming.

They stepped into a vast open chamber in the heart of the woods, rimmed by trees so ancient they had become little more than silhouettes, tall, still, and dark as midnight carved into shape. Above and below, rivers of starlight drifted freely, spilling across sky and ground with no beginning and no end. They weren't bound by gravity or logic; they moved as though guided by their own will. Silver braided with molten gold. Sapphire twined through threads of violet fire. Ribbons of opal glided like exhaled breath, and delicate lines of crimson wound through the currents, bright as living runes.

The light didn't merely shine; it shifted in slow, steady waves, carrying the quiet awareness of something sentient. I was as though the stars themselves had spilled their dreaming into this clearing and left it glowing with intention. This was the Veil of the Cascading Stars. Magic vibrated at the edge of sound, too ancient for language, too deep for hearing, yet Frankie knew it instinctively. It wrapped around her like the soft echo of a song she had once known in childhood but forgotten somewhere along the way. The light gathered around her, rising and sinking like gentle tides. It brushed her hands, curled across her shoulders, and rested against the hollow beneath her throat, settling there with the ease of something returning home.

She stepped forward slowly, breath caught between awe and trepidation, half afraid the light might shatter if she moved too quickly. All around them, the drifting rivers of starlight crossed and parted, weaving through the air like silken pathways, while others glided beneath their feet in mirrored streams. Silver twined with gold. Sapphire touched by violet flame. Traces of opal, crimson, and firelight threading the space as though someone were painting the air in real time. The glow did not flicker or beat, it deepened, attentive, as if sensing her presence. The ground itself seemed to hum in response, a quiet vibration that curled around her ankles like mist drawn from ancient stories. Frankie felt it rise through her as a recognition, intimate, startling, certain. She didn't just witness the Veil. The Veil regarded her in return. It marked her. It welcomed her and somewhere within the drifting light, something that had waited a very long time finally stirred.

She swallowed hard. "This is… incredible."

Aoife nodded, eyes alight with starlight. "It doesn't reveal itself to just anyone." Then her expression changed, some shadow of memory slipping through the awe. "Few find it," she said softly. "Fewer still return."

Nyx ruffled his wings uneasily, feathers catching motes of silver light. "So what? We just walk in and hope we don't end up stardust soup in some magical wormhole?"

Griffon's gaze stayed locked on the Veil, his jaw tight. "No," he said, voice steady "We wait."

Frankie glanced at him. "Wait for what?"

"For it to decide," he replied, calm and certain. "This place was never ours to just enter. It has to choose us."

They stood in silence, the weight of it thickening the air around them. Frankie shifted, restless, the energy of the place coiling tighter with every breath she took. A sidelong glance at Griffon revealed him utterly unmoved, gaze fixed on the cascading light ahead like some ancient figure carved from sheer, immovable resolve. Time lengthened, stretching in slow, syrupy increments until the stillness felt close to suffocating.

Even Nyx, usually quick with a barb, perched silent on Griffon's shoulder, feathers fluffed like he was bracing for impact. He gave an exaggerated sigh, loud in the quiet.

"If it's deciding, it might want to get on with it," he muttered. "I'm not getting any younger."

Frankie bit back a groan. Her fists clenched at her sides.

"Seriously? What if it decides we're not good enough? What if it just... tosses us out?"

Griffon didn't look away. "Then we go back home and start over."

She huffed, glaring at the Veil. "Brilliant plan. Stand here and let a glowing curtain of cosmic light play judge and jury while we turn into moss."

Nyx ruffled his wings. "I'm voting moss over vaporized, thanks."

Frankie shifted again, hard enough that her boot scraped loudly across the ground.

"Oh, for stars' sake," she muttered. "How many tests does one witch have to pass? First the gateway, then the grove twisting itself inside out, then the forest trying to read my soul like it's a diary, now this? If this cosmic... light-curtain... portal-thing doesn't decide soon, I'm knocking. Or kicking. Probably both."

Aoife hid a smile but Griffon did not. He turned his head slowly, one brow arched. "Because provoking ancient, reality-bending phenomena always goes well."

Frankie threw her hands up. "What's it going to do, deny me access harder? Add another cryptic warning? Send me on another side quest with a riddle no one wants to explain? I'm tired, I'm starving, my hair's plotting treason, and I am done with mystical metaphors!"

Griffon's mouth twitched, not a smile exactly, but close enough to soften the air around them. His gaze lingered on her, warm in a way that made her pulse trip.

"What?" Frankie whispered, suddenly self-conscious.

He stepped closer, slow and careful, like the air between them was fragile. His hand lifted toward her hair. She stiffened. "What are you … ?"

"You've got something," Griffon said quietly.

His fingers brushed her curls, light, sure, and freed a tiny object. He held it up between them: a small, iridescent feather, blue fading into gold, catching the Veil's strange glow.

Benoît.

Frankie blinked… then laughed, tension cracking like dry twigs.

"Of course he'd leave a piece of himself behind."

Griffon's smile deepened, warm and unguarded. "Looks like he wanted you to have a souvenir."

Frankie took the feather and twisted it into one of her curls, letting it settle there. "I'll keep it," she said softly. "For luck."

When she lifted her gaze, Griffon was already watching her, really watching her. The Veil's light caught the sharp line of his jaw, but the warmth in his eyes was all him. His hand rose again, slower now, brushing a stray curl behind her ear. His fingers lingered just a heartbeat longer than necessary.

"There," he murmured, voice roughened by something he wasn't hiding anymore. "Perfect."

Before a word left her lips, the Veil stirred. Light bent, not as idle streams but as awakened currents, coiling with intent, shaped by hands unseen. Beneath their feet, runes sparked to life, emerald, amethyst, and moonstone, cool flames rippling along ancient fault lines. Threads of verdant green, twilight violet, and molten silver shimmered like roots beneath the forest floor, racing inward with a breathless purpose. At the Veil's base, the threads wove together, forming a luminous heart that pulsed in rhythm with Frankie's own.

"It begins," Aoife whispered.

The Veil didn't part, it dissolved, unraveling like morning mist drawn into the breath of the deep earth. Light loosened in long ribbons, drifting with the slow majesty of caverns waking after ages of stillness. This was no doorway. It was a seam in the world's foundation, where time thinned and magic remembered itself. Beyond it stretched a sanctum carved from living crystal. Its walls glowed from within, lit by currents of wandering light that moved as if following a music too old to be heard. Threads of radiance drifted lazily through the chamber, echoing the earliest stirrings of spellcraft, before language, before lore, when magic was simply the world dreaming aloud.

Frankie stood at the threshold, wonder blooming through her, quiet at first, then bright, uncontainable. Not hidden, not hushed... rising into daylight where it belonged. There was no fear now, only a steadying certainty. Griffon stood beside her, firm as carved stone, and between them a gentle tension lingered, a promise held in breath and nearness.

She stepped forward, not the girl who once froze in the dark, but someone reshaped by loss, power, and the courage to keep walking anyway. Behind them, the Veil folded closed with the softness of settling dust. What lay behind no longer mattered. Ahead stretched only the unknown, unyielding, untamed, and waiting for her hand upon its door.

Magic lived here.

In the breath between stones.

In the hush where roots traded secrets.

In the stillness where silence learned its name.

It did not beg to be wielded, it simply waited to be understood.

There he was, Zyphirion the Unbound. A shape woven of smoke and starlight, argent fire braided with gold and shadow-blue older than any map. He was the moment before a flame decides to rise, the hush that gathers just before creation takes a breath. Light bent around him, unable to settle, as if it recognized a presence beyond its own making.

"Come, seekers of the hidden." His voice did not move through air but through bone and memory. "You ask for truth. But truth is a black flame. It reveals and devours in the same breath. It weighs the soul and names what you would rather not see."

The air thickened, pressing inward like fog heavy with unspoken grief. No easy answers lived here. Only the unraveling of what was false, so what was real could stand uncovered. Frankie's breath caught, but she stepped forward all the same, drawn not by fear or bravado, but by a pull as sure as gravity.

Zyphirion lifted a hand, woven light and shadow, silk and ash, and the gesture brushed through her without ever touching her skin. Soul met soul. Magic threaded inward, winding through her breath. Warmth blossomed through her, claiming space she hadn't known was empty.

She remained herself and yet… more. A single strand of radiance stretched between them, delicate yet impossible to break, brightening for one long, echoing moment, then fading as though it had passed its message into her keeping. Frankie exhaled and opened her palm. A sigil glowed there, etched in living light, shifting like tides beneath a silver sky. Not beating. Not flickering. Simply alive.

Zyphirion leaned close, his voice as old as dust. "This is a *Gift of the Everveil*." he said.

Frankie swallowed hard. "What… what is it?"

Zyphirion regarded the sigil glowing in her palm, the drifting strands of starlight bending toward it as if drawn by breath.

"A bond," he said. "This is a covenant with the raw, unshaped magic of the first breath. It does not obey. It becomes. It shifts with you, your choices, your fears, your courage, your shadow." He tilted his head, studying her as though reading an invisible script threaded beneath her skin. "Know this to be true *Francesca Caelith,* you were recognized by the Everveil, not for who you are now… but for what has always lived within you."

The words struck deeper than she expected, rooting themselves in places she didn't have names for.

"Why me?" she whispered. "There had to be others. Someone stronger. Someone trained. Why me?"

Zyphirion's expression did not soften, but something in it shifted, like a lantern turned toward a long-forgotten truth.

"Because the Veil does not choose at random," he said. "And it does not choose twice. When it remembers a soul, it is because that soul once remembered it."

Frankie blinked. The air felt too thin. "What do you mean?"

Zyphirion lifted his hand, and the chamber brightened, light bending, curling, forming visions within the drifting cascades above them. Silhouettes. Echoes. The shapes of women standing where she stood now, centuries apart, their eyes bright with the same living sigil.

"The Verdant Witch is not a title," he said. "It is a returning. Each is reborn when the world begins to fray, when root and star pull in opposite directions, when the old balances slip."

He nodded toward the mark in her palm.

"The Everveil recognizes its own across lifetimes. Not merely lineage. Essence. Will. Spirit.These are all woven from the same ancient thread."

He stepped closer, gaze fixed on the glowing mark. "You carry the echo of every Verdant Witch who came before you, their strength, their burden, their promise. The Veil called to that echo long before you drew breath in the Greyvale."

Frankie's fingers curled inward, instinctive, protective. The sigil warmed beneath her skin, a quiet, waiting thrum. A current coiled deep, like a river she had never realized she was standing in.

"So this..." she breathed, "...this isn't something I earned."

"No," Zyphirion said. "It is something you are." His voice dropped, low as shifting stone. "A vessel that has finally become wide enough to hold what has always sought you."

The truth settled inside her with the weight of prophecy, and the terrifying possibility that none of this had ever been accidental. Frankie stood very still, her hand curled around the glowing sigil, the edges of Zyphirion's truth dragging long shadows across the inside of her thoughts. She had always believed her life had begun in ordinary soil, in mistakes, in second-guessing, in small choices that never felt like enough. Now she wasn't sure anything about her life had ever been small at all.

Behind her, Griffon shifted. It wasn't loud. It wasn't dramatic. But magic caught the motion and held it, casting him in soft, fractured starlight. Frankie didn't look back, but she felt him, felt the way the world seemed to settle differently when he braced himself. Like he was preparing to carry something he hadn't asked for, but would take anyway if it meant she wouldn't break under the weight of it.

Zyphirion's words hung in the air like prophecy suspended in amber. Aoife stepped forward then, her eyes bright. Pride lived in her expression, but so did fear. Not of who Frankie was becoming… but of the cost she knew waited on the far side of this truth.

"Aye, love," Aoife murmured, reaching out but stopping just short of touch, as if one wrong brush might tip the moment into something too vast to contain. "This is why Velhollow stirred when you crossed the threshold. Why the pixies bowed. Why the forest opened doors it hasn't opened in lifetimes. It didn't happen because you were ready. It happened because the world could wait no longer."

Frankie's breath trembled at the edges. "So this was always going to happen? Even if I never wanted it?"

Zyphirion inclined his head. "The Veil is patient, but patience is not the same as mercy. When the pattern frays, it calls for the one who can mend it. Willing or not, understanding or not."

Frankie felt the sigil's warmth seep upward, spiraling into her, a quiet, undeniable certainty. A calling she had never agreed to, yet could no longer pretend she didn't feel. Behind her, Griffon exhaled, a steadying sound, low and rough, like stone deciding not to crack. He stepped closer, close enough that his presence brushed the back of her awareness like the warmth of a hand without ever touching her.

"If the Veil recognized her," Griffon said, his voice edged with something fierce and protective, "then we will stand with her when the cost comes due."

It wasn't a threat.

It wasn't a plea.

It was a vow, quiet, unpolished, and deeply real.

Zyphirion's gaze flickered toward him, unreadable. "The Veil stands with those who stand with her. It binds what is chosen. It shelters what is true."

Griffon didn't look away. He simply lifted his chin in a way that said he'd take on a realm of ancient magic if it ever asked too much of her.

Frankie's throat tightened. "Griffon…" she whispered.

He finally looked at her fully then, no shield, no half-hidden restraint, just the weight of someone who felt the earth shifting beneath them and had already decided where he would stand.

"You're not facing this alone," he said softly. "Not now. Not ever."

Aoife looked between them, the smallest smile tugging at her mouth, sad, knowing, and full of pride she no longer bothered to hide. Frankie glanced down at the sigil in her palm. It glowed steadily now, not demanding, not consuming, simply there. A thread woven straight into the core of her.

A thread stirred within her, one that had waited lifetimes for her name. For the first time, through the fear, through the doubt, she felt it clearly, steady and unmistakable. This was a path she could walk. Not because it was easy or foretold, but because it had opened in response to her choosing it. She could meet what lay ahead without being unmade by it. She could carry what the Veil remembered and remain herself. And perhaps most importantly, she understood this truth at last: whatever came next, she would not face it alone.

"You are not yet whole," Zyphirion murmured. His words carried no judgment, but something shifted within Frankie, like a seed splitting underground, aching toward a light it had never seen but somehow remembered.

She stepped forward, the sigil on her palm glowing softly, steady as a quiet lantern. The light wasn't urgent, it simply waited for her to speak. "There's something I need to ask."

Zyphirion shifted his attention fully to her, silent and listening.

"When we left the cottage… something found us." The memory tightened her voice. "It felt like the forest turned itself inside out. Like everything familiar went still in the wrong way. The air pressed in. Even the light dimmed, like it was being drained toward something hollow."

She drew a breath, grounding herself. "It came from the shadows. One moment it was smoke, twisting and stretching, and then it formed a body. Human-shaped, but too exact. Too still. The kind of stillness that watches without eyes." Her fingers curled inward. "He didn't speak aloud, but I heard him. Everywhere. He said his name was Veyrath." Her throat tightened. "And I knew he wasn't observing. He was waiting. For me."

Zyphirion's form shifted, as if the name had stirred deep memory rather than fear. Something sharpened in the air around him.

"You encountered a force bound directly to your rise," he said at last. "Veyrath was never meant to remain hidden. His return is tied to yours, as thread is tied to loom." The light within him flowed like deep water under starlight. "He is not a creature driven by hunger or territory. He is a reckoning entwined with the prophecy itself. When the Verdant Line awakens, so does its opposition. Veyrath does not conquer, he unravels. He seeks to remake the world in the shape he believes it should bear."

The sigil on her palm warmed, as if agreeing... or warning. Frankie's breath caught. "So... it really is about me."

Zyphirion's gaze dropped to the sigil on her palm, still glowing softly. "It was never about who you are, Frankie. It has always been about what you are. The Verdant Witch steadies the weave. Veyrath is the tear that waits to undo it. Your rising didn't summon him, it revealed him. He's been watching, waiting, because your name was once spoken in the same breath as his. And though the world forgot... he did not." He paused, and when he spoke again, his voice was quieter, edged with something nearly tender. "You're not wrong to fear him. But what wakes in you may be the only force that can meet him at the edge of the unraveling." His gaze lifted, meeting hers with sharp, crystalline clarity. "The dark remembers what the light forgets. He stirs not by accident, but because you do. Your becoming tugs at the oldest bindings. And he... has always been waiting for that pull."

Zyphirion stepped back, and for a moment, sorrow threaded through the starlight in him, a flicker of mourning for something long gone, or not yet born. "You asked why your rising calls to him," he said. "Because your names were once bound together in the oldest tongue, and the world has only just begun to remember."

He flared and the chamber seemed to shift around them, aligning to a truth too old for language. Then came his parting words, etched not in sound, but in knowing, meant to follow her beyond this place.

"*Where shadows fall and whispers dwell,*
A hidden truth the light won't tell.
A bloodline's curse, a family's stain,
To break the chains, embrace the pain."

A rush of warmth surged through her, like something unseen had marked her again. Her vision blurred and when it cleared, Zyphirion was still watching.

"You've been given the tools," he said. "Look closer to home. The answers are nearer than you know." He raised a hand and light and shadow twisted into runes that danced across the chamber. The sigil on her palm flared in reply.

"Another gift of the Everveil," he said.

Then Zyphirion unraveled, his form dissolving into threads of starlight, folding back into the Veil. Light spiraled upward and collapsed inward, but his voice lingered, woven into the hush.

"*Beware the shadow that knows your name.*"

The light withdrew slowly, as though reluctant to release them, and the Veil loosened its hold with a quiet grace that felt more like a warning than a farewell. The glow thinned by degrees until the chamber of starlit currents dissolved, leaving only the muted colors of the waking forest. The air settled heavier around them, charged with the sense that something vast had shifted direction and now watched from a distance, waiting for its moment to return.

When Frankie exhaled, she realized the path beneath her feet was the same one they had walked hours earlier, though it no longer felt familiar. The stones seemed older. The trees leaned closer. Every shadow clung to its place as if considering whether to step forward or remain hidden. Even the breeze had changed, carrying a faint tremor of magic that brushed her skin like a whispered thought she could not decipher.

Beside her, Griffon walked in silence. He kept close enough that she could feel the heat radiating from him, steady and grounding in a world that felt subtly rearranged. She glanced at him, only for a heartbeat, but his answering look was different now, more searching, more certain, as if he, too, felt the shift the Veil had wrought in her. Something unspoken tightened between them, not pressing, not demanding, but undeniable. The forest felt it as well. The leaves rustled with a curious hush, as though the world itself had paused to witness whatever lived in that glance.

Aoife stepped ahead of them, but Frankie sensed her listening, her awareness stretched through root and branch, attuned to every tremor in the unseen. The elder witch's posture was firm, though her silence carried the weight of knowledge she was not yet ready to share. Frankie looked down at her palm, the sigil glowed with a steady, patient light, as if marking not just her skin, but every path she would take from this moment forward. It did not flare or demand attention. Instead, it waited for whatever future was already gathering beyond the trees. A soft chill threaded through the canopy above them, bending the branches in a slow, deliberate arc. Something in the forest seemed to shift its gaze to the east, as though watching a storm approach from very far away. Frankie felt the echo of it settle in her bones, an instinct, a warning, a call. It was not fear. It was recognition, the quiet understanding that the world she had stepped into would no longer allow her to be anything less than who she was becoming.

When she lifted her head, Griffon was still watching her. His voice was barely more than a murmur, but it threaded through the dusk with a certainty that held her still.

"The Veil didn't simply mark you, Frankie. It aligned itself with you. Whatever waits ahead will meet us on its own terms... but it will seek you first."

She felt the weight of his words settle against her, not heavy, but irrevocable. The threads of destiny had begun to tighten, weaving themselves around her steps, around Griffon's steady presence, around Aoife's vigilance, and around the danger coiling in the dark places of the realm. The forest listened. The magic held its breath. Somewhere far beyond the treeline, something stirred in answer.

Frankie drew a slow breath, letting the night settle around her like a cloak. She stepped forward with the quiet decisiveness of someone who had finally recognized the path beneath her feet. The gateway behind them did not close; it lingered, faint and watchful, as though it, too, waited to see what she would become.

The forest exhaled.

The path darkened ahead.

And destiny, patient and inexorable, shifted one step closer.

Chapter 20

The forest didn't feel quite right anymore. It wasn't dangerous, exactly, just... different. Like it had seen too much and didn't know how to pretend otherwise. They walked quietly, as if their footsteps might wake something best left dormant. The path softened beneath their steps, the damp leaves shifting as hidden roots stirred restlessly below, as if the forest were drawing a long, guarded breath. The air smelled of old rain, iron tang and something unknown. Overhead, the light wove through the canopy in sleepy threads, unsure if it still belonged here. No one spoke. The silence had grown thick, stitched through with memory and something that felt suspiciously like a warning. Frankie walked in the middle of it all, the sigil on her palm glowing softly, no brighter than a candle flame, but steady, like it meant to stay. It was Nyx who finally broke the silence, his voice scratchy and full of feathers.

"So what does that even mean?" he muttered. "'The *shadows fall and whispers dwell. A bloodline's curse. A family stained. To break the chains, embrace the pain.* What hidden truth?" He gave a disgruntled flutter of wings. "That's not a riddle. That's a death sentence written in rhyming couplets."

Griffon made a quiet sound, somewhere between a sigh and a hum, as if rolling the words over in his head like stones in a pocket.

"Zyphirion doesn't do straightforward," he said at last. "He's a bit... layered."

Aoife's eyes were on the trees ahead, but her thoughts were clearly elsewhere.

"It's not a riddle," she said softly, like the words had weight in her mouth. "It's a warning."

Frankie didn't reply, but the words rang inside her like a bell clanging through fog. There was something buried in them, something that scratched at the edge of her thoughts like roots nudging through soft soil.

Griffon spoke again, quieter this time. "The bloodline's curse… does that mean the Verdant line?"

That was when Frankie stopped. She hadn't meant to, her body simply locked in place, bones going rigid before her mind had time to understand why. Heat flared across her palm as the sigil ignited, first with a faint glint of gold, then deepening beat by beat into a richer crimson. It didn't throb, but it quickened, growing brighter with each breath as though it had caught a scent on the wind and recognized it.

Chalupa was the first to notice. "Uh, kid?" he said, padding back toward her, tail flicking sharply. "You're kind of… glowing."

Frankie didn't answer. She couldn't. The forest had quieted in a way that felt wrong, too sudden, too complete, as if the world were holding its breath for the wrong reasons. Above them, the canopy shivered, but beneath their feet the change was stronger. Aoife slowed, her gaze fastening to Frankie with sharp, knowing focus. Her hand hovered near her pouch, fingers flexing as though she were already calling power into them. She didn't need to ask what Frankie felt. She sensed the rise in the air too, an unseen force gathering from root and soil and shadow, pulling toward one point.

The sigil brightened again, steady and insistent, not painful but charged, like a herald announcing itself through her blood. Her limbs grew heavy. Her breath shortened. Her heartbeat thundered in her ribs like far-off drums echoing in a cavern. Even the ground beneath her boots trembled with a faint, rhythmic shiver. This wasn't merely magic, it was a summons, or a warning. Ahead, the trees warped subtly out of shape, their outlines smearing as though the world couldn't quite decide what form they belonged in. Darkness pooled at their roots, thick as tar, and it shifted with deliberate intent. These weren't shadows cast by anything around them. They moved with their own purpose, stretching and folding inward as though preparing to reveal whatever lurked beneath their surface. Frankie felt it rising, an approach, a presence threading through the forest's skin, and she knew, with a certainty that hollowed her stomach, that whatever reached for her had not come from this side of the Veil.

Frankie's magic surged, not all at once, but in ripples, rising through her like a tide pulled by a moon no one could see. It wasn't chaotic, but it wasn't calm either. It was alive, shifting beneath her skin like wind through tall grass. She felt it in her fingertips first, a prickling warmth that traveled up her arms and into her chest, where it settled behind her ribs and pressed outward. The sensation was more like pressure not pain, like something vast and ancient had awakened inside her and was stretching for the edges of her being. It moved in her blood, ready to rise, but not yet called. Not yet commanded. And still it waited, humming with purpose. It was strength, but unshaped, a storm behind glass.

Griffon stepped beside her, steady and silent, his presence grounding as ever. But she could feel the tension rolling off him in waves, like heat before lightning. His eyes flicked toward the tree line, narrowing as they caught on something just out of place.

"Look," he said, voice tight. "There, by the roots."

Frankie followed his gaze. At first, it looked like nothing, just shadows gathered beneath the trees, thick and harmless. But then her eyes adjusted to the gloom. There, at the base of a twisted elder tree, tucked beneath a drift of damp needles and trailing ivy, the earth was disturbed. Footprints. Not leading forward. Not backward. Just circling, slow and deliberate, as though something had been moving around them in silence for hours, days, perhaps. Watching. Then she saw the eyes, dozens of them. Pale and low to the ground, catching the faintest threads of light. They didn't blink, they just stared at them.

Griffon's voice dropped again, this time edged with something sharp. "They've been here the whole time. Watching us."

Aoife turned, her hand brushing the silver runes stitched into her belt, her stance suddenly sharper. "Aye," she murmured. "They weren't hiding, they were waiting."

Frankie squinted into the dark, her heartbeat hammering louder than the forest around them. "What are they?"

Aoife's voice was low, almost reverent. "*Hollowbind*," she said. "Spirits of the Everveil. Sentinels born of old magic. Older than even I've seen."

Chalupa crept closer to Frankie's side, his fur puffed, his eyes never leaving the tree line. "They don't move unless the balance is at risk."

Frankie swallowed, her throat dry. "Are they dangerous?"

Aoife hesitated. "Only to those who forget what side they're on. The Hollowbind don't come for victory or vengeance. They come when the old laws are teetering, when the veil between what should be and what should never meet has grown too thin. Their presence means the world is tipping, and someone, somewhere, will be judged."

Suddenly, from the gloom beneath the trees, the shadows stirred like the darkness itself had flinched. A ripple passed through the underbrush, thick and oily, and the world tilted, not in sight or sound, but in the gut, as though reality had taken a wrong turn and refused to right itself. The forest seemed to stretch and shudder. Branches bowed unnaturally and time itself felt suspended, pulled thin like fabric about to tear.

Then it came. The dark coiled inward, and from that collapse, a figure emerged. It didn't walk, it unfurled. Smoke curled where limbs should be, and its outline shifted at the edges, never settling, as if it wore indecision like a second skin. It cast no clear shadow of its own, only deepened those already present. The longer it stood, the more the world recoiled, as if nature itself didn't dare move too close.

Frankie's gaze snapped to Aoife, searching for something, anything that might undo the moment. But Aoife didn't move. Her face had gone pale beneath the canopy's mottled light. Frankie hadn't seen her like this. The woman who met fire with fire now stood hollowed out, as though facing a nightmare dragged from the deepest part of memory, a memory she'd fought to bury.

The figure solidified. The smoke stopped flickering. The uncertainty drained away. The darkness parted like curtains drawn too fast, and at the center stood a man. Frankie's breath caught. Her heart stuttered. Her eyes locked on his face, and her stomach dropped like stone.

"No..." The word slipped from her lips, small and broken. "No."

Frankie's thoughts scattered, her mind a cyclone of disbelief, confusion, and a rising dread that curdled beneath her skin. Every possibility unraveled, every memory of her grandfather's clipped silences, every unexplained moment, every glance too sharp or too distant. It all cracked under the weight of this new truth. The world around her lost its edges. The ground felt unreliable beneath her boots, as if it too was reeling.

Nono.

Griffon stepped in close, silent but unwavering. His presence wrapped around her like a cloak thrown over trembling shoulders. He didn't speak. He didn't need to. He took her hand, steady and sure, not in comfort, but to keep her anchored. A quiet magic sparked at the contact, low and warm, threading up her arm like a tether cast from sanity. It wasn't enough to stop the storm, but it was enough to keep her from drowning in it.

Her grandfather stood before her, exactly as she remembered him, yet nothing like the man she had known. The angles of his face were the same, the lines time had carved remained familiar, but everything beneath had shifted. His presence no longer held quiet patience or distant affection. It carried something darker, intentional, knowing. The magic that moved around him wasn't wild or gentle. It was coiled, forced into shape, honed to a single, focused edge. Shadows gathered at his sides as though he commanded the absence of light itself. He didn't glow. He erased the glow from everything near him.

Frankie staggered back a step, her palm over her heart as if to cage it. "Is this like the mirror?" she asked, her voice breaking. "Is this a test? Some twisted vision? Do I have to face everything I've feared? Are my parents next?"

Nono tilted his head then he smiled. It was slow and deliberate, but joyless, a thing of inevitability, not warmth. His eyes, once stern and cold, now glinted like cracked ice.

"This is no illusion, Francesca," he said. His voice was calm. Measured. "No dream. No spell. I am here. I have always been here and no… your parents will not be joining us."

The trees shivered. The light thinned and with each breath she took, the truth carved deeper. He wasn't here to help her, he never had been. Her body felt foreign, numb, untethered, as if her bones had lost their shape inside her skin. The trees around her blurred, their edges bending in a slow, awful tilt. Something primal stirred beneath her ribs, not panic exactly, but grief laced with fury. This was the man who'd taught her how to mend a fishing net, how to tie knots that held. The man who'd never once spoken of magic. He had watched her grow, silent and unmoved, and now stood wrapped in shadow like a king of ghosts. She didn't know whether to scream or beg or run. But her feet wouldn't move. Her heart wouldn't stop. She could feel herself spiraling, pulled under by the weight of what couldn't be undone and then....

"Frankie," Griffon said, his voice a lifeline in the chaos. "Stay with me."

She didn't look at him, her voice cracked, barely a breath. "It's him."

Griffon's brow furrowed, eyes narrowing on the figure ahead, tension rippling through him like a drawn bow. "Who?"

Her throat tightened, the truth like iron, but she forced it out. "Dominick DiLegna, my grandfather," she whispered.

Griffon's gaze snapped to hers, his brow tightening with disbelief and confusion. He looked to Aoife, as if expecting her to deny it, to explain it, to do something that would make sense of the impossible. But Aoife remained silent, her expression carved from stone. The truth hung there, sharp and raw. He turned back to Frankie, his voice low, urgent.

"That's your grandfather? I don't understand."

He didn't move away, his grip stayed firm, one hand anchoring hers, the other settling gently on her shoulder. The warmth of him was steadying, but his eyes remained locked on the shadow-cloaked figure ahead, searching for something that might make sense of it all.

Frankie's body trembled from the storm gathering within her. The magic no longer stirred like a whisper. It rose like a tempest drawn from the bones of the earth, raw and ancestral. It surged through her with purpose, braided with betrayal, fueled by the revelation that had cracked her world open. This was not panic. This was power awakened, old as root and stone.

"He was always there," she whispered, barely able to hear herself over the thunder building inside. "So cold... so distant. Like I never mattered."

The air shifted, sharp, metallic, wrong. Power gathered at the edges of Frankie's vision, warping the light the way heat bends the air above desert stone. It crawled across her skin in thin silver fissures, bright enough to cast trembling reflections along the roots and trunks around her. Beneath her feet, the ground responded in a sudden flare of brightness, thin shards of light racing outward like living runes desperate to find a place to settle. And still, her grandfather stood cloaked in shadow, unmoving. Watching. As if he had been waiting for this exact moment, and nothing unfolding surprised him in the slightest.

The magic inside her wasn't rising, it was breaking open. It tore free in jagged bursts, wild and uncontrolled, the world around her wavering as though even the forest struggled to bear the force spilling from her. The sigil on her palm burned crimson-gold, its glow faltering under the weight of too much power. Sparks snapped along her fingertips, quick and restless, small streaks of lightning searching for release.

The earth gave way in thin fractures, lines of light clawing outward like roots hunting for a place to anchor, only to crumble into dust before they found one.

"Frankie, breathe!" Nyx called, wings snapping wide as he lifted himself into the air, feathers bristling with warning. "She's flaring!"

"She's about to blow," Chalupa growled, stepping in front of her with his back arched, every hair standing on end. His voice was low, protective, eyes locked on Veyrath.

Frankie couldn't hear them. The pulse in her ears was deafening, a war drum. The heat within her was unbearable, holy, alive. Magic curled from her like smoke from a burning sigil, untamed, glorious. Leaves spiraled into the air, dust danced in sudden whirlwinds, and stray light fractured into colorless brilliance. A halo of force spun outward from her in concentric waves, rippling through the forest like a bell struck at the heart of the world.

"Frankie!" Aoife's voice cracked through the rising storm like lightning splitting the sky. "Control it! Control yourself!"

But the command slid through her like wind through reeds. The magic had no interest in restraint. It fed on her fury, her hurt, her knowing and it climbed. Light fractured around her hands, shards of radiance scattering like broken glass in water, dazzling and deadly.

"Your emotions aren't in control of the power, you are!" Aoife shouted again, stepping forward, her hands glowing, runes racing along her sleeves.

Frankie was lost in it, the whirlwind, the rising storm inside her, magic and emotion tangled, impossible to tell apart. Her hair whipped around her face, caught in a current she hadn't summoned. Light seared the air at her fingertips, wild and aimless.

Griffon's presence was steady, unwavering, a rock against the tide. He moved closer, forcing himself into the storm's eye, ignoring the sparks that lashed at him.

"Frankie." His voice was low, fierce, right at her ear. "Look at me."

She couldn't, her eyes burned, her breath ragged, the magic still rising. His hands didn't leave her, they slid to her face, cupping it, holding her still. His touch burned with her power, but he didn't pull away.

"Feel me," he whispered, his voice thick with something more than just magic. "You're not alone. You never have to face this alone."

The light flared again, brighter, hotter.

"Emotions and magic don't mix, Frankie!!" Chalupa barked, fierce and unyielding. "You want to end up as a glitter bomb? Because this is how glitter bombs happen. And we all hate glitter!"

The absurdity of Chalupas comment cracked something in her. Her eyes flew open, just as a surge of laughter, panic, and power collided inside her. The magic buckled, then shattered as a blinding flash tore through the clearing, a gust of wind roaring outward, scattering leaves and sparks, and then, silence.

Her knees gave way, but Griffon caught her, pulling her tight against him, holding her as if he could keep her from breaking apart completely. Her head pressed to his chest, the steady thrum of his heart anchoring her as the last tendrils of power flickered and died. Aoife lowered her hands slowly, sleeves still glowing faintly, her breath sharp but controlled.

Chalupa remained where he was, his stance low, protective. His gaze was fixed on Veyrath.

"I knew something was off about him," he muttered. "Always looked like he'd smelled something awful... and now I know why."

The tension didn't break, it tightened, coiling around them. Frankie's breath steadied, but only just. The tremor beneath her skin still hummed, a wild thing not yet tamed. Her magic had stilled, but the truth inside her remained jagged, raw. Veyrath's gaze held her, sharp and knowing, as if he could see the weight of her thoughts, the crumbling of everything she had believed.

"You are... more powerful than I expected," he said, his voice smooth, gilded with cold satisfaction. "And yet... still so unaware."

His eyes slid to Aoife, the smile that curled his lips both cruel and intimate, like a blade sliding slow. "All that power… and she never even knew."

Frankie's gaze snapped to Aoife, and the truth hit her like a blow. Her grandmother hadn't taken a step, but the magic around her had shifted violently, as if it could no longer hold its shape. The runes along Aoife's sleeves brightened with an unstable, shifting light, no longer simple gold or green, but a fractured brilliance, like dawn forcing itself through storm clouds. A tremor crossed her fingertips, barely visible, yet the air reacted instantly. Sparks leapt in thin, jagged lines, weaving through the space like vines made of lightning. The runes writhed, struggling to settle, as though they recognized something too terrible to contain. They weren't answering Veyrath's presence. They were answering a truth that had torn straight through Aoife's defenses and struck at the core of her magic. Aoife's face remained composed, carved with the stillness she had worn through every danger they had faced. But her eyes, those storm-green eyes, were wide with a grief so raw it hollowed her.

Not just confusion or shock. Devastation.

Frankie turned back toward Veyrath, but all she could see was a face from the distant corners of her childhood, always watching, always cold, always just outside the reach of warmth. The man she had once called Nono. The man who had stood in every doorway like a shadow that refused to leave.

Dominick DiLegna was not swallowed by darkness.

He *was* the darkness.

He stepped forward, and the earth recoiled as if it recognized him too well.

The forest floor groaned, roots twisting away in retreat. Leaves blackened at the edges. Ferns collapsed mid-breath. Even the ancient stones of Velhollow, the ones etched with light and memory, dimmed where he passed. Cracks split through them, their enchantments unraveling as though the land itself refused to bear his weight.

The realm did not rise greet him. It remembered him and it trembled. Veyrath smiled then, slow, empty, assured of his own inevitability.

"Oh, Francesca," he said, his voice like oil over flame, "let's not pretend anymore. There is no Nono. There never was. You saw what I allowed you to see, what served my purpose." He moved closer, and the golden light that clung to the trees began to flicker and fade. Shadows spilled from his boots like rot spreading through soil. "The man who walked beside you, who tucked you in and offered silence in place of affection, that was a construct. A useful lie. Nothing more."

Frankie staggered back a step, the breath torn from her lungs as if the truth itself had teeth. The memories she'd clung to, those quiet moments she'd mistaken for care, were suddenly hollow.

"You, lied to me," she choked. "You lied to everyone."

"I needed the Verdant Line protected," Veyrath said, eyes gleaming with malice, "but muted. Drowned in softness and confusion, just enough to delay what you might become. Until now." His gaze locked onto her, unblinking, a weight she couldn't outrun, couldn't hide from. "You were never theirs, Francesca. Not of their world. Not of their fragile ideals."

The word *theirs* struck harder than it should have. He didn't need to say their names, she knew who he meant. The ones who raised her in the Greyvale, her parents. The ones who had smiled and nodded and gone through the motions of family but had never truly seen her. Never truly loved her. Not in the way she'd hoped. Not in the way a child deserved. They had called her dramatic when she cried for the woods. Strange when she spoke to shadows. Dismissed her wild dreams, her fierce empathy, her aching pull toward a world she had no name for. All this time, she'd wondered why they felt so distant. Why they always seemed like actors reading lines from someone else's script.

Now she knew.

"They were never meant to keep you," Veyrath said, his voice curling like smoke around the edges of the circle. "Only to dull your light. To keep you comfortable, numb, harmless. The house, the silence, the empty affection, they were a cage dressed in quiet smiles."

The air darkened around him, and even the birds had gone still in the trees beyond. A hush fell, the kind that coils before something terrible steps through.

"You carry the Verdant Line in your blood, yes," he said, "but deeper still flows mine, the Obsidian Line. The kind of magic that does not ask, only takes."

She felt the truth rip through her like a blade drawn slow beneath the skin, no mercy, no warning. Veyrath moved closer, and the shadows surged to meet him like loyal hounds.

"You were forged in the in-between," he said, voice low and rich with something ancient. "Not to bring balance. Not to heal. But to break."

His words slithered around her like smoke laced with ash, thick and clinging. "You are the hinge, Francesca. The hairline fracture in the bones of the world. And when the pressure comes, and it will, you won't seal the breach. You will widen it."

The trees groaned, their limbs creaking as if straining to pull away. Stones cracked beneath his feet. Even the air shuddered. Velhollow, a realm of light and memory, buckled in his presence like a wounded animal. The ground did not welcome him. It recoiled.

"You were never meant to save them," Veyrath said, almost gently. "You are not the answer to their prayers. You are the thing they forgot to fear." His smile deepened, sharp as a broken crown. "And I," he breathed, "I am the one who remembered and who has waited."

Frankie stood frozen, heart hammering against her ribs, as the forest warped around her. There had never been a Nono, only this shadow that had worn his face like a mask and now, the mask was gone.

Chapter 21

The world hadn't shattered, but something inside her had. Frankie stood in a stunned quiet, the truth settling over her like cold ash. The man she had called Nono had been real. Dominick DiLegna. Aoife's husband. Her father's father. A presence that had hovered at the edges of family stories like a smudge no one quite wiped away. There had been a grandfather once… but whatever piece of him had belonged to them was gone. What stood before her now was not the old man she knew. It was Veyrath. And somewhere along the way, the mortal man and the monster had become the same.

The fracture didn't stop with him. It ran deeper, splitting open the seams of every memory she'd ever tried to make sense of. Her childhood, thin, gray, loveless. Her home, silent, pristine, airless. Her parents, moving around her like actors reading lines they didn't fully understand. They had never held her close. Never reached for her. Never seemed to see her. She used to think they were too tired. Or simply the kind of people who loved quietly. Now she saw the truth more clearly: they had been molded into vessels empty enough to leave room for someone else's design. A hollow ache opened inside her. She felt suddenly young again, small, unseen, standing at the bottom of the stairs, clutching a perfect report card and waiting for someone to care. No one ever had.

Her voice cracked like a brittle twig. "What about them?" she asked, barely louder than a breath. "My parents… did they know? About you? About magic?" Her throat tightened. "Was I the only one who didn't?"

The forest seemed to still, every leaf, every stone, waiting.

Veyrath's smile curved, slow and satisfied. "They knew nothing," he said. "They were convenient. Predictable. Hollow. Exactly what I needed."

Frankie flinched. The words felt wrong and true at the same time.

"They weren't designed for greatness, Francesca," he went on. "Despite your grandmother's best efforts, your father was taught to have no curiosity. No fire. No real warmth to interfere. Your mother was chosen for the same reason. Only routine and rigid schedules. The sort of people who mistake order for virtue." His voice dipped, smooth and cruel.

"Your parents weren't guardians. They were scaffolding."

Her breath trembled. "Why?" she whispered. "Why orchestrate my entire life?"

"Because you were the prize," he said simply. "The Verdant Line had stirred again, and the prophecy did not lie. Aoife's granddaughter would be the next to rise. When I traced her lineage to that dreary little house in the Greyvale, everything aligned."

Aoife stiffened beside her, but Veyrath didn't stop.

"When you fled Velhollow," he said, eyes gleaming, "you thought you had found your freedom, slipped beyond the reach of fate. But I watched you, Aoife. I watched your magic dim in exile. I followed the branch of your bloodline into the world above and waited. When opportunity came, I did what I have always done. I adapted." His gaze sharpened, hungry. "I did not need to steal a body. I already had one. I let Dominick fade. I let Nono become a mask. Quiet. Attentive. Harmless. A grandfather no one would question too closely." His smile thinned. "And when the prophecy whispered that your granddaughter would be the one the Veil marked, I ensured her childhood left… space."

Frankie's hands curled at her sides. "You starved me," she said, the truth finally rising. "Emotionally. On purpose."

"Of course," he replied. "Longing begets magic. Hunger readies the vessel. A child who feels full does not reach for destiny. But a child raised on emptiness?" His eyes glinted. "She becomes the perfect flame."

Memories reeled, her mother's clipped replies, her father's distracted nods, birthdays treated like calendar obligations instead of celebration. The house had never been peaceful. It had been numb. Her life hadn't been neglected by accident. It had been cultivated that way.

"You think they raised you?" Veyrath asked, almost pitying. "No, Francesca. They *housed* you. They kept you just nourished enough to survive, just ignored enough to believe you were the problem. That ache in your chest?" His smile cut deeper. "That was deliberate."

Frankie swayed where she stood. Aoife reached toward her, but the words were already carving their path. She had not simply grown up unloved. She had grown up engineered for someone else's use.

Aoife's stance tightened, but not from fury alone. The magic in the grove reacted first, threads of light rising along the ground, the air thickening with memory the way the Everveil sometimes displaced the present. Frankie felt it gather, a subtle pressure behind her eyes, insistent, like the forest itself was drawing back a curtain.

Then the memory surfaced. It did not appear as a vision or illusion. It arrived as intuition made visible, a resonance passing from Aoife into the space between them, shaped by her unraveling control. Frankie didn't see the past so much as feel the emotional imprint of it, raw, vivid, unmistakably real and suddenly, she understood. Aoife wasn't only angry, she was remembering. Not as a story told, but as a wound reopening.

The impression washed through Frankie with startling clarity: her grandmother young and unburdened, standing in a Greyvale park where sunlight sifted gently through the broad leaves of sycamores. Aoife was laughing then, her magic loose and unguarded, moving through her like breath rather than duty. This was her wandering year, the season Velhollow granted before a witch chose her path and accepted its weight. One year to see the mortal world, to taste it, to decide who she might become before the land and the old vows laid claim.

Seraphina stood nearby, bright-eyed and fearless, her laughter ringing as Arden spun her once and set her back on her feet. Their bags were piled on a weathered bench, half-packed and careless, the way people packed when they believed the world would make room for them. They were drunk on independence, on possibility, on the simple thrill of standing nowhere they were expected to be. Aoife felt it then, that sense of being unmoored in the best possible way, untethered from prophecy, from lineage, from the quiet pressure of becoming what others had already decided she must be. She had not planned on staying in the Greyvale. She had not planned on falling in love, either with a place or with a life that felt softer, messier, and startlingly her own. Frankie felt the ache of that moment from the inside out, not as memory but as emotional truth carried on Aoife's magic. There was warmth there, and hope, and the bright, dangerous spark of believing she had found something that belonged to her alone. It was the feeling of standing at the edge of choice, of daring to imagine a future shaped by want instead of obligation, and of not yet knowing what the cost of that choice would be.

Frankie understood then that Aoife's story was not one of abandonment or secrecy. It was the story of a woman who had once believed she was allowed to choose joy, and who would spend the rest of her life paying for loving something the prophecy had never intended to let her keep. Dominick had stood before her, offering a fallen notebook she'd dropped. His smile had felt gentle. His voice warm. His steadiness comforting in a way that seemed safe. It was the memory of who she believed he was, not who he had ever been. The realization carved itself across Aoife's features now: that none of it had been real. That the tenderness had been a mask. That the choice she'd believed she made freely had been shaped by the quiet hand of a predator wearing a mortal shell.

Frankie wasn't seeing the memory exactly, she was feeling the truth of it radiating through Aoife's magic like heat from a long-buried ember. Aoife's eyes burned with grief, anger, and something more ancient, a dawning clarity that stripped away decades of self-blame.

She had never been weak.

She had never been unlovable.

She had never failed.

She had been hunted.

She had been chosen.

Cornered by something wearing a smile that didn't belong to it. Aoife had not fled because she was weak. She had fled because she had been trapped with a monster pretending to be a man. The runes carved into her skin ignited, gold and deep green, sharp and erratic, surging upward like a storm remembered. Her fingers trembled with rage that had waited decades to find a voice. Leaves rustled above them though not a breath of wind moved. The forest felt her fury and braced itself. Her voice came low and shaking, not from uncertainty but from the strain of holding back power.

"All those years," she whispered. "I thought I wasn't enough for you. I thought if I tried harder, if I stayed quieter, if I loved you more, maybe you'd look at me the way a husband should." Her jaw locked. "And when Anthony turned cold, just like you… I blamed myself again. I thought I had failed him too." Grief creased her face. Anger followed, hot and rising. Then another emotion, older, hollow, sick with realization. "You orchestrated everything," she said. "Even my shame."

Veyrath's smile curled. "Of course I did."

Aoife's breath hitched with a sound that might have been a sob or the start of a scream. The magic around her sharpened, tightening like a bowstring. Her heart had been breaking for decades, and now she saw that every fracture had been engineered.

"I didn't love you," Veyrath continued, tone cold and precise. "I used you. I used your hope. Your loneliness. Your desire to be wanted." His smile thinned. "You were useful until you weren't."

She trembled as the full weight of revelation settled into her bones, a deep, rising quake of power waking in a woman who finally understood the wound that had shaped her life. Frankie's chest constricted. Aoife had carried all of this alone. The years in Grimwyck Manor. The marriage. The neglect. Anthony's mirrored coldness. And then Corrine, her father's high school sweetheart, perfectly suited to the DiLegna legacy of control and silence in a way Aoife never could be.

Aoife's eyes burned. "I spent years thinking I'd abandoned my family out of cowardice."

"You abandoned nothing," Veyrath said lightly. "I never allowed you a family to begin with."

The trees recoiled. Roots curled away from him. Stones dulled under his presence. Frankie staggered. Her stomach twisted.

"So what was I?" she whispered. "Just a better version of your miscalculation?"

"No," Veyrath said, stepping closer, voice velvet and venom. "You were the answer. Verdant magic shaped by shadow. A convergence planned long before you took your first breath."

He shifted his gaze to Aoife just long enough to twist the blade. "Your husband never loved you. Because he was never your husband at all."

Aoife's entire form shuddered. Light rippled wildly up her arms, no longer smooth or controlled, this was raw, old power, shaking free of decades of suppression.

"Dominick was your mask," she breathed. "All this time."

Veyrath inclined his head, as though discussing weather instead of lives he had shattered. "He decayed long before you understood the depth of the rot," he said. "I allowed the shell to persist because you were still useful to me. Anthony was a dead end, inevitable, really. The Verdant power has never passed through sons. It cannot. It threads itself through the daughters of your line, and only them. A son is a sealed door, incapable of carrying what the prophecy requires."

His smile thinned, cold and deliberate. "But through him… through his brittle, loveless pairing with that rigid little wife of his… you finally delivered what I needed."

His gaze cut to Frankie. "You."

Aoife made a sound between a growl and a cry, anguish and revelation braided into one. Frankie felt something collapse inside her. The world twisted.

Her childhood, her parents, and the man she had called Nono were never sources of comfort, and she had never pretended otherwise. They had been distant, withholding, and inexplicably cold in ways she could never name as a child. Now, standing before Veyrath, the truth landed with devastating clarity: their cruelty had never been accidental. Their indifference had been arranged. Every sharp silence, every clipped dismissal, every moment she stood alone in that house had been constructed with purpose.

Veyrath watched her with a satisfaction that hollowed the space between them.

"You were not shaped to protect Velhollow," he murmured. "You were cultivated to unmake it. Your lineage narrowed. Your destiny engineered. A flame coaxed into shadow until you became the instrument I required." He began to circle, slow and deliberate, the shadows at his feet rippling with each step. "The prophecy you were told? A half-truth. A bedtime fable to keep you tame. But prophecy, real prophecy, is a coin with two sides."

His hand lifted, and the air bent around it, pressure spooling like stormlight. "From the blood of the Verdant Line shall rise a daughter, neither light nor shadow. She will stand at the threshold… and darkness shall bow, or burn." He stopped before her, his gaze locking onto hers. "You bind yourself to their side. You choose softness. But you are also mine. Born of my darkness. Shaped by my design. You think your power is a gift of nature? It was curated. Cultivated. Every fracture in you made fertile ground."

From across the glade, Aoife's voice rang out, clear and unshaken. "Then why wait all this time?"

Veyrath did not look at her. "Because some power cannot be stolen," he said. "It must be chosen." He turned, slow and sure, facing them both now. "I am not bound by *your* Balance. I do not serve light, nor yield to its laws. I am the fracture in the foundation you sanctify. I am the truth your Circle buried."

The earth beneath them shuddered, stone groaning in protest. Trees bent, not to wind, but to warning.

"I was cast out," he said, voice deepening, wrapping around the clearing like fog. "Sealed in the hollow between realms. Banished, named unworthy, forgotten by design. But no seal holds forever. Time devours all things, chains, names, prayers."

The shadows at his feet surged, alive and writhing. "While the world forgot, I endured. While you whispered of harmony and clung to myth, I prepared. You thought the story ended. You thought I was gone."

Darkness coiled from his fingers, unfurling like ink through water, hungry and precise. "I am not a memory," he said, voice like stone splitting under roots. "I am here and I will not be cast out again."

"Well, someone rehearsed his monologue," Chalupa said, his voice low and edged. He stood at Frankie's feet, tail lashing in short, agitated sweeps, eyes locked on Veyrath. "Tell me, Sparklebones, do you always weaponize childhood trauma, or is this a special occasion?"

Frankie blinked, still stunned, the air sharp in her lungs. The ache behind her eyes didn't vanish, but it paused, thinned, as if Chalupa had cracked the darkness just wide enough to breathe.

Chalupa didn't take his eyes off the threat. "I swear, one more line about destiny and I'm biting ankles. Ancient evil or not."

Veyrath's gaze slid down with visible disdain. His eyes narrowed, glittering like stormlight on obsidian. "I should've known the day you showed up," he said, voice curling with contempt. "A familiar, cloaked in charm and insolence. Did Aoife send you to spy? Or were you just sniffing out the bloodline?"

Chalupa sat back on his haunches, slow and deliberate, his tail curling like punctuation. "Spy? Babysitter? Depends on the day," he drawled. "But I always had one job, keep her safe long enough to see through monsters like you."

Veyrath's smile thinned, knife-like. "You must think yourself vital, then."

"Oh, I know I am," Chalupa said, eyes narrowing to slits. "And judging by how uneasy you look, so do you."

Frankie's knees buckled slightly, but she stayed upright. The memories crashed in, her mother's distant eyes, her father's empty silences, the way she had always felt just outside of love. She'd spent years trying to shrink herself to fit into their world, blaming herself for not being easier, quieter, more acceptable.

Aoife stepped forward, fire building behind her eyes. "You let her suffer," she said, her voice trembling as power moved along her arms like a gathering storm. "You let her believe she was alone and unwanted."

"She wasn't ready," Veyrath replied, his tone disturbingly calm. "If she'd awakened too soon, she would have collapsed beneath the weight of what she carries. But now she is complete. She is exactly what I waited for."

The wind twisted sharply through the glade, though the branches above did not stir. Magic thickened in the air, dense enough to feel against the skin. Aoife stood at the center of it, surrounded by that unnatural stillness that settles over the world when a storm gathers its strength and every bird vanishes from the sky.

Beneath her feet, the stone gave a slow, splintering groan. Hairline fractures crawled outward in measured lines, threading through the clearing as if the land itself were bracing for what was coming. The scent of torn earth rose sharply, metallic and raw, as though Velhollow itself had been wounded. Aoife didn't speak again, but Velhollow answered for her. Ancient roots trembled. Bark cracked in thin seams. The forest reacted to her grief and anger as if they were forces capable of reshaping the ground beneath them.

Frankie watched her grandmother, unable to look away. Fury, disbelief, and sorrow tangled inside her so intensely she could barely breathe around them. Aoife's magic lit her skin in uneven flashes of green and gold, responding to pain that had been buried for decades. The trees leaned toward her. The forest listened. Even the air felt sharpened by something old that was clawing its way back toward balance.

Frankie finally found her voice. "You made my life a lie."

The sentence came out quieter than she intended, but it carried the weight of everything that had shattered. It felt small when compared to the magnitude of her ruined childhood, yet it was all she could force out. Veyrath's smile curved with a self-satisfied ease.

"I made your life matter," he said, as if it were a kindness he had offered.

The earth behind him responded before Frankie could. A split opened in the ground, not as an explosion, but as though the soil had received instructions it had long been waiting to obey. A dark seam widened with deliberate precision, revealing depth instead of violence. Pale silver lines traced its edges in slow arcs, glowing like deep-lit beneath stone. Something cold seeped out, carrying a tension that prickled across Frankie's skin. The darkness within the opening did not simply exist; it invited.

At Veyrath's feet, shadows tore free of their anchors. They did not creep. They launched themselves toward the opening with a hunger so immediate that Frankie flinched. Some plunged directly into the divide, while others rose into distorted shapes, faces forming and disappearing in the span of a breath, as if remembering the bodies they once wore and abandoning them just as easily. The divide widened, drawing in the dark as though feeding on it. The forest did not tremble this time. It watched. Every tree stood rigid, braced for the presence emerging below.

As Veyrath moved forward the land parted for him with an obedience that made Frankie's skin crawl. The shadows at his heels stretched long across the stone, drawn forward as though following a command they had waited centuries to hear. Griffon moved closer to Frankie, his presence grounding her with a quiet strength she felt even without touch. Aoife shifted too, her jaw tight, the runes along her skin flickering in uneven patterns, responding to forces she had no name for.

The opening deepened, spreading across the ground in delicate networks of light that formed patterns Frankie did not recognize. Cold air flowed out of the depths, carrying the scent of a place untouched by the sun. Frankie felt the sigil in her palm flare with recognition, as though something beneath the surface knew her.

Veyrath lifted his chin slightly and spoke as if he were delivering sacred truth. "Look closely," he murmured. "This is the first thread pulled from a tapestry that should have unraveled centuries ago."

The ground beneath them tightened. Light bent around him in unnatural paths. Frankie steadied her stance without meaning to. The opening was no mere fissure. It was a summons calling to something older than the forest itself. A shift rose from its depths, moving through the air like a distant presence brushing past the treetops. The trees bent ever so slightly toward one another, forming a canopy that appeared to brace for what was coming. A subtle vibration drifted over the clearing, skimming the line of Frankie's shoulders before fading again.

Griffon edged closer, the tension that moved through him unmistakable. Aoife's fingers curled, prepared to summon magic that might cost her dearly. Chalupa positioned himself in front of Frankie, low and coiled, every instinct telling him to guard her.

Veyrath's smile widened with slow, ominous certainty. "Do you feel it, Francesca?" he asked. "The world is rearranging itself around you."

Frankie refused to look away, though every part of her felt the wrongness radiating from the opening. The sigil in her palm glowed more intensely, meeting the dark with a strength she didn't know she possessed. Veyrath watched that glow with an expression that hovered disturbingly between pride and hunger. The dark below released another wave of energy, drawing the light of the clearing toward itself. Frankie tightened her grip on her staff as Griffon's shoulder brushed against hers in a wordless vow. Aoife's magic rose behind her like the first gust of a coming storm.

The seam widened once more, and something began to shift inside the depths. A mass of shadow gathered, the shapes within it moving with intent rather than chaos. Eyes formed in the dark, many and shifting, watching them with unblinking focus.

Frankie saw Veyrath's expression change one last time, softened by certainty, bright with the promise of ruin, and she knew he had been waiting for this moment longer than her lifetime.

"Welcome," he whispered, "to the unraveling."

The forest fell silent.

Chapter 22

The divide behind Veyrath widened with deliberate purpose, its edges glowing in thin silver lines that reached deep into the earth. A low vibration rolled through the clearing, steady and unbroken, as though the world had been split to reveal a depth that should never have been touched. Shadows streamed toward the opening in fevered waves, answering a summons older than the forest itself. Through it all, Veyrath remained utterly composed, standing before the widening abyss with the calm certainty of a man greeting a destiny he believed he owned.

Frankie held her ground. No one around her rushed forward, not out of hesitation, but because something within the forest had changed. Griffon stood ready beside her, wings angled like an encircling shield. Chalupa crouched at her feet, low and seething, his instincts baring themselves in every line of his body. Aoife's magic rose through the air beside them in quiet, escalating intensity. Nyx circled overhead, his silhouette cutting across the light like a spell cast in motion. Yet none of them struck, the forest would not allow it. What gripped them was not fear. It was recognition, the deep, wordless kind that lived in rivers, in roots, in the old breath of the land. Velhollow had not simply paused. It had turned its full attention toward one person.

Frankie felt it gather around her now, unseen but undeniable. The hum rolling from the divide wove through her like a thread tightening, not painfully, but with purpose. Her breath aligned with it. The world sharpened. The haze of fear thinned until clarity pressed through her like a presence she had always known and only now remembered. This moment was not something she had stumbled into, it had been waiting for her. The sigil on her palm answered that call. Light rose from her hand in a sudden rush, streaked with green and violet, alive with an energy that carried its own gravity. The magic did not ask for permission or direction. It recognized its purpose and moved.

Frankie stepped forward and the clearing erupted in response. Darkness recoiled from the force that spilled through her, tearing back from the light as though it had been driven from its own domain. The ground quivered beneath her as if the land itself acknowledged her stance. The trees leaned inward, gathering like witnesses drawn to the first crack of thunder.

Her arm lifted, steady and unyielding. The blaze surged, cutting through the space between her and Veyrath in a clear, unwavering line that split the clearing with the force of dawn transforming night. For the first time since he had revealed himself, Veyrath's expression changed, and it wasn't fear. It was recognition, sharp, unwelcome, and dawning too late to stop what was rising in front of him. The balance of the clearing shifted with that realization. The power in the air no longer leaned in his direction; it gathered around Frankie instead, closing the distance between her and the forest's will until she stood at its center, claimed rather than chased.

"I will not be shaped by anyone's will except my own." Her voice came low and unwavering, carrying across the clearing with the same quiet authority that settles after thunder rolls away.

Heat flared through her palm as the sigil ignited, releasing power that unfurled in steady waves, each one stronger than the last. The magic didn't rush; it rose with purpose, gathering behind her ribs, threading through her limbs, filling her until she felt too small and too vast all at once. The air tasted different, brighter somehow, sharp with possibility, and every breath drew more of the forest's wild strength into her. The darkness in front of her hesitated, recoiling as the ground beneath her feet lit with thin lines of living color. For a fleeting moment, Frankie sensed the entire clearing brace, as though everything rooted or winged could feel her rising.

Then the words began, they came without effort, without thought, called from a place so deep it felt carved into her soul. Each syllable flowed like something remembered rather than learned, ringing through the glade with the resonance of a forgotten bell. The trees carried the sound. The stones carried it. Even the sky seemed to lean closer. A current surged through her, fierce and certain, and she felt her magic align, no longer scattered, no longer searching. It gathered into shape, tracing ancient pathways inside her as though it had been waiting her entire life for this moment. Frankie wasn't merely casting a spell, she was stepping into the truth of who she was meant to be and becoming the spell itself.

"*Light, eternal, pure, and deep,*
Shall rise where shadows dare to creep.
By root, by flame, by sky, by stone,
The dark shall bow, and stand alone."

Warmth surged within her, the light she carried was a force. Enduring, unyielding, and now it roared through. She stepped forward, the blaze from her palm cast long spears of gold into the suffocating gloom. The sigil didn't burn with pain, it burned with purpose.

"*By the old ways, with balance sound,*
I call the light from sacred ground.
It claims me now, as I claim flame,
In verdant truth, I speak its name."

The ground shook with a summoning. Shadows pulled away from her presence, their edges fraying, flickering like flame-starved wicks, as if some unspoken law kept them at bay. And still, Veyrath stood tall.

Aoife turned sharply, eyes gone wide with memory awakened. Her voice came as a whisper laced with both awe and dread.

"*The Oath of the First Light*," she breathed, her hands trembling at her sides. "It hasn't been spoken in an age… not since the sky cracked."

Frankie didn't answer. The words hadn't been taught to her. They had always been there, hidden in her bones, etched into the cradle of her bloodline. She locked eyes with Veyrath, and her voice rose from someplace beyond memory, clear and unyielding.

"Your shadow will not claim this realm. Light will rise, and I will not falter."

Her sigil flared, no longer a symbol, but a scar of truth, and the night around them recoiled. It wasn't brightness that emerged, but reckoning, a cold, wild radiance born of vow and defiance. The very shape of the world seemed to hold its breath. Aoife stepped beside her, a second flare of light answering the first. Her own sigils ignited, green and gold, fierce and burning with intent. The air cracked with raw force.

"You will not have her," Aoife said, voice low and commanding. "Not while I draw breath."

She thrust out her hands, and a barrier of light erupted, wild, jagged, serrated with intent. It didn't unfurl gently; it snapped into being like a command. The radiance flared in sharp, uneven bursts, each one honed as if shaped by defiance itself. It circled her with deliberate precision, forming a brilliant coronet that held its ground with a will as ancient as the forest breathing around them. Veyrath strode through the dark as though the shadows bent to clear his path. The barrier's brightness grazed his features, slicing his expression into sharp planes that made the cruelty in his smile unmistakable.

"Silly witch," he murmured to Aoife, voice smooth as polished steel. "Nothing you do can halt what has already taken root."

Above them, a low tremor rolled through the canopy, a sound like roots adjusting in deep earth. The forest fell silent. Stone tightened beneath their feet. Even the air carried the brittle tension of something bracing for impact. Branches arched inward. Leaves curled at their edges. The cavern walls tightened as though narrowing their gaze. Light didn't simply dim, it fractured, splintering into shards that broke across shadow like glass dropped in slow motion.

Then the Watchers emerged.

Golden eyes appeared throughout the dark, blooming one by one like predatory stars piercing a midnight sea. Too many to count. Too still to mistake for anything familiar. They ringed the glade, half-hidden among the twisted boughs, each pair bright with quiet menace. Their gaze held the hush of old gods, the patience of creatures that linger beneath centuries and wait for their moment to rise. Some blinked, slow, deliberate, appraising her as though weighing her very breath. Others watched without movement at all, their attention heavy enough to feel like a touch across the back of the neck and every single one of them had turned their eyes toward Frankie.

They didn't move but their presence pressed in, undeniable, ancient, sentient. They weren't merely spectators. They were part of this, watching Frankie with anticipation, like witnesses at a coronation, or vultures at a wake and they whispered. Not in language, but in cold that slid behind her ribs. In the faintest tremble at the edges of thought. The golden eyes had no mouths, no faces, but they hissed without breath.

They offered no speech, only impressions carried on the air, blunt, unfinished, reaching for her like half-remembered echoes. The meaning refused to settle into anything precise, but the threat within it settled easily into her bones. The whispers curled behind her ears like smoke from burned parchment, threading through her pulse, watching, waiting, wanting.

Beside her, Aoife's barrier thickened. Griffon shifted, bone and stone grinding like distant war drums. His skin silvered, wings unfurling in a span too vast for reason. He moved forward as a protector and a bastion. A cathedral of defiance forged from magic and will. Overhead, Nyx wheeled through the storm, a raven turned ember, feathers aglow. His caw split the dark, sharp as a blade. He dove, talons tearing through shadow like glass through silk. At Frankie's feet, Chalupa bristled, his body trembling with held power. His fur stood in spiked rows, his eyes twin suns of defiance.

"Nobody's touching her," he snarled, the words low and sharp as broken bone. "Not unless they'd like to be clawed back to the void."

Frankie stood at the center, breath shallow, stance unshaken. She didn't glow, she surged. Light and shadow rippled around her, two tides locked in tension. Her sigil felt alive not just with magic, but memory. The forest didn't shield her. It bore witness. She was no longer the girl who wandered into prophecy. She was becoming what prophecy dared not name. Veyrath only smiled. Not a grin or a sneer, this was something colder. Calmer. His eyes never left Frankie, but they flicked, just once, to the golden gaze of the Watchers.

"You hear them, don't you?" he said softly, voice curling around her like rot wrapped in velvet. "The whispers in the dark. They've always known you."

She didn't answer, but she heard them, felt them, those eyes not merely seeing, but weighing on her. A pressure sliding through her spirit, a hush settling deep inside her. His words weren't speech. They were invasion.

“You weren’t born to deny them,” Veyrath said, and his voice changed. It fractured, layered now with echoes that didn’t belong to this world.

The moment Veyrath drew breath, the forest reacted with a shudder that rippled through every branch and root. It was not a shift in wind or temperature, but a deeper change in attention, as though the entire realm recognized a threat rising and braced against it. The great trees angled their limbs away from him, leaves curling inward in a slow retreat. Moss receded against the bark, and ferns pressed flat to the soil, trying to hide from what they sensed. Even the stones seemed to dim, their faint inner glow fading as if they wished to disappear entirely.

Above the clearing, the canopy darkened into a bruised violet, and the light thinned so sharply it resembled a held breath. Roots hunched deeper into the ground, drawing back from the surface as if they feared being touched by whatever Veyrath was about to release. The entire glade tightened in on itself, shrinking from him with the instinctive recoil of a living world preparing for harm.

The Watchers responded next. Their golden eyes brightened all at once, illuminating thin rings of light around each shadowed form. They did not blink or shift; instead, an uneasy awareness settled over them, heavy and unified. Every gaze turned toward Veyrath, pulled by the gravity of inevitability. Their stillness stretched the air so taut it felt as though the glade itself had frozen in place to witness what came next. When Veyrath finally spoke, the sound carried the weight of something far older than speech. His voice did not rise; rather, the world around him seemed to withdraw, clearing a path for his words.

“You were born to command them,” he said, each syllable unfolding with a measured certainty that made the shadows lean closer.

He lifted his arms slowly, with a deliberate confidence that suggested long practice. The darkness at his back shifted with him, reshaping itself in jagged coils that reached toward the Watchers as though acknowledging a master they wished they could deny. They lowered their heads in a single, synchronized motion of recognition, an ancient response that made the glade contract with dread. A deep murmur traveled through the clearing. Bark split along the nearest tree trunks, releasing thin ribbons of sap that glowed faintly before dimming. The ground tightened underfoot as if trying to keep itself from tearing open. Above them, the sky pressed heavier against the canopy until the entire clearing seemed to exist under a dome of gathering storm. Only then, when the forest was held in the tension of a realm resisting the inevitable, did Veyrath speak the prophecy he had carried like a blade sharpened across decades.

"*When moonlight wanes and shadows rise,*
A child of root and ruin cries.
Not born to break, nor born to bind,
But forge anew what lies confined.
Blood of the Verdant, blessed and cursed,
A fate entwined, for best or worst.
Blood of Noctis, deep as night,
A child of shadow, a child of light.
She stands where midnight's fire burns bright,
A queen of dusk, a wraith of light.
From realms forgotten, from lines revered,
A storm untamed, a fate unclear.
Two paths before her, one must take,
To heal, to shatter, to mend or break.
If hand extends, the dark shall bow,
If heart resists, the world shall drown.
A throne in ruin, a crown in flame,
The choice is hers, to rule or reign.
One path to rule, one path to rend,
And Balance bends where she descends."

The words fell like hot ash, soft, but scorching. Frankie felt them burrow deep. Her ribs ached from the weight of them. Her bones remembered them before her mind could grasp the shape.

"In all things, Francesca," Veyrath said, voice a velvet blade, "there is a choice. You were born to command the darkness, not fight it. You are not solely one thing, you are both. Darkness and light. Flame and root."

Tears pressed at the corners of her eyes, but her jaw did not waver. They weren't tears of surrender, but of fury too long unspoken, grief scraping against bone, truth rising where lies had once taken root. Her breath caught, but she didn't look away. She shook her head slowly, as if trying to dislodge something crawling under her skin, a lingering doubt, a seed of fear he'd planted long ago that now shriveled in the light of her refusal. Her voice came soft, but sure, the syllable formed from something deeper than language.

"No," she whispered. A word small but immovable.

Veyrath tilted his head, just slightly, the way a predator measures a final move. It wasn't surprise that flickered across his face, it was calculation, the moment before a snare is sprung. The air shivered around him, pressure dropping like the pause before lightning strikes.

"That," he said, almost gently, his voice brushing the space between them like silk laced with iron, "depends entirely on how you choose to use what you've become."

Then a vision claimed her, it seized her, utterly, and without permission.

She stood upon a vast, ashen plain beneath a sky stretched thin between dusk and the brink of ruin. Light fractured across the horizon in long, broken ribbons, while clouds spiraled overhead like ink dissolving through water. All around her, shadows gathered, drawn, not driven. They did not strike. They knelt. Their shifting forms, half-shaped and nameless, bowed low before her as though answering an ancient summons.

Frankie did not recoil. She stood at the center of that desolate expanse, cloaked in dusk made living and flame that smoldered with slow, deliberate purpose. Her eyes burned gold, unblinking and unafraid, too steady, too knowing to belong to the girl she once was. Her hands remained poised, directing the forces that circled her.

Magic rose in coils around her form, light and shadow intertwined, neither seeking dominance, neither recoiling from the other. They moved in concert, drawn to her as their axis, as though she alone completed the design. There was no internal struggle, no fracture of will. She held both realms within her, balanced and unhindered, the calm at the center of an oncoming storm.

Frankie gasped as the vision shattered like brittle glass. She staggered back into the clearing, lungs burning. Magic surged beneath her skin, no longer quiet, no longer tame. It pressed against bone and breath, wild and waiting. Veyrath stepped forward, slow and certain, as if he too had seen.

"You feel it, don't you?" he said. "The power. The truth. It's not a lie, *Francesca Noctis Caelith*, it's your birthright. Etched in blood. Forged in bone." He didn't reach for her. He offered a hand, open. "Why deny it? The world was never made for you. Not a child of light, nor shadow. You're something between. That vision wasn't a threat, it was a promise. You don't have to fear the dark. You can rule it!"

Frankie drew back instinctively. She would not be a queen of cinder and ash. Griffon moved before she could. In Stonewing form, he stepped beside her, massive, silent. His hand found hers, reminding her, she was still here. Still herself. Still whole. Her jaw tightened. The heat in her chest was not hunger, it was defiance. Her fists curled. Magic flared, roaring away from darkness and reaching for the light like wildfire through dry roots.

"No," she said, voice raw but sure. "That's not my path. That's not who I am."

Veyrath's smile faltered, barely. "Such a shame," he whispered.

Then the shadows moved, they lunged like intent given form. From the void, they emerged. Long-limbed, broken things. Their limbs bent wrong, their motion graceful but sickening. Golden eyes locked on Frankie, void born, shaped by Veyrath's will. One blinked forward, crossing the clearing in a breath, claws outstretched.

Griffon met it mid-air, flame bursting from his limbs. He tore through shadowed flesh, fire searing it from within. His snarl split the night, savage and unrelenting. Another creature lunged. Griffon turned, claws glowing, flames rising. She was behind him, his reason to burn. Aoife was a tempest unleashed as magic ripped through the air, her runes igniting in gold and green. Chains of light shot from her palms, binding the creatures in searing coils. They writhed, silent but shrieking, as Velhollow itself rejected them. The land stirred, the air shifted and an ancient force awakened.

Griffon's fire flared brighter, no longer just his, but the fury of the earth rising with him. Where he struck, flame lingered, refusing to die. One shadow slipped through. It leapt for Frankie. Aoife cried out. Her hands rose. The sky tore open like ancient cloth, and from her palms surged a rift of raw starfire. It struck mid-flight, unmaking the creature in a burst of blinding brilliance.

"You shall not have her!" Aoife thundered, and it was not hers alone, but the voice of every witch of the Verdant line who had ever lived. Their power flooded through her like a rising tide, old as root and storm, bound to blood and oath. She bore the gift of the *Linekeeper*, the one who could summon the strength of her foremothers in full and in that moment, she did. Her fury became theirs, their light poured through her bones like molten dawn. From grove to grave, their voices rose in unison, woven through time itself, and the very earth seemed to lean toward her, listening.

Nyx screeched from above, wings slicing the sky in jagged arcs, each beat a tempest forged in ancient wind. Air bent to his will, rushing in gales that tore through the dark. He dove with lethal grace, talons extended, cutting through shadowed forms with the precision of a blade honed by storms. Where he struck, the shadows unraveled, spun apart by the very force of his command. Below, Chalupa's growl built from deep within his chest, low, guttural, ancient. Then he launched, a streak of golden fury. He moved like lightning drawn to earth, weaving between towering beasts with uncanny precision. Claws slashed with purpose. Teeth found the seams between shadow and form. He didn't fight wild, he fought knowing.

Frankie stood at the center of it all, a conduit and catalyst. She didn't simply watch the storm, she became its axis. She felt it surge beneath her skin, threading through her like wildfire and ocean tide. It wasn't just hers. It was Griffon's fire, Aoife's will, Nyx's wind, Chalupa's speed. It was the breath of Velhollow rising through the earth, ancient and indivisible. Elemental magic answered her call, not as a servant, but as kin. She aligned with it and channeled the rhythm of the realm.

"Move!" she shouted, and her voice struck like thunder, it didn't shake, it commanded.

Her hands lifted, forged in fury and purpose. The sigil on her palm flared gold, light pouring from it like dawn breaking through storm. The air thickened, pressure mounting as power gathered. The current of her magic rose, shaped by clarity. She knew what she had to do and she did not hesitate.

Power ignited in her palms, brilliant and blinding, a blast of raw force, white-hot and alive, streaked with gold and silver like lightning threaded through creation. The energy erupted forward, a radiant spear hurled by the heart of the world itself. It struck a lunging shadow mid-air, collided, and the result was annihilation. The creature didn't fall, it shattered. The impact tore silence open. The golden-eyed beast splintered into ash and smoke, its scream swallowed in the unraveling dark. The mist curled away, thread by thread, until even its memory was gone. Then Veyrath spoke, and the world seemed to close around them.

"This is what you choose?" His voice cracked like thunder, edged with disbelief, seething with fury. "To fight for them?" His eyes bore into her, hollow with promise. "When you could have had everything?"

No one had defied Dominicus Veyrath Noctis, until now. Frankie stood tall, breath burning in her lungs, the sigil on her palm blazing like a star refusing to fall. Her magic rose to meet his, not out of fury, but clarity. She squared her shoulders, grounding herself in the one truth he could not twist.

"I choose me."

Veyrath's expression shifted, his eyes hollowing with something ancient and shadows coiled tighter around him, thickening into a mantle of midnight.

"So be it," he said, voice low and absolute. "By the hour of midnight, on the Festival of the Black Veil, your power will be mine, one way or another."

The ground convulsed beneath them, as if the earth itself recoiled from his vow. Roots groaned, the soil shivering with unease. Trees bent without wind. The very air compressed as Veyrath lifted his hand, and the darkness collapsed inward with a soundless detonation. Pressure flattened the clearing, then emptied all at once. He vanished. The shadows with him. But relief didn't come. What remained was worse, a void in the shape of a man, a silence with teeth. It felt like the breath before a scream.

The glade stood too still. The wind returned in a hush, carrying the scent of scorched magic and the breath of forgotten crypts. The place where Veyrath had stood didn't close behind him. It yawned open, a wound in the world. Watching. Waiting.

Frankie exhaled slowly, rolling her shoulders like she could shake the last of him from her skin. Sparks still flickered at her fingertips, reluctant to fade. When she turned, her voice was calm but edged with iron. She swallowed hard, Zyphirion's warning now stripped of riddle, echoing sharp and clear,

Beware the shadow that knows your name.

Chapter 23

The forest had not quieted, it had shifted its awareness toward them. Every branch felt taut with listening, every stretch of earth braced as though preparing to absorb what came next. Even the breeze had withdrawn. This was not empty silence, it was anticipation. The kind that pools before revelation. The path ahead no longer resembled a wandering woodland trail. Its meaning had sharpened. Time around it felt tight, funneled forward, refusing to unwind.

Frankie walked carefully, each step sinking into soil still scarred by Veyrath's casting. She kept her eyes forward, but the memory of him clung to her thoughts like a shadow she couldn't shake. Irritation flickered beneath her calm, growing sharper with every step. The truth gnawed at her: nothing about this path had been accidental. Every so-called discovery, every sign she'd thought she had followed by instinct, every moment she believed she'd chosen for herself, he had been there first, arranging the board.

"He was waiting for us," she said at last, the words edged with disbelief and rising anger.

Griffon moved beside her, wings drawing in with a quiet sweep. "You're certain?"

"I have no doubt." The answer left her easily, carved from clarity she wished she didn't have. "He didn't wander into our path. He built it. The house, the chest, the timing, every piece of it was placed exactly where I would find it. I thought I was following Aoife's trail... but he laid his own breadcrumbs beside hers, counting on me to step where he wanted."

Her gaze hardened on the path ahead. "It makes me question everything I thought I knew. Every choice. Every instinct."

Her voice dropped. "How much of it was ever mine?"

Aoife slowed until she faced them, the last traces of her spellwork drifting like softened fire light along her sleeves. She drew a steady breath, though her eyes held the weight of someone measuring too many truths at once.

"That's what unsettles me," she said quietly. "He didn't strike today to win. He struck so we'd understand just how long he's been shaping this, and how close he already is."

Chalupa walked ahead, tail twitching with agitation, muttering under his breath the way only a disgruntled familiar could. Nyx circled high, wings banking sharply, his silhouette sharp against the dimming sky. Even the forest itself seemed to inch closer in its stillness.

Frankie frowned, frustration tightening her voice. "So this Festival is important, but no one has explained why. What actually happens during it?"

Aoife slowed, her expression shifting. "The Festival of the Black Veil," she said, "comes once every fifty years, when the Veil thins on its own accord, when the old magic stirs whether we're ready for it or not. People will call it tradition, or revelry, or remembrance... but it is none of those things. It's a convergence. A reckoning. A season when realms overlap and the world listens too closely."

She stepped closer, her voice threading through the stillness. "For three nights, power surges through Velhollow like a rising tide. On the final night, at midnight, the Veil thins to its weakest point. Spells cast then carry farther. Oaths bind tighter. Magic behaves like it remembers being wild. And every creature, witch, fae, beast, ghost, or wanderer, feels that pull. Some come for celebration. Some come for politics. And some come because they hope to steal a little power before the Veil closes again."

Her expression darkened. "That's why Veyrath wants the festival. Not because it's beautiful... but because it's dangerous. One misstep on that final night, and the Balance could break for every realm tied to ours."

She walked backward so she could keep her eyes on Frankie.

"It's when the old ways wake. When wards breathe easier. When prophecies tug at their threads. For three nights, intention grows teeth. Wishes grow roots. Spells stretch farther than they should."

Her mouth curved with dry humor. "And some folk get drunk on the excess magic the way others get drunk on mead. Truly a menace."

Chalupa chimed in with a sniff. "Last time, a selkie tried to wed a barrel of elderberry wine. Said it understood him. It did not."

Aoife continued, warm exasperation flickering in her voice.

"The festival isn't dangerous by design. It's joyful. There are lantern parades, treats that float when you laugh, ballads older than the forest, games that only work when the veil is thin. Folk from every corner of Velhollow gather in the village square. Even a few from neighboring realms sneak through."

Her expression turned more serious. "But where magic gathers, ambition gathers too. The festival is ripe for mischief. Bargains. Power grabs. Secrets traded in shadow. Some come to heal old wounds. Others come to sharpen new ones."

Frankie absorbed this slowly. "So… it's more than food and music."

"Aye. Much more. On the final night, at midnight, the Veil thins to its deepest point. For a breath, everything listens, ancestors, old magic, forgotten oaths. Anything spoken then can cling to the rootlines for years. Anything taken then can't easily be returned."

She let that settle.

"That's why it matters. That's why Veyrath wants it. Midnight on the last night isn't just a moment. It's a doorway and if he moves then… his reach will be felt in every realm tied to ours."

Frankie's frustration returned, sharper this time, edged with something almost like resentment. "So even this, this festival I knew nothing about, was on his timetable?"

Aoife nodded solemnly. "He timed everything around it. Veyrath was playing the long game."

Frankie exhaled, the truth settling cold. "It feels like every step I've taken was already counted by him. Every choice I thought I made on my own… every instinct… manipulated or used."

Griffon touched her shoulder gently, grounding her. "You're not wrong," he said. "But you're not trapped in his design either."

Aoife's voice gentled. "That's why we prepare. That's why we go home."

As they walked, time slipped past them unnoticed. Finally, the glow of the cottage flickered through the trees, warm, steady, waiting. Behind them, the forest whispered as though it already sensed the countdown. Chalupa walked ahead, his eyes gleaming with mischief.

"Alright," he said, flicking his tail. "So, no cookies then?"

Frankie glanced at him, eyebrows raised.

"What?" He sighed, dramatic and continued. "Well, Veyrath didn't win, which means no joining the dark side… which means no cookies."

Nyx fluttered down to a low branch, eyeing Chalupa with theatrical dismay. "If cookies decide the fate of the realms," he announced, "we're doomed. He'll switch sides for a cinnamon bun."

Chalupa gasped, scandalized. "I have standards."

"Please," Nyx said. "Your standards are flaky and iced."

"You're both impossible." Frankie laughter was quiet but real, the heavy air around them lifting just a little.

Chalupa trotted ahead as if he'd lifted the tension with a flick of his tail. Nyx swooped low, then settled atop the old iron gate just as it creaked open, its hinges groaning a familiar welcome.

They crossed into the herb garden, where rows of thyme and marigold blinked with dew, and the worn stones of the path gleamed in the firefly light. Wind stirred the wind chimes hanging from the eaves, their tones soft and metallic, like old coins tumbling in a velvet pouch. It should have felt safe. It almost did.

Griffon reached for the cottage door first, his hand pausing on the handle. A veil of wardlight brushed over the frame, quick and assessing. It recognized him, then eased aside like curtains parting at a familiar touch. The latch clicked softly, and warmth, tinged with rosemary, ash, and old secrets, rolled out to greet them.

Frankie entered last. Her eyes swept the room she had come to know so well. The floorboards creaked in their old, familiar way. The same dried bundles hung from the rafters. The same chipped teacups waited on the shelves. Yet the air felt different. Charged. As though the cottage itself had roused from a long, careful sleep.

The hearth glowed softly, but its fire didn't quite warm the space. Shadows stretched long across the stone walls, drawn thin as if something unseen had unsettled their usual rhythm. The cold lingered despite the flames, clinging to the corners, threading through the beams overhead. A quiet tension lived in the timbers, the old enchantments woven through them faintly stirring like threads shifting in a loom. Bundles of lavender, sage, and star-bright blue ferns hung above her, their scents rising in gentle waves, sweet, sharp, grounding, yet even they couldn't quite mask the undercurrent left behind by Veyrath's presence.

Velhollow's magic gathered close, aware, the way a forest becomes aware of someone stepping off the path. Frankie felt it settle around her, not hostile, simply intent, like a place that understood more than it was willing to say outright.

She tugged her sweater tighter, though she knew it alone couldn't chase off the chill inside her. That cold came from memory, his voice, his certainty, the deliberate way he had shaped her life long before she understood it. The echoes of his promises clung to her like smoke that refused to clear, drifting through thoughts she could no longer silence.

Finally, Aoife spoke, her voice a quiet murmur.

"It's the timing," she said, fingers trailing over the worn pages of an open tome. Her silver eyes darkened. "This is no coincidence."

Frankie sat up straighter, the weight of those words pressing into her chest. "Timing?" she asked, her voice tentative.

Griffon, sitting in a chair near the window, leaned forward then, elbows resting on his knees, his voice low and steady. "The Festival of the Black Veil," he said, eyes locking with hers, "only happens once every fifty years, Frankie. One night when the Veil between realms thins more than any other, and the oldest magics wake."

Aoife nodded, her expression grave. "Most festivals are for song, dance, a bit of mischief," she said, voice tightening. "But this one… this one changes things. For one night, certain spells can be cast that could shift the Balance itself. Spells that can't be undone."

Frankie's stomach twisted. "And it's just days away?"

"Aye, three days time." Aoife said, her mouth a grim line. "We don't have seasons to prepare, we have but hours."

Griffon exhaled, rolling his shoulders as if shaking off the weight that had settled there.

"Still," he said, "there's some fun to be had before the world threatens to end. The Festival's full of spectacle, enchanted food stalls, illusion duels, misfired love charms, shape-shifting bards… and of course, the unicorn jousts."

Frankie blinked. "Unicorns?"

Griffon chuckled, the sound low and unexpected. It broke the tension like sunlight through clouds. "Not as graceful as you'd hope. I once saw one launch its rider headfirst into a pie cart. The pie survived. The rider, less so."

The fire snapped in the hearth, warmth flickering briefly into the room. But Aoife's tone dipped, anchoring the moment back to truth.

"It's not all games. When that much magic gathers in one place… things can tilt sideways fast." Her eyes softened, yet grew distant with memory. "One year, someone tried to enchant a weather charm for the rain dance."

Griffon groaned, dragging a hand down his face. "Turned half the festival square into frogs."

"Not just frogs," Aoife corrected, her mouth curving into a grin. "Singing frogs."

Frankie shook her head, somewhere between disbelief and wonder. "Sounds… chaotic."

"Aye, it was," Aoife said fondly. "Wild, beautiful chaos."

As the fire crackled down, the warmth no longer reached the corners of the room. The levity slipped away, replaced by the quiet weight of something vast and urgent.

Frankie swallowed hard, her throat dry as splintered wood. "We need to be ready."

"Aye," Aoife murmured, her voice soft as damp wool. "And we can't do it alone."

She moved to the table, unrolling a parchment with the slow care of someone revealing something that mattered deeply. The vellum crackled like dry leaves, its edges curled from age and countless midnight consultations. As it unfurled, faint runes along its surface stirred to life, glowing softly as if warmed by firelight and memory.

"We need to call the Cairn Circle," she said.

Frankie raised a brow. "The what now? Who are they? And why would they help us?" Her tone dipped. "The villagers didn't exactly welcome me when I walked through town. Unless passive-aggressive glaring counts as confetti."

Aoife's gaze lifted, steady as moonlight on still water. "They're the ones who kept Velhollow's magic alive when the rest of the world forgot how to listen. Seers, hedge witches, lore-keepers, the kind who talk to trees and argue with the moon when she's being difficult. Elders who remember not only what was, but what was nearly lost." She leaned in, voice threaded with fond exasperation. "They're not always kind, and never predictable. One insists on speaking only in riddles and collects cursed teaspoons for fun."

Frankie blinked. "Cursed… teaspoons?"

Aoife didn't miss a beat. "Aye. One sings sea shanties during thunderstorms, another flung itself at Chalupa's head."

From his place by the hearth, Chalupa cracked one eye open and let out a long-suffering sigh, like a feline who had endured far too much cutlery-based nonsense for one lifetime.

"These are the people we're counting on?" Frankie asked, half-disbelieving.

"Aye, but they're not all from the village," Aoife replied, smoothing the parchment as if to calm it. "The Circle doesn't meet in tidy halls or send polite invitations. Some haven't set foot in Velhollow in decades. They come when the wind shifts, when the trees lean a certain way. Root-walkers from the North. Duskbinders who speak with wind and shadow. Even a Whisper-witch from beyond the Withering River who communicates entirely through cryptic embroidery and once hexed a squirrel for interrupting her stitch count."

Frankie squinted. "You're joking."

Aoife arched a brow. "Am I?"

"The squirrel deserved it," Chalupa muttered darkly.

"The Circle will come," Aoife continued gently. "Not just for you, love. For the Balance. When the old signs stir, they feel it in their bones. Even the cranky ones. Especially the cranky ones. They'll argue, yes, loudly, with passive-aggressive scones and the occasional hex threat. But they'll come. They always do."

Frankie rubbed her temples. "So, we're summoning a semi-retired league of magical grumblers who might show up out of spite and bring weaponized baked goods?"

"Exactly," Aoife said with a smile. "Now you're catching on."

Across the room, Griffon folded his arms with a sigh. "If anyone brings those lemon bars again, I'm not responsible for what happens."

Aoife shot him a look. "They were dusted with *truthroot*. Honestly, one bite and you confessed to using my hair oil."

"It smelled like oranges," he muttered.

Frankie laughed despite herself. "Fine, let's summon the goblet of grumbles. Or whatever they're called."

"The Cairn Circle," Aoife corrected, already reaching for the high shelf.

"Sorry," Frankie said, holding up a hand. "But doesn't that name sound like a band of druidic pirates?"

Aoife's lips curved faintly as she pulled a long wooden box into the light. Carved with spiraling runes, its edges were worn smooth by generations of hands. The moment her fingers brushed the lid, the air shifted, as if the room itself had straightened its spine.

"They're not pirates," she said softly. "They're the memory of this place. And when we open this box, the land will call them home."

Chalupa groaned. "If the box starts singing, I'm out."

Frankie sobered, the weight of wary glances and whispered warnings pressing on her ribs. "Are you sure they'll come?"

Aoife's gaze didn't waver. "Aye love, the villagers may whisper. They always have. But the Cairn Circle is older than their fences and fears. The Circle is not the village, it's the bones beneath it. They come from far corners, bound by vows made when Velhollow was more legend than land."

"This is how we call them," Aoife said, voice hushed. "The Cairn Circle doesn't answer small things. When they gather, it's because the realm itself demands it."

Frankie tilted her head. "How will we know they're coming?"

"You'll feel it," Aoife said. "Long before their feet touch the path."

"There's a shift," Griffon added. "In the light. The wind changes. Even the birds go quiet."

"The wards bloom," Aoife murmured. "The iron gate swings open without a hand to touch it. The sugar bowl fogs. The tea goes cold."

"And then," Griffon said solemnly, "you'll hear the goat."

Frankie blinked. "Excuse me… a goat?"

Aoife sighed, as if haunted by experience. "Aye, there's always a goat."

Griffon nodded gravely. “Every time. No one knows where it comes from. It just… appears. A hard-hearted omen with no respect for property lines.”

“Once,” Aoife muttered, “it kicked a banshee clean off the roof. Didn’t blink. Just trotted away like it had somewhere better to be.”

Frankie stared. “You’re serious?”

“Don’t make eye contact if it’s chewing,” Griffon said without blinking.

Frankie couldn’t help smiling. Her worry bent under their absurd seriousness. “So… chaos, omens, and an emotionally unavailable goat.”

Aoife rested her hand over Frankie’s, grounding her. “Magic and memory, love. They’ll come and when they do, this cottage will know it before we do.”

Griffon leaned back, voice warm but steady. “They’re not just answering us. They’re answering the realm.”

Frankie turned to the window, outside lantern light filtered through the trees like silver breath. “So… we send the call now?”

Aoife gave a slow, certain nod. “Aye. Let’s begin.”

The moment hung suspended, neither breath nor time daring to move, as the hush of what came next wrapped itself around them. The fire in the hearth gave a soft pop, as though the cottage itself were listening. Even the shadows seemed to still, drawn inward by the gravity of old magic preparing to wake. No fanfare. No thunder. Just the silence of something stirring from sleep.

Aoife turned to the wooden box resting on the table, the spiraling runes along its surface glowing in a slow, steady rhythm, like a heartbeat remembered. With a practiced flick of her fingers, she lifted the latch. A soft exhale of air slipped out as the lid rose, carrying the faint scent of old forests and distant storms, as if the box had been waiting to be opened again.

Inside, nestled against velvet the color of deep twilight, lay the tools of summoning. Six slender candles rested in a neat row, each carved with whisper-fine glyphs that caught the light and held it. Beside them sat a small vial of luminous oil, pale gold, flecked with drifting sparks that moved like fireflies trying to decide whether to rise or settle. A feather lay next, black as midnight water, its edges soft as soot yet ending in a quill honed with deliberate intent. Near it, a smooth, palm-sized stone glowed gently beneath etched runes, the markings responding as if they recognized the presence of those in the room. Finally, there were cords of silver thread and dark vine, braided and knotted into intricate patterns. Each twist held the quiet tension of old promises, the kind that never truly loosen with time.

They worked in silence. Aoife dipped each candle's base into the vial's oil, her fingers moving with unhurried precision. She handed two to Frankie, who followed her lead, placing them one by one outside along the path to the green, each wick catching the moon's gaze. The glyphs glimmered as they touched the earth, aligning in an unseen pattern only the land and the old magic seemed to know. The candles formed a quiet corridor of light, marking the way for what was about to come.

Aoife returned to the table, reached for one of the cords, and placed it into Frankie's hands. "Hold it steady, love. Let the land feel you." Her voice had gone soft, but it carried the weight of trust and invocation.

Frankie cradled it in both hands. The cord was cool to the touch, but alive beneath her skin, thrumming like a heartbeat, or like something listening for hers in return. Not just a tool. Not a symbol. A message waiting to be awakened, one that didn't need translation, only truth.

Aoife stepped back, closing her eyes. Her voice dropped into a chant, low, rhythmic, ancient. The words moved like wind through standing stones, a melody older than language. As she sang, the glow from candles on the table caught the silver runes and glinting in the curves of the feather and stone. The air thickened, not heavy, but full. Frankie didn't hesitate, her voice rose beside Aoife's, uncertain for only a breath before finding its shape. It didn't feel like remembering so much as being remembered. Like the song had always been written in her bones, waiting for … the right night and the right magic.

"By root and river, by stone and sky,
By oath once sworn and never broken,
Come forth, children of the Old Way,
Answer the call, the magic has spoken."

The cords pulled slowly as they lifted into the air. As if exhaling magic, they unraveled into delicate leaf-shaped offerings, each one flickering gold and green at the edges like candlelight caught in a forest breeze. They hovered over the table like tiny folded flames, swaying slightly, pulsing with breathless anticipation. Aoife whispering in a tongue older than any inked page, a language woven from root and star. Griffon struck a match, its hiss sharp in the hush. One by one, the flames came to life, green, silver, deep blue, warm gold, each flickering to its own rhythm, casting shadows that danced along the walls like ancestral echoes. The room was dense with energy and magic, soft and velvet-rich. It curled across the floor like rising mist, creeping into every seam and hollow, until even the air hummed with waiting.

Aoife turned to Frankie and offered her the black feather. "The breath of the Circle," she said. "You'll send the call."

Frankie nodded once. Her hand trembled slightly, but her grip remained firm. She closed her eyes and whispered the final words of the spell, letting them slip from her tongue like leaves carried downstream. She swept the feather through the candle flames, slow and deliberate. The fire rose in a brief surge of color, bright with purpose, then steadied into a quiet, waiting glow.

From its center, a thin ribbon of smoke unfurled, soft, luminous, pale as moonlit water. It drifted upward, curling through the rafters before gliding toward the door with an almost knowing grace, as if it recognized the path it was meant to take.

Aoife gave Griffon a small nod. "Now, lad."

Griffon stepped forward and unlatched the door. It opened with a long creak, the sound of old wood waking from deep rest. A breeze swept in, cool and sharp with pine, damp earth, wild mint, and something stranger still, an echo of starlight, of memory older than language.

The smoke slipped out into the night, and the forest shifted in response. The spell had taken root. They followed it outside, Frankie first, the feather still warm in her hand, the others close behind as the air thickened with anticipation. Night wrapped around them, deep and velvet-dark, holding a hush so complete it felt like breath caught between heartbeats. Outside, the feather's smoke had stretched into a slender trail of light, drifting just above the path like a thread woven from moonbeam and song. It moved with purpose, steady and sure, as though guiding them toward something waiting in the bones of the forest.

They stood together beneath the eaves of the cottage roof. Above, the wind rustled through the leaves like secrets trading places. No one spoke, they simply watched as the smoke curled higher, paused, then spun once, twice, then unraveled into a shape not quite smoke and not quite feather. For a moment, it hovered there, suspended in possibility.

With the barest whisper of sound, the smoke-thread drifted into the treeline and vanished. A weighted silence followed, thick, expectant, as though the forest itself drew nearer to listen. Then, from between the trees, came the first flicker: silver-winged, no larger than a thimble. A wispwing darted into view like a spark flying backward into the dark, drawn not by light, but by the echo of the spell that had called it. Dozens more followed, weaving around one another in bright, darting spirals, their wings catching hints of moonlight like tiny bells ringing without sound.

From the deeper shadows came heavier footsteps. A tall, horned dryad stepped forward, bark-textured skin mottled with lichen and moss. Her gown, stitched from dew-beaded leaves, shifted with every breath she took, catching glints of silver like morning light through a canopy. A river sprite emerged next, her hair a living fall of water that streamed and curled behind her, droplets drifting through the air in slow, drifting arcs. Her gown rippled as if stirred by tides only she could feel.

At the foot of the cobbled walkway, something else arrived, blinking into being rather than walking toward them. A creature shaped from fog and trailing vine wavered before settling into a form that was only mostly real. Its outline swayed gently, never quite one thing or another, its eyes gleaming softly in the dark, pools of deep, patient knowledge that seemed to watch straight through her.

These were not members of the Circle, these were emissaries of the Old Ways, drawn not by summons alone but by the deep thrum of oath and ancient balance. They arrived as forces woven into the land's oldest breath. Suspended before them, still floating in the air, were the spell-knots, leaf-shaped constructs spun from silver-threaded cord, delicate and glowing. Each bore a fragment of the invocation, the plea, the place, the tremor in the world's pulse. They were messengers, forged in magic, shaped by need and sealed in trust.

The emissaries stepped forward with quiet purpose, their silence deeper than anything spoken. No chants were required, no guidance offered, only the slow, steady hush of wild magic fulfilling what it had been called to do. One by one, each being approached the soft circle of candlelight and pressed claw, paw, wing, or brow to the waiting spell-knot. At the moment of contact, golden light rose and faded, gentle, sure, marking the transfer. In that suspended instant, each emissary changed. They were claimed by the land itself, bound to the message in a way no ward or forgetting spell could unravel.

"They'll carry the call," Aoife murmured, her voice low but certain. "They'll find every member of the Circle, no matter how far they've strayed. The land will guide them now. The magic has spoken."

As if answering that truth, the emissaries began to withdraw with the serene confidence of a duty completed. The dryad stepped backward into the trees, her leaf-woven gown releasing a trail of dew that glimmered faintly before disappearing. The river sprite lifted her face to the moonlight and dissolved into drifting mist, leaving only the scent of water and stone behind. The vine-creature blinked once, its eyes meeting Frankie's with soft, ancient recognition, and then unraveled into shadow and the faintest curl of green.

One by one, they slipped back into the wild that had shaped them. The final wispwing lingered a heartbeat longer, its wings flickering like a candle poised between flame and breath. It dipped in a graceful bow, then darted into the trees, leaving behind a thin trail of pale light that faded as quickly as it formed.

The clearing quieted, then, like wind moving through branches far above, the hush shifted. Leaves whispered in patterns too deliberate to be random. Magic settled around them with the steady certainty of a vow accepted.

Aoife rested a steady hand on Frankie's shoulder. "Well done, love. The word is loose on the wind now."

Frankie nodded, the weight of what they'd done settling into her slowly. She felt Griffon beside her, silent but steady, his presence as grounding as stone beneath moss. When she turned, she found him watching her. Like the way the earth listens to rain, not because it needs to respond, but because it wants to receive. He offered a rare, crooked smile that was entirely disarming. It was real and it made something flutter in her chest.

"We did our part," he said, his voice low and even, but softer now, tinged with a gentleness that had nothing to do with the ritual. "Now we see who answers."

She held his gaze a heartbeat longer than she meant to. There was something in his eyes, steady and unguarded, that made the world feel smaller, closer, like they were standing inside the same breath. She parted her lips to speak, but the words slipped away between her skin and his. He didn't look away.

Chalupa cleared his throat, loudly. "If you two are going to exchange elemental eye-gazing rituals, I'd like to request dinner first. I cannot witness this on an empty stomach."

Nyx flapped once, preening a wing with deliberate flair. "Honestly, the tension between them, you could cut it with a butter knife and spread it on toast."

Frankie blinked, startled into laughter, and Griffon exhaled a quiet breath of his own, one that curled at the edges like smoke off kindling. Even Aoife, standing a short distance off, allowed a quiet, knowing smile to ghost across her face, the kind that belonged to someone who had seen the wheel of the world turn more than once, and recognized what this was becoming.

Stars help them, they hadn't quite seen it yet, Aoife thought. The way they moved, his silence anchoring her whirl, her laughter cracking through his quiet like spring thaw. She could already see it, her granddaughter just down the path, in a home kissed by ivy and within shouting distance if needed, and close enough that fate wouldn't have to shout. It was not safety, not entirely. But it was balance. And that, in these days, was rarer still. As they reached the cottage threshold, the door eased open on its own, slow and deliberate, as though the house had overheard Aoife's thoughts and agreed. The warmth met them first, herb-thick air and old wood, the perfume of rosemary, ash bark, and something faintly metallic, like magic waking in the walls.

Inside, the fire had burned low. Shadows danced along the beams, and the ritual tools laid out earlier seemed to hum faintly in recognition. It was not comfort they stepped into, but a kind of familiarity that came from having crossed a threshold, one that wouldn't easily un-cross again. Aoife moved first, brushing her hands against her apron like she was shaking off the dust of half-forgotten centuries.

"We'll need the salt," she said, already striding toward the shelf. "And the stones from the northern ledge. The blue ones. Not the orange. The orange ones bite, and they remember."

Frankie opened her mouth to ask whether any of that had been a metaphor, then closed it again and reached for a bundle of dried rue instead. The leaves crackled softly in her hand, the sound too loud in a cottage that suddenly felt smaller than it had moments before.

Outside, the wind shifted. It stirred, slow, intentional, brushing against the eaves as if testing the wards for weak seams. The herbs hanging from the rafters trembled in answer, their scents sliding through the air: rue, rosemary, ash, and something stranger, something that did not belong to any garden. A hush followed, the kind that did not settle so much as descend, thick as dusk before a storm. It carried weight. Memory. Warning.

Inside the cottage, the hearth flared without a spark or touch, flames rising in a sudden, unnatural swell that threw long, skeletal shadows across the walls. They stretched and leaned, as if listening.

Frankie's breath stilled.

Aoife's hand paused mid-motion.

Griffon shifted in quiet readiness and far beyond Velhollow, past riverbeds older than names, past groves where ancestors walked, past the thin edges of what the world allowed … something woke.

It did not roar.

It did not rise.

But the air itself knew.

The Festival of the Black Veil was coming and whatever had answered the summons was already moving toward them.

Chapter 24

The quiet that lingered in the wake of the summoning was not silence, not truly. It was the kind of quiet found between heartbeats, between the final note of a song and the breath that follows. In the old magic places of Velhollow, where lichen crept like script over stone and roots remembered stories older than speech. The cottage itself seemed to hold its breath, as if even the walls were listening. Time curled in on itself, candles flickered, their flames tugged by a wind that didn't stir the curtains. Even the dust motes moved slower, like they, too, understood that something had just passed through the room. Outside, the wind shifted in the trees, rustling like a page turned gently by invisible hands.

Then a high-pitched warble broke the stillness, followed by a chaos of flapping wings, squeals, and something suspiciously like the chime of tiny bells being smuggled through a very small riot. A wispwing burst through the open window like a comet drunk on moonshine and bad decisions. It glittered obscenely, wings iridescent and flapping with the erratic precision of a sugar-crazed thimble sprite. It smelled faintly of cinnamon and the sort of chaos that usually gets banned from respectable festivals.

Nyx didn't stand a chance. The raven managed a single horrified squawk before the creature executed a reckless loop-de-loop, zoomed past his beak, and, without pause or shame, plucked a tail feather clean from its root like a pickpocket lifting a royal seal. Nyx froze mid-flap, scandalized into silence, wings splayed and dignity in free-fall, as if he'd just been pantsed by the moon.

"Oh no," Chalupa muttered, already crouching like a war general anticipating magical detonation.

Nyx erupted. There was fury. There were feathers. The air became a theater of affront and molting vengeance as he spiraled upward, shrieking with the kind of betrayal typically reserved for operatic finales. Chalupa launched after him with the harried grace of a feline chasing destiny and a diplomatic incident. His leap struck a lopsided stool, already precariously burdened with drying herbs, forgotten spells, and one badly folded prophecy. The stool sighed. It quaked. It gave up on life entirely. Chalupa skid across the floor in a spectacular explosion of mugwort, thyme, lavender, and existential regret. He landed sprawled like a dethroned monarch, tail puffed to maximum plume, glaring with the withering disdain of a knight who had not fallen in battle, but in basil.

Meanwhile, the wispwing, victorious and vibrating with joy, dive bombed from the rafters and crash-landed in Chalupa's fur with the triumphant thunk of a creature that had declared squatters' rights. Atop its head perched a crooked circlet of twigs and firefly-lit stones, which now tilted at a rakish angle. Aoife lunged forward just in time to catch a beeswax candle midair, her braid swinging like a warning.

"By the roots," she hissed, steadying it. "It's crowned. Don't insult the royal caste."

Nyx, still orbiting overhead in deranged figure-eights, screeched, "It stole from me!"

"It's nesting in my tail!" Chalupa yowled, writhing. "Do I look like a chaise lounge for the sparkly elite? Am I cursed now? I smell like tea and inherited privilege!"

Frankie couldn't stop it, laughter burst out of her like startled sunlight, sharp and helpless. She clapped a hand over her mouth, but her shoulders shook, giddy joy fizzing up like a popped cork. Across from her, Griffon had doubled over, shoulders heaving with silent, wheezing mirth, his hand braced on the hearth like laughter had stolen his balance.

The crowned wispwing, clearly pleased with itself and its new kingdom, gave one final smug pirouette on Chalupa's haunch before launching back out the window in a trail of glittering dust and crushed chamomile, like a royal decree written in confetti.

Chalupa flopped dramatically onto his side. "This is how it ends," he groaned. "Toppled by glitter. Tell my tale with honor. Make me sound taller."

Nyx fluttered down beside him, beak still parted in appalled silence. "I want my feather back. It plucked me. I am marked. Scarred"

Aoife straightened, brushing herb fragments from her apron.

"Welcome to the first signs of their arrival," she said dryly. "The scouts and the Circle never comes quietly."

Frankie wiped a tear from her cheek, still grinning. "Do they always send scouts this dramatic?"

"Oh no," Griffon said, stretching out a hand to help Chalupa up. "This is actually quite tame."

Chalupa didn't move. He simply stared up at the ceiling, glassy-eyed with exaggerated resignation.

"I want it noted," he murmured, "that I remained elegant under duress."

Frankie's laughter, spilled out of her, even Aoife's lips twitched into a reluctant smile as she knelt to gather the herbs the wispwing had scattered in its wake. Aoife nodded once, fingers closing around a sprig of crushed lavender.

"Now we prepare."

She moved to the long wooden table and opened the old tome again. Its spine creaked in protest, pages parting with a weary sigh, like something roused reluctantly from a long sleep. Candlelight wavered across the parchment, catching on ink that glinted with a muted, metallic warmth. The script didn't sit still; it shifted in subtle, liquid strokes, leaning toward her in a quiet acknowledgment she could feel more than explain.

"The Circle won't gather unless the old protections are honored," Aoife said, her voice low and deliberate. "They're not just tradition, they're a signal. A pact between the land, the line, and the magic. Without them, the gathering space won't hold."

"Why?" Frankie asked, watching the letters glint like forged starlight.

"Because the Circle isn't just people," Aoife replied. "It's trust, anchored by rite. Those protections bind the space, keep it from fraying, from being seen by what shouldn't see. They hold the veil steady. They let the old ones know it's safe to come."

Griffon moved at once, striding to the back shelves where coils of braided cord lay curled like serpents at rest. He gathered several lengths, then reached for the linen-wrapped talismans beside them, their edges worn soft by time.

"We'll mark the four thresholds," he said, his voice calm and practiced. "North, south, east, west. The clearing between our cottages, it's the heart."

Aoife nodded again, flipping to a marked page. "That land remembers. The trees lean inward there. The moss grows thicker than it should. It's already listening." Her finger traced the lines of a diagram inked in copper. "We'll place the offerings at the basin, as the text says, salt, ash, root, and feather. Each one calls something specific. Each one seals part of the circle."

Griffon pulled on his jacket and nudged open the door, letting in the scent of damp soil and woodsmoke. "We'll need stones for the corners," he added. "Marked with glyphs. Carried by hand. No shortcuts. No spells to lift the weight, intent matters."

"And don't forget the iron bells," Aoife called as she followed him out. "They go high in the trees. The wind will find them, and they'll sing the warding. Keeps the boundary firm. Keeps out what doesn't belong."

Frankie lingered a moment longer, eyes tracing the open pages before her. The glyphs still glowed faintly, as if reluctant to be left behind. Something quiet and certain rose inside her, guidance without instruction. She didn't need Aoife to tell her what to gather; the knowing was simply there. She collected several scrolls, choosing the most timeworn without hesitation, and tucked them into the crook of her arm. She pressed the old tome to her chest and reached instinctively for a pouch of salt and a woven cord from the shelf above. A bundle of dried rowan leaves caught her attention, and she added it without a second thought.

When she stepped outside, the air shifted around her, thicker, watchful, aware. Between the cottages, the clearing seemed to tighten its focus, as though the forest itself recognized what was forming. Roots seemed to settle. Wind leaned in. Starlight folded closer to the earth. Griffon looked up as she crossed into the open. Something in his gaze held her, steady, warm, quietly sure. Her breath slowed, not from surprise, but from the weight of the moment settling into place. Branches curved overhead, twined with vine and moonlit leaf. At the center of the small glade, the old stone basin gleamed faintly with gathered rainwater. Everything felt hushed, suspended, waiting for the next breath. She stepped forward, and the clearing seemed to welcome her. Griffon paused near the edge of the gathering space, his attention sweeping the perimeter.

"This ground carries its own power," he murmured, almost more to the land than to her. "Not because anyone blessed it, but because the years themselves have made it so. The Circle always meets here for a reason."

He moved closer, head tilted as though listening to something deeper than sound. "Aoife's cottage sits on wild magic, alive, shifting, always in motion. Mine rests on stone, steady and grounding. But here…" He scanned the moss-covered earth beneath their feet. "Here the two magics braid together. They rise under the roots. If you stand still long enough, you can feel it. Like the breath of something ancient… asleep, but waking."

Aoife joined him, brushing her hand along the low stones at the clearing's edge. "They marked it once," she murmured. "A spiral carved into the flat rock by the alder tree. You won't see it unless the moonlight hits just right. But it's there, waiting."

Without another word, she turned and headed back to her cottage gesturing Frankie to follow. The air inside still carried the sharp tang of burnt herbs and spell-smoke. With swift, practiced motions, she cleared the table, sweeping aside bundles, vials, and tools. From a narrow cupboard, she pulled out a stack of vellum scrolls and thick, leather-bound books, their spines cracked, their pages whispering of rites that hadn't been spoken in generations. Dust clung to them like sleep. Now, they stirred.

"Let's not waste the quiet," she said. "We've only got a small window to get everything ready."

Frankie opened the tome carefully, its parchment thin with age.

"What exactly needs to be done?"

"Plenty," Griffon replied, returning with a fresh bundle of cord and small clay markers. "The summoning ground needs to be cleared. Anchoring cords braided by hand. Glyphs drawn in ash and salt. We don't just ask the Circle to come, we have to prove we're ready."

Aoife nodded. "The protections must hold. If the rites aren't completed, they won't cross the veil. And we can't risk calling them into chaos."

Griffon stepped beside her. "We start with the ground," he said gently. "Clear the space, nothing dead or broken. It has to breathe. The Circle doesn't stand on rot."

Aoife pulled out a folded length of pale linen from a chest beneath the bench. "And we'll need the basin scrubbed and refilled. Spring water only, no rain, no well. It must come from a source that still runs."

Frankie's hands moved almost on their own. She gathered what felt right, cord, a sprig of rosemary, the pouch of ash. The old symbols still flashed behind her eyes, even when she looked away from the page. They weren't just instructions, they were reminders. Outside, the last of the twilight clung to the treetops. The clearing stretched out before them, quiet and waiting. The moss had thickened near the center, and the old stone basin glistened with a film of yesterday's storm.

Frankie knelt beside it, brushing leaves and twigs aside, hands working without hesitation. She didn't remember being taught any of this, but she knew it all the same. There was rhythm in the gestures, some deep, ancestral choreography written into her bones. Aoife stood just behind her, voice low.

"That's it. Let the clearing know your touch, let it feel you mean no harm."

Griffon moved through the trees, setting down one glyph-marked stone at a time. *North. East. South. West.* With each placement, a slight pressure shifted in the air, barely there, but felt.

Frankie turned toward the center and began uncoiling the cords. "How do we anchor them?"

"They're braided with intent," Aoife said. "Each one must be knotted at a point of power. Wrap them around the base of the boundary stones. They don't tie the Circle in place, they remind it where to land."

Frankie's fingers moved through the cords, weaving them slowly, murmuring under her breath, just her own thoughts, threaded through the work. Let this be safe. Let this be right. Let them come, and see me for who I am, not just whose blood I carry.

A stillness settled over the clearing, a pause brimming with intent. It was the kind of stillness that didn't fall, but rose. The woods leaned in, breath held in attention. Something ancient had heard the call.

Griffon stepped back from the final threshold, his expression unreadable. He studied Frankie for a moment, then gave the smallest nod.

"You're doing fine."

She didn't answer, but the corner of her mouth lifted, barely, briefly.

Then it began.

Fog unspooled from the forest floor, rising as if exhaled by the earth itself. Tinged gold at the edges like lantern light caught in smoke. The runes at the threshold glowed. The wind hesitated. With a sound like a sideways bubble pop and the faint scent of burnt sage and theater dust, something arrived in the way omens do, all at once and slightly off-center. A towering figure stood at the eastern threshold, haloed in haze and half-light. Cloaked in layered pinions like lacquered beetle wings, deep bronze, sea-glass green, dusk-violet, he looked carved from myth and contradiction. A crown of antlers rose from his brow, woven with frost-laced thistle and glinting shards of honeyed quartz. In one elegant hand, he held a floating porcelain teacup that refilled itself with each sip.

"Right on time to be on time," the being announced at last, voice rich with strange vowels and entirely too much self-importance. He swept forward like royalty at a festival no one remembered to host, casting a withering glance at the stillness, as though deeply offended by the lack of trumpets. "I would've arrived sooner," he added, adjusting a floating monocle that hovered by one eye and radiated mild disapproval, "but the woodland navigational sprites are completely unmoored. The thinning has them in tatters, emotionally scrambled. One attempted to direct me via interpretive dance. I've yet to recover."

He drifted forward, unhurried, every step curated for an invisible audience only he could see. A porcelain teacup floated near his lips, steam curling like enchanted ribbon. He sipped as if the fate of realms depended on the steep. Meanwhile, his staff, polished driftwood inlaid with silver thread and shards of sea glass, tapped once against the earth. Not out of necessity, but for effect. The clearing seemed to tilt around his presence, the forest itself pausing to decide whether to bow or laugh. The runes at the circle's edge flared in polite recognition. Somewhere above, a raven wheeled once and promptly veered away, clearly deciding it wanted no part of this.

The Circle had answered the call… and this was only the first. From the north came the rhythmic thunder of wings, vast, heavy things that stirred the canopy like a drumroll. Then came the sharp report of hooves on stone, echoing through the trees. Leaves rattled, branches shivered, and then a thud, heavy and unapologetic, as if a small star had decided to land without filing the proper paperwork.

A centaurish creature with the head of an owl and two monocles trotted stiffly into the clearing, muttering about spoiled ink, astrological sabotage, and how time distortion was so last century. On its shoulder rode a tiny, luminous being no bigger than a mushroom, scribbling furiously on a clipboard with a quill that sparked whenever it was annoyed.

They were followed by others, a man emerging upside-down from a knot in a birch, still holding a half-melted ice cream cone; a woman made entirely of candle wax, smelling faintly of rosewater and mild regret; a sentient vine dragging a harp behind it like a grumpy toddler.

And then... the goat. It arrived not by walking in like a normal animal, but by bursting from the treeline with the full fanfare of a minor deity who knew its reputation preceded it. Bells clanged wildly from the garland around its neck. Confetti, where it came from was anyone's guess, rained from its horns. It skidded to a halt in the very center of the clearing, eyes glinting with the weary cynicism of one who had kicked a banshee off a roof and would do it again without hesitation.

Frankie blinked. "Is that..."

"Aye," Aoife said grimly. "There's *always a goat.*"

Griffon nodded with solemn gravity. "Remember, don't make eye contact if it's chewing."

The goat, of course, was chewing. Something crackled between its teeth in a way that felt vaguely threatening. Without breaking eye contact with anyone in particular, it sidestepped toward the harp, placed one hoof on it, and strummed a single, deeply judgmental chord. No one spoke. Somewhere in the distance, a sprite dropped a plate. The goat snorted, as if the moment had passed beneath its standards, and trotted off to investigate the ice cream cone.

Chalupa sat up straighter. "I hate it when I'm the most normal one," he muttered.

A soft crack split the air, sharp, delicate, like a teacup breaking in a distant room, and the light parted. Not dramatically, but with the quiet certainty of something ancient resuming a paused breath. From within it stepped a figure none had expected, though some would later insist they'd sensed her approach, the way one feels the air shift before a storm or the hush before a story takes its first step.

She did not walk. She glided, soundless and unhurried, as though her feet remembered gravity only out of courtesy. Her robes were deep twilight, sewn through with constellations that moved of their own accord, stars drifting across silk with the patience of ages. Her hair floated around her like threads of storm cloud, shifting as if caught in a slow, underwater current, luminous without throwing light.

The clearing sank into stillness. The centaur squinted, as if staring at a ghost. The wax-figured woman gasped so hard her ear curled into steam. The sprite with the clipboard dropped their pen. A hush swept through the gathered crowd, fragile and crystalline, like frost lacing its way across glass.

"It's her," the centaur whispered, almost to himself. "Wendolyn Thistle-Thread."

Her name passed from one being to another with the weight of old magic. There had been rumors, of course, of a half-mythical woman who had once led the Cairn Circle through the Age of Thirteen Moons and then vanished, leaving only folklore and a badly-behaved pocket dimension in her wake. She held a goblet in one hand, its contents glittering like effervescent starlight, and surveyed the gathering with the disapproval of someone who expected better posture from legends.

"Oh, do stop staring," she said crisply.

She ignored the murmurs that followed and fixed her gaze on Frankie. That look landed with the weight of pages turning in a book no one else could read, sharp, precise, and unsettlingly aware. Her eyes twinkled, not with kindness, but with knowing. She didn't study Frankie like a girl. She studied her like a turning point.

"You are the axis upon which this improbable gathering pivots," Wendolyn said.

Frankie's spine tensed, heat blooming in her cheeks. Every eye in the Circle was on her now, some with curiosity, some with wariness, none blinking. She stood her ground, fingers curling against the worn fabric of her trousers. Wendolyn took one more step, her presence both grounding and unmoored.

"You carry the blood of Aoife Ní Talún, daughter of the earth," she said slowly, "and of Dominicus Veyrath Noctis. Light and dark in a single vessel. You are not the prophecy they feared, you are the hope they dared not speak aloud and now you're here. Everything begins to shift."

Frankie swallowed. Her voice came low but steady. "I didn't choose this story," she said. "But I'm not walking away from it, either."

Wendolyn tilted her head, her gaze sharpened, her eyes catching the candlelight like moonstone. "Child," she said, her tone neither soft nor stern, "that is a beginning."

The mist along the edges of the clearing stirred with curiosity, small and nosy, like a cat peering through lace curtains. The ancient stones marking the Circle's bounds were meant to discourage wandering eyes, but Velhollow had never placed much stock in boundaries, magical or otherwise.

Beyond the ward-line, half-shrouded in mushroom thickets and ferns fat with dew, a clump of townsfolk had gathered, quiet as ghosts and just as opinionated. They weren't part of the Circle. They had no formal invitation but if there was truth to be unearthed, prophecy to be sniffed at, or scandal to be aired like laundry on a breezy morning, you could count on Velhollow's finest to appear with flask, field guide, and a fair bit of skepticism.

Mrs. Hedra hunched like a toad, her crimson shawl knotted beneath her chin and glittering faintly with protective sigils stitched in elder thread. She held a smoky glass flask that smelled faintly of wild mushroom brandy and strong opinion.

Her breath fogged in the air as she muttered to the bramble at her feet, "Mark my words, she's of the Verdant's blood, but that does not mean the land will keep her."

Beside her, Jasper Dullfoot tugged absently at the rope tethering his thistlehog, a squat, bristling thing with beetle-black eyes and a jaw built for spite. The creature chuffed at the clearing and took a half-hearted bite at Jasper's boot before resuming its grudge against the nearest mushroom.

"It's not the witchling part that worries me," Jasper muttered. "It's the other half, Veyrath's name is like a bad seed. You can plant it in good soil, but it'll still try to twist and rot."

Nearby, crouched behind a hollowed log like a spy disguised as a daffodil, a girl no older than ten cradled an enchanted viewfinder nearly half her size. Brass-banded and humming faintly with old tech-magic, it clicked softly with every adjustment.

"She doesn't look dangerous," the girl whispered to the lens.

Frankie heard them, each murmured doubt, every rustling dismissal. It didn't stop her, it couldn't. She stood in the center of the clearing, the sigil on her palm still glowing faintly like memory made light.

Wendolyn lifted her staff and with a single arc, wide and deliberate, light following in its wake, a ribbon of silver smoke trailed through the dusk. The Circle fell silent. Her voice rang out, clear and unhurried, stitched with the kind of magic that didn't need to shout.

"Then let us ask the question properly," she said, turning, not to the Circle, but toward the treeline, where the villagers huddled in suspicion and shadow. "Not from the mages, not from the old rites, but from the land and those who live upon it. You, who've whispered her name like a warning. You, who have judged her with eyes full of memory and mouths full of myth." The staff glowed at its tip, soft but steady, and Wendolyn's gaze narrowed. "You've watched her climb toward something ancient. You've spoken of her blood, her face, her fate, always behind doors, always behind hands. But this girl, this witch, she stands here, and she listens. So speak."

A stillness settled, fine and taut as spun thread. "You fear what she carries," Wendolyn said, her voice like a frost sweeping low over the ground. "So speak it, not in whispers. Speak it where she can hear you."

Slowly, reluctantly, the villagers shifted forward, the old earth quiet beneath their feet. What followed wasn't a clamor, but a cracking open, the sound of a community exhaling something long held. At first, only the rustle of cloaks and the embarrassed crinkle of someone trying to unwrap a sweet too quietly stirred the stillness. Then came a voice, dry as tinder, sharp as flint.

“What if she turns as he did?” Mrs. Hedra of the baker’s stall stepped out from the tree-shadow, her shawl wrapped tightly as though it alone might ward off fate. Her scowl was carved deep, weathered by winters and worry alike, but it was her voice that carried, a brittle thing, long starved of ease.

“What if the power takes her, and we are left to mourn what she leaves behind?” she said, not cruelly, but like someone who had seen too many seasons end badly.

Her words hung in the air, brittle and echoing. Then another voice rose from the shadows, rougher, rawer, the kind born from calloused hands and sleepless nights.

“We’ve buried enough beneath the Greyvale,” a man said. “We’ve lit too many lanterns to guide souls home. This Circle comes with bells and brightness, but will they stay when it all burns again?”

Frankie didn’t move. She stood exactly as she was, chin lifted, and the weight of their words pressed down like stone. Still, she held. A ripple passed through the gathered crowd, subtle at first, then spreading like wind stirring tall grass. One villager stepped forward, then another, and another still. Their faces carried fear, yes, but also something steadier, something that had been missing only hours ago.

“It’s starting, isn’t it?” murmured a beekeeper from Lowbank, wringing her hands as she stepped closer. “The thinning. We felt it in the hives.”

“Our lanterns wouldn’t stay lit,” said the butcher’s husband, voice shaking. “The flames kept bending toward the river. That’s never happened before.”

A young potter with clay still on her sleeves swallowed hard. “My grandmother’s mirror cracked down the center at dusk. She said the last time that happened was during the Old Warden’s rise.”

Others stepped closer, forming a loose half-circle around Frankie, their concerns weaving together until they became almost a single voice.

“The roots under our barn shifted,” someone said.

“The sky blinked wrong,” another whispered.

“My dreaming went loud,” said an elder, eyes bright with warning.

"The river reversed its eddy."

"The crows refused their roost."

"The wards on the hill shook."

No one shouted. No one panicked. Their voices rose in overlapping threads, like a tapestry being spoken into existence, fear, yes, but also trust. Trust in Aoife. Trust in Griffon. But most of all, trust in Frankie, who stood at the clearing's heart with the mark of the Everveil still warm on her palm. More villagers pressed in, not crowding her, but aligning themselves with her.

"If he's rising," a stonemason said quietly, "then we'll rise too."

"You're not alone, child," whispered the apothecary.

"We've lost enough to shadow. Tell us what must be done," urged another.

Their voices gathered like a tide, a chorus of lived lives bound by fear and love of their home. And as they spoke, something in the clearing shifted, an old kind of strength settling into place, choosing its moment to reawaken. Frankie met their eyes, one after another. They were afraid, every one of them. But they were also ready and she felt it, not as pressure, but as inheritance.

Wendolyn turned to her once more, her voice soft but solemn. "Now, child of two truths," she said. "What say you to those who do not forget? What will you give, not to us, but to those whose fear bears roots as deep as memory?"

The clearing stilled.

Frankie drew breath, deep and steady, feeling her heartbeat echo in her bones. "I will not vow to be perfect," she said, her voice like the first wind through an open crypt. "Nor claim to hold all answers and I will not beg pardon for the blood I did not choose."

The clearing was silent, even Mrs. Hedra stood unmoving, arms still crossed, but the lines of her face had shifted, drawn now not in scorn, but in something closer to uncertainty or perhaps reluctant thought.

Frankie turned once more to Wendolyn, her voice quiet but firm. "I didn't come here to be feared," she said. "And I don't want to be put on some pedestal or treated like I'm above anyone else. I came because this place, these people, this land, it's become part of me. It matters. And if danger's coming, I won't back away from it." Her fingers curled slightly at her sides, her eyes steady. "I'll stand between. Whatever it is, whatever comes, it can go through me first."

Before Wendolyn could reply, a goose stepped forward with all the dignity of a retired general in sensible shoes. He wore a tattered blue ribbon around one leg and a look that suggested he'd seen far worse than witches and wayward prophecy. With a single, judgmental honk, short, sharp, and slightly accusatory, he flapped his wings once and planted himself beside Frankie's foot as if to declare, in goose terms, that her case was accepted, pending further review and perhaps a snack.

Wendolyn gave no explanation, but something in the goose's stance made even the wind hesitate. Then the mist above the clearing flared with sudden light. Sigils hung in the air, spinning slowly at first, then faster, their lines weaving into threads of silver and green that arced outward like petals unfurling from an unseen bloom. A low hum thrummed through the glade, deep and resonant, as though the earth itself had drawn breath, and was waiting to exhale. One by one, the members of the Circle inclined their heads toward Frankie in recognition. Even one of the sprite emissary paused its gentle orbit and hovered. The owl-centaur gave a thoughtful *hoo*, adjusting his second monocle with unexpected delicacy. The sentient vine rippled in place and bowed, shedding a single glowing leaf in quiet approval. From somewhere near the back, the candle wax woman clapped once, her palm squishing faintly against her half-melted wrist.

"Well, I like her," she declared, dripping on her own foot.

Griffon stood at Frankie's side now, quiet and grounded, his hand just brushing her arm. There was warmth behind his usual stillness. No words passed between them, but none were needed. Aoife stepped forward as well, her silver braid catching the sigil's glow, her gaze proud and searching.

"If they're nodding," she murmured, "they're not just agreeing... they're witnessing."

The sigil thrummed once, twice, then split open like a flower bursting into bloom. From its center, something descended, a shard of crystal, faceted and gently spinning, lowered into the space above the basin. It radiated a soft violet glow that brightened with each turn, casting slow-rolling waves of light across the moss and stone.

The Circle stirred and for the first time, they spoke in declaration. The voice that rose was not one, but many, layered and resonant, echoing like a song sung through stone halls, like memory pressed into the bones of the earth,

"*She bears the shadowed blood, yet she walks in light.*
She bears the name of sorrow, yet stands against the night.
She is not ruin. She is the reckoning."

The crystal flared white-gold and, with a single beat, released a beam of light that struck the stone at the clearing's center. Where it touched, a new symbol burned itself into the earth, interwoven circles, mirrored glyphs, and the ancient mark of summoning, a spiral nested within a crescent, ringed with binding lines and elemental runes.

Wendolyn lowered her staff. Her smile was faint, but true.

"Well," she said, "it seems you've answered the real question."

She turned to the villagers, some still watching from beneath their hoods, others peering out from behind root-pillars and bramble thickets.

"This is the one you doubted. Yet here she stands, not asking for your favor, but offering you her strength. Not by demand. Not by duty. But by her own will, and that," her voice softened, "is the kind of power that outlasts all others."

Wendolyn raised her staff and struck the earth. The sound that followed carried, low and resonant, like thunder tucked beneath velvet, a sound meant for stone and root, not ears. The air thrummed. Leaves stilled. Even the shadows seemed to listen. She turned to Frankie and those who had stood with her from the first crack in the veil.

"To you who bear the weight," she said, her voice laced with something both ageless and immediate, "to you who were not chosen by accident, but by the weave of the world itself..."

Her eyes swept from Griffon, silent and watchful, to Aoife, spine straight with purpose, to Nyx aloft in the branches, his feathers twitching in a hush only birds could hear. Then, finally, to Chalupa, who stared back, unblinking, as if he'd already lived this moment in a dream and was only mildly annoyed to be doing it again.

“And to you,” Wendolyn said, eyes resting on Frankie. “It is you who must now prepare.” Her words settled like ash and starlight, strange and final. “For the Circle has spoken.”

She drew a slow breath as though weighing the cost of what came next. “And with it comes a summons, long avoided. Sarithis must be called upon.”

The rune over the basin brightened in quiet response. Its glow rose and fell once before fading, but not before it found its echo. A matching glow stirred in the mark on Frankie’s palm, that slow, silent throb like something breathing beneath her skin. The light from the crystal curled inward, folding itself away like a drawn breath. One by one, the Circle vanished, some with a rustle of wind, some slipping through the seams of the world like forgotten dreams, until the clearing held only moss and memory. The last ember of light from the sigil curled into the night, and the forest exhaled.

Frankie stood still, palm warm, heart louder than it ought to be. Aoife exhaled beside her, slow and deep, the kind of breath that had waited through lifetimes. Griffon remained at her side, gaze unreadable but steady.

Nyx gave a twitch of his wings and cleared his throat with dry flourish.

“Well,” he said, “I’ve witnessed stranger council meetings, but never one that ended with assigned group work and a looming sense of doom.”

Chalupa gave a slow blink, tail flicking with theatrical disapproval. “Brilliant. Let’s poke the ancient forces and see what bites back.”

Frankie didn’t answer. She was still staring at the place where the sigil had hovered, where something old and unseen had leaned in to take measure. Her mark glowed faintly beneath her skin, no longer a warning, but a rhythm she hadn’t yet learned to move with.

Aoife placed a hand on her shoulder. “Come, love,” she said gently. “The work doesn’t start here. It starts at home.”

They turned from the clearing, no longer strangers beneath the trees, but something forming, something called. Behind them, the glade stilled again, closing its secrets in silence and shadows. The path was quiet as they walked, the night watchful. Frankie didn’t speak, but each footstep felt different now, less like wandering, more like returning.

Chapter 25

The cottage smelled like a cacophony of herbs, old books, and tension. It pressed close around Frankie, walls too low, air too still, every herb-draped rafter seeming to rustle with suspicion at her pacing. She clutched a mug of tea gone cold. Once it had smelled like comfort; now it only clung uselessly to her fingers. Chalupa crouched beneath the table, ears angled sharply, listening, coiled like a cat waiting for the other cauldron to boil. His whiskers twitched.

"One day," he muttered, "I'd like to face a crisis that doesn't begin with cryptic riddles and end in potential combustion."

Griffon stood near the hearth, arms crossed, the firelight catching on the edge of his blade.

Frankie exhaled slowly. "When we left the clearing, just before the light faded, Zyphirion said something to me." Her voice was hushed, as though repeating it might stir something listening. "'*Cast the net smaller;'* he told me, '*closer to home'*."

Aoife paused with her hand over a bundle of sage, her expression unreadable. "He didn't say it to all of us."

Frankie nodded. "Only to me. Quietly, like a thread he meant me to follow alone."

Nyx, perched on the mantel, tilted his head, feathers rustling like dry leaves. "Then what's the net?" he asked. "And what are we casting for?"

Aoife laid a piece of chalk beside a worn ritual tome and moved to clear the floor. "A summoning," she said. "That's the next thread. Zyphirion didn't just warn us, he pointed us. The Gift wasn't the end, it was an opening."

Frankie moved instinctively to the open floorboards, reaching for dried bundles of hemlock and wormwood, brittle, bitter herbs that cracked softly in her hands. Their scent rose quickly, sharp and earthy, curling into the lavender smoke still lingering in the corners. The space grew close around them, thick with breathless anticipation. The circle wasn't yet sealed, but the air had already begun to shift.

Griffon stepped forward, a clay bowl balanced in his palms. Inside, the black witch's salt glinted softly, coarse and dark, steeped in protective herbs, clove oil, crushed nettle, and powdered iron. It smelled of scorched leaves and storm-soaked stone. He knelt at the northern point of the circle and began to scatter it with slow, practiced care. It fell like dark snow, catching bits of candlelight as it spiraled down. Where it touched, the floor seemed to settle. The ward drew in around them like a breath held in the dark.

Chalupa, fur bristling like a feather duster caught in a storm, muttered from his perch, "Don't be shy with the salt. Anything that remembers before time was written down deserves a generous pour."

Griffon didn't look up. "I'd salt the stars if it kept the dark from reaching her. They won't touch her. Not while I'm breathing."

The salt poured steadily from his hand, slower now, each pass deliberate. It sank into the floor's grooves, mingling with carved sigils, curling into the pattern like ash into bone. The air rippled where the salt touched, releasing a breath of iron and stormlight, the kind of old magic that wakes only when called.

'Salt to mark the boundaries. Salt to anchor the summoners. Salt to hold the darkness at bay.'

Above them, Nyx shifted on a crooked rafter. With a flutter of feathers, he intoned in a sing-song rhythm, "Salt to bind and salt to stay, no slipping through or sneaking away!"

Chalupa groaned, tail twitching in a rhythm that screamed dread. "Brilliant. Rhyming, that's never a good sign."

Nyx's eyes gleamed. "Cadence keeps the wards from unraveling. Unlike you, I don't nap through impending doom."

As Griffon poured the last of the salt, the room changed. The stillness deepened. Candlelight bent slightly inward toward the circle, drawn by the pulse of magic starting to stir. Frankie stepped back, breath hitching. Her gaze moved from the glowing lines of chalk and salt to the shadowed edges of the room.

Aoife looked up from where she knelt at the center of the circle. Her hand hovered above the final sigil. When her gaze met

Frankie's, it held the steady weight of a thousand names whispered through ritual.

"It's ready," she said, voice low and sure. "Step back now, loves. From here on, the circle speaks for us." She turned fully toward Frankie, and for a heartbeat, all else dropped away. "Once we begin, love… there's no stopping. Do you understand?"

Frankie's nod came small, but certain. Her voice didn't rise, but her spirit did.

"I do."

Griffon stepped beside her, silent and steady, a coil of braided cord in his hands. He didn't offer it, not right away. Instead, he reached for her wrist with a gentleness that caught her breath. His fingers moved with quiet intent, wrapping the cord around her wrist, once, twice, a third time. Each loop was measured, protective, deliberate. His touch was warm, grounding like he was binding more than just thread, like he was anchoring her to the moment… and to him. When he tied the final knot, he looked up. His silver-blue eyes met hers, darker in the flickering light, but luminous with something unmistakably tender.

"For protection," he said, voice low, as if speaking a vow meant only for her. Then he leaned in and pressed a kiss to her forehead, slow and lingering. "For luck," he added, so softly it trembled between them like a secret.

Frankie couldn't speak, her throat ached with the weight of everything she felt and couldn't say. The world narrowed to only him, the warmth of his hands, the way the air itself seemed to still around them. The runes beneath their feet pulsed gently, stirred not just by magic, but by the truth blooming quietly between their hearts. For a single heartbeat, the danger they faced vanished. The summoning, the prophecy, the looming dark, all of it faded. There was only his touch and the quiet, the undeniable knowing that whatever came next, they would face it together. Then the runes flared brighter and then the moment passed, but it did not fade, the feeling lingered, woven into her. Griffon's fingers stayed at her wrist for a breath longer, as if reluctant to let go. When he finally spoke again, his voice was softer, deeper, threaded with something raw and real.

"When this is over," he said, "when the world isn't burning around us… we'll talk. We'll have the space to say it all." He lifted her bound wrist gently, like it meant something profound. "Mark my words, *Lady Francesca Caelith, Blood of the Verdant Line, Heir to the First Mother*, this story has not yet begun. What comes after..." He paused, eyes steady on hers, voice lowering into something close to a promise wrapped in longing. "Will be ours to shape."

Just like that, beneath the weight of prophecy and ancient power, a thread of hope stretched between them, bright, living, and unbreakable. The moment held, suspended like a breath not yet released. Then, as if the magic itself had exhaled, the light shifted. The warmth between them folded back into the stillness of the circle, and the air grew heavier, expectant, watching.

Aoife picked up a candle, its wax worn smooth with age, the surface etched with delicate sigils that glowed faintly when touched by the flickering light. She stepped forward, her movements fluid, purposeful. Kneeling at the center of the circle, she whispered something too soft to hear, words that carried through the air like a breath of something ancient, something neither entirely forgotten nor fully remembered. As she placed the candle onto the floor, the flame came to life, the light an eerie, steady blue.

The ritual had begun. She handed Frankie a small parchment, its edges crisped, as if already kissed by fire, she said, "When I tell you to, drop this into the flame. Not a second before."

Frankie took it carefully, the paper surprisingly warm against her palm. Aoife inhaled deeply, exhaling in a slow, practiced rhythm. Then, she began, her voice dipped into something melodic. The air listened, the candlelight flickered wildly, as if sensing what was coming. Chalupa's ears flattened, his tail curling tight against his body. Even Nyx, usually unbothered by magic, let out a low, uneasy caw from his perch. Aoife's storm green eyes flicked to Frankie, a final chance to turn back and then, the incantation began.

"We call thee forth, O veiled and forgotten,
Bound yet unbroken, lost yet not gone.
Through shadowed echoes and whispers untold,
By fire and blood, by fate and the old.

Through paths unseen and gates unsealed,
Where time stands silent and truth lies concealed,
We call to thee, O watcher of fate,

Step through the dark, unbar the gate.

By the stars that have burned and the ones yet to rise,
By the oath unwritten, by the unspoken ties,
By the hour that bends, by the veil growing thin,
Come forth, Sarithis, let the calling begin!"

The words rang out with the clarity of a bell struck in the dark, sending a silent vibration through the floorboards, through flesh, and into the deeper chambers of the soul. It wasn't sound in the ordinary sense; it moved like an echo carried on bone, threading itself through the room until the air shifted around them. The space seemed to stretch, thinned by something unseen, as if reality itself had drawn in a long, anticipating breath. Every candle flame steadied at once, holding its shape in an unnatural stillness. Aoife lifted her chin, her silver eyes catching the dim light with the sharp gleam of tempered moonstone, and she fixed her gaze on Frankie with a focus that felt like a summons.

"*Now!*"

Frankie stepped forward, the flickering blue flame casting shifting shadows across her face. The parchment trembled in her hands, whether from the draft curling along the edges of the circle or the thunder of her own pulse, she couldn't tell. For a heartbeat, nothing happened then the fire moved. It twisted once, like a breath inhaled, and surged violently upward, rising in a column of unnatural flame, blues deepened to violet, violet to black, licking toward the rafters in long, clawing ribbons.

The moment the parchment touched the fire, the candle exploded in a soundless burst, wax spilling out like spilled ink, thick and glistening, pooling in the carved lines of the floor like hot channels of power rushing to fill whatever called them. But the flame didn't die, it burned on nothing, burned through everything. A bloom of black fire writhed in the air, untethered and growing, flowering open like a gate that had not been opened in a thousand years. Without warning, the darkness collapsed. It gathered into a single point at the center of the circle, sharp as a needle, and pulled everything with it, breath from their lungs, light from the flames, even the sound from the room itself. The silence that followed was not empty, but saturated.

Aoife's voice lowered, quiet and weighted, carrying the kind of truth that didn't need volume to be felt. "Sarithis sees without eyes," she murmured. "She serves no light and bows to no shadow. She is whim and will, a force that stirs only when she chooses."

Her gaze stayed fixed on the circle, where the violet flame shifted in a slow, deliberate rhythm, as if drawing breath from a realm that didn't belong to this one.

"She does not guide, though at times she chooses to. She does not warn, yet she has been known to reveal what others refuse to face. And whatever she offers," Aoife continued, "comes with a cost no one can predict."

She drew in a steady breath, shoulders lifting, bracing. "If she judges us worthy, we may leave this circle whole."

No one moved. Even the flame seemed to falter, its glow dimming, then flaring again, as if something vast and unseen had turned its gaze their way. The air quivered, taut with expectancy, charged with the weight of a name never meant to be spoken aloud. It was like the silence before a thunderclap, the instant when every leaf seems to hold its breath. Frankie felt it press against her ribs and wrists and throat, as though the world itself had drawn in a breath and refused to let it go.

Then, the circle trembled, and she came.

Sarithis spilled into the summoning ring like ink in still water, too fluid for form. The air buckled beneath her arrival. Light stammered at the edges of her shape, where her presence touched the world, gravity loosened its grip. Dried petals rose from their careful arrangements. Pollen hovered midair like golden static. The flames in the hearth danced wildly, shadows flung like streamers across the walls.

Her robes billowed like storm clouds sewn from dusk, stitched with threads of starlight long extinguished. They moved without breeze, trailing behind her in tendrils of hush and half-remembered lullabies. The fabric pooled across the summoning ring like memory spilling into the present. She drifted, untethered, her feet never touching rug or board. Her hair, blacker than the hollows between stars, flowed around her in slow-motion waves, shifting to a rhythm no longer found in this world. Even the old beams of Aoife's cottage groaned as if in awe.

Light bent near her in uncertainty. The summoning circle glowed faintly beneath her feet, and when her gaze settled on Frankie, time thinned at the edges as though the room remembered something it had once forgotten. At the corner of her mouth, a hint of amusement curled like woodsmoke rising from a chimney at twilight, quiet and knowing.

"Ah…" The sound slid out like breath slipping through a keyhole between worlds. "You called."

Aoife lowered her head in a gesture shaped by root and ritual. Her hand hovered just above the boundary of the circle, fingers parted like petals preparing to bloom. When she spoke, her voice carried the hush of deep forests and the gravity of oaths that never truly break.

"Sarithis," she said. "We do not summon. We seek. If your will stirs, grant us your presence… and your insight."

Sarithis's gaze sharpened, casting the room into a hush so complete it felt woven from stone and shadow. Then she spoke.

"High Warden of the Verdant Line, Aoife Caelith."

The name resonated through the cottage like a bell in a long-abandoned chapel, clean, ringing, impossible to ignore. The rafters seemed to still. The hearth dimmed. Even the dried herbs hanging from the beams grew motionless, as if every leaf strained to hear.

"You have not gone unnoticed," Sarithis continued, her voice velvet-wrapped but edged like a blade that had never dulled. "Velhollow leans toward your steps more than you admit. You call yourself a garden witch, gentle-handed, soft-spoken, but the land remembers the truth of you. So do I."

She moved as if the world shifted out of her way, drifting forward with unhurried certainty. Shadows pooled neatly at her heels, gathering close like hounds waiting for a signal. "You were born of wilder things," she murmured. "How long will you pretend the roots beneath your feet are tame?"

The words hung in the air, dew-laced and heavy. Sarithis turned slowly, circling them, Frankie, Griffon, the firelight, the flickering edge of breath. Her feet never touched the ground, yet the floorboards remembered her weight, like an echo from lifetimes past.

"You call with only mere days until the festival," she murmured, her voice threading through the room like smoke from a just-struck match. "Three nights before the Veil thins. Before magic begins to fray… and what lies bound slips its knots."

She drifted past Frankie, her silky motion stirring the air like wind through wheat. Light bent faintly in her wake, and though her expression remained unreadable, something in the room stilled, expectant, breathless. Even the shadows waited, as if the very walls listened. Aoife did not move. Her posture remained composed, gaze steady. But beneath that calm a thrum like wind through the hollow heart of an ancient tree, both wild and rooted.

The flame in the hearth gave one final flicker, violet and strange, then vanished with a soft sigh, like a breath exhaled through centuries. For a heartbeat, the cottage held its breath. Even the rafters seemed to still. The hush that followed was not empty, but waiting, thick with portent, like the silence before the first snow touches down. Then the door began to stir by an unseen hand. The runes beneath its grain flaring to life as though the door itself had remembered something ancient. The iron handle quivered. A low chime whispered through the room as the hinges flexed with eerie grace. The door eased open slowly and magic spilled in first, threading along the floor in curls of luminous fog drawn from the earth itself. The air shifted, cooler now, fragrant with damp fern, crushed violet, and the sharp tang of something that had slumbered too long and was beginning to wake. Outside, the mist thickened into spiraling ribbons, glimmering with threads of green and opalescent pearl. Lanterns bobbed in the dark like sentient stars, dancing between the trees with quiet urgency, casting halos that bent.

Sarithis turned toward the opening. Her robes, stitched from silence and starlight, barely brushed the floor, but where she passed, shadows tilted and the light recoiled, folding sideways around her. She stepped forward, the magic parting like a veil before her, and the cottage seemed to lean ever so slightly in her wake. At the threshold, she paused, half in lamplight, half in legend, then slipped into the mist without looking back.

The others followed, wordless and compelled. Frankie moved as if called, not by duty alone, but by a thread of knowing that tugged from somewhere deep. Griffon fell into step beside her, their strides different but their paths aligned. Nyx dropped from the rafters in an elegant arc. Chalupa padded behind them with a twitch of his tail, muttering something about "ominous dew" and "getting mud in his fur."

Aoife lingered a moment longer. Her gaze drifted from Griffon to her granddaughter, this girl spun from stormlight and garden roots, and the man whose silences rumbled like thunder and a knowing smirk tugged at her mouth, quiet and fond. It pleased her, deeply, that Frankie would be just down the path, tucked into that half-wild cottage Griffon called home. The one with sheet-shortening gremlins and spices that reorganized themselves according to the moon. The one that always smelled faintly of pine, woodsmoke, and poor impulse control. Close enough to quarrel over the best way to dry thyme. Close enough to stand beside him when shadows pressed near. Close enough to matter, in all the quiet ways they hadn't yet dared name.

"Come," Sarithis called, her voice coiling from the mist. "The rest have gathered."

Beyond the cottage, the clearing waited, lanterns swayed from crooked branches and shepherd's hooks, casting golden halos into the dusk. Shapes stood in the half-light, some familiar, some strange. Aoife didn't flinch. Her spine stayed straight, her eyes steady, but beneath that calm, something ancient stirred. Not broken, not lost. Merely buried deep and waiting. The flame at the circle's center flared violet, then stilled.

Sarithis let the silence stretch, her gaze sweeping over the gathered faces, witches and craftsmen, healers and hunters, elders with eyes like weathered stone, and children clutching charms in nervous hands. Lantern-light painted their features in gold and shadow, every flicker catching on the uncertainty threaded through the crowd. Then she turned, and the shadows turned with her, obedient as hounds behind a sovereign. Her voice rang clear, low but carrying, the kind that settled into bone.

"The Verdant Witch does not rise alone," she said. "This is not her burden to carry while others watch from shadowed thresholds. When the final bell tolls at midnight, three nights hence, and the Veil falls, it will not be prophecy that decides what endures. It will be your hands. Magic remembers, but will reshapes the world to come."

A murmur rippled through the villagers, as if the weight of her words had found purchase. Some straightened their spines. Others reached instinctively for the hands beside them. Above, the lantern flames leaned toward her, drawn as though the air itself was listening. The clearing held still. Overhead, the canopy swayed not from wind, but awareness. Leaves tilted inward to catch her words. Beneath the circle, the ground hummed low and deep, as if the bones of the land had heard and understood. Shoulders straightened. Eyes shifted. Even the unseen leaned closer.

Sarithis's voice turned sharp. "Heed the call," she said, "or be swept beneath it. Stand idle, and you forfeit your place in what follows, mortal, mage, and forgotten alike."

Frankie stepped forward, moving gently to the circle's edge, no longer flinching from its glow. Her hands stayed at her sides, open but tense, as though she had to remind herself not to curl them into fists. When she finally spoke, her voice emerged low, steady, but threaded with effort.

"I'm not here to command anyone," she began. "I'm only standing where I was meant to stand… even if I'm still trying to understand what that means."

The next words caught in her throat. She swallowed, hard, forcing them out, each one scraped clean of pride.

"I don't offer this easily," she said, her voice thinning at the edges. "But a few days ago, none of this existed for me. Not Velhollow. Not magic. Not the truth of who I am. I was walking blind, pretending the ground wasn't moving beneath me."

Her gaze flickered downward, then lifted with resolve. "I never grew up with prophecy. I didn't know about spells or histories. I didn't have the years you had to prepare. Asking for help doesn't come easily for me. But even without the lessons or the lineage or the certainty… something here recognizes me. Like it's been waiting, even if I have only just begun to listen."

She drew in a slow breath, grounding herself in the hush. "The Veil is thinning. We all feel it and when it reaches its thinnest, when the last night of the Festival comes and the midnight bell tolls, what we choose will matter. Not just for me. For all of us. If Veyrath moves then, if he takes what doesn't belong to him, he won't stop with me. He never meant to."

The name landed in the clearing like a stone in still water. Not Nono. Not Dominick. Veyrath. The name that carried no illusion. Only truth. And the quiet, steady power of speaking it aloud.

Sarithis turned to her fully. Her expression did not shift, but the shadows behind her leaned in. "So," she murmured. "You have begun to understand." Her voice softened, though the edge remained like the curl of a blade. "You no longer call him grandfather. You've burned the illusion. You speak the name he keeps in shadow."

Frankie lifted her chin. "Dominick was the mask, Veyrath is who he truly is, and that's who I'll face."

Sarithis smiled, slow and curling, like smoke winding from a long-doused fire. "Then clarity has found you. You will need it."

A soft rustle answered her, cloth, leather, broom-bristle against boot. From the edge of the gathering, a villager stepped forward. An elder, bent with years and wrapped in a patchwork scarf stitched from old seasons and stories, trailed the scent of lavender and rain. Sprigs of herbs peeked from its folds, and tiny charms, buttons, feathers, bits of ribbon, swayed gently with each step like whispered memories. He moved with the deliberate grace of someone who knew the weight of gesture. With quiet ceremony, he knelt just beyond the ring and placed a weathered palm to the earth. Fingers splayed. Head bowed. A silent vow, older than language.

A younger woman followed, her apron still dusted in flour, a sprig of rowan tucked behind one ear. Then a child, clutching a ribbon-wrapped stone as if it were treasure. One by one, others emerged from the quiet, menders and mushroom hunters, candle-makers and nettle-charmers, faces lined with wisdom or wonder or wind. They did not speak, there was no need to. They came in silence, one by one. In their hands they carried offerings, bundles of rosemary bound in twine, hand-carved charms worn smooth with handling, fragments of honeycomb glistening like amber, and tiny folded notes inked with smudged hope. They placed them gently at the circle's edge, forming an uneven garland of intention, humble, human, and achingly sincere.

The stillness that followed was not emptiness but a rising weight, a hush thick with meaning, like the moment before water spills over the rim of a full cup. Something shifted deep inside Frankie's chest. It wasn't awe, not exactly. It was older than that, an instinctive tug of belonging threading through breath and bone, a recognition she had never asked for but could no longer deny.

Solidarity. The sense of being seen in a way that reached down to the hidden places she had kept guarded all her life. The circle, once motionless and waiting, began to glow with a low, steady radiance. It expanded outward in slow rings, each one drifting across the floor like ripples spreading through a scrying bowl disturbed by truth. It felt as though Velhollow itself had leaned in, had listened, and had chosen to respond. Candlelight tilted strangely, drawn inward as though the room held its own gravity now. Shadows stretched along the wooden planks, winding through the grain like tendrils seeking warmth. They were not menacing, only attentive, present, aware, almost breathing. The air thickened, velvet and charged, vibrating with a tension that reminded Frankie of a violin string moments before the bow touches down. It wasn't dread rising in the room.

It was expectation.

Sarithis turned her gaze toward the heart of the circle, her expression unreadable. Ancient. "The path is not safe," she said softly. "It never was." Something in her voice made the leaves shift and whisper, as if she'd spoken a truth the forest had been guarding in its roots. "The land remembers every footfall," she murmured. "Every trespass, every promise broken beneath its boughs. The Balance does not forget."

Her eyes flicked toward the trees beyond. "What walks beside you is not always seen and some shadows do not wait for nightfall." A wind stirred, though not a leaf moved. It smelled of iron and old smoke, hearths gone cold and fires never tended. "The path is ancient," she went on, more to the circle than to them. "Twisted with grief that grew thorns and oaths that learned to bite. It does not warn twice."

Then the world shifted and the edges of the circle pulled outward, thinning like cloth worn soft with age. Luminous threads unraveled from the seams of reality itself, like breath being drawn from a long-sleeping dream. Walls dissolved into mist. The ground became suggestion and the sky folded like an opened letter.

Shadows bled through the veil, swallowing the edges of what was real. This was no echo of the past, no softened memory wrapped in dreamlight. It was older, rooted in something that watched long before Velhollow took its first breath. Time itself seemed to lean aside, as if making room. The light thinned, wary and uncertain, and the air held its breath. What unfolded was not a dream, but a warning, an unblinking glimpse of the Festival yet to come, should the Balance strain… and finally break.

The festival.

Torches burned black, their flames licking hungrily at a sky devoid of stars, only an expanse of swallowing nothingness. The air trembled beneath unseen power, thick with the scent of smoke, scorched earth, and something wrong. Low, guttural chanting slithered through the void, a sound that did not belong to human tongues. It was endless, rhythmic, not words, but a force. A voice belonging to the world itself, singing a song of ruin. Figures loomed in a perfect circle, draped in robes of deep obsidian, their faces lost in the abyss beneath their hoods. They did not shift, did not waver. They stood unnervingly still, like statues carved from darkness itself. They were not merely present in the world but pressing against it, their very existence tilting the balance.

At the center stood Frankie. She was frozen, her wrists bound in tendrils of shifting darkness, the inky strands curling and tightening with each breath she took. Her head tilted back, her mouth slightly parted. Something was being pulled from her, something deep, something vital. The shadows coiled around her like a predator savoring its prey, patient, methodical. Then she felt it…The Hollowing.

A cold emptiness seeped through her bones. Pain had edges, a beginning and an end. This was something else, an unraveling, not just of magic, but of identity, of existence itself. Like delicate threads being plucked from the fabric of her soul, one by one, until there was nothing left to hold her together. Frankie fought to hold onto something, anything, but the harder she struggled, the faster the emptiness spread.

Then light flickered, at first like a dying star gasping against the vastness of the dark. Without warning, it flared like a firestorm igniting in the abyss. The vision lurched and a battlefield erupted before her, vast, seething with magic. The hooded figures were no longer standing. They were falling, collapsing into the fray as forces clashed in a maelstrom of power. Fire and shadow collided in violent bursts of light, rippling outward like shockwaves through the chaos. Spells arced like jagged lightning, slicing through the air, splitting the ground apart as molten cracks raced across the earth. Spectral figures streaked through the battlefield, wielding weapons of pure energy, striking and vanishing like ghosts. Above them, the storm did not rage, it obeyed. The ground beneath its feet didn't tremble in fear, but moved at his command.

The battlefield churned with chaos, spells arcing like shooting stars, their impacts splitting the ground, sending molten cracks racing through the earth. Shattered stone and embers swirled in the air like dying stars, caught in the vortex of magic ripping through the battlefield. Blades of light and shadow clashed in bursts of violent energy, sending shockwaves across the ruined landscape. Creatures of nightmare surged from the darkness, twisted, unnatural things molded from the void, their forms shifting, fluid, unbound by mortal shape. Distant at first, then it flared, furious and gold. The black torches roared, flames turning molten. The chanting faltered and the shadows recoiled and the vision shifted and a battlefield erupted in flame and fury. The robed figures collapsed as fire and shadow collided. At the center of the storm, he stood. Wreathed in shadow, standing untouched in the eye of chaos.

Veyrath.

Frankie's voice tried to rise, to warn, to scream, but the sound never left her throat. The vision shattered like glass underfoot, splinters of fire and shadow still burning in her mind. Breath caught hard in her chest. This wasn't just a vision, wasn't just some omen to be pondered over tea, it was a possible future, too vivid, too real. One she had to stop.

Veyrath was the storm.

The forest pressed close around her when she came back to herself, the air stretched thin, taut with the weight of what had just passed through it. Her pulse thundered in her ears. She forced her hands to unclench, forced her breathing to slow, though each inhale still scraped like frost in her lungs. Across from her, Sarithis studied her with an almost feline stillness. Her gaze traced Frankie's face, taking in the tremor in her breath, the way her knuckles whitened. Something shifted in that ancient expression, a flicker of recognition, almost satisfaction.

"So," Sarithis murmured, her voice curling like smoke, "you've seen it."

Her lips curved in a smile that hummed with something ancient and sharp. A dry chuckle followed, brittle, echoing like bone tapped against stone.

"Veyrath waits for midnight, in three days' time," she said, each word deliberate, tasting them as if they were rare fruit. "The only hour when magic belongs to no one."

Frankie's brow furrowed, the warning pressing against her ribs like a second heartbeat. "I don't understand."

Sarithis's gaze narrowed, catching the weight of unseen stars. When she spoke, her voice carried the solemn of ancient courts and the gravity of oaths sealed in the depths of the world.

"The Veil does not thin often. Not like this. Once every fifty years, the boundary between realms, above, below, and beyond, grows gossamer, threadbare as spun moonlight. And for a single turning of the sun, what is divided may meet."

She moved through the circle like wind wrapped in smoke, her presence warping the air. "The Festival is no mere celebration. It is remembrance, reckoning and renewal. The great gathering of the gifted and the old-blooded. Spell-crafters and seers, oath-keepers and storm-singers, all drawn to Velhollow by the pulse of something deeper than time. It is the only moment in an age where the ancient and the ascending may speak as equals." She paused beside the sigils, her voice ringing clear and deliberate. "It is when treaties are reforged, when laws may be rewritten, and the old Councils reshaped. Elections held for elder seats once bound by lineage may now be decided by merit. Ancient knowledge, long hidden, is traded in the open. Spells lost to silence are taught again, carefully."

Her gaze flicked toward Frankie. "To some, fifty years is a lifetime. To others, a mere breath. For the Fae, for the elemental-born, for the timeless ones who sleep in stone and surface only when the world changes, this is the blink of a great eye, a rare hour in which decisions may shift the course of centuries."

Sarithis's gaze lingered on Frankie, eyes deep and still as moon-pulled tidewaters. "You ask why he waits," she said, voice low and edged with the knowledge of old seasons. "He waits for the hour when Verdant magic is no longer tethered by lineage or memory. When the current forgets its banks."

Frankie's breath caught in her throat. "Because that's when it's vulnerable," she whispered. "When it can be taken."

Sarithis inclined her head, slow as winter's thaw. "Magic, in all its forms, has always chosen. It bends to those who know its weight. Who can hold it without flinching. But during that final hour, between the eleventh chime and midnight's breath, it forgets. The Veil leans open, and magic drifts untethered, unclaimed. In that hour, there are no bloodlines, no birthrights. Only will."

The shadows seemed to deepen around her as she continued.

"Most forms of magic may be conjured, commanded, or called. But Verdant magic is lived. It is not worn like a cloak, nor wielded like a wand. It roots itself in one's soul. Once it takes hold, it cannot be separated, not by force, not by fear."

Her voice curled like smoke around the circle. "There have been only a handful who could embody it fully. The last walked lifetimes ago, so attuned to the magical realms that her footsteps stirred rivers, and her grief brought storms to their knees. That kind of bond cannot be forced. It must be accepted. Woven."

She stepped closer, robes trailing behind her like dusk unspooling. "And to weave it, thread to thread, soul to soul, there must be a binding."

The words settled like a bell's final chime, low and irreversible. Sarithis looked to Frankie, her voice now soft, yet ringing with irrevocable truth. "Without the binding, the magic will drift and he will reach for it. I fear that this time… it may not resist."

Her gaze held, neither cruel nor kind, but rather knowing. Aoife's throat tightened. Her voice, when it came, was scarcely more than breath, fragile and trembling, as if pulled from the roots of something buried long ago.

"A binding." The word settled and a fault line cracked open, and for the briefest moment, she saw him again.

A face in silver moonlight, fingers twined through hers, rough with work, warm with promise. The tremble of wild magic drawn between two hearts bound by trust. That night, beneath lantern-lit branches and a sky that seemed to hold its breath, she had bound herself to him. Not just her power, though she gave that freely, but her heart and hope. This was not for glory or even for love alone but for protection. Long ago, after the ruin of her union with Dom DiLegna and the false promise of a different life in the Greyvale, she had returned to Velhollow, not in triumph, but in truth. The greener grass had withered, the veil of comfort had lifted and what remained was the truth of her blood, her purpose. Aoife of the Verdant Line, came back not to reclaim anything, but to become what she had always been.

He had been from Velhollow, too, one of their own. When she returned, when the shadows began to gather around the girl who would one day rise, she chose to do what no prophecy had asked of her. She bound her power to him. She folded it into his bones, sealed it in silence, and sent him into the Greyvale to protect the child who was not yet awakened but already watched. He had not wanted to leave and by the gods, she had not wanted to let him go. But love was not always tender. Sometimes, it asked everything of you and gave nothing back but the ache of distance. So she let the world believe she was a quiet garden witch, content among herbs and riddles, her life small and unremarkable. But that had never been the whole of her. She had sown herself into him, not just her magic, but her memory. Binding is a living tether between what was and what must be. Someone who had stayed near Frankie's path without overstepping. Always near, always watching. She had let him go once, but maybe, just maybe, if the fates were gentle, he might yet come home.

The vision folded itself away, like a pressed flower returned to the pages of a long-forgotten book. Aoife blinked, once, but behind her eyes, something shining remained. The glint of a vow that had never been broken, only buried, flickered behind her gaze. Her silence was full of all the things she had given up to keep Frankie safe. Then the light in the circle was insistent, like a heartbeat quickening, like magic remembering its purpose. It caught in the edge of Aoife's vision, tugging her gently back from the quiet corridors of memory. She turned toward it, breath held, as the shift in the circle grew unmistakable.

"A true binding does not tether, it rewrites. It burns the name you once carried and inscribes a new one in the bones of the world. It is not a promise. It is a surrender."

Aoife stepped forward, and the summoning circle responded, its runes flexing, tightening, as if drawing breath with her.

"If Veyrath succeeds," she continued, "he will not merely wield your magic. He will become it. The Verdant force will find a new shape in him, your essence consumed, your name forgotten. The line that bloomed through you will wither, and in its place, something darker will take root."

Griffon moved, one step, then another, before he even realized it. He came to stand just behind Frankie, as if his nearness alone could shield her from what had been spoken.

"No," he said. The word was low, rough-edged. "There has to be another way."

It wasn't fear that had moved him. It was dread. For one fractured moment, he thought the binding would be to someone else. That Frankie would be asked to offer herself, her spirit, her magic, her very being, to a stranger. That survival might demand a surrender more intimate than death. The thought of her belonging to anyone else, tethered, bound, remade. It cracked something open in him.

Sarithis turned to him, slow and certain. Her gaze was not unkind, but it was vast, unfathomable, the kind of knowing that spanned beyond mercy.

"There are always other ways," she said, her voice low and resonant. "But not all paths leave you whole."

Griffon did not speak, yet the weight of his silence reverberated like a wound the room could feel. The runes beneath Frankie's feet ignited, white-hot, blinding, casting fractured light across the stone floor. The air shifted, dense with the scent of cedar, ash, and something final. Sarithis turned once more, her voice no louder than a breath, yet it fell into the hush like prophecy.

"You must bind yourselves first."

The clearing stilled, even the candle flames stilled, bending toward the center as if listening. Frankie felt the words land, not with understanding, but with gravity.

"Binding?" she echoed, breath shallow. "I don't... to what? How do I bind myself?"

Sarithis's eyes, ancient and unblinking, glinted with something just beyond mortal knowing.

"Not to yourself," she stated.

Then, without another word, she turned toward Griffon. But it wasn't Sarithis who stirred what followed, it was the space between. The air changed. The ground held its breath. Light shifted sideways and in that pause, something unseen slipped free of its hiding place. The space between them tightened, drawn in as though the very air recognized what was forming. A thread emerged, thin as breath, bright as first light over water. It unfurled from Frankie's chest and reached toward Griffon, settling into place with the quiet certainty of something that had always been there, waiting for the right moment to reveal itself. Its color shifted in ways the eye couldn't quite follow, more emotion than hue, more truth than pigment. The magic rose, old as the key lines and beneath their feet, the runes carved in earth and stone began to move as if remembering an old dance. Lines unspooled and spiraled inward, twinning and mirroring, coaxed by the silent rhythm of fated recognition. At the circle's center, two glyphs rose, each a mirrored echo of the other, lifting like starlight blooming from soil. They drifted closer, drawn by gravity older than time. Frankie turned slowly toward Griffon, her breath catching as if the world had tilted to make room for this one truth.

"Do you feel that?" she asked, her voice barely a whisper, afraid that to speak too loudly might shatter the spell.

Griffon's eyes were fixed on her. He nodded once, slow and sure, as if to say, I've always felt it. Above them, the Balance took note. He inclined his head, his gaze still fixed on the spiraling glyphs.

"I do. It is as though we have crossed some unseen threshold… as if something vast has taken notice."

Her brows drew together, breath catching. "Whatever this is… it knows us. Like it's been waiting."

He looked at her then, steady and unflinching. "No," he said softly. "It remembers."

They stood like that for a moment, not touching, but bound by the invisible thread humming between them. Around them, the clearing held its breath.

"Two fates," Sarithis said, her voice low and ringing, "intertwined by choice, not chance. Sword and shield. Instinct and discipline. The binding must be more than power, it must be trust. Willingness. A joining that reaches beyond spell work or ceremony."

She stepped forward, and the firelight leaned toward her, drawn by something deeper than heat. The clearing between the cottages quieted, as if even the trees were listening.

"This bond will ground her magic not only to the land," she continued, "but to you. To everything you are. Her wildness, her strength, her storm, it will root itself in you. Your steadiness must hold. It must shelter her, steady her, guard what cannot be carried alone."

Frankie swallowed. "So this isn't just protection," she said slowly. "It's… alignment. A merging of something deeper." Her gaze slid to Griffon. "But if we get it wrong…"

Sarithis's silence was answer enough.

"Well," Chalupa announced, tail flicking like a banner behind him, "I'll be the one to say it. Are they magically married now? Because in the Greyvale, this kind of talk usually ends with a honeymoon or a shared bank account."

Frankie groaned. "Chalupa…"

He preened a whisker, entirely unbothered. "Look, I'm just trying to understand the logistics. Do I send a gift? Do I get a plus one? Is there dancing?"

Griffon didn't speak, but the twitch at the corner of his mouth gave him away.

Sarithis's gaze held steady on Frankie. "When the bell tolls midnight, three nights hence, in the final hour of the Festival, when revelry dies and the Veil thins to a whisper, he will strike. Mark my words." Her voice dropped, rich with something ancient and grim. "Not to claim what is his, but to take what was never meant to be his. Power still awakening. Magic not yet sealed. He will reach for it, twist it, turn it to serve his will, and in doing so, break the balance that holds the realms apart." The fire shrank inward, curling low as if recoiling from her words. "We do not yet know how. Only that he is coming, and he will not come gently. If the bond remains unmade… if the power lies unguarded… he will unmake this place and crown it his own. Velhollow, darkened and bent, an echo of the realm he seeks to spread across all worlds."

Her eyes narrowed, distant now, as if listening to time itself unravel. "Know this, time flows differently in the realm where he was bound. What passes as fifty years here is nearer to five hundred where he waited, feeding on silence, fury, and rot, long before he donned the mask of Dominick. His hatred has not faded, it has fermented. And now, with the Festival upon us and the Veil thinning, he believes the moment is ripe. He will not wait another five centuries for a Verdant Witch to rise. That is what makes him dangerous. He has run out of time… and so he means to take power by force, bend it, break it, claim it all for himself."

"Once he holds the magic," Sarithis continued, her voice dipped in something terrible and true, "the Veil will shatter. Velhollow will fall and the mortal world will not be far behind. He seeks not only dominion, but devotion. All realms bent to his will. All creatures made to kneel." Then, softer now, grave and final, she turned to Frankie. "You and your Stonewing must bind yourselves to each other. Your powers must choose one another freely, for the good of all."

Frankie turned to Aoife, but her grandmother said nothing. Her silence was not hesitation, it was knowing. So Frankie turned to Griffon, and his gaze met hers. What storm once lived behind those eyes had settled into calm conviction. Something passed between them in that moment, quiet and wordless. A silent yielding to whatever the fates would place in their path. It was not resignation, but readiness and when Griffon reached for her hand, it was not with urgency, but with the steadiness of one who had already chosen. He closed his fingers around hers, warm and sure, anchoring her like a lifeline in deep water.

"We do this together," he said. His voice was soft, but it did not waver.

Sarithis's gaze lifted, past them, beyond the treetops, into something unseen. The air around her fluttered like gossamer wings, and ancient forces stirred just out of reach, brushing the edges of the world like a cold breath through stone. It wasn't the chill of winter, it was the cold that lives beneath time. The earth beneath their feet shifted, the stones and beams of the cottages groaning in response. As if the very bones of this place remembered this hour, and all that came with it.

Sarithis smiled, slow and knowing, her voice barely more than a breath. "Ah," she whispered. "So it begins."

She didn't explain what had begun, she didn't have to. The answer was already written in the hush that followed, in the way the shadows coiled inward as if beckoned. The flame at the center of the circle no longer danced; it held steady, silent and alert, as though it, too, were listening..

Aoife stepped forward, her voice meant only for Frankie.

"You've always belonged to the wild," she said, her words soft as linen dried in the sun. "But now the wild will belong to you. Just... don't forget who you are beneath it." She reached up and brushed a curl behind Frankie's ear, her touch as light as wind through lavender. "I couldn't protect you from this, love," she whispered. "But I see you and I am proud, more than words will ever hold."

The first chime rang out.

Frankie startled, not at the dainty tinkle of porch chimes caught in a stray breeze, but at something far older. This was a sound meant for beginnings and endings. It came from the heart of the earth, from roots deep beneath Velhollow, and from places far beyond it, realms above, below, and hidden between. The note rolled through the clearing like a wave, moving up through the soil, into her bones, until her heartbeat seemed to echo its toll.

Lanterns strung from branch to branch swelled brighter, gold spilling over the gathered faces. Garlands of ivy shivered, scattering pale blossoms that drifted through the air like slow-falling stars. The villagers stood motionless, as if leaning toward something they could sense but not see, their breaths caught in the same invisible tide.

Then came the second chime... and the third. The air thickened with the scents of crushed thyme, woodsmoke cooling in the dark, and a faint metallic edge, like a blade polished for a war no one dared speak of. Magic rose with purpose, drawn from every hollow and hill of Velhollow, from caverns where the air glittered with minerals older than language, from mountaintops and riverbeds, from worlds that had never known mortal feet. Frankie felt it slip over the grass, coil around her boots, and wind upward along her jeans, soft, deliberate, and alive.

Her vision wavered, like looking through glass just before it shatters. She thought she saw a sweep of golden desert under a sky with two moons. A city of black stone towers rising from a sea of clouds. A silent forest where the trees wore crowns of frost and whispered in a language older than the sun. The sights were gone before she could focus, replaced by the night around her, but they left a taste on her tongue, metallic and sweet, like rain falling on hot iron.

The Veil had begun to thin. Not only here, but everywhere. Between light and dark, far and near. Between realms tethered to the stars and those rooted in the soil. Between the bright courts of magic and the shadowed dominions that waited beyond sight. The walls between them were loosening, folding into gossamer that could be drawn aside with a whisper. And this time, something older stirred in its depths, older than prophecy, older than Velhollow itself. The night did not just hold the moment, it shaped itself around it, as though unseen hands were preparing a doorway. The old ways were rising… and they had not forgotten.

Sarithis lifted her face toward the treeline, her gaze piercing past leaf and shadow into realms unseen.

“Know this,” she said, her voice carrying across the gathered villagers, “when the Veil thins… it does not open one way.” Her words wove into the night, binding themselves to it. Then she was simply… elsewhere. Not gone. Not fled. Just stepped sideways into a place that had always been beside this one, leaving only the echo of her warning to hum through the clearing.

Frankie’s pulse drummed hard enough to feel in her fingertips. Breath snagged in her throat, caught between instinct and omen. Something was watching. The shadows no longer lingered at the edges, they pressed closer, curious or hungry, she couldn’t tell. From deep in the treeline came a groan, low and splintered, like old roots tearing free or stone grinding in the dark. The forest had gone still.

Then, a new sound began to thread its way toward them. It moved like wind yet carried weight, a resonance stitched into the bones of the land. The kind of sound that rose only when something long-buried began to stir, stretching toward the memory of its own name.

Beside her, Aoife tilted her head, eyes narrowing as if listening to something just beyond mortal range. “The bells,” she murmured, the words barely air. “They shouldn’t still be ringing.” Frankie turned, searching her face for an answer that didn’t come.

Aoife’s gaze stayed locked on the treeline, where the night had thickened and the stars seemed frozen in place. “They’re not marking the start of the Festival,” she said at last, voice low and deliberate. “They’re warning of what’s coming with it.”

Frankie hadn't heard that tone in Aoife's voice, not even in the Hub. It was the sound of someone measuring the space between now and disaster. In Velhollow's oldest records, there were only two other times the bells had rung beyond the opening chimes. Once, in the Year of Hollow Fires, when the Great Ash swept through three realms and left forests burning for a decade. And once, during the Night Without Footfalls, when every bird dropped silent from the sky and the rivers ran backward until dawn. Both times, the bells had not stopped until what had crossed through was either driven back or claimed what it came for.

Tonight the bells did not stop.

Chapter 26

Chalupa gave a long, theatrical sigh.

"Wonderful," he muttered. "Summoning bells. Not good, that never ends in tea and a nap."

No one laughed.

The sound had become a presence, low and resonant, threading through bramble and leaf, slipping under cloaks and into ones bones. It didn't clang or echo, it pressed, like a palm laid against the chest of the world, feeling for its heartbeat. It wound through the hollows of trees, curled around the stones, rang down into the roots, and stirred something sleeping in the soil. Each chime came slower now, drawn out like the pause before an answer you don't want to hear… like the moment before a door opens by itself. Frankie stood still, her hands curling unconsciously at her sides. Even the fireflies had gone quiet. The light didn't dim so much as pull inward, as though the forest itself were bracing.

Aoife moved slowly, her skirts whispering like wind through corn husks. She knelt beside a patch of clover and drew a spiral in the soil with her fingertip.

"Wards won't hold if the bells keep calling," she said, her voice barely above the chirp of crickets. "And they are calling, not to us, but to something that remembers how to listen."

Griffon's hand hovered near Frankie's back, steady, close enough to anchor her.

"Why now?" he asked. "What's changed?"

Aoife's gaze lifted to the trees, to the starlight caught in their highest branches. "The Veil has thinned… but something's pressing back."

From deep within the forest, that strange sound stirred again.

"I don't like this," Griffon said, his voice low and taut. "There's shadow in the bell's echo now. It feels like something's trying to ride it through."

His eyes darted toward the far-off flickers of the Festival, where lanterns danced too sharply and shadows stretched too long. Chalupa's fur bristled as he slinked closer to Frankie's boots.

"It's not just the chimes," he muttered. "Something's inside that sound."

Nyx shifted uneasily on a branch overhead, his feathers ruffling. "The trees have stopped whispering," he rasped. "When they go quiet, it's because they're waiting to see what steps through."

Frankie turned slowly. The trees no longer stood in welcome, they leaned in, their limbs knotting like the brows of old men in warning. Between their trunks, shapes moved, half-formed, unwilling to be seen. Some carried the lanternlight of celebration. Others had no light at all. They waited, patient as stone. Watching.

Griffon's hand found hers, warm and firm. "Inside," he said, his voice pitched low, the way one speaks when the dark is listening.

She didn't argue. The bells still rolled through the clearing, each chime heavier than the last. The air between the cottages had shifted, thick with the copper-salt taste of magic being pulled from far-off places. Frankie could feel it tugging at the threads of her own pulse.

They crossed Aoife's threshold, stepping into the oldest kind of shelter, the kind built as much from trust as timber. The door closed behind them with the slow groan of old wood remembering storms. Inside, the magic was not gentler, but deeper, like a current running under still water. The air was close, scented with sage, ash, and the metallic tang of power drawn too long from its moorings. The floor seemed to hum faintly, the bell's resonance threading up through the soles of Frankie's boots. Even here, the sound had found them.

Griffon stayed near the door, his gaze fixed on the treeline beyond the glass. "The Veil's always thin during the Festival," he said, "but I've never felt it push like this. Why now?"

Aoife moved through the cottage with the purposeful grace of someone who had done this a hundred times before but never under these conditions. A sprig of rosemary was laid beside a silver bowl; a clay vial was uncorked and set where moonlight could catch the rim. She placed each piece on the altar table in a widening spiral, bone beads, a shallow dish of salt, a folded square of green cloth.

"Because something is pressing back," she said, voice even but edged. "And it's listening for the bells."

The fire in the hearth shifted, its pop and crackle swallowed into quiet. The summoning circle etched into the table's surface dimmed from a steady glow to a slow as though it, too, was bracing for what came next. Frankie's gaze lingered on the relics, ordinary-seeming objects that thrummed faintly with their own kind of life, realizing these were the tools of the binding, the magic that would tether her to what came after.

Then Sarithis's voice resonated from the beams, the floorboards, the grain of the wood itself. Her voice curled from cracks and corners, rich and steady. "*Forget not*," she said, "*three nights hence, when the clock strikes twelve for the final time, the Veil will yield. Magic will forget its masters. It will hunger for a new tether.*"

Frankie's gaze darted about the cottage, but there was no figure, only the voice, threaded into every shadow. "*You must choose,*" it went on, "*not only what you fight for… but how you fight, and with whom. Magic does not answer to bloodlines or legacy. It listens to certainty.*"

The shadows on the walls deepened. "*Do not underestimate what walks beside you,*" Sarithis whispered and the quiet that followed was like expectation, like the forest outside, holding its breath for whatever would cross through next.

The stillness didn't break so much as shift, like a deep root adjusting in the soil. The fire in the hearth gave a single, slow crack, and the circle of light in the cottage seemed to lean toward the altar table. The air felt thick with intent, as though Sarithis's voice had left threads behind, invisible but tugging them all toward the same point. Frankie could feel it in her chest, the sense that something had been set in motion and could not be called back.

On the table, the relics caught the low light in quiet, deliberate gleams. Frankie set down her rose-and-rowan wand first, its pale grain warm under her touch, the carved vines along its length seeming to shift in the corner of her eye, like they were listening. Beside it, a shallow bowl of spring water reflected not her face, but drifting images that rose and vanished: a flower bruised beneath a crimson moon, a shadowed doorway opening to someplace she had never seen. A vial of oil sealed with wax and thorn rested nearby, its contents swirling in slow, thoughtful currents. At the center of it all, suspended just above a handwoven cloth stitched with living sigils, hovered the Thread of Fates, a strand of silver and shadow, delicate as breath, alive with intention. It stirred faintly, as if testing the air, gathering itself like a thought on the cusp of forming. Even the light around it bent softly inward, careful not to press too close. Around it lay the tools of the rite.

Aoife finally spoke, her voice low. “It speaks to you, doesn’t it, love?”

Frankie didn’t answer at first, she couldn’t. The space between them and the table had narrowed without her meaning to move. Her eyes had locked onto the Thread, and her breath came lighter, slower, as though some unseen current had begun to draw her toward it. The rest of the room blurred at its edges, the hearth’s glow, the smell of sage, the faint copper taste of magic, and only that single silver strand seemed to remain.

“What is it?” she asked, her voice no louder than a leaf brushing against a windowpane.

Aoife stepped closer, her silver eyes catching the flicker of firelight. There was something ancient in them now, something vast and unblinking, like the still heart of winter.

“The Thread of Fates is not somethin’ made, but somethin’ remembered,” she said softly. “Woven at the world’s beginnin’, before time had a name, before the first tree drank from the first river.”

Her fingers hovered above it, never daring to touch. “It binds what must be. It does not command. It does not force. But it recognizes what already is. Every choice, every turning, every soul bound to another by truth, these it knows. These it holds.”

Frankie’s throat tightened. The Thread called, quietly, patiently, like a fire’s warmth felt through stone. “Why do I feel… like it’s drawing me in?”

Aoife’s gaze softened, though her voice carried the weight of something storm-heavy, old as river stone, steady as winter dusk. “Because it carries the weight of what has always been, love,” she said, the words gentle but rooted deep as oak. “Threads do not choose. They do not dream. But they know. And you feel it because some part of you has always known this path. This choice. It was never chance." She held Frankie's eyes, silver reflecting the flicker of the hearth. "Ye were always meant to stand here."

Frankie drew in a slow, steady breath. It wasn't fear that tightened her chest, it was recognition, deep and quiet, rising from a place inside her she had never known how to name. The same part of her that had been stirring since the moment she stepped into Velhollow now came forward with startling clarity, as if everything in the room, including her own magic, had aligned. She glanced at Griffon. He hadn't spoken since Aoife arranged the relics on the table, and he didn't need to. His silence wasn't distance; it was intention. He stood beside her like a pillar shaped by time and choice, still and steady, his gaze fixed on the circle forming before them. This was his world, not just the land or the ritual, but this kind of threshold. A moment where magic demanded truth as much as strength, where the outcome depended on who you were at your core. His face revealed nothing, yet his presence was unwavering. Whatever this calling required, he had already committed himself to it. A quiet descended over the cottage, not empty but charged, as though the very walls understood the weight of what was about to begin. The hearth glowed low, shadows drew long across the floor, and even the air seemed to hold itself still, waiting for the next word.

Aoife released a slow exhale. It carried more than breath, it carried the last unspoken warning, the one every witch gives before a rite that changes more than the night.

"Aye," she said, voice low and unshakable, "there is no turnin' back once the bindin' is sealed." The words landed with the gravity of prophecy, like a door swinging shut behind them and locking without sound.

Frankie felt the moment root itself in her, slow and sure, like rain soaking deep into loam. It didn't crash down. It claimed. It was the kind of moment that coaxed roots to stretch and seeds to remember their shape. This was not a path that could be *unwalked*, nor a circle one could step back from once crossed. It would mark her, forever and it would mark him, too. Whatever paths they wandered from this day forward, the thread between them would remain, woven into the breath of their magic, stitched into their own becoming.

She looked to Aoife and gave a small, steady nod. A knowing, settled deep in the bones. Because somewhere in the quiet hollows of her spirit, she understood. This choice had always been there, waiting like a gate left open beneath moonlight. It had been hers to step through. Griffon turned to her at last. There was no flicker of doubt in his gaze, only stillness.

"We're ready."

Aoife moved with quiet purpose, her hair slipping loose from its braid, trailing behind her like mist caught on morning air. Frankie raised her hand halfway. Then lowered it. Then raised it again.

"Okay. So… once again, explain this to me like I'm five. What exactly does this binding do? Do I get to be a Stonewing?"

Chalupa, opened one eye. "Please say yes. I've always wanted to ride into battle on a Frankie-dragon. Preferably one who brings emergency tarts!"

Nyx gave a sharp-edged chuckle from his perch. "You with wings and tarts? Stars save us. We'd never fit in a bakery again."

Aoife pressed her lips together, fighting back a smile. Instead of answering, she looked to Griffon, one silver brow rising in silent prompt. Well?

Griffon shifted his weight, boots scraping gently against stone.

"No," he said at last, gentle but sure. "You wouldn't be a Stonewing. That's passed down through the males in my family. It's… inherited."

Frankie sighed. "So no wings. Sadness ensues."

He offered a crooked half-smile. "But if we were… mated, " the word fell between them like the soft drop of rain before thunder "… you'd share some of my traits. Senses. Strength. A bond."

Chalupa's ears twitched. "Ah, the soul-bonding, life-altering, destiny-entwined sort of bond. Very romantic. Often results in forest crying and overly poetic declarations."

Nyx ruffled his wings. "Still better than being magically tethered to a kraken. That was a logistical nightmare."

Aoife, adjusting a sprig of mugwort at the circle's edge, finally rose with quiet steadiness. She smoothed her apron, hands marked faintly with sage and ash. Her gaze found Frankie.

"Magic like this isn't for show," Aoife said gently. "It's not about titles or spectacle, it's about truth. A binding is a vow, it isn't marriage, though love may find its way in. It's deeper. Older. It makes you sword and shield to one another. Anchors. Mirror guardians." She stepped closer, voice low but clear. "It cannot be broken. Not by time. Not by distance. Only death severs the thread. You might go on to love others, build lives elsewhere… but you'll always be tied. Because this bond asks more than affection. It asks duty."

From a carved wooden bowl, Aoife gathered three slender bones wrapped in green thread, a curled pomegranate peel still red with memory, and a bundle of iron twigs tied with waxed linen. Her movements were practiced, as familiar as kneading dough or folding linens still warm from the line. She reached up to the rafters, brushing the hanging herbs. Vervain bound in gold, a twist of rosemary dusted with salt, and a braid of mugwort, dark and pungent with oil. One by one, she fed them to the hearth. The fire hissed, flared, blue, then violet. The scent that rose was sharp and sweet, like lavender tucked into drawers or stone after summer rain.

With her arms full of offerings, Frankie returned to the table and set everything down with deliberate care. She spread the relics across the woven cloth, arranging each piece as Aoife had shown her, tools placed not by habit, but by intention. Then she lowered both palms to the tabletop, fingers splayed across the etched runes as if recognizing something that had been waiting for her touch. The cottage stilled around her. The runes responded in a measured blooming of gold and violet, widening across the cloth in gentle waves. Nothing flashed or flared; the magic simply awakened, calm and attentive, like a listener lifting its head after a long rest. Patterns shifted across the surface, graceful and slow, the symbols drifting into new shapes as though guided by memory rather than motion.

Aoife reached for the ashwood branch. Her fingers hovered above it for a heartbeat, then settled along its length. The carved symbols along the wand kindled with a soft radiance, small, steady sparks gathering along the grain, as if acknowledging her touch and the rite she was preparing to call forth.

"Even wood remembers," she whispered, fond and old. She stepped back with the calm gravity of someone who had waited a lifetime for this moment. The memory returned, quiet as mist curling over stone.

A morning stitched in dew and birdsong. Kettle humming, bread rising beneath linen, lemon balm drifting through shutters. She'd just returned from the Greyvale, city-worn and hollowed, hands more used to antiseptic light than wildflowers. But Velhollow had taken her back as surely as moss takes stone. She'd stepped barefoot into her garden, apron still dusted with flour and ash, the scent of rising bread clinging to her like a benediction. The earth was damp with morning dew pooled in the petals of marigolds, and the sky had that pale, held-breath hush just before the sun properly claimed it. She hadn't meant to pause at the gate, but something in the quiet pulled her. And there it was, nestled like an offering between a braid of honeysuckle and thorn: a parchment, mist-damp and curled at the edges, sealed with bone-colored wax. The ivy root twined through its fold had grown around it, not to conceal, but to keep.

She'd known before her fingers ever reached it. An echo of what was to come lay in wait. No fanfare, just there, waiting for her. It did not sing in riddles, only in rhythm. Of a granddaughter born of two worlds, one foot shadow-kissed, the other steeped in bloom. Of the Verdant Witch returning not to conquer the land, but to remember it, and to let it remember her. And of another, whose wings bore dusk and stone, ancient in silence and yet still becoming, whose thread would bind to hers by something older than choice, older than time. A convergence of becoming. Aoife had wept from the sudden joy of knowing that her story had more meaning than she had imagined. She had gone inside at once, lit three beeswax tapers, one for the past, one for what was yet to come, and one for whatever miracle would rise in the space between. Then she returned to the garden and planted feverfew in a ring around the gate. She sang as she pressed her palms into the soil, low and sure, a lullaby from the old tongue, the kind that asked nothing but promised everything and then she waited. Seasons passed. Leaves turned. Shadows lengthened. But one day, the wind began to carry their names, first Frankie's, clear and soft as water over stone. Then Griffon's, slower, heavier, like thunder remembering its own name. Aoife brewed nettle tea and sat by the window with both hands wrapped around the mug. Listening. Waiting. The land would tell her when it was time.

For a long time, Aoife had believed she was meant to be the shield, the one who stood between her granddaughter and the coming storm. But the threads had whispered another truth. Her purpose wasn't to guard the path… it was to prepare it. To clear the way when the hour struck. To make space for love, even when it came cloaked in dusk and carved from stone… even when it wore wings. She stood in the circle's glow, the runes breathing beneath her feet, and said nothing. She didn't need to. The cottage held its hush like a hymn. Only Chalupa, ever-watchful on the hearth rug, caught the flicker behind her eyes. He blinked once, slow, certain.

Frankie exhaled and reached forward, Griffon followed, his movement quiet, steady. The Thread stirred. Light traveled through Aoife's fingers, silver strands spiraling outward across the etched stone. The runes kindled one by one, soft as fireflies at dusk. The silver thread lifted between them, weightless. Griffon's hand hovered close to hers, and the thread brightened in response, its glow deepening to violet and shadow-laced silver.

Aoife remained still, her eyes reflecting the light of the circle. She had waited a long time for this moment. Now, she let the magic choose for itself. The binding had begun, not with thunder or decree, but with two hands, one thread, and the kind of vow that needed no words. She turned to Griffon.

"Stonewing," she said, her voice woven with an echo older than language, "do ye take this binding freely, with will unshaken, and soul unguarded?"

His gaze held steady. "I offer myself freely," he said, voice low and resolute. "In strength, in shadow, in soul. I bind not in duty, but in truth. As sword to shield, I stand beside her, not by force or fates choice, but by *my* choice."

Aoife nodded, pride flickering beneath the weight of magic. She turned to Frankie. Her voice shifted, heavier now, thick with emotion.

"Verdant-born," she said, "do ye take this binding freely, knowing it shall weave ye into the great Loom, to be read not only by seers and spells, but by fate itself? Do ye offer what cannot be reclaimed, your power, your purpose, your name, as oath and offering?"

Frankie lifted her chin. The firelight caught her eyes. Her fingers trembled, not with fear, but with clarity. This vow would thread through bone and memory, through future and ash. She thought of Velhollow, of Veyrath's shadow, of the bells tolling, of the ache in her chest that had never been fear… only longing.

"I too, offer myself ," she said. "I offer what is mine, freely, fully, not to be lost, but to become something more." Her breath was steady. "I bind myself not for glory, nor prophecy, but because the land remembers me… and I remember it. I give my power, my name, my breath, so what comes after may rise from what I choose now." Her gaze turned to Griffon. "I do not bind alone."

Aoife lifted the blade. Leaf-shaped iron glinted with faint silver lines, waking only when magic skimmed its surface. She pressed it first to Griffon's palm; he didn't flinch. Crimson surfaced in a bright, steady bloom. Then she touched the blade to Frankie's hand. The sting broke through her breath, sharp but distant, swallowed quickly by the rise of power moving through her. Aoife guided their hands together over the Thread. Where their blood met the silver, the strand brightened in a sudden flare, as though awakened by what it had been waiting for.

When Aoife spoke, her voice sank into a deeper cadence, shaped by the weight of every witch who had ever bound their strength to another.

"By fire that tempers,
By oath unbroken,
By will unyielding,
Spill only as freely as ye bind.
Let magic bear witness.
Let fate do the weaving.
Let the tether be forged in truth,
and remain unshaken by time or trial."

Their mingled blood sank into the thread, and the magic answered. A column of violet and gold ignited from the circle's heart, spiraling upward in a helix of light. The air roared, rich with cedar smoke, charged stone, and the scent of rain on soil. The thread shivered once, then lifted, unraveling into a thousand strands, each gleaming with its own magic, some soft as dawns light, others dark as starless sky. They moved with purpose, not clinging to skin but diving deeper, coiling around wrists, slipping beneath ribs, wrapping through bone and breath until soul met soul. The strands braided around Frankie and Griffon, binding them as one.

The cottage quaked gently, shadows huddling like quiet witnesses, and still the weaving continued, light and dark threads fusing into something whole. Frankie felt something open inside her, like a door that had been waiting. Through it, she felt Griffon, not beside her, but within. His magic touched hers with gravity and heat... and then something older stirred. His beast. Ancient, elemental, vast. It brushed against her soul like wings through flame. Griffon shivered, breath catching for a moment before it smoothed out again. She felt his surprise, his readiness for less, and his awe at the wild flood of her.

Her magic surged, uncoiling like roots through stone, like a storm learning its name. Her edges blurred. She no longer ended at skin. The beat of her heart became a drum that echoed beyond her, a rhythm the land answered. She felt the roots beneath the cottage, the trees swaying beyond, the silver-threaded river humming through the dark. Not beneath her, but through her.

Aoife's voice carried through the silence. "It is decided."

Griffon's eyes widened, just a breath, just enough. His voice, when it came, was low and playful. "How mortal," he asked, "do you feel now?"

Frankie opened her mouth, but no answer came. There wasn't a single word for what she felt. She was still herself, yet something inside her had widened, deepened, intertwined. Her own magic remained, wild and root-bound, but now it moved in tandem with something newly awakened. Secondary and tertiary gifts she'd never possessed stirred gently beneath the surface, subtle ripples of Griffon's strength, his stone-born resilience, his quiet tether to deeper planes of magic. She sensed them not as intrusions, but as doors she'd never realized existed, doors that were no longer locked. She could see things flickering just at the edge of vision, threads in the magic itself from the realm between realms. As if the binding had not only tethered them to each other, but opened her to the forgotten places where magic listens with its teeth bared and its heart wide.

She turned to him, and though his expression remained steady, she could feel the resonance, like a bell struck once, still humming. The bond was forged. As the last embers of magic settled into the air, the silence stretched, thick and unbroken. The ritual was complete. Frankie and Griffon knelt within the fading circle, bound by something ancient, something unshakable. Then, a voice cut through the solemnity like a blade.

"So… what happens now?"

Frankie turned just in time to see Nyx standing at the edge of the circle, one dark brow arched. Beside him, Chalupa perched on the table, tail flicking lazily.

"In the mortal world," Nyx continued, "when two people are bound together, they usually throw rice or confetti."

Chalupa huffed, flicking an ear. "I don't see any confetti, and if anyone so much as thinks about tossing rice in my direction, we're going to have words." He sniffed at the fading glow of the summoning circle. "So, what's the tradition? Bonfire? Group interpretive dance?"

Aoife opened her eyes, the glint of old knowing settling behind them like stars returning to a twilight sky.

"Now," she said, stepping forward, her boots brushing through the last wisps of magic, "the binding begins to take root. What you set in motion cannot be undone, not by doubt, nor by fear. The forest has heard you. The magic has answered."

She glanced between Frankie and Griffon, her voice low but resolute. "From this moment on, you walk a path braided in fate and consequence. It will test you. It will change you, but it will not lie." Then, softer, with the weight of memory, she added, "That truth will carry you when the light grows thin." Her mouth curved with the ghost of a smirk. "And if it doesn't… try not to die in the first five minutes."

She stepped back, the fading edge of the circle ghosting across her boots like cold mist.

"You have until the second tolling of midnight bells in the village square. Two more days and nights, no more. In that time, you must learn to move as one, to thread your magic like silk through thorns, swift and sure. Only then will the path home reveal itself. Fail…

and the forest will seal its gates, and the Festival will end without you."

Her gaze lingered on Frankie, steady as starlight. "And remember, time moves differently here. Waste it, and you may find the hourglass emptied before you even know the sand began to fall."

Before Frankie could ask what that meant, the circle flared. Light coiled around her and Griffon's hands, racing up their arms in spirals of silver and violet.

"Brace yourselves love," Aoife said, voice dry as kindling, even as the room tilted. "And do try to land on your feet."

The summoning circle spun faster, its runes igniting like a wheel of fire and then, everything fell away. The last thing Frankie heard was Chalupa's indignant yowl and Nyx shouting, "Well, this escalated," before the world folded inside itself and vanished.

Chapter 27

Frankie plummeted through a swirl of light and wind, tumbling end over end through a tunnel of magic that didn't follow the rules of up or down. Threads of silver snapped past her like shooting stars; the air howled with something ancient, wild, laughing. She wasn't falling, she was being delivered.

Then came impact, she hit the earth with a spectacular lack of grace, knees buckling as she skidded into a carpet of leaf rot and damp earth. A root caught her shin, a vine tangled her braid, and a startled "*oomph*" escaped her lips as she landed face-first in the moss. Somewhere nearby, a cluster of startled mushrooms promptly exploded into bioluminescent spores. Griffon landed beside her with infuriating poise, his boots barely making a sound. He stood slowly, eyes scanning the dark.

Frankie groaned. "That felt personal."

She got up and brushed off her jeans with as much dignity as she could muster. She looked up, and froze. Towering trees loomed around them, their bark blackened and marbled with glowing cracks, like lightning scars still burning. Mist curled low to the ground, silver and restless, coiling around her boots as though trying to get a better look at her.

Griffon's expression shifted, wariness settling over him like a long-shadowed truth. "This is the heart of Velhollow," he said quietly. "The heart of the realm. Once you cross into it, it judges you, whether you stand here as kin… or as a trespasser."

The mist thickened around Frankie's boots, curling higher, twining like it meant to shape itself. For a heartbeat it formed the outline of a girl, her outline, shadowed and ringed with thorns. Her stomach lurched, and she blinked hard. The shape unraveled back into harmless fog. Still, her skin prickled as though the forest had shown her something true and quickly taken it back.

They stood in a forest unlike any she'd seen in Velhollow. Towering alder trees surrounded them, trunks silver-streaked and twisting skyward into a canopy of low-hanging fog and starless dark. The bark of each tree was slick and blackened in places, like it had once burned and then decided to heal backward. Strange fruit glowed faintly in the distance, and clusters of firefly-colored light hovered between the branches, blinking in no recognizable rhythm.

Griffon exhaled slowly. "The Aldervyn Forest," he said. "We're deeper in than I've dared to tread. We're still in Velhollow, but this part... this is older, wilder."

Frankie stood shakily, brushing spores from her sleeve. "This is one of the places Aoife warned us about, isn't it? The ones that... move?"

Griffon nodded. "Indeed, and it tests you. It remembers your intentions and it rarely forgets trespassers."

Something shifted behind the trees. He gestured toward the claw-like roots tearing up from the ground.

"Aldervyn doesn't follow rules. It changes with every step." His voice darkened. "The land here isn't enchanted, it's alive."

Frankie's voice came soft, nearly a whisper. "You know this place?"

Griffon nodded once, eyes flicking over the trees. "People don't walk into Aldervyn and come out the same, if they come out at all."

Their eyes met, something unspoken sharpening in the air between them.

"Stay close," he said, and though his voice was quiet, it left no room for doubt.

Frankie arched a brow, defiant and amused. "Is that an order?"

He smirked. "A strong suggestion."

She took a step closer, tilting her head, voice low. "And if I ignore it?"

Griffon's mouth curved, but there was something hungry beneath the grin. "Then I suppose I'd have to catch you."

Frankie's breath hitched. Her heart skipped, then thudded harder in her chest, but she met his gaze, steady.

"Maybe I'd let you."

He laughed, but it was softer now, like it had folded in on something quieter.

During their decent, she'd reached for him instinctively, and now, surrounded by dark magic and ancient trees, that instinct remained. Her hand hovered near his sleeve, unsure whether to reach again, but Griffon made the choice for her. His fingers brushed hers, the contact hummed between them, warm, fleeting, and full of ache. Something about this place made every touch feel like a question, every glance a thread pulled tighter.

Frankie looked away first, but the tension lingered, the distance between them charged like the forest itself was watching, waiting. Somewhere in the branches above, a whisper stirred the air, neither wind nor voice, but memory.

He turned then, eyes scanning the trees. "Most in Velhollow don't speak of this place but those who do call it the *Forest That Remembers*."

Frankie's brow furrowed. "Remembers what?"

Griffon's voice dropped. "Everything. Every person, spell, every truth and lie ever told." He gestured to the gnarled trees towering above them. "It doesn't just exist, it observes. It judges." He pointed to the twisted canopy. "This part of the forest has no past, because it never lets go. It holds every oath ever spoken, every betrayal ever whispered beneath its branches."

Frankie turned slowly, taking in the eerie stillness. No wind stirred the trees, yet their branches swayed, as if reacting to an unseen breath. The undergrowth shifted subtly at their feet, curling like it was aware of them. Griffon's voice lowered, touched with wariness.

"They say Aldervyn has no true edges, it shifts as you move. Walk straight, and you'll find yourself looping in circles. Paths disappear the moment you glance away. Time unravels, landmarks change. Nothing remains where it was, unless the forest wills it."

Frankie's eyes swept the trees. There were no visible trails, no bent branches or signs of passage. The forest was impossibly old, yet untouched, preserved, almost like a memory caught in a photograph.

"There's an old tale," Griffon murmured, his voice dropping like a stone into deep water. "Long ago, a caravan tried to pass through Aldervyn, just travelers, merchants mostly, with wagons of goods and a hired mage or two for protection. They thought the tales of the forest was exaggeration, stories told by village elders to keep children close to home. They ignored the warnings. Laughed at the sigils carved into the bordering stones."

He paused, gaze narrowing as the shadows deepened around them. "The forest didn't attack them. It simply... watched and waited. First, their maps failed. The moss grew on every side of the trees. Then the birdsong repeated the same note over and over, like a lullaby being unwritten. Campfires refused to light unless everyone was silent. They tried to leave, but couldn't find the forests edge because it had moved."

Frankie's brow furrowed. "Did anyone survive?"

Griffon's jaw tightened. "No one knows. The story ends the same in every telling. One day, the trees opened just enough to let a single relic be found." He paused. "Just an ox shoe, half-buried in the middle of an open clearing."

Frankie blinked. "That's it?"

He nodded. "No cart. No beasts. No sign of safe passage, just that single iron shoe, like the forest let it remain as a... warning."

Frankie exhaled through her nose. "That's comforting."

Overhead, the canopy rustled. She stepped closer to Griffon without thinking, her hand brushing his forearm.

"Do you feel that?" she asked, voice barely more than breath.

Griffon didn't speak right away, his eyes scanned the trees, their bark etched with glimmers of bioluminescent scars, like old wounds half-healed by starlight. A branch creaked overhead, no breeze stirred it. The underbrush shifted without movement. His beast stirred beneath his skin, restless, spine prickling with recognition.

"Something's watching," he said, voice low and distant, as if the words belonged to another time.

Frankie turned, brushing a stubborn leaf from her hair with a sigh.

"Alright," she said, glancing over her shoulder, "any clever plans for charming our way out of a forest that clearly has its own agenda?"

"That depends," came a voice, gravelly, sprightly, and far too smug for its size.

Frankie let out a yelp, spinning on her heel. Perched atop a twisted root was a figure no taller than her knee, arms crossed like he was about to issue a verdict on her entire existence. His bark-like skin was knotted in places like wind-warped wood, and his beard looked like a small garden had exploded on his face, moss, twigs, even the delicate skeleton of a leaf tucked behind one ear like a badge. His ears, wide and leaf-shaped, twitched with every sound. His eyes, though, gleamed with the sharpness of old magic and the mischief of someone who knew more than he'd ever admit.

"Well then," he said, his voice like a thistle in a teacup. "Two bigfolk trampling through Aldervyn like lost lambs with no shepherd and even less sense."

"Who..." Frankie started.

"Name's Bramble," he said, puffing out his chest. "Keeper of the quiet places, whisperer of roots, and enthusiastic saboteur of the ill-prepared. You're lucky I found you before the forest got bored and turned you into compost."

Griffon narrowed his eyes. "You're a... "

"Bog sprite," Bramble cut in sharply. "But not just any bog sprite, *The* Bog Sprite. Capital letters, please and thank you... proper respect, don't you know. There's only one of me, thank the roots." He gave a sniff that managed to sound both wounded and smug. "And if you're bumbling through Aldervyn without a guide, which, judging by the way you've been stomping around like a pair of blindfolded badgers, you clearly are, then I'd say your chances of finding the way out are somewhere between slim and swallowed whole by an hidden vortex."

Frankie blinked. "You're offering to help us?"

Bramble tilted his head, beard bristling like moss in a breeze. "Offering is such a generous word. Let's call it... professionally intervening. Besides, if I left you to your own devices, the forest would either eat you, confuse you into becoming a bush, or make you walk in circles until your bones grew moss."

Griffon arched a brow. "And in return?"

The sprite's grin turned sharp and leafy. "I knew you were the practical one. Don't worry. I haven't decided on the favor yet. I prefer to save those little surprises for just the right moment. Builds character."

Frankie exhaled through her nose and shot Griffon a long-suffering sideways glance.

"We're really about to follow a tiny woodland menace with a beard full of twigs and an ego bigger than his boots, aren't we?"

Bramble, utterly unbothered, smoothed his mossy beard with pride. "You're lucky you found this tiny menace. I'm the reasonable sort, most of the others bite."

Frankie pinched the bridge of her nose and sighed. "Alright," she said, eyeing Bramble warily. "If you really know the forest, then lead on."

At that, Bramble puffed up like a smug toadstool basking in a sunbeam. "Wise choice," he declared. "You may address me as Bramble the Magnificent, Keeper of the Quiet Places, or simply Bramble, if you're feeling unworthy. I'm flexible."

He turned without waiting for approval, strutting into the underbrush with the self-importance of someone who knew the trees would part for him, and they did. The vines curled aside. The ferns bent low. Even the moss seemed to shift under his feet like it had been saving him a path.

Frankie glanced at Griffon, her expression caught somewhere between disbelief and resignation. "Let's just hope he actually knows where he's going."

Griffon gave a dry chuckle. "At least he walks like he does."

"This is either the best idea we've ever had," Frankie muttered under her breath, "or it's how we end up in a cautionary tale."

Griffon's mouth twitched with the ghost of a smile. "Probably both."

With that, they followed the bog sprite, grinning, rooted in mischief, and undeniably real, into the forest. Around them, Aldervyn shifted. The trees leaned in, trunks whispering secrets in groans of bark and creaking limbs. The path wasn't straight, or even really a path, more a suggestion of direction shaped by Bramble's whims and the forest's tolerance. Frankie stepped carefully, half-expecting the roots to slither underfoot, but so far, they held.

"So," Bramble said over his shoulder, without looking back, "shall we talk about the part where the forest is watching you?"

Frankie stiffened. "What do you mean?"

He stopped abruptly, turning to face them with a sly gleam in his eyes. "You didn't think you could wander into Aldervyn without stirring its attention, did you?" He tapped his temple. "You two are glowing like torchflies to the trees. Magic knows its own, and right now, yours is humming loud enough to wake old things."

Griffon stepped slightly in front of Frankie, instinct crackling beneath his skin.

Bramble raised a hand. “Relax, Stony. I didn’t say the forest meant you harm. But it is curious and when it gets curious… strange things tend to happen.”

Griffon crossed his arms, but the forest responded before he could speak. Beneath them, roots stirred, shifting like restless serpents, and the ground exhaled in a deep, earthen sigh. Overhead, vines curled inward, tasting the air like sentient things. Shadows elongated unnaturally, as if something just out of sight had begun to stir. Beside her, Griffon’s body tensed, his hand hovering near his blade as he instinctively stepped closer to her.

“What…” Frankie began, but before she could finish, the ground lurched. The path beneath their feet collapsed into itself, vanishing with a low, hungry groan. Trees shifted with creaking menace, trunks pressing close, branches weaving together into a dense, unbroken canopy. The forest swallowed the trail whole, the way forward was gone.

Griffon’s jaw clenched. “What did you just do?”

Bramble, utterly unfazed, hopped up onto a thick root that rose like a throne beneath him, as if the forest itself had made it for his amusement. His eyes glittered with mischief.

“Me? Nothing, but the forest here doesn’t take kindly to outsiders,” he said with a casual stretch, like he had all the time in the world. “It decides who walks its paths… and who gets swallowed whole.” He tilted his head. “You want me as a guide?” His voice took on a teasing lilt. “Prove to the forest why you deserve to be here first.”

Frankie’s heart thudded in her chest. In her short time in Velhollow, she’d already learned this much, nothing in the magical world came with a straight answer. Questions led to riddles, directions turned into tests. Every path forward required more than logic, it demanded instinct, resolve, and sometimes a willingness to leap before you looked. Magic loved its games and it rarely played fair.

“How exactly are we supposed to do that?” she asked, pulse still hammering.

Bramble grinned wide. “Simple,” he said, drawing out the word like it tasted sweet. “Find the path.”

The silence stretched.

Then he winked. “Course, if you can’t, I could help. Or…” He tapped his chin thoughtfully. “I could sit back and watch you wander in circles till the trees get bored and turn you into compost.” His grin sharpened. “Wouldn’t be the first time I’ve seen folks ask directions from boulders and argue with moss.”

Griffon’s gaze swept the trees. “The path’s gone.”

Bramble gave a dramatic gasp of mock offense. “Gone? Nah. Just playin’ shy.” He waved a lazy hand at the tangled woods. “Aldervyn Forest doesn’t lose things. If it wants you here, it’ll show the way. If not…” A low groan echoed through the trees, long, wooden, final. A sound like a door closing somewhere behind them. He grinned wider. “Let’s just say this place is real good at… removin’ complications.”

Frankie raised a brow. “So, what, a charming maze of magical doom?”

Bramble beamed. “Not doom, darling, a selective invitation.” He rocked back on his heels, crossing his arms. “If you belong here, the forest will know. Eyes won’t help you. You’ve got to feel the path, not find it.” Then, with the giddy energy of a ringmaster, he flung out his arms. “So, play smart, trust your gut, and above all…” He paused, grinning. “Don’t get eliminated!”

She glanced at Griffon. He exhaled slowly, tension rippling through his frame as his gaze cut to Bramble.

“If it wants us here,” he said, “we’ll earn our place.”

Bramble chuckled. “Atta boy.”

As if answering the challenge, the forest shifted. Vines slithered across the mossy ground like serpents. Bark stretched and groaned. The glow of the bioluminescent mushrooms dimmed, flickering like nervous fireflies.

“Alright,” Frankie said, steadying herself. “So how do we do this?”

Griffon’s voice dropped, low and sure. “We don’t force it, we listen.”

Bramble perched on a twisted root, tail flicking with delight. “Now you’re catchin’ on.” He tapped his temple. “Aldervyn don’t take orders. Doesn’t care about your bloodline, or how shiny your magic is. It listens. If you want it to open, prove you’re worth hearing.”

The mist thickened, coiling with a strange intelligence. Then, without warning, a voice, no louder than thought but felt in every bone. "*Prove yourselves.*"

A rush of movement, not seen but felt, swept over them. The world twisted, then blurred, and vanished. Frankie stumbled as her boots struck unfamiliar ground, the breath catching in her throat. She and Griffon froze in place, the world around them transformed. They stood in a clearing that hadn't existed a heartbeat ago, perfectly circular and cathedral-still, with trees arched inward like pillars of living silver. Their trunks glowed faintly, pulsing like distant stars through bark. The mist that had followed them so stubbornly now curled at the edge of the glade, hesitant to enter, as though even it knew better than to intrude. The air held a silence too deep for even birdsong.

Even Bramble stilled, his ears twitching. "Oh… stars above," he whispered with unease. "This bit's new."

The moss beneath their feet thrummed. A living rhythm, as if the land itself were drawing a breath. Shapes emerged from the trees, tall and otherworldly, cloaked in flickering threads of wind, flame, stone, and shadow. They didn't walk so much as form, coalescing from shadow and light, born of air and memory.

Four of them.

One glowed like moonlight caught in water, its edges constantly shifting, impossible to pin to any single shape. Another burned with the slow intensity of molten gold beneath bark-slick skin, its fissures lit from within by the steady heat of an ancient forge. The third wore a crown of thorns that bloomed and withered in the same breath, roses of ash falling into petals of memory that never touched the ground. The last moved on wings woven from soot and flower-petal light, each beat dissolving into drifting smoke that reformed a moment later.

Frankie turned back toward the figures. "What are they?"

Bramble's voice dropped. "Elemental messengers. The forest doesn't waste breath on riddles when it can send something like this."

Griffon's jaw flexed. "Why now?"

"To ask what the trees cannot," Bramble murmured. "To ask if you deserve to stand where you are."

The figures traveled across the clearing with the hush of something exhaled from the deep belly of the world, weightless and unhurried, as if they had been shaped from breath, twilight, and the first spark of creation. They did not claim a single form. They were not wholly flesh nor wholly spirit. They were what the forest remembered from before language: elemental, unbound, alive in a way nothing mortal could ever be.

The first figure turned its gaze onto Frankie, not piercing, but unveiling, seeing through her rather than at her. When it spoke, the forest bowed in a single ripple of branches, a slow cascade of leaves acknowledging something older than themselves. Its voice wasn't sound at all, but cadence, rhythm drawn from bark and bone, a rhyme carved into the memory of the realm.

"*Granddaughter of root, of ember and bloom,*
Born not from comfort, but shaped from loom,
Of thread line woven in verdant fire,
Heir to oath, to blood, to pyre,
Stand now, child, and know your name;
You walk beneath a crown of flame."

Frankie's breath hitched. "What... what does that mean?"

The second figure drifted forward, its feet never fully committing to the earth. The ground settled into a deeper quiet beneath it, soil and stone listening as though the forest itself held its breath. A faint ripple crossed the air around the being like a subtle folding of space, the way heat bends the horizon on a far-off road. It paused before her, gathering its attention with the gravity of a storm centering itself.

"*She is of Caelith, thorn and grace,*
Of royal bloom in hidden place.
Grandchild of the Verdant Flame,
Whose shadow bends, yet bears no shame.
Blood of the Court that walks between,
The Lirathian Crown, the Ashen Queen."

Frankie turned, stunned. "Aoife?"

The being's glow deepened, its voice settling into the hush of leaves and distant storm.

"Aoife Caelith, Warden of Flame,
High Crown of the Lirathian Name.
The Rose Unfallen, Thorn Unbroken,
She who speaks where none have spoken.
Keeper of the Skybound Vow,
The forest bows before her now."

Frankie swayed a little, the truth spiraling outward like a stone dropped into deep water.

"Aoife is... royal?" she whispered.

She turned instinctively to Griffon for something solid, something known. Before he could speak, the third figure drifted toward him. Its attention sharpened, its voice ringing like metal forged in moonlight.

"And he who stands beside her,
Griffon Thorne of the Stonewing Line,
Guardian born of mountain spine,
Shield-forged heart and oath-bound mind,
Last of the Skyward Guard who swore
To rise when Verdant magic stirs once more.
Wing and root, flame and stone,
No fate she walks she walks alone."

Griffon stilled, the words settling over him not as praise, but as a mantle being returned after too long buried.

A Verdant Witch rising.

A Stonewing Guardian restored.

A prophecy shifting toward its true shape.

The first being moved toward them now. Its form bent like smoke in a breeze. Where a mouth should have been, petals spilled, violet and green, drifting to the ground in slow spirals, soft as a forgotten prayer.

"One of earth, and one of flame,
Bound by magic, not by name.
If you seek to find the thread,
Prove your heart, or leave it dead."

Frankie's pulse surged. "Is this... a test?"

Bramble voice carried a hush that even the trees seemed to heed. “No, witchling. This isn’t something you pass or fail. This is where truth comes to the surface, where masks fall away and what’s left must stand on its own. The forest doesn’t ask for perfection.” He hopped off the root, voice low and old as root stone. “A test, you can study for. A trial, you might endure. But this, ” his tone grew thin and hollow, like wind through a ruined chapel, “this is when the truth comes calling. No masks. No excuses. Just the heart of who you are… and whether you rise, or come undone.”

Then, the clearing shifted, subtly at first, then all at once. The glow beneath the moss dulled, color draining from leaf and bark alike. What had moments before felt whole now carried a brittle tension, as if something vital had been stripped away. Shapes darkened. Edges blurred. Even the light seemed to retreat.

The fourth figure dimmed, its form unraveling into shadow, edges fraying like charred parchment touched by unseen flame. The others flickered in response, their glow withdrawing inward, as if shielding themselves from what stirred. The trees stiffened, their branches straining upward as if reaching for something forgotten or feared.

“*There is another,*” the figure said. The light around it collapsed until only its outline remained, a silhouette scorched into the clearing like a wound.

“*He walks with forgotten names upon his tongue,*
The Unforgiven, the Undone.
Blood that mirrors, breath that binds,
He is the fracture in the lines.
One coin. Two faces. One must fall.”

The figure’s focus fell upon Frankie like a curse long buried and now unearthed. It seeped into her being like slag, molten and merciless until her bones ached with it. Her limbs went cold, not from fear, but from recognition.

“*He knows the thread, he hunts your flame.*
He calls you blood, he speaks your name.
Steel your soul, for paths will split,
One shall rise, one shall submit.

The forest keeps the vow you gave,
But he will come, with blade and grave."

Griffon stepped nearer to Frankie, his shoulder brushing hers, steady as the stones beneath them but didn't look away from the shadowed figure. The wind rose, it smelled of scorched bark and distant thunder and of hot metal. The fourth figure, still and burning at its edges, spoke one final rhyme, softer than breath but clear as death.

"*The time grows thin, the light grows low,*
The path home calls, yet none may know.
Verdant flame and shadowed wing,
Must rise in truth, or lose everything."

The figure's final words left a silence that wasn't stillness, it was anticipation sharpened to a point. It wrapped around them like tension before a storm, coiling through the trees, threading under the skin. Frankie didn't dare move. Griffon stood beside her, jaw clenched, arms locked like pillars braced for impact. Even Bramble, usually a murmuring blur of wit and twitching limbs, was still, his expression unreadable, his body held taut. Whatever had passed between the elemental messengers and the waking world wasn't a warning. It was a line drawn and now... now came the consequence.

Veyrath.

He didn't merely *arrive,* he tore through. One moment, the space beneath the trees was empty. The next, it bent, ruptured, and from that rupture he stepped, like a wound opened in the world. The forest didn't part for him. It fled. Branches gnarled themselves away, bark splitting in protest. Leaves shriveled on the stem. Roots shrank from his tread. Shadows didn't gather, they surrendered, rushing to him like loyal beasts returning to a master. They wrapped around him, not as cloak or smoke, but as sentient memory, sorrow given claws. Light stuttered at his edges, warped and unwilling. His magic wasn't earned. It was stolen from the essence of things that had once lived. It didn't hum or blaze, it drained. It pulled at the world like rot beneath gilding, like thirst that could never be quenched and then he smiled. It wasn't a warm greeting. It was a fracture. A soft, deliberate tear in the shape of a man. The clearing recoiled from it. Time seemed to drag, thick and off-tempo, as if the world itself flinched.

"Such potential," he murmured. The air thickened, rippling into an image, familiar and wrong all at once. Frankie saw herself, but not as she was. This other Frankie stood cloaked in ruin, thorns coiling like serpents around her shoulders, her eyes a green gone sharp and merciless. She moved like someone who had stopped asking permission from the world and had started taking what she wanted. For a heartbeat, Frankie's chest clenched with recognition. She had felt shades of that self before, in the sharpness of her temper, in the hunger that sometimes startled her, in the way her family's cold stares had convinced her she was too much, too dangerous. This shadow-self was all of that, unbound.

The man's gaze slid past the flickering vision of dark Frankie, lingering only long enough to acknowledge it, before landing on the real one with chilling clarity.

"You feel it, don't you?" he said, soft as sin. "That fire in your bones? That ache in your soul? The hunger? You weren't meant for potted herbs and whispered spells in garden sheds. You were made to command."

Then he tilted his head, eyes narrowing with something not quite amusement, more like a predator puzzling over prey that hadn't yet bolted. "Tell me, granddaughter," he said, the word slick with venom and silk, "does my truer self rattle your bones? Do I unsettle the soft thing you are?"

Frankie didn't blink. "No, not really," she said, her voice dry as sun-scorched lavender. "Bit more mildew and melodrama, maybe. But you've always looked like that, haven't you? Even when you wore my grandfather's face like a clever mask."

She stepped forward. Her boots whispered across the earth like truth breaking free. "You haunted me for years. Not because of what you are, but because I couldn't figure out why I never measured up. Why I always felt fractured, like a song with no final note." The shadows around him stirred, agitated, but halted, held back by something unseen. She didn't flinch. "But you don't live there anymore. You don't get to rot inside my story. You never earned that place."

His smile flickered, just a tremor, just enough to know the words had landed and still, she stood taller. Around them, the clearing waited. The forest had not made peace. It had merely drawn breath, holding the weight of the moment on its bark and root. Something knew.

Veyrath raised his hand, not in invitation, but in declaration.

"Come," he said, and the shadows behind him surged like smoke pulled toward a pyre. "Step off this path of trials and chains and I will crown you in truth. You are heir to the Noctis line of the Forgotten Realm, to the darkness itself where fear becomes power, and power bows to none."

He stepped closer, his smile widened. "Rule beside me, Francesca, and there is no throne you will not touch. Refuse…" His voice dropped, iced and precise. "And I will peel Velhollow apart, root from rune, song from soil. I will make a hunting ground of your precious woods. And your beast," His gaze flicked to Griffon, slow as poison. "He will know rage and only rage. He will burn through what he is until he becomes ruin."

He turned back to Frankie, smile thin as a crescent blade. "And you? I will leave you hollow, just full enough to remember what you could have been. Power without purpose, magic without joy, a queen without a crown."

Griffon stepped forward, voice a growl. "She's not going anywhere with you."

Veyrath laughed, low and indulgent. "Ah, so the beast bares its teeth." He tilted his head, studying Griffon with a dark glint. "You feel it too, don't you? That ache deep in the bones? That itch to break the shape they handed you and become more than legend ever allowed?" His smile was almost tender. "That's not fear, that's freedom."

Bramble gave an unimpressed snort. "Here we go," he muttered. "Trade your soul for dominion, skip straight to the end of the story where the villain monologues for six pages."

Veyrath ignored him, his attention was fixed, wholly, on Frankie. "You've felt it," he said, voice curling like shadow-smoke. "That call to cast off the leash. To stop playing all soft and small. They told you who to be. I'm offering you the truth of what you are. All you have to do… is stop pretending it isn't already in your bones."

Frankie didn't step forward because she wanted power, she stepped forward because she refused to let him define her. The forest shifted in support; branches arched closer, vines coiling as if to lend her their strength. Her sigil flared, soft yet unyielding, a glow of green-gold like sunlight spilling through leaves.

"You think I care about being big or small?" she said, her voice calm but cutting, like the whisper of a blade through silk. "I'm not afraid of power, Veyrath. I'm afraid of becoming something that forgets who it's meant to protect. That's you, isn't it?"

The shadows twitched, recoiling for a beat as though her words had struck deeper than any spell. Veyrath's smile darkened, sharp as frost cracking through glass.

"Roots," he said with a sneer. "Roots only keep you buried."

Griffon's wings flared, obsidian feathers bristling with silver light. "You talk too much," he growled, stepping forward like the shield he had become.

Veyrath's shadow lashed in response, coiling around Griffon's talons with a hiss. "And you, beast, think your loyalty will save her? You think love will keep her from being pulled apart when the choice comes?"

Frankie's chin lifted. "The only choice I have to make is mine, and it won't be to align myself with you." Her words fell soft as loam, but the ground seemed to listen. "I don't choose for dominion or power. I choose for what I might learn, for what I can give, and for those I would protect." Her gaze didn't falter. "It's like knowing the difference between apathy and empathy, and choosing which one you want etched beside your name when the wilds remember."

Beneath her boots, the earth gave way in welcome. A hush swept the clearing as though the forest itself had paused to bear witness. From the soil, green rose like memory exhaled. Vines uncurled, trembling toward the sky. Petals opened with the slowness of old truths remembered. Her magic didn't strike. It bloomed. It wove through the clearing like an ancestral hymn, threading root to branch, stone to stem, not as conquest, but as communion. It moved like morning overtaking shadow, steady, inevitable, alive. The land didn't kneel to her, it recognized her.

Something shifted. The clearing changed its breathless rhythm. Whatever had lingered in waiting began to stir, vast and unseen, like the slow unfurling of a storm no charm could stall. The edges of the world sharpened and her magic surged again, luminous and wild, anchoring her. She was not called to choose a side for power.

She chose because she knew the cost of silence, and the worth of protection. She had seen what fear could do, and she would not be its vessel. She didn't crave dominion, she walked with purpose. That was her truth. And it was enough to wake what slept.

Frankie stood rooted in the forest's rhythm, around her, branches bent subtly closer, leaves trembling as if to catch her breath, the air rich with the scent of green things awakening. The earth beneath her boots steadied, firm and sure, as though the land itself was lending her its weight. The clearing itself seemed to lean, ever so slightly, toward her and away from him, an unspoken choice, subtle but undeniable and yet he smiled, face-to-face with her, a sharp promise of violence curving his mouth. It wasn't warmth. It wasn't welcome. It was a blade unsheathed.

"You cannot fight what you are," Veyrath said. His voice slid through the clearing like velvet soaked in rot. He lifted his hand in a gesture that pretended to be an invitation but carried the unmistakable weight of command. "Choose."

Frankie did not answer immediately. The world around her dropped into a deeper quiet, the kind that belongs to oceans before they rise. The clearing held a stillness that felt deliberate, the same eerie retreat of breath and tide before a tsunami gathers its full force. It was not peace; it was pressure. It built in the ground, in the air, and most of all inside her. She felt her magic coil beneath her skin, like an animal pacing the edges of a cage it had never been meant to inhabit. She had no spell to rely on because no one had ever taught her one. She had no ritual to draw from because she had never known a world where they existed. She had received no training at all. Everything inside her felt too large and too unshaped, as if she carried a storm in her ribs without knowing where the sky ended and the lightning began. The uncertainty frightened her. Admitting that fear frightened her even more. But she reached inward despite it, because she finally understood that fear was not a summons to retreat. It was a signal that she stood at the edge of something important.

She searched for the thread of her own center, the quiet place where instinct lived. At first it eluded her. All she found was turbulence, a swirl of heat and color and pressure that refused to take shape. Her magic surged without direction, tugging hard at her breath, untempered and determined to be felt. It pushed against the edges of her control, wild and impatient, reminding her that she was still learning, still stumbling, still new. Yet beneath that chaos, she sensed something familiar.

Magic itself was new, but the possibility of it had lived in her for years. It had flickered at the edge of childhood, in moments she couldn't explain. It had stirred in her chest during long sunsets, in dreams she had written off as imagination, in the quiet certainty that she was meant for something she could never quite name. She had spent her life doubting that feeling, shrinking from it, convinced it was foolish to believe she was more than ordinary. But here, in the heart of Velhollow, the truth rose with a clarity she could no longer deny. That pull she had always felt wasn't childish fantasy. It had been the first whisper of her own magic calling to her. It had been her birthright trying to reach her across years of silence. Here, in a place that recognized her as surely as she recognized herself, the truth settled through her with quiet certainty. She wasn't unraveling. She was opening from within, like a seed that had waited years beneath dark soil and had finally found the season it was meant to rise in. A part of her she had never trusted, never dared to believe in, stepped forward at last, steady and real.

Frankie steadied herself and reached inward once more. This time she didn't resist the rising power. She allowed it to move, listening to the quiet hum beneath her feet, the whisper of root, stone, and river carrying the memory of everything that had lived and died before her. She leaned into the truth she had always been afraid to admit: she wanted this. She wanted to know who she could become. And the earth answered. Not as a teacher correcting a child, but as an equal rising to meet her. The roots shifted. The branches hushed. Something ancient settled its attention upon her, patient and vast, as if Velhollow itself waited to see who she would choose to be.

She drew a deeper breath, and with it released the burdens that had shaped her life. She let go of the prophecy that had never belonged to her, the bloodline she had never asked to carry, and the expectations others had draped across her shoulders. For the first time, she allowed herself to stand without anyone else's story defining her. In choosing herself, she granted her magic permission it had never been given. The change began quietly, like the first swell beneath deep waters. Then it rose.

Vines burst from the ground, spiraling upward in fierce, blooming arcs. Emerald light threaded along her spine, lifting her hair as though carried by a rising current. Gold gathered around her arms, weaving through the air with slow, deliberate strength, as if dawn itself were learning how to take shape around her.

Her magic did not wait for instruction. It recognized the moment she let go of fear and moved toward her with unmistakable certainty. For the first time, she was not drowning in it. She was rising to meet it. Light gathered behind her eyes. Green flame curled along her fingers. The forest shifted first. Branches arched downward in a sweeping bow, leaves trembling in recognition. Roots stirred beneath the soil in allegiance. Even the shadows pulled back in a single, unified ripple, as though the clearing itself refused to hold space for Veyrath any longer. The realm turned toward her and Velhollow answered.

Frankie felt the response rise through the earth and into her bones, a steady surge of power that did not overwhelm her, but met her exactly where she stood. The clearing grew brighter around her, not with flame or spellwork, but with the quiet certainty of a realm choosing its witch. She stood at the center of the storm she had become, and the land stood with her. The air thickened with recognition. Branches quivered. Stone hummed beneath her boots. The world aligned, as if something ancient had waited years for this moment and had finally opened its eyes.

Veyrath recoiled. Smoke spilled from his mouth in twisting, venomous threads.

"Pretty weeds," sneering, he stepped forward, but the vines rising at Frankie's command struck like living blades, their thorns bright and unyielding. They drove him back a full pace, his form wavering, unraveling like soot caught in a wind determined to disperse him. Frankie's magic was not polished. It was not refined but it was hers, and it was enough to make the world take notice.

Bramble stared, every trace of mischief wiped clean from his moss-bright features. Awe reshaped him, raw and unguarded, softening even the wild edges of his bog-born face. It struck him so completely that the clearing itself seemed to quiet around him, as though his silence carried a weight powerful enough to carve stillness through the air. Frankie felt the shift before she fully understood it. Something in her, instinct, magic, recognition, turned her toward him. When she met his eyes, she saw no jest, no bluster, none of the theatrical bravado he usually wrapped himself in like armor. Instead she saw reverence edged with disbelief, a wordless certainty that whatever she had just become was far beyond anything he had ever expected. In that breath, he wasn't Bramble the loud, Bramble the chaotic, Bramble the bog-sprite who threatened to bite ankles as a greeting. He was Bramble the witness and he was seeing her, truly seeing her, for the first time.

Griffon stood at the center of the glade, mid-transformation. This was no simple shift of flesh and bone. His shoulders bowed, spine lengthening as if mountains themselves pushed upward beneath his skin. Stone cracked along his arms, glowing with silver fire that sealed itself into living armor. His wings unfurled by the inch, shedding ash as new pinions formed, obsidian dark vast enough to eclipse the clearing's glow. The scent of scorched earth thickened as sparks hissed where his talons struck soil, splitting the ground in slow, deliberate cracks that radiated outward like a command. His face was still his, familiar in its lines, in the shape of devotion that lived there. Yet something ancient rose within him, something rooted in Velhollow long before he drew breath. It had not been called by force. It had been called by recognition and his soul had answered.

Veyrath's snarl ripped through the clearing.

"No!" His voice cracked like stone under strain. "Not him. He is mine!"

Veyrath slashed his hand through the air and shadows tore loose in violent ribbons, hurtling toward Griffon with the force of a command sharpened over decades. Yet the moment the darkness touched the forming shape, it withered, collapsing into smoke as if scorched by a truth the world itself refused to deny. The land recoiled from Veyrath's will, rejecting him with a force older than prophecy, and in that instant he understood the magnitude of what had slipped beyond his reach. He had not merely lost a pawn on a board he believed he controlled; he had lost both sources of power he had spent decades shaping his schemes around. Frankie, whose magic he had intended to corrupt and bend into shadow, and Griffon, whose Stonewing lineage he had hoped to twist into a weapon, now stood beyond him, aligned in a bond he had neither predicted nor prepared for. They had chosen themselves, they had chosen each other, and the land had chosen with them, sealing a truth that shattered the foundation of every plan he had ever laid.

For the first time, fear thinned the edges of Veyrath's smile. Frankie's sigil blazed across her palm, bright and fierce, but the heat that surged through the clearing no longer belonged to her alone. A second mark ignited across Griffon's skin, identical in shape, matching her light in perfect symmetry. The glow sprang between them like a single chord struck on two strings, resonant and commanding, so strong the glade itself trembled around them. Magic surged outward in a thick, rising wave, no longer wild or directionless, but braided, hers, his, and the land's.

Fire climbed Griffon's frame as though it had been waiting for him, rising with slow, deliberate certainty. His obsidian wings unfurled in a single sweeping motion, the sound echoing like mountains shifting their weight. Each feather brightened along its edges with molten silver. His talons pressed deep into the earth, not in aggression but in declaration, and bands of rune-light spiraled across his basalt skin like constellations awakening after centuries of sleep.

Veyrath staggered backward.

"No," he whispered, smoke curling from his mouth in frantic threads. "Not him. He cannot bear that mantle. He is not a vessel. The realm does not choose without cost." His voice frayed, sharp with dawning horror.

Frankie's breath caught as she saw it, the change settling into Griffon as if truth coming home. His spine straightened, shoulders expanding with an ancient weight. The fire around him shifted tone, burning with purpose. His eyes opened, and the world stilled. One iris gleamed silver, the other gold, both lit from within by an older fire that seemed to recognize the very soil beneath them. For a moment, Griffon's form flickered. He was Stonewing, yes, but layered atop that was something larger, more primal, the echo of a legend Velhollow had nearly forgotten.

A Berserker.

Bramble's jaw dropped, his mossy curls quivering. "By the bog's own bones," he breathed. "He's really becoming it."

Frankie barely heard him. Her heart pounded with fierce recognition, because she could feel it, the realm was not overtaking Griffon. It was choosing him.

Veyrath reeled. "The mantle cannot awaken without a king's blood," he hissed. "It cannot take root without ritual. It cannot, " His words broke, and his eyes widened with a terror so sharp it hollowed his voice. "He's been claimed. The realm has claimed him."

Griffon inhaled deeply, the breath shaking the branches overhead. Currents of firelit gold threaded down his arms, across his ribcage, and along the sweeping curve of his wings. The transformation did not devour him. It strengthened him, shaping itself around who he already was. Stone cracked, reshaped, and regrew in living patterns, each piece clicking into place with the certainty of prophecy. Heat shimmered off him in a slow, rolling tide, carrying the scent of cedar, granite, and storm-forged metal.

Frankie watched, her pulse racing, her palms trembling. This was no fury-fueled monster from legend. This was her Griffon. Loyal. Steadfast. Fiercely protective. Now amplified a thousandfold, sharpened by a power that had slept beneath Velhollow for centuries. She sensed him through the live-wire connection of their twin sigils. His mind was still his. His will was still his. His heart, steady and resolute, was still his.

Veyrath clawed at the air, shadows ripping forward at his command. "No vessel holds that power! None survive it! He must burn!" More smoke tore from him, desperate and wild, but every strand that touched Griffon's blazing silhouette disintegrated into drifting ash. The realm itself refused Veyrath's claim.

Griffon rose taller, wings spreading so far the edges brushed the treetops. The ground trembled. Leaves bowed. Roots surged beneath the soil as if greeting him. His neck arched back and for a breathless instant, the clearing glowed with his presence alone. He was guardian and storm and oath made flesh.

Frankie pressed a hand over her sigil, stunned as the heat in her palm synced with the beat of his power. Their magic braided, alight and alive. He turned his gaze toward her, just briefly, and she saw him, truly saw him, Griffon as he had always been, carved of loyalty and endurance, now revealed in full. The glade leaned toward them. Branches bent, roots hummed low underneath, and even the moonlight seemed to still.

Veyrath retreated, smoke boiling from his frame. His eyes, coal and void, snapped to the tether of light between them, and his face twisted with fury.

"You mistake this for triumph," Veyrath murmured, his smile thinning to something surgical. "Berserkers burn bright, but they do not last. The realm devours its champions as readily as it crowns them."

"And you, Francesca... do you truly believe you can hold him together when the fire turns inward?"

Griffon stepped fully into the shape the realm had carved for him, wings lifting in a sweeping arc that washed the clearing with molten light. The air thickened around him, charged with a gravity that made even the trees bow their crowns. When he spoke, his voice rolled through the glade like distant thunder crossing the ribs of a mountain, deep, resonant, threaded with something ancient that had slept too long beneath stone.

"This realm knows my name," he said, every word carrying weight and heat. "It has called me to rise, and I rise for her."

His gaze locked onto Veyrath, steady and unbroken. "You sought to claim us," Griffon continued, "but the land has chosen and so have I."

The silver-gold fire along his wings swept outward in a slow, controlled flare, not a threat, but a declaration.

"I am her shield," he said, voice sharpening, "and her storm."

Roots stirred beneath Frankie's boots. Branches leaned inward. Even the shadows withdrew. The realm agreed. The words cut through Veyrath's smoke like a blade, quiet and undeniable. The rot shrank back, coiling tighter, as if even he could not withstand that recognition. And in that moment Frankie saw him in all his wildness, in every form he had ever been and every form he was still becoming. Something shifted in the space between them. Frankie's magic stirred, steady and sure, reaching out like a hand extended. Griffon's power rose to meet it, older now, deepened by what he had become. His magic was no longer only the Stonewing's strength, but the echo of the storm that carves mountains and the silence that follows. It answered her call with grounded force, ancient as stone split by lightning.

When their magics touched, the air flickered with something curious and becoming. Energy wove between them like ivy climbing weathered stone, like flame discovering warmth instead of destruction. The two currents twined, learning each other in real time. Power spiraled around them, lifting leaves into the air, spinning petals in slow arcs, threading song through the hush. The trees did not pull back. The clearing did not resist. Even the wind grew still, not from fear, but respect.

Veyrath snarled, thrashing against the unseen tide, but his strikes found no purchase. His smoke-lashed tendrils unraveled the moment they touched the spiraling bond, unmade by the resonance of bloom and stone. This was no longer just Verdant magic or Berserker might, this was something both in-between, a meeting place of earth and fury. A collective was forming, alive, untamed, and still unfolding. Whatever it was becoming, it had not yet found its edge, and at the center of it all, stood the two of them.

Frankie's sigil pulsed at her palm, no longer a mark of singular power but a living tether. It glowed with promise, gold and green entwined, spiraling like ivy through sunlight. It reached beyond her body, beyond her breath, and found its match across the narrow space between them. The mirrored sigil on Griffon's chest glowed in response, etched into his skin as if carved there by the will of the realm itself. The glow was subtler, deeper, a heartbeat of amber beneath the surface, as though a second sun stirred behind his ribs. This wasn't an echo. It was resonance, harmony born of truth.

"This... this wasn't just me," Frankie whispered.

Griffon's gaze met hers, steady and glowing from within. "It's us," he said softly.

"Whatever this is... it belongs to both of us now."

The words lingered like spellwork between them, delicate and undeniable. The air shifted, no longer merely heavy with magic but changed by it. Something old and watchful stirred through root and stone, through vine and sky, as if the land itself had drawn a breath and was holding it, listening. The bond was not only between them. It reached outward, into the soil, into the trees, into the quiet spaces where ancient things still remembered how to feel. Around them, Velhollow breathed. Trees bent low in acknowledgment. Somewhere far off, a bell rang, though none had been rung. The realm had seen, and it had answered.

Something ancient had awakened, and it had chosen them. Energy cracked through the glade, bloom, root and wing, thunder softened by ivy. Velhollow felt it, the raw, unchecked force of their bond as a promise. One that would need tending. Shaping. But it was theirs. Together, they had awakened something vast and powerful.

Veyrath's scream ripped through the clearing, but it no longer carried power. His rot thrashed uselessly against the living bond, smoke dissolving into the air, his decree broken, his claim denied, still Frankie and Griffon stood, the center of it all. For a moment, it seemed Veyrath had been unmade entirely, his scream fading into smoke that the glade itself consumed. But rot is not so easily banished. His voice lingered, thin as cracks in stone, curling through the roots like frost that refused to melt.

"You bind yourselves in light," the shadow rasped, hollow and vast, "but every bond carries its shadow. When the green turns to ash and the stone to dust, it will not be my hand that breaks you, it will be your own."

As the words unraveled into silence, the ground where he had stood blackened, roots curling in on themselves, brittle and burned. A stain spread outward in fractures of light, seared into the earth like a brand, before the glade pushed back, vines creeping over it, moss rushing to cover, but the mark remained, faint and smoldering, a wound in the living green. Only then did the air release its breath. The last of Veyrath's smoke bled upward into nothing, leaving behind only the echo of a curse, the promise that ruin could come from within.

The glade shuddered, as though exhaling the last of him. Light filtered back through the canopy, thin and hesitant, brushing Frankie's shoulders like a question. Her pulse still hammered with borrowed fire, her sigil throbbing against her palm in time with Griffon's. For a moment, neither of them moved. The silence pressed so deep, the kind that follows thunder before the world remembers how to breathe. A single feather spiraled down through the still air, landing on the blackened scar in the earth. The glade did not consume it. It only lay there, stark and waiting, a reminder that shadows had not gone so easily.

Griffon's voice broke the silence, low and steady.

“This isn’t over.” His gaze stayed fixed on the smoldering wound in the ground, silver and gold burning in tandem. “He’ll return. Rot doesn’t vanish, it waits. It seeps. And when it finds a crack, it spreads.” His wings flexed once, obsidian and silver catching the fractured light. “We held him back that’s all.”

The words rooted in Frankie like iron. She wanted to protest, to claim the realm’s answer was enough, that the tether between them had changed everything. But the scar in the earth still smoldered, and deep in her bones she felt the echo of Veyrath’s curse, cold as frost beneath her fire. Griffon was right. This was not the end. It was only the first battle.

Bramble blinked up at them both, breathless. “Well,” he murmured, “I’ll be spun into a spider’s dream. You two might just be the real thing. You don’t see that every day.”

The wind stilled, as if the land itself had paused to listen. Even the birds were quiet, feathers tucked, songs forgotten. A single leaf drifted sideways, caught mid-air like it, too, was waiting to see what would come next. Frankie looked at Griffon.

“So,” she breathed, “does this mean our magic knows how to play nice now?”

Griffon didn’t answer right away. His breath came hard, shoulders rising and falling in deep, shuddering rhythm. Smoke curled faintly from his skin, and his eyes flickered like they hadn’t quite settled back into human stillness. The weight of what had just happened clung to him like soot, his body not only shifted, but reshaped by something ancient. A breath, then another. He huffed a soft laugh that sounded more disbelief than humor.

“Play nice?” he rasped, voice hoarse, raw with magic still echoing through his bones. “I’m not even sure what just happened knows the rules.”

He looked at her then, really looked, and something in his posture eased. He dragged a trembling hand through his hair, still streaked with faint glints of silver, and gave a crooked, exhausted smile.

“But yes,” he said, catching his breath. “I do think we are on the right course.”

The quiet held for a beat longer, like even the world was waiting to see what they’d choose next. Frankie watched the wild magic begin to settle in his eyes, still storm-lit, still not entirely still. Frankie's fingers tightened.

"Are you okay?"

He looked down at his hands, flexed them slowly, as if relearning the shape of being whole. No flame danced there now, only a quiet, ancient strength beneath the skin. Something settled. Something wild. Something rooted deep. He met her eyes, steady and sure. His lips curved.

"Better than okay."

He lifted one hand to his chest, to the place where her sigil had marked him. The skin held a faint gold glow, a breath of living magic etched into him. Without hesitation, he stepped closer. His hands rose to cradle her face, gentle despite all he'd become, and Frankie barely had time to draw a breath before his lips met hers.

BANG!

Magic surged, wild, radiant, and certain. A golden wave unfurled from where they stood, spreading outward like sunlight breaking through an ancient canopy. Ivy curled skyward along nearby trunks, twining in slow, joyful spirals. The air shifted, velvet-rich and spell-sweet, as though Velhollow itself had paused, just for a breath, to bear witness. From the soil, tendrils of green and gold unfurled like rising smoke. Leaves quivered on their branches, lit from within by quiet awe, while motes of pale green and soft gold drifted through the clearing like a lullaby made visible, warm and remembering.

Bramble let out a delighted cackle, stumbling back a step. "Now that's how you seal a spell! Reminds me of the *Midsomer Fête*, fewer coconuts, more combustion. Last time I saw magical kiss like that, someone lost their eyebrows and a salamander developed an existential crisis."

Frankie, blinking hard and breathless, turned to him. "Was that... supposed to happen?"

With a jaunty whistle, Bramble turned and bounded ahead, his mossy beard bouncing and his eyes bright with mischief and old magic.

"Honestly," he called over his shoulder, "that was gloriously excessive. A Berserker blooming, ancient magic hollering through the trees, and a kiss loud enough to wake the fern-folk? Oh, the storytellers are going to lose their mossy minds over this."

The trees shifted, bending as though yielding to something profound. Branches arched high overhead like cathedral beams, bark groaning softly, the quiet ache of old doors remembering how to open. The undergrowth parted without a rustle, revealing a winding path worn smooth by countless forgotten footsteps. Bioluminescent moss lit its curves in soft shades of blue and green, and the very air seemed to hold a low hum of welcome, as if the realm had adjusted its breath to match theirs. Along the path's edge, a rare bloom stirred. At first it appeared simple and faintly luminous, but when its petals unfurled, the forest leaned in as though recognizing something long awaited. Violet and gold rippled across each delicate surface, shifting in the exact hues of Frankie's sigil… and then, with a second breath, warming into the amber threaded through the runes along Griffon's skin.

Frankie froze. "What… is that?"

Bramble crept closer, squinting as though trying to decide whether the flower might suddenly talk back. "Well now," he muttered, awe slipping into his mossy voice despite his best effort to sound unimpressed. "That's a *Verdant Crownlily*, that is. Nasty thing to find unless the forest's in a telling mood."

Frankie looked at him sharply. "A telling mood?"

"Indeed" Bramble said, scratching his ear with a twig-like finger. "Crownlilies don't bloom for fun. They bloom for recognition… or when the land decides two magics just braided themselves into something worth paying attention to."

Frankie's breath softened, her chest tightening with something she didn't dare name yet. The bloom brightened again as she stepped forward, petals opening fully, turning toward her like a greeting. But when Griffon drew nearer, the colors deepened, shifting into an amber glow that mirrored the fire living beneath his stone bound skin.

The forest wasn't simply acknowledging her.

It was acknowledging them.

Bramble gulped. "Well," he whispered, eyes widening until they looked more leaf than iris, "that's a first. Verdant and Stonewing, both marked in the same breath. The realm's makin' statements tonight."

Griffon plucked it carefully, the stem cool beneath his fingers. He turned to Frankie, his expression unreadable, but his eyes said more than words could carry. She looked up at him with a soft smile, curious and unguarded, and for a moment, neither of them moved. Then, with a gentleness that surprised even him, he stepped closer and tucked the bloom behind her ear. His fingers lingered near her cheek, just long enough to feel the warmth of her skin, just long enough to anchor the moment.

She blinked, a little breath caught in her throat. "What was that for?"

He shrugged, eyes not leaving hers. "Seemed like it belonged there."

Frankie looked away then, not out of shyness but to catch her breath, to make room in her chest for the way his voice settled into her like rain in dry soil. She touched the bloom gently, as if afraid it might vanish if she held it too tightly. Griffon stood silent beside her, watching the light catch in her hair, in her eyes, in the glow of the Crownlily nestled just above her cheekbone. Something in him eased. Not everything was solved. Not everything was safe. But in this one sliver of time, something had aligned and Velhollow knew. They didn't speak, they didn't need to, as they walked forward, Frankie with the bloom tucked like promise against her temple, Griffon steady beside her, and Bramble dancing a few paces ahead, singing softly to the night. Behind them, the trees closed gently, and ahead, the forest opened wide, vibrant, beckoning, home. Frankie paused at the edge of the clearing, her hand brushing against Griffon's.

"So are you coming home with us?" she asked, turning to Bramble.

He blinked, caught mid-skip as if the question had startled something loose. "Back to the witch's hearth? Absolutely." he leaned in, eyes gleaming with mischief.

They followed the path, together, Griffon with a strange new steadiness in his step, Frankie with golden sparks still clinging to her fingertips, and Bramble humming something that sounded suspiciously like a waltz for root vegetables. They walked on without speaking. They didn't need to. Behind them, the trees closed with quiet intention. Ahead, the forest opened wide, vibrant, beckoning, unmistakably home.

Griffon broke the quiet at last, looking like someone had just been handed a riddle written in fire. "So. The Ashen Queen?" he said, incredulous. “Once she made me chop onions with a butter knife and told me to toughen up. That’s not queen behavior. That’s warlord energy.”

Frankie huffed a quiet laugh, still reeling. “Velhollow really does love its titles.”

Bramble glanced sideways, uncharacteristically serious. “They call her Ashen Queen because her rule was forged in fire and loss. She gave up her place in the Lirathian Court to walk with mortals, to guard the line. That crown didn’t come from blood,” he said softly. “It came from sacrifice.”

Frankie swallowed. “Any other monikers I should know about?”

A flicker of mischief returned to Bramble’s eyes. “She has a few,” he admitted. “But I’m not brave enough to speak them.”

As they walked a thought occurred to Frankie. “Bramble, just how far to we need to walk to get back home?”

“Don’t worry about that. The path will take you to where you need to be,” replied Bramble.

As if on cue, the trees began to clear. As the cottage came into view, the air shifted again with quiet certainty. Velhollow had opened its arms, and something deep within its heart whispered,

You’ve made it… for now.

Chapter 28

Frankie stepped into the clearing, and the air changed. Behind her, the forest stilled. Its part was done for now and there, at the heart of it all, stood Aoife's cottage, glowing like a lantern tucked between tree roots and moonlight. It wasn't waiting. It was calling. The roof bowed beneath ivy, softened by time and threaded through with old magic. Stones leaned into one another like gossiping elders. Windows flickered with firelight, golden, alive, warm as a memory half-remembered and wholly welcome. Smoke curled from the chimney in slow, fragrant spirals, rosemary, dried apples, a hint of thunder tea. Wind teased the chimes on the porch, old thimbles, cracked glass, a spoon bent by a spell gone sideways. They sang like laughter caught on a breeze.

By the door, a lopsided bench sagged with the sort of wear that only came from stories told under stars and boots kicked off in relief. Somewhere inside, a kettle had already begun to sing, as if the cottage had sensed her approaching.

Griffon moved to her side, he didn't speak. He was simply there, steady and real, as if summoned not by words but by knowing and that, somehow, was enough. Frankie paused. The kind of stillness a moment asks for when it knows it's about to become memory. Then, with a breath that felt both ancient and newborn, she stepped forward.

She was home.

Not Grimwyck Manor, all marble and silence and lemon-polished constraint. Not the beige, buttoned-up house where her parents lived like emotion was something you scrubbed off the counters. No. This place wanted her. Her tangled hair, her wild boots, her soul that never quite fit anywhere else. The magic stirred in her chest. Not rising, but settling. Her ribs no longer braced. Her heart no longer flinched. The walls of the cottage breathed like they remembered her name. Then the door slammed open with all the grace of a kicked beehive.

"By the gods' tangled beards, did you stroll through every cursed glade in Velhollow to get here?" Aoife barked, bursting barefoot into the clearing like a storm dressed in linen. Her silver curls flared like bramblefire, her skirts swirled with the fury of unfinished tasks, and her expression could have withered a lesser witch at fifty paces.

Her eyes, green as storm-washed sage, swept over them both, sharp and assessing. Like she was already cataloguing damage, mood, and whether they'd eaten anything foolish along the way. She held the presence of someone who could fix you with a look, heal you with a pinch of thyme, or scold a tree into blooming early if she was in the mood. She looked them over for blood, for bruises, for even a freckle out of place, scanning like a woman who'd once lost too much to ever stop checking. Then she pulled Frankie into an embrace and she pulled back just enough to hold Frankie at arm's length, eyes glinting with unshed tears.

"Aye, love," she said, her voice thick with emotion. "Took your time, didn't you?"

Then her gaze shifted to Griffon. The humor in her expression eased, like moonlight sliding off steel to reveal what had always lain beneath. Something deeper crossed her face. Pride, yes, but also the quiet understanding reserved for those who cross a threshold and return changed in ways they have not yet begun to name.

"You look different, lad," Aoife said, her tone steady, almost casual, though her eyes missed nothing. "A touch taller perhaps... or perhaps the air just knows how to stand aside for you now."

Griffon folded his arms, his smirk slow and practiced, the kind meant to deflect rather than reveal. "Probably just the lighting," he said. "Or maybe I slept funny."

But the flicker behind his eyes betrayed him. A new weight lived there, not heavy, but certain, an unseen mantle settling across his shoulders. Frankie saw it too, the faint golden current beneath his skin, the quiet strength that seemed to hum with purpose. Griffon shifted as if adjusting to the feel of himself.

Aoife's lips twitched. "Aye," she murmured, "and perhaps stones grow softer in spring."

He looked at her, not challenging, but almost sheepish, as if acknowledging something he hadn't meant to reveal. A quiet understanding settled between them. Whatever had risen within him carried an ancient resonance, unmistakable in its depth. Aoife saw it at once, without effort. Griffon seemed to steady himself, not in refusal, but in the tentative acceptance of a truth still settling into his bones..

He exhale as though the world had grown a fraction lighter beneath his feet. "You knew," he said quietly. "Didn't you?"

Aoife did not step closer, but her presence filled the clearing all the same. "I knew the potential you carried," she said. "Not what you would become. That part was yours alone."

He studied her, brow furrowed as though she had just drawn back a curtain he hadn't realized was there. "You might have told me," he said. The words held no anger, only a long ache of things learned late.

"What purpose would it have served?" she asked, shaking her head. "If I'd spoken of it, you might have chased it… or feared it. Power like yours wakes only when it is met with something worthy. You had to discover yourself in your own time." Her voice gentled, losing none of its strength. "And you did."

Griffon's smirk returned, smaller now, almost vulnerable. "So I'm not imagining it," he said. "The… shift. The way the forest keeps watching me like it expects something."

Aoife's eyes glinted. "The forest watches those it trusts. It watches those it claims." Her breath left her in a slow measure, threaded with relief. "And you, lad… have finally stepped into the truth Velhollow always knew lived in you."

Griffon absorbed that, shoulders lowering as if learning the contours of a new shadow he had yet to grow into. Frankie watched him, feeling the steadiness of him settle through her like an anchor she hadn't known she was missing. At last, he inclined his head, the tension in him easing by a small but certain measure.

"Fair enough," he murmured.

Aoife returned the gesture with a quiet nod, the kind of wordless acceptance that passed between people who understood one another without needing explanation. It was not fanfare. It was truth, plain and steady as breath.

A crisp breeze whispered through the clearing, stirring the ivy that clung to the cottage walls. The air carried the distant hum of festival, the rhythmic clang of stalls being set up, the occasional enchanted lanterns winking to life in the trees. Here, in the quiet glow of Aoife's doorstep, the weight of what was coming pressed against them like an unseen force. Aoife let out a quiet breath, then turned, just as Bramble stepped forward, brushing moss from his sleeves with exaggerated care.

Frankie gestured toward him. "Aoife, this is Bramble. He guided us through the forest. He's... something between a bog sprite and a nuisance."

Bramble swept into a deep, theatrical bow. "*Bramble, of the Aldervyn*," he announced. "Whisperer of roots, collector of secrets, and reluctant guide to the magically entangled....present and accounted for."

"A bog sprite," Aoife mused, voice softened. "It's been many years since one of your kind crossed the threshold and warmed at my hearth." She stepped forward, lowering her head slightly. "You are most welcome here, Bramble of the Aldervyn and you have my thanks."

Bramble blinked, visibly caught off guard, then tilted his chin. "Well, I might stay awhile."

From within the cottage, Chalupa slinked out first, his narrowed eyes scanning the clearing like a cat personally offended by every leaf out of place. Behind him, Nyx emerged without sound, wings wide in the lantern light. He glided forward and landed upon Griffon's shoulder, talons gentle, gaze sharp. The raven studied him in silence, a long, weighted stillness that felt like the pause before an omen was spoken. Then, with a slow dip of his head, Nyx spoke, voice low and grave, like wind moving through an ancient chapel.

"The realms have seen you, Stonewing and they do not give lightly." His eyes glinted, catching the firelight like obsidian struck by storm. "You've been given a gift. The kind that roots itself in the marrow and answers to no name but your own. You carry the mark now. And the wild knows its own."

Griffon met his gaze without flinching. Between them passed something weightless and unbreakable. An accord that did not need to be spoken aloud. Nyx gave a final solemn nod, then tucked his wings and settled against Griffon's shoulder with quiet finality. The silence that followed was not empty, but full. Full of the forest's breath. Full of what had been awakened.

Chalupa snorted, flicked his tail, then deadpanned, "Who invited the goblin?"

Nyx tilted his head, considering. "Goblin? No, no... too loud for that." His beak clicked thoughtfully. "More like a wayward porch ornament. You know, the unfortunate kind people leave outside in bad weather."

Bramble pressed a hand to his chest, eyes wide with mock wounded dignity.

"*GOBLIN*?! *PORCH ORNAMENT*?! You wound me, truly."

His already wild hair looked even more unruly as he bristled, the sharp points of his ears twitching beneath the mess of curls. His deep brown skin darkened slightly with indignation, and his sharp gaze darted between Chalupa and Nyx as if debating whether to defend himself or plot revenge. His usual smirk faltered, his mouth opening, closing, then opening again.

Frankie nudged Griffon, barely suppressing her grin. "I don't think we've seen Bramble flustered before."

Griffon folded his arms, smirking. "Ah, now this promises to be entertaining, like a duel, but with more magic and significantly more fur."

Bramble scoffed, rolling his shoulders. "I am not flustered." His voice cracked slightly at the end. Chalupa's tail flicked with obvious enjoyment.

Nyx cawed, tilting his head. "Oh, he's flustered."

Chalupa stretched luxuriously, his eyes gleaming with mischief. "Mmhmm, positively rattled."

Nyx preened a feather. "Like a pixie caught in its own trap."

Bramble bristled, crossing his arms so tightly he practically folded into himself. "Well, if you lot are done tearing apart my flawless reputation, I'll have you know I am both a delight and an essential part of this grand endeavor."

Chalupa yawned. "Mmhmm. Essential."

Nyx just clicked his beak.

Bramble groaned, muttering something about being surrounded by ingrates before dramatically flopping onto a crate, arms still crossed. "Ungrateful. The lot of you."

He then pressed a hand to his chest, scandalized. "I'll have you both know, I am a dignified emissary of the forest!"

Chalupa snorted. "You're a walking compost heap with opinions."

Frankie stepped between them before the fur and feathers could fly. "He guided us through Aldervyn."

Aoife's eyes twinkled, amused. "Aye, then he's earned his place, hasn't he?" She turned back toward the door and pushed it open wide. The firelight inside flickered gold against the threshold. "Come, come," she said warmly. "Tell me what the forest showed you." The silence that followed wasn't empty, it thrummed with old truths, still settling in the bones.

As if on cue, Bramble cleared his throat. "Beautiful moment, really," he said, hopping onto his feet with theatrical grace. "Ancient bloodlines, long-lost secrets, broody revelations, all very stirring." He waggled his fingers. "But if he starts glowing again or sprouting wings without warning, I will insist on hazard pay." He squinted at Griffon, then stage-whispered to Frankie, "You do realize we can't let it go to his head."

Aoife turned and stepped inside, the door creaking softly on its hinges. One by one, the others followed, Bramble muttering about dramatic exits, Chalupa striding in like he owned the floorboards, and Nyx sweeping past in a silent blur of black feathers.

Griffon's hand brushed Frankie's, no flourish, no words, just steadiness. A quiet promise, spoken skin to skin. His fingers lingered, anchoring her in the now, even as her thoughts drifted toward whatever waited beyond the trees. She paused at the threshold, gaze drawn to the distant woods where festival lanterns glimmered faint as stars. The world felt suspended, caught between memory and becoming. Without looking at him, she laced her fingers with Griffon's, an echo of trust. When she met his eyes, her expression was soft, but beneath it burned something quieter, stronger. A steadiness, shaped by everything they had survived and all they hadn't yet spoken.

It had been just over a week, though it felt like lifetimes tucked into a single breath. She'd packed a satchel, filled her Jeep with questions, a tabby cat with too many opinions, and left behind everything familiar. She didn't know then the breadcrumbs were left by the very man she'd have to stop. Or that her cat was far more than he seemed, enchanted, ancient, and more than capable of sarcasm. Still, she went, because something inside her whispered go and every crooked turn since had led her deeper into herself.

She found family she never knew she had and more than that, she found belonging, quiet and steady, the kind that wraps around the bones and stays. She became the witch whispered about in prophecy. Not because she chased power, but because she didn't turn back. For every risk taken, every door stepped through blind, she had chosen the uncertain path, the one tangled with mystery and thick with magic and it had made her more.

Distant music stirred the air, delicate and bright. The festival had begun again, laughter rising like birdsong, bread baking, cider steeping. Lanterns bobbed above the trees like floating spells. The Festival of the Black Veil never truly slept. Now with Veyrath's final call looming, its rhythm shifted. Joy lingered, but tension threaded beneath. Spells cast in laughter now wavered with unease. Light lingered too long. Shadows pooled in places once safe. It wasn't the revelry that had changed, but the space between. Time thinned, meaning bent, as if the world itself had softened around the edges, less a door, more a seam between realms. Something old was stirring. Whatever watched from beyond the Veil... had begun to move.

When Frankie stepped through Aoife's door, the weight on her shoulders lifted, if only for a breath. Warmth met her like an old friend. The scent of crushed herbs and firelight wrapped around her like a familiar shawl. The cottage smelled of stories and secrets, of home. Aoife's cottage had never known emptiness. It held magic and solitude, not loneliness. Now, the hush had given way to laughter and voices, to footfalls and lives colliding.

The hearth glowed with presence. Around it gathered a trickster sprite with wild opinions, a raven spun from shadow and ink, a sarcastic familiar, and a warrior newly claimed by myth. At the heart of it all stood Aoife herself, Ashen Queen, Royal of the Lirathian High Court, High Warden of the Verdant Line, her silvered presence both fierce and rooted, a sovereign cloaked in bramblefire and truth and Frankie, blood of that line, legacy of prophecy, stood like a match struck in the dark. Aoife welcomed it all. But there were things still unspoken. She turned, eyes sharpening like a blade through mist.

"Aye," she said, voice low and commanding, "come now and tell me everything. What you saw. What you felt. Let no detail be swallowed by silence. Let the story breathe in full, speak with your eyes, your hands, your breath. Engage all your senses, children. The old magic listens best when nothing is withheld."

A beat of silence.

Then Chalupa's nose twitched. He sniffed once, then again, nose wrinkling in offense. Slowly, he turned his head toward the rafters. "Before we dive into doom and destiny," he said, dry as driftwood, "is anyone else catching a whiff of... burnt peppermint? With a hint of scorched socks and terrible life choices?"

Nyx dropped from a high beam, wings stirring the air in a quiet ripple. He landed without a sound, feathers catching firelight, his head tilted in scrutiny.

"It followed us in." he said softly.

Chalupa gave a low hum. "Residual magic?"

"Maybe," Nyx said, eyes narrowing. "But it doesn't behave like anything I've tracked. It clings like a spell that failed to anchor, or worse, was never meant to."

Griffon frowned. "What would that even mean?"

Chalupa tapped a claw against the wood. "Experimental enchantment, half-born invocation, maybe a summoning no one finished. Or..." He trailed off, expression pinched. "Or something trying to forget itself."

Nyx glanced toward the door. "There's something familiar beneath it, though I can't name it. Like a forgotten chord or a word caught behind your teeth. Whatever it is... it doesn't belong."

Aoife's gaze sharpened. "Is it still here?"

Nyx inhaled again, slowly. Then exhaled. "Fainter now. Dissipating."

Chalupa's eyes tracked the curling steam rising from a teacup.

"Good riddance," he muttered. "Smells like a spell that didn't pass inspection and left its soul behind to ferment."

Frankie glanced toward the door, unease settling into her chest like a chill. "Could it be a warning?"

Nyx didn't answer at first, then, quietly he said, "Possibly. The festival has begun, it could mean anything."

No one spoke for a long moment and then, as if on cue, the scent vanished, folding in on itself like a page turned too quickly. Gone. But not forgotten.

Aoife didn't hesitate, with a flick of her wrist, the fire flared, and she turned toward the shelves, hands moving with practiced purpose. Dried herbs, ceramic cup, this was ritual made casual by use.

"Tea first," she said. "If we're to untangle the threads of fate, we'll do it with steady hands and clear minds."

The room answered, wood creaked and firelight danced. Griffon ducked beneath a crooked beam, settling in near the door like a quiet sentry. Frankie followed, trailing her fingers along the back of a carved chair. She took the seat beside him, their shoulders brushing. Bramble circled the room like a bard selecting a stage. He poked a chair, tapped a cushion, muttering things like "too smug" and "this one has secrets." Finally, he collapsed onto a crooked stool near the fire with dramatic flair.

"Perfect. Slightly unbalanced, just like me."

Nyx perched on the windowsill, still as sculpture. Chalupa leapt to the bench, curled into his usual spot with a satisfied sigh. "If this doesn't involve snacks," he declared, "I will be dramatically offended."

At the hearth, Aoife worked in silence. Herbs crumbled between her fingers, honeyroot, lemon balm, frostbloom. Steam rose in fragrant spirals, curling through the beams like a ward. When she turned, cups had already appeared, filled with tea that looked faintly like moonlight stirred into water. They passed the cups between them, hands brushing, glances meeting, silence settling like a soft cloak. The world outside could wait, the storm still gathered, but inside this cottage, something steadier held. They were together and that mattered. Aoife sat last. Her fingers curled around her cup. Her gaze met Frankie's, and something in the air stilled.

"Now," she said, quiet but certain. "Tell me everything."

Frankie drew in a slow breath, meeting Griffon's gaze before they began. They spoke of the shifting paths, of how the Aldervyn Forest had moved with them, around them, watching, waiting, judging. How it had tested them, how it had decided to let them pass and then, the vision, it hadn't been just a glimpse of what could be. The Verdant Witch, power woven into the very bones of the earth, magic flowing as effortlessly as breath, a force of balance and creation. She had been radiant, commanding, alive with the heartbeat of the realm, her magic not just wielded, but understood. She was everything the prophecy had foretold, a guardian of life itself. But if that magic had been twisted? If Veyrath had reached her first? Frankie swallowed hard, her voice steady despite the weight of the words.

"If I wasn't who I am, if I didn't have the heart of the Verdant Witch, he could have turned me." The admission settled like a stone in her chest. "If he had tainted me, if he had gotten to me before I understood my magic, I could have been twisted into something else entirely. Not a protector, but a queen of ruin, ruling at his side in the Dark Court." Her fingers curled into fists at the thought. "Because magic doesn't choose morality, it follows the will of the one who wields it."

Griffon's jaw tightened, but he nodded. "Veyrath kept pushing the idea that power itself is neutral, just like the prophecy. That it's not about what the words say, but how you choose to interpret them."

Frankie exhaled. "He's not wrong."

Aoife's expression darkened, but Frankie pressed on. "Magic is like people, it can be shaped, guided, even deceived. Twisted into something unrecognizable, made to serve a purpose it was never meant for." She exhaled. "It can be convinced of a truth that isn't truth at all. The Verdant Witch isn't just a savior, and the Berserker isn't just a destroyer. They're forces of nature, fire and earth, storm and stone. It's not the magic that decides fate, it's the choices of the one who wields it."

For a long moment, Aoife studied them, her gaze unreadable. Then, at last, she nodded, something softer flickering behind her eyes. "So... do you understand now?"

Griffon met her eyes. "We do."

Chalupa stretched out with slow feline ease, his tail flicking with lazy amusement. "Good. So we're not all doomed, then?"

Bramble shrugged, flashing a grin. "No promises."

Chalupa eyed Bramble with practiced suspicion, especially when, without so much as a sleight-of-hand, the bog sprite produced a generous wedge of nut-crusted honey cake from somewhere entirely unclear. Whether he'd pilfered it from the table, swiped it from someone's plate, or conjured it through sheer gall and pastry-based manifesting, no one could say. He tore off a bite with theatrical relish, chewing like a man whose salvation lay in frosting.

Chalupa's gaze drifted to the cake, his whiskers twitching. "You eat like someone who survived the Great Crumpling."

Bramble paused mid-chew. "Well, excuse me for having cake-based trauma."

Frankie blinked. "The what now?"

"The Great Crumpling," Nyx intoned, puffing up with ceremonial gravity. "Year of the Ever-Sour Harvest. Half the realm's supplies turned to sawdust overnight, the other half exploded. It's a long story."

Bramble jabbed a thumb toward himself. "I was there, thank you. You learn to guard your snacks when cursed flour starts detonating mid-muffin."

Chalupa narrowed his eyes. "You planning to share that cake, or just inhale it like a starved trash goblin?"

"I am not a *GOBLIN*!" Bramble huffed, though his mouth was full again. "And no, I was not planning on sharing."

Chalupa sighed with the weariness of a soul long burdened. Then, lazily, he extended a single claw and hooked the edge of Bramble's plate with practiced ease.

Bramble yelped, jerking it back. "Oi! That's mine!"

"You seem to misunderstand how this works," Chalupa said smoothly. "You bring food into my presence, it becomes communal."

Nyx clicked his beak in smug agreement. "It's written into forest law, page four, post-crumpling revisions."

With perfect precision, Chalupa extended one claw, poked Bramble squarely in the hand, and Nyx plucked a chunk of honey cake straight from his fingers.

"This isn't thievery," Bramble snapped, hugging the plate like a scandalized dowager. "It's collusion!"

Chalupa purred, biting into the stolen prize. "Delicious. Tastes like entitlement."

"You menace!" Bramble cried.

Aoife shook her head, though a smile tugged at her lips. She listened without comment, but the air around her seemed to hum, a low, restless stir, like the first tremor before a spell wakes. She exhaled slowly, rolling her shoulders as though casting off the weight of something unseen. Then, with a sharp clap of her hands, the moment shattered.

"Right! Enough brooding. The festival's on, and we've work to do. Eyes open, ears sharper. We'll learn more from the crowd than we ever will from staring at old words."

Around the room, the others stirred to life, Nyx ruffling his wings with solemn flair, Bramble humming something as he tucked the last of the honey cake into a pocket that may or may not have been real, Chalupa stretching with the regal disdain of a creature certain the world revolved around him.

Frankie crossed to the door, her palm resting against the frame. The wood was warm, as if the cottage itself acknowledged the shift. Outside, laughter rose from the hills like woodsmoke, curling low and lingering. Lanterns bobbed in the dusk like will-o'-the-wisps called home for one night only. Music, bright, wild, and strangely ancient, threaded through the breeze, carrying the scents of sugared almonds, bonfire smoke, and something sharper… something that didn't quite belong. She lingered, breath catching from wonder. Something was waiting beyond that door, something bigger than riddles or relics, something she couldn't yet name but could feel, thrumming beneath her ribs. Revelry, certainly. Magic, always. But also… a pull. The sense that tonight the forest might whisper secrets only the brave or foolish would dare to hear.

Griffon stepped beside her, quiet as breath. "Are you alright?"

She turned to him, a spark in her eyes. "Yes. Just a little excited," she admitted, a grin betraying the flutter in her chest. "And just enough worried to know I'm not dreaming."

His smile was slow, crooked, almost conspiratorial. "Then you're ready."

He reached down, his fingers brushing hers, not accidental, not hurried, and for a moment they simply stood there, joined by that small, steady touch. It was not grand, but it was grounding, like clasping the root of a tree before stepping into deep water. Frankie laughed, the sound light as wind through leaves.

She opened the door and Velhollow opened with it. Music bloomed, lanterns swung, and magic thick as honey spilled into the night. Somewhere, far off, low at first, like a single note drawn from a bow over the world's oldest string. It swelled, deep and resonant, until it was less a sound and more a presence, rippling through the trees, down into the soil, and straight into her bones. It was not a call to gather, nor a warning to flee, but something stranger… a reminder that the forest knew its own, and that tonight, it was listening. Then, just beyond the spill of lanternlight, at the edge of the trees, a figure stood, still, watching. The distance blurred their features, but the shape was unmistakably familiar. She had felt it before, lingering at the edges of her vision, always gone when she tried to look too closely.

By the time her gaze locked on the shadow, it had already slipped back into the treeline. She told herself it didn't matter, that tonight belonged to music and laughter and the wild promise of the Festival. But the feeling clung, quiet and constant. Something was watching and waiting.

Chapter 29

Outside Aoife's cottage, the world stretched into form around her, alive, listening, and impossibly awake. The night breathed against her skin, cool and fragrant with spice and spellwork, as though Velhollow itself had released a quiet tide of magic just for this moment. Lanternlight pooled in gold and amber along the cobbled paths, catching on rain-kissed ivy and glimmering like liquid honey where the stones curved toward the square. Somewhere, a fiddle laughed its way through a quick reel, twining with the hum of voices and the soft chime of bells she couldn't see but could feel in her bones.

A shiver traced her shoulders, not from cold, but from the heady sense that the village had leaned closer to greet her. Before she could reach for warmth, something soft and weighty settled over her like an embrace. Aoife, standing just behind, deftly adjusted the shawl.

"Here, love," she murmured, her voice threaded with an unspoken knowing, "this just might come in handy."

Frankie looked down. The shawl was deep green, the color of forest shadow at twilight, shot through with the thinnest strands of platinum that caught the lanternlight like morning light caught in frost. When she brushed her fingertips over it, the weave felt alive, soft, yes, but faintly thrumming, like a heartbeat pressed close.

Aoife's hands lingered, smoothing the fabric with almost ceremonial care. "Moon-dyed wool, for warmth and grounding. The gold will protect you from stray magic, and the binding threads..." Her voice softened into almost a hush. "...are spun from a unicorn's mane."

Frankie's brows lifted. "An actual...?"

"Mmhm," Aoife confirmed, as casually as discussing the weather. "Collected with her permission, mind you. Very particular creatures, unicorns. This one's mane was given freely on the solstice to protect a Verdant Witch." Her mouth twitched, eyes glinting. "Just... keep it away from Steve."

Frankie tilted her head. "Steve? The Bigfoot?"

Aoife's brows arched. "So you've heard of Steve."

"Darrow mentioned him." Frankie said, fighting a grin. "Called him 'a *lovesick legend with big feet and bigger feelings.*'"

Aoife smirked. "Aye, its fair and accurate. He once courted a unicorn. Left her bouquets of star thistle, sang ballads so off-key the owls complained, and stood outside her glen in the rain until his fur went flat."

Frankie winced. "And?"

"She ran off with a kelpie," Aoife said briskly. "Better singing voice, if I'm honest. Steve's never quite recovered. Best not to bring it up unless you've got a spare hour and a strong pot of tea."

With a final pat, Aoife let the moment go. "Anyway, these threads aren't hers, before you ask. They'll hold against wind, weather, and a fair bit of magical meddling and if someone tries to hex you, well... the shawl will hex them back."

From the porch railing, Chalupa hopped down with lazy elegance, his tail curling like a plume of smoke. "Boho witch aesthetic," he declared. "Solid choice."

Frankie snorted. "Oh, shush."

Aoife's bracelets chimed like wind-bells as she tapped one of the shawl's platinum threads. "Protection, warmth... and a little something extra, just in case."

The cottage door clicked softly behind them as Griffon stepped out, closing it with the quiet finality of someone who carried both strength and care. He offered Aoife his arm, an old-world courtesy that suited him more than she'd expected. She accepted with a small, knowing smile, and the three of them started toward the village center, where the hum of music and laughter was already blooming.

Above them, Nyx adjusted his perch on the porch beam, feathers catching the lanternlight. "I do love the first steps into festival night," he said in a low, pleased rumble. "It's when the magic hasn't shown its hand yet, but you can feel it shuffling the deck."

The moment they turned the corner, Velhollow greeted them like an old friend. A fire juggler in a velvet waistcoat tossed kaleidoscope colored flames that squealed in delight before bursting into glitter. Beside him, a man on a unicycle, its wheel perfectly square, rolled with baffling ease over the cobblestones. He wore a crimson fez tipped at a jaunty angle and sang in a booming baritone about the tragic romance between a turnip and a tea kettle, his chorus punctuated by the wheeze of an accordion played by an elderly sprite perched on a barrel. Frankie laughed before she could stop herself.

The path ahead twinkled as if powdered with moonlight. Cobblestones glowed faintly underfoot, their rhythm syncing with her own steps like an old song remembered. Cottages leaned in close, their thatched roofs draped in bunting stitched from mismatched ribbons and faded festival cloth, each one fluttering like memory on the breeze. Chimneys curled up smoke rich with rosemary, honeyroot, and the slow promise of something sweet rising in an oven. Every open window spilled golden light and the low hum of conversation, as if the entire village was breathing in harmony.

The air was a tapestry of scents, each thread spun from something familiar and wild. Sugared almonds roasted on open flames, their scent caramel-warm and clinging to the breeze like laughter. Sweet cider bubbled in copper kettles, its spice-rich steam winding between stalls and shawls and small, eager hands. Bread baked in stone ovens, its crust crackling, scent golden and grounding. But beneath it all, like the base note in a song, came the perfume of night-blooming flowers, jasmine and moonvine, valerian and ghost lavender, unfurling their fragrance into the dark, releasing what they had gathered in silence all day. It wasn't just fragrance, it was story. Each scent a thread, woven into the next, looping around memory and promise, warmth and wonder. Together, they stitched the air into something textured and alive, like a quilt passed through generations, patched with joy and dusted with enchantment. Frankie breathed it in and felt it settle against her skin like belonging.

Sprites zipped overhead trailing ribbons of silver dust that curled like spun sugar. Their laughter was high and bright, like chimes stirred by playful wind. To her right, three hedge witches lounged against a crooked fence, sipping from mugs that caught the light with each sip, warmth blooming at the rim like a shared secret. Across the lane, two enchanted gnomes bustled past with garlands and jars of glowing jam, muttering over whether the honey-berries this year were "too smug" or merely "confident."

Everywhere she looked, the festival was a living painting, colors richer than daylight could hold, edges softened by enchantment. Even her heartbeat seemed to fall into step with the rhythm of it all, drumbeats from somewhere unseen, the shuffle of dancers' feet, the rustle of leaves overhead swaying to the same ancient tune.

Drawn by a subtle glow, she wandered toward a stall beneath a canopy of woven ivy. Pots lined the table, each holding something stranger and more beautiful than the last, leaves like dragonfly wings, flowers that sighed when touched, and buds that opened only when someone whispered to them. One vine caught her eye, twilight-blue blossoms in opalescent silver. As she leaned closer, a tendril unfurled toward her, brushing her fingertips in a feather-light caress. Frankie didn't pull away. She let it linger, her throat tightening with a sudden rush of something unnamed, part joy, part ache, wholly alive in this moment.

"Pete would've loved this," she murmured, voice soft as breath. "He used to talk to his plants like they were old friends. Said the trick wasn't getting them to grow, it was convincing them they were safe enough to try."

A beat of silence.

Griffon shifted beside her. "This Pete," he echoed, carefully. "A f*riend* from home?"

She nodded, eyes still on the vine. "He was my boss where I worked and lived back in the Greyvale. But really… he looked out for me. The only one who did, I think." She smiled faintly. "He never said much, but I think he knew I didn't belong there. Not really."

He was quiet for a moment, then, gently he asked, "Did you love him?"

Frankie blinked, surprised, and turned to look at him. His gaze didn't flinch, but there was something in it, curiosity, yes, but something guarded too, like he wasn't sure if he wanted the answer.

"Yes, but not like that," she said gently. " Pete was… safe, he was the only family I had. He reminded me there was goodness in the world."

Griffon nodded, smiling slightly, as if weighing her words like stones in his palm.

"Sounds like he'd have fit in here."

Frankie's smile wobbled as she blinked back tears. "Yeah. I think he would've loved Velhollow. Especially the plants with opinions."

Somewhere nearby, a cluster of mushrooms gave a chorus of delighted giggles.

Griffon chuckled low in his throat. "We should keep moving, before the shrubbery starts asking for introductions."

She elbowed him gently, and together they stepped forward, toward the glow of lanterns, toward the hum of magic and music, into the wild promise of the festival. Behind them, lanterns unfurled like golden blossoms, opening in slow, luminous rhythm. The path ahead wound into celebration, mischief, and perhaps mild disaster. Frankie inhaled deeply. The air was heady with the scent of sugared almonds, bonfire smoke, and something stranger, like charmed cinnamon and possibility.

She could almost hear his voice again, gruff and yet full of quiet wonder. "*Now that's a beauty. See how it listens? How it moves? That's not just a plant, it's a conversation.*"

A tight ache rose in her chest. Pete would never walk this path. Never stand beneath lanterns strung like constellations, or watch vines reach of their own accord. He'd never touch the earth here or see the flowers that hummed in languages older than prayer and yet, he was part of it. Somehow. He hadn't shaped her in traditional sense, but in the way gardeners do, by waiting, watering, believing, by seeing what others missed. Where others saw wildness, he'd seen potential. Where others saw weeds, he'd seen a beginning. There's a saying, she remembered, about how it takes a village to raise a child. Pete had been her one man village. Just a man and a greenhouse, steady hands and dirt under his nails. He'd pruned her into something green and reaching. Something ready to root elsewhere. The scent of spiced cider and smoldering lanterns wrapped around her and laughter laced the air, threaded into songs played on instruments no one could see.

The music wove through the air like dew strung across spider silk, pipes and strings drifting with the ease of birdsong from another world. Above, floating lanterns brightened and softened in slow, rhythmic breaths, their colors deepening and fading as they drifted in time with the revelers below.

Younglings of every kind, fae, sprite, shifter, and stranger still, dashed between legs and stalls, chasing winking lights that darted just out of reach. Their laughter spun spells in the air, bright and untamed. A trio of windwalkers whirled in time with the music, their feet never quite touching the ground. They twirled through invisible currents, their silver sashes trailing stardust, their voices rising like spell-bound bells that carried through every corner of the village. The cobbled streets shone with enchantment. Lanterns floated like dreams unmoored, some shaped like moths, others like tiny dragons, great beasts of legend curling above rooftops and chimneys. Market stalls burst with wares both wondrous and weird, hawked by vendors whose smiles sparkled with mischief. The scent of roasted nuts, honey-dipped pastries, and wild berry mead curled through the air like temptation. Promises flew from every corner, tokens of beauty, luck, or whispered truths meant only for the brave and as the festival bloomed around her, Frankie felt it again, that quiet certainty. Pete would never see this place but she carried him with her, root-deep and sunlit, in every breath she took beneath Velhollow's spell-lit sky.

Banners wove themselves between rooftops, alive with magic, depicting past festival champions in glowing runes and shifting images. Spell infused confections sat temptingly on display, glowing candied apples that made your voice chime like a bell, pastries that hovered just out of reach until you said please, and blue chocolates rumored to grant the temporary ability to speak to animals. Frankie took it all in, feeling the sheer wonder of it settle deep in her bones.

A murmur of excitement rippled through the square as a towering warlock strode into view, his long cloak billowing dramatically behind him. He came to a stop at the center of the crowd and, with an exaggerated flourish, unfurled a parchment so long it rolled halfway down the street. The onlookers leaned in, eager, the air buzzing with anticipation.

"The Great Illusion Duel shall commence in two hours!" he bellowed, his deep voice carrying easily over the chatter. "Participants must dazzle and deceive with their finest illusions, may the best trickster triumph!"

A cheer went up from the crowd, and a few illusionists smirked at each other, already sizing up the competition. Without missing a beat, the warlock pressed on, his tone turning wry.

"Next, we have the *Levitation Relay*, no brooms, no wings, just pure magical control and a strong stomach!" He let the words hang for a beat, before adding with a knowing smirk, "During the last festival, one poor fool floated upside down for three days. Who among you dares to break that record?" Laughter and groans echoed through the square as some festival-goers clapped while others shook their heads, muttering about the infamous mishap.

Then, with a dramatic pause, he scanned the crowd, his eyes gleaming with mischief. "And now, the *Shapeshifting Challenge* returns! Before anyone asks, no, you cannot stay in your new form permanently." He raised a single brow. "I'm looking at you, *Cauldron the Cunning*, we all remember the chicken incident."

The square erupted into laughter, several voices calling out playful jabs toward a rather sheepish looking warlock near the back. The energy in the village shifted, the festival spirit taking hold. Children darted between legs, trailing enchanted ribbons that looked like liquid gold.

Frankie blinked, glancing at Aoife and she smirked. "Aye during the last festival, poor Cauldron, spent a week clucking before he admitted he had no idea how to shift back."

Griffon sighed. "I'd still take a wayward shapeshifter over another *Goblin Sack Race* disaster."

Frankie raised a brow. "Dare I ask?"

Aoife chuckled, shaking her head. "Let's just say goblins are sore losers and have an alarming aim when throwing bags of enchanted mud. Some poor souls hadn't even realized they'd been hit."

Bramble cackled, delighted. "I, for one, am thrilled to witness whatever chaos unfolds this year. Nothing like a friendly magical duel to liven up the day before inevitable doom."

A group of gnomes bustled past, their beards braided with tiny charms, herding crates that floated weightlessly beside them, the wood wobbling eagerly as their whispered spells coaxed it along. A unicorn stood at the edge of the clearing, its pearlescent coat catching the glow of dawn as though the light itself chose to rest along its skin. It stood at the edge of the square, lowered its head as a young witch traced gentle fingers along its mane, the strands shifting between silver and deep sapphire. Further down, a centaur adjusted the straps on his armor, his hooves striking the cobblestone with a steady rhythm.

The scent of magic drifted through the air, burnt cinnamon, storm-kissed earth, and the lingering embers of last night's festival fires weaving together in a warm, uncanny haze. Overhead, glimmerwings darted between rooftops, their iridescent wings catching the morning light like liquid moonlight. No taller than Frankie's hand, their tiny bodies pulsed with shifting colors, soft gold for curiosity, deep indigo for scheming delight. They whispered in rapid, clicking voices, an ancient language known only to their kind.

A stall nearby erupted in a flurry of movement as two witches bickered over a potion gone wrong. The cauldron between them bubbled violently, shifting from violet to green to an ominous shade of black before belching out a puff of smoke that smelled strongly of burnt sugar and regret. One of the witches flailed her arms in frustration while the other merely crossed her arms, unimpressed.

"That is not what I asked for," the first witch hissed, jabbing a finger toward the cauldron.

The second witch scoffed. "You said you wanted a good luck charm."

"I wanted a charm for fortune, not a potion that might summon a plague of enchanted frogs!"

As if in response, the potion gave one last gurgling heave before a single frog, bright blue and faintly glowing, plopped out of the cauldron and onto the counter. It blinked at them. Then, with the tiniest, most judgmental croak, it promptly vanished in a puff of glittering smoke.

Frankie snorted, nudging Griffon. "We should probably move before something worse crawls out of there."

They passed beneath banners stitched with charm-light and embroidered starlace, their edges catching the breeze like whispered spells. Lanterns bobbed on threads of air above velvet-bearded gnomes selling marmalade, while a chorus of singing mushrooms harmonized beside a bubbling cauldron. Treefolk watched from high limbs, bark fingers curled around garlands of glowing moss. Moss-backed tortoises offered prophetic tea. A hedgehog in a velvet waistcoat tipped his hat to Bramble, who returned the gesture with such a theatrical bow he nearly tripped on his own feet. But beneath the laughter and spell-sparkled light, something tugged at Frankie's awareness, a shift in the current.

"Something feels off," Griffon murmured, just loud enough for their circle to hear. "Like the air's turned too still between breaths."

Aoife nodded, her smile still painted on for the crowd's sake, but her eyes had narrowed. "There's a wind from the east," she said softly. "Velhollow's currents don't bend that way, unless something's pulling them."

Nyx let out a low rasp from above, circling once before gliding down to perch on a banner post beside them. "I've been watching the glimmerwings. They're flocking too close together, nervous. One darted straight into a lantern and didn't even flinch."

"That's not just odd," Chalupa said, padding along beside them with ears twitching. "That's omen-level strange."

Frankie glanced around again, more carefully now. The joy of the festival still burned bright, but she could feel it, thin slivers of wrongness glinting beneath the surface. Magic brushing too sharp against her skin, whispers in the wind that didn't belong.

"We have to learn the shape of what's coming," Frankie said, her voice threaded with unease. "If Veyrath's dark magic is already seeping through, it won't look out of place, not right away. We'll have to feel the shift before the world shows its cracks."

Griffon eyes scanned the crowded square, but his focus was distant, drawn inward, to the magic coiled beneath his skin. "It's already shifting," he said, voice low. "I can feel it... like the current's pulling sideways. Like something's breathing beneath the ground, but not in rhythm with the land."

Nyx ruffled his wings above them, letting out a soft rasp. "The wind's wrong too. Carried the scent of smoke and river salt a moment ago. There's no salt water for miles."

Aoife's jaw tightened. "Aye, the ley lines are thinning, or they're bending. Either way, it doesn't bode well."

A hush fell over them, the kind that settles when the world itself is listening. Just ahead, the Moonthread Stream caught the festival light in long, liquid ribbons, silver-laced and luminous as it wound through the heart of Velhollow. It did not mirror earthly stars; instead it reflected the realm's living canopy, a sky of drifting spore-lanterns and soft phosphorescence that rose and fell in harmony with the land's quiet breath. The stream had always been more than water. It sang with ancient magic, carrying truth, possibility, and warning in its current. Children whispered wishes into it during festival rites, and witches sought it when their spells unraveled, hoping its glow would reveal what they could not. Tonight, the surface didn't flow. It hovered, still, suspended, not with peace, but as if the stream itself had forgotten how to breathe.

Two robed vendors bustled past just beyond the bridge, arms full of glittering charms and bottled breezes. Their voices, though quiet, carried sharp unease. "Did you feel it near Mossbarrow Crossing?" one muttered. "The ground hiccuped. I dropped a whole tray of moonberries.... they rolled *uphill!*"

The second snorted. "A gust of wind whispered my childhood nickname and insulted my posture. I'm not saying it was a ghost, but it knew my business."

Frankie blinked, watching them vanish into the crowd. The exchange should've been funny, but her arms prickled with gooseflesh. The air around her buzzed with enchantment, music spilled like sugar through the streets, and lanterns bobbed above. Yet beneath it all, something had shifted, the festival's magic, normally vibrant and spiraling like ribbons through the revelry, felt off. Not broken, not absent. Just... wrong. Like a melody that had slipped a few notes off-key, subtle enough to miss, unsettling enough to feel.

Frankie scanned the crowded square, unease prickling along her arms. "There's too much going on to tell what's real," she murmured. "If Veyrath is moving pieces through all of this... how are we supposed to see it?"

Aoife's eyes narrowed beneath the lanternlight, their green depths sharpening like a blade drawn slow. "We stop relying on sight alone," she said. "Old magic doesn't shout, it hums. It slides behind curtains and waits to be noticed. Look for stillness where there should be motion. Listen for silence in places that should sing. The land knows when something begins to turn."

Frankie followed her gaze. The wind had curled and vanished. Birds had fallen silent in the trees, a hush swept the far edge of the square, not of peace, but pause.

“Start with what feels wrong,” Aoife murmured, voice threaded with old knowing. “Moments that stutter. A step taken twice. Laughter before a mouth moves. Bells that chime out of sequence.” She gestured toward a nearby market stall where a witch counted coins.

Nyx landed overhead, wings folding with a sound like wind against parchment. “The shadows,” he rasped. “They’re pulling the wrong way.”

Griffon stepped to the stream’s edge, his expression distant.

“So we’re not approaching the distortion,” he said quietly. “We’re inside it.”

Frankie’s voice came thin. “Could he be here already hiding beneath a glamour?”

Aoife turned to her, eyes sharp and dark as cracked glass. “No lass, not glamour or illusion. This is erasure, a spell that doesn’t hide, it unthreads.”

She glanced at Griffon.

“It doesn’t just fool the eyes, it rewrites perception.” He said.

Frankie shivered. “Then if something feels wrong…”

“It is,” Aoife confirmed. “Trust it. Especially in Velhollow and most especially now.”

As they passed a fruit vendor’s stall, Frankie caught a flicker at the edge of her vision, the table stretched, just for a blink, and the apples split into doubles before collapsing back into one. The moment snapped shut like a trap.

She turned to Aoife. “Did you see …”

“Yes,” Aoife murmured, her voice tight.

Nyx ruffled his wings. “Something is testing the seams.”

They pressed on, Velhollow’s festival still humming around them, lanterns drifting overhead, laughter echoing between the stalls, bright magic woven through every breath of air. But beneath all that color and noise, Frankie felt a slow tightening, a hush coiled under the festivities like a creature waiting to exhale.

Then the crowd parted and the Moonthread Stream came fully into view, silver-bright, winding through the heart of Velhollow. But tonight, the water did not dance or sparkle. Its surface lay unnaturally smooth, stretched thin and perfectly flat, as though light itself had been pinned in place. Frankie stopped. She had grown up near rivers and streams; water always moved. Always murmured. But this stillness felt wrong. Intentional. Like a single note held too long.

Griffon moved ahead, his posture shifting with a quiet certainty that needed no magic to announce itself. His shoulders eased into a balanced, ready alignment, and the cadence of his steps changed, lighter, quieter, deliberate. It was the kind of movement that came from years of reading danger before it took shape. He scanned the banks with a steady, disciplined gaze, taking in every shadow, every flicker of light, every place where sound should have lived but didn't. The stillness wasn't lost on him. He studied it as a soldier studies an omen.

Aoife murmured, "The stream is listening."

Frankie's pulse fluttered. "Listening for what?"

Griffon didn't look away from the water. "For whatever touched those apples."

He crouched near the bank, fingertips hovering just above the unnervingly smooth surface, testing the air the way a hunter tests wind direction. The lanternlight overhead flickered across his jaw, but nothing disturbed the stream. It remained flat and bright, refusing to reflect the world around it.

Frankie stepped closer, breath catching. Beneath that thin, silver sheen, she felt a depth that didn't belong, an ancient, waiting depth that had nothing to do with water at all.

"It feels aware," she whispered.

Griffon nodded slowly, tension coiling through him like a drawn bow. "Something is pressing against the veil. Close."

Aoife stood between them, her expression carved from old knowledge. "Then this is where we begin looking."

Griffon turned to Frankie. "Do you see what I see?"

Frankie didn't answer him right away. She stood at the rail, staring into the stream. Its surface no longer moved, not even a flick of light from the living canopy reflected above.

"It's not reflecting," Frankie whispered.

Aoife stepped closer, calm but alert. Her hand hovered over the surface, fingers spread, reading the currents of a silence that felt wrong.

"This isn't stillness," she murmured. "It's severance. The stream has been cut from remembering, something's disrupted its link to the realm."

Chalupa's tail gave a twitch. "If it starts showing what doesn't belong, step back."

"Aye cat, I do know what I'm doing," Aoife said, her tone gentle, not dismissive.

"I know," Chalupa replied sullenly. "I don't like that it's doing nothing."

Nyx tilted his head, talons tightening on the beam. "The stream reflects what the realm feels. If it's gone blank... something's cloaking more than light."

They all stilled. Then the water twitched, not a ripple stirred by wind, but a disturbance from below. The stream shivered, once, and split and from the depths, a vision rose.

Bone surfaced first, pale and luminous, slick with shadow, ribs arching like a cage forged to hold ruin. Smoke coiled upward from the hollows, thick and slow, drifting like ash in air that dared not move. Then came the violet flame, flickering with eerie grace, its pulse a war-drum heard in reverse, steady and inevitable, echoing with the rhythm of something ancient waking and then the face appeared. Blurred, but known. Hollow-eyed and half-formed, but watching. She felt it before she understood it, a subtle recoil in the water, as though the stream recognized what lingered nearby and instinctively drew back.

Veyrath but not in flesh, not yet, but formed in intent. His features writhed beneath the water's surface, caught between becoming and being, flickering like a memory too dangerous to name. But he knew, he knew they had seen him. Knew the realm was soft with celebration. Knew the veil was thinning, and that his moment was nearly upon them. That knowing rippled outward, through the stream, across the ley lines, into the bones of Velhollow itself. Behind him, the vision widened, not of what was, but of what could be, should Veyrath rise unchallenged. Darkness surged, vast and rising, with armies of shadow and bone flooding the landscape, cloaked in flame and rot. Wraiths rode beasts with no eyes. The sky split like porcelain, spilling black starlight that swallowed the constellations whole. Trees bled sap the color of ash. Magic screamed as it unraveled, pulled backward through time like thread torn from the hem of the world. The ground fractured beneath the weight of a war not yet written, hovering just beyond the now, waiting for midnight's permission. In the stream's reflection, a clock emerged. Its hands, carved from light and shadow, crept toward twelve with the aching slowness of dread. Each tick echoed through the water like a heartbeat. The future waits for no one. Tick. Tick. Tick.

The clock dissolved, but the echo clung to her bones. After midnight on the last night of the festival wasn't simply a mark in time, it was the hinge upon which Velhollow's fate would turn.

Aoife pulled her hand back as if burned, her face pale, her eyes dark with knowing. "That wasn't just a vision," she said softly. "It was a warning."

They all felt it then, a heaviness settling over the air, thick and inescapable. Griffon's jaw tightened, the muscle in his cheek ticking. His voice came low, clipped.

"He's not casting illusions, he's feeding his magic into the ley lines, weaving himself through Velhollow like barbs under the skin." He stared at the stream as one might study a wound. "That water doesn't just hold memory, it carries doubt and dark possibility. The ley lines run through it like blood through a heart. If he poisons it, even a single thread, he touches everything it reaches."

Frankie's throat tightened. The image in her mind sharpened, Veyrath's face in the water, not fully formed, but watching. Not clawing from the outside, he was already inside Velhollow, whispering through the realm. The realization hung between them, vast and unspoken, while the forest seemed to hold its breath. But Velhollow did not pause. Above the weight of what they had seen, festival laughter still rose like startled birds. The light shifted, music swelled, and the scent of something sweet and impossible curled through the air.

Behind them, the festival gleamed on, golden, radiant, oblivious to the fracture blooming beneath its feet. Ahead, the shadows listened. And something in them had begun to move. Aoife walked slightly ahead, her silver hair unbound, catching lanternlight like moon-thread. She paused at a stall hung with wind chimes made from crystal-boned feathers, her sigh edged with memory.

"The festivals weren't always so loud," she murmured. "Once it was lanterns and quiet prayers, not phoenix rides and deep-fried stardust rolls."

Frankie blinked, trying to reconcile the vision of what had once been with the wonder before her. Magic was still new enough to feel like a dream she hadn't quite woken from, lanterns that whispered to one another, creatures stitched from mist and starlight, pastries that might hum if bitten too quickly. She took a slow turn, letting the night press against her senses. The cobblestones were warm beneath her boots, their edges dusted in fallen petals that glowed faintly, as if kissed by moonlight. The air smelled of roasted chestnuts, spun sugar, and woodsmoke curled with something rarer, wild thyme and stardust, drifting from a cart where tiny, flame-winged moths hovered over cups of steaming cider. A troupe of masked dancers spun past, skirts flashing in impossible shades, sea-glass green, storm cloud violet, firefly gold, each step scattering sparks that winked out before touching the ground. Children chased floating ribbons that darted away like playful sprites, their laughter braiding into the music rising from a square where fiddles and drums tangled with the deeper hum of some unseen instrument. She let the sensory tide wash over her, and still, the thought wouldn't settle. She looked at Aoife, incredulous.

"You're telling me this used to be quiet?"

Aoife's gaze gentled, though memory and myth curled through her tone like old roots rising to the surface. "Aye, love. Long before festivals learned to shout, the lanterns rose and fell with the realm's own dreaming. They drifted by the breath of river and stone, not music and merriment. Each light carried a whisper. Warnings, blessings, truths the land wished to share. Folk would stand here for hours, watching the lanterns move as steady as tides. It wasn't silence. It was listening."

Griffon's mouth curved in a faint smirk. "She's waxing poetic again."

Aoife's eyes twinkled, sharp and amused. "Och, listen to him. One flare of moonbeast fire in him and he thinks he's too grand for a good story." She nudged him with her elbow. "Your mother would've cuffed you for interrupting."

Frankie fought a smile, and Aoife turned her knowing look on her next.

"And as for you, mo chroí," she said, her voice warm but pointed, "don't pretend you wouldn't have stood here wide-eyed as any young witching seeing her first omen-light. You've the look of someone who still half-expects a lantern to drift close and whisper something meant only for her."

Frankie flushed, and Aoife softened, ancient affection woven through her sigh.

"It wasn't just spectacle. It was how we spoke with the world when the world still whispered back."

Her voice lowered, myth thickening like mist across the stream.

"When the lanternlight shifted, we listened. When it dimmed, we prepared. And when it glowed bright as dawn..."

She tapped Frankie's wrist lightly. "That meant someone nearby was meant for more than they yet understood."

Frankie tried to imagine the festival the way Aoife described it.

"So, how long ago was that?" she asked playfully.

Aoife's eyes glimmered, the lanternlight catching threads of old memory. "Long enough," she said, lifting her chin with a soft, knowing smile. "And not nearly long enough to be telling tales about counting my years."

Frankie huffed a quiet laugh. "So it's a secret?"

"Hardly," Griffon murmured, scanning the crowd while a faint smile curved at the corner of his mouth. "But in Velhollow, time behaves like the wind. It shifts, circles back, carries what it pleases. Asking someone to pin it down is... complicated."

Aoife gave an approving hum. "He's right. Time is measured differently here."

Frankie studied them both with a half-smile, sensing more in the spaces between their words than in the words themselves. "So you're avoiding the question."

Aoife tapped her fingers lightly against the rail, a gesture both playful and evasive. "I'm choosing the proper moment for an answer, love. Time reveals itself when it wishes, not when it's cornered."

Griffon's voice softened, threaded with quiet warmth.

"Besides... some stories are best told after the battle, not before it."

The three of them continued along the lantern-lit walkway, the teasing still lingering between them like a shared secret, gentle, affectionate, threaded with the weight of everything unsaid, and everything still to come.

Chalupa trotted up, tail flicking. "Well, I vote we regroup, with snacks and fewer visions that end in doom."

"Seconded!" Bramble crowed, practically bouncing as he rummaged through the charms at his belt, sending half of them jingling in protest. "And let's choose a spot with cushions, yes? All great plans are born on cushions!"

Nyx landed lightly above them, talons clicking once against the beam. "Snacks won't slow what's coming."

The shift began so subtly she almost missed it. A ripple, too small to name, passed through the crowd. Laughter thinned, pulled just out of reach, like the joy had taken a step back to watch. She glanced up, frowning, as the music began to fray, one note slipping loose, then another, until the melody unraveled into silence. Lanterns caught mid-sway froze where they hung, their glow sharpening into something too still, too deliberate.

A prickle threaded up her spine. The air felt… occupied. Dense and intent, as though it had decided to watch her rather than be part of her. Low in her chest, something tugged, sharp, sudden, and achingly familiar. Recognition, but the kind that came with teeth. Movement near the fire jugglers drew her gaze. A figure stood just beyond the circle of light. Tall. Motionless. The kind of stillness that was wound tight, waiting for its own cue. Shadows clung to its edges, concealing its face. It could have been a statue, a specter, or something older still. Her breath caught when it tilted its head. Through the thick air, a voice broke, warm with teasing, cutting through the hush like a clean blade.

"Still looking for trouble, I see. Some things never change."

The tension snapped, but her heart didn't. It beat harder, caught between disbelief and a dangerous flicker of relief. She knew that voice. Knew it deep in her marrow, from a life untouched by prophecy or shadow.

Aoife stilled, her eyes narrowing to a lethal point.

Chalupa's tail flicked once. "Well… took you long enough," he said, sounding smug enough to make her want to throw something at him.

Frankie turned toward the sound. The festival blurred, the crowd dissolved, the lanterns and colors dimmed to nothing. Only he remained. The man stepped forward into the lantern-light, real and smiling.

Chapter 30

P*ete.*

Frankie stood beside Aoife, her posture drawn tight, like a wire strung between hope and disbelief. Griffon stood a half-step ahead, every muscle coiled in quiet readiness, his gaze locked on the figure breaking through the thinning edge of the crowd.

Frankie's breath hitched. "Pete?"

But it wasn't Pete, not exactly. The man who stepped forward wore the same face, the one she'd seen grinning through greenhouse steam and mumbling about mulch, but everything else had transformed. Gone were the flannel shirts and soil-crusted boots. He was robed now in deep emerald, silver embroidery glinting across the fabric like frost caught beneath moonlight. His beard was neatly trimmed, streaked with silver like comet trails, and though his hair still curled rebelliously at the edges, it had been swept back with a deliberate, almost regal touch. But it was his eyes, those warm, cedar-brown eyes, that undid her. They were still Pete's. Still kind. Still steady. And yet, behind the quiet patience, something new gleamed

Power.

Not wild or volatile like Griffon's, nor bright and electric like Aoife's. Pete's magic thrummed low and ancient, like tree roots twisting deep beneath the world, unseen but undeniable. He smiled, just a little, just enough, and that was what truly broke her.

"Aye, lass," he said, his voice now laced with a soft Irish lilt that hadn't been there in the nursery. "Tis me."

Frankie took a single step forward, slow as breath, as if movement might undo the moment. "How are you here?" she whispered.

It wasn't accusation, it was awe. The question floated between them like dandelion fluff, fragile and full of wonder. Of course he was here. His smile widened, mischief flickering beneath the tenderness.

"Have you learned so little in Velhollow?" he asked. "This is a realm where truth wears a hundred faces, and the oldest secrets like to sleep in the open. Expect the unexpected, child. Here, even the ordinary might be something extraordinary in disguise."

And with that, he stepped forward and wrapped her in a bear hug, solid, warm, and entirely real, and Frankie melted into it. He still smelled of smoke and soil and something timeless, like rain moving through deep woods. This was Pete, who spoke in leaves and silences, who made stillness feel like safety. The one who'd always steadied her when the world blurred at the edges. But now he looked like something lifted out of old lore, cloaked in emerald and silver, as unshakable as bedrock and thrumming with the quiet strength of ancient trees. He no longer seemed merely a man, but a truth the world had buried and forgotten how to describe.

Then he turned and moved toward Aoife with the unhurried grace of someone returning to the place he had always belonged. When he knelt before her, every movement held a deep, grounded respect, deliberate, certain, whole. And when he spoke, his voice carried the calm weight of long years and lived memory, clear, steady, and unmistakably his.

"*Lady Aoife,"* he said, *"Stormbearer of the Lirathian Court, Keeper of the Old Way, Mistress of Tempests, Guardian of the Sacred Vale."*

The titles rose like an invocation, each one a thread in the tapestry of who she had been, and still was. They wrapped around her like wind and thunder, stirring something ancient in the air. Aoife's eyes glistened, and when she finally spoke, her voice trembled with memory, low, raw, and shaped by years she had never dared to recount aloud.

"*Seamus Aedán Caelthas of the Verdant Reach,*" she said. "*Oathbound of Root and Storm… Warden of the Hollow Grove… and sworn Captain of the Royal Guard.*"

The titles did not hang between them like boast or badge. They settled into the clearing like truth rediscovering its shape, ancient and steady, echoing through root and stone as though the land itself remembered him.

She paused, and then her voice softened, breaking just slightly. "My heart's echo, hidden far, but never forgotten."

The name rang like a chime struck by the wind, not just a name, but a memory called home, a vow, a bond rekindled.

"Aoife," he said hoarsely, as though tasting the name for the first time in an age. "My stormlight. I would've crossed every world to hear you say my name again."

He rose not as Warden or warrior, but as the man who had once been hers, proud, unyielding, bound by love and ancient duty. He took her hand in both of his and pressed a kiss to her knuckles, a gesture more intimate than royal. Even the air between them seemed to still, as though the forest remembered the shape of their bond.

Frankie looked from one to the other, awe tightening her throat.

"Seamus?" she whispered.

He turned toward her again, and the change in him was subtle but undeniable, like seeing the true outline of someone who had been standing in half-light for years. The man she had hugged moments earlier was still present, warm and steady, but beneath that warmth lay the full measure of who he had always been.

"Aye, Greenling," he said. Then his posture shifted, straightening with a quiet authority that felt older than any title she had known. When he spoke again, his voice carried a calm, deliberate gravity.

"*Lady Francesca Caelith*," he said. "*Blood of the Verdant Line. Heir to the First Mother. Verdant Flame of the First Grove. Keeper of the Balance. Light to the Fire. Shield to the Sword.*"

Every name settled around her like truth finally spoken aloud. Then he bowed. When he faced her fully, the formality softened, not into sentiment, but into recognition.

"You were never only Pete," Frankie said quietly.

He inclined his head, the gesture quiet but unmistakably regal. "Not quite, child," he said, his voice was calm. "I've worn many monikers, across many roads but to you, I was Pete, and that meant more than you'll ever know." Then, with a crooked smile that broke through the centuries, he added, "I'm still me. Though I suppose I owe you an explanation or two."

He turned back to Aoife, voice low, raw. "I told you I'd find my way back, love, when she was ready. The mortal world held nothing for me." Beneath the steadiness, there was something fragile in his tone, something only she could hear.

Chalupa, tail twitching, stretched with theatrical flair. “Well, isn’t this heartwarming?”

Seamus chuckled. “I see your voice returned, old friend.”

Chalupa smirked. “I see you finally ditched the ‘*humble gardener*’ routine.”

Frankie stared between them, realization dawning. “So you both knew?”

Chalupa’s ears flicked back slightly, his voice lowering just a notch.

“Of course we knew, witchling.” His gaze held hers. “You were never alone, we made sure of that.”

Seamus had turned from Aoife, his gaze settling on Griffon for the first time. The air shifted between them, subtle, but certain, as though something ancient in the soil stirred to bear witness. Two men, shaped by old power and older purpose, stood facing one another across the glow of firelight and moss-laced memory.

They didn’t speak at once. They didn’t need to.

For a breath that stretched too long, they simply studied one another, not with suspicion, but with the solemn gravity of recognition. As if each saw the weight the other had carried and understood it in kind. Griffon stepped forward, shoulders squared, each movement deliberate. The light caught the curve of his jaw, the tension coiled in his stance, and the quiet fire in his gaze, a look honed by battles notched into bone and spirit both. Seamus’s expression didn’t falter. His eyes gleamed with pride and knowing, as though he’d seen this shape forming from afar and was only now witnessing it take its true form.

“You’ve grown into it, then,” he said, voice low and sure. “The mantle fits.”

He didn’t name it, *Berserker*, but it lived between them, unspoken and undeniable. The old force that had risen in the Aldervyn Forest, claimed not by blood alone, but by choice. Griffon gave a single nod, slow and rooted.

“It was a surprise,” he admitted. “But I think it knows me now and I think… I know it.”

Then, in a motion smooth as instinct, they stepped forward in unison. Arms extended, not for a handshake, but for the warrior’s clasp, forearm to forearm, grip strong and sure. The kind of greeting carved into the marrow of oaths long kept. A gesture older than thrones and bloodlines, one that spoke of storm-forged respect, of pacts made with steel and silence. But they did not stop there. Their brows came forward, foreheads pressed gently together. It was not ritual. It was remembrance. The meeting of old magics that had waited too long to touch.

No one spoke. Even the trees seemed to still. For a heartbeat, Frankie stood frozen, watching the two most vital men in her life, one who had tended her roots in secret, the other who now walked beside her through fire, meet as keepers of the same ancient trust. What passed between them was consecration. When at last they broke apart, Seamus released Griffon's arm with solemn grace, and the nod he offered was not merely respect, it was permission. The end of one long vigil. The passing of a mantle worn through time.

He didn't look away when he spoke.

"See her well guarded," Seamus said. As the echo of a promise once made to the land itself and then, with breath drawn deeper, his voice dropped. "I have watched over her since the day the stars turned and the winds carried her name. I held her in silence while others hunted shadows. I kept her close when the world would have scattered her like ash on the wind. Not because I was told to, but because love and honor do not seek glory. They shelter. You are not asked to carry her for she is no burden. But the path ahead will demand more than strength or fire. It will ask for sacrifice. She will shield the realm, aye, but even a shield needs something to stand behind it. Be that, stand as the sword she does not wish to wield, but must trust at her side and when the darkness calls her name, let it find you standing there first."

Griffon bowed his head in vow, the gesture quiet and solemn, like the drawing of a blade meant only for purpose. When he lifted his eyes, they held the weight of storms stilled only by love.

"She will never stand alone," he said, his voice low but unwavering. "Not while breath lives in me. Not while the stars hold their place. I'm not here by chance," he said, softer now. "I know that now. Every battle, every scar, it all led me to her."

He stepped forward, closing the space between them, his gaze never leaving Seamus.

"She is the shield, the light. I was not forged for peace, but for the reckoning to come. Let me be the sword that answers when the dark comes knocking, the line they do not cross." Then, softer he added, "I was not made for gentleness, but I would learn it … for her."

Frankie's breath caught. The world felt too vast, too full, to hold. Emotion surged in her chest, sharp, golden, impossible to name. She stepped toward the both of them with a shaky laugh, blinking fast against the warmth rising in her eyes.

"You two are making it very difficult not to cry in front of the whole village," Frankie said with a laugh that cracked beneath rising warmth.

Seamus smiled, and something in his eyes softened at the edges. Whether it was like a father's pride or a guardian's surrender, Frankie couldn't tell, but it warmed a part of her soul she hadn't realized was still waiting to be seen.

Aoife moved forward then, slow and sure, like the tide returning to shore. She'd said nothing through the exchange, only watched, silent as stone, still as starlight. But now her breath came slower, heavier, and when she finally spoke, her voice came thick with feeling, her brogue rich and unmistakable.

"Ah, mo chroí," she whispered, a term from the old tongue, *my heart*, spoken like a blessing, like a wound. "There are moments the realm tucks away like pearls, aye, but this?" Her voice trembled, just for a breath. "This is a thread the land'll carry in its bones long after we're dust. A vow spoken in truth, in love, in the oldest magic we've left to give."

She looked between Griffon and Seamus, and then to Frankie, her eyes shining, her voice firm as the roots beneath the cottage floor. "The ground remembers, child, as does the wind. And when all else fades, it's moments like this that echo loudest."

The words settled into Frankie's bones like morning sun into stone. She was the shield, not by steel or spellwork, but by nature's quiet insistence. Her magic was to protect, to preserve, to endure. Griffon was the sword, honed in stormlight, tempered by purpose, forged not to lead but to stand beside. A breath passed, then Frankie blinked, the spell of the moment breaking just enough to let disbelief slip back in. She turned to Seamus, her voice half-wonder, half-demand.

"Wait, how are you even here?"

Seamus smiled softly, the weight of too many years threading through his voice. "Wouldn't miss a Festival of the Black Veil, lass. Haven't yet."

Frankie stared. "Seriously? This happens once every fifty years. You expect me to believe you've been to more than one of these too?"

He gave a one-shouldered shrug, mischief flickering in his eyes like moonlight off wet leaves. "Time keeps different rhythms here."

She looked to Aoife, then to Griffon, shaking her head with a half-laugh. "So I hear."

Seamus had already turned to Aoife, the warmth fading from his face like dusk chased by an oncoming storm. "Catch me up, love. I walked in on prophecy and reunions. Now tell me, what are we up against?"

Aoife's smile dimmed, shadows gathering at the corners of her expression like storm clouds folding in. "Not here," she said softly. "Not with so many eyes and ears, not while the veil's still dancing." She turned toward Seamus, her tone deceptively casual, though the air around her had begun to tense with the weight of truths unspoken. "Come on then, back to my cottage. You do still remember the way, don't you?"

Seamus gave her a long look, his smile crooked. "I could find that path blindfolded, love," he said, voice low and rough like stone worn by wind. "Though I wouldn't mind getting lost, if it meant following you a bit longer."

As Aoife turned, lanternlight catching in the silver strands of her hair, Seamus's gaze lingered, soft and full of something unspoken. There was an ache in his eyes, the kind forged by memory, weighty and worn from years spent looking back too often and too long. He watched her move with the quiet grace of someone shaped by wind and rooted in stone, the arc of her spine as familiar as a forgotten song. She walked like she belonged to the path itself, like the earth remembered her steps even when he could not. And though every detail struck him as known, it struck him just as sharply as new.

Aoife arched a brow over her shoulder but didn't bother hiding the smirk tugging at her lips. "Careful, Seamus. Keep that up and I might start thinking you missed me."

Frankie leaned toward Griffon, her whisper featherlight.

"Okay… tell me that sounded like flirting."

Griffon didn't miss a beat. "If it wasn't, then I've misunderstood a lot of poetry."

Chalupa groaned. "If this turns into a slow walk down memory lane, I'm throwing myself into the soup pot."

Nyx fluffed his wings and tilted his head. "Nothing like rekindled romance while the world teeters on the edge of doom. Warms the feathers."

Aoife said nothing more, but the look she gave Seamus over her shoulder spoke volumes, an unspoken invitation layered in memory and defiance. She stepped off the path with the quiet confidence of someone who belonged to every root and stone beneath her feet, and the rest followed without question. The sounds of the festival faded behind them, laughter softening like the last chime of a bell, firelight giving way to the silvery hush of moon-washed leaves. Music lingered in fragments on the breeze, but even that began to unravel into the hush of old magic waking. The air cooled, kissed by dew and the faint metallic tang of unseen power.

Overhead, the lanterns strung through the boughs shifted hue, from golden amber to a gentle, argent glow like starlight caught in crystal. The path narrowed beneath an archway of branches, and the trees leaned close, their leaves rustling not with wind, but with breath, ancient and watchful. Will-o'-the-wisps bobbed lazily between roots and stones, and from the underbrush came the soft clink of fairy bells, laughter like wind chimes, and the brief flicker of wings no larger than an acorn cap. A chorus of night-sprites darted between the moss-laced tree trunks, trailing threads of silken light that vanished as quickly as they appeared. The whole forest felt expectant, as though holding its breath for what came next. The ground itself seemed to beat, gently, like a heartbeat beneath the moss. Magic coiled in the air, denser now, tasting of rosemary and rain, green things pressed between the pages of time.

By the time they reached the ivy-wrapped gate of Aoife's cottage, Velhollow had fallen away entirely, left behind like the fading remnants of a safer story. The gate creaked open with a sigh, and even that sound felt steeped in history. The cottage welcomed them with its usual warmth, shutters aglow, smoke curling from the crooked chimney in spirals of violet and sage. The roof sagged beneath a patchwork of moss and creeping thyme, and above the lintel, a pair of thistle sprites whispered and scattered as they passed beneath. The stone path was faintly lit, runes woven into the mortar flaring briefly with their steps.

Inside, the air was thick with the scent of rosemary, dried lavender, and the deep, comforting tang of woodsmoke. But beneath that comfort was a silence layered with something deeper, like the earth had drawn in its breath and was waiting to release it.

Seamus stood in the center of the room as the door clicked shut behind them. His silhouette cut against the hearth light, broad, unyielding, but frayed at the edges, like parchment gone brittle with use.

"All right," he said. His voice was low, but it carried. "Tell me everything."

A hush settled in the cottage, thick and pressing. Shadows curled tighter along the walls, and the flames in the hearth shrank low, their golden tongues flickering with unease. Even Chalupa, perched like a coiled question on the mantel, said nothing.

Frankie felt the breath of the room shift, magic stirred under her skin, like the first crack of frost across glass. Griffon stood beside her, quiet and grounded, his presence a steady weight in a world tilting toward something darker.

Aoife hadn't moved, but she felt taller now, still as an old tree before a tempest. Her fingers brushed a dried sprig of sage hanging from the beam above her head, and the air immediately sharpened with its scent. She drew in a slow breath, then another. Aoife's expression darkened, and when she spoke, her voice came with the weight of thunder trapped in granite.

"Dom DiLegna *IS* Dominicus Veyrath Noctis of the Forgotten Realm."

The words cracked the air like lightning, impossible to unhear, and for a moment, time itself seemed to halt. Seamus froze, his once-easy stance stiffened, the warmth leaching from his face like flame pulled into ash.

"What?" he breathed, not a question, but a jagged fragment torn from his chest. His gaze flicked between Aoife and Frankie, searching their faces for some cruel jest. "You're telling me..." His voice faltered. "Dom, that cold-hearted shadow of a man who treated kindness like it came in rations, is Veyrath?"

Aoife gave a single, grave nod. Seamus staggered back a step, as if the name alone had struck him. Seamus looked at Frankie, his face awash with concern and empathy.

"Dominicus Veyrath Noctis of the Forgotten Realm," he repeated, the name falling like iron into deep water. "I've only heard it in fragments, in old songs no one sings aloud anymore, in warnings carved into the foundation stones of ruins no map dares mark. He was the one who made magic bleed. Turned spells into weapons, hope into poison. Drained ley lines until they were nothing but marrowless bone."

"What do you know about him?" Frankie asked.

His voice dropped lower, steadier, but no less haunted.

"There's no full account of where he came from. Not anymore, most of it was lost, or scrubbed clean, on purpose. Some say he was forged in the wake of the First Fracture, when the veils between worlds were still new, still bleeding, and the boundaries of creation had not yet settled. That he rose from the splinters of unshaped realms, shaped not by birth, but by rupture. Others claim he was once a man, brilliant, broken, too curious for the gods' liking, who delved beyond the last thread of light and never came back whole. But the oldest tales..." He hesitated, eyes narrowing as if the air itself might betray them. "The oldest don't call him a man at all. They say he was conjured in the dark before language, summoned by grief and greed and something older than intention. Not born, no. Cast. Like a shadow without source. A curse given form. Malice given mind."

He turned to Aoife, fists clenched, knuckles pale. "The Forgotten Realm wasn't exile, it was containment. A prison built from time itself, sealed with blood-oaths and elemental law. His name was struck from every archive, erased so completely even speaking it became dangerous. Just a whisper could draw his attention."

He shook his head. "But stories find a way. In the mutterings veiled as the Babbaman, in the riddles of shadow-folk and root-singers, those who speak in dream and metaphor because truth like this... truth like him... burns too bright to name outright."

He swallowed, jaw tight. "The realm did everything it could to forget, but forgetting doesn't mean he stopped existing."

Aoife's voice followed his, quiet but carved from stone. "And now... he walks among us again."

The silence that followed wasn't empty. It held its breath. The air felt brittle, thin and sharp, like it could tear under the weight of a name no world should ever speak again.

Seamus drew in a jagged breath. "Sweet roots and ruin." He raked a hand through his hair, eyes burning. "How did he keep it buried? You lived with him. Shared a hearth. Had his child. And I, I walked the same streets for decades and yet I never saw through it." His voice cracked, raw and thundered open. "What kind of spell could veil him from us?"

Aoife stood, her hands clasped tightly before her like she was holding something broken in place. "The kind we helped make possible."

Seamus looked up sharply. "What?"

"We dulled ourselves, Seamus," she said. "You and I... we weren't just hiding. We buried who we were so deep, we started to forget. Our names, bloodlines, the very power in our bones. Every day, we poured energy into shielding ourselves. The more we veiled our magic, the dimmer the world became and our senses dulled." Her voice caught, and she forced it steady. "There's a cost to living small when you were born of something vast. He didn't need to outmatch us, just to slip through the cracks we left behind. We made ourselves blind to stay safe. And in that blindness... he thrived."

Seamus's eyes flashed to Frankie, his expression now fierce.

"Then why didn't he act? He had her right there. All that time. Why wait?"

Frankie inhaled, but it was Aoife who spoke first, her voice soft, but shaped by the weight of knowing. "Because he couldn't."

Seamus blinked. "Why not?"

Aoife's gaze didn't waver. "The Verdant magic doesn't yield to force," she said. "It opens. Slowly. Deliberately. It roots itself in trust, not conquest. It protects what matters, especially from darkness. He couldn't touch what hadn't awakened. She wasn't ready."

"So he watched," Seamus murmured, the truth starting to thread through him. "He waited."

“And schemed,” Chalupa muttered from his perch, tail twitching. “Like a squirrel hoarding cursed acorns.”

Seamus turned to Frankie. “And now?”

She lifted her chin. “It’s too late now. We bound the magic.”

Seamus went still. For a heartbeat he looked younger, struck by the weight of understanding. “A true binding?” he asked, his voice low. “Not ceremony… but an actual fusion of power?”

Frankie nodded, steady and certain. “My magic isn’t mine alone anymore. It’s ours. Shared. Alive in both of us.”

She turned toward Griffon then, unable not to. The firelight caught his features in warm gold, carving strength into every line of him. Frankie reached for his hand, fingers brushing his before she intertwined them fully. His grip closed around hers, firm, grounding, and something in her eased as though it had been waiting for that single point of contact all along.

Her voice softened, but it did not waver. “The rite didn’t bind our choices. It bound what was already true between us. Two magics moving in the same direction. One current, not two.”

Griffon’s thumb swept once across her knuckles, slow and reverent, and she felt the answering hum of their connection rise between them like a breath drawn in unison.

“If I rise, he rises,” she said, meeting Seamus’s gaze. “And if I fall…” She glanced up at Griffon, the certainty reflected back at her in his quiet, fathomless eyes. “…then he falls with me.”

Griffon didn’t speak, but his hand tightened gently around hers, a silent vow stronger than any oath spoken aloud.

The room held still, Seamus said nothing, but something shifted in his face, like memory rising from the deep, recognition of the power she now carried. Frankie pressed a hand to her chest, where the pulse of magic still thrummed low and constant. “The magic didn’t just wake,” she said. “It chose me and when it did, it didn’t stop with me. It moved outward, through bloodlines, through ley-lines, through the very heart of the land.” Behind her, the fire gave a single flicker, slow and deep, like the cottage itself had drawn breath.

Seamus stared at her, and whatever doubt had lingered melted from his expression. “You outwitted him,” he said softly. “You did what the old protections couldn’t do and you chose your path, not with force, but with knowing.”

He stepped forward, voice rough with feeling. "That's not just magic, lass. That's prophecy made flesh."

The words struck something deep. Frankie felt them echo through her, not as praise, but as recognition. The air around her shifted, heat rising at the base of her neck, the kind that always came before something important. The hearth crackled behind them, but the warmth no longer came from flame alone. Magic stirred. Old. Watching. Alive.

She stepped forward, and the room seemed to shift with her, not in a dizzying sway, but in a quiet realignment, as though the cottage itself recognized the moment. The stones underfoot, the rafters overhead, even the fire in the hearth drew still, waiting. Chalupa straightened on the mantel, tail curling in a perfect arc, his golden eyes fixed on her. An unseen presence gathered at the edges of the room, attentive and intent, as if magic had leaned close to hear what she would say.

When Frankie finally spoke, her voice was low and steady. It carried none of the stiffness of something practiced, none of the echo of something recalled. The words rose from a place deep within her, woven through breath, shaped by instinct, guided by a truth she had never dared to look at directly until now. It felt less like speaking and more like revealing something that had lived in her all along. Aoife's head snapped up, stormlight flaring in her eyes. Seamus froze and even Nyx fell silent, feathers puffed in wary awe. And Griffon, Griffon knew. His breath hitched beside her. His hand tightened gently at her elbow. He knew these lines too. Though neither had spoken them before, they remembered. Frankie's voice rang clear, anchored by truth.

"*Beneath the endless, skyless glow,*
Where unseen rivers of magic flow,
Two paths converge, destined to meet,
Where ancient earth and wild hearts beat."

Her gaze found Griffon's, and he moved to her side without hesitation. His voice joined hers, deeper, steady, braided with something fierce and old.

"*One bound to witches' roots, to green life's bloom,*
A healer's hand to chase back gloom.

One shifting form, unbound by name,
A fleeting shadow, a flickering flame."

Their voices twined then, river and root, echoing through the beams and stone like a bell struck true.

"*In shadow's dance and nature's grace,*
Together they'll mend the fractured space.
By bloodlines woven, by fates aligned,
A bond shall rise to heal, and bind."

The fire stilled, as if bowing to the verse. Outside, the wind hushed, and the very walls of the cottage seemed to hold their breath. Frankie's voice steadied again, the next lines pouring through her like breath returning to lungs long denied air.

"*Where twilight lingers and veils wear thin,*
Their journey starts, but won't begin
Without the leap, the trust, the fall,
When courage dares to heed the call."

Griffon's tone deepened, pulled from the depths of the earth itself.

"*Yet even light must walk through night,*
Where wrong feels right and truth takes flight.
A choice must come, a price be paid,
Where hearts are tested, and lines are frayed."

Together, they gave the final verse, not as recitation, but as vow.

"*The dark will rise to claim its due,*
With poisoned charm and paths askew.
And she must stand where good men break,
To save the world or be the quake.
In shadow and light, their strength will grow,
To face the tide, to ebb and flow.
Two souls entwined, a single thread,
To hold the balance where all may tread."

The last syllable hung in the air like a struck bell, its echo trembling through stone, through skin, down into the heart of the realm itself. Even the fire bowed low, its flames drawn inward, listening. Aoife moved. She didn't speak at first. She crossed the room in measured steps, skirts brushing the floor like a hush made tangible. At the hearth, she knelt, not hurried, but with the calm certainty of someone stepping into a familiar ritual. She laid a sprig of rosemary across the coals. The flames rose at once, curling in tendrils of green and gold, and the scent that followed was rich with memory, warmth, and protection, the kind of love passed down through hands rather than words. The fire lifted for a breath, then lowered again, as though settling into acknowledgment. The rosemary hissed softly, releasing its fragrance into the quiet like something long-held finally being spoken. The words they had summoned still moved through the walls, through the beams, and through their bones.

Frankie stood utterly still, the taste of the last verse lingering on her tongue like iron and honey. She couldn't feel her heartbeat, or maybe she could, too many of them. Hers. Griffon's. The realm's. All of them strung together like beads on a thread suddenly pulled taut. She turned toward him, and he was already looking at her with the calm steadiness of someone who had finally remembered his own name. Something old passed between them in that silence. A recognition that ran deeper than shared words.

"I felt it," she whispered, voice low, throat tight. "Not just the words, the truth of it. Like it's always been waiting in me. In us."

Griffon nodded once, slowly. "It wasn't just prophecy," he said. "It was instruction. Warning. Oath." His gaze drifted toward the fire, though his hand found hers again. "It's telling us what's coming. What we have to do."

Frankie swallowed. Her voice was steadier now, even as her thoughts spun. "The two paths, that's us. Our magic, our bond. But it's not just about power. It's about choice. That part... 'where wrong feels right and truth takes flight', that's not metaphor. That's a test. A trick, maybe. Veyrath's going to twist everything."

"We'll be pulled in opposite directions," Griffon murmured, his brow furrowed. "Challenged where we're weakest. I think the 'fall' isn't just danger, it's the moment we doubt ourselves. Or each other."

Frankie's lips parted as realization bloomed, sharp and undeniable. "And the line, 'she must stand where good men break'… that's the point. That's the hinge. The place it all turns." She glanced toward Aoife, who still knelt at the hearth like a sentry in prayer. "It's not about surviving. It's about choosing right, even when right looks like ruin."

Griffon's grip on her hand tightened. "And we do it together. Every verse pointed to that. Not just balance. Fusion. We're the thread. Entwined."

Frankie exhaled, but it wasn't relief. It was understanding. Weight settling into place. "If we fail… the fracture deepens. The balance slips. We lose more than the fight. We lose the realm itself."

Outside, the wind had quieted, as though even the trees were listening. Inside, the fire burned low but bright, the scent of thyme curling upward like breath. Aoife moved, her head lifting slowly, the stormlight in her gaze tempered by something gentler. Her voice, when it came, was low and firm, as if replying not just to the prophecy, but to everything that had brought them here.

"Enough for tonight," she said. "The realm has had its say."

She reached for another bundle of herbs, thyme bound in twine, and fed it to the fire. The flames flared gently, warm and golden, and the weight in the room shifted again. Not gone, not dulled, but grounded.

"We'll speak of what's to come," Aoife continued, "but not in this hour." She paused, her gaze flickering over each of them. "Food, anyone?"

The magic of the moment didn't vanish. It settled. Sank into the seams of the floorboards and the spaces between heartbeat and breath. The prophecy still hung like mist at the edge of thought, but it no longer pressed. It folded itself gently into the rhythm of the room. Frankie exhaled. Griffon moved closer, settling beside her, their shoulders aligned. She hadn't realized how tense she'd been until his presence reminded her how to be still. Somewhere behind them, Bramble was already shuffling toward the pantry.

"Just saying," he muttered, "if there were ever a moment for pie, this is that moment."

Chalupa's whiskers twitched, his velvet voice dry as ash. "You think of pie as strategy."

"Pie is strategy," Bramble replied solemnly. "You think armies march on glory? No. They march on full bellies and small comforts.

You think magic holds its shape in fear? No. It anchors itself in sweetness, in ritual, in oat crusts laced with nutmeg and defiance."

Nyx's feathers rustled, halfway to a chuckle. "A flimsy strategy," he murmured, "but consistent."

Bramble sniffed, utterly unbothered. "Call it flimsy if you like. But no war was ever won on an empty stomach. And no prophecy was faced properly without dessert."

Even Seamus's hard mouth softened, the ghost of a smile tugging at the edge before he ground it back into stone. The heaviness broke by a thread, enough to let breath move again. Aoife bent to the hearth and coaxed the embers to life once more, slipping a final sprig of herb across the stones until the room filled with green brightness. Honey warmed in a small pot on the edge of the flame. Bramble rummaged noisily in the pantry until he unearthed a jar of oatcakes with a victorious noise. Chalupa leapt onto the mantel, curling himself into a crescent of fur, eyes narrowing in regal approval. Nyx preened one wing and muttered a dry critique of Bramble's "culinary strategies."

The cottage settled around them, wood and stone steeped in listening quiet, the kind of hush that feels less like silence than love holding its breath. Frankie sat close to the fire, her tea cooling between her palms. Griffon lowered himself beside her, the boards groaning beneath his weight. For a while they said nothing. Then his hand found hers, large, steady, closing over her fingers as though to anchor her in place. Neither of them knew what the days ahead would bring, only that the world had shifted, and the path before them would not be kind. Frankie's throat tightened. But when she turned, his gaze was waiting, fierce and gentle all at once.

"I don't know where this road ends," Griffon murmured, voice low and roughened with truth. "But I know this. Whatever comes, dark, storm, fire, I'd rather face it with you than walk a thousand safe paths alone."

Her breath caught. The words settled with the warmth of the fire itself. She leaned into him, shoulder to shoulder, root to stone.

Around them, Bramble's triumphant exclamations over pie filled the air. Chalupa issued tart rebuttals. Nyx judged them all with lofty disdain. Even Seamus's voice rumbled low, softer than stone had any right to be and for a fleeting moment, prophecy loosened its grip, making room for something gentler. The night turned from thunder into warmth. From prophecy into preparation. From fear into the small, stubborn comforts of family. But beyond the laughter, beyond the pie and the honeyed tea, something watched. It pressed at the edges of the realm like smoke beneath a closed door, seeping, seeking.

The festival lights still glittered in the distance, but their cheer rang hollow now, a song off-key. Frankie could feel it, just beneath the noise, magic twisted, out of rhythm, as if the forest had swallowed a breath and forgotten how to let it go. She wished she could strip the air of the festival's distractions, peel back the revelry, and listen, truly listen, to the woods.

To the hush between heartbeats. To the warning nested in wind. Because something had shifted and it hadn't shifted back.

Chapter 31

After food was shared and stories wound long through the hearth-lit room, the evening exhaled into something softer. Laughter clung to the air like steam on a windowpane, faint, warm, familiar. Bramble had conjured an extra round of honeyed root pies "for morale," and Nyx, smug on the rafters, had declared them "acceptable for a creature with no palate." Even Chalupa had dozed on the mantle, his small, dignified snore an endorsement of the company. The fire had burned low, and most of the cottage had gone quiet, save for Bramble snoring gently into a lavender-stuffed cushion and Nyx muttering in his sleep about improper sentence structure. Frankie lingered near the hearth, her tea long gone cold, watching shadows stretch and curl against the stone floor. Seamus leaned back in his chair with a sigh, one arm draped across Aoife's shoulder. He absently twined a lock of her silver hair around his finger, as if the act tethered him here.

"Well now," he murmured, soft Irish lilt curling through the hush, "with Councilor Elyen gone, the High Seat of Hollowmere sits cold and waiting."

Aoife turned toward him, one brow sharp as a hawk's wing.

"And how would you be knowing that, my love?" Her tone was light, but not without challenge. "You haven't set foot in Velhollow since you were tasked to watch over our Frankie."

The words slipped easily from her, but Frankie caught the difference, *my love*. Not a fond phrase like she used with Bramble or Nyx, but something claimed. Frankie glanced toward Griffon. He had noticed too. His eyes flicked to Aoife and Seamus, then back to her, the faintest smile curving the edge of his mouth. Not teasing. Just a quiet recognition of truth.

For a moment, even the fire paused, gilding Seamus's hands where they rested against Aoife's arm. Frankie felt it then, that strange ache of wonder braided with relief. Love didn't always arrive with grand declarations. Sometimes it came in the quiet, in the familiar, in the choosing. Griffon's fingers brushed hers beneath the table. A simple touch.

Seamus continued, his gaze still on Aoife. "I was far, but never gone. A whisper here, a well-placed stone there. Old friends in low places. And now and then, a breeze bringing word from a wind that hadn't forgotten my name."

Nyx flapped from the rafters, feathers rustling like dry parchment. "He means eavesdropping."

Seamus didn't blink. "Ah, but a bountiful harvest it's been, whispers and half-truths, ripe for the plucking."

Frankie blinked, her spoon hovering. "Wait… there are listening stones?"

Griffon leaned in, his grin crooked. "Of course there are. Half the stones in Velhollow hear better than its council. Walls may not have ears, but the rocks certainly do."

Seamus chuckled, low and warm, though his hand never left Aoife's hair. "I may have lived in the Greyvale," he said softly, "but I never turned my ear from here. And never from her. If danger had come, even a whisper of it, I'd have known. Not as a spy in shadows, but as a man who's never stopped keeping watch over what he loves most."

Aoife's chin lifted, but she reached up to still his fingers in her hair. "Even from afar, you never truly left," she whispered. "I felt you. Always. Just beyond the veil. Like a memory that refused to fade."

Frankie glanced across the hearth. Griffon's eyes met hers, steady, golden, unflinching. There was pride in his gaze, but beneath it. Something that said, I would do the same.

Griffon cleared his throat, pulling them gently back to the moment. "So… who's throwing their cloak in the ring for the Hollowmere seat?"

Seamus's expression darkened. "Quenric Wren. Archivist to the Royal Guard. He put forth his bid last solstice."

Frankie tilted her head. "Archivist?"

Seamus leaned forward, bracing his elbows on the table. "The Guard isn't only blades and battle lines, lass. Quenric minds the relic repository beneath the barracks, a vault so deep it brushes old bedrock. Every cursed blade, every whispering mask, every coin or charm that's drawn too much blood or bent too many minds is bound there. It's not a museum. It's a prison for magic too wild, too treacherous, to leave loose."

Bramble wrinkled his nose. "All that magic locked underground… sounds less like a vault and more like the world's crankiest pantry."

Nyx clicked his beak. "Cranky pantry or not, those relics have undone kings."

Seamus nodded grimly. "And at least one steward. Poor man tried to polish what he thought was a decorative moon-dial. Brass base, glass top. Looked harmless enough. But it was a sleep relic once used by a dream mage. Put the entire southern wing into a trance for eight hours. Snoring like mountain bears, mid-formation, spears and all."

Aoife's brow furrowed, expression turning sharp. "Quenric may keep the keys, but his eyes have always been on a higher prize. He would trade the lockbox for a throne if given the chance."

"His son serves there as well," Seamus said, more thoughtful now. "Calem. A scribe. He tends the tomes, scrolls older than kingdoms, parchment frail as breath. If Quenric is the jailer, then Calem is the interpreter. He unravels the curses woven into the ink itself."

Aoife tilted her head. "And what do you make of him?"

Griffon spoke before Seamus could answer, voice steady and low. "Calem listens where others dismiss. He doesn't carry a blade, but he sees how battles are lost before steel is drawn. When the Guard faces forgotten magic, it's his ink that shows us the shape of danger. He sees patterns no one else does."

Seamus gave a slow nod. "Mark my words. That lad will matter more than his father ever dreamed."

A quiet followed, deep and deliberate. Heavier than normal silence. The kind of stillness that settled before a spell spoke itself into being. Even Chalupa stirred on the mantle, blinking as though something unseen had passed through him. Frankie's hand tightened around her cup. Just a moment ago, they'd been wrapped in warmth, laughter blooming like steam from the hearth, stories shared in the hush between embers. There had been honeyed root pies, teasing glances, the gentle cadence of kinship. But now the room had shifted again. Not visibly. Not in anything said aloud. But in the way the air sat heavier against her skin, the way her magic prickled along her collarbones like warning. The hearth still burned, casting golden breath across the beams, but the warmth no longer reached her fingertips. It was as if the fire, too, had turned inward, bracing itself.

The logs cracked sharply, a single pop loud in the silence. Frankie flinched. She looked toward the window, drawn by something she couldn't name. The trees outside moved, but not from wind. Their limbs swayed slowly, deliberately, like sleepers rolling toward a dream they couldn't escape. No breeze kissed the glass. No gust stirred the leaves. And yet the forest moved.

She didn't know what to call the feeling rising in her chest. It wasn't fear, not exactly. Yet it moved through her with a quiet insistence, like a forgotten truth stepping forward to be seen. Not threat. Not danger. Recognition. As though the world had subtly shifted its attention and she now stood at the center of its gaze.

Griffon's voice broke through the hush, low and steady, shaped by a kind of strength that felt born of purpose rather than bravery.

"Come with me."

She turned toward him. His gaze was unwavering, fixed on her with the certainty of someone who had already chosen where he would stand. The weight of prophecy clung to her still, wrapped tight around her like damp cloth, heavy, unexpected, impossible to ignore.

"Where?" she asked, though part of her already knew.

It wasn't escape he was offering. It was alignment. A shared breath before the plunge. A moment pulled from the storm. Griffon didn't smile. He stood by the door already, cloak in one hand, the other extended toward her.

"To my cottage," he said. "Just for a while. There are things I need to gather, and something I want you to see. It'll be tomorrow before we know it."

She arched a brow, a smile tugging at the corner of her mouth despite the tightness in her chest. "You're a Stonewing, and a Berserker at that. What could you possibly need? Extra thunder? A second scowl?"

He didn't flinch. "You'd be surprised." A breath passed between them, heavy with unspoken things. Then, softer, "Besides… I want to show you my home."

The word home landed strangely. Frankie realized he'd said it with a kind of emotion that startled her. He wasn't just taking her to a place. He was offering her a piece of himself he hadn't let anyone touch. Not really. Not in a long time. Maybe ever. Something in his voice made her go still. It wasn't a request. Not really. More like a tether pulled tight between them, stretched across whatever was coming. She studied him for a breath. His eyes were steady, his shoulders squared, but beneath all that armor, something flickered. Something raw. She nodded once, and set the empty mug on the windowsill.

"All right."

They stepped outside. The door clicked shut behind them like a seal pressed in wax, and the warmth of the cottage exhaled behind them in a quiet farewell. Outside, the world was shifting. The night blushed with more than moonlight. Dark magic hummed at the edges, threading through the trees like a second wind, brushing the leaves, stirring the moss, seeping into the heart of Velhollow. It wasn't loud, not yet. But it was moving. A soundless thrum felt more than heard, like breath held too long beneath ancient stone.

Somewhere behind them, the festival still hummed with life, drums rolling in distant waves while flutes braided their melodies through the lantern-lit branches. The sound was meant to be comforting, a heartbeat of celebration. But even joy, when echoed through shadow, could become something eerie. Something fading. The forest greeted them with stillness. A quiet too intentional to be peace.

They walked in tandem, their boots brushing frost-softened moss. Mist coiled at their ankles, and the branches overhead quivered with delicate bands of magic that flickered like warnings left hanging in the air. Frankie felt Griffon's nearness before she fully registered it, his stride matching hers, his warmth steady against the cool breath of the forest. Every time their shoulders drifted close, the air between them shifted as if the realm itself leaned in to listen. She didn't look at him, not yet. Looking meant acknowledging the pull, the tether, the way her magic settled whenever he was near.

But she felt him, quiet, certain, watching the path ahead as if guarding her had become instinct rather than choice. And when his hand brushed hers, just a glancing touch, soft as breath on glass, the forest seemed to still… waiting to see what they would do next. Moonlight filtered through the canopy in broken ribbons, silvering the path ahead in strange, shifting patterns.

Frankie's pulse quickened. Not from fear, but knowing. A deeper kind. The kind that lived in the bones before the mind could name it. Something had changed since they'd walked this way earlier. The magic was thicker now. Hungrier. It wasn't just pressing in, it was curling, sliding between the trees like oil on water, unseen but unmistakable. The beauty of the forest remained, moss luminous beneath their steps, glowing with its own soft logic; owls blinked like lanterns from high boughs, their golden eyes slow and ancient. But every lovely thing was now threaded with something darker. The space between branches had gained weight. It no longer felt like quiet. It felt like breath held too long. Like something just beneath the surface was poised to rise.

Her senses stretched like threads in the dark, taut and seeking. There it was again, that bitter, back-throat tang of burned cedar, sharp and ancient. Not the hearthfire kind, but older, heavier. The scent of something that had blistered its way through bark and soil and memory. Frankie paused, her breath hitching as the air thickened around them. The forest here felt different. More disturbed. Like a garden uprooted, a silence bruised. They moved deeper into the woods, and the path dissolved beneath their feet, replaced by spongy earth laced with fallen leaves and frost-kissed moss. The trees arched above them like cathedral vaults, branches bare but humming, somehow, with the memory of green. Here, the world breathed differently. Frankie could feel it with that quiet, deeper sense that had been growing inside her since the moment she set foot in Velhollow. Like a tuning fork struck against her ribs. Moonlight slicked the forest in silver, illuminating pockets of mist that curled like thoughts half-formed. Pale fungi clung to bark like glowing runes. A fox darted across their path, tail flashing white at the tip, and vanished again without a sound. The beauty of it stole Frankie's breath. But beneath it all, the wonder was threaded with unease. The light in the air wasn't just moonlight. It was something darker, something coiled beneath the moss and frost, leaching up through the roots. She could feel it now, more pronounced than before. The dark magic didn't rush. It seeped. It settled. It waited.

Griffon said nothing, but his hand found hers, warm and steady in the chill. He didn't pull her forward. He just held on, like a grounding line cast in deep water. Frankie tried to name what she was feeling. It wasn't quite fear. But it was kin to it, something ancient that made the hair along her arms rise, something that whispered, *You're not alone anymore*.

There was a kind of stillness in the trees, but not a peaceful one. Not this time. It felt… suspended. Like the woods themselves were waiting to see what came next. A breath held too long. She glanced at Griffon, about to ask if he felt it too, but then she saw his jaw was tight, his shoulders tense beneath his cloak. He felt it. Of course he did. A sudden gust of wind stirred the trees, not loud, but sharp, and she turned toward it instinctively. Her breath caught. Along the trunk of a nearby ash tree, vines had blackened. Not the natural rot of season's end, but something unnatural. The leaves had curled inward, dark as ink and nestled between two roots, the soil glistened, not with dew, but with something too still. Too slick.

A cluster of mushrooms pushed up through moss-slick loam. But their colors all wrong, they glimmered with the green of curdled moonlight, like they'd drunk something rancid from the roots below. They stirred faintly, not like light, but like warning and then, just ahead, nestled between the gnarled roots of a tree twisted too tightly to be natural, something gleamed. Frankie stilled. It wasn't dew nor was it sap. What glistened there between the roots held no reflection, too dark to catch moonlight, too dense to scatter it. Slick, yes, but not wet. It pulsed with slow, deliberate rhythm, like something dreaming its way awake. Not the heartbeat of a creature, but of intent. Of presence. The bark surrounding it had blackened, warped inward in brittle curls as if the tree itself had tried to reject whatever had been seeded into it, but failed. The gleam coiled like ink spilled into velvet, a stain in the world itself. Too slick for resin, too alive for shadow. Not just magic gone wrong, a wound pretending to be substance. It was anchored, buried into the forest like a spike of will. A tether of something dark, insidious. Not alive in the way of beasts or men, but aware. Listening. Waiting. And now, knowing. Her breath hitched as her knees threatened to give way. Then Griffon's hand closed around hers, warm, steady, solid. The heat of it snapped through the chill curling around her limbs, and the pressure in his grip said what he didn't, *I see it too.*

"It wasn't here earlier," she whispered.

"No," Griffon said, his gaze sharp and unblinking. "It wasn't."

"What is it?"

He was quiet for too long. When he finally spoke, his voice came gravel-soft, each word shaped with weight.

"A rootmark," Griffon said, his voice low, threaded with something dark. "That's what this is. A marker, yes, but more than that. It's how he spreads. How he feeds."

Frankie turned toward him, unease settling deeper in her chest.

"Feeds?" she echoed, the word tasting wrong on her tongue.

Griffon didn't look at her. His gaze stayed locked on the glistening wound in the earth, the slick of shadow magic coiled between the roots.

"Veyrath doesn't draw power the way most mages do. He doesn't siphon it from stars or tides. He feeds on unraveling. On old magic left unguarded. Memory, grief, imbalance, he sows rot into places that still remember what came before. The wild places. Hallowed ground. Anywhere the weave runs deep enough to ripple when disturbed."

Frankie's throat tightened. The forest around them suddenly felt thinner, more fragile, like they were standing on skin stretched too tightly over bone.

"He plants these things like burrs under the world's skin," Griffon continued. "They fester. Foul the ley lines. He doesn't have to tear the veil open, he just has to weaken it enough that the land forgets how to resist. And once it forgets…" His jaw tensed. "He feeds on the loss. On the unraveling of what should've held."

Frankie's stomach turned. Griffon looked at her, and what she saw in his eyes made her breath catch. Certainty. Quiet and grim.

"If it roots too deep," he said, "the land stops remembering what it was. It forgets the balance it once held. Rivers turn bitter. Trees grow twisted. Magic frays at the edges, starts obeying different laws. His laws."

She stared at the mark between the roots. The thing didn't move, but it didn't have to. It had been planted like a seed and now waited for harvest.

Griffon's voice dropped, roughened by anger. "That's how it begins. Not with armies. Not with fire. With one place forgetting. Then another and another. Until the realm doesn't recognize itself anymore."

"I thought magic was..." she faltered, eyes locked on the unnatural gleam, "wild. But good wild."

"It usually is," Griffon said gently. "But wild things can be turned. Everything has the ability to rot."

He crouched near the roots, watching. His voice dropped lower.

"A rootmark isn't just a claim, it's a corruption. It drinks from the land, leeches its memory, hollows out whatever balance was there. The wardlines fray. The protections fade and we don't even see it happening until it's too late."

Frankie's stomach turned. "It's not just watching. It's... doing something to the forest."

Griffon gave a slow nod, jaw tight. "It doesn't just sit. It spreads. Quietly. It threads itself into the root systems, hijacks the memory of the land. The trees, the moss, the very soil, they don't know how to fight it, because it doesn't strike. It whispers." He glanced at the bark, now warped and black near the mark. "The forest still breathes around it, but not for long. This kind of magic doesn't just infect, it rewrites. It convinces the land that rot is part of its rhythm. That the sickness belongs."

Frankie's gaze flicked back to the strange gleam between the roots. Her skin prickled. "So it's not just a message."

"No," Griffon said. "It's a seed. A lie planted deep enough to take root in truth. And if it's not burned out or severed... it blooms."

Her magic flinched at the word. The thing in the roots stirred again, bolder this time, almost... pleased. It had chosen to be seen, and now it answered her. The surface rippled, barely a flicker, and then a deeper movement rolled outward through the ground, a slow, echoing rhythm that throbbed like a distant drum pressed into the earth. Frankie gasped as it surged toward her, swift and sharp, like a serpent catching scent. Not physically, there was no shape to strike, but the magic coiled fast and tight, invisible and predatory. It lunged for her chest, not for her heart, but for her core. For the place her magic lived. She arched back, a ragged cry catching in her throat. Cold fire wrapped around her ribs, threading into her aura, sharp with hunger, with purpose. It wasn't just touching her. It was trying to take.

"Frankie!" Griffon's voice was close, too close, but the darkness drowned it. She couldn't speak. Couldn't scream. The thing was already inside her wards, threading between her thoughts like rot seeping through the grain of old wood.

Griffon moved, instinct rising like a tide. The shift stirred in him, deep and primal, stone and wing and fury, but something pulled at his magic, held it steady. He stilled mid-breath, teeth clenched, every muscle poised to rend, but the shift didn't come. Something else did. Where his hand still clasped hers, light flared. Verdant and storm-born. Their magic surged, braided without command. It wasn't cast. It was called. A force awakened by need, by bond, by something more ancient than either of them had named. The energy lashed outward in a single arc, pure, radiant, rooted. It struck the thing in the roots like a blade made of every vow they'd never spoken. The forest shuddered. The ground heaved once. Leaves lifted from the earth in a soundless gasp. And the dark presence recoiled. It snapped back like a hand burned by fire, ripping itself from the edge of her soul with a hiss that shivered the underbrush. Dead leaves scattered. The gleam dulled, wounded.

Frankie staggered, lungs heaving, her vision full of after images, green fire, stormlight, the echo of something vast and feral and theirs. Griffon caught her before she could fall, arms firm around her, holding her steady.

"Are you hurt?"

She shook her head, lips parted, but the words wouldn't come. Around them, the air still crackled, soft, invisible sparks dancing across their skin. Their magic hadn't faded. It simmered between them like coals under ash.

"I didn't mean to do that," she whispered, her voice hoarse.

"Neither did I," Griffon said, wonder threading through his voice like silver through dusk.

Their eyes met. And in his, she saw no fear and no confusion, only awe, deep and unmistakable. It was the kind of awe that rises when something long-hidden steps into the light, when truth shows its face and the world must rearrange itself to make room.

He reached up, brushed a strand of hair from her temple, and let his hand linger there. "That's the bond," he said softly. "When magic recognizes magic. Yours and mine. Together."

Frankie drew in a quiet breath as the night seemed to narrow around her, pulling her into a stillness that felt impossibly intimate. A warmth rose through her, steady, like a truth that had been waiting for the right moment to reveal itself. It moved through her with purpose, threaded with the unmistakable echo of Griffon's magic. Their powers intertwined with instinctive precision, not battling for space but finding shared rhythm, as though they had always been meant to meet. Green wove through gold. Root met storm. The connection deepened in a way that felt both startling and deeply familiar, as if she were touching a future she had already lived in dreams.

Griffon's presence pressed close, not physically, but through the tether of their magic. She felt him as clearly as a hand in hers, steady and unshaken, guiding her toward a certainty she had long feared to name. The forest stilled. The air brightened. And Frankie understood, with a clarity that left her breathless, that this bond wasn't an accident of ritual or prophecy. It was choice layered upon choice, woven into something neither of them could unmake and in that recognition, something inside her, and inside him, aligned with fierce, irrevocable grace.

Not because fate demanded it. Because they did.

"I felt you," she said, the words steady and rich with realization.

Griffon's thumb skimmed along her cheekbone, a touch both grounding and reverent. "And I felt us."

Behind them, the gleam at the tree's base flickered, smaller now, drawn back, but unmistakably aware.

Frankie turned toward it, her focus sharpening as the truth settled into place. Her voice wavered with the force of understanding, not with fear.

"It wasn't only watching," she said. "It reached for me."

"I know," Griffon answered. His tone held certainty, threaded with something fiercely protective. "But it couldn't claim you."

"Because of the binding?"

He inclined his head. "That, and the way you stood your ground. You didn't bend. You met it on your feet."

Frankie stared down at her hands. They didn't feel entirely like hers, not after everything they had done, but they were hers. Steady. Certain. She hadn't seized the power; it had come to her because something in the world recognized her as its own. The silence around them shifted. The forest didn't breathe, but it listened. Griffon's hand remained in hers, warm and anchoring. They were both trembling, yet none of it was fear.

"We need to go," she said softly.

He didn't argue. They turned from the tree, boots whispering across moss. The thing in the roots didn't follow, it didn't need to. It had been seen. Worse, it had seen them together.

Frankie reached inward as they walked, testing the edges of her power. It hummed through her, reshaped and resonant, and beside it, woven through it, was Griffon's. Not touching her magic. Braided with it.

Griffon's cottage was close, barely a few minutes' walk, but Velhollow did not always give the same path twice. As they made their way toward the slope that led home, the world bent subtly around them. Trees that normally framed a clear route stood closer now, roots curling like half-finished thoughts. A familiar mossy boulder appeared where Frankie swore a fallen log should have been. Time didn't stretch; it folded. Distance didn't lengthen; perspective shifted. Still, she never felt lost. The forest seemed to usher them gently, guiding them along a route that wound deeper than memory, yet always remained within the small ring of woods near Aoife's hearth.

A pair of foxes appeared on a low rise, eyes glowing like embers. They watched without blinking, then vanished, not into brush, but into thin air, dissolving like mist. The air thickened, the hush deepening until the forest felt like a held note and then, something unexpected rose to meet her.

A scent.

Summer dew over dry pine needles. Lake water clinging to old windbreakers. The damp cotton of socks that had run through wet grass at dawn. It hit her with the force of memory, the liminal mornings of sleep away camp when she'd been ten, silvered with dew, suspended between night and day, steeped in the ache of believing anything could still happen. Her boots scuffed softly through moss. Griffon walked beside her in steady silence. Mist curled at their ankles as if greeting them by name.

"Time slips here," he said quietly. "Hours fold. Seasons stutter. I've seen saplings bloom, wither, and grow again in a single breath."

She gave him a sidelong look. "And you live here?"

His gaze softened; even in the dim, the gold in his eyes warmed. "I choose to. Not because I enjoy solitude, but because nothing pretends here. The forest tells the truth." His mouth curved, almost sheepish. "And it's close enough to Aoife that she can feed me."

Despite everything, she laughed under her breath. They crossed beyond Aoife's garden and followed the rise of a longer hill, the path bending in subtle ways that stretched the walk without announcing it. Time seemed to thin as they went, the world narrowing to root and breath and quiet footfall. Only after the land had taken its due did Griffon's cottage reveal itself, tucked deep in a sheltered hollow, half-swallowed by ivy and old stone, as though it allowed itself to be found only when it was ready. Familiar. Yet the magic between here and there made the world feel dream-thick.

The cottage looked grown rather than built, its moss-covered roof dipping gently under the weight of dew. Ivy draped over the stone walls, leaves glistening in the faintest mistlight. The chimney curled a ribbon of smoke skyward, and as Griffon brushed his hand over the carved sigil on the wooden door, the etching responded in a soft glow. Frankie stepped closer. A vine reached playfully toward her, curling around her finger in a gentle loop. She stiffened, then relaxed into it. The vine tightened once, like a handshake, and released a puff of golden pollen that drifted into the air, fragrant and warm, something like nectar warmed by sunlit leaves after rain.

She inhaled, and understanding whispered through her, not just welcome. Invitation.

Griffon watched her quietly, his expression unreadable but softened at the edges. He stepped aside as Frankie crossed the threshold. The cottage was small, warm, packed with books, jars of herbs, maps curling at the edges. Bundles of dried plants hung above the rafters.

The entire cottage breathed like a held exhale, quiet, cluttered, and alive. Candles guttered in sconces fashioned from horn and copper, casting soft gold across the wooden beams overhead. Bundles of dried sweetgrass and yarrow hung from hooks by the chimney, gently spinning as if stirred by breath, not breeze. There was a kitchen nook built into the stone wall, nothing grand, just a kettle resting on a blackened iron ring and a basin stacked with mismatched mugs, each one etched with a rune or chipped from use. But it was the far wall, tucked beneath a row of low, arched shelves, where wonder bloomed in miniature.

A miniature door, only a foot high, painted buttercup yellow with tiny birch-bark shutters. Beneath the door, a small staircase curved up from the floor like it had been carved by time and care rather than tools. Its steps were worn smooth, scaled for someone no taller than a teacup. At the top, a windowsill had been transformed into a garden, thread-spool pots sprouting moss and forget-me-nots, a pebble path lined with walnut-sized lanterns that flickered like caught fireflies.

Frankie blinked, then stepped closer, breath catching. "Is that a… dollhouse?"

Griffon didn't even glance up from where he was unlacing a leather satchel on the bench. "Do *not* call it that. Erma doesn't like it."

The correction came with such deadpan finality that Frankie instinctively straightened, just as the miniature wooden door nestled in the hearth's stone base creaked open with theatrical precision. Out stepped a tiny figure, her presence somehow managing to command the space like someone three times her size. She wore a cape fashioned from dried petal scraps and a strip of old lace, pinned at the shoulder with a bead that caught the light like foxglove resin. Her hair was a wild tumble of pale green curls, bound loosely with a strand of twine, and her wings, translucent were etched like young leaves, folded neatly behind her. She gave one brisk flutter, as if shaking off the air itself.

Frankie inhaled sharply, startled, but thoroughly enchanted. "Erma?"

The sprite paused on the threshold of her hand-carved stoop, hands planted firmly on her hips like a librarian preparing for chaos. Her voice, though no louder than a whisper, rang with unimpressed authority.

"You brought someone home," she said, narrowing her eyes at Griffon like he'd tracked in mud on freshly swept stone. "Is she the reason your boots have been wandering in circles for a week in the Gloaming and who-the-stars-knows-where else?"

Griffon flushed. Actually flushed. The man who'd faced down shadows in the woods without blinking looked briefly, and blessedly, guilty. Frankie let out a strangled laugh, caught somewhere between horror and delight.

Erma turned to her next target. She looked Frankie over slowly, appraisingly, not like one might greet a guest, but like a hedgewitch inspecting a potion mid-boil, trying to decide whether it would heal or explode. Her wings gave a single twitch, delicate and sharp as dew-tipped thistle.

"Well," she muttered. "She doesn't sparkle yet."

Frankie blinked. "I, what?"

"You heard me. The key to life is to sparkle, not farkle. No one trusts a dull witch."

Griffon straightened beside her, voice calm but grounding.

"Erma, this is Francesca *Caelith*."

The name struck the space like a stone cast into still water. It rippled, resonant and true. A name spoken in its full tongue. Frankie felt it land around her like a charm stitched into the seams of the world. Francesca Caelith. She liked how it sounded. She liked how it felt.

"Granddaughter of Aoife Caelith," Griffon continued. "*Blood of the Verdant Line. Keeper of the Balance ...*"

Each title landed like a stepping stone across an invisible bridge, from prophecy into presence. Even the cottage seemed to hold its breath.

Erma stilled and something flickered behind her sharp eyes, recognition, chased by awe. Her wings fluttered once, like leaves stirring in the wind, then she bowed, not a curtsy or a nod. A full bow with her arms tucked, head lowered, wings dipped like a banner in allegiance. Frankie's heart slammed against her ribs. When the sprite rose, the sharpness in her manner hadn't vanished, but it had softened, curved into something shaped like respect. She studied Frankie anew, voice lower now, gentled.

"Ahh," she breathed. "So it's true. The Verdant Witch has, in fact, risen. And the threads of prophecy are no longer waiting. They've begun to weave."

Frankie opened her mouth. Closed it again.

Erma's gaze flicked to Griffon and she sniffed. "Took you long enough."

Then, with a huff and a toss of her green curls, Erma turned and marched back to the buttercup-yellow door. At the threshold, she paused.

"She may stay," the sprite declared. "But only if she keeps her hands out of my pantry and stops alphabetizing my tea. You reorganized my licorice root and teas last time, and frankly, I found it invasive."

Frankie blinked. "I've literally never been here before."

"Mmm," Erma sniffed. "We'll see."

She vanished inside with a flourish, her door clicking shut behind her like the period at the end of a very opinionated sentence. Griffon let out a long breath, dragging a hand down his face as Erma's door latched behind her with finality. For a moment, silence bloomed. Then Griffon turned to her, still wide-eyed.

"She bowed to you."

Frankie exhaled, pulse fluttering like a lantern in wind. "Yeah," she said softly. "I noticed."

So quietly she wasn't sure he meant her to hear, Griffon murmured, "Francesca Caelith."

The name curled into the air again, softer this time, and Frankie felt it root inside her. She liked how it sounded here. How it sounded in his voice. Griffon smiled, just barely, as if he knew, sooner or later, that name might change again. Frankie blinked, still reeling. She wasn't sure what she'd expected from a forest sprite, pixie dust or riddles, maybe, but not bureaucratic approval delivered with the flair of a town clerk issuing permits for emotional occupancy. And yet, somehow, it felt like a truth grown patiently over time, the kind that settles into bark and memory.

Frankie stared at the nook again, still half-expecting a tiny eviction notice to slide out from under the door. "I still stand by what I said. That is absolutely a dollhouse."

Griffon groaned. "She's going to hear that."

"She already has," came a muffled voice from behind the door.

Frankie laughed, and Griffon watched her, the edges of his expression softening into something tender. Not everything was light tonight. But the moment held a glint of quiet magic, one of those rare, steady truths that lived in root and hearth and in the simple fact of being wanted. He moved past her then, gathering a few things into the leather satchel salves, folded maps, and something wrapped in deep green cloth that throbbed with a muted glow beneath his fingers, as though the magic within it recognized the touch.

"All right," he said, shouldering the bag. "Let's go back. Seamus will want to strategize and I'd rather not leave the planning to that cat."

"Smart," Frankie said, following him to the door. "Chalupa's revenge plans tend to involve killer bees and minor arson."

They slipped back into the forest, the path narrowing beneath their steps. Fog curled at their ankles like breath held too long. Around them, the everything seemed to lean in, curious and listening. The hush that followed felt as if the forest itself understood something had shifted.

Griffon slowed as they crested a rise, boots brushing through moss that glimmered faintly with mistlight. The forest leaned in around them with that quiet, watchful presence Velhollow always held when it knew something important was about to be said.

"There's something I need to ask you," he murmured, his voice low and deliberate, like he was summoning the courage to name something that had lived unnamed for too long. Frankie glanced over, brows lifting slightly, but she didn't speak. She felt it too, whatever this was, it carried weight. Not danger, no this was true heartfelt meaning.

"In Velhollow," he said, "when two people feel the stir of something deeper, not just affection or fate, but was magic moving between them, there's a tradition." He paused. "An old one. It's called the *Aelmath Dainn.*"

The words curled around them, foreign and beautiful, like a spell spoken into snow.

Frankie tilted her head. "Aelmath Dainn?"

"It means '*the shared hush*,'" he said. "A season of living side by side. Not a binding. Not a claim. Just... witnessing. The quiet parts. The truth between the words. The way you carry yourself when no one's watching but the trees."

He drew in a breath, as if steadying something inside him. "In the Greyvale, I believe they call it a cohabitation. As if hearts are contracts to test. But here, it's older. It's rooted. One full moon cycle, and a fortnight beyond. No oaths. Just presence. Shared hearth, shared hours, shared silences."

Frankie's breath caught. The way he said it, like it wasn't just something he wanted, but something he cherished, something he hadn't thought he would ever get to want.

He still wasn't looking at her. Not yet. "When this is over… whatever remains after Veyrath has had his last say… I'd like you to consider it. To come back with me. Not to visit but to stay."

She opened her mouth, but no words came. Her pulse beat like a drum in her throat.

Griffon's voice deepened then, softer, steadier. "I've walked alone a long time, Frankie, most Stonewings do. We're built to survive isolation. To carry burden without flinching. But that's not living. That's weathering. And I didn't even realize the difference until you."

He looked at her then, and the weight in his eyes nearly undid her.

"If we weren't fated," he said, "if we weren't meant, then why would our magic have bound so quickly? So cleanly? Why would it recognize yours as something I've been missing?"

They walked in silence for a time, side by side beneath the cathedral hush of the trees. But it wasn't the kind of silence that begged to be filled. It was the kind that healed. Frankie's fingers brushed his as they walked, tentative at first, then certain. He turned his hand and wove theirs together without hesitation. He didn't rush her. He didn't press. He let the forest hold the quiet while the meaning settled between them like pollen on spring light.

Then, after a stretch of path bent by root and memory, Griffon slowed again. The mist curled in silver ribbons around their boots, parting just enough for moonlight to gather on his shoulders like a blessing. He didn't turn to face her fully, he didn't need to. The weight of his presence was already enough.

"So," he said softly, the words threaded with a depth that felt older than hope itself, "you'll give it consideration, then? The Aelmath Dainn."

Frankie didn't pause. "Yes."

It was a simple answer. But nothing about the way she said it was small. Because the way she looked at him, steady, curious, already a little undone, wasn't the look of someone weighing a choice. It was the look of someone who had already chosen, and just hadn't realized how quietly the decision had rooted in her bones. Griffon turned then, fully, as if the moment called for more than silhouettes and shadow. The expression on his face was all softness now, astonishment worn like armor finally loosened. She smiled, faint but real, and he reached for her hand, lacing their fingers slowly, like drawing a sigil into warm earth. When their palms touched, the forest shifted around them with quiet acknowledgment. The moss at their feet brightened, faintly aglow and leaves rustled overhead in a wind that didn't touch their skin. Somewhere, a nightbird sang a single clear note, as if in benediction. Even the hush between the trees felt lighter now, threaded with something new. As though Velhollow had been listening all along, and approved.

Frankie exhaled, breath misting in the cool air, her lips twitching into a lopsided grin. "I just hope Erma's okay with this. She seems like the kind of landlord who checks your tarot cards before handing over a spare key."

Griffon let out a low, startled laugh, the kind pulled from somewhere deep and good.

"You're not wrong."

They stood there a moment longer, hands twined, magic humming quiet and alive between them. Neither one moved to break it and when they finally stepped forward again, the path did not resist. The forest made space, like it already knew.

By the time Aoife's cottage came into view, its windows lit like lanterns in the dusk, woodsmoke curling from the chimney, thyme and something sweeter threading the air, Frankie felt it like a chord pulled taut through her ribs. This place. This man. This bond. It wasn't just fate, it was her choosing. As they stepped toward the light, shoulder to shoulder, heart to heart, she realized the question had already begun to root its answer deep inside her.

Griffon reached for the latch, then paused, his gaze finding hers again. "Are you ready for this?"

Frankie exhaled. "Not even close."

The garden, once wild and welcoming, seemed to watch rather than greet, its night-thorn blossoms drawn tight, their petals closed like fists. Even the moon orchids glowed only faintly, their usual radiance muted, as though they too were bracing for what was to come.

The air around them shifted, cooler, tighter, stretched like skin over a drum. There was no wind, but the trees whispered anyway, dry voices brushing against bark, too low to name, too old to ignore. Magic wasn't just present, it was unsettled. It didn't curl in soft spirals or hum with promise, it pressed in from all sides, twitching at the edges of perception. Frankie's skin prickled beneath her sleeves.

She couldn't explain how she knew something had changed. She hadn't grown up listening for this kind of silence, the kind that throbbed like a held breath. But she felt it anyway, in her bones, in the weight behind her sternum, in the hush that vibrated between heartbeats. Something had shifted. And whatever it was, it wasn't finished. She glanced at Griffon. He hadn't said a word, but his grip had tightened slightly around her hand, not protectively, but with recognition. He felt it too. Still, Frankie didn't pause. She squeezed his hand once more, then let go, because whatever waited inside, they would face it together.

They stepped inside, and the door shut behind them with a soft click, sealing out the cool night air. The cottage of warmth and rosemary-sweet air. Frankie shed her cloak, fingers stiff from mist, and hung it by the door just as Griffon did the same. Across the room, Seamus and Aoife sat close at the table, their heads bent over an open tome, a scroll unspooled beside it, weighted at the corners with stones. Two mugs sat forgotten between them, the dregs of tea long cooled, but the conversation had clearly not.

Frankie paused, breath catching. Seeing him like this, armored in purpose shook something loose in her chest. He wasn't supposed to be here. He had been part of the life she left behind: mornings in the nursery, quiet talks over chipped mugs, the steady presence who never asked her to explain why the world felt too loud some days. Of all the things she thought she'd lost by coming to Velhollow, he was the only one she mourned and yet… here he sat.

Seamus looked up first. The stern lines of the Royal Guard eased, softening into something achingly familiar. For a heartbeat, she saw not the man cloaked in titles and centuries, but Pete, the one who used to slap ridiculous warning labels on her leftovers, as though the fridge were a battlefield and her stew a weapon best handled with caution.

"*Lady Francesca*," he said, though mischief sparked bright in his eyes, betraying the formality of the words.

Frankie's expression twisted immediately, half a smile, half a warning.

"No," she said, pointing at him as if scolding a wayward toddler. "Absolutely not. I am not '*Lady Francesca*.' I'm Frankie. If you call me that again, I swear I'm putting special mushrooms in your tea."

A slow smile crept across Seamus's face, warm as sunrise and twice as fond. "Aye," he murmured, amusement threading through the softness. "There she is."

Her laugh wobbled then, shaped more by emotion than humor. "You know you're still Pete to me, right?"

His smile deepened, quiet and full of something she didn't yet have a name for. "I would expect nothing less."

"It's just…" Frankie swallowed, the truth catching lightly in her throat. "I never imagined you'd be here. In any of this. And now that you are, it feels… steady. Like something that should have always been."

Something gentle passed across Seamus's features, pride, affection, relief, and the entire room seemed to soften in response. Aoife's mouth curved with quiet approval, touched by decades of knowing, and warmth unfurled through Frankie's chest in slow, blooming waves. After everything she thought she had left behind, here was the one piece she mourned most… returned to her in a way she never could have predicted. The ache she'd carried since crossing the veil eased, slight but unmistakable. The moment lingered, warm and weighty, then shifted, subtle as the cottage itself exhaling. Frankie stepped deeper into the room, and the hush followed her, settling into place like something long displaced finally finding its true shape again.

Aoife looked up next, her eyes carrying that uncanny ability to see more than she ever voiced. She studied Frankie and Griffon for a long, quiet breath, as though measuring not only the magic that clung to them, but the people they were becoming.

"Well, loves," she asked gently, "did you find what you needed?"

Griffon nodded once. His jaw remained tight, his gaze sweeping the cottage with a warrior's vigilance, checking corners and shadows as though still unconvinced the world had stopped tilting beneath their feet. Only after a long breath did he step toward the hearth, letting the low flame anchor him. Firelight brushed the faint glow beneath his skin, the quiet reminder of what Velhollow had awakened in him and what he now accepted. In the quiet that followed, Frankie understood it was not only the forest that had shifted. All of them had turned in their own way.

Aoife no longer carried her power as a quiet, solitary burden. For years, the weight of the Verdant Line had lived inside her, woven into her breath, her posture, even the way she listened for danger in the wind. She had been a placeholder for a destiny meant for another, guarding a prophecy she feared she might never see fulfilled. Now, unmistakably, the rightful heir stood before her, and the truth of it settled through Aoife like the slow release of a long-held breath. The shift was subtle but profound. Her magic didn't drain away; it simply no longer pressed so sharply against her bones. Its balance had shifted toward Frankie with the natural certainty of roots finding earth. A new role unfurled within Aoife, one she had longed for and feared she'd never earn the right to hold. She could be Frankie's guide now, her mentor, her grandmother in both love and legacy.

Seamus, too, had changed. He no longer carried the weight of his title like a man trapped beneath it. The years settled around him like armor rather than chains, fitting again, familiar, as though returning to Velhollow had restored the piece of him that had gone quiet in the Greyvale.

And Griffon... he stood differently now. A steadiness had rooted itself in him, a quiet certainty in the way he drew breath, as though the earth itself had accepted him as one of its own. The Berserker mantle was no longer a myth rising unbidden from his blood, it was something he embraced. Strength, fury, purpose... all of it lived in him without consuming him, and he bore it with the calm of someone who had survived the fire and understood what it meant to rise from it.

Frankie felt her own shift just as clearly. Only days ago she hadn't known Velhollow existed, hadn't imagined magic could live beneath her skin like a second heartbeat. But here, in this place that had chosen her as surely as she had chosen it, she no longer feared what she was becoming. Her magic didn't feel like a stranger anymore, it felt like a door she had finally stepped through. She embraced it now: the wildness, the wonder, the responsibility. Velhollow wasn't just a realm she'd stumbled into; it was hers, threaded through her breath and her becoming. They were no longer reacting to the world around them; they were shaping it, side by side, their choices rippling through the realm with the quiet certainty of roots taking hold. The world had begun to shift in ways none of them could ignore, and each of them was shifting with it, changed not only by magic, but by the simple fact that they no longer walked their paths alone.

Griffon finally spoke, his voice low but steady. "We found more than we expected," he said. "There was… something on the path. A rootmark."

Seamus's pen stilled mid-stroke as Aoife straightened, every line of her body answering the change.

Frankie moved slowly toward the bench by the fire, lowering herself with more care than usual, the weight in her limbs heavier from exhaustion. She swallowed.

"It wasn't just magic. It was seeded dark. Sentient."

Griffon nodded grimly. "Veyrath's reach. It tried to take her."

That made Seamus lift his head. "How?"

Frankie met his gaze. "It attacked. No shape. No form. Just… force. It went for my core. Wrapped around my magic like it knew me. Knew how to unravel me."

Aoife rose from the table slowly, as if every movement mattered. "And yet… you're here."

"Our binding pushed it back," Griffon said, voice low. "Instinct. Neither of us called it. It just… flared and repelled."

Aoife's eyes sharpened. "You flared together?"

Frankie nodded. Her hands still trembled faintly, as if the magic hadn't fully settled. "We didn't mean to. It just happened. It felt... ancient."

The room went still. Even the fire seemed to bow inward. Seamus leaned back, arms folding. "That's no minor tether, then. That's the land answering."

"It knew me," Frankie said quietly. "Whatever it was, it saw me."

"And it feared you," Aoife murmured. "Or at least... what you're becoming."

Frankie leaned back against the long bench, sinking into the cushion like she might never get up again. But her chest, her heart, held something steady now. A warmth she hadn't known she needed.

Aoife reached for a fresh page but paused, her eyes narrowing slightly. "Did she meet Erma?"

Griffon let out a low chuckle, the edge of tension finally giving way. "She did. Erma approves."

That made Seamus look up. He blinked once, then again.

"Erma approves?"

"She bowed," Griffon added, his voice touched with the kind of disbelief usually reserved for falling stars or talking stags. "Full wingspan. No sarcasm."

Aoife's hand froze mid-reach. Her brows rose.

"She bowed?"

Seamus leaned back in his chair like he needed structural support to process the information. "That sprite hasn't bowed to anyone since the *Moss Trial of '84*. And that was only because she tripped."

Aoife pressed a hand to her chest in mock dramatics. Frankie smiled faintly, she was starting to realize that in Velhollow, the smallest things, like a bow from a forest sprite or a flare of shared magic, could mean everything.

"Didn't throw a single acorn at her," Griffon added, as if this were proof of divine intervention.

Aoife's lips twitched. "Well then," she murmured, "miracles abound."

Frankie smirked, stretching her fingers toward the flame. "She said I could stay. As long as I don't organize her tea again."

Aoife glanced up, curious. "Have you?"

“I’ve never been there,” Frankie said, deadpan. “I have no idea where her tea even is.”

Seamus barked a short laugh, the sound unexpected but welcome. “Doesn’t matter. She’s already convinced you did it in another timeline.”

Aoife shook her head fondly. “Sprites keep odd ledgers.”

“And long grudges,” Griffon muttered.

Frankie leaned back, warmth slowly sinking into her bones as the firelight caught the curve of her cheek. “I liked her. She’s completely unhinged. But honest.”

Aoife met Griffon’s gaze over the rim of her teacup. “She bowed.”

Griffon just nodded, slow and steady, as if the gravity of it was only now beginning to register. “She knows who Frankie is. And she’s not the only one.”

The silence that followed was thick, like the hush that falls after a name is etched into stone. The fire crackled softly and Frankie felt it in her chest, that shift in the air, subtle but undeniable. The kind of shift that meant something had begun.

Griffon rose from the bench and crossed to the hearth. “There’s a magical storm coming,” he said, voice quiet but certain.

Aoife didn’t flinch. Her fingers stilled on the spine of the ledger, tightening slightly. She unrolled another chart, this one marked with the territories of Elderglen Reach, its rivers and valleys inked in fluid lines, familiar and deceptively calm. But the real focus was etched in red, sigils marking the thresholds where ancient protections once held firm. Now, some flared dimly. Others had gone dark altogether. The page looked like a wound.

Seamus leaned forward, his voice dropping to gravel. “We’ve been tracing the ley-lines that once sealed the Forgotten Realm. Not just boundaries, but living threads of magic woven to keep the worst of what lies beyond from ever crossing into our world.”

His finger landed on one of the fading sigils, the ink thinned to the barest shimmer. “The cracks aren’t theoretical anymore. They’re here and they seem to be widening.”

Frankie leaned forward, studying the map with new eyes. It was more than terrain; it carried a quiet current, a living network etched into the skin of the realm. What she’d once imagined as invisible threads were now laid bare, unmistakable in their presence. Some lines held steady, bright with resilience. Others flickered uneasily or had faded to near-nothing, like pathways in danger of being lost.

"These aren't just lines," she murmured, voice soft with dawning understanding. "They're arteries."

Griffon nodded from the hearth. "Exactly. The ley-lines were never just boundary markers. They're conduits. Ancient ones. Magic once ran through them like blood, binding the land, the trees, the spirits, all to a shared heartbeat."

"And when they weaken…" Frankie began.

Seamus's gaze didn't lift from the map. His voice, when it came, was low and rough as worn stone. "They don't just fail. They fray. Like a binding spell unraveling from the inside out. And when they fray long enough…" He tapped one of the sigils with a knuckle, and the parchment seemed to shudder. "They tear. And through those tears, the worst of what was once sealed can begin to creep in."

Aoife reached out and tapped a section of the map, just north of Dawnmere. "These lines were woven long before Velhollow had a name. The first Verdant Witches didn't craft them alone. They heard them. Coaxed them from the land itself. The lines aren't just spell work, they're covenants. And if enough of them break…"

She trailed off, her mouth tightening. Griffon picked up the thread, his voice low. "If they collapse completely, the Forgotten Realm won't need to breach the veil. It'll bleed into ours. Like rot through bark. Like ink spilled in clear water."

Frankie shivered, her eyes scanning the reddened markings on the chart. "And Veyrath?"

Seamus stabbed his finger toward the southern quadrant where three ley-lines once intersected. Only one remained.

"He's not trying to break through from the outside. He's corrupting the inside. Threading himself into the weave. Turning the magic against itself."

"Which means," Griffon added grimly, "he doesn't need to knock. He's already found the cracks, and now he's learning how to widen them."

Frankie felt her skin prickle, her breath tight in her throat. "Then it's not a matter of *if* he comes through."

Aoife nodded solemnly. “No. It’s only a matter of how much destruction will fall in his wake before we stop him.” Her brow furrowed, fingers brushing the rim of her teacup before setting it aside, forgotten. “We’ve long suspected he would try to breach the veil,” she murmured, eyes drifting toward the window where the trees pressed close. “But now… I fear he already has.”

Seamus leaned over the table and tapped the map with a knuckle, his voice rough. “The ward lines used to flare when danger drew near. Now… they barely flicker. They’re worn. Stretched too thin, like parchment left too long in the sun.”

“Aye, he’ll wait,” Aoife said grimly. “Until midnight on the last night of the festival, when the veil thins to thread, when deep magic breathes shallow and the old magics open their eyes.”

“To collapse the defenses,” Griffon added, his voice like gravel smoothed by gravity.

Frankie studied the spread of maps and sigils. What once looked like ink now felt like bloodlines, vulnerable with unspoken urgency.

“So what do we do?” she asked. “There’s barely a day left.”

Seamus turned one of the maps toward her, rotating it so the red sigils faced her fully. “We hold the ley-point at Dawnmere Crossing. If Veyrath breaks through there, he won’t stop at Velhollow.”

Aoife’s hand brushed the edge of the parchment. “That’s where the Verdant Grove first met the river,” she said. “It’s where my grandmother’s grandmother began the original stitching of the balance, where the first Verdant spell was cast into soil. If Veyrath taints that place, he doesn’t just win this battle. He rewrites the past that made you.”

Frankie felt the breath catch in her throat.

Griffon moved beside her and placed a hand at the small of her back, grounding. “Then we hold it,” he said, quiet but certain.

Seamus nodded. “We will.”

Even as the words settled into the old wood and stone of the room, a heavier stillness followed, thick and deliberate. Something unspoken passed between Griffon and Seamus.

Frankie noticed. “What?” she asked.

Seamus hesitated. Then, in a voice coarse with years and memory, he said, “The repository.”

Frankie turned to him, the word ringing with more weight than she expected. "The one beneath the Guard barracks? What's actually sealed down there?"

Griffon crossed to the hearth and his gaze held steady on the flame, though his voice seemed to speak from a deeper place.

"A vault," he said. "Not of this age. Ancient. Older than the first treaties, older than the war lines drawn in ash and oath. It was carved from the bedrock before the last great convergence, before language was whole, before magic wore names. When the ley-lines first began to fracture and the sky whispered in tongues no mouth could mimic. Before Velhollow was Velhollow, when this valley was still wild and half-feral, cloaked in fog, haunted by stars, and spoken of only in prophecy." He paused, the firelight glinting in his eyes. "They built it when magic stopped behaving like a servant and started hungering like a god. Warded it with blood sigils, bound it with iron taken from stars that fell in the old storms. Seven keys, seven seals, each buried beneath a different moon cycle. It holds what couldn't be destroyed... and what dared not be remembered."

He turned then, eyes shadowed. "These aren't just relics and artifacts," he said softly. "They're echoes with teeth. The kind of things that look back when stared at. Magic that learned to survive by binding itself to grief. Power that remembers the first scream. And should they ever be freed... they wouldn't just shift the balance. They'd remake it."

"What sort of relics?" Frankie asked.

Seamus's voice dropped lower, darker. "Not the polished kind displayed in halls. These are remnants of the Forgotten War, objects carved from vengeance, betrayal, grief. Cursed things. Living magic bound in bone and iron. Some older than even the Verdant Line."

"Magic that's still awake?" she asked softly.

"Aye," Seamus said. "And still listening. Too dangerous to wield. Too aware to bury."

Griffon's jaw tightened. "The vault is more than a prison. It's a sanctuary of the unspeakable. Only the High Seat and the Commander of the Royal Guard hold full access. But even under lock and ward, there are relics down there Veyrath could turn loose. Or worse, has already begun to twist."

Seamus's mouth pressed to a hard line. "We don't know what's safe anymore."

Aoife rose slowly, the weight of thought pulling her upright. She tapped a finger against the map, each beat a drum of quiet urgency.

"Then we station a silent guard. No word passed. No chain of command. Just eyes that understand what they're watching for, and hearts steady enough not to flinch if it stirs."

Frankie's breath hitched. "Do you think he's after something specific? A relic powerful enough to change the course of … everything?"

Aoife's gaze met hers, unwavering. "Anything is possible, Veyrath doesn't just want to conquer. He wants to unmake. To thread a new beginning through the oldest seams. And yes… there are relics that could aid him."

Griffon's voice darkened. "The *Mirror of Thorns, The Bone of Ashelain,* the last sigil from the *Hollowmoor Accord*."

Frankie shook her head. "I don't know what those are."

"Aye witchling and you don't want to," Seamus murmured.

"But you should," Aoife said gently. "Because Veyrath could easily thrive where we hesitate to look."

The fire snapped behind them, scattering sparks like fireflies caught in the wind. Shadows danced along the carved beams above, no longer idle but attentive. Nyx stilled in the rafters, feathers tucked. Bramble watched from beside the pantry, expression unreadable. Chalupa opened a single eye, unblinking. Velhollow was not quiet. It was bearing witness. And far below the moss and meadows of the valley, in places where the stones still remembered war, something ancient had begun to turn in its sleep.

A hush bloomed in the wake of her words, deep and wide as the roots beneath their feet. No one moved. No one needed to. The silence wasn't empty, it was full. Full of thoughts too heavy to speak, of fears not yet named, of memories that had begun to stir like dust in a closed room. The kind of silence that only follows truth. Frankie could feel it pressing into her chest, into her breath. The fire's warmth didn't quite reach the corners now. Even the air seemed to listen differently, like the room itself was drawing breath alongside them, waiting. Then, at last, Aoife exhaled slowly, like a tether releasing. She reached for the scrolls and began to roll them with quiet, precise care.

Aoife's voice came low, but resolute. "We prepare, but not idly," she said. "Now, my girl, there are spells you'll need to know. Wards. Shields. The old evocations. We won't go deep. Just enough to make sure what you already carry can answer when it's called."

Something shifted inside Frankie. It wasn't a spark, nothing sudden or sharp. It was older than that, quieter. Like a door creaking open in a house she hadn't known she lived in. A flutter along her spine. It was as though a part of her had heard Aoife's words not with ears, but with blood. Something stirred and turned toward the voice like a flower to sun. She didn't speak. Didn't need to. Aoife felt it too, Frankie saw it in the way her aunt's gaze flicked up and caught hers, steady as a lodestar.

"There," Aoife said softly, not smiling but close. "You felt that."

Frankie nodded. Slowly. "I… I don't know what it was. But yes."

"It was your magic," Aoife said.

Frankie's brow furrowed. "But I've always let it in. I wasn't blocking it on purpose, I just… haven't known how to listen."

Aoife's eyes gentled, her voice slipping into the space between silence and spell. "And now it's beginning to listen back." A quiet stillness fell in the space between them.

Frankie felt it then, that flicker inside her, newly understood. Not a flare of power, not a jolt of force, but a sensation she recognized. That flutter of warmth in her palms when she touched old bark. The weightless prickle behind her eyes when she stood alone in the garden and the wind changed direction. The way her heart sometimes quickened when silence deepened, like something unseen was waiting just beneath it. Frankie leaned closer to the map, though her attention had begun to drift inward. A thought rose through her like a tide returning to shore.

"I've felt this before," she said softly. "Long before Velhollow. Before any of this. When I was little in the woods behind our house… there was a pull. Something brushing past me, almost familiar. Like the air remembered something I didn't."

Aoife's lips curved with a warmth shaped by recognition. "Of course you did, mo chroí. That was your magic. It has whispered to you your entire life. You didn't stumble into it. You were born speaking the language. You simply didn't know you were fluent."

The truth settled through Frankie with a quiet, radiant weight. Relief and wonder moved through her in equal measure, as if vines inside her finally found sunlight. All those strange moments she had tucked away, soft tugs at the edge of thought, the certainty that she was not entirely alone even when no one stood beside her, had never been imagination. They had been this. They had been hers.

"So it's not foreign," she said, voice lowered in awe. "It's not something I have to become. It's something I've always been."

Aoife stepped closer and placed her hand gently over Frankie's sternum. She didn't press, only rested her palm there as though touching a story returning to its first line.

"Exactly that. It has always belonged to you. It grew with you, learned with you, waited with you. Now it rises because you are ready to rise with it. You're not trying to welcome it anymore, love. You're remembering it."

Frankie closed her eyes. Inside her, warmth gathered and unfurled. It met her where she stood, curling around her spirit like a vine finding its trellis. Not something she needed to shape. Not something she needed to control. Only something she needed to let be.

"It's syncing," she whispered. "With me. With everything I am."

Aoife nodded, her hand steady over Frankie's heart. "And that, my girl, is the beginning of every real spell."

Frankie looked up, her voice shaded with dawning certainty. "It moved through me earlier. I didn't call it. I didn't even try. But it knew. It recognized something before I did."

Aoife's smile softened, touched with memory. "That is how you know your magic is truly awake, mo chroí. It doesn't always ask. It doesn't always knock. When something does not belong, your magic will rise of its own accord." Her gaze deepened with quiet understanding. "And you've felt it many times, even if you never named it. Those moments you called instinct, or dread, or a strange tightening in your chest… that was your magic, trying to speak."

Frankie stood very still. The weight she carried didn't vanish, but it settled differently. It shifted from burden into belonging, something rooted, something known, something that had always been waiting for her to finally turn toward it. She breathed in slowly, and the world seemed to meet her halfway.

"Griffon," Aoife added, "you and Seamus will walk the lines. Go over the wards. Test them. Speak them aloud. Strategy by firelight is still strategy. We'll sleep, but only just."

Griffon's jaw tightened in affirmation. Seamus was already nodding, drawing a fresh sheet of parchment from the pile.

"But before morning comes," Aoife added, her gaze finding Frankie's once more, "we'll go into the village. To the heart of the festival."

Frankie tilted her head, curiosity sharpening beneath the weariness. "Why then?"

Aoife's expression sobered. "Because what lingers after the revelry ends is often more revealing than what dances in the lanternlight. When the last song fades, and the fires burn low, the land is honest. It hasn't yet put its face back on."

Griffon spoke quietly, his tone steady but weighted. "The veil doesn't close cleanly with sunrise. There's always a thinning just before the light fully claims the hills. If Veyrath's influence has taken root, among the villagers, the wardstones, or the festival grounds, we'll feel it then. The dark threads shimmer most when no one's watching."

Seamus didn't look up from the map, but his voice came rough, graveled with warning.

"The mistake is thinking midnight is the end. But it's the quiet before, the breath between dark and dawn, when magic slouches low and minds go soft... that's when the blade slips deepest."

Frankie's stomach twisted. She could still feel the ache beneath the roots, the way it had reached for her, not blindly, but with eerie precision, like something that already knew her name. And her magic had answered. She rose slowly, her muscles aching, exhaustion woven deep into her bones. She turned to Griffon, who was already watching her. His voice, when it came, was low, meant only for her.

"One more night."

She nodded. Just one more. And then everything would change.

The others drifted to their corners of the cottage, Seamus to his old chair, Aoife to her writing desk. Chalupa leapt from the mantel and curled beside Bramble, who was already half-asleep. Nyx took to the corner rafter, one eye open, feathers fluffed in wary silence.

Frankie and Griffon found a spot near the hearth, their hands still laced. The fire had burned low, casting the stone in soft golden hushes. Its glow stretched like lullabies spun from ember and root. And though the shutters were latched and the hearth still breathed warmth, every soul within could feel it, that slight tilt in the air, like the earth itself had turned its ear. Velhollow was not quiet. It was listening. And far beneath ward and woodgrain, below frostline and memory, something ancient began to stir. It would not sleep again and by dawn… it would rise.

Chapter 32

A blur of of striped fur swept past them with all the gravity of a creature on a divine mission. Chalupa darted between Frankie and Aoife like a feline magistrate inspecting his constituents, then vaulted onto a chair, and from there to the table, landing beside the butter dish with the practiced grace of someone who absolutely belonged there. He paused, leaned in, and gave the butter a single dignified sniff, then recoiled with a theatrical shudder that would've embarrassed a Shakespearean understudy.

"By the salted stars of the Seventh Veil," he declared, nose twitching in offense, "why is there a dagger in the butter?"

Aoife didn't look away from Frankie, but one brow arched, dry and knowing, as if confirming a long-held suspicion. "Bramble."

From the far end of the table, Bramble's voice rang out with chipper indignation. "In my defense, the butter attacked first."

Nyx, perched like judgment incarnate atop the bookshelf, gave a ruffling squawk. "You were carving runes into toast."

Seamus merely sighed, tugging his gloves snug. "I warned him about enchanting food."

Nyx made a noise that could only be described as avian disapproval. Chalupa licked a paw with performative detachment. Bramble, undeterred, continued buttering his toast like a man at war with convention. Around them, Aoife's cottage stirred, the lamplight pooled like melted amber, and the hearth sighed low, casting its warmth in waves. Bundles of rosemary, lavender, and lemon balm swayed gently from the rafters, stirred by the quiet updraft of simmering magic. The scent of thyme clung to the air, layered with smoke and a trace of wintering sage. Wax dripped in slow arcs down stubby candles, the flames dancing gold over shelves lined with jars and hand-written labels curling at the edges.

Outside, darkness cradled the village in its palm. It was the kind of hour when dreams clung like fog to the edges of thought, and magic hovered in the stillness, uncertain which way to lean.

They hadn't slept, only closed their eyes for a few borrowed moments, stolen from a night too full of watchfulness. There hadn't been time, and even if there had, the quiet in the room wasn't the quiet of sleep.

Frankie reached across the table without thinking and scratched gently behind Chalupa's ears, right where his fur was thickest and warmest, the spot she'd learned long ago was his undoing. He made a low sound, something between a hum and a purr, and leaned into it before catching himself. His tail twitched once in slow protest, like he hadn't meant to enjoy it quite that much.

She smiled, her hand lingering. "Is this still okay?" she asked quietly. "You're… more than a cat. I don't want to overstep."

Chalupa's eyes didn't open, but the tip of his tail curled like a lazy question mark. "It's fine," he said, voice drowsy. "If it helps you feel better."

She huffed softly, but didn't stop. "You sure?"

A beat passed, then, grudgingly, "I didn't say stop."

Frankie grinned, her fingertips moving in small, practiced circles. "You do like this."

"Don't ruin it," he muttered, sinking deeper into the tablecloth, all regal loaf and barely disguised contentment. "Just… carry on."

Her chest ached with something tender and old. She had no idea what she'd done to deserve him, but she was glad the stars had given her the chance. And then Chalupa yawned, baring small, perfect teeth, and glanced at her sidelong, his tone returning to casual.

"So… the Stonewing finally asked, did he?"

Frankie blinked. "Asked what?"

He gave her a look, the look….The one that said *Don't be dense, darling, it doesn't suit you.*

"The Aelmath Dainn," he said, as if she were forgetting something as obvious as her own name. "Trial tethering. Magical courtship. You know. The quaint old tradition where people decide if they can tolerate one another's laundry habits and spiritual baggage."

Frankie flushed. "Oh. That."

Chalupa sniffed, pleased. "So, did he ask?"

She smiled, ducking her head. "Yes. He did." A silence stretched between them. Then, softly, she added, "Would you come with me? If I stayed there?"

Chalupa stilled. The flick of his tail slowed. He looked up at her with something harder to name. His gaze held the weight of watchfires, of paths shadowed and guarded in silence, of years spent curling at her feet not just because he was a cat, but because he was her sentinel.

"I guess," he said finally, voice dry. "Someone has to keep Erma in line and you are hopeless without my supervision."

Frankie's laugh broke like light through mist. She leaned forward and pressed her forehead gently to his, a moment brief and infinite.

"You've always been more than you let on."

"And you've always needed someone to knock your tea over at pivotal moments," he replied, but he didn't pull away. Not until the fire popped and Bramble sneezed behind them.

Frankie drew back, brushing a knuckle under one eye. "You'll really come with me?"

Chalupa curled back into his loaf with regal indifference.

"Assuming you both survive."

She smiled, crooked but steady. "We will."

Griffon stepped beside her, warmth brushing against her like sunlight on a cold morning. He didn't speak, just touched the back of her hand. A quiet vow. He didn't see her as unraveling, but becoming.

The air in the cottage stilled, not with peace but with pressure, like the earth itself was holding its breath. Even the fire gave a low sigh, its glow dimming as though reluctant to cast too much light. A silence unfurled between them, but it wasn't empty. It was full, swollen with everything unsaid, everything approaching. A reverent calm that belonged to churchyards and old forests and the final page of a story just before it's turned. Outside, the dark pressed tighter against the shutters. Frankie felt it before she heard it. A strange awareness blooming behind her ribs, beneath her skin, under the oldest part of her name. Magic, hers, rising not in response to fear, but to recognition, something was coming.

She turned slightly, gaze catching Aoife's. The older witch's eyes had gone distant and silver-bright, like a storm seen far across a field. Chalupa's tail flicked once, slow and measured. Nyx, for once, made no sound at all. In that breathless beat, the air grew heavier, tinged with iron and pine and something darker, like the scent of wet stone split too deep, of root systems torn from the belly of the world. The hour had shifted. Not forward. Not backward. But sideways and suddenly Frankie understood when they said time moved differently in Velhollow, she'd thought they meant pace, slow mornings and second cups of tea, a place where the days meandered like streams over mossy stones. But this was something older. Wilder.

The clocks in the cottage, old things with wood-carved faces and bone hands, began to tick erratically, some forward, some backward. One spun in silent circles as if trying to remember where it belonged. Shards of light pierced the seams of the room, slipping under the door, spilling down through the chimney, curling out of tiny cracks and fairy doors that hadn't been there a moment before. Colors shifted where they shouldn't have. Shadows pooled in the wrong corners. The fire popped, but gave no heat.

The festival lanterns might still be burning. The villagers might still be laughing, unaware. But something ancient had leaned closer to listen, beneath that listening… something else had begun to stir. Frankie moved to the doorway. The wind clawed at her sleeves, sharp and dry. Beneath her boots, the floor felt thinner than it had before, less like shelter, more like a skin stretched too tight. Outside, the forest bent inward. Branches tilted. Leaves stilled. As if everything green was holding its breath.

"Is this Veyrath's doing?" she asked, her voice tight.

Frankie stood still. Her spine did not bow, her gaze did not falter. He had stopped being Nono the moment she'd learned his true name …Veyrath.

The name Nono bore no familial warmth. It did not echo in her bones with longing. It did not stir memories of dappled sun on garden benches or stories told in low voices near the fire. It carried only the sharp tang of iron and betrayal. Recognition, yes, but not the kind that rooted. The kind that warned. It was a name braided with shadows. A name that belonged to someone who had not merely lost his way, but had carved a path in the dark and called it destiny. She had felt it for years, though she hadn't known what to call it, why her skin crawled when he entered a room, why the silence around him was never peace, only pressure. As a child, she'd avoided his presence without knowing why. As a teen, she'd hated how the air seemed to still around him, how his gaze made her feel like a puzzle he meant to solve and discard, now, finally, she understood.

Aoife and Frankie stood at the long wooden table beside the hearth, its surface cluttered with small glass vials, worn scrolls, sachets of herbs tied with twine, and the runes etched in salt and powdered bone. Aoife's fingers moved with quiet precision, plucking dried wisterthorn, measuring sprigs of yarrow, whispering incantations into the folds of folded silk. The room smelled of rosemary and lavender, something metallic and green, like magic still wet from the earth.

"These you'll carry in your satchel," Aoife said, her voice steady as she tucked each item into place. "This one wards off unspoken charms. This, for reversing blood-borne hexes. This… " she paused, holding up a tiny jar glowing faintly from within, "… for if all other light goes out."

Frankie had tried to memorize every name, every use, every whispered phrase laced in languages older than paper. But Aoife had stilled her hand, placing a palm atop her wrist.

"You won't need to remember everything," she said gently. "Magic listens when it matters. Just make sure you're listening back."

Above the hearth, a bundle of vervain crumbled without cause, shedding dust and shadow onto the stone below like the first quiet crack in a ward long-held. Beyond the walls, the laughter of villagers still rose faintly, out of step with what had shifted here. The creak beneath her boots was no longer simply wood, it was warning.

When she found her voice, it was quieter than before, but steadier. "What's happening?"

Chalupa's answer came low and sure, his usual sharpness stripped down to something older. He stepped forward, tail flicking once, slow and deliberate.

"What you felt, that pressure, that wrongness, that's the rot he planted. The dark rootmark is growing."

Frankie's brow furrowed, the ache behind her ribs tightening. "You mean like the thing that attacked us near the crossing?"

He nodded once. "Exactly like that. It's not him directly but it's because of him. His magic seeded these fractures long ago, knowing the Veil would thin during the festival. Add in the surge of magic flooding Velhollow from every hedge witch and charm-carver lighting candles and tying wishes to trees, and now those seeds are feeding."

He glanced toward the dark window. "They're drawn to power that's unfocused. Untethered. Loose magic burns brightest and hungriest. What you're feeling is what rises when no one's watching, when everyone's playing at magic and no one's minding the roots."

Frankie's stomach twisted. "So they're feeding on the festival itself."

"On the residual magic of it," Chalupa said, his voice sharp with warning. "The joy, the grief, the spells strung from whim and wine. They feast on raw edges. It's not a breach in the Veil. But it's what waits to crawl through when it finally tears."

The wind outside shifted again, sharper this time. Frankie's skin prickled. This was no ordinary chill, it was something deeper. A knowing. The scent of scorched leaves curled in through the eaves, mingled with ash and iron, memory and rot. Down in the square, the lanterns flickered. Their light faltered like breath trying to hold. Inside, no one asked what to do.

No one spoke again. The decision had already been made, braided into breath and bone, they moved. Seamus slung his satchel over his shoulder, hands aglow with restrained ancestral light, an old magic that flickered like coals banked deep beneath a mountain. Chalupa leapt to the window ledge, tail swaying like a blade deciding which way to cut. Bramble stuffed a bundle of dried wisterthorn into his sleeve, grumbling about vinegar, runes, and the butter-stabbing stupidity of lesser men. Nyx gave no cry, only the whisper of wings as he vanished into the dark like a warning loosed too late. Griffon was already beside Frankie, grounding her with his silence. Just there, like granite beneath storm-split sky.

Aoife's gaze swept the room like a warding spell, her voice a low incantation wrought of iron and wind. "Walk with your roots beneath you. With the stars at your back. Let the land know you come in truth. The wind is listening. And it does not come empty-handed."

Seamus gave a sharp nod. "We don't wait for fate to knock. We meet it in the dark. Where it thinks we won't."

Aoife turned, her hand rising to tuck a curl behind Frankie's ear, her palm steady against her cheek. "Let the dark come, then," she said, voice wrapped in thunder and memory. "Let it bare its teeth and claw the door. The prophecy never said you'd stand alone, mo chroí. You are the Verdant Witch, you carry the Verdant Flame."

She looked to the others now. "The Stonewing walks beside you, fierce and loyal. Seamus bears the mark of the Royal Guard, not by crown, but by choice. He'd face the void itself for you. Chalupa, for all his smug nonsense, is Moonlit Court-blooded and owes nothing to this realm but the truth. Nyx sees what others blink away. He's watched the Veil longer than any of us. And Bramble, well... clever as a fox and thrice as fast." She stepped back and then she spoke again. "This isn't your burden alone, Veyrath has made one mistake too many. He's underestimated you, my girl, and that will be his undoing."

Outside, the lanterns flickered, stuttering against a wind that had turned sharp and strange. Far off, thunder rolled like a memory being shaken loose. Magic thickened in the air. From the edge of the forest came a low, splintering groan, the kind of sound that rises from breaking stone. From time. From places where oaths had once been buried under ash and blood.

The hearthstone cracked, the rafters moaned and the wind surged upward, wild and dry, like something exiled finally remembering its name. Then the bells began.

One.

Two.

Three.

Each toll struck like a verdict, sharp, deliberate, unyielding. The sound didn't merely ring; it slammed into the bones of the cottage, vibrating through timber and ribcage alike, as heavy as iron gates locking behind something ancient and wrong.

These were not the bells of the village square. This was the Warden Bell, carved into the cliffs beyond the eastern ridge, an old magic cast in bronze and blood, bound to sound only when the ancient seals were threatened. It had rung only once in Aoife's lifetime. Her grandmother had spoken of a second time, barely, and only in whispers. A bell with no ropes, no gears, no hands to pull it. It was not tolled. It was triggered. By the weave. By danger so dire, even the earth could not stay silent.

The *first bell* was a summons, a call to the old bloodlines, to stir the Watchers and the hidden wardens scattered across the realm. It meant danger was near, not yet here, but approaching. It was a warning for those who could still fortify the edges.

The *second bell* meant the edge had been crossed. That something dark had moved from shadow into form. That it had touched the threshold of the realm. It marked a breach.

But the third... The *third bell* was never meant to ring. Not unless the old protections had been compromised. It sounded only when a seal had begun to falter. When the wards beneath the valley, etched in blood, bound in oath, and hidden even from memory, had been weakened from within. It was a bell rung by the land itself and the land had spoken.

The third note stretched long and low, inhabiting the very bones of the land. It vibrated through the rafters, the beams and the valley itself. It didn't fade. It settled like a blade being laid flat across the heart of Velhollow. The earth went still in recognition as Velhollow remembered. It remembered what had been buried deep beneath its roots, Veyrath's first attempt to corrupt the Verdant Line. His ancient spell work, once thought severed, had been too dangerous to destroy. So it had been bound instead, sealed in salt and name and blood, held fast beneath the ward stones by rites older than the language used to cast them.

Griffon's gaze never wavered. His stance held, firm as stone, but when he spoke, his voice bore the quiet finality of steel drawn across stone.

"It's begun."

The rafters above groaned, as though remembering the weight of older storms. A candle bent toward nothing, its flame leaning sideways, and beneath the floor, beneath root and relic, beneath moss and ward stone and the ancient bones of the valley, something vast leaned closer and the land... listened back.

Aoife lifted her staff and tapped it once against the stone. The sound rang out like a summons. "Come now," she said softly. "Best we move. Velhollow doesn't favor delay."

They opened the door, and the forest opened back. Above them, the illusion of sky, the enchanted dome stretched high above

Velhollow, began to fracture with silence so sharp it carved the light in two. A jagged seam tore across the vaulted canopy, not in cloud but in the ancient spells woven to mimic sky. It wasn't the real sky, but it bled like one. For a breath, no one moved. The air felt charged, caught between heartbeat and war-drum. Frankie stepped forward, and Griffon caught her hand. His thumb brushed the back of her knuckles then her jaw.

"If we don't come back," she whispered, voice tight.

"We will," he said, certainty threaded through every syllable. Then softer, "But just in case… "

He kissed her. Not tentative or hurried. This was a promise, fierce and unflinching. The kind that said, this is *real,* even if the world forgets everything else.

Behind them, Chalupa cleared his throat with theatrical precision. "Touching. Truly. I'll be sure to carve it into the prophecy margins: '*In case of impending doom, commence smooching.*'"

Seamus didn't hesitate. He turned to Aoife, cupped her face with quiet, unshaken devotion, and kissed her as though the battle could wait, as though she were the only force he would ever choose to follow into danger or into peace. When they parted, her fingers lingered at his collar, soft and sure, as if anchoring them both to the moment before the world shifted again.

"You stayed in the shadows for too long," she whispered, voice threaded with both ache and knowing.

His smile was quiet. "I was where you needed me."

"And now?"

His hand found hers, grounding and certain. "Now I walk beside you."

Bramble blinked. Slowly. Then turned to Nyx. "So?"

Nyx cocked his head. "I have a beak."

Bramble huffed and turned to Chalupa. "You?"

Chalupa didn't answer. He simply sauntered past the bog sprite, tail flicking like punctuation, and bumped his head lightly against Bramble's leg, the feline equivalent of a head butt, dignified but unmistakable.

Bramble's eyes went wide. "You do care!" he gasped, scooping the cat into his arms like a mossy missile. "I knew it! You love me, you fluffy curmudgeon!"

Chalupa let out a strangled sound, all wheeze and offense.

"Unhand me, you damp cabbage."

Nyx let out a low, raspy caw that could only be described as laughter.

"Gods above, what is in your pocket?" Chalupa gagged, pawing at the air. "It smells like pickled toadstools and poor decisions."

"It's a warding poultice," Bramble said cheerfully, squeezing tighter. "Or possibly lunch." Bramble crooned, nuzzling him.

Chalupa muttered something vile in a language older than shame, then set about furiously grooming his shoulder, as if indignation could be scrubbed away with enough spit and spite. Bramble beamed, utterly unrepentant. Nyx cackled like storm wind through rafters, sharp and delighted. But the mirth thinned quickly, as laughter does when it strays too close to the edge of something watching.

Ahead, the forest exhaled, not in welcome, but in warning. The wind no longer stirred the branches for sport. It threaded through them with intent, sliding along bark and leaf as though counting breaths. The dark was no longer still. It had found its shape, and it waited. As they moved deeper into Velhollow. The forest did not close behind them so much as absorb them. Sound dulled first, not silenced, but pressed flat, as though the air itself had thickened enough to hold it. Lantern light softened, filtered through branches that arched too close together, their pale bark striated with mineral scars and half-erased markings older than any road. The ground sloped and shifted beneath their feet, sometimes firm, sometimes yielding to root and shadow.

Aoife set her staff to the stone. The ring of it traveled farther than it should have. "From here on," she said quietly, "the land decides how you pass. Velhollow has a long memory in places like this." She tapped the staff once more, slower this time. "It's not fond of haste."

The path narrowed. Frankie felt the distance begin to tell, not in miles, but in weight. Her legs burned sooner than they should have. The sigil on her palm warmed, not painfully, but with a steady insistence, as if it were keeping count of every step taken toward something that could not be avoided.

Griffon stayed close, his presence steady and deliberate. Seamus ranged ahead and behind in quiet arcs, never allowing the group to compress too tightly. Nyx flew low beneath the vaulted dark, a moving shadow among shadows. Bramble walked with unusual care, muttering charms under his breath, adjusting his pack like someone who knew exactly which ground might give way without warning.

Chalupa broke the silence at last, tail flicking. “So,” he said, “is it just me, or does this stretch of Velhollow feel… judgmental.”

Bramble didn’t look up. “The realm isn’t offended.”

“That’s a relief.”

“It’s deciding.”

Chalupa groaned. “That’s worse.”

The farther they walked, the more the forest leaned in, not threatening, but attentive. Moss darkened beneath their boots, slick with cold. The air carried the sharp tang of iron-rich stone and deep water hidden far below, a mineral bite that coated the back of Frankie’s tongue. Somewhere beneath them, pressure gathered, not the rush of a river, not yet, but the unmistakable sense of something being drawn tight, as though the land itself were holding its breath.

She took it in slowly, letting unease settle where curiosity usually lived, then asked softly, “How far to Dawnmere Crossing?”

Aoife hesitated before answering. “Close enough that it already knows we’re coming.”

Ahead, the forest thinned just enough to reveal a place where the realm grew taut, stretched too thin and never fully healed. Behind them, the path they’d taken was already knitting itself closed, roots easing back into place. Above, the enchanted dome of Velhollow groaned softly, the sound traveling through the trees like a breath held too long.

They had barely cleared the last lantern posts when footsteps joined theirs. First one pair. Then another. A baker fell into step beside a hedge witch, flour still ghosting his sleeves. Two Wardens of an old river line emerged from the mist, their sigils faded but their eyes sharp. A pair of shifters followed in quiet human skins, boots scuffing stone in unison. Others came more slowly—hands empty, shoulders squared, faces set with the calm resolve of those who had decided that standing still was no longer an option. No one spoke. They didn’t need to. Velhollow knew how to answer a summons without needing to being asked.

Frankie glanced back, breath catching as she realized how many had come, not to watch, but to help. Bramble paused, frowning as though struck by sudden inspiration. He plunged a hand into one of his many pockets. A cascade of debris spilled out, a bent copper spoon, three unidentifiable seeds, a thimble that had no business existing, and something that hissed before scuttling away. At last, he tugged free a crumpled tea towel, shook it out, looped it around his neck, and tied it into a cape. The knot sat crooked. The fabric was stained.

Bramble straightened anyway. "Well," he announced, hopping onto a stone marker like it was a stage, "if this becomes a heroic march, I want it on record that I dressed for it." The cape immediately snagged on a low branch and nearly yanked him backward.

Chalupa snorted. "A magical storm's brewing and you're worried about your wardrobe."

Bramble sniffed, smoothing the tea towel. "If we're walking toward destiny, we may as well walk like we mean it."

Nyx gave a low, amused caw from above. "If this were a ballad, this is where the chorus joins."

A ripple of laughter passed through the gathered villagers, quick, but real. Someone muttered, "Gods help us," and someone else answered, "They usually do," with the weary affection of someone who had lived long enough to mean it.

They moved as one now, the road narrowing as it led away from the homes and hearth light and into older ground. The air sharpened with every step. Frankie felt it press against her senses, more insistent than threatening, like a tide drawing breath before the pull.

The forest thickened. Roots crowded the path. Branches knitted overhead.

Some villagers slowed then, their steps faltering as the land made its preference clear ... this far, but no farther. Hands reached out in passing touches, to Frankie's shoulder, to Aoife's sleeve, to Griffon's arm, to claps to Seamus's shoulder. Grounding gestures. Quiet blessings offered without ceremony. Not all turned back. A solid group pressed on, wardens, hedge witches, shifters, elders whose magic ran deep enough to answer the land's scrutiny without flinching. They closed ranks behind Frankie and Aoife, not crowding, not leading, just simply *staying*. Walking with the calm resolve of those who had already chosen their sides.

Ahead, the trees parted just enough to reveal a shift in the air, a wrongness that did not belong to soil or shadow. Something stirred beyond the bend, seeping into the world. Smoke folded around sinew. Bone surfaced and sank again, undecided. The path fell silent. Whatever waited near Dawnmere Crossing had felt them coming and it was waiting.

Chapter 33

The forest did not wait. The moment they crossed its threshold, the ground convulsed beneath their boots, a violent shudder that rolled from root to ribcage. The sound wasn't thunder, it was stone screaming, the memory of something once broken clawing to break again. Above, the false dome of sky warped. Distortion bled across it, a pallor bending like glass under strain. A seam split wide, jagged and wide, like a revelation, a glimpse into something raw and wrong, seething with intent. Branches writhed against a wind that carried no scent of season, only ash and iron. Trees bent low, as if in mourning. From their shadows, dust devils spun themselves thin, spirals of leaf and ash glowing for a heartbeat before vanishing, the residue of the realm's warning. Velhollow itself was shivering.

Then the ground lurched harder, violent and deep. Roots groaned beneath the soil. Ancient timbers snapped like bones under a weight too vast to bear. Far off, village or veil, it was impossible to tell, something shattered. Glass. Spell. Silence. The bones of the earth were stirring with intent. Frankie staggered. Her breath caught sharp between ribs and throat, but magic steadied her. It rose from within like a second spine, heat and cold braided together, ancient and alive. It threaded through her without panic. Only purpose. She did not need to call out. She felt him, before she turned. Before the wind curled and broke against the arc of obsidian wings. Before firelight caught the glimmer of his skin and reflected the gold that lived beneath it. Griffon was already in motion. Shifting.

The transformation wasn't abrupt. It was elemental. Stone rippled beneath skin. Bone answered blood. Power rose in deliberate layers, first through his spine, then his shoulders, until his silhouette darkened into something forged by mountains, not men. The wings unfurled behind him, wide and sharp and echoing with the memory of flight. The runes along his forearms lit faintly, old marks of the Stonewing line, awakening. He didn't roar. He didn't bare his teeth. He stood and in that stillness, the storm found its anchor. He hadn't summoned the full Berserker, she could feel it, pacing just beneath the surface, waiting for the call, but this version of him was no less fearsome. It was the sentinel. The shield. The calm before the wildfire.

His eyes found hers across the rising wind and held. Steady. Certain. A vow without words, spoken in silence older than language. She breathed him in. Cedar. Char. Iron warmed by the sun. Her hand found his, larger now, roughened with power, talons curling where fingers used to be, but still warm. Still human enough to steady her and gods, steady her he did. She looked down at their hands, fingers laced like a promise. The moment felt surreal, crystallized against the weight of everything that pressed in around them.

"I always think you'll feel cooler," she said softly, almost surprised.

A slow smile curved his mouth, rare and unhurried. "There's nothing cold about me when you're near, *Lady Francesca.*"

From the ground at her feet, Chalupa flicked his tail, voice dry as tinder. "Excellent timing. Nothing says 'ready for battle' like shameless flirting on the doorstep of doom."

Then, with the poised grace of a knight greeting his sovereign and blatantly ignoring Chalupa, Griffon bowed and lifted her hand to his lips. The kiss was light as breath but steady as gravity, a quiet promise wrapped in warmth. When he rose again, a glint sparked in his eyes and a subtle smile tugged at his mouth.

He winked. "Besides, stone remembers the heat that shapes it."

Around them, Velhollow stirred with purpose. The witches, shifters, spirits, and old blood were still with them. Some wrapped in mist. Others cloaked in nothing but resolve. Wardens from forgotten lines. Guardians from buried courts. Magic hummed in the air, waiting. Listening. They had come to stand, not to solely bear witnesses, and what waited beyond the trees, the rot, the breach, the unraveling, was no longer reaching. It was here. They moved forward together, breath held, the air pulled taut around them like thread on the verge of snapping.

The forest answered their approach with hesitation. Not with challenge, not in welcome, but an uneasy pause. Light ahead thinned and warped, distance bending oddly, as though the land itself were unsure how to hold what waited there. Whatever lingered beyond the trees didn't move to meet them. It remained still and the realm braced around it.

Frankie's voice caught in her throat. "That's not... natural. Even for Velhollow, this is wrong."

The thing oozed from the breach like oil over shattered obsidian, slick and glistening, shifting with grotesque grace. Its form never settled: skin rippled between scale and sinew, limbs jutted where none belonged, joints bent wrong. For a breath its shape faltered, a torso splitting open, dozens of mouths gaping, none aligned, all teeth. Eyes blinked too fast, too many, a ribcage flexed inside-out before snapping back with a sickening lurch. It moved the wrong the way, like an echo is wrong when it arrives before the sound. Frankie stumbled back, breath caught shallow, sparks of magic flaring at her fingertips.

Aoife's voice rose, low and steady. "It's not a beast. It's a remnant."

"A remnant of what?" Frankie whispered.

Aoife didn't flinch. "Of war. Of rot. Of the burning age when the old wilds turned on themselves. When witches and warlords tore the Veil and fed magic with their own dead. What you see is what was left behind, corruption-born things that learned to live on rot and ruin. They crawled through battlefield ash, drank fear like mead. I thought they were sealed when the Veil was bound." Her gaze flicked to the breach, iron-hard. "Seems I was wrong."

The creature opened one of its mouths, jawless and yawning, and something like a word spilled out, more felt than heard, like scraping bone.

Griffon stepped in front of Frankie, wings snapping wide. "It clawed back from where it was meant to stay buried."

The beast lunged. Griffon met it mid-stride, obsidian wings slamming forward like twin shields. His talons twisted through its limb, such as it was, and the thing shrieked through all its mouths at once, a howl that bent flame sideways. Frankie thrust her hand down. Verdant magic surged, vines bursting from the soil, thorned and grasping. They lashed around its shifting mass, binding limbs that flickered in and out of shape. For a heartbeat it was caught, snarling, twisting.

Nyx swept overhead, his voice sharp as his shadow. "It's reckless! Strike now while it falters!"

Frankie flung raw power forward. It hit the creature with a crack like lightning through ice. From behind a splintered cart, Bramble popped up, bog light glowing faint.

"Don't waste your flashy bits on him! Hit where the shadows cling. Follow the ripple when it flinches."

The beast ripped free, pieces tearing off and regenerating mid-motion. It pivoted sideways, lunging again. Chalupa darted forward, claws gleaming.

"Left side's weak," he snarled. "It's leaking essence!"

Frankie dove under a barbed tail, slammed her palm to the ground.

"Griffon, drive it back!"

"Gladly." His wings flared, power surging. He launched skyward, dust spiraling in his wake. Nyx shadowed him like a second heartbeat, swift and precise. One flew with brute force, the other with razor-edged grace.

Above the treeline, Griffon arced and folded into a dive. His claws, etched in faint runes, struck deep into the writhing mass. The shriek that followed bent the air, high and wrong, before the creature split open. From the wound crawled darkness thick as tar, alive with slithering shapes. Faces surfaced, some contorted in grief, others grinning with too many teeth. One wept shadow from its eyes; another sobbed with a mouth that never closed. Not real, yet every one turned toward Frankie with predatory precision. Whispers snagged the air, until her name slid from their mouths in a hundred voices.

Bramble froze, voice low. "Oh stars... echoes."

"What?" Said Frankie, eyes wide.

Aoife's eyes sharpened, voice carrying the weight of history.

"Echoes. The oldest magic remembers, Frankie. It devours cries, fears, souls, and wears them. They are hunger given form, the cast-off remnants of every war this realm has endured. They whisper with voices you long to hear, wear faces you ache to trust. Step too near, and they take what is left of you and make it their own. That is why they were bound with the Veil. That is why they should never walk here again."

The air warped. Frankie smelled honey thick as drowning, saw faces flicker into ones she knew, Aoife, Griffon. Even her parents. Their voices whispered her name, calling to her. A hand stretched toward her, warm, familiar. Her fingers trembled forward.

Nyx's shadow crossed her face. "Frankie!"

His cry cracked the spell. The hand dissolved into smoke, the face collapsing into darkness. Frankie staggered back, heart hammering.

"They nearly had you," Bramble muttered, grim. "Never meet their gaze. Not even for a breath."

The ground shook. Griffon landed, wings half-spread, a wall between her and the rising tide.

"Eyes on me," he growled.

Her hands blazed green fire. "Let's finish this."

They moved as one. Frankie's feet rooted, Verdant power curling down her arms. She hurled green-gold fire; it struck one echo's face, which collapsed like scorched parchment.

Chalupa's voice rang behind her, sharp and commanding.

"*Now, witchling*!"

She didn't need more. The word itself was a spark. Frankie thrust both hands down. The vines that rose were not healers' threads, but the old ones, deep-rooted, glowing with runes unsung since the Founders. They struck true, piercing illusion and flesh alike. The echoes shrieked, unraveling. Shadows tore like threads from a cursed tapestry. Griffon saw the flaw, a seam of weakness. His claws drove through it, stone-light flaring. The creature hissed like a nightmare exhaled, then folded inward, collapsing into nothing. For a breath, there was silence.

Nyx angled east, wings tightening. The forest there rippled unnaturally, brush crushed low, branches bowing as several forms threaded through the trees together, fast and disciplined,.

"Look," he called down, voice edged with iron. "Eastward, through the trees ..."

Griffon turned at once, shadows along his shoulders tightening.

"They're hunting in packs," Nyx continued, banking hard.

Below him, the forest to the east churned with movement, branches moving, undergrowth collapsing inward as shapes slipped between trunks too fast, too coordinated to be chance. Before Griffon could answer, other sounds rose. Commands. The clang of iron. It was the villagers. At the forest's edge, lanterns bobbed and steadied. The eastern border met resistance, not panic.

Nyx circled once more, satisfied enough to report, "They're holding. Not cleanly. Not easily. But they're not breaking."

Griffon exhaled, a low, grounding sound. "Good," he said. "Tell them we see them."

Nyx dipped a wing in acknowledgment and vanished back toward the treeline, a streak of black against the bruised sky, while the forest ahead drew tighter still, as if deciding where the true reckoning would fall. The soil trembled with many footfalls. From the treeline, shadows poured in, half-formed, many-eyed, slick with rot. They didn't howl. They stalked.

Bramble ducked low. "Oh splendid. An organized apocalypse. They are the worst. Last time, it took three covens, a wind elemental, and a very confused goat."

Chalupa's ears flicked. "They'll come fast. They'll keep coming."

Aoife stepped forward, voice iron. "Frankie, anchor yourself. Let the Verdant roots remember your name. Don't reach, call."

Seamus turned to Griffon. "Hold your magic open. Don't shield it. Let it braid."

Frankie met Griffon's eyes. Together, they sank into the earth's hum. Magic answered, eager, waiting. Light glinted across Griffon's wings. Roots stirred beneath Frankie's hand. Verdant magic met shadow fire and did not waver. For one breathless instant, the clearing held, as though waiting to see which force would break. Then it surged, a reckoning made visible. A current snapped into place, green-gold and searing, threading from Frankie's chest to Griffon's wings, down into the soil. A union of power. Frankie gasped words she did not know, not from memory but from an invocation rising like flame.

"Root to flame, breath to bough, Verdant Light, awaken now."

Her voice rang clear through the thickened dark, and her side, Griffon's voice joined hers, low, steady, old as the stones beneath them.

"By oath unbroken, by bond made true, Verdant Flame, we call on you."

The ground shuddered in answer as the Verdant Flame roared to life. It was a blaze, wild and it erupted in a spiral around them, green-gold fire surging upward and outward, scorching the very breath from the air. It ripped through smoke and illusion like dawn cleaving fog, racing across the ground with the certainty of truth rediscovered. The nearest Shadowforms screamed as the flame tore into them, their shrieks swallowed by light too ancient to be denied.

Griffon moved with her, step for step, breath for breath, his presence not just beside her but interwoven. His wings snapped open, catching the blaze that surged around them and bending it, forging it into force. He drove forward through the thick of the fray, claws alight with the ancient runes of stone, slashing through the flank of a lunging creature mid-leap. It dissolved before it could land, reduced to ash that spiraled upward, swept into the wind now rising with purpose.

Frankie followed without hesitation, her magic no longer erratic or flaring wild, but honed, steady as the tide, fierce as the storm it had always been becoming. With each measured turn of her wrists, the earth responded, obedient and alive. Vines erupted from root and stone, glowing at their tips with molten green-gold heat, like lightning distilled into sap. Along each twisting length, the runes of the Elders rose into motion, ancient script that brightened with power and memory, as if the land itself were reclaiming the truth of her name. One vine struck, clean and final, spearing through the nearest Shadowform with a sound like splintered ice. It gave a single, broken scream, then folded in on itself, unraveling as though some unspoken truth had tugged loose its seams. The earth dragged it backward toward the breach, as if the lie could no longer bear to stand in the presence of what was real.

A Shadowform veered left. Griffon saw it and turned it to vapor with a burst of flame. Another lunged for Frankie's blind side, he moved before she had to call for him. Their magic didn't just align. The Verdant Flame expanded, radiant and wrathful, curling through the clearing like judgment written in fire. The ground did not retreat, it answered. Roots stirred below. Stones glowed dimly at their edges. And the very Veil between realms pulled taut, as if it, too, was bracing for what came next. The creatures faltered and the breach groaned. Frankie raised both arms, the magic rushing through, bright and blistering. Her voice cut through the smoke and dark with clarity and command.

"*Back to the rot that claimed you. Back to the dark that made you.*"

The words rang with the weight of old oaths made new and the flame obeyed. It surged forward, fed by the Verdant magic and Stonewing strength, bound and blessed by the realm itself. Frankie's light poured outward, fierce as spring's first blaze and Griffon stood with her, shaping the fire into something elemental, something inevitable. Together, they became more than the sum of their parts, they forged the Verdant Flame. She flung her arms wide, calling the last of her gathered magic. Griffon stepped behind her, one hand at her back, wings arched to shield, to steady, to send. Their power entwined, not pushed, but released, a command spoken in unity.

"Your tether to this realm is undone," Frankie intoned, her voice deep with the cadence of the earth.

"By root and flame, by sky and stone, we cast you out," Griffon said, his words ringing like ancient iron struck true.

The Verdant Flame surged forward, no longer a shield but a sentence. It swept through the clearing with purpose, delivering judgment. Twisted remnants of shadow were purged in its wake, banished, driven back through the breach like poison drawn from a wound. This was no battle cry. It was a reckoning. One by one, the echoes fell. Some dissolved into vapor with a hiss like wet leaves on fire. Others burst apart in shards of fractured light, their remnants vanishing as if the earth itself refused to remember them. The last of them twisted as they died, their form contorting into Frankie's likeness, mirror-eyed, hollow-mouthed, whispering falsehoods in her stolen voice.

But the Flame knew better, knew her. It knew the braid of her magic like a river knows its bed, like roots know the shape of stone. It felt the ache behind her defiance, the weight of every promise carried in her soul. It saw the lie for what it was, a hollow mask woven from windless memory and brittle fear, a mimicry stitched with breath not its own. And it burned it clean with the steady truth of wildfire meeting drought.

Then the breach snapped shut. The sound wasn't a crack, it was the forest drawing breath and holding it. A closing not of triumph, but of tension, like bark knitting around a wound still fresh beneath. Relief stirred, but it was cautious, cautious as deer in deep thickets. Silence fell, soft and heavy as moss, the silence of portent. The grove held its breath in spellbound stillness. It was the hush of ancient things listening. The kind of quiet that falls when a fox melts into shadow, when birds vanish mid-flight, and the wind forgets the way forward. This was not absence, it was presence cloaked in secrecy. A silence rooted in the old earth and unseen eyes behind bark. Old magic hung thick, earth-scented and heavy, not bright or playful like the spells of earlier days, but dense with memory. Beneath it all lurked a sharp, metallic tang, like blood on old iron or rain on stone, unsettling and out of place, as though the land itself braced for something it could not cleanse.

Far off, a hollowbeak sang out, its voice high and strange, like a lullaby remembered wrong, and no voice rose to answer it. Something deep in the realm twisted and turned, as if the bones of creation themselves remembered what should have stayed buried. From the smoldering mouth of the first breach, still thrumming faintly like a wound that refused to close, darkness began to unspool like memory taking form. It seeped through root and ruin, coiling into the forest like ink into clear water, silent, searching, certain. It did not feel like fear. It felt like recognition. Magic unbound. Magic betrayed. Without warning, the corruption surged, not from above or below but from within. As if the world itself had grown ill, and he was the sickness rising.

Veyrath rose, not as a man, but as a monument to corruption. Towering and warped, he seethed with a power that was never meant to touch mortal form. Magic bled from him in waves, blackened, hungry, devouring all it brushed. His limbs stretched too long, his shape cloaked in something that breathed like smoke and moved like tar. Where his eyes should have been, twin coals of starving flame burned. Lanterns went out. Runes carved into ancient thresholds sparked once, then died, as if their oldest purpose had been fulfilled and spent. Even the trees recoiled, their limbs splintering like ribs around a heart too dark to beat. The protective wards flared faintly, as if trying to remember what strength felt like. Then they, too, faded, recognizing him for what he truly was.

Dominicus Veyrath Noctis had never been a name draped in silk or civility. Dom DiLegna was the illusion, the polished smile, the steady hands, the quiet voice stirring sugar into tea, pretending at gentility. But this, this was what had always lived beneath. There was no mask now. No elegance. No trace of the grandfather Frankie had once avoided with polite discomfort. He was power unbound, ruin risen from the depths of the forgotten. His presence carried no mercy, only devastation, ancient and seething, inevitable in its descent. Veyrath had not returned to lead, nor had he come to rule. He had come with one purpose alone: to consume.

For the first time since arriving in Velhollow, Frankie could finally see it. Each time she had crossed paths with Veyrath, the mask had been slipping. Not all at once, but steadily, like something rotten beneath a gilded veneer. The illusion had frayed at the edges, the polish dulled, the cracks spreading where even light refused to go. With every encounter, the seams had split further. He had grown darker, larger, less man, more myth, more hunger, more hollow. And now, the final mask was gone. What remained was the final revelation. This was the ruin that had waited, festering behind every velvet word and false kindness. This was the ancient hunger, the rot beneath the civility. This was the truth that had always been, stripped of pretense, unbound by charm, and it was far, far worse than any disguise. The illusion had finally decayed. What stood before them now was raw and ravenous, a force no longer clothed, but shaped by need. Predatory, primal, and real.

Around her, the others felt it too. Griffon's wings arched, curving protectively toward her with silent resolve. Aoife clutched her staff so tightly the wood strained under her grip. Seamus whispered something in the old tongue, his fingers trembling as he traced a protective rune across his chest. Even Bramble, irreverent, quick-witted Bramble, stood in stunned silence. Frankie stood without a word, her fingers laced with Griffon's, steadfast, unwavering. In that quiet gesture, her choice was unmistakable. She had chosen connection over conquest, compassion over control. And Veyrath, watching, recognized it for what it truly was, defiance.

"Such sentiment," he said at last, his voice a slow toll of disdain. "Clinging to borrowed warmth, how quaint."

His eyes, twin coals of devouring flame, fixed solely on her.

"You've wasted it," he hissed, each word sharpened like a drawn blade. "All that power, the Verdant flame, the bloodline, the birthright. The realms didn't choose you to cradle the wounded or tend wildflowers. They chose you to burn the blight from its roots. To wield power like a scythe, not a salve."

"And you," his gaze slashed toward Griffon, sharp as a curse, "you leashed that fire with love. You dulled it with mercy. You poisoned it with hope." His stare fixed, molten and pitiless. "You are a creature born of fury, now curled like a pet at her heel. Do you think that bond will spare you when the world begins to bleed?"

Frankie started forward, chin high, power storming beneath her skin, but Griffon's grip held fast, anchoring her in place. Her silence rang like thunder waiting to break.

Veyrath stepped fully from the breach, and the glade itself seemed to flinch. Darkness no longer drifted around him; it adhered, allegiance made flesh. He raised one hand and the air warped around him. Cold power bled from his palm, ancient and unyielding.

"I offer something greater," he said, each word savoring the curve of threat, as his gaze swept over the everyone. "A world without fracture. No Veil. No exile. No sacrifice. Power unchallenged, restored in full."

His gaze flicked to Griffon, voice sly. "You, with your Berserker always caged, always leashed. Do you not tire of being feared? Serve me, and your fury becomes law. The world will kneel before you, whisper your name in ash and awe."

Then to Frankie, tone shifting to steel wrapped in velvet. "And you, Verdant Witch, rule beside me. No more pretending gentleness while the world demands fire. No more hiding in dead forests and broken lines of love. Not beneath the mercy of a realm that used you and never asked what it cost to survive. This is the final offer. Join me, rise above the rot. Refuse…" His gaze swept the glade. "And fall with Velhollow. I will leave nothing to mend."

The grove held its breath. Lantern flames froze mid-sway. Then the earth responded, with purpose. A thrum coursed through root and stone, older than language. Across the glade, the people of Velhollow began to shine: witches, shifters, healers, children of the old ways. Power welled in them like spring from stone.

Frankie's gaze never wavered.

"No." she said at last, voice calm and full of iron.

The single word sliced through silence like a blade through fog, carrying the weight of roots splitting stone, vows spoken beneath moonlight, every act of quiet defiance that had ever taken hold and refused to move.

Griffon's wings unfurled with storm-forged grace and the ground cracked beneath his step as he growled, low and steady, "I rise in her light and I will burn the world before I ever serve you."

The glade hushed, listening, from a moss-draped stone, Chalupa flicked his tail. "So just to confirm… still no cookies on the dark side? Tragic waste of tyranny."

Bramble snorted. Nyx's wings rustled like a smirk in the rafters of the dark.

Veyrath sneered, eyes narrowing. He stepped back, not retreating, but calculating.

"So be it," he rasped. "You have chosen ruin over reign."

Frankie stepped forward, the breath of Velhollow rising at her back.

"No," she said again, soft as moss, firm as mountain stone. "We've chosen truth, and what is right."

The land stirred. Fir needles bristled. Power rose from the soil like breath returned to long-lost lungs. The realm itself replied:

We are still here. We are not yours to consume.

Veyrath lifted his hand, shadows writhed, his mouth curling into another declaration, but the words snagged, stuttered, as though even his tongue faltered beneath the weight of the realm's refusal. The breach pulsed behind him, half-formed shapes flickering like lies unable to hold. The light itself hesitated as the world held its breath. Then the trees parted and a presence stepped from the western glade. Moss brightened beneath his boots. Roots reached to greet him. The canopy thinned, casting him in green-gold dapple like the memory of spring. Silence bent, breathless with recognition.

Darrow Quinlan.

Chapter 34

He came unarmed, no blade in sight, no shield raised, carrying only a velvet bag clasped in his hand, as though the realm itself had cleared a path just for him. He crossed into the glade without hesitation, and the ground, root, moss, and stone, leaned subtly toward him in recognition and welcome. Behind him followed witches, wild-kin, farmers, and healers, but it was Darrow who held the moment's center. He walked into the glade as though he had never left it.

Veyrath reeled back at the sight of him, smoke coiling from his mouth like venom dragged through flame. His form crackled violently at the edges, unraveling and reforming in frantic bursts.

"You," Veyrath snarled. "I expected you to still be skulking in the mortal realm after the defeat at Hollowmere."

Darrow stepped forward, the velvet bag glowing against his palm. "I didn't hid," he said. "I remained where I was meant to be, until the rightful heir arrived. Lady Aoife set the path. I merely held its course."

A gust of hot air ripped through the clearing as Veyrath roared, hurling a spear of shadow wide as a hall and jagged as shattered obsidian. It shrieked across the air, ripping through lanterns, extinguishing flame in a single violent breath. But before it reached Darrow, it disintegrated, shattering into harmless ash that blew backward into the breach as though the realm itself rejected the attack. Darrow lifted the velvet bag higher. The breach convulsed. The air screamed. Veyrath's form buckled like heat-distorted glass.

"You cannot hold me!" Veyrath spat. "Nothing ever forged has the power to contain what I am."

Darrow loosened the drawstring. A silver glow seeped through the velvet like moonlight remembering itself. Aoife gasped, one hand flying to her mouth.

"The Vessel of Maw..." she breathed. "I thought it lost when Hollowmere fell."

Darrow drew the relic free. Its surface shone with runes older than the Veil, lines alive with root-light, each mark breathing in time with the valley beneath their feet. The villagers whispered, the glade shuddered, and even the breach seemed to recoil as though recognizing an ancient predator.

Veyrath convulsed, his form warping as shadow tore itself apart and tried to reassemble. The scream that ripped from him was not pain alone, but outrage.

"That cannot hold me!" he shrieked, smoke tearing from his body in violent, unraveling ribbons. "You dare to try to use that relic against me?"

The Vessel flared in Darrow's grasp, its ancient runes tightening, locking into alignment as if answering a long-remembered command. The air around it thickened, the light sharpening rather than spreading. Darrow did not raise his voice. He did not need to.

"You've had your fill," he said evenly. "You've taken what you could. But you do not get to stay."

The breach behind Veyrath shuddered, its edges distorting as if the realm itself were pushing back. Trees bowed away from the tearing sky. Roots wrenched free and coiled upward, not to imprison him, but to deny him purchase. Rivers surged against their banks, the land recoiling in rejection. Veyrath thrashed, shadows lashing outward in frantic arcs, striking stone and air alike, but nothing answered his call. Rage twisted his features as understanding finally took hold. This was not a binding. Not yet. It was a severing.

"This is not over," he snarled, his voice breaking into echoes as the void began to collapse inward. "I will take what is owed to ..."

The pull seized him mid-threat. Shadow folded in on itself, dragged backward into the tearing light. His scream tore across the glade, stretched thin, then cut off abruptly, snapped like a cord pulled clean through stone. The breach sealed, light shattering inward before vanishing entirely. The forest held still, as though waiting to see if he would force his way back through. When nothing came, the roots sank slowly into the soil. The rivers eased. The sky knit itself closed.

Darrow stood alone at the center of the clearing, the Vessel now dim in his hand, its runes cooling to a steady, watchful glow.

He released a slow breath, shoulders settling, not in relief, but resolve.

"He's retreated," he said quietly. "For now."

A shudder moved through the ground beneath their feet, subtle but unmistakable, like the last echo of a door slammed far below the world. Frankie felt it along her spine, a cold recognition settling where triumph should have been.

Veyrath was gone, yes, but not undone. Whatever had been torn open had not healed so much as closed its eyes. The quiet that followed felt watchful, coiled, as though the realm itself understood the difference between banishment and escape.

Aoife's jaw tightened. Griffon's stance remained braced, weight balanced, every instinct refusing to stand down. Even the forest did not celebrate. Leaves stayed still. Birds did not return. Somewhere deep beneath root and stone, something had withdrawn to lick its wounds, and the land knew it. This was not an ending. It was a pause drawn in blood and breath, a promise deferred rather than broken.

Darrow turned toward Frankie, Griffon, and Aoife with a rueful, almost sheepish tilt of his head. "Sorry it took me so long," he said. He lifted the velvet bag slightly. "I had to fetch this. Good thing I did."

Aoife walked towards him, her posture lifting with old pride and new ache and the glade leaned with her.

"Well," she said, crossing her arms, "look what the forest dragged in."

Darrow bowed, crown of vine and root tilting rakishly. "Lady Aoife."

"You're late," she scolded, though her mouth betrayed a smile. "You missed half the screaming, all the dramatic wind, and I'm fairly certain Chalupa cursed someone in Old Velhollow."

"Ah, but I always arrive precisely when I mean to," Darrow replied, straightening with theatrical dignity. "In time for the grand finale, devastatingly handsome and questionably prepared."

"You didn't even bring a blade."

"Better. I brought wit, this vessel, and a flask of elderberry cordial. Arguably more dangerous."

Aoife snorted. "You'll be the first to die."

"And yet I always survive," Darrow said, winking at Frankie, at Griffon, at anyone willing to share the joke. "Charm, you see. Indestructible."

Aoife and Darrow exchanged a look, the kind shaped by decades of shared camaraderie, danger and unspoken plans. A familiar flicker of mischief passed between them, then, as one, they turned toward the treeline. Their shoulders aligned without instruction, two who had survived too many storms to need words now.

The quiet deepened.

It did not relax.

It tightened.

Griffon stepped closer to Frankie, his presence shifting, shadows tightening along his frame like smoke drawn toward heat. He did not unfurl his wings, but every line of him braced for impact. Seamus's hand settled on the hilt of his blade, fingers curling with practiced restraint. Above them, Nyx crouched low on a twisted branch, feathers slicked tight, a glint of storm light burning in his eye. Even Bramble, usually restless, humming, half-lost to curiosity, stood utterly still, the glow of his flask dimmed to a dull ember. Chalupa's tail lashed once, sharp and deliberate. A promise. A warning.

Then the bell tolled.

Slow.

Measured.

Unforgiving.

Eleven strokes echoed through the valley, each one landing heavier than the last. Only one hour remained before the Festival's end, and with it, the final thinning of the Veil. One hour to finish what had begun beneath root and star, through fire, blood, and choice. The sigil on Frankie's palm burned through the folds of her cloak, green-gold light bleeding into the air around her. It did not simply glow. It answered. The mark sank deeper, not just into flesh, but into the realm itself, threading through soil, stone, and breath. Something ancient loosened beneath their feet, a knot long bound finally beginning to give.

Across the glade, the Veil shuddered. The air grew thick again and sounds dulled. Voices from the villagers faltered, then thinned, as if swallowed by fear. Frankie felt it first in her feet. The ground beneath her shifted, not moving, just... bracing. Aoife went still beside Darrow, every line of her body gone sharp with knowing. Darrow's hand closed around the velvet bag, not lifting it, just grounding himself to its weight. Seamus's fingers slid to his blade without thought. Griffon stepped in closer to Frankie, close enough that she could feel the heat of him, the quiet tension gathering through his frame like a storm choosing its moment.

Around them, Velhollow held its breath. Leaves stilled mid-whisper. Lantern flames stretched thin, their glow paling as though they'd been asked to look away. Somewhere behind them, a youngling whimpered and was quickly hushed. Villagers edged back, not fleeing, just retreating, hands finding something solid as a touchstone. Fear settled low and heavy, not panicked, but old.

Darkness began to gather. The breach widened only as much as it needed to, as if whatever stood beyond it knew the shape of this place too well to force its way through. Then Veyrath stepped back into the clearing. Smoke clung to him in slow coils. His form wavered now, fissured by dark seams that glimmered faintly, scars where something had tried, and failed, to bind him. The crown of bone and shadow sat tighter against his brow, drawn inward as though feeding on his fury. His gaze swept the glade without haste, a conqueror's measure. He took one step forward, and the shadows moved with him. At his heels waited the remnants of his dominion, warped echoes of ancient beasts and specters stitched from the hunger for power and old dark magic. Beneath his skin, black fire shifted restlessly, lightless and unstable. The air fouled around him, thick with soot-dark power, as though the world itself recoiled. Flame tore loose from him in violent bursts now, sparks scattering like falling stars before snapping back into his orbit. The power around him no longer flowed cleanly. It buckled.Turned in on itself as if struggling to obey.

"You gathered," Veyrath said softly, and that was where the mockery sharpened into something dangerous. "You bound yourselves together. You called on land and blood and bond, and you mistook that communion for victory."

Lightning cracked again, striking so close the villagers staggered, the smell of scorched stone and metal filling the air.

"I did not return to test you," he said. "I returned to finish what began long before you learned your own name."

His eyes fixed on Frankie then, and the storm around him shuddered in response.

"You stand there believing the world has chosen you," he said, voice dropping, venomous and precise. "But choice cuts both ways." The fire around him surged, brighter now, hotter, uncontrolled. The air screamed as power compressed inward, straining against itself.

"And now," Veyrath said, fury finally bleeding through the arrogance, "we will see what you are willing to lose."

Frankie did not flinch. She stepped forward, and the moment her boot sank into the moss, the ground shifted. She pulled her wand from her satchel, rose and rowan wood aged by centuries, tempered by fire, etched with runes passed down through generations of witches who had stirred cauldrons, blessed thresholds, and wrapped the dead in rosemary and song. Aoife had crafted it herself from ancient materials, shaping it with care and foresight, knowing this moment would one day come. Frankie's fingers gripped it like an anchor, her knuckles whitening as her breath steadied. Energy moved through the grain beneath her palm, answering her hold. The glade began to spiral around her, light fracturing in the air, threads of green, copper, and gold unwinding outward, magic rising through the mist as if long-buried paths had finally been stirred awake.

Veyrath snarled, the sound guttural, too jagged for any mortal throat. He flung out his hand. A spear of shadow burst from his palm, jagged and seething. The moment it reached her, it disintegrated. Rejected. The realm itself refused his touch near her. Veyrath stilled. His sneer wavered for the briefest instant, a fracture in the mask. His gaze slid past Frankie, toward Darrow, and there, his eyes widened.

Seamus stepped forward, his blade half-drawn, voice taut with recognition. "He's calling everything he's ever broken."

Griffon's wings flared, obsidian and starlight slicing the air, his eyes catching fire. "Then we break him."

Veyrath's gaze locked on Frankie. His words fell heavy, each syllable carrying the gravity of a spell spoken in true tongue.

"*Francesca Caelith.*"

The sound struck the air like iron hammered on an anvil, ringing until even the trees seemed to tremble. His voice poured through the square, swelling with both triumph and venom.

"Granddaughter of Aoife Caelith. Blood of the Verdant Line. Keeper of the Balance… and yet more. Francesca *Noctis* Caelith. Sovereign of the Hollow Flame. Daughter of Twilight. Breaker of the Balance. Heir to the Forgotten Realm. My blood threads your marrow. My shadow stains your name."

The villagers gasped. The words fell on them like stone, each title a weight they had never heard but somehow recognized in their bones. Mothers pressed trembling hands to their young's hearts. Elders lifted their chins, eyes wet and wide. A ripple ran through the crowd, fear first, then something else, something steadier.

Whispers broke. Names carried. "*Francesca.*" Again, louder. "*Francesca.*"

The chant built like a tide. Faces turned from him to her. The villagers pressed their hands to their hearts, voices joining until the square throbbed with her name. Roots stirred beneath the cobbles. Lanterns flared, their flames silver-threaded, as though the stars themselves had bent to listen. The air thickened with recognition, the old covenant called aloud, undeniable now. Veyrath's sneer faltered, cracking around the edges. He felt it: the land, the people, the realm bending not toward him, but toward her.

"You choose her?" he spat, disbelief warping into rage. His body shook with fury too great to contain. "A child of the Greyvale? Untutored, untested? She doesn't even understand what she wields!"

The villagers' voices rose higher, steadier, each syllable a thread of power weaving into Frankie. She staggered from the force of what they gave her, trust, kinship, a strength older than blood.

Aoife's voice cut through. "They're answering her."

The realm itself stirred, roots coiling tighter in the soil, the river's current quickening, the air trembling with a harmony no throat could sing. It was no longer just Frankie standing there. It was every hand that had ever planted seed, every heart that had ever bled for Velhollow and for the first time, Veyrath's eyes flickered with something dangerously close to fear.

The energy around them beat like a living heart. Threads of light, green, purple, gold, and silver, wove from villager to villager, then leapt from their palms into the air, gathering, braiding, and pouring into Frankie.

The cobbler still streaked with soot lifted his cap, lips moving in silent vow. The beekeeper raised a jar of amber honey that glowed as though lit from within. A seamstress held her spindle high; a gardener cupped soil still damp with dew. One by one, they gave what they had: small tokens of life, love and labor. None of it insignificant. All of it power. The earth shuddered, then answered. Runes ignited in spirals beneath her, glowing through soil and stone, a map written in fire. A column of wind burst upward, scattering leaves and carrying motes of golden pollen that spun like stars. Frankie's hair whipped back. Her eyes no longer held hazel, but fractured into storm light, bark and bloom, root and flame. Veyrath shrieked. His minions lunged forward, their bodies twisting into spears of shadow, jaws unhinged to bite the light from her.

Griffon didn't hesitate. He stepped in front of Frankie as the ground split, planting his boots into stone that buckled beneath him, and drew a breath so deep it sounded like the mountain itself inhaling through his lungs. His shoulders rolled once, a final human motion, and then his wings snapped free. They burst from him in a sweep of obsidian and starlight, vast and serrated, scattering fire in a roaring arc that slammed into the dark like a living wall. The impact drove shadow-creatures backward, smoke tearing apart in screaming ribbons as flame and stone claimed the space he stood upon.

"With me," he growled.

The words were not invitation, they were a command that Frankie didn't question. She surged forward and took his hand, and the moment their palms met, the bond between them ignited. Not two forces standing side by side. They became one. Stone and storm locked together. Root and fire braided so tightly they could no longer be separated. The land recognized it instantly. The cobbles split beneath their feet as ancient roots tore upward, thick as wrists, then as torsos, dragging shadow-things screaming back into the soil that had rejected them centuries before. Stones wrenched themselves free from the ground, jagged spines hurling through the air to pierce and pin what tried to flee. The river twisted violently in its bed, abandoning its course to rise in towering arcs that slammed down with the force of falling stars.

The villagers did not run in fear, they stood in solidarity. Witches raised hands blistered from spell craft. Shifters braced, human skins cracking at the edges. Elders pressed palms to the earth, voices lifting in old languages meant for storms and endings.

Aoife stood rooted at the heart of it all, staff blazing, her magic moving not to dominate but to hold, to keep the realm from tearing itself apart under the weight of what Frankie and Griffon had become. Seamus moved like a shadow between strikes, blade singing, guarding the edges where the dark tried to regroup. Nyx wheeled overhead, lightning glinting in his eye, crying warnings that cut through the chaos like bells.

Without thought, Griffon reached beyond the limits of the Stonewing form, and this time the power answered in full. The change did not stop at his wings. It took him, every bone, every breath, and rebuilt him from the ground up. Stone rolled beneath his skin like continents shifting. His frame expanded, shoulders broadening, spine lengthening, muscle stacking upon muscle until he rose far beyond the shape of any being Velhollow had known. The earth groaned beneath his feet as he grew, not in a sudden burst, but in a deliberate claiming of space, as though the land itself had decided he required more room to stand.

When the motion finally stilled, Griffon stood immense, well over seven feet, nearer to eight now, his presence mammoth and unmistakable. He was stone-winged still, yes, but now he was something more than a shifter, more than a guardian. He looked carved rather than born, as if some ancient sculptor had taken a mountain and decided to make it walk. If not for the ferocity etched into his posture, the sheer scale of him beside Frankie's much smaller frame might have bordered on absurd, like a legend who had stepped a little too far out of proportion with the world around him. This power was still new. The Berserker is still untested, he wasn't sure how it would answer the call. Now he had an idea. Even now, it did not seize control. It waited for his intent and his intent was clear.

He positioned himself in front of Frankie without looking back, his body angling instinctively, creating a shield of stone and will.

The message was unmistakable, nothing reached her without going through him first. Not shadow. Not ruin. Frankie stood steady behind him, unafraid. Velhollow breathed beneath his feet, battered but alive. This was why the Berserker had risen, not merely for conquest born of rage, but for protection. For the realm that had shaped him. For the woman who had chosen to stay and fight. For the balance that still mattered enough to defend.

He drew a breath, deep and seismic, and when he moved again, it was with the weight of something that could not be pushed aside. This was not frenzy. This was focus, sharpened and terrible, a living bulwark forged to hold the line while the Verdant Witch brought the storm.

Veyrath reeled from recognition. The flames around him surged out of control, black fire ripping through bone and shadow in violent bursts as his form destabilized. Lightning cracked outward from him in jagged arcs, slashing through the glade and tearing the ground apart as though the land itself were an insult he needed to punish.

His gaze locked on Griffon.

On the Berserker.

"You dare to try to intimidate me *Stonewing*?" Veyrath snarled, his voice fracturing the air, echoing too many times at once.

The realm buckled under the force of his rage, reality folding inward as he tore the world open rather than face what stood before him. Stone and root dissolved. Sound vanished. The glade fell away. For a single, suspended heartbeat, Frankie stood alone with him again.

The void stretched endless and ash-choked, filled with the echoes of half-buried memories and ruined promises. He loomed across from her, vast and terrible, his grin splitting too wide, teeth jagged as broken stars. Fire coiled around him now, not controlled, not triumphant, but lashing, turning in on itself as though it could no longer decide what it wanted to destroy first.

"You could have ruled beside me," he hissed, stepping closer, the void warping around his presence. "Blood of my blood. Verdant fire bound to shadow. Together, we would have been inevitable."

His voice softened, sharpening into something crueler.

"Instead, you hide behind *them*."

Frankie didn't look away from him. For so long, his voice had lived in the margins of her life, quiet judgments, stories sharpened just enough to wound. She saw it clearly now for what it was, not lineage, not legacy, but hunger wearing the mask of birthright. Veyrath did not seek to claim her line, that had never truly been possible. What he wanted was what the Verdant line carried. There were only two ways to take it from her, by breaking her entirely, or bending her until she moved at his command, a willing puppet hollowed out and repurposed. That had always been the plan. He had mistaken silence for weakness. He had watched her grow and assumed she would fold the way others had, that she would doubt herself long enough for him to slip the leash around her throat and call it destiny.

Frankie met his gaze and felt no fear rise to meet it, only clarity.

"You thought I wouldn't see it," she said, her voice steady, carrying through the broken air. "You thought I was so small that I'd never question you. That I'd never push back."

She lifted her chin. Light gathered at her skin. Verdant green braided with molten gold, the color of growth that returns even after fire. It did not burn the dark away all at once. It outlasted it.

"You underestimated me my entire life," she said. "And that was your mistake. Blood does not make a family," she went on, each word striking true. The words echoed outward, through the watching villagers, through the land that had been listening to her.

"Blood can bind," she continued, voice steady, carrying the weight of truth hard-won. "But it can wound. It can lie."

Veyrath's fire lashed higher, lightning snapping from him in violent arcs as if he could tear the words apart by force alone.

Frankie did not falter. "Family is a choice. It's who stands when the ground breaks," she said. "Who walks with you when the path turns dark. Who chooses you back."

"I choose them," she said, and the land answered with a deep, resonant hum.

"I choose this land," she went on, and roots stirred beneath stone, rain scent rising sharp and clean.

"I choose love over ruin," her voice rang, brighter now, surer.

"I choose light, not because it is easy, but because it endures."

The fire around Veyrath began to turn inward, folding, devouring itself as though it could not bear the shape of her certainty.

"You are my past," Frankie said quietly, and that, somehow, was the cruelest blow of all. "And you will not be my future."

The void cracked. Light surged through the seams, reality rushing back in as the world reclaimed its breath. Veyrath reeled, fury tearing through him, not because she had rejected him, but because she had rendered him irrelevant. She had chosen and the realm had chosen with her. The illusion shattered. Light tore through the ash, seams splitting wide as reality rushed back in. Veyrath screamed, his form unraveling into tattered ribbons of shadow.

"Frankie ... now!" Darrow's voice thundered. He raised the velvet bag, and the Vessel of Maw unfurled like a silver bloom forced open by destiny.

Instinctively, Frankie reached for Griffon's hand. Together, they pressed their palms to the ground. Runes erupted outward in a sealing circle, Verdant magic surging in waves the realm. The Vessel answered with a cry of its own, runes blazing as it drank the light hungrily. Veyrath shrieked. Shadows ripped loose from him in great streaming banners as his essence was torn free. For one terrible instant, Dominic DiLegna's face flickered through the storm, cruel, familiar as the mask he'd never wear again.

They stood united, Griffon's wings beat once, and a thunderous sound rolled outward in a single, devastating wave. The force of it rushed through the clearing, flattening grass, shuddering stone, driving the air back on itself, yet Frankie did not stagger. The sound passed through her like recognition, not impact, her breath syncing instinctively with his as the echo threaded through bone and soil alike. Where the shockwave touched her, it did not bruise or break; it settled, warm and steady, as though his strength had wrapped itself around her spine and said, I have you. The ground answered them both, humming beneath their feet, and in that shared pulse Frankie knew, this power was not something she stood beside. It was something she stood within.

Their combined strike came down like a verdict. Root and flame, sword and shield, fused into a single force that did not rush or falter, but arrived, absolute and unyielding. The impact tore through Veyrath with the full authority of a world reclaiming itself. Shadows and flame screamed as they were driven backward, the false shape he wore collapsing under the truth of their union.

The Vessel of Maw answered.

It was still small in Darrow's hands, but the moment the power struck, it ceased to obey the rules of scale or space. It's runes ignited, roaring to life, and the air around it split open as though the world itself had been folded and torn.

Reality bent to it.

A vast hollow yawned open at the heart of the glade, an absence so profound it pulled at breath and light alike. The ground bowed inward, colors draining as the Vessel's call rippled outward. Veyrath felt true panic, which fractured his composure. Shadows tore loose from him in great streaming banners as the pull seized hold. He raged, flung fire and lightning in all directions, the force of his own magic turning wild, imploding against itself as he fought the inevitable.

"NO ..." he roared, the word splintering as the Vessel drew closer, closer, closer.

The pull intensified but Frankie and Griffon held fast, their power locked together, feeding the force that drove him back. The glade shuddered as Veyrath was dragged toward the widening void, his form unraveling, centuries of hunger and ruin ripped from their false cohesion.

The Vessel of Maw drank him in. Not all at once, but in a terrible, deliberate pull, as though the prison itself were tasting what it had been forged to hold. Shadow, flame, fury... everything Veyrath had stolen, everything he had twisted and fed upon, was torn from him in a screaming torrent. His essence stretched thin across the glade, clawing for purchase, for memory, for control, leaving scorched impressions in the air like afterimages burned into the world itself.

"*Francesca!*" The last cry broke free, not command, not plea, just the splintering of centuries undone.

As he unraveled, something broke loose. A fine dust shook free from the storm of his unmaking, heavy and dark. It glittered briefly as it spilled outward, catching the light like powdered obsidian and dead pollen, before drifting low and wide instead of rushing toward the Vessel. It did not scream. It did not burn. It simply fell, settling into the grass, into the cracks of stone, into the waiting soil, unnoticed in the violence of the moment.

The last of Veyrath stretched, thinned to a single, writhing filament of will. It trembled once, a soundless vibration that set teeth on edge, and then snapped.

The hollow collapsed inward. The Vessel sealed with a sound like a cavern roof giving way deep underground, stone folding over stone, ancient and final. Its glow dimmed, shrinking back into itself until it was once more small enough to be held in two hands, silent and whole, as though nothing had ever disturbed it.

The silence that followed wasn't empty, it was as if everyone and everything was collectively holding their breath.

Then the glade exhaled. The wind eased. Roots settled back into the earth with low, weary creaks. The air cleared, leaving behind the clean scent of rain-soaked stone and something faintly bitter, like leaves crushed too early in the season. Somewhere nearby, a lantern guttered and steadied.

Frankie felt it then, not a threat, not yet, but a wrongness, subtle as grit between teeth. She glanced at the ground where the dust had fallen, now indistinguishable from shadow and soil, already sinking from sight. Whatever had escaped notice did not feel alive. But it felt patient. She sagged forward and Griffon caught her and all around them, Velhollow stood tall.

Darrow cinched the velvet tight around the Vessel, its faint starlit pulse beating steady against his palms. He looked to Frankie, to Aoife, to Griffon, sobered by what had just been contained.

Frankie stood rooted in the silence, the world subtly realigned, as though the balance itself were choosing where to set its weight. Her chest rose and fell with careful breaths. Griffon's hand was still warm in hers, solid as stone after the storm. She turned, and the silver-blue of his gaze caught her like a tide. Whatever lived there needed no name. It had been building between them from the first moment they stood side by side, and now, at last, the land had listened to them both.

"It's over?" she whispered.

"It is." he answered, his voice the first warmth after a bitter frost, something she could step into and never wish to leave.

Exhaustion tugged her knees toward the ground, but he held her against him without hesitation. Their foreheads touched, and for a moment they simply breathed together, their magic braided so tightly it refused to release. When he kissed her, it was not the frantic press of survival but the steady claim of recognition. Rain clung to her lips, cool against his warmth, and when they parted, the world itself seemed steadier beneath her feet.

It was not the end. It was the beginning of everything. The Vessel of Maw glimmered faintly under its shroud, silver threaded with rootlike seams. Shadows writhed against the confinement, Veyrath's essence slamming like storm-surf against unbreakable walls. Each strike only brightened the relic's glow, as though it drew its strength from his defiance.

Seamus stepped forward, eyes narrowed, hand already reaching.

"Gods above and below," he murmured. "He's in there." He glanced sidelong at Aoife, his mouth tugging into a grim curve. "We'll need more than a shelf in the bastion. A cell. Reinforced. Layered in wards until they hum."

Aoife's lips curved, sharp despite the shadows of exhaustion. "Aye. We'll build it. I'll etch the wards myself, blood and bloom, iron and stone. He'll not slip through."

Seamus accepted the Vessel from Darrow with care, as though holding a blade older than kingdoms. Aoife steadied the weight with one hand, and for a breath the glade itself seemed to bow around them. Witches, familiars, villagers, even the weary soil recognized what had been contained. Above, the wind sighed through the trees, a release. Lanterns flared, silvered with starlight. The river's roar softened into song. Balance had not ended. It had been reclaimed.

Nyx's dry voice drifted from the ruin of a broken arch. "Could've done without the bit where reality nearly collapsed," he said, ruffling feathers dulled by exhaustion.

Chalupa padded up beside Frankie, tail flicking with deliberate patience. "Took you long enough," he murmured, tone sharp but lined with something softer.

Frankie laughed, the sound breaking from her chest like light after a storm. "You're insufferable."

“And yet,” Chalupa replied, whiskers twitching, “you’d be lost without me.”

Bramble grinned wide, flask already in hand. “Celebration feast, anyone?”

Laughter rolled through them, light and unguarded. For the first time since the veil split, joy returned not as defiance but as release.

Frankie turned to Griffon. He smirked, lazy and certain, his hand still firm around hers. “Think we’ve earned a break?”

“A break?” she snorted. “I think we’ve earned a lifetime of peace.”

Chalupa stretched long and slow, eyes gleaming. “Don’t count on it. We live in Velhollow now.”

Frankie rolled her eyes, but his words lingered, a reminder of how this strange, impossible place had pulled her fully into its currents. She glanced around: Nyx preening a wing, Bramble humming, Aoife and Seamus steady in the glow, Griffon warm at her side. What they had just come through was more than survival. It was kinship. It was belonging.

Aoife’s voice slipped into the moment, low and certain, like the burn of a hearth fire. “Aye, love... you are amongst family. This is your home. Truth be told, I never thought you’d leave once you found your way.”

Frankie’s chest tightened. “I’ve no plans to go anywhere,” she said softly. “I just... don’t know where I’ll be. You and Seamus, ” her eyes flicked between them, catching the way his hand lingered on Aoife’s shoulder “perhaps the cottage is better suited to the two of you. I’d like to give you the space.”

Before Aoife could scoff, Griffon’s hand tightened around hers. His gaze held her, steady as the roots themselves. “You do remember the *Aelmath Dainn*?”

Her breath eased. Of course she remembered, the shared hush he had spoken of before. No oaths, no claims. Just presence. Witness. Roots choosing where to grow.

“Yes,” she whispered.

“Then don’t trouble yourself over cottages or walls,” he said. His silver-blue eyes softened, twilight-steady. “We’ll begin there. One moon and a fortnight. Shared hearth. Shared hours. Shared silences.”

Her heart answered before her mind could intervene. "Then my place is with you."

Chalupa sighed, long and theatrical. "I hope he realizes we're a package deal."

Nyx cawed sharply. "Where the furball goes, I go."

Bramble crossed his arms, mock solemn. "Fine. I'll split my time fifty-fifty between Aoife's cottage and yours. Someone has to keep both households stocked with gossip and baked goods."

Frankie's laughter rose again, this time light and sure. Around them, the Festival surged back to life in full glory, fiddles climbing high, dancers spinning until skirts blurred, ribbons catching lantern light like sparks. The square hummed with resilience.

Someone laughed aloud, calling, "How long will the revelers last?"

"As long as they are inspired." another replied, and cheer rose like firelight.

Aoife emerged first, stepping out from between the festival stalls with the unhurried certainty of someone who knew the night had already bent around her will. The square behind her still rang with music and laughter, mugs raised high, skirts spinning, joy stubborn and hard-won. She scanned the crowd once, then her gaze settled on Frankie and Griffon.

Before either of them could speak, another presence slipped in beside her. From between the lantern-lit booths, a woman stepped into view. She moved with the ease of someone who knew precisely how to be seen and exactly when not to linger. Silver rings winked on her fingers, etched with symbols Frankie couldn't read, and a long braid lay over one shoulder. Her eyes were a deep, liquid green, sharp, observant, and far too calm for a night that had nearly torn the world apart.

"Walk with me, children," she said.

The square behind them was still alive with sound, but the moment the words left her mouth, the noise dulled, as if the air itself had leaned closer.

Frankie hesitated. She looked at Griffon, then back at the woman. Griffon's expression had shifted, not wary, not surprised. Familiar.

He leaned in slightly. "Frankie," he said quietly, "this is Seraphina Mornveil. I'm surprised you haven't met her yet. She's Aoife's oldest friend."

That alone made Frankie straighten.

Seraphina arched a brow.

"Oldest?" she repeated mildly. "Really, Griffon. I leave you alone for one apocalypse and that's what you land on?"

Aoife snorted. "Aye, you might try most enduring, or least tolerable," she offered.

Seraphina smiled faintly. "See? Growth."

She gestured with two fingers. "Come along."

They followed her into a narrow pocket of shadow behind the stalls, where the lantern light thinned and the music reached them muffled, like sound heard through water. The air smelled of cider, smoke, and crushed herbs underfoot.

Seraphina stopped beneath a swaying lantern and turned to face them. Her gaze rested on Frankie, not unkindly, but with unnerving clarity, as though she were looking at what lingered just beneath the skin.

"Now is not the time for details, yes, the shouting's over," Seraphina said. "The vessel held. That matters."

Frankie exhaled without realizing she'd been holding her breath.

"But," Seraphina continued, "don't confuse quiet with mended."

"Veyrath took more than what we realize," Seraphina said. "He siphoned magic. He meddled where no one should have lingered." Her gaze slid briefly toward the lantern-lit edges of the square, toward the ordinary-seeming night. "Some of what he damaged will correct itself. Some of it will not."

Frankie swallowed. "Like what?"

Seraphina met her eyes. "Like souls that should be whole." The pause was deliberate. "Like Arden," she said softly.

The words landed gently and struck hard all the same.

"He should have returned fully," Seraphina continued. "When I brought him home, the balance should have restored."

"And it didn't," Aoife said.

"No," Seraphina agreed. "Which tells me Veyrath was feeding longer than we knew."

A hush settled between them, thicker than silence. Seraphina's eyes narrowed slightly. "There's something else."

Frankie followed her gaze toward the trampled earth near the edge of the treeline. For just a heartbeat, she thought she saw it, a faint scatter of dark particulate, not ash, not soil. It shimmered, like jet black glitter, against the lantern light before dissolving into nothing.

Frankie frowned. "Did you see …"

"Yes," Seraphina said at once. "And no, we're not naming it tonight."

Frankie stiffened. "Why?"

"Because some things grow louder when you give them a word," Seraphina replied. "And I'd rather they stay quiet a little longer."

The festival sound swelled again behind them, someone laughing too loudly, a fiddle striking up a faster tune. Relief, fragile and real.

Seraphina stepped back, already half-vanishing into the light. Her gaze flicked once more to Aoife, something old and unspoken passing between them.

"Enjoy the night," she said. "You earned it."

Then she was gone, folded back into the festival as seamlessly as she'd appeared. For a moment, Frankie stood still, letting the music wash over her, the unreality of it all settling at last. Griffon's hand found hers, solid and grounding.

"Are you okay?" he asked.

Frankie nodded slowly. "I think so," she said. "I think Seraphina was right … I don't think everything ended tonight."

Griffon's thumb brushed her knuckles once. "No," he said quietly. "But some things did, and for that I am grateful."

They stepped back into the square, into spinning skirts and raised mugs and the stubborn joy of people who had survived. Music swelled, laughter catching and spilling over itself, lanterns flaring brighter as if the night itself had decided to loosen its grip.

Aoife found Seamus near the edge of the firelight. He didn't speak. He simply reached for her, and she went to him without hesitation. The kiss they shared was quiet and certain, the kind that didn't need witnesses, steady as breath after a storm.

Frankie turned back to Griffon, the moment softening between them, the world narrowing just enough for the rest to fall away.

"Before anyone commits to lingering eye contact and questionable life choices," Chalupa announced loudly, "I'd like to point out that we just helped vanquish an ancient terror and no one has offered so much as a biscuit."

Nyx landed on a nearby post with a sharp flick of his wings. "It is customary," he added dryly, "to replenish one's strength after apocalyptic exertion."

Bramble popped up between them, hands already clasped hopefully. "I'm not saying I *require* a snack," he said. "But I am saying that watching you all wrestle doom into submission worked up a heroic appetite."

Aoife snorted. Seamus huffed a laugh into her hair. Griffon groaned softly and pressed his forehead to Frankie's for half a heartbeat longer before surrendering the moment.

"Fine," Frankie said, smiling despite herself. "Snacks first. Kisses later."

"Now that," Chalupa said, tail flicking, "is leadership."

Frankie and Griffon walked hand in hand around them, the festival danced on. For tonight, there was warmth. There was music. There was the fragile, hard-earned joy of survival.

She lifted her face to the night. She had seen ruin. She had seen love. She had walked through doubt and found belonging where the wild things bloom.

Epilogue

By the time the last banners and ribbons from the Festival of the Black Veil had been tucked away, life in Velhollow had folded itself into a new rhythm. Frankie and Aoife's tea and tonic shop, *The Rose & Rowan*, had opened in the heart of the village square, a place where remedies came with honeyed smiles, and gossip steeped alongside chamomile. From morning until twilight, its windows glowed gold, the air perfumed with lavender steam and cinnamon bark.

The biggest change, however, was the double wedding, though calling it that made Griffon roll his eyes and Seamus laugh until he nearly dropped the ceremonial broom. In Velhollow, marriage wasn't sealed by papers or rings but under the Bloomveil, an ancient, shy enchantment that only unfolded its pale, star-shaped flowers when it decided the match was worthy. The town gathered in the meadow to watch as two blooms opened at once, one curling above Aoife and Seamus, the other above Frankie and Griffon. The officiant, an elderly brownie named Mister Thistledown, kept losing his place in the vows because Chalupa and Nyx were heckling from the front row, and Bramble insisted on "translating" for the flowers in an overly dramatic voice. It was perfect, which was to say, it was theirs.

Weeks later, Griffon was pulled into the Royal Guard's headquarters on the cliffside, with Seamus named as co-captain. Frankie and Aoife visited one windswept afternoon with a basket of rosemary scones and a vial of headache tonic. The place was a storm of clanking armor, muttered reports, and the sharp scent of ink. Griffon met her with that small, quiet smile, the one he never offered to anyone else, and steered her toward a desk half-buried in scrolls. That's when she met him. Calem Wren, Royal Scribe, sharp-eyed and sharper-tongued, his sleeves rolled to the elbow and a quill tucked behind one ear.

“So you are Lady Francesca Caelith,” he said without looking up from his parchment. “Good, I have questions.”

It wasn’t exactly a warm welcome, but there was something in the way his eyes finally lifted, storm-gray and far too curious, that told Frankie trouble tended to find him. She didn’t see Seraphina watching from the far corner, her expression unreadable as she exchanged the barest nod with Aoife. That would come later. For now, Frankie only knew that life had grown full, of tea and spice and laughter, of love that bloomed like magic and magic that behaved like love. But high above the cliffs, where the wind twisted wild, something stirred in the clouds, black petals unfurling, slow and deliberate. A new storm was already waiting on the horizon.

The End...

About the Author

(as told by Chalupa, Who Is Very Real, Thank You)

Let's get one thing straight before we begin: I am real. I do not live in Velhollow. I live in Nevada. This is important, because people keep asking.

My human is Lily Mackenzie Duffin. She writes books about magic, forests, witches, and talking cats, which frankly raises expectations I cannot always meet in the mortal world. Still, I do my best. I supervise. I judge. I nap directly on her notes.

Lily is an east coast girl at heart who relocated all of us to the high desert of Nevada, where the sun is aggressive and the vibes are… dry. She is married to Travis, her favorite human, who edits her work, keeps her going when others are unkind, and has earned my respect by not pretending he understands cats. He knows better.

She is surrounded by familiars. Three cats (obviously the most competent beings in the house), one very large dog named Barnaby who believes he is subtle (he is not), and Mongo, a tortoise who moves like a prophecy unfolding. There is no bog sprite wandering the kitchen. Benoît does not drop by with commentary. If he did, I would have words.

Mongo will be properly introduced in Book Two of the trilogy. Barnaby, against my objections, will appear in Book Three as a cantankerous capybara. I warned her this would have consequences.

Lily writes stories about old magic, stubborn women, found family, and the quiet truth that belonging is not granted, it's claimed. Verdant Witch Rising is the first book in the Verdant Witch Trilogy. It contains danger, warmth, mystery, and at least one talking cat who is far more reasonable than the humans.

Again, for clarity: I am real.

Chalupa
Senior Familiar, Reluctant Muse, Keeper of Reality

www.ingramcontent.com/pod-product-compliance
Lightning Source LLC
LaVergne TN
LVHW100459110826
845146LV00002B/458
9798994637111